Also by Kate Jacoby in Gollancz:

EXILE'S RETURN
VOICE OF THE DEMON
BLACK EAGLE RISING
REBEL'S CAGE

TRIAL OF FIRE

Fifth Book of Elita

KATE JACOBY

GOLLANCZ

LONDON

The right of Tracey Oliphant to be identified as the
author of this work has been asserted by her in accordance
with the Copyright, Designs and Patents Act 1988.

First published in Great Britain in 2002 by
Gollancz
An imprint of the Orion Publishing Group
Orion House, 5 Upper St Martin's Lane,
London WC2H 9EA

A CIP catalogue record for this book is
available from the British Library

ISBN 0 575 06888 4 (cased)
ISBN 0 575 06889 2 (trade paperback)

Typeset at The Spartan Press Ltd,
Lymington, Hants

Printed in Great Britain by
Clays Ltd, St Ives plc

For Aaron, with love

Acknowledgements

Thank you as always to my family and friends, for their endless patience, support and encouragement. More thanks to Leslie Gardner and especially to Jo Fletcher, for letting me tell the story.

And so we come to the final chapter in this saga. This was a time of confusion, of uncertainty, of faltering hope, and yet those at the heart of this story knew their time was fast approaching.

This was the time Robert Douglas had most feared, for it was his hand that would divide fate from hope, his destiny to find an answer to the Prophecy, or, while delivering his country from evil, destroy the very thing he loved most.

History had always worked against him. He'd returned from his self-imposed exile to find Lusara struggling under the rule of Selar, the conqueror; the Church floundering, the powerful Guilde growing stronger under Proctor Vaughn. Vaughn knew Robert was a sorcerer – and hated him for it.

The secret Enclave, hidden high in the Goleth Mountains, was home to sorcerers who no longer dared to live in the country, fearing for their lives from both Guilde and the evil sorcerers, the Malachi. The Enclave was protected by the Key; it was this powerful talisman which had given Robert the Prophecy.

While the people needed a release from tyranny, those within the Enclave, the Salti, begged Robert to help them, but Robert, a man of honour, could not reconcile the responsibilities placed upon him with his oath of allegiance to Selar, nor with the terrible fate of the Prophecy. This conflict raged within him for more than thirty years, becoming a dark stain inside him he could neither control nor destroy. In his own mind, he called it the demon.

The one person who understood both Robert and his demon was Jennifer Ross, abducted as a child and sent to live in Shan Moss forest. When, fourteen years later, Robert rescued her, he discovered she was not only a sorcerer, with powers vastly different to any other magic-wielder in Lusara, but the daughter of the Earl of Elita. Robert returned Jenn to her father as he had promised, but even as he realised his feelings for her were changing, he discovered that she was also a part of the Prophecy, named the Ally – and he knew that if he allowed it to come true, *she* would be the one he would destroy.

King Selar had a new friend, Samdon Nash. A sorcerer of incredible power and evil, Nash was known as Carlan to his people, the Malachi. He would stop at nothing to posses the Key – and Jenn, the Ally.

And then fate took hold of Robert and his brother Finnlay once again, and the secret of sorcery died. Word flew across the land.

Nash secured his position at court, using a hideous perversion of the ancient Bonding to tie Selar to him, so the King would lose all free will and become Nash's puppet.

Robert helped the Queen to safety, but it was Jenn's impending marriage that finally broke him. Despite all his promises to himself, he spent the night with her, giving into the Bonding foretold by the Prophecy. Then he went into exile once again – this time determined to stay there and harm no others.

Though heartbroken, Jenn understood Robert and went through with her marriage to Duke Teige Eachern, Selar's brutish cousin. When she found she was carrying Robert's child, she kept the secret, allowing her husband to believe it was his.

Robert exiled himself in a remote abbey where he met Bishop Aiden McCauly, hiding there after escape from imprisonment on false charges of treason. The seeds of a deep and powerful friendship were born between the two. They were drawn from their sanctuary by threats to Robert's brother and an attack on Jenn at Elita.

Racing across the country, they arrived at the castle in time to discover those besieging were Malachi, under control of the Angel of Darkness, the third protagonist in the Prophecy. Even as Jenn went into labour, as her father was killed and her son born, the enemy was closing in, threatening to overrun the castle. Exhausting all his defences, the demon within Robert finally cracked and broke, flooding through him with a fury that would not be denied. From the highest battlement he let loose the Word of Destruction, obliterating the Malachi and severely wounding the Angel of Darkness.

Five years later Robert returned again to Lusara, on an urgent mission: Selar was determined to invade neighbouring Mayenne, but his success would mean the end of Lusara. Robert set about gathering loyal men to stop Selar in his tracks.

With her husband's death, Jenn took her son, Andrew, to live with her sister, while she joined the rebels. She and Robert travelled to the southern continent in search of answers to the Prophecy; though answers eluded them, the trip healed the rift between them, and Robert vowed to marry her . . . but on their return to Bleakstone, Robert's allies insisted instead he marry Selar's daughter, Galiena, and, upon victory, that he take the crown. Jenn insisted that he agree; Lusara was more important than their love.

After the wedding, word arrived that Selar was advancing to the border and the rebel forces were mobilised.

Jenn headed to the Enclave, where she was chosen by the Key to replace the dead Jaibir, the leader of the colony. Robert arrived too late to stop it: with Jenn now joined to the Key for life, Robert could no longer trust her; he left to rejoin his army.

Still determined to help, Jenn joined Robert's army. That night, when their camp was attacked by Malachi, one young woman was captured, Sairead, the girl Robert's closest friend had fallen in love with.

At dawn the battle was engaged. Both sides fought hard, but there was no clear winner, even though Robert killed Selar.

As Robert slept fitfully that night, Malachi crept into the camp, freed Sairead and abducted Micah, her lover, Robert's closest companion. When the armies lined up for battle the following day, Robert faced his bitterest enemy, Nash, the Angel of Darkness.

Robert rescued Micah, but was stabbed in the back by Sairead. Believing Micah had betrayed him, Robert turned to fight Nash, who was severely wounded, his power virtually gone. Robert too was hurt, but Jenn felt the build-up of power and knew Robert was preparing to use the Word of Destruction to kill both himself and Nash – he would defy the Prophecy he hated with his *own* death.

Jenn rushed between them, using her own awesome powers to split them apart. Nash was spent, but alive, and Kenrick's men rescued him from the field. Robert remained standing long enough to see Kenrick's army racing away in terror and to hear the cheers of his own men. Then he collapsed into Finnlay's arms.

The war was over, and Kenrick – now King – fled back to Marsay with the wounded Nash and the dispirited Malachi. Micah, desolate to be banished from Robert's side, left to play bodyguard to his friend's son, Andrew. Robert's army buried its dead that night as Robert himself lay dying, his wounds severe, the demon inside him making them worse.

Finnlay fetched Jenn, hoping she would tell Robert that she loved him and that Andrew was his son so Robert might have something to fight for. But Jenn's choices were too limited; the only way to save Robert was with another lie: she told him that she had never loved him – and the demon struck out at her, but with Robert so weak, it could do no damage. Now the demon was working to heal him, but he looked at her with hatred. She left for the Enclave, knowing that she had irrevocably lost his love – but that he was now free of her, free to fulfil a destiny his country cried out for.

For the next eight years, Robert worked in the background, carrying out small raids against the Crown and Guilde, gathering support and information. Though he achieved much, he was not yet ready to move against Kenrick, who had grown into an even worse tyrant than his father – the boy was a powerful, though untrained, sorcerer firmly under Nash's control.

Though the country was desperate, Robert couldn't move until one last piece was in place. In a monastery in Flan'har, and with his most trusted allies around him, Robert announced that he was placing Jenn's son, Andrew, on the throne of Lusara. He would fight and destroy Nash, while Andrew dealt with Kenrick, his cousin. Bishop McCauly and the others would remain in Flan'har, ready to support Andrew when the time came.

Andrew, growing up strong in the care of his mother in the Enclave and Micah at home, knew nothing of Robert's plans until Robert kidnapped him one night. In his secret home buried inside the caves under Nanmoor, Robert detailed enough of his plans to horrify the fourteen-year-old boy before returning him to his home at Maitland. Here Robert saw Jenn for the first time since the Battle of Shan Moss, eight years before.

After his fight with Robert at that same battle, Nash was broken in body, but not in spirit. As his life had been sustained by the blood of others, his wounds required more to heal – and this blood he found hard to obtain. Crippled but unbowed, he set out to place his Bonded Malachi spies in the courts of southern princes, and to capture Jenn's son with an eye to replacing Kenrick with him, if the King did not obey.

But even as he sent his men south to kidnap Andrew, another more desperate struggle erupted and, to his surprise, Nash discovered that he had a daughter of his own blood. With all haste, he set out to find her, imprisoning Valena, the mother, and using the child's blood to repair his injuries, increasing his power tenfold. For three days he lay vulnerable while his body was rebuilt, but at dawn on the fourth he rose, strong, whole and more powerful than he'd ever thought possible.

Nash's Malachi attacked Andrew and Micah, but Jenn and Robert intervened, rescuing the boy. In revenge, Andrew's aunt and uncle were murdered by the Malachi and, fearing more reprisals, Robert took them all back to the Enclave.

Though they were now safe from Nash, the Malachi and even Kenrick, Robert felt the evil had followed him, in the shape of the demon nestling inside him, burning with anger and hatred: if he lost control, he would use the Word of Destruction as he'd been told in the Prophecy. But even as his ability to contain the demon cracked and broke, Jenn's love held him secure. He saw at last that she'd been his all along.

Robert presented Jenn with the one thing they'd always believed could help their struggle against Nash: the Calyx. But as they took it before the Key, hoping for the answers they desperately needed, disaster struck. Key and Calyx joined to become one and, in the process, the protective walls around the Enclave fell away, leaving them open to discovery by Nash. With his new powers, Nash cried with delight, promising to cross the country to find them, kill Robert and take the Key – and Jenn. His victory was assured.

In the act of salvation, you will become desolation itself, destroying that which you love most . . . So said the Prophecy to Robert, when he was just nine years old. From that day onwards, everything he did to prove it wrong only proved it right. Every attempt he'd made to free Lusara, to help his people, the Salti, ended in the destruction of something – and always by his hand. Now he knew; there was nowhere else for him to go. He had to accept the fate handed him; he had never had a choice, and never would.

But for Robert Douglas, torn across layers of history he could never understand, victory and failure had become one. He could not know that courage alone would not be enough, that the answers he needed were closer than he thought, nor that history itself would be his salvation. And he could certainly never know that the Ally of Prophecy had yet to speak.

He could be absolutely sure about only one thing: if it took his last, dying breath, Lusara *would* be free.

Excerpt from *The Secret History of Lusara* – Ruel

This eerie tale of evil grows
Its tail around the wind and blows
A course through good and willing breath
To stab and hack hard hope to death

O, wonder ye with eyes so wide
Wherever men of good do hide
They stand but here, with courage sure
To fight the dark for ever more

He listened hard, with eyes of tears
Such tales of woe for these long years
And with that strength of eons born
He gathered all before the storm

His savage gale swept o'er the land
Slew deadly dark, his bloody hand
And blinded, fuelled further by his ire,
True Prophecy, his trial of fire.

TRADITIONAL

1

John knew he was going to die, but since he could no longer feel his fingers or toes, or most of his extremities, he could be reasonably assured that his death would be relatively painless. But to die in such a manner, in the middle of the night, lost in a snowstorm, somewhere in southern Flan'har, was not quite the hero's demise he might have hoped for. Of course, he'd never actually hoped for any kind of demise, hero's or otherwise, but the truth was, if he had to die, then he would have chosen to do so pursuing the cause of his people's freedom. Instead, it appeared he was going to die pursuing the end of a road lost some moments after dark, many hours ago.

Nobody had warned him about the weather. In fact, at the inn where he'd stayed the previous night, he'd been assured the worst of the winter was most definitely over and that setting out on foot at dawn the next morning would gain him his destination by nightfall. It was true that black clouds had mocked the morning sunshine, but he was a priest and had never really had much cause to learn to read the weather . . . or maps, or how to tell the direction from the sun – assuming there was one.

This was his first pilgrimage; it was fast turning into his last. He'd known there would be risks when he'd left Maitland, and Andrew, bless his soul, had been worried, had given him advice that no ordinary fourteen-year-old boy would normally offer. The young Duke had urged him to be careful, while pretending there was no envy in his eyes. He'd seen John's trip as an adventure, and wished he could have one of his own, but Andrew's foster parents, his Aunt Bella and Uncle Lawrence, would have preferred their precious boy to remain at home, and not even cross the country to see his mother, a woman they both knew was a sorcerer.

Of course, they'd never known that John was also a sorcerer – though to look at his current predicament, he would be embarrassed to admit to such skills. But John hadn't practised much, concentrating instead on his vocation, knowing in his bones that he was born for the Church – even if that same Church's laws against sorcerers would have him executed if he were ever discovered.

Times had changed, though. King Kenrick had overturned the laws against sorcery because he had abilities himself, and both Guilde and

Church claimed they would not slaughter anyone they found with talents . . . assuming they could know just by looking, or assuming sorcerers would be stupid enough to confess their abilities even now . . .

His mind was drifting. Though he placed one foot in front of the other, though he pushed the air in and out of his lungs, his mind couldn't hold onto his place, his moment, his night of dark, his black and white death.

John had wanted so much to make this pilgrimage, to find this man and place himself into his service. He'd done all he could for Andrew, but the boy had grown up and for John, there were other paths he knew he had to follow, so he'd left all his comforts behind, packed a few meagre belongings and set out on foot to cross the border into Flan'har. He had no idea where he should look, but he was positive he was needed to help a man whose spiritual leadership he knew would one day free not only Lusara, but also Lusara's sorcerers.

John's foot came down hard on something and twisted sideways. The rest of him followed and he landed spread-eagled in the snow, fresh flakes landing softly on his face. He could see nothing now as he looked up, just the frame of snow around his body where his landing had created a hole and a black nothing above. So, this was his death. He needed to make his confession, to release the regret that he had waited so long to find Aiden McCauly, not to mention the hubris that the great man would have need of a man who couldn't even follow a road after dark—

'You there! Are you alive?'

John frowned. Was that a real voice, or simply his mind playing evil games before it gave up the ghost?

'Are you hurt? Can you move?'

A face appeared in front of him. Though it was dark, he could make out deep lines, a thick beard and a frown of concern. A hand reached out and shook his shoulder.

'Are you dead yet?'

'I . . . don't think so.' John managed. He tried to convince his body to move, but he could feel no more than the inside of his mouth now; the rest of him was happy to just lie there in the soft, warm snow.

There was movement around him, and in the distance he could hear the jingle of horse reins, the hard thud of other feet landing on the ground. It appeared there were people around here who had no trouble keeping track of the road.

'You're a very lucky man.' Hands came around him, lifting him up, wrapping him in something he couldn't feel. 'We almost didn't come out on patrol tonight. We were about to turn back when we saw you fall. What in the name of Serin are you doing out here on your own, on foot? What's your name?'

'John . . . Father John Ballan. I was . . . looking for . . . looking for . . . Bleaksn—' The words got much harder to find all of a sudden. He looked into the face of the man holding him up, caught the shadows of a dozen horses behind him, and something that might have been lights far in the distance. Then abruptly everything went dark.

'I think he's one of yours.'

'But where did he come from?'

'He didn't say, but he was clearly alone and he's definitely not armed. Nor did he exhibit any signs that he's been Bonded by Nash.'

'That we know of.'

'Was I wrong to bring him in?'

'No, of course not! Still, I can't help wondering what he was thinking. Do you think he was looking for us?'

'Well, the last thing he said was something that sounded like Bleakstone Castle.'

'What do you think?'

'As I said, Bishop, I think he's one of yours.'

'Very well. Let me see him. Did you find out his name?'

'Father John Ballan.'

'Father?'

John blinked, but his eyes were too sore to keep open. He was comfortable, that much was certain. And he was warm. Oh, so warm! Warm and comfortable. Now if only those people would stop talking, he'd be able to get some more rest and—

The bed dipped and he opened his eyes a little again – and gasped in shock. 'Bishop!' Desperately, he struggled to sit up, but Aiden McCauly placed a firm but gentle hand on his chest and kept him down.

'You stay right where you are, Father. I don't think you'll be getting up before tomorrow.'

John blinked again, his eyes still sore, but he couldn't close them now if his life depended on it. Aiden McCauly was sitting on the side of his bed, alive, well and with a small smile playing across his face. John prayed silently that he wasn't still lying in the snow somewhere, breathing his last and dreaming this.

McCauly had aged since the last time John had seen him, fifteen years ago. The brown hair was mostly grey, and the lines on his face were deep, though few. Still, his gentle brown eyes were as perceptive as ever. For a man in his sixties, living in exile, Aiden McCauly had done better than most.

3

The truly elected Bishop of Lusara was now holding a cup of something hot to John's lips; he dutifully sipped. The aroma of the spiced brew drifted into the room, making him sleepy again.

'Now,' McCauly began, holding the cup between his hands, 'Deverin tells me you were on foot? The last I heard, you were living at Maitland Manor, tutor and chaplain to Andrew Eachern, Duke of Ayr. What brings you here? And on foot?'

'Forgive me, Your Grace.' John tried again to sit up, but at the Bishop's gesture, he settled once more. 'I came to . . . to find you. I want to—' He paused. Suddenly his deep desire to be instrumental in the freeing of his people seemed an exercise in self-indulgence. He'd already had an important role, and he'd forsaken Andrew to come here, and be a burden on the one man who—

'You want to?' McCauly prompted.

'I want to help you, Your Grace.'

'Help me?'

'Yes. If you will allow it.'

'Help me how?'

And there it was, the moment he had been dreading. He knew when he left Maitland, even when he had first contemplated this pilgrimage, that he would have to confess this most secret of secrets. Though his body ached, he took a deep breath. 'You have been working with Robert Douglas.'

'Have I?' McCauly was noncommittal.

'Yes. And you've been writing books and papers, disseminating them throughout Lusara. You've been writing about sorcery and how the Church needs to question all we've been told about it. That there are questions about the old Empire and the Guilde's ancient attitude to sorcery. That every priest must search his conscience and ask what it is we most fear, and how best we should address those fears. How simple prejudice only breeds more fear and hatred.'

Surprised, McCauly sat back. He put the cup on the side table and laced his fingers together. His expression gave nothing away. 'You have certainly kept up with your reading. So tell me, why would this make you want to join me?'

'Because, Your Grace, I . . . I am a sorcerer.'

There was nothing in McCauly's gaze, not a hint in his movements; just a pause and no more. Then, abruptly, he got to his feet and moved away a little to poke at the fire. For the first time, John noticed the rest of the room, but he couldn't take in details other than the warm ochre colours, the sparse furnishings.

'You recall,' McCauly began softly, 'Everard Payne, Earl of Cannock-burke?'

'Of course, Your Grace.'

McCauly turned and faced him squarely. 'He told me you had been instrumental in aiding my escape from prison. He never actually said, but I had to assume the only way you could do so was to use sorcery.'

'I'm sorry, Your Grace.'

'For what? For having the courage to take such a risk on my behalf? If you'd been caught, Father, you would have been burned at the stake! And now you've come all the way here – on foot – to help me?'

John was taken aback at the fierceness in the Bishop's gaze. It lasted only a moment, then McCauly was calm once more, his hands folded again into his woollen sleeves. 'By all means, Father, if you want to help, then I am not the man to dictate in what manner you give that help. For my part, I am glad to have the company of another priest. Tomorrow we will celebrate mass together. In the meantime, I ask that you get your rest. You will be sore tomorrow for your trouble.'

As he turned to go, he paused, showing John his face in profile. 'And you being here has given me the opportunity to thank you personally for your part in my rescue. You are indeed a very brave man, Father John, and our cause is the stronger for your joining it. Good night.'

'Good night, Your Grace,' he breathed into the silence. Then the door was closed behind the Bishop and John lay there with a grin on his face, his aches and his sore eyes completely forgotten.

John had no idea what time it was when he woke. There was some daylight, a few misty clouds, and a gusty wind that whistled under his door now and then, but beyond that, he could only guess.

He got out of bed gingerly, his muscles protesting even that little effort. But he needed to relieve himself and was delighted to find a corner curtain hiding a garderobe. After that, he found a bowl of warmish water, a towel and some plain clothes – not clerical, but they were warm and since the Bishop hadn't worn any kind of habit, John had to assume that was the wisest move.

He washed and dressed quickly, not wanting to lose this dearly won heat. Some kind soul had left him some food on a tray. He ate only enough to quell his grumbling stomach, then, a little excited, a little daunted, he opened the door of his room and peeked into the passage. It was dark except for a slit of weak sunlight from a narrow window further along which marked the wooden floor and half the opposite stone wall. He tried to get his bearings, to gauge from the smells and noises of this place his best option for finding other people, but Bleakstone sounded horribly silent for a castle well-inhabited with rebels.

John closed his door quietly. Choosing at random he turned to his right, heading for the narrow window and what looked like a staircase beyond it. It wasn't a staircase, but rather, an angled turn in the wall, which he followed. It was lit by more narrow windows which looked down onto a courtyard. An open door showed a room with two tables, one long, one round. The long table had piles of books, scrolls charts and other things he recognised. The round table had a beautifully carved book stand, a thick tome resting upon it, and at the side, an inkwell, a pen, a sheaf of papers and a heavy eye-glass. Curiosity burned within him and, despite his years of discipline as a priest, he took a step inside.

'Ah, there you are!'

John started at the Bishop's voice coming from behind the door. There was a fireplace against that wall; McCauly had obviously been reading while warming himself. He was watching John with a smile. 'I'm glad to see you up at last. Did you sleep well? Do you feel better for your rest? We were wondering if you'd even wake today.'

'I feel well, Your Grace. Thank you.'

'Did you have something to eat?'

'Yes, I did.'

McCauly took one more look at the paper he was holding, then moved to the long table, placed it on a particular pile and turned his attention on John. 'So. You've decided to become a rebel.'

John didn't need to answer.

'You know,' McCauly continued, 'the others have questions regarding the wisdom of embracing you into our circle. I'm sure you understand that what we are doing here is very . . .'

'Sensitive?'

'Exactly.'

John swallowed hard. 'Do you wish me to leave?'

'No – and besides, that wouldn't make them feel any better.'

John took a fortifying breath. 'Then the only other alternative you have is to imprison me here.' He folded his hands together. It was not what he had wished for, nor what he had hoped, but if this was the only way he could serve, then so be it. 'I can act as scribe for you as easily from a cell as anywhere else. I am also proficient in a number of ancient languages and although I have not practised as well as I might, I am a fair Seeker and can scan on an hourly basis to warn if there are Malachi in the near vicinity. I also have some skills in treating minor wounds, though I hope that won't be necessary.'

When McCauly said nothing, John went on, 'I assure you I have no abilities to bend metal bars or burrow through stone. If I am to be imprisoned – which I think is your only option – then the sooner I am secured away from sensitive material—'

'That won't be necessary.' McCauly picked up a log from the rack and placed it on those burning in the fireplace. 'The others have questions – I do not and, for what it's worth, my word carries some weight in this place.' He turned back, his serious expression softened by a smile. 'Now, suppose I show you around Bleakstone and introduce you to your fellow rebels? There are not that many of us here as yet, but there are reasons for that.'

'And Robert? He is not here?'

'No – and please don't ask me where he is. I understand he is in Lusara, but I have no idea where. More than that I think should wait until you've got your bearings. Come, this way.'

Aiden couldn't help watching the younger priest as he showed him through the castle. He was so very earnest, so serious, Aiden was tempted to deliberately say something to make him smile at least, if not laugh. There was an innocence to Father John Aiden hadn't seen outside St Julian's, the kind of innocence usually found only in children and cloistered monks.

But he had seen things, this priest. He'd been Jenn's Chaplain at Ayr during her marriage, giving what support he could when the Duke had beaten her. He'd helped Robert get Jenn and the boy out of there and safely to Maitland. He'd stuck faithfully to Andrew ever since; Robert had often said how glad he was that John had chosen to stay at Maitland, that they had somebody they could always trust inside the house.

Of course, the others at Bleakstone weren't actually suspicious of John; they were just naturally wary of any newcomer at a time like this.

Aiden took him through the rooms in the main keep, mostly accommodations currently empty. He did show John the tower room Robert normally used when he came here, but following a brief walk across the courtyard, and an even briefer wander through the barren castle gardens, Aiden finally took him to the council chamber.

This room was not the biggest in Bleakstone, but it was probably his favourite. The walls were covered in rich wood panels, the carvings depicting hunting scenes and dances with the gods. The floors were tiled in roan and white marble, cool in the summer, icy in winter but for the thick Alusian carpets thrown down, their colours adding to the warmth. The painted ceiling panels were decorated with key moments from the lives

7

of previous dukes of Flan'har and, together with the rich furnishings, the deliberate light from north- and south-facing windows, there was not a day when this room was not welcoming.

Aiden spent a lot of time here, working with men who now looked up as he entered, John a step behind him. Aiden didn't tarry with the introductions. 'Father John Ballan, you remember Payne, Earl of Cannockburke?'

'Of course.' John bowed as Payne got to his feet and approached.

The Earl was taller than John, young and handsome; his eyes appraised the man. 'It's good to see you again, Father. You are well after your . . . er, trip?'

John blushed a little, but matched Payne's smile with a hesitant one of his own. 'Yes, thank you, my lord.'

Aiden turned to the oldest man in their group. 'This is Sir Owen Fitzallan.' Owen had a patch over one eye, lost fighting at Robert's side at the Battle of Shan Moss. He'd been a servant of the House of Douglas since a boy; now an old man, he lent his wisdom, along with his ability to read the weather.

'And this is your rescuer, Sir Alexander Deverin.' As John bowed to the big man, Deverin clapped the priest on the shoulder. Like Owen, Deverin had been with Robert's family since a boy. Now with a new family of his own, Robert's Master at Arms was anxious to be able to return home to Lusara, to settle down and enjoy the peace they all craved.

'There is one more of us,' Aiden continued as John finished thanking Deverin for pulling him from the snow. 'Lord Daniel Courtenay, but he is away visiting family and isn't due to return until the end of the week. Everyone who works at Bleakstone is a refugee from Lusara, and we stay here thanks to the beneficence of Grant, Duke of Flan'har.'

'He is a good man,' John offered.

'He's a brave man.' Payne added dryly, turning back to his seat at the table. 'I'm not yet convinced Kenrick won't one day bring an army over the border, though I suppose the cost might be enough to make him pause. So, Bishop, have you told him yet?'

The others looked equally enquiringly at Aiden, who said, 'I wanted to ensure I had your agreement before I said anything. Do I?'

Payne looked once at John, then nodded. 'Aye, you do.' With that, he sat down again and drew the book he'd been reading towards him. The others took that as a signal. Owen returned to his window seat where he picked up a tally sheet and a marking board. Deverin sat at the table opposite Payne and resumed sorting through a pile of papers.

Recognising that their behaviour was anything but a dismissal, Aiden ushered John to the opposite end of the room and explained, his voice low enough not to disturb them, 'This is where we do most of our work.'

'What about your study upstairs?'

'That's my own work – this is . . . I suppose you could say Robert's work, the work of Lusara's rebellion.' Aiden pulled out a chair and gestured for John to sit. 'The last time he was here, he charged us with these responsibilities. He'd been years planning this and he left us with the paperwork and detailed instructions of what we are to do for the rebellion. He will come when he is ready for the men gathered here, and for all our other plans to be put in motion. If another comes in his place, then we will know he is dead and we must go on without him. Our role will tie in closely with his – though he has insisted we not cross the border until he gives the word.'

John frowned a little, and looked at the others. 'Why not? Surely he would need his strongest allies to help—'

'His plan,' Aiden continued carefully, 'is not to wage a war, but to fight a battle – with Samdon Nash.'

'But what about Kenrick? He has powers and he supports Nash completely. How does Robert plan to—'

Aiden could see the questions flash across the priest's face, along with concern, worry, ideas and, he was pleased to note, only a little fear. Already this newest recruit was thinking of solutions. Aiden answered as many of those unspoken questions as he could at once, summing them all up with one sentence. 'Robert's ultimate goal is to remove Nash and Kenrick and place another on the throne.'

For a moment, John didn't move, though his eyes widened in surprise. Moments later, his face drained of colour as his agile mind got to work. He rose slowly to his feet, and whispered, 'Andrew? He's going to put Andrew on the throne, isn't he?'

'Yes.' Aiden stood too, John's deep shock setting off alarms in his own mind. This was more than mere surprise. 'Why? Is there something we don't know?'

'But he can't! He doesn't—' Abruptly, John's mouth shut and his eyes snapped to the others, who were now staring at him openly. He blushed and dropped his gaze. 'Forgive me, I . . . '

Aiden moved quickly, taking hold of John's elbow and ushering him from the room, not pausing until they were outside in the brown and lifeless garden. 'Tell me, Father. Whatever it is, you must say. Thousands of lives depend on your honesty.'

'Forgive me, Your Grace.' John held up his hands, then clasped them together, gathering himself. 'I was just surprised. I thought he knew . . . but obviously— By the gods, what am I to do? What am I to say?'

Steeling himself, Aiden took a few steps away from the distressed priest, keeping his hands joined behind his back. 'Is it something held under the seal of the confessional?'

'No, no, that's not the problem. I'm not supposed to know this, but it never occurred to me it could be a problem, though of course, I was blinding myself really.'

'Father?' Aiden insisted gently.

John shook his head. 'You must understand, Robert can't put Andrew on the throne.'

'Why not?

'Because . . .' John paused, steadying himself. Then he looked up, his eyes dark with worry. 'Because, Your Grace, Andrew is Robert's son.'

There was a bench in the furthest corner of the walled garden where a trellis framed the area with a barren arch. In spring, this place would be moderately pretty, but now, with that season still a week or so away, there was nothing but bleakness in this place, the only colour coming from the red stone walls of the castle and the patchy blue of the sky above.

John followed the Bishop, sitting on the bench in silence while the older man paced for a while. Then came the questions. 'You know this for sure?'

'I was with the boy's mother from the weeks after Andrew was born until she killed Eachern, almost six years later. I never asked, no. Nor could I, not even as her priest. I think she wanted me to know, but didn't dare tell me.'

'But I need to know for certain! The entire rebellion rests on Robert putting this boy on the throne, on the people accepting him as a legitimate heir, both through Jenn's House and through Eachern's kinship to Kenrick. Have you no proof?'

'How can there be proof? Do you think Jenn would leave something like that around? And if there were, Jenn would ensure it was destroyed.'

'Would she do such a thing?'

John could only sigh. 'Your Grace, you should know – Jenn will do anything she deems necessary to protect her son and her country, to survive and fight another day. That is perhaps her greatest gift.'

McCauly shook his head again, 'You must explain how you know, why you are so positive.'

John ordered his thoughts. 'I cannot give you evidence, Your Grace – all I have is fourteen years of knowing the boy, of watching him grow up, of seeing his relationship with Jenn and with the man he thought was his father, Teige Eachern. I don't know Robert that well, but I do know him enough to see him in so much of what Andrew does. It's there in his voice, in the way he thinks. His choice of words and his . . . deep sense of right and wrong. I believe his Aunt Bella is aware as well. I know she has no love for Robert, and there are moments when she looks at Andrew and despairs.'

John paused and found McCauly's hard gaze on him. 'You would have to see them together, Father. You would have to see Andrew. His looks are his mother's. His hair is dark, almost black. His eyes are a vibrant blue, the shape of his face oval, but strong. He is already tall, and will grow more, his build tempered both for speed and strength. In his eyes, you see his mother. In every other aspect, you see his father – and you know it must be Robert. Eachern never looked like that.'

'Are you,' McCauly whispered harshly, 'absolutely sure, without any doubt whatsoever, that Andrew Ross Eachern is the son of Robert Douglas?'

John said, 'Yes. I am.'

McCauly raised his hands in frustration, 'Then how is it that everybody doesn't know? If it's so obvious to everybody who looks at him.'

'But it isn't. Since his mother is not around to compare him with, and Eachern dead almost ten years, nobody would guess. Only those who know either Robert or Jenn well would be able to tell, and even then, if they didn't expect it, they wouldn't see it.'

'Oh, by Mineah's teeth, I can't tell anyone about this! Robert doesn't know, does he?'

'Apparently not – and nor does Andrew.'

'But why—'

John held up his own hands. 'I can't say. So much of what happens between them is directed by the Prophecy. There is a point past which I never dared go, with any of them. I don't know Robert all that well, but I do know Jenn. She was afraid to tell him, afraid of what he would do. Perhaps she was also afraid of what Andrew would say – though she should have known better. Andrew worships Robert as a hero. It would not be so great a step to love him as a father.'

McCauly put his elbows on his knees, his face in his hands. 'By all that is holy, Robert will put that boy on the throne.'

'Surely Jenn will stop him.'

'You think so? I don't know her that well – and I've never met Andrew.' The Bishop got to his feet and continued, 'There's nothing we can do about this at the moment. I can't contact Robert, and I don't know what I'd say if I could. And as to the others? I don't think it's prudent we say anything for the moment. Not until I have a chance to think on this more. Do I have your word, Father?'

'Of course, Your Grace.' John stood. 'I'm sorry to—'

'Bishop?' They both turned at the call from the gallery door to see Payne coming towards them, Deverin, Owen and somebody else holding back. 'Daniel's just come back early. He checked the drop points and picked up a letter. It's from Godfrey.'

Payne held the letter out to McCauly who took it, his gaze suddenly wary. As if in answer to a question, Payne nodded, putting his hands on his hips. 'It's what we've been expecting. Bishop Brome is dead.'

Without thought, Aiden drew the sign of the trium over his forehead and shoulders, his whisper emerging from habit alone. 'The gods grant him peace.' He paused only a moment. 'Who is elected Bishop in his place?'

'There was no election. Brome appointed his successor. The synod ratified the appointment the same day.'

'Oh, sweet Mineah, not another—'

'The new Bishop is Godfrey.'

Aiden's eyes widened in surprise. John himself was delighted. If another man had to stand in McCauly's place, he would prefer it was his old friend Godfrey than any other.

'And Kenrick?' McCauly barely moved. 'He has accepted Godfrey as Bishop?'

'It seems he expected it. Godfrey anticipates no trouble, though he writes only the day after his enthronement. There is more in the letter.'

'Of course.' Aiden opened the pouch and extracted the single sheet of paper. He read in silence, then folded the letter up, handing it back to Payne, his expression clearly disturbed.

'Thank you for letting us know. Father John and I will go to the chapel and say prayers for Bishop Brome's soul, and for Godfrey, that the gods will guide him in his new role.'

As the last breath of incense died away, Aiden got to his feet, keeping his hands clasped together. At his age, his knees should be shaky with the hours he'd spent on them, on cold stone floors, praying – but somehow, his body remained strong, as though the gods were determined to ensure he survive long enough to win this fight. In dark moments such as this, that gave him hope.

He sensed rather than saw John moving around the chapel, putting things away, blowing out candles until just two were left, along with the presence light suspended above the altar.

This was a tidy building of round arches and clear glass windows, though not really big enough for Bleakstone. There were memories here, of him marrying Robert and Galiena, before the poor girl was murdered by her brother, Kenrick. Memories of others, too, men who had fought and died at the Battle of Shan Moss.

Brome. The man who had supplanted Aiden as Prelate of the Church in Lusara. The man who had destroyed a Church so needed by the people, and had done so out of his own vanity. But that man was now dead and facing the judgment of the gods. Who was Aiden to judge? Had Brome had any more choice than he? If Aiden had not been imprisoned, would he have had the strength and the skills to hold the Church together? To do what was right? To fight the evil on the throne, and that which lurked behind it?

No. The truth was, Brome, like them all, was a man of the times. He'd had no more choice than Aiden, no more power to change his fate than anyone else.

And equally, there was nothing Aiden could do to stop Robert putting his own son on the throne. By the gods, if he knew . . . Aiden knew Robert and Jenn had spent one night together before her wedding, how Robert had seen that as a weakness in himself, an inability to withstand the Prophecy. For fifteen years he'd believed he had betrayed Jenn that night. Aiden could well understand why she'd never told Robert, why doing so now would scare her. But would she say something when she discovered Robert's plans?

The truth was there really was no alternative to Andrew, no other way for Robert to free Lusara and be left with something other than civil war. Still, it seemed appropriate that the bastard son of a rebel and a sorcerer should go on to rule a country known the world over for its vengeful stance against sorcerers.

Straightening, he signed the trium over his forehead and shoulders, then turned and led John from the chapel. He paused long enough to close the doors behind him, then looked up to find Payne waiting for him, leaning a shoulder against the wall, arms folded. Patient.

Long ago, before any of this madness, Everard Payne, Earl of Cannock-burke, had been one of Robert's closest friends. Though living something of the life of a dilettante, his heart had never wavered from the cause of freedom, though his methods might sometimes have been a little unconventional. Even so, despite the years, Payne was certain Aiden could still surprise him.

'You never say,' Payne said after a moment, his tone conversational, 'what it is that's really worrying you, deep down. After all this time, I can't help wondering why. More to the point, I wonder why it is you won't confide in us – or is it perhaps that you can't?'

'Deep down?' Aiden heard John move away a little to give them some privacy. He took a deep breath and laced his fingers together. He had always known that one day he would be expected to answer these questions. Nevertheless, he said, 'You know my concerns. I have voiced them often enough.'

One side of Payne's mouth curved up in an ironic smile and he gestured vaguely. 'Ah, but you see, that's my point. You only ever voice the concerns we would expect you to have. I am no priest, nor am I a sorcerer – and even I can see you're hiding something. I simply want to know why you don't trust us enough – surely by now we have proved ourselves worthy?'

A deep weariness rippled through Aiden, making him sigh. He turned to the diamond-paned window beside the earl and rested his hands against the rough stone embrasure. 'You should know that trust is not the issue here. Serin's blood, Payne, you know what Robert's like.'

'So you admit you are hiding something.' Payne tilted his head back to study the ceiling a moment. 'And Robert won't let you talk about it? Am I right? Damn him! He's been doing this too long on his own. He's forgotten how to treat his friends, how to work with us. Doesn't he know—'

Aiden watched the younger man quickly fold up his anger with sharp-edged discipline. There was once a time when such discipline would have been beyond him.

Payne returned to the point. 'You're worried about Robert, and him fighting Nash. You think Robert won't survive? That he can't beat Nash?'

Aiden swallowed hard. These were the shadows of his nightmares, not things to be spoken aloud, even to this man. He straightened up and began to turn away, but Payne's hand shot out to stop him. Aiden ground out a reply. 'I can't know what will happen between them. Not even Robert knows. How can you ask me?'

Payne raised his voice a little and called, 'Father John?'

'Yes, my lord?'

'Robert – is he or is he not supposed to be the most powerful sorcerer ever born?'

John remained where he was. 'Aye, he is. At least, as far as we know.'

'And Andrew's mother?' Payne's gaze bored into Aiden then.

'She is very powerful, my lord. Robert believes as powerful as he. But—'

'But?'

'Her powers are different to the rest of us. Her skills are in different areas.'

'But you'd say they'd . . . complement Robert's? Would that be a fair judgment?'

'Yes, my lord.'

Payne dropped his hand, but his gaze didn't falter. 'You know all this, Bishop. So what are you hiding? If trust is not the issue, then what is it? Is it not in all our interests for us to know? Will Robert mind so much if you tell me?'

Aiden almost laughed at the silliness of that question, but it did at least break the moment for him. He sighed and turned back to his window where nothing but the dark night could be seen. Stray snowflakes stuck hard against the corner glass. This was not about Andrew at least, and for that, he was grateful. 'He didn't want you all to know because he's not entirely sure about it himself. There was no point in worrying you unnecessarily.'

'And yet, here we are . . .'

He'd warned Robert this moment would come one day. 'There is an ancient Prophecy. Robert was given it as a child and it's haunted him since then, driven so many of his actions and dominated his decisions. In it, he is told he is destined to fight some one called the Angel of Darkness. And there is another mentioned, called the Ally, which we know to be Andrew's mother, Jennifer.'

'And Robert? Is he named in this Prophecy also?'

'He is called the Enemy.'

'Enemy, eh?' Payne pursed his lips. 'And all this is something to do with Robert being a sorcerer? And Jenn as well? And Nash, I assume you mean he is this Angel of Darkness?'

'He is.'

'Then is not Kenrick named also? And what of Andrew? If this is to be the stuff of Prophecy, then surely they are also a part?'

Aiden spread his hands. These questions had plagued him for years, and Robert too. 'Unfortunately, we know too little about the Prophecy. Robert has spent most of his life studying the history of sorcerers, and I the last eight years. We are desperate to learn its true meaning, and perhaps gain some clues as to what we can do to increase Robert's chances of beating Nash. Robert even sent his friend Patric to Alusia in search of the last rogue tribe of sorcerers in the hope they might be able to help. It's been almost a year since we last heard from Patric and to be honest, I have given up hope that he will ever return, let alone bring us good news.'

'What kind of news could he bring?'

'I don't know.' Aiden paused, the truth sitting in the pit of his stomach like lead. 'All I do know is that Nash knows more than we do, more than Robert does, and in this game, knowledge is everything.'

Confused, Payne tilted his head. 'How so?'

Aiden sighed. 'You mentioned Jenn, how strong she is and how her powers complemented Robert's?'

'Yes?'

Unable to watch the as the truth sank in, Aiden turned and began walking back to the main keep. 'Nowhere in the Prophecy does it say she's *Robert's* Ally.'

2

A frantic banging on the door woke John out of a nightmare. He sat up panting, trying to clear his head, but the noise didn't stop. With a groan, he rolled out of bed, stumbling on the rug, and reached the door in time to wrench it open before the next bout of banging. 'What is it?'

Lord Daniel stood before him, his sandy hair all over the place, trying to push his arm into the sleeve of a jacket. 'Sorry, Father, but there's a beacon lit on the cliff. A ship has foundered on the rocks and we're on our way out to help.'

'Just let me get dressed. I'll meet you down there.'

Lord Daniel was gone before he'd finished speaking. Pushing his own hair down, John grabbed the first clothes he found, barely able to see in the inky night. The last week had been a challenge as he tried to learn as much as he could, but early on, he'd been told of the beacons and the cliffs along the southern coast of Flan'har. It was an unwritten law: when ships were in trouble, everyone living within sight of the beacon would go to help. At this time of the year, pilgrim ships crossed the Gulf in flotillas, the better to ward off pirates; if just one of these ships went down, there could be hundreds of lives at stake.

John grabbed his cloak and ran down to the courtyard, taking two stairs at a time. The yard was already full of mounted men and soldiers, along with the Bishop, Payne, Deverin and Daniel. Owen was giving orders for things to be made ready in case wounded needed to be brought back to Bleakstone; already lights were glowing through scattered windows.

Shouting commands above the clatter, Payne soon had the gate open. John took the horse handed to him and swung up into the saddle; as they cleared Bleakstone's gates the bitterness of the night really hit him. The cold was enough to freeze the breath in his chest, but worse than that was the fog. He could see nothing and, from habit, immediately reached out with his Senses, hoping somebody better than he was responsible for keeping them on the road.

In the furthest distance, he could see the beacon glimmering, a faint yellow glow in the coal-black night. He rode hard, determined to keep up and not be a burden; though it wasn't long before his fingers froze in his gloves and he lost feeling in his feet, still his horse galloped on steadily, warming him with its movement. As the glowing beacon grew nearer John could finally smell strong salt on the air.

Without pausing, Payne led them towards a rocky beach nestled between two tall cliffs. They were not the first rescuers to arrive. Already torches stood along the beach, while men rowed tethered boats into the pounding waves. John dismounted and frowned into the night, hoping to see the wreck, but there was nothing out there other than darker shadows, which his Sight could not penetrate.

He had no time to wonder then as more people were pulled from the water, injured, freezing, half-drowned. Fires were built high above the waterline; he gathered driftwood to keep them stoked, and tore up bolts of cloth for bandages. From time to time he manned the ropes and his hands grew raw hauling boats back from the sea, laden with people too cold to cry, too scared to move.

He had no way of knowing how long they worked, only that the fog finally cleared just before dawn. By then, they were clearing salvaged cargo from the boats and the wreck had all but disappeared. Now and then he caught sight of the others, and more than once he saw the Bishop on his knees, signing the trium over some still form. Did these people know who he was – or did they care only that a man of the gods was prepared to give them absolution?

John didn't need the dawn to see the strain on the Bishop's face, the deep grief for those dead, and the genuine joy that so many had been saved. It was not so common to find a priest who was still able to love the people from whom his vows kept him apart, and to show that love so openly.

As the last threads of night disappeared, John pulled his cloak around him and headed to where the others were making ready to mount up again. He'd long since lost his gloves and his belly was cranky for want of food, but he was, for the moment, still warm and that was a lot more than many of those poor pilgrims, most of whom had been put upon carts and taken to Colteryn, or nearby farms. Two cartloads had gone to Bleakstone, where they would be fed and rested before being helped on their way.

The ring of steel on steel broke him out of his reverie. He turned around to find Deverin stepping back, his hands raised in a gesture of peace. Before him stood a young man, long hair wet and bedraggled, tossed by what wind was left. He held his sword easily before him, a mark of quality training. His clothes were foreign, long robes rather than jacket and trousers, and they were torn and ragged, still dripping water from the sea.

'Easy now,' Deverin soothed, not moving, keeping his voice gentle. 'I just wanted to take a look at your friend. I can see blood on his face. His wound will need attention. I mean you no harm.'

John could see the other Bleakstone men were tense, ready to move if necessary, anxious to protect the Bishop – but the young man could also see that. His eyes scanned them all, his stance not softening. He made small shifts to keep himself between Deverin and his friend, who lay unmoving on the ground behind him. Then the man spoke, a word John didn't recognise.

A chill rippled down John's back.

'I understand you're frightened,' Deverin continued. 'But we just want to help your friend, that's all. Can I come closer? Just to look?'

For a moment the young man didn't move, then, slowly, he took a step to the side, his sword no less of a threat than before. McCauly moved up close behind Deverin, but not close enough to jeopardise the delicate balance. He watched the young man as Deverin knelt down and reached out a hand to the injured man's face. With a glance at the sword, Deverin pulled a cloth from his jacket, folded it and held it in place over the wound.

'Father? He needs to see a Healer. This is deep and he is unresponsive. I fear he may—' Deverin stopped suddenly, his whole body stiffening. Then, urgency in his voice, he added, 'Father, come here!'

Eyeing the young man warily, McCauly threw him a smile and moved to Deverin's side. He looked down at the injured man.

'Do you not recognise him?' Deverin whispered.

Aiden froze too. Unable to stop himself, John moved forward until he could see the face of the injured man. The pale skin was tanned by years on the southern continent, there was the nasty gash over the right eye and his hair bleached almost white, but it was impossible not to know the man who lay before them, badly injured from the shipwreck.

'Sweet Mineah's breath,' Aiden whispered in a prayer of thanks. 'Patric!' He reached out a hand to Patric's shoulder, but his movement was halted by the sword neatly slid before his throat. Immediately, Deverin moved, his own sword drawn as he sprang to his feet, but Aiden moved quickly, desperate to avoid bloodshed.

'Deverin, no. He's just trying to protect Patric.' He rested back on his haunches and raised a hand to the blade. Carefully he pushed it away, his eyes rising to meet the young man's. 'Somebody go fetch some clean water and a bandage of some kind. Everybody else stay back.'

'Father,' Deverin murmured in warning, but he did move back a little, putting his sword away.

Forgetting the others, Aiden kept his gaze on Patric's protector. 'Do you understand my language?'

The young man narrowed his gaze and said nothing. His eyes were pale, a glittering grey, his skin olive, tanned. He might have been about twenty-five, but no older. Fine dark eyebrows and a small cut on his bottom lip were the only distinguishing marks on his face, but there was such intelligence in those grey eyes that Aiden tried again. 'We are friends of Patric. Friends. We want to help.'

The stranger frowned a little, his eyes darting to Patric for a moment, then back to Aiden. He opened his mouth, his lips forming a word, but making no sound. Then, as one of Deverin's men returned with a bowl of water and some cloth, the young man finally spoke, his word a question directed at Aiden.

'Malahi?' For a moment, Aiden didn't understand. Then the stranger spoke again. 'You – Malahi?'

'You mean . . . are we Malachi?' Aiden shook his head, spreading his hands to indicate his peaceful intentions. 'No. We are not Malachi. We are friends. Patric's friends. Will you let us help him? Bind his wounds,' Aiden indicated the bandages, 'and we have a safe place to take him, where it is warm and—'

'Warm?' Suddenly the man's expression changed. His eyes widened and he took his first proper look at the other men standing behind Aiden, Deverin, Payne and Daniel, John and the twenty soldiers they'd brought with them. 'Robrt?' he asked.

Again, Aiden shook his head. 'No, Robert is not here.'

The stranger turned his gaze back on Aiden again, his sword now hanging loose at his side, though still not sheathed. 'B . . . Bi'ship?'

Aiden smiled, unable to help himself. He nodded vigorously. 'Yes, I am the Bishop. Patric's friend.'

The young man lifted his sword and slid it into the scabbard. He nodded once, then stepped back. Immediately, Deverin moved forward; he knew more of healing than the others. Shortly, they were ready to travel and, with his eyes on the stranger, Aiden mounted up, his burning curiosity in check. His questions could wait until they got back to Bleakstone. They would have to wait until Patric awoke.

But all the way back, Aiden prayed – both in thanks for his friend's safe return, and that the return heralded a turn in their fortunes. But pray though he might, he did not yet dare to hope.

John stood back, well out of the way of the men who carried Patric into the bedroom and laid him gently on the bed. A fire had been lit and hot food was on the way up. John had to swallow his excitement and wait for the room to empty a little.

'Just be careful there, John,' the Bishop murmured, his tone wary. 'Patric's friend is a little protective. Keep all your movements open and visible.'

John nodded, barely glancing at the others before stopping at the bedside. He'd been unable to get a proper look at Patric on the journey back to Bleakstone; even now, his memory did him no service: the man was almost blue with cold and the bandage over his forehead didn't help. 'We need to get these wet clothes off him and get him warmed up. Then some soup, I think.' He reached out and pulled the blanket away from Patric's shoulder, and would have kept on – but a hand shot out, gripping his wrist so hard he recoiled.

The stranger stood over him, grey eyes glittering in the firelight, long hair ratty and tangled. But there was something in that gaze, something . . . intangible, but too akin to that ripple over his Senses. John paused.

That something intangible abruptly filled his awareness, sparking his Senses until his skin almost burned. With a hiss of pain, he jerked his hand away from the other man, who matched his surprise, and his equal awareness.

This man was not Salti, nor was he Malachi. But if not, then *what* was he? How had he come to be travelling with Patric, and *where* had he come from?

'John?' The Bishop was at his side, his voice steady and easy. 'What is it?'

'I . . . don't know. This man is . . . I don't know what he is but—'

'Is he a danger to us?' Payne queried from the open doorway where the others waited, out of the way.

'Danger?' John frowned, unable to think in those terms. He'd never experienced anything like this before and knew not how to judge if it were a danger. 'I can't tell you; all I know is that he is some kind of . . . sorcerer.'

'*Some* kind?' Payne's dry question slid into the silence. 'How many kinds are there?'

'What do you Sense?' Aiden spoke softly, his gaze moving between John and the stranger. 'He's not a Malachi?'

'No, it's not at all like a Malachi. But I think he feels it as well. He knows I'm a sorcerer too.'

'Well, we still need to get Patric changed before he gets a chill. Why don't you—'

He was cut off by a moan from Patric. The Bishop moved to his side, the young man with him; John went round to the other side of the bed. Patric moaned again, his hand coming up to his head where the bandage covered his wound. He murmured something that John didn't recognise, then suddenly his hand reached out and his friend took it, as though Patric was dizzy and needed it to gain his balance.

Then the Bishop spoke. 'Patric? Do you know where you are?'

Patric frowned, but didn't open his eyes. For a moment, John held his breath, then, slowly, Patric smiled. 'Aiden? Is that you?'

'Yes, it's me.' McCauly was grinning hard now, looking at the others. 'Welcome back.'

'I'm at Bleakstone?'

'Yes.'

'Thank the gods!' He relaxed a little then, swallowing.

'How do you feel?'

Patric's forehead furrowed against some pain. 'Not so good . . . Cold.'

'Well, we'd like to get you changed into dry clothes, but your . . . ah, your friend is very protective and won't let us near you.'

'My . . . friend?' Patric shook his head slowly, then stopped as the pain took him again. He gasped and the stranger moved closer, his stance menacing. Then Patric's expression changed completely. 'Oh, you mean Joshi?' Patric was silent a moment, then he continued, 'Joshi kept me alive. We were . . . attacked on the ship . . . coming over, and—'

'Easy, Patric,' Aiden said, still smiling, 'you've plenty of time to tell us everything. Right now, we need to get you changed and warmed up. You've got a nasty cut on your head.'

'Jus . . . feel tired.'

'Then you sleep, Patric. Just sleep. John, can you help Patric into warm clothes? I'll try to get Joshi to change before he also catches a fever.'

'Aiden!' Patric sat up, reaching out for McCauly's arm and gasping again in pain. 'I need to find Robert! Is he here?'

'No, he's in Lusara.'

'I have to find him . . . it's important—'

McCauly urged him back down onto the bed. 'I can send him messages, but I have no idea where he is, or when he'll get them. I'm sorry, Patric, but we'd given up hope you'd come—'

Patric grabbed his arm again, this time opening his eyes. 'Find him!'

John bit back a gasp of surprise; McCauly frowned. Patric's eyes were as white as his hair, as though the colour had been bleached from them by the sun.

McCauly spoke again, his voice soothing now. 'Rest, Patric. Don't worry about Robert. Just rest.'

Patric was back in one piece – but he was completely blind.

*

Aiden stepped into the corridor and closed the door behind him. Almost instantly, the questions began.

'What did Father John mean by Joshi being some kind of sorcerer? What if Patric has changed sides?'

Aiden turned to Daniel and shook his head sharply. 'We have no reason to suspect him. So far Joshi has done nothing but try to protect Patric. John didn't say he was a threat.'

'No,' Deverin grunted. 'He said he didn't know if he was. That doesn't mean—'

'We have too much at stake here,' Payne hissed. 'Is it wise to take in a complete stranger with sorcerer's powers? What if he's just waiting until we're all asleep? What if—'

'Enough!' Aiden interrupted. 'It is exactly this kind of fear that has driven sorcerers into hiding and made them afraid of us. I repeat, Joshi has done nothing to threaten us; in fact, he's done us a huge favour by returning to us a man we know to be a friend and ally – one who has spent the last nine years risking his life to find something to help Robert. Are we going to repay that with suspicion?'

There was silence for a moment, then Deverin, who was personally responsible for Aiden's safety, said, 'Be that as it may. I will still have a guard posted outside this room and the young man will be followed wherever he goes until we can be sure.'

'Do what you must,' Aiden nodded. 'I understand your concerns – but I beg you, treat Joshi with the respect he deserves or you will do both Patric and Robert a great dishonour.' Aiden waited until he got a nod of assent from all of them, then he turned back into the room.

Though he'd been at Bleakstone a week, it still took John a few extra minutes finding the kitchens. For a place this size, they were horribly small, though, oddly, only half-used. But there was a roaring fire, and tables of food mid-preparation, and smiles on the faces of those who worked there. He quickly explained what he had come for, and he was given a tray. He gathered bread, cheese, pickled herrings, sliced red onions, a tub of mustard and some hard winter apples. Cups and a pot of brew filled the tray; he was about to ask for some help when the Bishop appeared at his side, refreshed from his nap and ready to face the evening.

'Stocking up for the next winter, Father?'

'I . . . they were hungry.' John hefted the tray and McCauly carefully removed the cups and pot, making it substantially lighter. 'Thank you.'

'I take it both Patric and Joshi are awake?'

'Yes, Your Grace.' The kitchen door was held open for them and as he called out his thanks, Aiden followed behind. 'Patric has a fever, but he's not too ill at the moment. I wouldn't like to see him travel, though. He wants to talk to you. It's hard to keep him in bed.'

'And Joshi?'

John lifted the tray to see the stairs beneath his feet. 'He says nothing, but he has removed his sword and is constantly there to help me with Patric.'

'And you Sensed nothing further from him?'

'No. But then, I haven't really tried.'

'Oh? Why not?'

John stood to one side as McCauly elbowed another door open for them. 'The truth is, I'm not all that skilled as a sorcerer. I've spent my life trying to be a good priest. I've had very little occasion to use my abilities and, as a result, I have little training and rusty talents. I know enough to see what he is, but not enough to tell you more. If Robert were here . . .'

'If Robert were here we wouldn't have this problem in the first place.'

'No, I suppose not.'

'Here, put the tray down a moment.' McCauly placed his burden onto a table set against the wall. Aiden peered down the corridor towards Patric's room, then back the way they came. His voice soft, he asked, 'What do you know of the Prophecy?'

John shrugged. These were mysteries that had concerned those who lived at the Enclave, things he'd not given much thought to. 'Only what I have been told. When Robert was nine, the Key spoke to him, and from that moment onwards, he claimed the message was personal and for him alone. Then, fifteen or so years ago, it spoke to him again, only this time everybody in the Enclave heard it. It gave him the rest of the Prophecy and the secret was out. In her letters, Jenn said that Patric had gone to Alusia in the hope of finding another group of sorcerers who might know more about the Prophecy.'

The Bishop looked down the corridor again. They couldn't see the door from here, nor the guard standing outside. He dropped his voice to a whisper. 'We believe that group quarrelled with the Cabal, who were at war with the Empire. Jenn thought the Prophecy was at the heart of the dispute.'

'But?'

'But if the incarnation of Mineah who then rose and fought with the Empire was none other than a sorcerer from that group, then that same splinter group betrayed the Cabal and brought them down.'

A cold hand gripped John's innards. 'And you think . . . Joshi could be one of these?'

'It's entirely possible. And though he's made no threatening move since he's been here, his bond to Patric is all too obvious. There is no way we can be sure of where his loyalty lies except with Patric, and we have no understanding of that. Since you are the only other sorcerer we have at hand, I would appreciate it if you could do all you can to ensure that—'

'Of course, Father.' John nodded vigorously. 'I'll do my best.'

'Hopefully, I am alarming us both for no reason. Still, I wanted you to be prepared. Come, let's feed them and see if we can learn something for our troubles.' With that, he handed John his tray and picked up the cups and pot and the two men continued on their way.

Aiden kept to his comfortable chair by the fire and watched. Though John was supposed to be feeding Patric, Joshi didn't leave him alone long enough. He never said a single word, but it seemed as though he didn't need to: more times than he could count, Aiden saw a faint smile pass between them, and occasionally a frown of concentration on Patric's face. All very odd indeed.

Once the meal was done, John cleared away the scraps and refreshed the fire, while Joshi got Patric settled once more. The fever was clearly visible through Patric's tan and his breathing was laboured. Aiden needed to be careful not to tire him.

'How do you feel?'

'Awful. Comfortable bed, though.'

'What happened?' Aiden asked. He'd put off the question long enough.

'When?' Patric frowned, then waved his hand in the air. 'Oh, you mean with my eyes? Well, that's a long story and all very boring, I'm afraid.'

'I'm sorry.'

'No, it's all right. It happened five years ago, old news to me. If it hadn't been for Joshi, I wouldn't have survived. I was forced to spend some time in a salt mine. I thought I wrote to you and said . . . oh well, never mind. There were things there, dark crystals in the soil, acids I couldn't avoid. Half of all the slaves who work in those salt mines go blind. I was lucky; I escaped. Most of them die.'

'How did you escape?'

Patric gave a short laugh. 'I pretended I was dead.' He paused to cough, starting lightly, and ending up having to sit to breathe. The moment he began, Joshi was there, holding him steady, a cup of water ready for him to sip. It was amazing, as though Joshi knew what Patric needed before he did himself. Aiden hadn't seen anything like this before, except—

'You're mindspeaking with Joshi, aren't you?'

Patric froze and John sprang to his feet from his corner seat, out of the way.

Aiden continued, determined to learn what he needed to know. 'Well? Is that something else that happened on your journey? You recall Robert and Jenn headed into Budlandi, to find out more about the Prophecy, but as they left the Palace of Bu, they encountered a group of people called the Generet. Jenn said they were all mindspeaking. Joshi is of the Generet, is he not? And somehow, you have become—'

Patric sipped the water Joshi gave him, then lay back once more. Joshi returned to his seat by the door, as relaxed as ever, as though he hadn't understood a word that had been said.

'You're suspicious. I understand that. And with good reason. Joshi is Generet. His truename is Jo'shiminal'ya Borai. It means "eyes of shimmering light". He has saved my life countless times and I would have died in the shipwreck if it hadn't been for him. He has . . . left his people to—' Patric coughed, carefully '—stay with me, to help me return here. I promise you, he would never harm you or anyone else. His people are lovers of peace and abhor violence of any kind.'

'Yet he carries a sword.'

'He is trained to protect, like all his people. Like people anywhere would protect what they are, what they have. Trust me, Aiden; he could have killed you all a dozen times over if he'd wanted to.'

Aiden didn't doubt that. 'And yet, Robert and Jenn were in danger from the Generet.'

'No, only Robert. They all make a vow upon attaining adulthood that they will seek to kill the Angel of Darkness wherever they might find him. Jenn was perfectly safe, and they would have—'

'What?'

Patric paused, tilting his head a little. Joshi watched him with a frown. Patric shook his head, as though to clear it. 'John?'

The priest was already halfway across the room. 'Yes. I feel it, too. A tremor, but not in the ground. I thought I was imagining it. It's odd. Like thunder, only—'

'What?' Aiden asked again, this time for a different reason. The other three were moving as though they could hear sounds he was deaf to. John stopped by the bed, his eyes closed, head turned towards the window where the new morning was spread out across the hills of southern Flan'har. 'Patric? John? What's going on?'

He got to his feet when neither answered, but it was Joshi who was giving him greatest concern. The young man had drawn his sword, his eyes fixed on something Aiden couldn't see. Then he let out a high-pitched keen, dropping his sword and pressing his hands to his ears. Before Aiden could move to him, both Patric and John doubled up, as though listening to something deafening.

The door banged open and the guard rushed in. Calling for help, Aiden moved first to Patric, then to John, who had fallen to the floor. The noise continued; none of the men moved, but just as Payne and the others reached the room, Joshi's keening stopped. Almost immediately, John and Patric relaxed, Patric letting out a groan of pain.

'What in the name of the gods has happened?' Payne knelt down by John, Aiden stayed with Patric, trying to get some water into him.

'This is madness. Patric, can you hear me? What has happened? What is this about?'

'Madness . . . yes—' Patric whispered, tears now flowing down his cheeks. 'I know where Robert is . . . The Enclave! By the blood, no, no—'

'John?'

The priest, a little younger and not handicapped with a fever, was quicker to recover. He sat up with help from Payne, but a mouthful of strong wine did nothing to return his colour. He just sat there shaking his head. 'We are lost. Robert has—'

'What?' Aiden demanded, now terrified to his core. 'What's happened to him?'

'He has . . .' John swallowed hard, his voice shaking, 'You know our people, sorcerers, the Salti, live safely in the Enclave. They . . . can't be Sensed there, because there is a barrier protecting them . . . Oh, sweet Mineah—'

'Go on,' Aiden urged.

'Robert has . . . has . . . broken the Enclave! He has destroyed the barrier and now the Enclave is no more. Our people are unprotected – and Nash . . . sweet Mineah, *Nash has found him!* Nash knows where the Enclave is! He will go there and—'

As the priest fell silent, only Patric's hoarse whisper could be heard in the stunned room.

'*Oh, Robert, no . . .*'

3

Robert!

Silence surrounded him; stillness filled him.

A gale of emptiness swept across his icy flesh. His body had no substance, no life of its own, no space it could occupy. He was here and somewhere else and nowhere at all; even so, he felt solid, like stone, like time, as though he would never move again.

Where had this peace come from; where, in the midst of battle, had he found such contentment?

A trickle of breeze drifted downwards, fluttering over his face, making his lips quiver, his eyelids tremble. A sweet breeze, lacking in menace, wholly without substance or force.

This space went on for ever. Endless white, placid and inconceivably infinite. Smooth, blank, entirely without expectation and failure.

Where was he?

Robert?

If he tried, if he pushed hard against the overwhelming lethargy, he could open up his Sight. It yielded pictures he could barely analyse: the great cavern of the Enclave, a huge natural hole in the mountain from which ran dozens of man-made tunnels, connecting smaller caves, home to the Salti Pazar, both sorcerers born and those with no power. This was their sanctuary, sitting beneath the peak of the Goleth Mountain, buried beneath rock and centuries of ignorance and blessed apathy.

Robert!

It was all so plain, soft and peaceful. So near, so intimate.

The cavern was full of people, their faces screwed up in anguish, something he couldn't touch, or be touched by. The whiteness protected him, cushioned him, let him feel nothing.

There were others closer to him, people he knew. His brother, Finnlay, face ashen, kneeling beside him. Andrew, the boy he would make into a king. Friends: Arlie and Martha, Finn's wife, Fiona. His mother, Margaret, and the old librarian, Acelin. So many more now, crowding around, pressing closer, looking down at him, even as he looked down at them from some height he couldn't measure.

Was he dead?

Robert!

This was the place to be, where the softness was endless and no time burned his edges; everything was wrapped up in the same whiteness, the same veil. His eyes saw better now than ever before.

There was his country, his Lusara, bleeding to death. There were his people, Lusarans and Salti alike, gasping for life. There was the face of evil, laughing within the deep caverns of his mind, as though the Angel of Darkness were here, inside the Enclave.

And . . . there was—

Robert, please, I beg you, let it go!

And there was . . . his—

His Sight flickered. He'd missed someone, a shape in his field of vision, a face beloved.

There was his hope: Jenn, with tears in her eyes, holding his hand, her lips moving, making no sound.

He must be dead, or he would hear her. Only death would keep them apart now. He'd promised her so. After so many years, he'd finally made that promise.

Robert, you're running out of time! Please, you have to let it go! Do it!

Jenn wasn't alone. The others crowded in around her, faces darker, more fearful, more angry, urgent. They were shouting in his silence, breaking it up, making him think he could hear when he was deaf, making him think he could see when his eyes were closed, making him think he could feel when he floated on whiteness.

Making him think he was alive when he was surely dead—

Noise shattered the silence in Jenn's head, but she couldn't pay any attention to it, not yet, not until she got that monstrosity away from Robert, until he started to breathe again, until she could be sure Nash couldn't find them any more.

She turned her head, not taking her eyes from Robert, nor her hand from his, and shouted over the noise, 'Finn, help me!'

She barely saw him lurch to his feet, shocked: he'd been expecting a miracle, a gift from their ancestors. Instead, they'd been cursed again, this time, devastatingly.

Jenn squeezed Robert's hand once more, urging him to let go the Key/Calyx. He held it clasped to his chest, the shape as it had just formed: the Key, an orb of matter she couldn't define, the Calyx moulded around one half of it, gold and silver, unreadable glyphs moving across the surface so fast the shapes were dizzying. They were one now, and she couldn't begin to understand what that meant. It was inconceivable that it would kill him, but he was not breathing, and he would end up so weakened he would be unable to travel, and they had to get out of here fast.

Nash was on his way. Nash. The Angel of Darkness. He who would destroy them all.

Finnlay's voice rose above the deafening cacophony bouncing off the cavern walls. Gradually the noise abated a little as Finnlay tried to make sense of what had happened: that the one thing they'd always trusted had just betrayed them in the worst possible way.

She shut her eyes, wishing she could shut out the noise with it, shut out the reality and concentrate on Robert alone. But their words darted into her like arrows, and the horror drove her to her feet to face them.

'You have to listen!' Her voice stunned them – and shocked her as well. The resonance was deep, multiple, so like the Key it was frightening. She sounded as though she were speaking through the Key itself, though the words were her own. But she had no time to think about this: they had to move, now, and they wouldn't without her orders.

With Finnlay's wide eyes on her, she continued in the uncomfortable silence, 'We don't have time for this! The Enclave is no longer protected and invisible. Nash knows exactly where we are, and staying and fighting him would be suicidal.'

A rumble of noise rose at that, but she spoke over it, relentlessly driving them to silence once more. 'He's no more than a week away, possibly less. We have an evacuation plan already set up. Now we need to put it into motion. Please, go now!'

With that, she turned and knelt down beside Robert once more, taking his hand, touching his motionless face, feeling the cold flesh beneath her fingers. She closed her eyes, reaching out, whispering mindspeech to him, but it was like talking into nothing. He couldn't hear her, couldn't feel her, couldn't be touched by her. The Key had him at last, and it wasn't letting go. She could only pray that he would prove to be the stronger.

Finnlay raised his hands to still the noise after Jenn's short speech. She'd already turned back to help Robert, leaving him to deal with the chaos and terror of a people suddenly bereft of their security. He knew he had to say something. They needed more from Jenn, but until Robert was safe, she was unable to give it. He could see the other Councillors trying to get to him, so there would be some order, some framework to this escape, but he was trapped on the dais, shock still rattling through him.

How could he tell these people what to do when he didn't know himself?

But the decision was taken from him: a voice spoke up, young and a little

29

shaky, but very brave, a boy he had thought unfit to rule. 'Please, you need to start moving now. If Nash is only a week away, that means those headed east need to be gone by tomorrow in order to be clear of the mountains in time. We can't afford to leave anything here he can use against us.'

'Against *us*?' a voice rose from the crowd.

Andrew frowned a little, but pushed on, his voice growing stronger, his expression intense, as though he could read these people's innermost thoughts and was speaking directly to them. As he spoke, his confidence grew, and so did theirs. 'You're all afraid, and with good reason. You've all had experience out there, been hunted yourselves, lost those you loved. It's been a long time since you could leave the Enclave in safety, but . . .'

Finnlay held his breath, hearing the silence in the great cavern, almost hearing the heartbeats of the five hundred souls listening.

'But out there, it's not as bad as you think. There aren't Guildesmen with Bresails behind every hill, waiting to capture and torture you. Sorcery is no longer illegal. If you take care, if you follow the plans, if you stick to your stories, you'll get to safety, I promise. You don't need to be afraid. We do have time to get away. Let's make the most of it.'

Before he finished, Finnlay was there, his arm around the boy's shoulder, supporting in a way he'd never dared before. He wanted to express his pride in his nephew, but the moment was gone. Martha stepped onto the platform, her calm methodical approach giving form to the work they had to do.

'Very well, people. You all know what you need to be doing. Those heading south can take another day, but be careful; you've got more of the mountains to cross through. Those taking the heavy baggage west, meet me in the Council Chamber and we'll set out the order of transport. Within the month, we all meet up again at Bleakstone Castle, in Flan'har. Let's get moving. Now!'

And just like that, the tide shifted and turned; people shuffled off, then began to walk more purposefully as they realised how much they had to do and how little time they had.

'Robert!'

Finnlay turned back to Jenn to find her still intent on his brother. He rushed to Robert's side to see his chest rise and fall a little. Robert was finally breathing, shallow and sharp perhaps, but breathing nonetheless.

'Jenn? How is he?'

She shook her head, eyes moist but focused. 'He can't mindspeak me, but I think Nash still has some link to him.'

'What happened?'

Jenn was silent a moment, her eyes on Robert, her gaze turning inwards.

She frowned, drawing dark brows together. 'I'm not sure. I felt him fly, completely connected to the Key, as though they were made for each other, but then . . . the barrier began to drop—'

'How? Why?'

She looked up sharply. 'I don't know. Perhaps the Calyx needed the power, or— I don't know. But Robert tried to stop it, tried to separate them, and that's when . . . Serin's blood, Robert, please wake up!'

'Jenn, what happened? We need to know.'

'He tried to stop it.' Jenn shifted, gained a better grip on Robert's hand. 'And the Key did something, I couldn't see what – and the next thing I knew, Nash had found him. He must have been Seeking at that moment . . . I wish I'd never . . .'

Finnlay reached out and squeezed her arm, keeping her focused. 'Is that the problem? Is that why Robert can't wake up?'

'I don't know!' Jenn snapped, taking a deep breath. She looked up in apology, but he waved it away. 'I can't even work out what he's doing. He's stopped trying to separate the Key and Calyx at least. But it's projecting in some way, and that's how Nash can see him – us. I think he's trying to break that connection, between the Key and Nash.'

'What's the point? If Nash already knows where we are?'

'Oh, Finn! Are we going to leave the Key here? We'll take it with us. If Robert can't break the connection, then no matter where we go, Nash will follow, and with Robert in this condition, we will have no means to fight him. I don't know what to do.'

As Andrew came up behind her and put his hands on her shoulders, Jenn leaned back into his strength for a moment, giving Finnlay time to think.

This had all begun because Robert had finally found the Calyx. It had been hidden in the shape of a book, but when Robert and Jenn had touched it together, the shape had shifted and changed, revealing the Calyx, bowl-shaped, glittering and ancient. He'd thought – they'd all thought – that the Calyx would give them answers, would show them how they could live outside the Enclave in peace. But it hadn't had enough power to work for more than a few moments, so Jenn had said they should take it to the Key, because everything they knew suggested the two were supposed to work together.

But the moment Robert had approached with the Calyx, the Key had taken over, driving him forward until the two had joined, and tragedy had struck, bringing the wrath of Nash down on them all.

Finnlay knew what the answer was; he just wished he didn't. He met Jenn's gaze. 'I think the only way to get it away from Robert is if you take it.'

'He'd never let me.'

'No. But you might be able to help him break the connection.'

'How?'

'By touching the Key. By going to wherever Robert is. He can't do it on his own, can he?'

Jenn shook her head slowly, her gaze going back to Robert.

Finnlay pressed her. 'Do you know what he's trying to do?'

'Make some kind of mask, as though he can recreate what the Key did to protect us. I don't know that he can do it, and not in time. I just wish—'

'You have to intervene, Jenn. There's no other option.'

'Mother.' Andrew knelt beside her. 'If the connection is with Nash, what if you can't break it? What if you get trapped like Robert?'

Jenn didn't seem to hear him. Her hand moved out, reaching to the glistening surface of the Key, held so close against Robert's chest.

It never got there. Andrew snatched her hand away, pulling her around to face him. His voice was harsh and urgent, sounding much older than normal. 'Mother! Listen to me! Robert said . . . he said he couldn't trust you, because you were joined to the Key and he couldn't trust it. He said you weren't on the same side. What if . . . ?'

Jenn touched the side of his face gently. 'I can't leave him there. Finnlay's right. Even if we know nothing about this, the one thing of which we can be certain is that everything here must be done by Robert and me. Please, love, move back.'

Andrew began to shake his head, but a hand appeared on his shoulder and Finnlay looked up. His mother, Lady Margaret, was urging Andrew to his feet, her face worried, her lips moving as if in prayer.

Finnlay looked around. They were almost alone now, but he could hear noise coming from all directions as people began the awesome task of evacuating a home the Salti had had for almost six hundred years.

'Finn,' Jenn whispered, dragging his gaze back to hers. 'If this doesn't work—'

'It will.' He said with a finality he dredged up from somewhere. 'It has to.'

She nodded slightly, her eyes fathomless. 'I'll make sure it does.' With that, she closed her eyes, reached out and touched the Key.

Cold instantly filtered through her fingertips, along the palm of her hand and swept up her arm to fill her from head to toe. In a moment, she was frozen, barren, solid and immobile.

She could see nothing, feel nothing, hear nothing. No, not nothing. There was something there, in the whiteness. A half-familiar rhythm, pounding in the background, softly. A heartbeat? But whose was it – Robert's, or hers?

Was he here? Of course, that required an answer to where *here* was, and she didn't have one. Over the last eight years, since she'd become Jaibir of the Enclave, since she'd been chosen by the Key and joined to it, she'd spent hours with it, talking, constantly linked to it, always feeling it in the corner of her mind. Not once in all that time had she ever been truly alone, and the Key never let her forget that. So why couldn't she feel it now? Why, when she was actually touching the Key for the first time ever, was there no sense of that connection? Had Nash done this, or the Calyx? Or was Robert—

Can you hear me? Robert? Can you answer me? She sent the query out gently. There was no way to guess how much Nash could use the connection, and they were already in enough trouble as it was. *Robert?*

There was no response, but an overwhelming feeling of his presence, as though he was there, but couldn't talk yet.

Robert, let me help. I know the Key, I understand how it works. We're joined. It's supposed to respond to me. If you let me, I know I can help. But you have to let me. I know you're trying to block Nash's access, but in doing so, you're blocking my connection to the Key and I think we need that now. Robert? Please, Robert, I need an answer. I need to know you're—

J . . . Jenn?

The word came out with so much effort, Jenn instantly felt guilty for forcing it from him. If he'd been using his voice, he would have sounded as frozen as she, as though the cold were making him stutter. But it was more than that. It was the effort he was making, the power it was taking from him to do this small thing.

J . . . Jenn. He tried again and this time she could feel him closer, as though he were standing just behind her. She opened her eyes and tried to See, but the white affected everything, pulling mist over shapes so thick they became invisible. Except . . . There! A shadow, something she could focus on. It shifted and fluttered, lifted and sank, the surface rippling constantly, as though it were alive.

She knew what she was looking at, though how, she couldn't guess. This was how Robert was protecting them, why Nash was no longer talking to them. Somehow he'd used raw power to form a tight mask around the aura of the Key/Calyx, so that whatever connection it had to *anything* was utterly blocked. And the effort to keep it going was killing him.

Robert, she began quickly, seeing and Seeing what needed to be done, *you can't do it this way. I know it's your first instinct, to use your own powers to shield and protect everyone, but this won't last long, and you'll be dead at the end of it.*

33

No choice. Can't . . . stop.

No, but we can find an alternative together.

Alternative? How?

Remember how every Salti uses their powers through an ayarn*? They use it to focus and shield? The* ayarn *prevents a power backlash but also provides just enough power to do the work, without draining the user?*

Yes. In his tone, she could tell he was already understanding what she wanted to try. Good.

If you can relinquish control just a little, to let me in, I think I can use the Key the same way.

But you never used an ayarn.

No, but you can show me what to do, how to make one.

Can't make the Key . . . ayarn. *Not possible.*

Then how?

Silence for a moment as he thought, and in that silence she could hear his heartbeat falter a little, feel the thickness of the fog grow more dense. They had no time left.

Robert . . .

Can do it . . . won't last, but it will work.

How long will it last?

Perhaps a few days? After that—

We'll worry about that later. What do I do?

There was a long pause, then finally he spoke again, and the tone in his silent voice was full of regret. *This is going . . . to hurt.*

Finnlay knew he needed to get moving, to help Fiona and the girls, to start packing up all the books and papers he'd been working on over the last . . . by the gods, how long had he been living here? Sixteen years? A lifetime! He'd been married, had three daughters, lost many friends, fought in a war and known the depths of despair and heights of happiness in that time. And now he was packing up his life here and leaving. He'd always wanted to leave the confines of the Enclave, but he'd had in mind to take his children and his wife back home to Dunlorn, where they could enjoy the comforts and privileges of the noble House to which they belonged. He'd planned to take them on a scenic tour of his beautiful Lusara and show them all the places he'd loved as a boy. Instead, they were running from an evil he had seen with his own eyes, an evil which had nearly destroyed him. There would be no triumphant return to Dunlorn, no life spent in freedom. If they made it to Bleakstone alive, they would be very lucky indeed.

He got to his feet, stretching out cramped muscles. Now the initial shock had worn off a little, he could begin to think, remember what he'd noted down, what steps he needed to take in the event they needed to evacuate. Family first, then library, school and . . .

Jenn moved. She was kneeling beside Robert, holding his hand, her other hand on the Key. She began to sway, her face pale, a line of sweat on her forehead. Robert looked like a ghost. His strong face was white, his skin as translucent as the wings of a moth. His dark hair clung to the sweat on his forehead. The rest of him, so powerful, so commanding, lay prone and unmoving; struck down by a power they'd all feared for a long time. He lay on the stone platform beside Jenn, barely breathing, the Key/Calyx clasped to his chest as though it would become part of him.

Suddenly, Robert hissed and Jenn frowned. Jenn let out a moan, in pain. Finnlay sank to his knees once more, but before he could say anything, the air around them began to shimmer, trembling like new leaves on a windy day, glittered with silver and frost. The shimmering spread out directly from the Key, in a spherical shape, moving faster and faster, further and further until, with an audible snap, it vanished.

'By the gods!' Jenn breathed, opening her eyes. Instantly, she moved down to Robert, but he was looking up at the ceiling, blinking rapidly, breathing harshly.

'Help me.'

The words were barely out of his mouth before Finnlay was there, Andrew and Margaret with him. While Robert clutched the Key/Calyx to his chest, they helped him to his feet. He swayed, closing his eyes, breathing hard through his nose, as though he was about to be sick.

Jenn stood before him, her fingers lightly on his arm, her gaze fixed on his face, but it was to Andrew she spoke. 'Go fetch a chair, or a small table or something. And a cushion or blanket. Something soft.'

Andrew turned and ran into the Council Chamber, returning moments later with a wooden chair and a cushion. He placed the chair down before Robert, the cushion on the seat. Then Robert, as though he could see through his closed eyes, turned slowly, bent and laid the Key/Calyx on the cushion. He stood over it, maintaining his touch, then he let it go; instantly, his knees buckled, but Finnlay caught him and eased him into another chair. A cup of wine was pressed into Robert's hand and he took two long swallows before looking up and studying each of them. He frowned, and glanced around the cavern, noticing the increased noise echoing through the Enclave. For a while his eyes were barely focusing before moving on again; a few more deep breaths and they began to steady.

'They're getting ready to leave,' Jenn said quietly, her fingers once again resting lightly on his arm, as though she were afraid to lose physical contact with him. 'What do you want to do first?'

'Wait. Wait a moment.' Finnlay held up his hands. 'Are you going to tell me what happened? How did the Key and Calyx join in the first place? I thought the idea was to simply use the Key's power to operate the Calyx. This wasn't supposed to—'

'Finn.' Robert rested his head on the back of the chair. His colour was returning a little and his voice grated, but he still looked like he'd fought a terrible battle; it was impossible to guess whether he'd won or lost. 'I wish I could explain everything that just happened – but I can't. Not yet. Not until I can . . .' He swallowed hard and Jenn moved closer.

'Is it holding?' she murmured.

'Yes. It's just not so easy, that's all. We need to get moving as soon as we can.'

Now Finnlay remembered what it was like being around these two. Not only did they mindspeak; some of the time, they didn't even seem to need speech of any kind. 'Nobody's going anywhere until I get some answers. What is holding? What did you just do?'

'A trick.' The ghost of a smile drifted across Robert's face. He ran tired hands through his long hair and shook his head as though to clear it. As each moment went by, his strength seemed to be returning. 'I . . . Jenn made the Key believe she was turning it into an *ayarn*.'

'What? But that's impossible – the power required would be simply enormous!'

'Only if she actually *was* turning it into an *ayarn* – assuming she could. No, she's just made it think she has by performing the first four of the seven steps required to make one.'

'And?'

A dry chuckle escaped Robert at that moment. He looked sideways at Jenn and she shook her head, acknowledging the humour in the situation. 'Because I was attached to the Key at the time, I can use it like an *ayarn* and make the mask through it. It will hold for a few hours at least.'

'Serin's blood!' Finnlay swore. He put his hands on his hips and walked away for a moment. This was stupid. 'You mean to say that after all those years when I begged you to Sand the Circle and let the Key choose you, when you deliberately did everything you could to avoid contact with the Key, when you virtually ran away from the power you could have had, you are, right now, actually—'

'In complete control of it? Yes.' Robert was laughing, although there was fear mixed in with the mirth. 'Ironic, isn't it?'

Jenn added, 'He can't control all of it without actually joining with the

Key. At the moment, the join is about half what I have with it. It's enough for Robert to create a stable mask over the Key. Enough to stop Nash from seeing it – and us.'

'A mask? Then you can't move the Key?'

'Yes,' Robert said, getting to his feet. 'Of course I can move it. I just have to move the mask with it. And that means I can't go anywhere without it.'

Finnlay looked at Jenn, but her eyes told him nothing. When he turned back to his brother, he could see the lines of effort etched around his eyes. 'And what happens when you can't hold it any more?'

'Why, then Nash will be able to see us again. So—' Jenn murmured.

'So,' Robert's voice turned hard, 'we need to leave tonight, before dark. Heading due east, directly for Bleakstone. If I can hold the mask long enough, we'll find an alternative means to hide it before he can find us.'

'And if not?'

Robert smiled grimly at him. 'Then we could be in a little trouble.'

4

A rattling wind creaked through the treetops, knocking ancient branches together, sounding like old bones echoing in a pauper's forest. The house beneath the scraping branches stood alone and quiet. Inside, in the room bare of any furniture, Nash lay on the wooden floor, still, naked, and more whole than he'd ever been in his life. He gasped in a deep breath, then another, bringing his eyes open. Shock left him dizzy, nauseated and trembling.

The connection feeding him, sweeping him up into the heavens, making him fly: it had been broken somehow.

By whom – the Enemy? Or the Ally, still determined to have a say in her own fate? No person alive other than they would have the power to sever that connection.

Unless it had been the Key itself cutting off the lifeblood . . .

But how thrilling, how incredibly exhilarating it had been, for those precious few moments: to fly so far, so high, so fast. To soar through the nothing between them, to keep going, to hold his breath and then to see, in the Seeker's mist, to actually *see* the Enemy, the Douglas, holding onto the Key, actually touching the thing he'd been chasing all his life—

To finally *find* it – and to show the Enemy, at last, that he could never win.

By the blood of his ancestors, of Bayazit of Yedicale, who had helped create the Key, who had made the Word of Destruction, down through all those who had followed him, by the blood of Thraxis himself: the journey was almost over. He was so close to victory that he could almost taste it, almost feel it in the fingers which tingled even now with new life.

The nausea subsided in the wake of his joy. Shaky with his new-found strength, Nash rolled to his side and carefully rose from the bare wooden floor. Again dizziness swept through him, but he was blind to it.

'Taymar!'

A heartbeat later, the door opened and his devoted servant slipped into the room, fresh clothes draped over one arm, a cup of wine in the other. As Nash dressed, Taymar kept his silence. It was not the first time this man had aided Nash in regenerating; perhaps it would be the last.

'How do you feel, Master?'

Nash smiled, emptied the cup in one swallow and handed it back. 'Invincible.'

Though his eyes were dulled by the Bonding, Taymar could match Nash's smile. 'Your men are waiting, Master.' With that, he stepped back and opened the door. Nash walked through, emerging into a small sitting-room, where an unexpected richness of quality in the neat furnishings brought him back to the present.

Valena. The woman who had pledged herself to his cause, who had shared his bed for many years, who had borne his daughter, had, in the end, betrayed him – just as he'd always known she would.

'Where is she?' he asked softly, almost enjoying not knowing. The prospect of what he would do to her was a pleasure just tasted and not yet devoured. He would take his time with her, because he could.

'Lady Valena is outside, Master.'

Nash's gaze flickered to the open door and the dank, grey view he could see through it. Wind kept the trees moving; all else was as still as death.

He stepped outside and lifted his face to the air, savouring the cool feather-touch upon his skin. He saw the wood and the hills. He saw his men and horses waiting for him at the bottom of the clearing. He saw the trees barren of leaves, their gnarled arms reaching to a sky they'd never touch. He saw that sky thick and grey, three days after the last time he'd seen it, before he'd taken in the blood.

Ah, such blood. Such power. His child, and Valena's. The blood still fresh, still warm, still bubbling with bright power. And now it was all his.

He laughed. The trees were old. He was young. Again. And this time, he would stay young. He moved, feeling his newly awakened body tingle with fresh life, needing to run with the dry wind, to stretch and push, to exert and expend the hidden energy within. He had so much strength now, so much power at his fingertips.

How could the child's blood have done this – surely all this was beyond Prophecy?

Of course, *this* child hadn't been in the Prophecy. No, the child he was *supposed* to use should have been born of his blood and the Ally, or better still, of Ally and Enemy. It was clear, in all he'd read, that such a child would give him immortality; he didn't know what this one would give him. It mattered not. Now he was more than young enough to sire another child; Valena herself was not yet too old to bear another – assuming he let her live.

'Bring her here.'

She did not struggle. Though bound hand and foot, though drugged half-senseless, her defiance shone through; her eyes pierced him. This was no betrayal to her but obedience to some higher truth.

Flanking her were two Malachi, *Bonded* Malachi, though whether she could tell the difference he didn't know. Even so, she would feel their devotion to him keenly. They drew her close, then forced her down on her knees before him. At his gesture, they removed her gag; she swallowed hard at its sudden absence.

She was still beautiful: lush honey-coloured hair, eyes of darkest brown, flawless skin, a mouth to invite seduction, a body to fulfill it. She had been the first woman he had ever touched, the first to make him weaken. Even as he'd taken her, he'd revelled in the danger in her eyes, the risk that one day she might try to kill him.

But even he had not thought her capable of infanticide. 'You failed,' he began with a shrug. 'You must know DeMassey is dead. That's why you . . .'

That was why she'd done it: because her protector was no longer around, though why DeMassey had gone to such lengths to protect another man's child, he couldn't begin to guess.

'You know you will be hanged for murdering your own child?'

Her eyes blinked slowly, the result of the sleeping drug which had kept her under control while he was busy. 'Hanged? You think I fear death after what you've just done? Hah. You underestimate me, as always.' She turned her head away, but couldn't stop the heavy tears which fell from her eyes. She neither blinked them away, nor moved to wipe them.

'Why did you lose faith in me?' Nash asked, genuinely curious. 'I never turned on you. I gave you all you asked for. I even left you alone these last few years, hoping that you would tire of DeMassey and return to me.'

'Liar!' The heat was drugged away from her voice, but the bitterness remained. 'I was of no use to you, that's all. Just as I will be the moment you get your hands on Jennifer Ross, your Ally. I was always destined to be cast aside, so don't pretend otherwise. I just wish I'd seen it sooner.'

'Or you would not have borne my daughter?'

Valena blinked slowly again, meeting his gaze, but seeing nothing of him. Her voice dropped to a weary whisper. 'I wish I'd killed her in my womb. She . . . she was a monster . . . just like her father.'

Nash laughed, triumphant. 'You hated her! Like you hate me! Now I understand.'

'You understand nothing!' Battling the drugs, Valena struggled to her feet, fury blazing from eyes which knew him too well. 'She was my child and I loved her. So did Luc, something you will never understand. I did it because—' she paused, swallowing a sob, 'because I knew what a monster like you would do with your own flesh and blood. After all, didn't you murder your own father and regenerate from his blood?'

Nash raised his hand to strike her, but paused. DeMassey had done this.

40

He'd lain in his bed, badly injured, deliberately taunting Nash, provoking him in order to— He would not put Valena out of her misery by conveniently killing her. This heinous crime, this *betrayal* demanded vengeance. She would suffer before he killed her. He would see that light of defiance in her eyes finally die; only then would he be satisfied.

He turned his back to her, facing the house. Raising his hands, he let loose the power which thudded through him, making his whole body sing. Shaking with the pleasure of it, he clapped his hands together – and the house exploded into flames. Even as a great cloud of smoke plumed into the air, he turned back to face her.

'You will never be free,' he murmured. 'There is no one left to save you. I am your only path to release.'

For a moment, she blinked at him, as though gathering her strength. Then, finally, she hissed, 'There is nothing left in this world that I love. You can do nothing to harm me more.'

Nash gestured to his men, his gaze still on Valena. 'And now you will see what I have always tried to tell you: love is irrelevant. I think you'll be surprised just how much harm I can do to you.'

He turned to his Malachi. 'Take her and drug her again. The man who lets her escape will die in terror.'

'Yes, Master,' the Malachi responded in harmony.

As they dragged Valena back to the waiting horses, Taymar approached. 'Master, the priest escaped. Do you wish to send men after him?'

'Priest?' Nash frowned. What priest? Oh, yes, the priest who had killed the child, hoping to keep her blood from Nash, when all he'd done was prepare it for him. So the priest had escaped. Godfrey, wasn't it? *Bishop* Godfrey? Murder came within his purview, did it? 'No, don't waste the effort. Chances are he'll just head straight back to Marsay, so I can find him when I need to.'

'Then you're not going to—'

Nash swung a fur-lined cloak over his shoulders. 'To what end? For a man like that, killing an innocent child will make him suffer more than anything I could do. And if I killed him now, then I would lose the sport later. Besides, I have something much more urgent to attend to.'

He turned back to the blazing wreck that was Valena's house. In the smoke he could scent hope. 'Send to Ransem Castle. I want all of my Bonded Malachi, every man and woman I have. They are to meet up with me on the ride west.'

'West, Master?'

'Yes,' Nash smiled, heading for his horse, 'west. To kill the Enemy and take the Key.'

5

Finnlay reached the door to his rooms to find it open and, inside, a mess of movement. Bags and boxes were already piled up. The bedroom doors were flung wide, his daughters running from one place to the other, their faces white with fear. The fire had been extinguished, leaving an ugly sickly smell that clung and lingered. All the shapes he'd become familiar with, the combinations of colours and patterns – all the things that had made him recognise this as home had gone.

'How long have we got?' Fiona emerged from their bedroom and placed another bag on the floor by the door. 'Are we taking your books with us, or will you leave them to go with the library tomorrow?'

Her voice was harsh, her gaze uncompromising. Her face, softened a little with the babies and age over the years since they'd married, was contained. Reality had never been so hard.

Without saying a word, Finnlay went to her, pulled her into his arms and held her close. A heartbeat later the stiffness in her body evaporated and she melted against him, needing to give comfort as much as to receive it.

Nobody but their daughters ever saw this gentle and vulnerable side to Fiona. Finn was glad: he'd never felt more loved. The embrace lasted only a moment, then she was pulling back, looking up at him, her eyes moist but full of tenderness. 'Your brother.'

'My brother,' he nodded, conceding.

'Again.'

'Aye, again. What can I say? At least he's consistent.'

She gave him an ironic smile, then asked, 'How much time have we got?'

'Two hours. We must travel light, so we leave the bulk of our goods to go with the carts. Take only those things we can't live without. Leave all the furniture.'

'Do you know where we're heading?'

'Flan'har, I should imagine, but we didn't really discuss it. How much more have we to do here?'

'Almost done.'

'Good. Then we get the girls fed, and rugged up for the ride. I'll organise provisions and get the horses saddled.' He paused, then kissed her lightly. 'I love you,' he whispered, then turned and left before he could see more tears in her eyes.

This was, after all, the only home she had ever known.

Andrew pressed himself against the passage wall, lifting his feet out of the way as two men carried a heavy wooden chest between them, followed by a woman with her arms wrapped around an enormous cloth bundle. Once they were past, he hurried on, some part of his head counting the seconds until he had to be back with his mother.

He couldn't just get back on his horse and ride away; he'd not even been here a whole day yet. He'd hardly had a chance to see anyone, even Liam's family; he had wanted to tell them how sorry he was about the boy's death. How could he forget that night when he'd helped Liam perform a dimensional shift? The older boy had looked at him with respect, had treated him like a friend, like he belonged here, with the rest of them, like he was Salti born and bred and that it didn't matter if he didn't have any powers of his own; they would accept him anyway.

Only it no longer mattered whether or not he was accepted by the Salti. The Enclave was dissolving before his eyes, melting like snow on a warm spring day. His chance to become a true member had vanished that easily. And all the people he'd once thought of as his friends by default were about to lose their home – the only chance of safety they could ever have.

Andrew had always had two homes: Maitland and here. When he rode down the mountain today, he would have none.

Horror lent his feet wings. He began to run, skipping down stairs he knew by heart, swinging around corners balanced without thought, climbing more stairs three at a time and landing at the top without breaking his breath. He knew this place, but now it looked different: now it felt different, smelled different and sounded different. He had to find Guy and talk to him before—

'Andrew?'

He skidded to a halt. Guy was standing in the doorway to his family's rooms. He wore a cloak and his riding boots and carried a saddle-bag weighted down by something angular – probably books.

'I came to find you,' Andrew gushed, suddenly breathless. It was so good to see his best friend again; he had so much to talk about – and there was no time at all. He needed to know what Guy thought about all this . . . and about the whole thing with Robert and Kenrick and this assumption that he would be the next King. Guy was bound to laugh himself silly at the idea, and if he did, Andrew would feel much better—

But there was no time for any of that, only for a goodbye.

43

'When are you leaving?' Guy rushed forward and dumped his bag on the floor beside two more. Andrew could hear Guy's parents moving around inside their rooms, gathering the last of their things.

'I have only a few minutes. My mother's expecting me. We have to head out with the Key . . . or the Calyx, or whatever it is now.'

'You're going with Robert?'

Andrew nodded, unable to dismiss the tiny, pleased feeling inside him at Guy's awe. Though he knew Robert better now, he still felt that same awe himself from time to time – in fact, knowing him better only made it worse, for now he was sure it wasn't all his imagination. 'Finnlay and Fiona and the girls are coming with us as well as Lady Margaret, Arlie and Martha and their children.'

Guy was almost jumping up and down with glee. 'Us too! Us too!'

'Really?' Andrew grabbed his friend's shoulder hard. 'But why?'

'You know my mother fought with Robert at Shan Moss. She said Robert needs a few strong fighters to protect the Key, in case the mask falls and Nash finds us. My father wouldn't let her go alone, and you know what a brilliant archer he is, and Robert said this was not the time to be splitting up families – so we're all going the same way!'

Andrew's face hurt, he was grinning so hard. 'I'd better go. I'll see you up there!' With that, he turned and ran again, this time his feet touching the ground more lightly. But as he reached one of the main corridors, he came to a complete halt.

The tunnel was choked with people, with bags and boxes, with trolleys and children. Up ahead were voices he recognised: Martha and other Councillors, calling out for calm, for order. Their words vanished into the deafening rumble of panic.

Andrew once again pressed himself against the wall to let people by, to avoid getting crushed, but he stumbled, and there were too many people around to stop his fall. Suddenly he was on the ground, with no room to move, no room to stand again, with too many feet shuffling around him.

Abruptly a hand grabbed his elbow hard, hauling him to his feet without ceremony. He barely had time to register who it was before the voice commanded silence. Seconds later, everyone came to a halt as every head turned to face Robert.

'Is this panic?' he asked without preamble. 'Is this what all our training, all our discipline is for? So that we can panic at the first test? All those hours we spent working out the best and most practical means of evacuating, all for nothing. Instead, we're going to allow a little panic to kill our children, is that it? Did none of you see the Jaibir's son get knocked to the ground?'

The silence had more depth then. Some eyes shot to him, others looked away. He didn't dare to guess which was shame and which anger.

Robert continued, 'Those of you who are scheduled to leave now, move to the walls. Those who leave in the next wave, head back to your rooms. I promise you, Nash is too far away to get here in less than a week, even if he barely stops to rest. We will have the Enclave empty in fewer than three days – because we refuse to panic. It will be your patience which defeats him here, not your urgency.' With his voice gentler, he added, 'Go, now.'

And the noise rose again, but this was subdued, more constructive. Andrew remained by Robert, saying nothing, standing there and watching a frightened people pretend they were, instead, very, very brave.

He knew exactly how they felt.

As the throng began to clear, Robert murmured in his ear, 'Let's get moving. Your mother will be waiting for us.'

Jenn moved from one horse to another, checking saddles and bags and straps and doing all she could to ignore the cold day, the sharp gusts of wind and the bare stone of the mountain-top around her.

She would never come here again.

Irritatedly, she pulled in her bottom lip, deliberately catching it between her teeth. The pain cleared her thoughts for a moment and she drew in a deep breath, willing calm. She had erred on the side of caution and chosen to wear a pair of boy's trousers; her hair was already bound up in plaits to sit beneath a cap. Sometimes her diminutive size was a curse, and there were moments like these when the instant disguise gave her more safety than anything else, and she would be able to move freely in these clothes where she would be trapped by a gown of any kind. Though she'd said nothing to the others, she knew this trip would be dangerous. It didn't matter that Robert was with them – being bound to the Key as he was at the moment, there was no way to guess how much his powers would be hampered if they should come across Nash, and if they did . . .

She walked towards the next horse as others arrived. There was already so much activity on the field, it was hard to see the order, but here and there a voice was raised, instructions were given and everything slotted into place. It all appeared so damned *organised* – and so unbelievably horrible at the same time. They were afraid, but they were still working, still ruling their own lives, working together for their freedom.

These brave people, these vulnerable souls had trusted her. *Robert* had trusted her, and she'd failed them all. Robert had warned there could be danger taking the Calyx to the Key, but she'd insisted, her confidence at winning Robert back blinding her to the possible consequences. But she had felt so sure that it was the right thing to do.

And now she was leaving. Leaving *them*.

She blinked, her eyes abruptly moist. Though she'd tried to stop it, she was staring at the mountain-top, the open field surrounded by a crown of stone, and the entry tunnels leading to the caves beneath. She would never see this place again, never feel at home in it, never feel trapped by it again.

With a gasp, her eyes widened. Had she done it deliberately, because, deep down, she'd felt trapped living here, tied to the Key?

By the gods! How could she have done something so—

'Stop it.'

Jenn started as a gentle hand squeezed her shoulder. She blinked away tears and looked at Martha, who was reading Jenn all too easily.

'It's not your fault,' she said compassionately.

Jenn laughed dryly. 'You don't know that. You weren't there. It is my fault. If I hadn't—'

'If you hadn't, Robert would have found a reason to sooner or later. You know that as well as I do.'

'And if he'd done it later, he would have ensured there would be no danger. The Enclave would still be intact and—'

'You can't know that, Jenn!' Martha came around and stood before her, voice firm but quiet. She knew what this day would mean to all Salti. 'From the sound of it, the Key and Calyx were meant to work together like this and nothing either you or Robert could have done would have changed that. Blaming yourself will only make you suffer.'

'They will hate me. They'll hate Robert.'

Martha's eyebrows rose. 'Possibly. Then again, maybe there are those here who welcome the push to get out of here. You know there are many Salti who have found living here as little more than a prison – Finnlay being one of the most obvious. Now there is no reason to stay and every reason to go.'

Jenn shook her head and turned to gaze once more at the stone peak above. Finnlay was the only Salti in history to have climbed it in winter; only twelve people had ever climbed it at all. Andrew was the youngest.

'Our strength,' she murmured, 'has always been seated in our need to stay together. To work together, to find solutions together. We have survived hundreds of years because of that. Even before Selar and Vaughn with his Bresail hunting us down, most Salti lived here, with only a few out there, in Lusara. We stuck together because we had to, because there was no choice, because we could never survive separately. Now . . . now there is no choice but to survive on our own, because staying together will be the end of everything, not just the Salti.'

'And so far, staying together has brought us nothing but further imprisonment.'

Jenn blinked at that.

'It's too soon to assume this can only end in tragedy,' Martha continued.

'Please, Martha. I appreciate the thought, but don't try to make this a good thing. Not today.'

'Jenn, not all change is bad.'

'Then why do I feel like—'

'Like what?'

She started at the deep voice which was like a warm touch on a cold day. Before she could even move, Robert was beside her, letting her feel his presence. Andrew was with him, looking scared and trying not to. By the gods, he'd lost so much in the last week. She could only pray he would lose no more for a while.

'You feel like?' Robert insisted, with a glance at Martha. 'Like you're deserting them?' Jenn met his eyes: deep green reflecting her own thoughts back to her. Yes, he would understand exactly how she was feeling. Hadn't he blamed himself for every evil in Lusara for the last thirty years?

When Jenn didn't answer, Robert turned to Andrew and Martha. 'You'd better mount up. We'll start heading through the gate in a moment.' As soon as they were alone, he put his hand on her arm, but she forestalled his words of comfort. With her heart thumping in her chest, she murmured, 'I can't go with you. I have to stay.'

His grip tightened. He looked around to see if anyone was watching them. They were surrounded by horses, and those who would accompany them; those from whom they would have to keep so many secrets.

Sure now that nobody would overhear them, Robert turned his gaze back to Jenn, who shook at little at the determination in his eyes.

'You're not staying here. I won't let you.'

'I'm the Jaibir, Robert.' Jenn tried not to hiss, but she felt so stretched: first Robert taking Andrew, then the attack on Maitland and the Malachi trying to steal Andrew from her, killing men to stop them, getting injured in the process, then . . . Bella and Lawrence being murdered by those—

And now this. The destruction of the Enclave. *She* had done this, and she should be the one to face up to this responsibility. Wasn't that what being Jaibir was all about?

'I *have* to stay, don't you see? I should be the last to leave. I did this to them. They need me now, especially when you take the Key away. Please, Robert. Don't fight me on this.'

He stared at her a moment, then let her go. He straightened up, a muscle in his jaw jumping where he was clenching it so tight. With a sigh, he closed

47

his eyes and shook his head. When he looked at her again, that sharp-edged determination was back, leaving room for nothing else. 'No,' he said quietly. 'You're coming with me. You'll stay by me until I say otherwise.'

'But—'

He leaned close once more. 'If you stay, I stay. If I stay, the Key stays and Nash comes to find us now, when we are least ready to face him. The choice is yours, but you should know, I don't care whose Ally you are.'

He turned away then and gave the order to ride. As those around them pulled away, Jenn stared at Robert with an open mouth. He shrugged. 'What are you always telling me about blaming myself? Well? Are we staying or leaving?'

'Damn you, Robert,' she grunted before turning to her horse. But there was less heat in her voice than there could have been; she owed him too much truth to deny his. She swung up into the saddle and watched him do the same.

And then he smiled. A small smile, just for her, and much of the darkness inside her lifted then. 'Let's get moving.'

It was only when he turned his horse for the gate that she saw the bag strapped around his shoulders: an old, well-oiled leather bag with a large, rounded shape nestled inside, carefully wrapped in something soft.

Of course, he had to carry the Key/Calyx like that. He had to remain in the closest possible contact, or else his fragile control over it would break and Nash would find them again. No matter how far they travelled, Nash would be able to follow and track them, and in the end, destroy them.

She barely heard Robert's call to ride, but her horse, well-trained and obedient, turned and followed him anyway. Only when she neared the gate did the world tip back again and she knew this was time to say goodbye.

As the group filed through the gate, she waited until they were all gone, then she turned once more, tears falling down her cheeks. Almost every Salti in the Enclave was there in the field before her, come to say farewell to the Key, and the Jaibir who was taking it from them.

'I'm sorry,' she whispered, though they could not hear her, nor under-stand why this had all happened. 'I promise . . .'

But there was nothing more to say, no vow to make, nothing left to give that could make this disaster any better. All she could do was to remove herself from Nash's path.

As she turned her horse into the gate tunnel and looked on the Goleth and the Enclave for the last time, she felt the cold, hard hand of Prophecy push her into the darkness.

After five hours, the straps began to dig into Robert's shoulders and the old pain in his side began to ache. The Key sat in the bag on his back, padded by plenty of cloth, but it burned his skin anyway. He'd noticed that the moment Finnlay had placed the bag on his shoulders; Finn had checked his skin, but the flesh was untouched: the burning was in his mind only.

He had no choice but to stay this close to the Key, nor could he let anyone else close. Until this morning, nobody had touched the Key in more than five hundred years, since it had been placed in the great cavern the day the Enclave had been founded. A mask was used to cover a stationary person or object; in carrying the Key, he was pushing the limits of what a mask could do. The only way he could ensure it continued working was to keep it this close, as though it were his own aura he were masking.

The weather warmed a little as they came down from the mountains. For the most part, they rode in silence, though the children talked amongst themselves; Robert could hear the underlying fear in their voices, but there was nothing he could do to erase it. He didn't need to urge greater speed; they all knew how desperate this flight was, how hopeless if they didn't get out of Nash's path.

It had been a long time since he'd travelled with such a large group. Apart from Jenn and Andrew, there was Finnlay and Fiona and their three daughters, Helen, Bronwyn and Anna. Robert barely knew his nieces, but this trip, if nothing else, gave him the opportunity to learn how to talk to them.

Martha and Arlie had insisted on joining them too; Martha had declared that Robert would be a fool to travel without a skilled and trained Healer, and with Robert tied to the Key and Finnlay unable to Seek without risk of Nash finding them, then her own Seeking skills would be required to assist Fiona. Robert could hardly disagree – nor did he dare, when Martha was in that mood.

Of course, Arlie and Martha had brought their two children with them: Damaris, a promising Seeker who, at sixteen, was the eldest, and Joey, a bright twelve-year-old who looked much like his tall, gangly father; it was a joy to watch them together.

Maren Stratton was a warrior, and her husband, Ronald, was a fearsome archer. Their son, Guy – also skilled with the bow – was Andrew's best friend.

Robert's old friend, Murdoch, had joined them, his good sense and swordsmanship both welcome on this trip. Murdoch's two nephews, Edain and Braden, both star pupils in Finnlay's combat school, had offered their skills too; Robert accepted. He needed all the help he could get.

And lastly, the oldest member of the group, his mother, Lady Margaret. She had made no entreaties; she'd said nothing at all. She had simply packed up her things to go with the baggage train, collected a few items in a saddle-bag and followed Finnlay as if nothing in the world would stop her.

Robert hadn't tried. She was sixty-two, and not in the very best of health, but she was strong, and full of a determination he could only admire. And besides, he wanted her there. She sat proudly on her horse, grey hair wrapped in a red wool scarf, quietly answering questions from the children. From time to time she took in the view, revelling in her first taste of freedom in far too long.

Eighteen of them in all: too many to travel quickly, but with a little luck, that might not be necessary. If he'd been a priest, he would have prayed; as it was, he could only hope.

Eighteen souls, and he could honestly say he didn't really know any of them, except perhaps Jenn.

Perhaps.

They followed the track down from the mountains, a path well-travelled over the years. Though it was officially spring now, there were still clumps of snow here and there, hidden in the corners between rocks, and in places where the sun could not reach. The worst of the bleak grey stone was gone now, and already there were small bushes readying buds for the new season. With each turn in the path, the view of the valleys below grew wider, a thick, rich green patched here and there with tilled fields and barren trees.

Now this he did know: this country, the land he had spent so many years defending, this he knew so well now.

With a sigh, Robert shifted the straps on his shoulders once again, trying for another spot that wasn't already abused. The new position worked for a moment, but then the now-familiar burning resumed.

'When we stop,' Finnlay trotted up alongside him and gestured at the bag, 'we should rig up something so it can sit on the saddle in front of you.'

Robert shook his head. 'I need to be able to move if necessary. I can't if it doesn't move with me.'

Finnlay looked at the group on the trail before them, then back at Robert. 'Are we going to Bleakstone?'

'Didn't I say?' Robert replied, hearing the evasion in his own voice.

'So we're heading somewhere else. I see,' Finnlay replied softly. 'Why not Bleakstone?'

They turned a corner in the path and the first valley opened before them, a vista full of awakening life. But this path had only ever taken him in one direction, no matter its twists and turns or the number of times he'd lost his way. As the valley spread out in front of him, so did Fate.

'I don't have time, Finn,' Robert replied, his voice a whisper, even though the words felt like shouting. 'I can't keep this mask going indefinitely, and I won't make it as far as Bleakstone. Not without finding another solution.' He stopped then, the words drying up as though he'd had no control over them. He turned to find his brother's eyes on him, dark and understanding. Was this what it looked like on the outside?

For a moment he thought Finnlay might argue, but he turned his attention back to the trail, his tone completely different. 'I see that things between you and Jenn have . . . improved.'

Robert looked at him sharply; Finnlay's expression was both innocent and smug at the same time. He smiled himself. 'How did you know?'

With a shrug, Finnlay grinned. 'You're my brother. She might as well be my sister. You think I wouldn't know?'

'But it's nothing. Not really. Not with the Key—'

'Of course.' Finn said. 'Nothing at all.'

'Yes,' Robert agreed softly, unable to deny how good it felt that things had . . . improved. Even with all the doubt in their lives, in this minute there was between them this bond of belonging. Now that it was there, and acknowledged by them both, he couldn't imagine how he had lived so long without it.

Finnlay pulled in front to negotiate a narrow part in the path. Robert smiled to himself: as much as he knew the country, so his brother knew him.

And he knew Jenn. Even as the thought formed, he peered downhill to find her waiting for him, watching him, her upturned face catching the late light, glowing a little. Were they together? Or would the Key keep them apart and if so, how far apart? Would their love stand the tests awaiting them, or would it turn out that what they had was little more than an incomplete Bonding and a Prophecy that wouldn't leave them alone?

Finally he drew up to her and she smiled at him, letting him know. 'How goes it? Is the Key behaving itself?'

'You can't tell?'

'To be honest, I haven't dared open the link. I don't want to distract it from the mask.'

'Good point.'

She rode alongside him in silence for a moment, then, without a word, she reached out and took his hand. Even through his gloves, he could feel her warmth. The path didn't allow contact for very long, but it was enough. By the time she let go, his questions were silenced.

He would have the answers soon enough.

6

The thunder of hooves on the hard road was a constant in Kenrick's days and nights. His impatience kept time, marking each minute until he could arrive at his destination, until he could find out what had happened, if his cousin Andrew had been killed – and whether Nash was about to betray him.

He barely stopped for rest. Instead, he'd driven his men on, telling them to sleep in the saddle, change horses at each tavern along the way, take food where they could. He'd seen the looks from the people as he passed: enough of them had recognised their king to be afraid of what his journey might mean; none had had the courage to ask.

He didn't care. All he knew was that the leader of the Malachi who worked with Nash, Baron Luc DeMassey, was dead. DeMassey's people had taken his body from Marsay back to their home – wherever that was. But the Baron had been killed in a fight at Maitland, which was where Andrew lived. And the reports Kenrick had received said that Andrew had also died in the fight.

Had Nash sent DeMassey here to protect Andrew, or to kill him – if to protect him, against whom? Andrew was more harmless than a butterfly, a boy to whom a malicious thought was inconceivable. He was no threat to Kenrick's throne, no threat to anyone, so why would Nash want him dead – why would anyone?

His soldiers slowed as they approached the crossroads. A busy tavern sat on one corner, a shrine to Mineah on the other. The shrine was decorated with what had to be the first flowers of spring, as though the peasants couldn't wait to pay the goddess homage.

This time he didn't stop. He was still too far away to allow distraction. In front of him rode Forb'ez, a man known for his consummate skill as a warrior, a man his father had trusted like no other. And yet, this man, who had spent his adult life protecting Kenrick's father had, in Selar's most desperate hour, deserted him.

Why?

Selar had trusted Forb'ez; Kenrick would not be a fool and make the same mistake his father had made, so he used what Seeking powers he'd developed to make sure he wasn't riding into a trap.

Of course, if his powers were *really* developed, he could be so much more confident of his own safety.

Once past the crossroads, the forest closed in. The thoughts continued to circle in Kenrick's head: Andrew dead? He was just a harmless, gentle, trusting boy; the only person who had ever shown Kenrick a moment's worth of genuine kindness. He couldn't be dead. Because if he was, then—

'Sire! There!'

Kenrick looked up at the shout, following the pointing arm to the right, where the forest thinned a little—

'By the blood!' Kenrick kicked his horse and turned into the forest. There, for all the world to see, were scorch marks on the ground, obvious evidence of an arcane battle. Three trees had burned to blackened stumps and another had fallen before being incinerated. Grass and bracken were shrivelled and burned, and all around was the acrid stench of burnt wood.

As he jumped to the ground his men spread out, forming a protective circle around him, but Kenrick knew there was no danger. He could feel it somehow. Whatever had happened here was two weeks old: there was no heat in the ashes, only marks from where it had rained. But there were other scars on the ground, dark patches and grass pressed flat where bodies had lain. Some person, long gone now, had removed and buried them.

Who?

Kenrick straightened up, pulling his gloves back on. He looked around to where the forest thickened again, then south. In the faint distance, he could see the outline of Maitland Manor.

Swinging up onto his horse, he turned back to the road.

With a grunt, Micah Maclean sank the shovel's blade into the fresh earth, then once loaded, he turned and dumped it into the last grave, patting down the dirt before getting more. Around him, the people of Maitland – those who had survived the Malachi attack – laboured with him. At least he had help now; if he'd had to do the whole thing alone, it would have been a nightmare. As it was, he could scarcely think of a more horrible task, but nonetheless, it had to be done.

Malachi had come to get Andrew, but Robert and Jenn had been there to stop them, and Finnlay and Micah had done what they could. Jenn had been injured, a dozen Malachi were killed and the rest had come here, to the Manor, burned the house and put to the sword not only fifty of its inhabitants, but also Andrew's aunt and uncle, his own surrogate parents. Micah assumed that was done in a fit of spite . . .

He'd wanted to burn the Malachi bodies, for what they'd done, but in the back of his mind, a voice scolded gently, reminding him that he was not the monster they were and that, as a good man, he should treat all creatures with respect – even those he'd had a hand in killing. He'd grown to hate that voice.

As he bent to pick up the shovel again a shiver ran through him. The memories were so close to the surface, too new to be easily forgotten. They'd haunted him night and day. Even the comfort of Sairead's presence had been denied him.

In the days that followed the attack, after Robert had hurried Jenn and Andrew off to the Enclave for safety, Micah had come here to begin this terrible work. At first he had toiled by himself, burying the dead, for the survivors had run from the terror the Malachi had wrought. They had seen sorcery at work that awful night; Micah could not blame them for staying away.

Alone, he had dug graves for Bella and Lawrence. He'd found remnants of the rich curtaining to wrap their bodies in; as he laid them to rest he whispered what prayers he could remember.

After that, he'd dug more graves in the shade of the huge oak tree which was so much a part of Maitland's setting. He'd been injured himself and sleep contained his nightmares; it was hard, sorrowful work as he discovered one body after another in the ruins of the Manor. After a few days some had come back, hoping it was safe. Then at last, he was no longer alone.

When he levelled off the last of the fresh earth, he straightened up, stretching the kinks out of his back. The others continued with their tasks, some burying, others putting up name-stakes, saying prayers, and mourning. Behind them stood the blackened shell of Maitland Manor, grim underneath the pewter sky. Once this day was done, the burying would be finished and he could finally rest.

A flash of colour caught his eye. He looked up and instinctively took a step back, but there was nowhere to run to, nowhere to hide. As the host of soldiers took the last turn in the road, everybody stopped work, their fear almost palpable in the air.

Micah did nothing. He tried not to hold his breath, tried to ignore the hammering in his chest. Why hadn't he thought that Kenrick might coming looking for his cousin? Word of the attack had obviously reached the capital; was Kenrick here to make sure Andrew was dead, or to find out if he was alive?

As the men spread out to secure the area, Micah frowned. Kenrick was asking questions of the people nearest to him. From the look on the King's face, it was clear that the attack had not been his idea; so Nash had done this without Kenrick's permission.

More to the point, was this something that could be used to their advantage? Robert would know how best to use this to drive a wedge between Nash and Kenrick; after all, that was why he needed Andrew in the first place, so the boy could take care of the King while Robert fought Nash.

If Micah said anything to Kenrick, he'd risk being recognised: Kenrick had seen him fight alongside Robert on the field at Shan Moss. Though eight years had passed, Kenrick might still associate him with Robert, and then all Robert's plans would be for naught.

Behind him, soldiers picked through the wreckage of the Manor, shouting to each other. As far as Micah knew, there were no more bodies lying cold amidst the ruins, and there was definitely nothing those men could find that would be a danger to anyone. Bella and Lawrence had lived blameless lives; their only crime was that Jenn, Bella's sister, was a sorcerer, and she'd left her son to live with them – but neither Kenrick nor his men would know anything about that.

'You!'

Micah started and turned back to find Kenrick before him, staring down at him from his horse. Almost too late, Micah gave a deliberately clumsy bow; it had been a long time since he'd bowed before a king and it would do nothing for his disguise as a farm worker to do so in a polished manner.

Of course, the king he'd last bowed to had been this boy's father, Selar. Kenrick resembled him in all the wrong ways: Kenrick was tall and broad-shouldered, with fair hair and smouldering brown eyes. He stared down at Micah with disdain, but there was caution there, and enough worry to give Micah hope.

'Sire,' he murmured, keeping his whole stance as subservient as possible.

'Who have you buried here? Those folk say Lord Lawrence and his Lady are amongst the dead. Who else?'

Micah swallowed hard, still unsure as to what to say. 'I know not, Sire. The fire burned most beyond recognition.'

Kenrick waved his hand in irritation. 'Yes, but what of His Grace, the Duke? Has anyone seen the boy? Was he here when the attackers struck?'

Consumed with indecision, Micah allowed a nervous glance towards the Manor. If he said Andrew was dead, what would Kenrick do? If he said Andrew was alive, would Kenrick go looking for him – would he challenge Nash for the sake of his cousin?

Would such an action precipitate Robert's own plans? Damn him for always relying only on himself and never trusting anybody else to help him.

'Well, man! Speak up! I want an answer! Have you seen the Duke since the attack?'

Honesty. That voice spoke up loud and clear now. And yes, he still hated it.

'No, Sire, I have not seen the Duke since the attack.'

'Then he is dead?'

Honesty? Why not? 'I could not say, Sire. I did not see the attack on the Manor.' All absolutely true. Not a word spoken in falsehood. This was too easy.

'Then he is alive? If he's alive, then where is he?' Before Micah could move, Kenrick reached out towards him, then clenched his gloved fist. Instantly, Micah was frozen to the spot, unable even to breathe.

By the gods, he had no idea Kenrick has this much power – did Robert know? Did Andrew?

Though he knew deep down it was futile, his body tried desperately to draw in air, to ease the growing pain in his chest, but nothing happened. Kenrick jumped down from his horse, came close to Micah and peered at his face, as though the answer could be found there. An unholy fury burned in his eyes, flooding his face with a kind of ugliness Micah had never seen on Selar.

'If my cousin is not dead, then where is he? Who has him? Why did you not protect your lord and master with your own life? Why are you still alive?' Frozen, Micah could do nothing to stop the blow to his face, but Kenrick's power released him at the same time and he fell backwards, stumbling over the grave he had just finished filling.

But at least Kenrick had lost interest in him. Even now the young king was calling to his men. He swung up into his saddle and kicked the horse savagely, galloping back towards the road, his men following.

It was only then that Micah noticed Forb'ez in amongst them.

Kenrick rode into the night, paying no attention to the fast-wearying horse beneath him. His men had the wisdom to say nothing, riding beside him in silence.

Andrew was nowhere to be found, although if he *had* been dead, then surely those remaining would have known, as they'd known of Bella and Lawrence's fate.

But Forb'ez's story remained the same: there had been a fight, and Kenrick had now seen the evidence. It was certain Malachi were involved, and they did nothing without Nash's orders – so, for one reason or another, Nash must have sent DeMassey's Malachi south to Maitland. The only question remaining was why. If Nash had wanted Andrew dead, then he'd seen some threat to Kenrick's throne. There was only one rebel in Lusara; Kenrick still shuddered even to think his name. But though Robert

Douglas had been a thorn in his side for a long time, not once had he ever made an attempt on the crown, and if he did, he would hardly use Andrew; he would take it himself.

So, if there was no threat, that left him with only one possibility: Nash wanted to use Andrew as he'd used Kenrick. Nash wanted to . . . *replace* Kenrick with Andrew. It made perfect sense. Andrew was not a sorcerer, despite the rumours about his strange mother; not only that, but he was the most amenable boy, still young enough to be manipulated and trained. Nash could place Andrew on the throne and control him without any effort at all. Then he could do away with Kenrick and his defiance – and most especially, his powers – without losing his control over Lusara.

Perfect – but only if Nash had succeeded in grabbing Andrew. Perhaps that's what Nash had intended all along with his Prophecy. There had been evidence of two fights: one in the forest clearing, and one at the Manor. The real battle had been in the forest; the attack on the house had been punitive only, suggesting the Malachi had *not* got what they wanted.

Kenrick smiled in the darkness. DeMassey had failed. Nash had failed. Somehow, Andrew had escaped. For the moment at least, that meant both of them were safe.

For the moment.

Until Nash came up with some other scheme, or until Andrew reappeared. Or until Kenrick finally grew strong enough to rid himself of Nash altogether. After that, neither he nor Andrew would be in danger again, and there was only one way he could do that.

Kenrick's smile widened, rumbled in his belly until it emerged as laughter: after all these years, he would finally make Nash *pay*.

By the time Micah was finished and the remains of Maitland was cleaned up, all the livestock were taken care of, all the people sent on their way, it was long after dark and Micah was ready to drop with exhaustion. Shutting out the images of his work, he trudged back to the cottage Bella and Lawrence had given him so many years ago. He'd come to protect Andrew and they'd seen his presence as a risk. Even so, they'd allowed him to stay. Now the irony made his heart heavy. In the end, Andrew had been the risk, and they'd paid for it with their lives.

He knew the way along the path well enough to see it in the dark; he knew the sounds of the woods around him, and the cold chill in the air still waiting for spring warmth to banish it. It had been a long winter this year, longer than any he could remember. Right now, he could hardly recall the last time he'd seen the sun.

The cottage was dark and lifeless when he arrived, as it had been every day for the last two weeks. He opened the door, felt along the window ledge for the candle and flint he left there. With the candle to show him the way, he lit a fire, then another lamp, and set about warming up the stew left over from last night.

It was done. In Andrew's name, in Jenn's name, he had buried Bella and Lawrence and taken what care he could with Andrew's inheritance. Now all he had left to do was to sit here and wait for Robert to return, as, inevitably, he would. And then?

He heard the sound more because he was expecting it than because the soft noise reached his ears. He was at the door almost before he'd registered his reaction. He pulled it wide open, and then hissed in a breath of disappointment.

'Gilbert. Come in.' Micah turned, leaving the door open for the other man to close behind him. From habit, he took down another cup from the mantle and poured brew from the pot hanging over the coals. Before he straightened, he gave the stew another stir. He didn't have enough to feed two. With luck, Gilbert wouldn't be here that long.

He turned to find the other man seated on a stool by the table. Micah handed him the mug, then began slicing bread ready for his supper.

'I see you had a visitor today. I take it Kenrick didn't recognise you?'

'Obviously not,' Micah muttered.

There was silence a moment, then Gilbert rose to his feet and placed his half-empty cup on the table before Micah. 'If you wish to change your mind, you should say so now. I'm risking an awful lot on your involvement.'

'I never said I'd changed my mind.'

'And yet, your enthusiasm wanes further each time we meet. Is it me? Or are you no longer certain you wish to do this?'

Micah put down the knife, rested both palms on the table top and looked up at the man before him. Gilbert Dusan was tall, but just as his niece was beautiful, Gilbert was almost too ugly for words. His complexion had been scarred by disease as a child; his hair, rust-red and streaked with dull grey, was long, plaited with a leather thong. Heavy eyebrows sat over small amber eyes, but his face was dominated by the large nose and crooked teeth. Micah could see a little family resemblance, though; the man was Malachi, after all.

'I am certain I wish to do this,' Micah stated firmly, the conviction sitting in his stomach like a rock, making him feel ill. The price was rising as each day went by. 'But I would be more at ease if you would allow me to see Sairead.'

'My niece is not entirely sure she wants to see *you*.'

'Then let her tell me that. How can I know those are her words? You sent her away and you prevent her from returning. Is it not enough that I have betrayed her? Betrayed my own friends? Must you separate me from my own wife? Especially now?'

The moment he said the words, he bit his lip, wishing he could take them back. But it was too late; Gilbert's gaze narrowed and the tilt of his crooked mouth altered to hint at a smile.

'Especially now? You know she married without her father's consent; without the consent of her family. This is not the Malachi way. We could have a priest annul the marriage for that reason alone. Did she not tell you this?'

A flash of rage whipped through Micah, shocking him with its intensity. He gripped the side of the table and shoved hard, pushing it into Gilbert's thighs, making the other man stumble back. He didn't bother doing more; he knew he was powerless against sorcery.

Gilbert raised his hands in supplication, his expression filled with genuine regret. 'Come, Micah, I never meant to suggest that we *would* do that, only that we could. Surely Sairead mentioned our laws.'

For a moment, Micah couldn't bring himself to speak. Then that damned voice whispered in the back of his mind again, and he took in a deep breath, allowing the anger to flow away into the night. Calm now, he met Gilbert's gaze. 'If you mean to control me by using my wife against me, then you are not the man you claim to be. You are not a man I would deal with and your threats will not keep Sairead from me. I *will* see her. I will know that she is well, that she is—'

The door opened. In the frame stood Sairead herself, her face still and white, her fine brows frowning at him. Before she entered, she glanced at her uncle. At his nod, she moved towards Micah, but still she said nothing.

Instead, it was Gilbert who spoke. 'No child does well not knowing his own father. You may have a few minutes only. When Douglas comes back to look for you, he must only find my niece here. I had a man follow Kenrick to the crossroads. He will let us know if the King returns, though I doubt that will happen. You and I will wait a little distance away, for safety. This area is already too busy for my liking. Hopefully, Douglas will arrive soon. We are running out of time.'

Micah heard the words, but didn't bother registering the meaning. All that concerned him was the fact that she was standing there, waiting for Gilbert to walk to the door, go outside and close it behind him.

The ensuing silence was broken only by the crackle of the fire and the damp logs he'd thrown on earlier to warm the cottage. Sairead simply watched him, as though she feared he might disappear. Even so, she made no move to come closer. She had not forgiven him.

'You are pale,' Micah began, his voice catching. 'Are you eating properly?'

'Yes. Of course.' Sairead looked away, as though enough had changed in the cottage over the last two weeks to make it worth her attention.

They'd been married almost seven years. They'd given their vows in secret and shared a few fractured, stolen moments together in all that time, because he served the Salti and Robert, and she was of the Malachi, a D'Azzir trained for combat. They were on opposite sides of the centuries-old war between their people – and he'd never told her that he was also working with her own uncle.

For all the years they'd been together, they'd kept their lives completely separate. Never had they asked questions of each other, nor demanded the other change sides, or make some decision that would alter that balance. And still Micah had betrayed her.

He knew. He could see it in her eyes. It was the same thing he'd seen in Robert's eyes at Shan Moss.

He could have prayed for hope, but even that was beyond him now. If he lost her because of this . . .

'Don't hate me, please,' he whispered. 'I couldn't tell you. Can't you see that?'

'No, Micah, I can't.' She met his gaze then, her left hand unconsciously going to her belly. He could see the smallest swelling there.

'Please,' he whispered again, moving to stand close to her. His hand reached up to her shoulder, needing to touch her, to regain his own balance. 'I love you, you know that. I'm sorry.'

Was this how Robert had felt when he'd had to turn his back on Jenn? Was this how he'd felt when, time and again, he'd had to step back from saving his country because he'd made a promise? He didn't need to answer the question. He already knew.

Sairead was watching him, her crystal blue eyes regarding him solemnly. On instinct, he reached up and soothed back the tangled curls from her forehead, breathing deeply of her scent at the same time. He studied the strands of hair as they filtered through his fingers, each moment making him calmer, making him as certain as he'd ever been that this was indeed the right path to take.

He leaned forward and pressed his lips to hers, gently, asking, rather than taking. After a moment, she responded, a reply, no more. But in that was the core of forgiveness.

When he looked at her again, she was just as solemn – but for them both this time. 'Do you need to lie to me again?' she asked levelly.

'I don't know,' he replied honestly.

She searched his face once more, then asked a question almost without breath, as though it scared her too much to use voice. 'Am I ever going to be the most important thing in your life? Is our child?'

Micah had to swallow twice to loosen his throat. Even then the words came with difficulty. 'Yes, my love, I promise you. I promise.' With that, he reached out and wrapped his arms around her, pulling her close. She remained stiff in his embrace, but she held him in return. This forgiveness would take time, but at least it would come. He knew that now.

And before he had had his fill of her, Gilbert banged on the door, calling out that it was time to go. As Sairead began to pull away, Micah pressed one last kiss to her cheek before he fled.

7

For the second night's camp, Finnlay chose a wooded slope where water ran clear at the bottom of the hill. By the time fires were lit and supper started, the camp was well developed, scouts posted and horses brushed and watered. With so many people, Finnlay was glad of Martha's ability to organise. Without her, so much would have been forgotten, making the journey both frightening *and* uncomfortable. They were in a hurry to cross the country, but Robert needed to rest too.

With a few words, he sent Andrew and Guy down to the stream to draw water, then wandered over to where Jenn sat with Robert, a little distanced from the main camp. Robert said it was for safety, that he had no idea what the Key/Calyx might do.

Finnlay knew better.

Jenn had lit a fire, small, but with enough warmth to draw the damp from the night air. She had Robert's blankets laid out, and a bowl of something by her side. Robert sat on the ground and Jenn knelt behind him. With the gentlest hands, she dipped a cloth in the bowl and then dabbed on Robert's bare back. Even in the flickering light, Finnlay could see his brother trying not to flinch with each touch.

Robert looked up as he approached, but said nothing. Steeling himself, Finnlay walked around until he could see the burns with his own eyes. There was a cluster of them focused around the centre of Robert's back, red and angry, overshadowing scars from older wounds – in particular, a wound to Robert's side that appeared awfully new. If that was where Selar had cut him, at the Battle of Shan Moss, almost nine years ago, why had it still not healed – or was there more his dear brother wasn't telling him?

'Ouch,' he murmured on his brother's behalf, silencing for the moment his darker questions. Jenn didn't take her eyes from her work. 'They're getting worse, aren't they?'

'Yes. Arlie's out now looking for some things for a salve, but really the best solution is for your stubborn brother to stop carrying the damned Key on his back.'

'I told you,' Robert grunted as Jenn dabbed one vicious burn after another, 'I need to be—'

'Able to move, yes,' Finnlay finished for him, 'you said that two days ago, and now you're almost crippled with it. We have to find another solution. At the rate you're going, it won't need Nash to defeat you.' He sank to the ground, crossed his legs and watched Robert's face. These days, they looked the same age, an odd feeling. But the Key had done something to both Robert and Jenn, to prevent them ageing the way everyone else did. It was as though the last eight or so years had never happened, at least on the surface.

Robert's hair was still long, reaching just beyond his shoulders, and still so dark it was almost black, but where Finnlay had a few threads of silver through his, Robert's was a thick, wavy sable. Even with his forehead beaded with sweat, Robert's face exuded strength. Level, expressive brows sat above eyes of forest green, below a straight nose and wide mouth which, when smiling, could make a person believe there could be no evil in the world. Six years older than Finnlay, Robert was also the taller; even grown up, he had retained a physical superiority over his younger brother. Finnlay was by no means small, but Robert was bigger, stronger and faster: and it always made Finnlay smile with pride. Robert had never been bested in a fight, though he'd had a few close moments. Finnlay intended to do all he could to ensure that was as close as it would ever get.

But watching as Robert shut his eyes against the pain, Finnlay saw the other reason why his brother slept a little apart from the others. It would do little for morale for them to see Robert so vulnerable. With all the work of moving nineteen people in relative secrecy, Finnlay had paid little attention to how the strain of keeping the Key hidden from Nash was affecting his brother; now he could see it clearly on Robert's face. The skin, beneath the usual tan, was grey, almost ashen, and there were new rings around Robert's eyes. When he brought his cup of ale to his mouth, his hand shook a little, making Finnlay frown.

'Robert?'

'Mmmn?'

'Have you slept?'

Finnlay saw Jenn's gaze dart to him momentarily, before returning to her work. Her lips pressed together into a thin line. 'He won't sleep,' she said quietly.

'I would love to sleep,' Robert said in his own defence. 'I just can't risk it.'

'Oh.' Finnlay sat back and folded his arms. 'And how long can you go without any sleep at all?'

Robert sighed, making Finnlay feel just a little guilty for giving him the usual arguments. 'Finn, what choice do I have? I have to keep the mask going or Nash will sense the Key and know where we're going.'

'But he's still, what, three days away?'

'Perhaps. I can't Seek to find out and even if I could, I'm not sure I'd find him.'

'Not even now?'

'No, not even now. He only found me at the Enclave because the Key and Calyx . . . well, pushed me out there, I guess. I can't think of another way to put it.'

Finnlay rolled his eyes and was rewarded with a quick smile from Jenn. 'So, if the Key isn't pushing you out there, you don't think Nash can Seek you?'

'Yes. Or no, depending on how you read that question.'

With a short laugh, Finnlay said, 'Ah, as pedantic as ever. Tell me, if Nash can't find you anyway, then the mask is only for the Key, right?'

'Of course. It was always only for the Key.' Robert opened his eyes then and fixed Finnlay in his gaze. It was only then that Finnlay saw the full extent of the strain on his brother. He'd said the mask would hold for a couple of days; now it had been almost three. Once again, Robert was holding to his word from sheer determination alone, and such determination was likely to get him killed.

'How much longer until we are where we're going?'

'Another three days perhaps. Possibly four.'

'Robert!' Jenn put down her cloth and laid an old, soft blanket over his shoulders. 'You can't go without sleep for that long! I won't allow it.'

'Nor I, brother,' Finnlay agreed grimly. 'We have to find an alternative.'

'Oh?' Robert moved so he could face both of them, then carefully sipped his ale again, keeping his back as far from the fire as possible. 'And who do you suggest should keep the mask going while I rest, eh?'

Finnlay paused at that. Robert was right, as usual, but there had to be an alternative. 'Do you need to keep the mask going all the time?'

'I can't guess when Nash might try to Seek for the Key. Without the mask, he *will* find it.'

'But there's a chance he'd be asleep at night as well, right? I mean, surely there's a few hours you can get a little rest.'

Jenn reached out and put her hand on Robert's arm. Even in the flickering firelight, Finnlay could see the effect that one touch had on his brother. Almost instantly, Robert stilled. His gaze drifted down to where her hand rested. A moment later, his eyes darted up to meet hers. There was a flash of a smile and then he was looking at Finnlay again as though nothing had happened.

'Finn, there's too much at stake for me to release the mask for even a moment. Don't worry, I can hold it until we get to our destination. If I can hold it that long, it won't matter if I'm not strong enough to fight Nash – he won't be there.'

'Fine,' Jenn nodded, 'in that case, you'd better tell us where we're going.'

Robert leaned his head back, stretching out his neck. 'We're going somewhere safe. Much closer than Bleakstone.'

'And if you become incapacitated?' Finnlay asked archly. When would Robert finally begin to trust others?

'Andrew knows how to find it.'

Finnlay blinked at that. 'He does?'

'That's right,' and the tiredness flowed into Robert's voice then as he started to relax. 'Just tell him I want to go home. He'll know where to go.'

With that, Robert lay down on his side, his eyes closing, his breathing even and steady, as though he were asleep. Finnlay had seen this before: Robert, though not awake on a superficial level, was completely alert as far as his Senses were concerned. This was as close to sleep as he would get, but at least his body was getting some rest. They would get no more talk out of him that night.

Finnlay got to his feet as Jenn collected her things together. As they headed back to the main camp, Finnlay didn't have to look hard to see the worry on her face.

'How bad are the burns?'

Jenn shrugged. 'There is a part of the Key which heals both of us. That part prevents lasting damage to him, and will help that wound heal quicker – but at the same time, the pain alone would break any normal man.'

'But as we know, my brother is not . . .' He didn't bother finishing. 'What about your injuries? How are you feeling now?'

'Still a little sore, but the worst has gone. Another few days and I'll have only the scars. That's how strong the Key is.'

Finnlay caught her arm, turning her to face him. Like Robert, she'd not aged over the last few years, but then, she was still young, yet to turn thirty-five. Her long, dark hair was still braided and kept up out of the way, leaving her oval face open to scrutiny. Her huge blue eyes told him more than he'd expected.

'And what about the Enclave?'

She raised her eyebrows, as though he'd just asked her about the weather. 'The Enclave?'

'Yes.' He gestured at the camp around them. 'How do you feel about leaving it?'

'Come on, Finn. How do you feel? Aren't you glad to be finally out of the caves? You never liked living there in the first place. You always wanted your freedom back. I should think you'd be happy.'

'I already know how *I* feel, I was asking about you. Though, by the sound of that little tirade, I don't think I'll pursue the question, even though that was your goal, wasn't it?'

For a moment, there was a smile in Jenn's eyes, then she seemed to remember why she shouldn't. Her gaze, inexorably, returned to where Robert lay on his own, beside his small fire, in pain and in danger.

Finnlay took the hint. 'I don't suppose Arlie can deaden Robert's pain at all?'

'Robert won't let him try, not with his close links to the Key open. Trust me, Finn, Robert really is worried about how much power there is in the Key, and how it might behave under certain circumstances.'

'What do you mean?'

Jenn reached her bags and began putting her things away. All the others were busy with their tasks, but even so, she kept her voice low. 'He won't let anyone else touch him, and he only allows me because I'm already joined to the Key. You have no idea how much effort it takes for him to hold this mask. That's why he's brought so many of us with him. There's no other way he can protect it. He can't Seek, he can't even mindspeak me, Finn. The smallest thing could jar his control. The moment the mask drops, Nash will find us, and no amount of running will help.'

Finnlay reached out and squeezed her shoulder, giving her the opportunity to take in a few deep breaths, to calm herself once more. He looked around to find only Martha paying them any attention at all, and he saw understanding in her eyes.

'Do you remember,' he began quietly, still watching Martha on the other side of the camp, 'years ago when I tried that tandem Seeking? I did it successfully with both Martha and Fiona.'

Jenn looked up, speculation in her eyes. 'Do you think you could adapt that to help Robert?'

'When we were in Kenrick's camp Seeking for Helen, we used a tandem connection because he wasn't sure of her aura.' An involuntary smile crossed his face. 'Though I have to tell you, working in tandem with Robert is an overwhelming experience. It took him a split second to find her and nearly blew me away in the process.'

Jenn frowned. 'But I don't see how you can use that principle to hold a mask for Robert.'

'Well.' Finnlay paused, taking a few steps towards the fire. He was making this up as he went along, and he wasn't afraid to admit it. 'It's not that nobody else of similar strength couldn't hold the mask, is it? It's that Robert doesn't dare let anyone else have that close a connection with it. So—'

66

Jenn was already ahead of him, 'So if *I* hold the mask, then you can use a tandem link to hold it as well, at the same time. Two of us working it would have to be at least as strong as Robert alone, and thereby split the exposure to the Key. Do you think that would work, Finnlay? Do you?'

He couldn't ignore the hope in her eyes. 'I think it's worth a try, and it's certainly something we can test before we talk to him. You feel confident enough with the mask process?'

'It's been a while since I made one, but if I practise first, I know I can do it. Hell, Finn, even if we can only hold it for a few hours at a time, that will give Robert enough rest to go on. That's better than nothing. Enough to save his life.'

'All right. Let's ask Martha to help.'

Since Andrew had better night vision than Guy, he led his friend down to the stream at the bottom of the hill. They'd already filled all the water bottles ready for the morning; now they needed to take the horses down, two each at a time, let them drink and wander in the water for a few minutes, then take them back up. By the time they were finished, supper would be ready – or at least, his growling stomach hoped it would be.

Andrew was tired. He couldn't quite escape the feeling that he'd been in the saddle for the last two months – largely because that was horribly close to the truth. But not only that; things just kept moving faster and faster and there didn't seem to be any way to make them slow down for a moment, so he could just get used to things. First Robert had abducted him, then the mad, secret trip to Marsay, then coming home and the Malachi attack, then . . . then Bella and Lawrence and then the flight back to the Enclave and now all this, the joining of the Key and Calyx and this crazy flight *from* the Enclave to some other place where— He had no idea what was supposed to happen next. And if Robert had his way, it would *never* be normal again.

'Andrew?'

'What?' He blinked to find Guy tugging on his sleeve, trying to get his attention.

'I don't think your mother would be too happy if you let her horse wander off.'

Andrew looked across the stream where the animal was happily munching on some tufts of grass, the reins he was supposed to be holding now dangling in the water. With a whispered curse, he splashed into the stream, getting both his boots and his feet wet. He grabbed the reins and tugged until the horse reluctantly followed him back. He came to a halt to find Guy shaking his head.

'You said we had lots to talk about, but you haven't said a word.'

'Neither have you,' Andrew protested, but it was half-hearted. It didn't matter what he wanted, only what he did. Even if he didn't want to do it.

'Something bad happened, didn't it? Something aside from your aunt and uncle?' Guy peered up the hill to where camp fires dotted the darkness. 'Helen said you were upset about something, but you wouldn't tell her what.'

'It won't help.'

'So, tell me anyway. Then,' Guy paused, giving him half a smile, 'then you can complain to me about it and I can at least sympathise. That's what friends are for, after all.'

Something inside Andrew wanted to smile, but memories tugged the corners of his mouth down.

Guy took a step closer, deliberately putting his horses between himself and the camp. 'Is it . . . something about your father?'

With a frown, Andrew shook his head, refusing to even think about *that* man. 'No, of course not! Why would it have anything to do with my father? He's dead, and you promised you wouldn't ask about him again.'

'Well, I just thought that, well, with you being so quiet and everything that . . . well something had happened. Sorry.' Guy didn't move away. 'Is it something to do with Robert?'

Andrew felt a flash of fear. 'Why do you say that?'

'Isn't *everything* about him?'

Without meaning to, Andrew laughed, surprising himself as well as his friend. While Guy was busy looking pleased with himself, Andrew wrapped the two sets of reins around the base of a scraggy bush and sat down on the nearest flat rock. As his friend joined him, he began to talk, his voice coming out no more than a whisper. He'd not talked about this with *anyone*.

'I don't think it's about Robert. But it is about something he wants me to do.'

With a conspiratorial glance over his shoulder, Guy shifted closer and whispered, 'He picked you? Wow! Why?'

Andrew frowned at his friend, surprised at the envy he heard. But a few weeks ago, his reaction would have been exactly the same. 'I don't know why he picked me, except that . . . well, he says it's because of my parents and my grandparents, and my ancestors way back to when nobody really cares about them any more.' Andrew bit his lip; he sounded petulant and he could hear it.

Guy heard it too. His tone softened. 'What does he want you to do?'

And then Andrew's throat dried up, as though the moment he said it out loud would suddenly make it irrevocable, as though his choice would be taken away. But Robert had said he wouldn't have a choice. When the moment came, he'd just have to do it.

'Robert wants me to kill Kenrick and take the throne.'

The gasp he heard came not from Guy, but from his own mouth. The words had spoken themselves, leaving him with no choice at all. Was this the kind of power Robert had over him? He needed to talk to Robert, badly, but Robert was tied to the Key, working on keeping the mask in place and in no condition to answer his silly questions.

'What are you going to do?' Guy asked after a moment. 'Are you going to do it?'

Andrew was gratified to find all traces of envy gone from Guy's voice, although now there was a touch of awe.

'I don't know.'

'Kenrick's your cousin, isn't he?'

'Selar was my father's maternal cousin, and Kenrick is Selar's son. I'm the only family he has left in Lusara.'

'You don't want to kill him?'

Andrew was shaking his head before he knew it, but he stopped when Guy sprang to his feet.

'But what about what he did to Liam? What he almost did to Helen! *I'd* kill him for that alone! How can you—'

Liam was dead, killed by Kenrick's men trying to defend Helen. And Finnlay and Robert had rescued Helen from Kenrick's clutches, her arm already cut and bleeding for some disgusting arcane ritual. She still woke with nightmares; she'd admitted that to him when she'd told him the story. That should have been enough for any man to want to kill Kenrick: to take revenge on a person who would do something like that to someone as sweet and gentle as Helen would be honourable—

And still the thought made him feel ill. If Kenrick were here now, he knew that he would never be able to lift a hand against him. How would killing him make what he did go away?

He was useless, not at all the kind of man Robert should be making into a king. He was too afraid, too hesitant, nothing like Robert, like what a king *needed* to be in order to rule Lusara. And despite having a mother who was Jaibir, he had completely failed to develop whatever powers they all thought he had. Kenrick was a sorcerer. If Andrew had to face him on the battlefield, the fight would be a short one.

Wearily, he got to his feet. Guy was still waiting for an answer, but Andrew had none to give. Instead, he took up the reins again. 'I'm sorry,' he murmured, then began the long walk back up the hill alone.

'Well?' Finnlay opened his eyes and watched Martha's face. 'Did it work?'

'Yes, it worked, Finnlay, but I'm still not convinced you should take this to Robert.'

Finnlay got to his feet and paced up and down in frustration. Jenn closed her eyes and breathed deeply, the way she always did after using her powers. They'd always known Jenn's powers were different to all other Salti, but they'd never had an opportunity to work out exactly how – or why. All he did know was that doing the normal things, those he took for granted, always seemed quite difficult for her, while things he couldn't even imagine doing were as easy for her as breathing.

The important thing right now was that she could make a mask – and, even more importantly, he could help her hold it using the tandem technique he'd developed more than a decade ago. Because he'd been trapped in the Enclave and too afraid Nash would find him to use his Seeking abilities, he'd never done more work on the technique, but now, at last, he could use it for something useful.

'Well, if we don't take it to Robert, and he finds out, it could get violent.'

Jenn stood. 'Don't exaggerate, Finn. We'll take it to Robert, Martha. We don't have much choice otherwise. If he doesn't get some rest soon—'

'But you have no guarantee this will work!'

Jenn took her hand and squeezed it. 'Thank you for your help. Go and have supper with the others. If he says no, we'll join you in a minute.'

'And if he says yes?'

Finnlay caught Jenn's elbow, unwilling to wait any longer. 'Then send a couple of bowls of broth over. It will be a late night.'

They left Martha still shaking her head at them. The rest of the camp was busy eating. He'd paused just long enough to explain their plan to Fiona, but his need was for haste; nobody was prepared to guess how much longer Robert would last before even his enormous strength failed.

They skirted the camp until they arrived at Robert's little spot. He hadn't moved, but his fire had died down. Finnlay built it up a little while Jenn knelt beside his brother and put her hand on his arm.

'Robert?'

At her touch, he opened his eyes, breathing deeply as his gaze focused. With a groan, he sat, dragging the bag containing the Key/Calyx close to him without thought. 'What's wrong?'

'Nothing's wrong. We just wanted to talk to you about something.'

Robert shook his head, frowning a little. 'This feels so strange, you know. I feel half blind not being able to use my Senses the way I usually do. Finn, we have people Seeking, don't we?'

'Every few minutes one of us does a scan, yes. Relax, if anyone comes near us, we'll know.'

'Good, good.' Robert turned his head towards the main camp. 'Mmn, supper smells wonderful. Who cooked?'

'Mother.'

'Really?' His eyebrows rose in genuine surprise. 'She cooks? Since when?'

Finnlay could have said a dozen different things about sons who stayed away from their mothers for eight years at a time, but Robert didn't need to hear any of them, so he said, 'Since Fiona got pregnant with Anna. Mother wanted to help and Fiona wanted to teach her.'

'Amazing.' Robert's smile was directed at the woman squatting down to ladle food into one bowl after another.

'Yes, she is,' Finnlay agreed. 'You need to talk to her, you know?'

Robert's gaze darkened. 'Yes. I know.'

'Listen,' Jenn began after a moment. Immediately, Robert's eyes returned to her, ready and alert. 'Finnlay's come up with an idea that might let you get some sleep. We've tested it and Martha says it definitely works. Now, it probably won't give you more than a few hours' break at any one time, but it would be better than nothing, and certainly enough to get us to this place.'

Finnlay was a little annoyed when Robert looked askance at him.

'This is Finnlay's idea?'

'Don't start,' Finnlay warned him.

'But you're always such an easy target,' Robert grinned at him. 'Even now.'

Jenn stopped the ensuing battle by holding up her hands. 'Fine, if you two want to fight, you can do it while I'm eating my supper. Right now, I want you to consider this solution, Robert. Finn, be quiet a moment, please?'

'But it was my idea!'

'And you'll just provide your brother with another moving target. Please, Finn?'

He sat back and folded his arms. 'Fine. Go ahead.'

Turning to Robert, she said, 'Since I'm already joined to the Key, this shouldn't present any danger to anyone. Finnlay's idea is that if I create a mask, and he supports me using the tandem link he developed, then you can dissolve your own mask for a few hours and get some sleep.' She paused, then continued, 'Martha also says that because of the tandem link, our connection to the Key is limited, so theoretically, any of us could do this and make it work. Because we're only doing it while we're stationary, none of us will need to physically touch the Key.'

Robert said nothing for a moment; he just stared, first at Jenn, then at Finnlay. Then he shocked them both when he said, 'You're confident you can hold the mask steady over the Key?'

Finnlay gaped at his brother. Robert usually argued against involving Jenn at all, because of the risk to her, because of his own vow to protect her – and now he was virtually agreeing to this?

'Yes,' Jenn replied, not as shocked as Finnlay, but certainly surprised. 'I can't hold it on my own, and if we were moving, I wouldn't have a hope. With Finn's help, I know we can do it.'

Long seconds of silence ended when Robert agreed. 'Very well. But I want Martha or Fiona here monitoring you both. At the first sign of difficulty, they have to wake me. And nobody else is to try this until you're sure it works without contact with the Key. Agreed?'

Jenn's smile flashed sunshine into the night, which made Finnlay question Robert's real motives for agreeing. She sprang to her feet and ran off to get Martha.

'I hope you know what you're doing, brother,' Robert murmured into the silence.

'So do I,' Finnlay replied, equally softly. He paused a moment, then whispered, 'You have to tell me, don't you find having that much power at your fingertips even a little tempting?'

Robert blinked once, then casually turned away, his voice almost inaudible. 'You have no idea.'

Jenn returned with Martha and Fiona. There were minutes spent explaining the process, when Jenn's mask would be established, when Robert could release his – and then they were all seated, and Finnlay was holding Jenn's hand, and watching her face, and her other hand as it hovered over the bag holding the Key. Robert sat opposite them, his tender back cushioned by blankets and resting against a tree, concern written all over his pale face, a little fear visible in his eyes.

Finnlay tore his attention away and back to Jenn. Then, just as they'd practised, he breathed deeply, focusing in on where his hand held Jenn's, on the shape and depth of her complex aura, and the pulsing power of the Key/Calyx before them. Second after second slipped by as he steadied his breathing, as he felt Jenn do the same. Then abruptly, as if a veil had been drawn over it, the bag seemed to fade for a moment, as though it had become transparent. But this was a mask only of the Key's aura, not of its actual physical appearance, and so the image became more solid as Jenn settled into it. Once it stabilised, Finnlay reached out and . . . *pushed*. He let the power flow through him, meagre though it was. Still, it was enough to fill in the gaps for Jenn, to give her a foundation she could lean back on; his greater expertise with the mask made it all the more solid.

Oh, it was such a pleasure to be working like this again – and to finally put this tandem link to good use! It lay there before him, like an open channel cut into the air, breathing of its own accord, and so easy to keep flowing. Afterwards, he'd have to ask Jenn how it worked for her, how she experienced it, whether it was hard to hold. The possibilities for its use could be endless . . .

'Well?' Martha whispered, kneeling before them both. 'How do you feel?'

'Fine,' Finnlay replied. 'Jenn?'

'Fine. It's not easy, but I saw how Robert did it and—' She opened her eyes and smiled a little. 'With practise, Robert, I think we could give you four, perhaps five hours' sleep.'

When there was no answer, Finnlay looked over at his brother, but even then he got no response. Instead, there was nothing but the soft hiss of steady breathing.

Robert was fast asleep.

8

Long drops of liquid light fell onto the lake, giving the sunset a feeling of time slowing down, of nearing its natural end. On the opposite bank, spiky thorns of young conifers stood black against the twilight, forming an inky, impenetrable mass.

The lake was too deep to cross, and there were no boats nearby large enough to take the horses. Though it would slow him down, Nash would have to go around.

He stood on the shore of the lake, where dry pebbles crunched beneath his feet. Above him, streaks of thick grey cloud obscured the sun, spraying the sky with layers of blue, orange, yellow and red. Behind him, if he'd looked, the heavens had turned a royal purple, forewarning a storm to come.

'Master, the horses are watered and ready to travel. Are we to camp here the night?'

'Here?' Nash frowned. He was still too far away. 'No, we'll go on further before we stop tonight.' He turned then, and without a glance to ensure his men followed, he swung up onto his horse, kicked its sides and galloped away, north, around the lake.

The wind rose an hour after sundown. In the copse where he'd chosen to camp, it whistled through the treetops and howled its way out onto the valley. The noise unsettled the horses and plagued Nash as he tried to concentrate.

He'd had three fires lit, just as he had for the past four nights since he'd found the Key. The fires formed the points of a large triangle amongst the trees. He sat on a blanket in the centre of them, legs crossed, breathing steadily. He kept his eyes open, however, for even now he didn't trust Valena. His men were on guard-duty, or resting. Either way, they left him alone. Bonded Malachi had little to talk to him about.

It was incredible how much stronger he felt; and how little he could do with all this power. Even so, he relaxed his muscles, allowed his Senses to reach out to the night, then began Seeking. Detached, he launched himself into the nothingness, ignoring the faint auras of his men, the brighter auras of his Bonded Malachi. He dwelt for a moment on Valena's aura; even drugged, there was a familiar tone and quality to it he could not ignore. But he pushed on, Seeking west and further west.

Where was he? Where was the Key?

Even with this newly regenerated body, even with all this power almost flowing from his fingertips, why couldn't he find them?

He ranged north and south, up to the Goleth mountains and beyond. Nothing. And all of it was so grey, so completely like every other time he'd been Seeking. No matter what he did, he could never recreate that one night when he'd found the Key, found the Enemy – and seen it all with his own eyes, as though he were there with them.

Fury dragged him back into his own body; he stood, wanting to hit something. Snatching his cloak from the ground, he swung it around his shoulders and stalked back towards camp. He ignored his soldiers, his Malachi, their food and fires. Instead, he made directly for the place where Valena was kept apart from the others, chained to a tree, even her hands bound to prevent her doing anything. She had it in her to end her own life, just to spite him.

He stopped before her. She lay on a blanket, on her side, hands up to cushion her head. Beneath the blanket was a layer of bracken, softening her bed. She had another blanket over her, keeping her warm where the night would freeze her. Her eyes were closed; ignoring him, no doubt. He couldn't trust her, so he kept her drugged enough not so she could neither move nor speak, but just enough to prevent her from using her powers against him. She would kill him if she could; one of the reasons he wanted to keep her alive: it kept him alert and ready for danger. With her so close, he could never become complacent.

By the blood, how he hated her. 'Tell me how he did it.'

She barely moved. 'Why do you think I would tell you anything?'

'Yet you know you will.'

Valena groaned and rolled over, using her bound hands to shift her body. Nash watched her discomfort with a kind of joy which almost erased his earlier anger. 'Come,' he said conversationally, 'wake up properly and talk to me. I'll delay your next dose of drugs if you behave yourself.'

That earned him a low laugh, her voice husky in the deadened wood. 'You want something from me? You want me to help you? You want me to talk to you?' Her laughter deepened, but eventually ended with her coughing. As she gasped for air, she sat up, opening her eyes. 'You already have everything I ever valued. I have nothing more to give. Leave me alone.'

Deliberately, Nash stepped closer, forcing her to look up, but even there, he could see no fear in her eyes, no suggestion that he had the ability to control her in any way at all. Even the drugs did no more than subdue her. And that wasn't enough, not for the one who had betrayed him, and in such a manner. Revenge demanded her broken, and to do that, he would have to make her give things she didn't have, things she didn't even know she cared about.

Reaching down, he took her elbow, forcing her up enough to sit on a fallen log. Then he grabbed her chin with one hand and held it hard. She grimaced against the pain, though her beautiful face lost none of its allure in the process. Only now was he immune to it – amazing: his regeneration had finally made him invulnerable to her.

His revenge had already begun.

He shook her face, revelling in the pain he caused. Then he began, 'You think that because you lost both lover and child that you have nothing else to lose. You think that there is nothing else I can take from you, nothing else that could hurt you. How narrow your perception.'

He let go and stepped back, folding his arms as something else occurred to him. 'Or is it that you expect the D'Azzir to come after you? You were DeMassey's mate and now he's dead. Surely his men will protect you, rescue you from my evil plans?' Nash laughed again; this was so much fun now that he thought about it. 'I'm afraid if they haven't found you yet, they never will. Besides, from what I hear, they've taken DeMassey's body back to Karakham for your traditional Malachi funeral rites, haven't they?'

'Of course they have!' Valena spat back. 'They loved and respected Luc. They would ensure all duties were paid to him.'

'Empty gestures! Taking his *dead* body back for a pyre when you are here, in need of rescue? Do they not see how preposterous that is? This is why your people have failed, year after year, to gain what they wanted from the Salti: not one of you has had the courage to stand against your idiotic traditions long enough to try something new, to see if there's another way that might get you what you want. Instead, you've left the way open and now *I* have found the Salti, *I* have found the Key!'

Valena gave him a slow smile at that. 'In which case, why do you need *my* help? Why not just kill me and be done with it?'

'Kill you?' Nash grabbed her arm again and hauled her to her feet. 'And end your suffering? But, my dear, that would be murder.'

She began to laugh again, untouched by his anger, his threats. The very sound made his skin crawl. 'Luc knew you were a monster. That's why he used poison on himself. That's what he did, isn't it? So you couldn't use his blood to regenerate. And now you think you'll use me, as you used my baby?'

Her laughter was like straw to the flames of his fury. He sank his fingers into her flesh, exerting enough power to make her skin burn. She hissed in pain, no longer laughing, but that wasn't enough for him. 'You think I can't hurt you? Really? Well, what about if I gave you to my men as sport for the night, eh? You think you would enjoy that? If you were bound and tied? If I let them use you like the whore you are? Knowing that I would give them explicit instructions on exactly what they were to do?'

She had stopped moving, her gaze downcast, her breathing harsh and stunted. In that moment, he felt his first real taste of victory. 'See?' he whispered close to her face, seeing her flinch as his breath flowed over her unblemished skin. 'It seems there are still things you are not willing to lose.'

He held her there a moment longer, then carefully released her, stepping back to give her time to think. She remained standing, her hands clasped together, ignoring the ropes binding her.

'Now you will help me,' he continued after a moment, his voice full of certainty. 'You will help me find the Enemy and the Key. Won't you, Valena?'

She was silent a moment longer, then she lifted her chin, keeping her eyes from him, denying him that. 'You can't find him, can you? You keep Seeking Douglas and the Key and you can't find either of them. Why do you think I know where they've gone? I was never on their side.'

'No, but you were with DeMassey a long time, and as Master of the D'Azzir, he was highly skilled in the ways of the Malachi. Somehow, Douglas has managed to hide the Key from me, and I need to know how he's done it.'

Valena was silent again, but he didn't push her this time. For the moment, he would leave her alone, relatively speaking.

'He must be using a mask of some kind.'

Nash frowned. 'But not even he has that kind of power! I couldn't do it myself, not even after I've regenerated! The Key has an aura that can't be masked, that's why it's so odd that I—'

'He might be able do it if he uses the power of the Key itself.' Wearily, Valena pulled her gown about her and sat back down on the log. 'I don't know the Key of course, but from what I understand, he could do it using the Key's own power – but how he would harness it, I couldn't tell you.'

She couldn't be right, and yet, there was no other answer. Tempting as it was to throw such an idea away, he'd done that before and regretted it. This time, he couldn't afford to be blasé, no matter how impossible it sounded. After all, he would never have thought it possible that the Key would give the Enemy the Word of Destruction – and after that, any concept, no matter how bizarre, was worth examination. And how had the Key managed to hide itself all these centuries?

'You have your peace for another night,' he allowed, feeling magnanimous. 'I might even send you some supper.' After that he turned away.

It would never do to spoil the fun by indulging too much in one day.

So a mask it was – but even with a mask, there was always the chance it might slip. Was Douglas strong enough to keep such a mask going, day and night, for ever? And what would he do the day he faced Nash – would he do so with the Key in his hand? If he did, he would lose without a fight.

Nash would keep Seeking. Not even Robert Douglas was strong enough to keep a mask going for ever – and when it did slip, then Nash would find him, find him weak, depleted, needing sleep and rest.

The best time to kill the Enemy was when he couldn't fight back.

With a laugh, Nash returned to his triangle of fires, his blanket, and his Seeking.

9

'Wait, wait.' Aiden raised his voice again, trying to get their attention. 'Please, gentlemen, we won't get anywhere like this. We have to take it one step at a time.'

One by one the others quietened, leaving the bedchamber heavy with expectation and light on explanation. It had taken them four days to reach this point. With Patric's fever sapping his strength, it had been difficult to get answers from him.

Finally, with Patric's consent, he'd called a meeting, though John had insisted that it be held in Patric's bedchamber, ensuring that he did not leave his bed and tire himself unnecessarily. Extra chairs had been brought in and the table pushed to one side and laden with bread and cheeses, some sweet fruit from the southern continent, wine and ale; the fire was banked with warming coals. Seated around the room were the others of Robert's council: Deverin, Payne, Daniel Courtenay, and Owen. Joshi never left Patric's side except to get him something. The others had found that disconcerting, especially since it appeared Joshi spoke little of their language.

'I'm sorry, Bishop,' Daniel said into the ensuing quiet, 'but I still don't know why Patric went to the southern continent in the first place. Why would what happened there almost six hundred years ago have a bearing on what's going on with Robert?'

'And why,' Payne added, 'is this the first we've heard about it? Damn that man! If he didn't work in secret so much . . .'

Aiden silenced him with a look. This was not the time to be tearing Robert's character apart. They could all indulge in that luxury after this whole war was over, and when Robert was with them to offer what defence he could. 'I know there's a lot you don't know. But we can remedy that. If you can contain your questions for a while, I'll try to explain what we know and then let Patric tell his story, so you know what he was doing and why.'

At that, Patric leaned his head back against his pillow, his voice coming out in a harsh whisper. 'By the gods, we're wasting so much time! I need to speak to Robert *now*! Do none of you know how I can find him? Is there no way you can contact him?'

'Not without pulling him away from what he is doing, no,' Payne replied. He sat back in his chair and folded his arms. 'Unless you can explain why you need to see him?'

'My lord,' John interrupted quietly, 'Patric is Robert's friend and has been since they were both boys.'

'I'll grant that,' Payne nodded, obviously not impressed, 'but he's also been out of this country for the last eight years. How do we know what happened to him in that time, or how his loyalties might have been affected? After all, he did bring this friend back with him.'

'A friend,' Patric shot back, 'who has done absolutely nothing to harm anyone here! Why do you insist on suspecting us? What have we done wrong? Why can't you at least allow us to explain? Don't you think there's a possibility that Robert will *want* to know what I have to tell him? Don't you think that's why he sent me to Alusia in the first place?'

For a moment, Payne was silent. Aiden looked at the others; although they'd said nothing, it was obvious they felt the same. Then Payne said, 'I don't doubt he will want to know what you discovered, but I will not allow you access to him until I am sure neither you nor your friend can do him any harm. I'm sure, as his childhood friend, you can understand my reasoning.'

Patric turned towards the window, where sunlight could hit his face. His eyes were open, but they saw nothing of the bright day. 'Then you choose not to trust me.'

'Yes,' Payne replied, unrepentant. 'But we have the safety of a nation to consider. We don't have the luxury of trust.'

Patric came back with, 'And yet you would complain that Robert doesn't trust you.'

'Arguing the point will not make me change my mind. Bishop,' Payne turned to him, 'tell your story, and let us be convinced. Until then, neither Patric nor Joshi will be allowed to leave Bleakstone, nor to speak to Robert.'

Aiden looked at the man on the bed, and the younger man seated on a stool by the window. It was unfair to assume they were a danger to Robert, but while he'd been left the position of leadership of this council, Payne had the responsibility of keeping them all safe, a role he took very seriously.

'It's hard to know where to begin, so forgive me if I touch on things some of you already know.' Aiden began, taking a sip of his brew. It was cold now, but he didn't bother getting another. 'Six hundred years ago, when the old Empire still stood, sorcerers were an accepted part of the world, and were called the Cabal. Back then, every prince, every lord with any power at all, had a sorcerer at his court. They were paid well, and their abilities highly prized. We don't have much detail on what else they did, but suffice to say the Guilde and Cabal worked together closely, with many of their ventures jointly led. Also too, the Guilde did much of the documentation of sorcery. As a result, many of the Cabal's most important works were written by Guilde scribes.'

'So what happened?' Daniel asked, leaning forward on his seat. 'Why did the Empire go to war with the Cabal?'

'Historically, it's never been clear – though of course, the Cabal was always blamed. My research suggests otherwise. However, we do know that a rift formed and the Empire eventually declared war, with battles and raids, palaces destroyed and the like, until over a year later, when the Cabal and the Empire's forces met on a field in Alusia.'

'A battle,' Payne added quietly, 'which the Empire won, sending sorcerers into exile.'

'Exactly,' Aiden nodded, surprised by the tone in the Earl's voice. 'At the time, the premier Cabal Palace was Bu, in Budlandi. It still stands today. Robert visited it a number of times, most recently, just before the Battle of Shan Moss, when he went with the Lady Jennifer.'

'I never did understand why he went,' Daniel said.

Aiden went to take another sip of his cold brew, then realised what he was doing and put the cup down. There was some part of him which didn't want to tell this story, knowing how personal it was to Robert, and how very private a man he was. Still, these men needed to know. 'Robert's powers began to develop when he was only nine, and so he made his first visit to the Enclave. You all know about the Key – well, it gave Robert a Prophecy that named him as the Enemy, Jennifer as the Ally and a third person as the Angel of Darkness—'

'Nash.' Payne growled.

'Yes, Nash. It's in this Prophecy that Robert and the Angel are supposed to fight. But Robert was also given an ending to the Prophecy that he's always hated and he's spent many years trying to prove the entire thing is false, or at least the ending. His trip to Bu was in the hope that he would find out more about the Prophecy and his and Jenn's roles in it.'

'And did they?' Payne was gazing steadily at Aiden, almost willing him to conjure up the right answers.

'No. Instead, they found the wall where the Prophecy was written had been completely defaced by the Guilde, not long after the battle with the Empire.'

Daniel frowned. 'I'm sorry – why would the Guilde destroy the Prophecy?'

'That's a good question,' Patric interrupted with some fervor. 'Another question is, how did they find out about it, since, as far as anyone can tell, the Prophecy was a huge secret, known only to a handful of people – and all of those sorcerers.'

'But didn't you say, Bishop, that the Cabal and Guilde had always worked together closely?' Daniel looked from one man to another. 'If they kept all the Cabal records, then wouldn't somebody have heard about the Prophecy, even written it down?'

'That is possible,' Aiden agreed, 'but we have no way of proving it. I only wish we could. That would have saved us a lot of time and effort.'

Payne came to his feet and walked over to the other window. He rested his elbow on the ledge and turned back to face the room. 'All this work, all this effort, just so you can find out the answer to this Prophecy, which affects nobody but Robert? Is that what you're saying?'

'Not exactly.' Aiden also stood, unwilling to get bogged down like this, but also needing to be clear. 'I said only the *end* of the Prophecy affects only Robert. The rest of it affects all of us: Lusara, Flan'har, Mayenne – everyone. The Angel of Darkness is evil personified and one way or another, Robert is destined to fight him.'

He accepted the cup of wine John brought him, took a sip and looked around the room before continuing. 'About the same time Robert and Jennifer decided to go to Bu, Robert sent Patric to Alusia. The trip was prompted by the same documents which said the Prophecy would be on that wall. These documents all but described another Cabal Palace, in Alusia, which had, for reasons we had to guess at, developed a rift with Bu a year or so before that last battle. This was the first mention we'd had of a Palace in Alusia. Robert had been there and found no suggestion of it, so it was worth investigation, especially with our need for information.'

'And what caused the rift?' Payne asked levelly.

'We had to infer that the cause was the Prophecy itself. That there was another version of the Prophecy which differed to the one Bu had. This was why it was so important to send Patric. That, and hopefully, that he would make contact with the remaining Cabal.'

To a man, they all looked at Joshi. The young man took in their scrutiny without flinching. As Deverin regained his seat, Aiden stoked up the fire a little, trying not to feel like he was on trial here. But it was hard with Payne watching him as he was.

'So, is that it?' Payne said after a moment, not moving from the window. A thread of sunlight crossed his head, making his light hair glow like a halo, an image which didn't suit his character at all. On any other day, Aiden would have smiled at the thought. 'Is that what this is all about? This Prophecy? Robert's run us all ragged over the last, what, thirty years, all because of a Prophecy? Because he doesn't like how it ends?'

'Don't trivialise it, my lord,' Owen spoke up. One eye was patched, the other glared at the younger man. 'You know full well there were many more pressures brought to bear on Robert other than the Prophecy alone.

His vow of allegiance to Selar for one. The same vow you yourself took, as I recall.'

Payne stared at him a moment, then turned his gaze out the window. He didn't move for a minute as the rest waited uncomfortably. Then the Earl turned back to the room, his expression no longer so hard.

'You hate the waiting,' Deverin ventured, 'as do we all.'

'Aye,' Payne agreed, 'I hate the waiting. Still, let's hear this story. After all that, Patric should be allowed his say.'

Dusty light streamed through the windows of the council chamber, bringing a feel of spring to the room for the first time. As the light hit the thick carpets on the floor, the colours came alive, awakening the painted ceiling and giving the whole room a warmth Aiden had never seen before.

He kept to one side, out of the way, as the others systematically cleared the table of books and papers and stacked them neatly in the chests along the south wall. As each was filled, Payne went along and turned a key in its lock. When all was cleared, Payne joined Aiden by the fireplace as servants came in and set the table for a meal. The Earl didn't look at Aiden, however, but instead, clasped his hands behind his back and feigned a complete interest in the menial tasks being performed in front of him.

Aiden had known this man many years now, and was not so easily fooled. 'You don't think it's a good idea to let Patric out of his bed?'

Payne raised his eyebrows a little. 'I think he's at least well enough to sit at table with us, and I'm sure he will appreciate the change of scenery.'

'Except that he can't see it.'

The Earl replied, 'I don't think that makes a difference.'

'What *will* make a difference?'

Payne frowned and half-glanced at him, not quite meeting his eyes. 'What?'

Aiden placed one elbow on the mantel stone, enjoying the warmth from the fire. 'To you. What will make a difference to you?'

'I don't know what you're talking about.'

'It's not the waiting, is it? You've always been restless, but in the last week or so, it's grown noticeably worse. And never before have I seen you so critical of Robert.'

'Oh, come,' Payne scoffed, 'I have never ignored his faults.'

'No, but you never used to advertise his failings, either. So what has changed? Is it since Father John arrived? Has his joining us changed something?' Aiden paused, watching the other man's face carefully. 'You know I have to ask these questions. We must be unified. If we are called upon to act as Andrew's council then—'

Payne sniffed, lifted his chin and turned his gaze out of the north windows where billowy clouds tumbled across the sky with abandon.

Aiden had his answer, though he could not afford to pursue this any further. Payne had noticed John had information about Andrew and was not sharing it with the rest of the council – though by the look of it, he hadn't said anything to the others.

After a moment, Payne did glance at him, a light of something indefinable in his eyes. 'You know my older brother fought alongside Selar during the Troubles?'

Surprised at the change of subject – and the direction – Aiden could only nod.

'The shame I felt at his betrayal of his country . . . there are no words to describe it. I still wear that shame to this day.'

'Nobody thinks you—'

'No, I understand that. But . . .' Payne kept his voice low so the servants wouldn't hear, 'but I am equally ashamed that I rejoiced the day he died. I took the title of Earl, became head of our House, and have done everything within my power since to expiate his sin. I *need* to see Lusara freed, Bishop. I need to have a hand in achieving that.'

'I understand.'

Payne paused then, turning once more to look out of the window. 'I'm just not sure I like where this is taking us. I'm no longer certain of what we will have once we win this war.'

Aiden caught in his breath, surprised a second time. 'You don't support Andrew for the throne?'

The Earl's response was a long time forming. Then he nodded, once, firmly. 'Yes, I do. He's better than any alternative. But that's not all a King should be, don't you agree, Bishop?'

Finally Payne turned and faced him squarely, allowing Aiden to read what he could in that open gaze. 'I do agree, with all my heart. But I also have faith in Robert, and in his ability to choose the right person.'

'Even if so much of his life has been dominated by a Prophecy he's kept secret from us? How can we judge what is right, or his ability to know what is right?'

Aiden kept hold of that gaze, struggling to find an answer, but he ran out of time. The others returned then, John and Joshi supporting Patric between them. As they took their seats around the table, food was brought in, and Aiden set aside his concerns for the moment in favour of hearing Patric's story.

'I will tell you now, before I begin, that I cannot divulge all the secrets I learned. Those must be for Robert alone. He will know what to do with the knowledge I gained.

'The day I left Flan'har on that ship was the last moment of peace I knew for a long time. I had no idea what the world out there would be like. You may not know this, but I was born inside the Enclave and until I rode on a mission to Robert at Dunlorn, I had spent my entire life inside the caves, with no real desire to leave them. But working with Robert, trying to solve the mystery of our people and this Prophecy, drove me beyond all I knew and out into the Gulf, on a ship that rocked so bad I was sick every hour of the journey.

'I won't recount every day of my trip to you – that would take much longer than your patience would endure. But I did arrive in Alusia safely, and spent some time learning the cities, gaining work to pay for my food and lodgings, and doing all I could to find out if there had ever been a sorcerer Palace in Alusia. It took me a year before I found enough threads to warrant a trip inland. I found a guide, but I discovered nothing. I mounted three other expeditions, all to no avail. I'm afraid I got something of an odd reputation in the city. People believed I was chasing after ghosts.

'After the second year, I gained more information, but I promise you, it was still all little more than guesswork, suspicion and rumour. I was persuaded to take another sea voyage north around the coast, stopping where all the pilgrims go. This was perhaps my biggest mistake. The ship was attacked by pirates. I was captured and worked as a galley slave for months, until, one night, a fearful storm drove the ship into rocks. The captain survived and sold those of us who still lived. We were sent to a salt mine where I met Joshi, and lost my sight.'

Patric paused in his story, and before he could so much as draw breath, Joshi leaned forward and refilled his cup, gently guiding Patric's hand to it so he could drink. Aiden took the time to see how the others were responding; when he had time, he would sit with Patric and learn all the detail that was being missed today.

'When I first met Joshi, I was confused. He appeared to be no more than what you see, and yet, my Senses were constantly on guard, the way they would be if he was Malachi, yet he so obviously wasn't. He also could not speak my language, and I could not speak his. He hardly spoke at all. Even so, we struck up a friendship. He worked at the mine, but was not a slave and could come and go as he pleased. I am sorry to say that it wasn't until my sight went completely that I was able to Sense him properly, and discovered that he was not only neither Salti or Malachi, but was in fact of the Generet, the very people I had been sent to find.'

Again, Patric paused, turning to face Aiden. 'Robert and Jenn happened upon a travelling group of Generet at Bu, didn't they?'

'Yes.'

'I didn't find out about that encounter until years later. As it was, it took another year of wandering the hinterland before I learned to speak Joshi's language enough to communicate my purpose. We . . . had some difficulty with some thugs in a tavern one night. I used my meagre combat abilities to gain our freedom. He decided that was something of sufficient interest to warrant taking me to his people. We had no horses, so the journey took months on foot. When we finally arrived I found he had taken me to a city in the heart of the desert, known the continent over as a capital for thieves. This, I was to discover some time later, was the place which unknowingly hid the Generet.'

'What is the name of this place?' Daniel asked quietly.

Patric didn't answer immediately, but instead, inclined his head slightly towards Joshi. Aiden knew they were mindspeaking; a moment later, Patric gave a half-smile in apology. 'Forgive me, but Joshi has asked me not to say where his home is to any other than Robert. Even then, he is doubtful. I'm sure you can appreciate, all sorcerers have for centuries lived in fear for their existence.'

'Of course. Please continue.'

'It took me a long time to meet with the Generet. They mistrusted me completely; despite Joshi's recommendation, they refused to speak to me for more than a year. In that time I got a job as a teacher of children to one of the more powerful thieves. I was accepted as harmless because I was blind, you see.' Patric smiled then; although he was still pale and his voice a little hoarse, he did not appear to be overly fatigued.

'Finally, when I had all but given up hope, one of the elders agreed to see me. Over the next few months, I gradually got to know them. They began to trust me, and took me to where their homes are, which is not a part of the city itself. Some of the buildings are very old, and it was one of these which started me on the path of discovery. At first, the elders were reluctant to answer my questions, or to allow me to study. It took a long time for me to learn anything because what I found was carved on walls, in symbols and pictures, and I had to learn this new language as well.'

'A new language?' Aiden couldn't help interrupting. 'Not one you already knew?'

'No, though there were similarities here and there in structure and grammar. Once I began to piece together what I learned, I took it to the elders and they told me what they knew. The more I learned, the more amazed I became.'

'But you can't tell us what you know?' Payne asked carefully.

'I must tell Robert before anyone else.'

'But does it involve the Prophecy?'

'Yes, it does. Not only that Prophecy, but also other prophecies we knew nothing about.'

'Other prophecies?' Aiden murmured, unable to help smiling. 'That's just what we need – *more* prophecies.'

'Oh, but, Aiden, you have no idea how many prophecies there have been,' Patric grinned, warming to this theme. 'Some of them go back beyond the Dawn of Ages, to when this world was formed, and the gods Mineah and Serinleth fought Broleoch for the heavens.'

A shocked murmur rattled around the table at that, but Patric continued, 'When I first heard about Robert's Prophecy, I wondered why we had so little in our heritage. I did my best to investigate, but all I could find was a vague mention of a Prophecy that was supposed to happen about three hundred years ago. I thought it was odd that nothing else seemed to be written down. Well, I learned from the Generet why that is, and why there was a split between them and the rest of the Cabal. Jenn was right on that score – it was the Prophecy which caused the rift.'

Steeling himself, Aiden asked one of the questions that had plagued him since the day Patric had left on his odyssey. 'What about the last Battle, the Cabal against the Empire? The incarnation of Mineah who helped the Empire defeat the Cabal? Did you learn anything of her?'

Patric turned his unseeing eyes on Aiden and said slowly, 'Yes, I did.'

Aiden was about to ask more when the door opened and a servant entered, a letter pouch in his hand. He made directly for Aiden and delivered it without a word. Every man in that room knew what this letter might be. Every man dreaded it.

Feeling the silence around him, Aiden opened the pouch and broke the seal on the letter. It was from Godfrey, and the first few lines made his heart stop.

Your Grace,

I have the worst news to impart. I beg you, do what you can to inform Robert as urgently as you can. Nash has used his evil abilities to regenerate his body, using the blood of his own daughter. He is now whole and healed, and far stronger than ever before. It is even possible that this blood will guarantee his immortality!

Again, I beg you, please send to Robert and tell him all I have set out. If you do not, then he will face Nash unprepared, and both he and our whole cause will be lost!

10

'Godfrey, tell me you didn't!'

Osbert reached out and caught his arm, forcing him to stop in the middle of the castle corridor, drawing the gazes of others passing in the opposite direction. Almost instantly, the Proctor recognised the awkwardness of their situation and let Godfrey go. Even so, he glanced around, chose a door almost at random and briskly ushered Godfrey into a darkened – but mercifully empty – room.

'Please, tell me you didn't write anything—'

'Of course I wrote something!' Godfrey snapped back, then drew in a breath, and his self-control with it. He laced his hands together and lifted his chin. Just whom he was defying, however, he couldn't quite pinpoint. 'Did you honestly expect me to say nothing? The Baron DeMassey died to give me that information so I could act on it. They need to know what happened. I wish I could tell the whole country, but who would believe me? My silence now could seal our defeat – is that what you want?'

'Damn it, Godfrey, don't be an ass.' Osbert took one long stride to the door and opened it a crack to see if anybody was close enough to listen. Satisfied, he shut it again and turned back, his face in half shadow and deeply unhappy. 'And what happens if your letter is intercepted? Eh? By Kenrick, or even Nash? What will you do then? Or if your courier is followed. How can you risk everything . . .'

'There is no risk. I've been using this system of couriers for years. They're protected so that—'

'But—'

'What risk worries you most?' Godfrey continued relentlessly. 'You think your timely rescue of me from that wood will somehow make Nash forget that I was there, that I was the one who—'

'Ssh!' Osbert clapped a hand over Godfrey's mouth. They remained frozen together like that for a moment, the Proctor's eyes screwed shut, as though he could erase the truth the way night would chase away the day. Godfrey did not fight him; instead, Osbert grunted and let him go, turned and walked away to a thin pencil window which looked out onto the east side of Marsay. The Basilica stood to the right, the Guildehall to the left.

Poetically, only he and Osbert, Bishop and Proctor, seemed to stand between the two.

'Nash still hasn't returned to court,' Osbert murmured, his hand finding the wall, his head dipped. 'Kenrick came back last night, but I couldn't find out where he'd been. At least, not for certain.'

Willing to take the peaceful route here, Godfrey asked, 'But you do have your suspicions?'

Osbert replied, 'My contacts say there are rumours that Malachi attacked Maitland Manor, that your friend, the young Duke, and his family were murdered.'

'No!' Godfrey gasped in a horrified breath, but Osbert was already turning to face him.

'I have doubts about how true those rumours are: however, I think that's where Kenrick went, to find out about his cousin.' Osbert blinked a moment, then added reluctantly, 'They have always appeared to the rest of the court to be very close. And now that Kenrick has returned, his presence rules out the possibility that he left to join Nash, wherever he is.'

'Wherever he is.'

'Yes.' Osbert drew the word out, his gaze going over the nondescript furniture in the room before finally finding Godfrey. There was a silence between them for a moment.

'We must stick together.' Osbert raised his hands, perhaps indicating the entire country as their joint enemy. 'If we don't . . .'

Godfrey could only shake his head. 'Nash knows it was me, Osbert. He will probably guess that you got me free. If he wants us dead, there'll be an end to us. My writing letters will not change that.'

In the space of a few heartbeats, Osbert's expression altered, his brow clearing, the lines of stress about his eyes and mouth smoothing out completely. Only his eyes showed all he felt: a bitterness and a fear held for far too many years. 'I don't know . . . what to do.'

And with those simple words, Godfrey felt the chasm open up beneath them, drowning them in an isolation that would most likely be the death of them. In this room, in Kenrick's castle, in Marsay, they were alone and surrounded by people who could only afford to be enemies. There was no comfort he could offer, no hope reality had not already spoiled for him. But still he reached out and patted the Proctor's arm, his voice emerging as softly. 'Nor do I, my friend. Nor do I.'

'Sire, the Guilde Proctor has requested an audience with you this morning.'

Kenrick looked up from his bath. Forb'ez had changed his clothes since they had returned last night, but at this distance, in this light, he looked exactly as he had when he had worked for Kenrick's father, his white hair cropped, and his fair eyebrows not breaking the absence of colour on his face. He held himself like the warrior that he was, as though there were no secrets he was hiding.

'Tell him to go away,' Kenrick grunted, turning back to the sheaf of papers he held above the water, but the moment he did he lost all interest and handed them to one of his serving men. The bath had felt warm and relaxing when he'd first sunk into it, but now the water was cooling and there was an itch to be up and at the day.

He had things to do.

He stood, dripping water all over the place, and was handed towels warmed from the blazing fire in the south corner of the room. Refreshed, he stepped out onto more towels and instantly, his men brought forth the clothes he had chosen earlier. He hadn't yet worked out how he would get out, but ultimately, that was irrelevant.

Forb'ez was still waiting by the door, yet not dismissed. As Kenrick thrust his arm into the worn jacket, he clenched his jaw and asked the question he'd been avoiding since his return last night. 'And Nash? Has he been back to court yet? Has he sent any message? Is there any word of when he will return, or when he plans to?' Each word fell out of him reluctantly. His stomach churned. It was a good thing he had yet to have breakfast.

'Of Nash I can discover nothing, Sire.' Forb'ez took a step further into the small room, his hands clasped before him. 'He departed, as you know, the day we left for Maitland, and has not been seen in the city since. But . . .'

'But what?'

'Most of those who worked with him seem to have left the city also.'

The Malachi? Gone? Then Nash had gone to fight Robert Douglas – and he'd not thought to tell Kenrick. Was this the battle they were to fight? *Now?*

No, it couldn't be, not without warning, not without a moment's preparation. Though he could barely trust Nash to tell him if the sun was shining, they were, for the moment, still allies.

So where in Serin's name was he?

Kenrick shrugged his serving men away and attended to buttoning up his own jacket. 'You said you overheard some men talking, when you heard of the fight at Maitland.'

'Yes, Sire.' Forb'ez might have looked surprised, but on that face, it was hard to discern.

'Where were you?'

'A tavern in the city. A place called the Two Feathers.'

Kenrick smoothed down the ordinary clothes he was wearing and took the dusty cloak handed to him. 'Good, you can take me there.'

'Now, Sire?' This time the surprise was visible.

'Yes, now. Come, let's go.'

Godfrey dipped the pen into the jar of ink, once, twice. Then he lifted it out, holding it above the jar to ensure no rogue droplet would fall upon the desk, or the pile of letters and documents he'd already signed. Content the pen was safe, he brought it across to the bottom of the next page and, slowly and deliberately, he scrawled his name: Godfrey Mawnus, Bishop of Lusara.

He sat at his desk, surrounded by an air of determined activity, both quiet and undisturbing in its intensity. Even as his eyes swept over each line of carefully scribed letters, he could feel the currents in the air as a small group of monks removed his heavy winter curtains and replaced them with lighter sets, ready for summer – should it ever arrive, should this long, long, dismal, cold, unfriendly, terrifying, soulless winter ever end . . .

Godfrey paused mid-signature, took in a deep breath and held it as he re-dipped his pen, using the moment to gather himself. He would *not* do this, and especially not when surrounded by men who looked up to him. He couldn't afford the luxury.

His pen made its way back to the paper, his title appearing once more before his eyes, an ever-present and beloved reminder of what he was, what he would never be, and of what he had done.

His private study was a comely room, and well-suited to his purpose. At the very least, it was a room his predecessor, Brome, had disdained. The walls were all of the same rose-gold sandstone, and vaulted, with each arm folded and folded again, to form each fan arch in the roof above. There were three graceful pillars along the centre line of the room; his desk stood against one of them.

And there were windows, long, wide windows, which let in much light during the dark winter days, two on each side of the fireplace, and two more behind him, at the end of the room. The other two walls held doors and provided space for bookcases, another, smaller desk, three chairs, a prie-dieu, and a corner garderobe. There was another table in the centre of the room, at which Godfrey ate, when he could get away with eating alone.

And there were other chairs and rugs and a single, brightly coloured tapestry above the fireplace. It hadn't been there when he'd taken up office. His predecessor had hidden it away, but Godfrey had put it back. Bishop Domnhall had loved it, and he loved it himself. It was a simple scene: a tall, sharp mountain in the background with a cap of creamy snow. In the middle ground were the sturdy buildings of a small village, surrounded by the lush green of Lusara. Then in the centre, with light gleaming from their faces, were the gods they all worshipped: Serinleth, astride his horse, with his sword of fire illuminating the darkness, and beside him, Mineah, her eyes all-seeing, her palms open to embrace the world, her horse eager to trample evil in its path.

This tapestry was rare, both in its artistry, and in the fact that it did not portray the other god, who stood against all Mineah and Serin represented. For this reason, the tapestry could not be displayed in the Basilica or any other church, for every priest was sworn to acknowledge the evil Broleoch along with the good Mineah and Serinleth. One could never exist without the other.

But in here, for the hours he toiled at this desk, when he was interrupted by the ghosts in his head who rattled their chains and refused him peace, he took comfort from that tapestry, offering up a small prayer each time. Amongst his very great crimes, this was as a breath of air.

He looked up as Archdeacon Francis appeared in the north doorway, hands folded in his sleeves, his cowl up to warm his bald head. Though his gaze met Godfrey's instantly, he bowed formally before entering the room, then stood aside as the last of the winter curtains, folded and laid over the arms of a puffing monk, made its way out of Godfrey's study. The new curtains were all hung now and, one by one, each monk passed Francis, bowed towards Godfrey and left.

The silence at their departure was only dispersed by the faint noise of the city outside the windows, all the more audible now the curtains were thinner.

'Good morning, Your Grace. Do you wish the door closed?'

For a moment, Godfrey longed for even more silence, and almost asked Francis to leave, but he held back the words and nodded. Francis shut the door while Godfrey busied himself with his last signature. When he was done, he found Francis waiting on the other side of his desk, a picture of perfect patience. Francis had been a priest for most of his fifty-odd years. He was able to hide his wily nature when he wanted to.

Godfrey put his pen down and pushed his chair back. As he got to his feet, he grunted at the ache in his hip from sitting still for too many hours.

'Are you in pain, Your Grace?'

'No,' he lied, then wished he hadn't. But more, he wished Francis would simply call him by his name. But he never would again. No priest ever would. 'Is something wrong?'

'Forgive me, Your Grace,' Francis's tone was that of friend, rather than secretary, 'but I was about to ask you the same thing. You have seemed unwell for these last three weeks. I would be more comfortable if you would agree to seeing a Healer. People are—'

'What?' Godfrey snapped, then raised his hand in instant apology. 'I'm sorry, Father. I am just a little tired. I haven't been sleeping well.' Such lies! Sleeping well? Sleep was nothing more than a fond memory. These nights he no sooner closed his eyes than his vision was filled with blood, his dreams replaying over and over again the moment when he plunged a dagger into the heart of that young girl, murdering her, feeling the agony of her death, breaking his own heart even as he sliced hers in two.

And she had died for nothing, he had killed her for nothing. Her blood was on his hands and so was his failure. DeMassey had warned him of the dangers, had begged him to kill the child, but he'd hesitated, needing to be sure for the sake of his own conscience – and in that moment of hesitation, he'd given Nash enough time to arrive, to take the girl's blood – his own *daughter*'s blood – to do the gods knew what with. But DeMassey had told him. DeMassey had known. Such blood would make Nash stronger than ever before, perhaps even stronger than Robert – and it would also make him immortal.

Dizziness swept over him, as it had done every moment he thought about this. His stomach lurched, threatening to embarrass him, and he reached out to the graceful pillar to steady himself. He'd promised himself he wouldn't do this – but then, he'd also promised DeMassey he wouldn't fail. What virtue did any promise have these days – especially those made by a man of the gods, a priest, who was sworn, on the Basilica's altar, never to use violence of any kind, against anyone, ever.

With discipline born of desperation he breathed deeply and looked up to the tapestry. *They* had defeated evil before. This was not the time to abandon hope.

'Your Grace?' Francis was at his side, offering a friendship Godfrey could not afford.

'I'm fine,' Godfrey said evenly, schooling his features to work with the lie. He turned to face his friend and even managed something akin to a smile. 'I finished what you left for me. Are there any other documents you wish me to review?'

Francis shrugged, his eyes searching and finding no obvious chink in Godfrey's armour. He matched the smile. 'There is so much work that was left undone because of Brome's long illness, so many things he would not attend to. I am trying to parcel a day's work up each time, so as not to tire you but—'

'It will take us until next Caslemas to clear the backlog?'

Again Francis shrugged, refraining from answering. 'There are also the courts you will need to hold, on the first day of summer. This year, I'm afraid, you will have to run at least three weeks, just to catch up – and that's assuming no further complicated cases need your judgment.'

'Very well,' Godfrey said, using the brisk efficiency of Francis's report to harden his own resolve. 'Let me look at what we have so far, then I can begin my reading.'

'Are you sure? You've already been working all morning.'

'Yes,' Godfrey said, heading back to the desk. 'I'm sure.' He had failed to stop Nash regenerating, but the Angel of Darkness hadn't won the war yet. And until he did, Godfrey would work with his tainted hands and his bruised conscience. There was, after all, much more at stake here than just his soul.

Moving through the city without pomp and ceremony left Kenrick with an odd feeling of emptiness he couldn't quite shake. But it was more than that. He'd travelled the streets before without attention to his rank, but this was the first time he had walked in complete anonymity. Not only that, but his only escort was a man who appeared to have betrayed his father.

Kenrick had felt fear before; most of the time he'd spent in Nash's presence he'd felt it.

Any time Robert Douglas's name was mentioned he felt it.

But this time the feeling rattled deep into his bones, as though he were risking more than his own life. But what good was his throne if he was dead? If he couldn't get Tirone to agree to the marriage with his daughter, Kenrick would have no heir to pass it to, so how could there be more to risk than his life?

He thrust his hands into deep pockets in his jacket. Forb'ez strode before him, a cap on his head to give him a little disguise. He paid no attention to where he was, nor the people who walked by him. For Kenrick, the journey was a miniature nightmare. The streets were filthy: rotting straw, dead vermin and the gods knew what else lay in the shallow gutters. Only the cold of the spring day prevented the smells he knew would rise in summer. The buildings Forb'ez took him past were little more than ruins, paint flaking, roofs tilted and falling down, shutters hanging off their hinges.

And the people: they were the worst. They were dirty and, by the gods, they smelled. They held themselves with little regard to dignity, their clothes ragged and caked in filth, as though they spent their time rolling in the streets in which they lived.

Kenrick quickened his pace. No wonder he'd never been through this part of the city before – and he never would again. If these were the people Robert Douglas would free, there hardly seemed any point. The inhabitants of this city were little more than animals, and deserved to be treated as such.

The smell got worse the further downhill he moved. Marsay was a city on a river island: the water should have taken the filth away. Instead, it festered below the city walls; Kenrick could see it through the archery slits built into the stone.

'How much further?' he grunted, hurrying to catch up with Forb'ez.

'Another corner, S—'

'Don't!' Kenrick hissed. 'I don't want these people to know who I am, don't you understand?'

He could tell from the sideways glance the man gave him that he didn't. It was on the tip of Kenrick's tongue to ask him the truth, about himself and his desertion of one King before he had a chance to betray another, but prudence stopped him. For the moment, Forb'ez was helping him, giving him access to something he'd wanted for a long time; this was not the time to be questioning such a gift.

'Here it is, S— Here it is.' Forb'ez cut short a gesture towards the inn and paused outside the door, waiting for instruction. The building was unremarkable, though clearly a hostelry of some nature. Above the door was a faded wooden sign, with the outline of two feathers only just visible.

Kenrick came to a halt, his fingers suddenly itching, his imagination abruptly darting from one thought to the next. He'd wanted to do this for a long time – had *needed* to do this, but until now, he'd had neither the opportunity, nor the means, and it had been far too risky for him to try. Now fate had given him this chance and if he didn't take it, then he would deserve whatever it was Nash had planned for him.

Forgetting Forb'ez, he reached out and pushed the door open. He stepped inside, remembering late that he needed to look more casual than he probably did. Even so, his gaze eagerly swept the room, seeing little in the darker corners beyond vague shapes that might be people. In the foreground a few men sat at tables, mostly eating meals from wooden plates. Only one looked up, and that briefly. The rest ignored him, sipping from ale mugs and tearing coarse brown bread apart. The room was as dirty as the street, the ceiling stained beyond his imagination, the floor something he dared not look at. Even the fireplace in the wall opposite gave out an air of poverty and filth. How anybody could sit in this place and eat was beyond him.

A wave of revulsion swept over him, but he swallowed hard and chose a table in a corner by the door. He took a seat with his back to the wall and carefully arranged himself there, using the arrival of Forb'ez as cover.

Leaving the other man to order if necessary, Kenrick then closed his eyes almost completely and sent his Senses out into the room.

He found nothing, but that didn't surprise him: he'd found nothing on the countless occasions he'd tried this since returning last night. But this time he had another weapon. Sure he was not being watched, he took hold of the small bag he had tied to his waist. Keeping it beneath the table, he put his hand into the folds of hessian until it could cup the glass seated there. Only then did he look down at the Bresail.

He'd had this one made for his own personal use; it was a small glass bottle almost perfectly spherical in shape, with a tiny opening at the top, stoppered by a piece of cork and a wipe of wax. Inside was the faintly coloured oil Nash had imported from the southern continent. Resting at the bottom of the bottle, surrounded by the oil, was, he'd been told, an *ayarn*, a stone once used by a Salti sorcerer to wield his powers – a Salti now long dead.

Kenrick had no idea how or why this device worked, only that it did. He'd seen it work week after week as it showed him how many Malachi he had at court, so that Nash could keep track of them, to ensure they were not planning on betraying their alliance. And he saw it work now as it began to glow in his hand, warning him of the presence of a sorcerer other than himself. More than one, in fact.

He almost laughed with delight, but his stomach twisted in anticipation and it was all he could do not to leap to his feet and declare his interest – but this was not the way to go about it. With his hands shaking, he settled back, letting the Bresail complete its task.

The glow increased and the glass began to feel warm in his hand. This was a good sign, as it meant that the sorcerers nearby were strong. Kenrick closed his eyes again, fumbling to allow his Senses to filter through the Bresail. He'd seen Nash do this once, but the older sorcerer had refused to explain how it was done.

But somehow, his clumsy attempt brought direction to his Senses. The men he wanted were sitting in the back of the inn, under cover of the shadows Kenrick could not penetrate.

He opened his eyes and looked up. For a minute he could almost see the faces he wanted, but the moment passed. Then, abruptly, there was movement, and his heart began to pound. Almost belatedly, he closed the hessian bag, hiding the presence of the Bresail, but it was too late. Footsteps came towards him and he turned to find a young man standing before him, of perhaps twenty years of age. His hair was cropped short, coppery, and matching that of his eyebrows and equally short beard. His skin was more olive than pale, as though he were used to much more sun than this. His entire bearing both warned Kenrick and sent a thrill through him. This young man held himself like a warrior who feared nothing – the same stance held by every Malachi Kenrick had ever met.

The man stared at him for a time, then looked briefly at Forb'ez. He took another step forward and returned his gaze to Kenrick. 'What cause have you to use such a device?'

Surprise flooded through him – he'd not expected a Malachi to *know* when the Bresail was being used. Nash had said nothing about—

But of course, there was a lot Nash kept to himself – and that, really, was why he was here.

Taking a fortifying breath, he straightened up, gestured to an empty chair and nodded to Forb'ez that he should wait outside. As the older man left, the younger took his place, never once taking his eyes from Kenrick's. Such steady scrutiny was not easy to bear.

'What's your name?' Kenrick began carefully, keeping his voice low. 'Why are you here on your own?'

'My name is my business, and so is why I am here. I ask again, what cause have you with that device? Is it to hunt us down? Surely you could leave such work to another and not soil your hands.' The tone was level, the expression gave nothing away, and yet there was nothing but contempt in the air around him. This young man knew exactly who he was, and more importantly, who was his ally.

It was time to take a chance. 'Where is DeMassey?'

'Dead,' the young man replied, blinking slowly.

'And your brothers?'

'Gone to bury him.'

'And you are left here alone?'

Another slow blink, but this time, silence.

'You are left alone here to keep watch? Or to effect revenge?'

The young man moved to get to his feet, but Kenrick reached out and caught his hand, exerting the smallest amount of pressure. He could not do this without taking a chance. He'd done so ten years before, and he'd made an ally of the most powerful man in the country – but that same man would also kill him at the first opportunity. He'd been a child then, unable to understand what he was doing, or the man he would help. He knew more now, could read a stubborn loyalty in this young man's eyes, in his brooding silence. He could do this.

'Just listen to me,' he urged in a whisper, looking swiftly around the room once before releasing the hand. 'You blame Nash for DeMassey's death? So do I,' he lied. 'But that's why I'm here.'

'You owe your throne to Nash; you are his friend.'

'Only until the day he kills me.'

The young man's eyes widened a little, surprise filling his face for a moment. 'What do you want?' he asked bluntly.

'I want you to help me.'

The young man shook his head. 'I am not allowed to speak for my people. You must address your request to Gilbert Dusan or Felenor Calenderi.'

'I only want *your* help.'

A flash of anger lit the young man's face. 'I will not betray my people.'

'Nor would I ask you to, unlike Nash.' Kenrick paused a moment, then took a deep breath. 'I want you to teach me.'

The young man stared at him a moment, looked to the back of the room, then to Kenrick again. He frowned and sat back. His eyes closed and remained that way for a few seconds, then he opened them again. Kenrick waited as their safety was confirmed.

'Well?' he asked, already knowing what the answer would be and barely able to stop himself from crowing in triumph. 'Will you teach me what you know about sorcery?'

'Will you help my people avenge the Baron?'

'At the first opportunity. If you can kill Nash for me, I will be for ever in your debt. I can't see that we have any goals that would cause conflict, can you?'

That gaze ran over him again, flinty hard at first, then softening to a satisfied grin. 'No. You have yourself a teacher.'

'Excellent!' Kenrick rubbed his hands together. His oldest dream was about to come true. 'What's your name?'

'Rayve, Sire. I was DeMassey's best student.'

'Good.' Kenrick got to his feet. 'Gather your belongings. From now on, you have rooms at the castle.'

He waited while the young man retreated to the back of the room, to where another man sat in the darkness. The two talked for a few minutes, then Rayve left and headed upstairs for his belongings.

Kenrick smiled and turned for the door. Stepping outside was nowhere near as hard this time as he'd expected.

11

'I don't like this.'

Margaret paused in chopping carrots and looked up at the man standing close. Murdoch was a powerful figure, aged somewhere around fifty, with the strength of an ox. His gruff exterior hid a gruff interior, but his sense of humour and genuine kindness had won its way into many hearts. He'd been one of Robert's most loyal and staunch supporters and had worked with him every summer for the past eight years. He alone had been Margaret's source of information about her oldest son throughout that period.

'What don't you like?' she replied, keeping her tone as soft as his. She looked around at the night's camp, which was buried in a nest of trees below a barren hilltop. As usual, everyone was about their allotted tasks; in an hour they would eat and soon after that, sleep. She prayed, along with everyone else, that tomorrow would bring them to their destination – wherever that was.

Murdoch pursed his lips; he barely glanced over his shoulder, though Margaret could tell which way his gaze went: the same as everyone else's, to the separated bed, Robert wrapped in his blankets, grabbing a few hours of sleep as Jenn and Finnlay held the mask over the Key to keep them all safe. The lack of direct leadership from Robert had an odd effect on the group. To see him so vulnerable made everyone – Margaret included – more than a little scared.

'Robert looks like he knows where we're going,' Murdoch murmured.

'But?' Margaret returned to chopping vegetables; she had hungry people to feed.

'But . . .' Murdoch looked up at the sky and the faint stars he could see through the trees. 'He's putting us directly in Nash's path.'

'What?' Margaret dropped her knife and turned to face him.

He met her gaze with unhurried concern and nodded slowly. 'Judging from where he said Nash started, and from where we started, our steady eastward journey—'

'We were heading more north today . . .'

'Making it even worse. If Nash was determined to find us at the Goleth,

99

he would have been heading due west and a little south. If we're not careful, we'll make the whole mask business a complete waste of time. Nash will stumble upon us as we sleep!'

Margaret bit down a gasp; her eyes turned to where Robert lay. 'Have you spoken to him about this?'

'He's barely able to function, Lady Margaret, let alone hold a conversation. If we don't find this place within a day, the mask will slip anyway. As soon as the others finish setting up camp, I plan to speak to them. Serin's blood, we don't even know where we're heading.'

'*You* don't know? But I thought . . .' Margaret's voice trailed off. She'd been afraid to ask. She'd sensed the tensions running between them all; for all that she'd lived at the Enclave for more than eight years, she was still very much an outsider in all this. Without the powers of a sorcerer, or the education they had, she could never be a real part of this coterie, but even so, her own gifts, meagre though they seemed some days, gave her the insight she needed. She would have loved to have spoken at length to Robert, but apart from a few words after his arrival at the Enclave, she'd been able only to observe him from afar. She'd known she would have to wait. 'You can't mean he's doing this deliberately.' Margaret looked back at Murdoch, unsure what to believe. 'He must have a plan.'

'If he has a plan, then he needs to tell it to the rest of us. If not?' Murdoch left the question unanswered. 'After supper, we'll talk with the others. I'll get you some more firewood.' With that he was gone, leaving Margaret with her supper.

'Andrew! Andrew, come on. Talk to me!'

Andrew put his hands over his ears, shut his eyes and curled up onto the rock where he was sitting. He was watering the horses again tonight, and they stood before him, ankle-deep in the stream, oblivious to his discomfort, huge black warm shadows in the darkness.

'Andrew!'

Even with his ears covered, he could still hear Guy's voice. Any minute now, his friend would find him and he would have to make some excuse and go back to the camp. He'd not been able to face Guy the last two nights, since he'd revealed Robert's plans for him. He couldn't get the picture of the shock on Guy's face out of his head, the dawning understanding and the horror at Andrew's refusal.

He knew; he felt the same things himself.

By the gods, what was he supposed to do? He only had two family members left alive: his mother and Kenrick. What kind of person was he that would kill his own cousin? What kind of man was he *not* to? Certainly he couldn't even think about what had happened with Helen without his stomach starting to rebel, but connecting that to Kenrick just seemed like some horrible fable conjured up to scare children.

But this wasn't the first time he'd heard of Kenrick's bizarre activities; he'd had nightmares as a boy – of course, that was exactly why he'd been told, so that he *would* be afraid, so that he would be obedient.

And the man telling him had been his own father. He remembered quite clearly sitting on his bed, his father on a stool before him, huge hands clasped together, his heavy jaw set in determination as, with little inflection in his voice, he'd told one story after another, until Andrew was certain he was making it up. But it had worked. He *had* been afraid – and not just of Kenrick.

So now Robert said he had to kill Kenrick – but what if he *couldn't*?

'Andrew?'

He froze. This voice was much closer – and completely different. Quickly, he uncurled himself and sat up, turning to find Helen standing there, a faint frown on her face as she looked at the horses, the stream and the distance he was from where the orange glow of fires lit the camp.

'What are you doing out here?'

'I just wanted some quiet, I suppose.'

Helen stared down at the forest floor beneath her feet. She was silent a moment, then whispered, 'Guy told me what you . . . what Uncle Robert—'

In an instant, Andrew was on his feet, though quite who he was ready to fight, he didn't know. Still his fists balled up and his heart pounded so hard Helen should have been able to hear it. 'He shouldn't have said anything. It was a secret! He promised—' though he couldn't remember whether he'd extracted a promise from Guy or not. 'You weren't supposed to know. I—'

Helen silenced him with a single, gentle look. It was obvious from her long dark hair, her dark brown eyes, the curve of her smile, that she was Finnlay's daughter. The shape of her face was her mother's, but the sweetness of her nature was all her own. Andrew didn't know a single person who didn't think the world of Helen. Including him.

'Uncle Robert,' Helen began softly and a little shyly, 'wants you to be King. And to do that, he wants you to kill—'

'Yes,' Andrew said so she wouldn't have to. He knew the memories were still painful for her. Kenrick had tried to drain Helen of her blood, use it to heal his own wounds, and he would have killed her in the process. If Robert and Finnlay hadn't rescued her, or if they'd been a minute later, she would be dead now. Why could he not feel rage when the life of one of his best friends had been so at risk?

'I don't think,' Helen said after a moment, her voice husky in the darkness, 'that I could just kill my own cousin either.'

He looked up with a start. Then he noticed Guy standing in the shadows behind her. With a sigh, Andrew sank back onto his rock. 'But it doesn't matter what I want, or whether I could kill my own cousin or not – Robert says I will do it regardless. I know I should want to, and I know what he's done, I just don't—'

'See how you *can* do it when you need to?' This came from Guy as he emerged from the brush and stood beside Helen.

'Exactly,' Andrew said solemnly. 'I feel like a coward.'

Helen moved and sat down beside him. She wrapped her arms around his shoulders and gave him a brief, fierce hug. Then she said, 'Who scares you more? Kenrick or Uncle Robert?'

Andrew snorted laughter at the silly question. 'Why, Robert, of course!'

'And yet,' Guy said, 'you keep fighting Robert on this thing, don't you? You keep standing up to him, no matter how scary he is. You can't do that and be a coward, Andrew. It's not allowed. I know. I've seen the rule book.'

As Andrew and Helen looked at him, Guy smiled and added, 'Seen it, memorised it, quoted from it . . .'

Andrew couldn't help a small laugh emerging from him, releasing some awful tightness in his chest – though he didn't know how he could feel so much better when nothing had changed.

Except that it had.

Andrew got to his feet and grabbed the horses' reins he'd anchored under a rock. Feeling more daring than ever before, he took Helen's hand in his and, with another laugh, led them back through the forest to the camp. For the first time since this had all started, he didn't feel alone.

'Robert, can you hear me?'

The heaviness sat on his back like a mountain, unmoving and unwilling. It was so hard to breathe now that he had to constantly remind himself to do so or he would die.

'Where are we?' Words were mouthed only; voice had long since deserted him as it required effort far beyond his present capabilities. Even mindspeech had become impossible.

'By the Warle River, at the flatstone bridge. Can you open your eyes?'

One breath after another, feeding the last threads of his energy. If he didn't get home soon, this would kill him, and then they would all die.

Little by little, light filtered in, dulled and shifting, faint and misty. Was that his sight, or the hour?

'Don't try to see too much, Robert. Dawn is still an hour away. Andrew is unsure which way to go from here and doesn't want to guess. Do we cross the river, or do we continue east?'

His eyeballs stung; his eyelids blinked rapidly to alleviate this small pain. The other, larger pains he didn't dare address. Another breath in, bigger, more determined, and he opened his eyes further, trying to see, trying to remember the last time he'd approached from this direction.

Too dark. Too tired to bludgeon up the memory he needed. But he had to, or they would wander around this place for days until Andrew found something he recalled. By then Nash would have found them. They'd been out in the open for too long as it was. This trip had taken a day, two days longer than it should have.

Everything had taken longer than it should have. Serin's blood, this whole war . . .

'If you can see down there, those two rocks hanging over the river, and that dead tree trunk, well, they look as though they'd make some sort of landmark. Do they seem familiar? Robert?'

Cool, soothing, silky touch, like ice upon his burning skin. Jenn's hand caressing his as though he were made of fine glass and might break under the slightest pressure. But she could give him no strength; she was using all she could to spell him this work, to allow him those few precious hours of rest, without which he would have been dead days ago. Though his vow had been to protect her, now she was protecting him.

He opened his eyes a little further, summoned the presence to swing his head this way and that. Somebody, probably Finn, had had the sense to turn his horse for him, to allow him a greater field of vision with the smallest amount of effort. It was enough.

'Cross,' he mouthed. He could see her turning to look at the flatstone bridge which crossed the ford. They would have to be careful, and he could almost feel her thinking that. Initially she had tried mindspeaking him, but she soon realised that even the effort of listening was almost enough to jolt his fragile control. He should never have attempted this in the first place. Better still, he should have found another way to hide the Key while he rested.

Oh, how he hated it. He had never embraced it, nor celebrated what it was supposed to stand for, and for all the Prophecy it had given him, and the Word of Destruction it had cursed him with, he had never before enjoyed such a hatred as this.

And the Key *knew*.

How, he didn't know, only that it did. But he didn't mind: wallowing in such feelings had helped keep him alert and aware, ready for any bump in the road which might rattle his mask. Masks had never been designed to be moved; that had always been their limitation. Moving a mask, strictly speaking, was impossible – assuming you followed all the usual rules about making one. Robert, of course, almost never followed the rules about anything. As a result, *he* had thought of making a moving mask while everyone else stood around and—

Laughter bubbled up inside him and he shortened his breath to kill it flat. Such an expenditure of energy would be enough to topple him. Years ago, decades, in fact, he'd gone out on a patrol with . . . Deverin. He'd been eleven? Twelve, perhaps? They'd had an interesting week and Robert had learned a lot from his favourite teacher. One night, they'd camped by a long lake and Deverin had taught him how to catch fish. They had, between them, caught enough for both supper that night and breakfast the next day; he recalled holding the fish to take the hook from their mouths, the way they wriggled and squirmed, slimy wet scales making a proper grip impossible, flicking up water, threatening to drive the sharp bone hook into his own fingers, tangling him in the catgut line, and at every moment, the heart-stopping danger that the fish might actually leap back into the water and escape—

'Robert?' Jenn's voice once more broke into the silent world he inhabited, fighting with the squirming Key in its desperate bid to be free of his hook. 'We're going to start crossing now. We've had to light torches; the horses aren't too happy. I'd prefer it if you dismount, but since I don't think you can walk, I'm going to have Finnlay and Murdoch flank you. Just hold tight and we'll get you across.'

He gave her a tiny smile from the corners of his mouth, all he could manage. He could feel the sharpness of the fisherman's hook.

He hated the Key; it could only hate him back. If he'd had more energy, he would have laughed at the awful irony of his current link to it. All those years, so determined to having nothing to do with it, and now – now there was no escape for either of them.

At least there was no demon rattling inside him, poking at the hatred and making it burn. He knew it was still there, but now he had Jenn in his life – no matter how tenuously – the demon had no power to grab hold of his hatred and use it against the Key. On that score at least, they were all safe. For the moment.

He could hear the first stirrings of birds returned for spring, beginning their morning chorus. From memory alone he could tell where east was, for it was still too dark to see. He could hear movement from the others, the slightly unsteady gait of horses crossing the flatstone bridge, the gentle words urging calm upon them. This bridge, unlike most others on the Warle, was unusually narrow and the river was swollen with melted snow and spring rains.

He would be the last to cross, with Finn on one side and Murdoch on the other – but if something went wrong, neither of them would be able to help, and if his control of the Key slipped, it would be far too dangerous for them to be so close. He opened his eyes again, waiting a moment to let the mists swirl and shift into place. Then he saw Finnlay before him, holding the reins of his horse, watching the last of the others complete the crossing.

'Finn, go.'

Finnlay looked up with surprise. 'Go? We're going right now. Just relax, Robert. Andrew said we're not far now, just another couple of hours' ride. Then we'll work out a way for you to have a good long rest, and Arlie can tend those burns—'

'No!' Pain rattled through his chest as the word came out, the loudest he'd spoken in more than a day. Shocked, Finnlay moved closer, allowing Robert to drop to a whisper again. 'You, Murdoch, go ahead. I cross alone.'

'But, Robert—' Finnlay began to protest, then stopped, his eyes flickering over Robert's face. What he read there seemed to unsettle him as, a moment later, he nodded and stepped back. 'Fine, but I'll stay on this side, Murdoch on the other, in case you do need help.' Finnlay took his brother's agreement for granted, handing the reins up to him and calling out to Murdoch to wait for them on the other side of the bridge. Then he moved back, giving Robert space to kick his horse forward.

The horse did not like the river, nor the bridge made of long flat stones supported by smaller low stone pillars. The edifice had stood for three hundred years without falling, but the horse wasn't to know that: all it could see was a too-narrow expanse of wet slippery rock and a river swirling around it, close enough to splash.

Perhaps it would be better if he tried the ford rather than the bridge – but in the spring this crossing would be too deep, hence the bridge. With determined hands, he patted and cajoled, and finally the animal walked forward, until it was standing on the bridge, where it stopped, shaking its head and snorting wildly. Robert wasted no time. He reached out and caught the animal's feeble will with his own overstretched powers, forcing the horse to move. His hands began to shake with the effort, but now the horse walked slowly and steadily, though each step raked pain up Robert's body. He held his breath now, unable to afford even that luxury and still keep control of the horse. A few more steps and then—

With a stumble, the horse gained the other side, its hooves sinking into the muddy earth already trampled by the others. He knew Murdoch was by his side, holding the horse as Finnlay quickly crossed, but he could see nothing, could feel nothing, could not even gain his breath . . . should not have done this—

He had to pull back now or he would have no reserve left to hold the mask, but he couldn't see the lines now, couldn't work out where the mask began and control of the horse ended. Dizzy now, the world tilted around him, and his whole body shook.

'Robert!'

The voice rose up out of the nausea and he reached for it, grabbing it as a lifeline, pulling back from the tight control. Agony shot through him like an arrow through his body. As he gasped for air, his frail control slipped. He recoiled from the deafening clamour and dizziness overtook him. With a groan, he tumbled from the horse.

Even as Murdoch and Finn caught him, he could hear the voice again, crashing around inside the Key, leaking out into him like poison.

Enemy! I have you again, so very close: you can't escape now!

Jenn left the others and ran back to Robert, but she couldn't stop him falling. As they got him safely to the ground, she slipped the bag straps from his shoulders and removed the Key. At once Robert moaned and collapsed back, his breathing harsh and hard. He blinked a few times and whispered, 'Lost the mask . . . He was Seeking; found us! He's close. Can feel it!'

For a second, blind panic rose in Jenn's throat, choking off thought. They couldn't fight Nash here and now – Robert was simply not fit; he couldn't win in this condition – Nash would kill him!

Robert reached out and seized her hand, his grip painful. 'Get them moving. Defence . . . Jenn, he's coming. I need time . . . to find a way—'

Even as he grunted and tried to say more, Jenn's panic was swallowed by need and the plea in Robert's eyes. Without pausing, she snapped off orders. 'Murdoch, help me get Robert back on his horse. Finn, defensive positions. Now! Nash is on his way and we need to buy some time.'

She didn't even see Finnlay go, but Murdoch came around and, with his hands under Robert's shoulders, got him to his feet. For a moment, Robert swayed, seemingly unable to take his own weight, but then he straightened.

'What are you going to do?'

He shook his head, his gaze drifting down to the bag at his feet and the Key it contained. 'I need to make another mask, but I can't if I have to fight him. There's no point in running away if he can follow the Key.'

'We can't get away without facing him.' The words fell into the silence between them. Robert's gaze was steady now in the growing light and despite the awful exhaustion around his eyes, he'd lost much of that deathly pallor. He was pulling himself together through sheer will alone; she marvelled at his unbroken determination. But no matter his powers of recovery, Nash would still kill him.

'Murdoch,' Robert said briskly, 'go help Finn. Make sure everyone is ready.'

As Murdoch ran back to the others, Jenn watched him go. Finnlay had everyone moving, taking care of the horses, stowing their belongings in case they needed to flee, arming everyone with the meagre supply of weapons they'd carried with them, and finding rocks and trees and anything else that would do as cover. The forest was thick along this side of the river, but forty feet from the bank, the trees thinned to open meadow.

'We can't survive this,' she whispered, feeling the gloom of the morning drift inside her and take up root. She knew if she'd closed her eyes and opened her own feeble Senses, she would feel Nash drawing closer – but did she really need to *feel* that? Wasn't the look on Robert's face enough?

'Listen to me,' his voice came out laced with urgency, his hands coming up to hold her shoulders, firmly, but not hard enough to hurt her. 'You have to promise me—'

'What?' She placed her hands over his. 'That I will do all I can to get away from him? To save *myself*? Would you promise me the same thing?'

Robert breathed deeply, then began again, 'Yes, I want you to promise me that – can you blame me? How can I know which decision I make is the one which makes the Prophecy come true? If I tell you to run, will that be your destruction? Or if I tell you to stay by my side—'

'Robert.' Jenn reached up and pressed her fingers to his mouth to silence him. 'No. You can't face him. Not like this. You won't last a minute.'

'Do we have another choice?'

The answer was so obvious, it made her ill. 'Yes,' she replied, her voice oddly steady. 'I can face him.' He was shaking his head before she'd finished speaking, but she forestalled his objections the only way she could. 'Look, if I go and talk to him, he's not going to attack you, is he? Or the others – and let's face it, apart from perhaps holding a grudge against Finn, he's hardly going to be interested in them.'

'Except as bargaining tools against us.'

'Exactly. So while I'm keeping Nash busy, you have time to do whatever you need to do.'

'And what if you can't get away?'

'He has no choice. *I* wield the Key – and *he* knows it.' When Robert said nothing, she added, 'He doesn't know you're not strong enough to fight him right now, either.'

'You don't think he'll be suspicious when you walk out there? No, Jenny, I can't allow—'

She squeezed his hands tight. 'Robert, we don't have a choice!'

He stared at her a moment, then stepped back, turning unsteadily to take a water-bottle from his saddle-bag. In profile, she watched him take long swallows, then wipe his mouth with the back of his hand. As he shoved the stopper in the bottle and put it away, he said, 'Fine. You face him. I'll tell the others what we're doing and be ready to start another mask before we get moving. If he can still Sense the Key while he's talking to you, he won't panic that we're getting away with it.'

'Moving where?' Jenn asked, feeling a little unsteady herself.

'We need to give him a false trail. So once you've spoken to him, we'll make it look like we're going to run. I'll take the Key, unmasked, and ride for a few hours. Then, when I'm a good distance away, I'll mask the Key and double back. If you get everyone straight to the cave, Nash won't realise his mistake until it's much too late, and by then there'll be no trace of us for him to find.'

'But if he sees us—'

Robert raised his eyebrows. 'He won't see us. If you go now, you'll come upon him beyond that turn in the hill.'

'And if you go now, then—'

'I can't. I need a few more minutes. He'll know we're still here, unless . . .' Robert paused and frowned over her shoulder in the direction she guessed Nash was coming from. 'Unless you can still create an image. Like you did years ago, remember? When you made it look like Finnlay was still in that prison cell? I know this is a much more complex illusion, but if you could make it look like the whole group is with me, if Nash sees that with his own eyes – hell, if *we* don't know how far your powers go, how can he? Then, when I go with the illusion, the others can mask their presence and Nash will ignore them. We just need your illusion.' He brushed a thumb over her cheekbone. 'Could you do that?'

An ironic laugh rumbled up from deep inside. 'Sure, I can do that while I'm talking to our most dangerous and bitter enemy. Anything else while I'm at it?'

'Yes,' Robert whispered, and before she could ask what, he caught her, drew her behind the horse and kissed her with such urgent gentleness, it took her breath away.

And just like that, his unshakable calm settled into her, like magic. 'The illusion is easy,' she murmured, stepping back for fear of what *she* might do. 'The challenge will be how long I can sustain it.'

'A guess?'

'At least an hour, if I'm not working in some other manner. If all is well, then four, perhaps five hours. Say to midday. Will that be enough?'

'Enough is all we have.' Robert half-smiled at his own brief wisdom. 'Go now. Take my horse. Say whatever you need to say to him and when you're done . . . come back to me.' He helped her swing up into the saddle, but as she looked down on him again, she couldn't miss the palpable fear in his eyes.

Had he just set the Prophecy to rolling?

'Be careful,' she whispered, then kicked the horse and galloped away, not daring to look at him. If she did, she would turn back and their single chance would be gone. The thick forest swallowed her up, and beyond that the meadow stretched grey and shadowed, like the man she rode towards.

Only now did she open her Senses.

12

Nash could almost taste victory. It sat upon the early morning air like a sweet scent, ready to be savoured and enjoyed. What, in the name of the Blood, were they doing here, in the middle of nowhere? Had they thought to hide from him? If escape was their plan, surely they would have known in what direction he'd be heading; the Enemy must have Seen him just as clearly as he had Seen the Enemy.

Perhaps they had allies out here, or they had planned some sort of trap. He closed his eyes a moment and sent his Senses further out, over the gentle hills surrounding him. He swept east to west, but came upon no large body of men, nothing out of place. There was only the Key, shining and glorious in front of him, and a small knot of people huddled next to it, no doubt ready to defend it with their lives.

It didn't matter. What did matter was that the Enemy, Ally and the Key were a hundred yards away and in a moment, he would have them all in his power.

He kept the gallop steady, not wanting to tire his horse in case a further chase was necessary, but he could *feel* the Key getting closer, could feel his men behind him, even Valena, trapped in her prison of drugs. It felt as if the closer he got to the Key, more of the world opened up to him.

His regeneration had made him powerful, but that was nothing compared to what the Key would give him – what the Ally would give him.

'Master! Look!'

Nash pulled his horse to a stop, signalling those behind him to do the same. He stared, hardly able to believe his own eyes. There, riding towards them, was a figure he couldn't help but recognise. She passed through the last of the forest, crossing behind a clump of trees to the north and then across an open meadow: Jennifer Ross, the Ally.

Even in the grey, predawn light, she managed to glow. Though her face was pale, her blue eyes were striking; he sat there and watched her come closer. It had been so long since he'd seen her: Shan Moss, when she'd gone looking for him, and he for her. And while their armies had fought one another, he had kissed her, and told her that one day she would come to him of her own accord.

But this couldn't be that day – at least, not in her eyes. And if it wasn't that day, then what was she doing?

Once more he sent his Senses over the area, double-checking that the Key was in the same place, that there was no trap or ambush here. Though he couldn't See the Enemy, it was obvious he was still back behind the hill, with the Key and the others. He kept his men behind him and remained where he was as she rode closer, as her eyes swept over the numbers behind him, as they lighted on Valena and finally, slowly, on him. Just as slowly, she came to a halt. Close enough to talk and no more.

Her horse snorted heavily, stamping its feet, but she held the reins with a loose grip, paying it no attention. Instead, her gaze returned to Valena where it lingered as she frowned. Yes, she would wonder whether he'd found another to love. Nash wanted to laugh, to shout for the sheer joy of seeing her again, after so many years, after so much effort to find her, after the despair of his terrible wounds and the news – albeit false – that she'd been killed. After believing that he might never have her.

He realised she was staring at him, but her expression was unreadable.

'Your wounds,' she said just loud enough for him to hear. 'You have recovered finally.'

'More than recovered,' he replied. There was no need for him to keep his regeneration a secret, especially not from her. 'I am restored to my former strength and more. I am once again a man of twenty-five, with more power than I have ever before enjoyed. Thank you for your concern. I see you also have not aged. You are just as beautiful as I remember, more so with that fire in your eyes.' As he was about to move closer to her, a roar from behind warned him and before he could move, a horse galloped in front of him as Valena rode straight for the Ally with murder in her eyes.

Nash raised his hands to stop her with his power, but his men were already after her. Even as the Ally pulled her horse out of Valena's way, the Malachi was brought to a stop, her bound hands caught, her horse contained. As one, they moved back behind Nash.

Valena's recapture did nothing to silence her. 'It's all your fault that he's like this,' she shouted at Jenn. 'Don't you understand? You've made him a monster – if it were not for you – everything was always for you! It's all your fault! I hate—'

And then she was silenced. Nash watched only as long at it took one of his men to put a gag over her mouth and then he turned back to the Ally, gauging her reaction to what she'd just heard. Jennifer, wide-eyed and extremely wary, said nothing. Nash told her, 'Pay no attention to her. She's a little deranged. She lost a child recently and that has unhinged her mind. I keep her with me to take better care of her.' Oh, how he loved picking out the truth in a lie.

Jennifer stared at him a moment, then raised her eyebrows. '*Your* child?' His smile dropped a little as she continued, 'She's Malachi, isn't she? Lady Valena de Cerianne, if I'm not mistaken.'

Now Nash frowned. 'You've not met.'

'No,' Jennifer said, 'but her beauty is much renowned amongst the Douglas men. I see their words did her justice, despite her grief.'

Nash could hear Valena continuing to struggle behind him. He looked once at Taymar and the man instantly turned and headed back to Valena. Jennifer watched as Valena was given a drug, as she fought it, as she calmed and became silent at last.

The silence drew out until Jennifer turned and met his gaze once more. 'And that is how you would treat me.' There was no question in her voice, only certainty.

He moved forward until it looked like she would back away. Then, his own certainty clear in his tone, he replied, 'But I do not *love* Valena. The death of her daughter has made her unbalanced. I keep her restrained for her own safety. She would harm herself if I set her free.' He deliberately let her see the absolute honesty of that statement; it was no lie.

'Now is not the time,' Jennifer said, 'to try to make me believe that you are the very soul of kindness and generosity. Would you have me think you were good when I know you are nothing but evil?'

Nash laughed a little. 'You once looked upon me in that light, once saw me as a friend. You did not think I was evil then.'

'Yes, I did!' she snapped back. 'I just didn't know that Nash the Guildesman was the Carlan, Angel of Darkness! You lied to me then, as you've always lied to me. My pain is your pleasure. You've killed my sister and her husband! For what? For being there? You killed their people, and so many more I can't even count them! The depths of your evil can't even be imagined!'

'I did not kill your sister.' Nash kept his voice light, knowing it would enrage her more. Oh, how he loved to see her like this! So beautiful, so utterly righteous. 'I merely sent DeMassey down to find your son and bring him to me.'

At the sound of her lover's name, Valena let out an anguished cry, despite the drugs, despite the gag.

Nash continued, regardless, 'It was DeMassey and his men who killed your sister, though they told me your boy was dead as well. I see they lied to me.' Her gaze darkened then, and for the first time in his life, he felt a *frisson* of fear. To hide it, he went on, 'But now you come to me, of your own accord, just as I said you would.'

His brazen words were enough to bring the fire back to her eyes. 'You should stop and count the number of things that don't happen just as you said they would. I come to learn what you want with my son.'

Now it all made sense. The light in her eyes at mention of the boy, the whole purpose for this meeting, though doubtless she imagined it would buy her time, she would be unable to exploit it. 'I wanted your son in order to keep him safe from the coming conflict. He is, after all, our King's cousin. I wanted to be able to guarantee his safety for you.'

Her face paled a little, but more with anger than anything else. She stared at him a moment longer, then hissed, 'Liar. Nothing but lies. How would you ever expect me to join you willingly?'

He laughed, softly and without rancour. 'Why not? Here you are, and the Key is just beyond the curve on that hill behind you.' He noted the flicker of her eyes and spread his hands in a gesture of peace. 'Come, join me now and let us stop this open conflict. You know as well as I do that the Enemy is not what everyone thinks he is: deep down, he is plagued with doubts, he walks a fine line between working for good and using his powers for evil.'

'More lies!' she hissed, but she was listening.

'You know him as simply a man, my dear. I know him as my Enemy, and believe me, I need no lies. Robert Douglas is afraid. He's afraid to face me, and afraid to fight me. Most of all, he is afraid of his destiny.' Nash paused, smiling a little at her open horror. 'Come. Surely Lusara will be better off if we two are friends? You know the Prophecy decrees that we belong together. Why continue to fight it when we both know there can be no other outcome?'

Jennifer opened her mouth, but didn't speak initially, as though she was at war with herself, with what she could and couldn't say. 'The Prophecy does not *guarantee* the future. We can defeat you, no matter what words you may use. What matters is only our actions.'

'Really? Then my ancestor, Bayazit of Yedicale should have called it the Action of Destruction rather than the *Word*.' Nash dropped his voice, inching closer to her. 'It scares you, doesn't it? That the Douglas has the Word to use when he wants to. That he killed so many people at Elita. That's why you stopped him at Shan Moss, why you wouldn't let him kill me with it.'

'But you said he *couldn't* kill you with it!'

Nash grinned, loving her confusion. 'Yes, I did. But *you* didn't know that at the time, did you? You still saved me from him, no matter what else you might say, and for that, you have my thanks.'

'I don't want your thanks!'

'Then what do you want?'

'Your . . . your—'

'Death? See? You can't even say it. Because you know it won't happen, and it won't happen because your hero is flawed – and ultimately, because the Prophecy will give him only one choice: to surrender you to me, or be the cause of your destruction. No matter what he does, he will kill you. Your only hope of surviving is to come to me.'

Robert would allow only Finnlay to help him. Together they adjusted the saddle on Jenn's horse; she was not heavy, so the animal would be fresher and more able to handle the coming ride. Robert ate some sweet dried figs and apricots, but couldn't cope with anything heavier, no matter his body's needs. He drank water only, needing to be alert and focused. He found extra padding to put between the Key and his back and ensured the horse ate nothing, but drank its fill. This was all the rest he would get, and it wasn't enough. The numbing waves of exhaustion which swept over him were almost enough to make him call the whole thing off. He tried not to pace up and down, and to ignore the growing terror coiling in the pit of his stomach.

He listened: to the forest around him, to the river rippling behind him, as though nothing of importance was happening. He listened for the signal Jenn would send, via mindspeech, that he should be ready to move. He listened for their conversation, though he couldn't possibly hear so far away.

He couldn't breathe properly; it hurt to fill his chest. He shouldn't have let her go, shouldn't have ever allowed her to become entangled in this whole nightmare. The day he'd met her, he should have – what? Left her to the Guilde to execute as a horse thief? Left her, a child of seventeen, to wander Shan Moss on her own?

By the gods, he just wanted this over, wanted her away from *him*. He wanted to go and drag her to safety and blast Nash's body into a million pieces . . . The others were all watching him from their positions, huddled in relative safety, eyes wide, fear clear on their faces. But there was a lot of courage, too, even amongst the children, Andrew included. He felt their eyes on him, their questions, their hopes. Their trust.

Finnlay's hand reached out and grabbed his arm, halting him. 'No, Robert, you must not go out there!'

He stopped and looked back – he'd marched a dozen feet from his horse without realising it.

'Jenn is safe as long as the Key is here. It *will* protect her. We're prepared to fight if we have to, set to flee when we can. We have masks all ready to slip into place the moment you leave. Now, please, Robert, try to rest.'

He agreed, returning to his horse, to where the Key sat in its bag on the ground, waiting for him to put it on his back again, for him to make another mask and hide its miserable existence. He *had* to be able to do this.

Jenn froze as the sickening truth rattled her. Nash sat there, almost vibrating with life, his dark hair blown by the wind, trimmed beard and black eyes framing his so-very-ordinary face. But it was those black eyes which gave away the evil inside, eyes which smiled at her now with ill-concealed triumph.

The Prophecy. Sweet Mineah, *no*! All Robert's fears, all his nightmares: all true. All these years, his hopes that somehow the ending had become garbled over time and lost its true meaning; his determination to defeat the Prophecy, no matter what: all this was for nothing. How could she tell him?

'You seem surprised.' Nash leaned closer; it was all she could do not to flinch. Instead, she again played upon her genuine discomfort, burying her fear and her fury, allowing her eyes to flicker once more over the soldiers in his band, at the woman, Valena, still bound and trussed like a slave – a slave to her past as much to her future.

Nash had regenerated. They had lost the advantage and now swung back the other way. She could not falter now. She was Robert's only hope. *The Prophecy does not guarantee the future.* Her own words seemed to echo across the meadow, soaking into the bright spring grass. Sunrise was just a few minutes away now; soon the field would be flooded with light: a force not even Nash could ignore.

Robert?

I'm here and ready.

Mount up and be prepared to ride when I say.

A moment later, *Done and ready.*

Robert, he's regenerated, and very strong. Please be careful.

I will.

'But how much of this surprise is genuine, I wonder?' Nash continued without appearing to notice her momentary shift in concentration. 'Did you truly not know the ending of the Prophecy? If he kept you in ignorance all this time, then he is more cruel than I gave him credit for. And you charge me with being evil? I ask you, my dear,' Nash looked into her eyes, 'is *he* everything you hoped for in a man?'

'He is more than you could hope to be if you lived a thousand years!'

Nash took the bait. 'The difference being, of course, that I *will* live to a thousand years, whereas—'

She didn't hear the rest directly. *Robert? He's distracted. Go now. The illusion will follow.*

On my way.

She wanted desperately to call after him, but she could afford no more risks. Nash was suspicious enough of her presence, and there were a limited number of things she could reasonably talk to him about without increasing that suspicion. She had gained Robert all the time she could; prolonging the inevitable wouldn't make it go away.

Though she kept her eyes on Nash as he talked about how superior he was, how destined he was to win, she once more reached out, as she had taught herself to do, into the air, into the ground beneath her, into the trees around her, into the song of the birds awaking the dawn. She drew them all into herself and twisted until they wound together. With the smallest of efforts, she reached out again, this time to place another image back upon the landscape: one lie to combat another.

Nash felt a wrench. The Key was moving. The Enemy was trying to steal it from him. The motion drowned his hearing and drew him into a pit of rage. With a roar, he called out to his men to ride forward in pursuit, then grabbed a strong hold on the link. He could *see* the Enemy riding with it, with his whole band galloping behind him—

But at least he still had the Ally.

Nash turned back to her, a hand raised, ready to ward off any sudden attack she might make – but she had disappeared. Literally. Even as his men galloped past him, he looked around, but as far as the eye could see, there was no sign of her, though she could not possibly have run all the way back to the forest in so short a time.

The link with the Key trembled in his grasp. He had no time to wonder where she was now, he had to follow the Key or he would lose it. Kicking his horse viciously, he galloped after his men, turning around the hill to see a flash of colour disappearing into the trees on the other side of the river. Without pausing, he shouted orders; his men immediately raced for the flatstone bridge.

As he crossed behind them, he could hear Valena laughing at him, calling out to him with a voice laced with drugs and hate, 'He's done it again! You are such a fool! So easy to trick, and all because of her—'

Robert kept his body low on the horse, setting his Senses to run before him, Seeking out the best possible route between the trees, making the most of forest paths and woodcutters' clearings, anticipating the fall and rise of the land. He could not afford a single mistake, or he would be dead, and the Key – and Jenn – would be lost for ever.

Only once did he glance over his shoulder, to find the uncanny image following him like a shadow, faceless and eerie. Jenn had obviously forgone accuracy in favour of longevity. Details in this image were kept to a minimum, but they would be enough to fool somebody in pursuit – and that was all Robert needed.

He burned to know what Jenn had said to Nash, or what he had said to her in return. She had sounded very shaken when she had mindspoken him, but asking about it was impossible. He didn't even dare try to mindspeak her; he had no way of knowing how much control of the image she had.

So he kept his head down, now and then looking up at the sun through the budding trees. He would go until her image vanished, or until Nash was well and truly lost behind him. Then he would find the nearest cover and mask both himself and the Key.

Nash had been easy to fool this time, but this trick would work only once. Next time, he would have to fight, Prophecy or not.

'Mother? Mother, please, open your eyes. Finnlay says we have to move.' Andrew squeezed her shoulder a little harder and shook until, slowly, her eyes opened. She blinked twice, took a deep breath, and focused on his face.

He'd found her sitting behind a small knot of trees north of the meadow. Her horse was tied to a branch and she was sitting on the ground, her back to the trunk, her hands folded neatly on her lap. She looked as though she'd been there for a while, though it couldn't have been more than half an hour since she'd ridden out to meet Nash.

'Mother?'

'Yes, Andrew, I'm fine.' She breathed deeply again and took his offered hand. Using her son as leverage, she got to her feet, brushing down her clothing before frowning up at the sky.

'How did everything go—' Andrew swallowed hard. 'I came out to get you . . . you didn't come back and you weren't with Nash. I was afraid you'd— he'd—'

She turned horrified eyes on him and, without a word, swept him up in a fierce hug. 'Oh, I'm so sorry! I had no time to warn you. Come, let's walk. Finnlay's right, we need to get away now, before Nash realises he's been tricked.'

'But you—'

She smiled at him and tucked her hand inside his elbow. Their horses walked on beside them. 'I was never out there, Andrew. I sent him an image of me, no more. Otherwise I wouldn't have been able to get away.'

Andrew, accustomed to the odd way in which her powers worked compared with the other sorcerers, smiled. Looking at the others already mounting up as they turned the corner of the hill, he murmured, 'Mother, are you and Robert . . .' He paused, his throat tightening as she turned wide eyes on him. Everyone said he had her eyes; was this what he looked like when he was surprised?

'Are Robert and I what?'

'I thought you were enemies,' he stammered, his eyes darting to where Finnlay was watching them, almost pacing in his urgency to get going. He looked back at Jenn to find her smiling.

'Robert has often said he and I are on opposite sides, but never once, since the day I met him, have we been enemies. But no matter what he says, we are both working for the same goal. Don't you ever worry about that, Andrew. Now come, before Finnlay breaks something.'

13

Night fell suddenly, with a cold wind whipping around the horse's tails and a moon quickly swallowed up by murky clouds. No matter how closely Andrew pulled the cloak about his neck, nor how firmly he pressed his hands into his gloves, he couldn't quite get rid of the shiver rippling down his spine.

This waiting made him feel ill; he knew he wasn't the only one who felt that way, and it was small comfort that he wasn't the worst at hiding it. Finnlay, wrapped up in his own cloak, his expression grim, stood in the shadows of a nearby tree, his gaze locked on the narrow gully leading to Robert's hideaway cave.

Robert was overdue. The rest of them had arrived shortly after noon and now, six hours later, there was still no sign of him. Inside, they were setting up beds, lighting fires, cooking their first real meal for more than a week. These caves were nothing like the Goleth: they were smaller, and not ideally shaped for people to live in, but they gave shelter, and for the moment, they offered a safe haven.

Andrew knew his mother was praying that the cave would be deep enough to hide the Key from Nash. Andrew was simply hoping Robert would come back so the Key's safety would be *their* main problem and not *his*.

Finnlay left his shelter and paced away for a few steps; all Andrew could see of him was his black outline against the dark night.

'Can't you Seek for him?' he asked quietly.

'What, and give away our position as well?'

Andrew swallowed hard at the reminder. Nash knew Finnlay's aura – if Finnlay tried to Seek Robert, Nash might be able to find them, and then they would have nowhere to hide.

'You should go inside,' Finnlay added after a moment, his voice softer. 'Get something to eat, get some rest. I can stand watch on my own.'

Andrew was a little hungry, but there was something horribly unsettling about the prospect of eating a normal meal, chatting to people when the man they all depended on so much was still out there, in the cold spring night, possibly at Nash's mercy.

The ensuing silence made Andrew fidget; he knew it irritated Finnlay, and his father had hated that in him as well and had punished him for it. Andrew took a deep breath. He simply couldn't imagine Robert not returning, nor a world without Robert in it somewhere. It didn't seem possible, and yet—

And yet both his mother and Finnlay were both now worrying that the worst had happened, that Robert had been caught by Nash and, in his depleted state, been killed.

It couldn't be possible – but that was what the Prophecy said would happen – or at least, it said that Robert and Nash would fight.

He began to fidget again, and the picture of Robert appeared once more: Robert, with his calm demeanour, his dry sense of humour, the way he never got angry – how could a man do that?

Well, if Andrew wasn't *actually* brave, then at least he could assume the outward appearance of it. 'He's not so late,' he said after a moment. 'Not if he rode due south of us to take Nash as far as possible from here.'

He felt Finnlay's sharp gaze on him and, for a second, Andrew wished the shadows would swallow him up: he'd obviously said the wrong thing. But then Finnlay turned his gaze back on the gully and replied, 'He wouldn't head due south – it would look too obvious to Nash.'

Frowning, Andrew pictured the map in his head: they had come from the west, but Nash would know they'd never head north, towards Marsay. If not south, then east? No, because they'd not been heading in that direction initially. But wouldn't Nash expect them to lay a false trail once he'd realised he'd been fooled? Of course, he could just as easily think that Robert would expect him to think that and therefore not bother to lay down a false trail.

The twists were dizzying, but even so, he came up with an answer. 'Robert would have headed northeast, towards Elita.'

He could see nothing, but the smile was evident in Finnlay's voice. 'Yes.'

'And,' he continued, encouraged, 'that will take Nash further away from the Enclave, giving everyone as much time as possible to get as far away as they can.'

He saw the faint movement of a nod. 'It's comfortably easy to allow other people to think for you. My brother plans to put you on the throne; it's time you started using your own mind. You'll find the exercise will do you good.'

'But what if I don't want to be King?' The words were blurted out before he could stop them and he winced as he awaited Finnlay's response.

To his surprise, Finnlay laughed a little, although it was very dry. 'You don't want to be King? Amazing. I do. I would love to be King. If Robert chose me, or even if he decided to take the throne himself, I would do all within my power to make sure it happened. And the moment I had that power, the moment the crown sat upon my head, I would do my best to make sure the poor were fed, to welcome the thousands of refugees back home, to bring back justice to the courts and prosperity to this battered country of ours. I would make sure no sorcerer was ever punished for being born with powers, and I would encourage the Salti to come out of hiding and give them the opportunity to become part of the community. Andrew, I swear, I would love to be King – no matter the cost.'

For a moment, Andrew was stunned into silence, but the prickles of his own conscience poked at him, urging him to do exactly as Finnlay had just instructed. 'So you think it's all right to murder one man in order to save others? Is that what the Church would preach? Would I have McCauly's blessing if I do it?'

'Who says it has to be murder?'

Andrew sighed. 'Kenrick is my cousin, my own family.' He would have gone on, but Finnlay strode up to him, and stood over him, his eyes glinting in the fragile light.

'Don't *ever* mention his name to me again,' Finnlay hissed, seething hatred. Shocked, Andrew kept silent as Finnlay continued, 'Your *cousin* took my daughter, cut her vein open between her wrist and her elbow and tried to drain her lifeblood from her. If you get the opportunity to kill him, then consider yourself fortunate, because if I get to him first, you will find nothing left of your precious cousin but ashes. Trust me, Andrew, you and that monster are *not* members of the same family!'

'Which monster?'

Andrew froze and Finnlay turned around at the sound of that voice, then, together, they rushed forward to where Robert was emerging out of the gloom. His horse stumbled on the rocky ground; Robert sat hunched over, trying to keep his body from contact with the Key on his back. As Andrew caught the horse's head, Finnlay moved around to the side, reaching up to help Robert dismount. In the darkness, the only giveaway to Robert's exhaustion was the slowness of his movements, the careful way in which he dropped the reins and swung his leg over the back. And then he was sliding down and Finnlay caught him.

'Quickly,' Finnlay ordered, 'get the door open and the horse inside.'

'What monster?' Robert repeated, his voice light and distracted. 'The one chasing us, the one we're going to go looking for, or the one on my back?'

'We were getting worried,' Finnlay grunted, throwing Robert's arm over his shoulder and half-carrying him. Andrew hurried to the massive stone covering the opening of the cave and pressed his hand against it, feeling it shift slowly. Under the noise, he heard Robert's response.

'Worried? S'no need to worry, Finn. S'all fine. Easy. Monster'll never find us now. Never.'

Andrew took the horse through the opening, moving it quickly to one side to let Finnlay bring Robert through. The older man was barely walking, and the moment Andrew pressed his hand against the stone to close the door again, Robert collapsed to the ground. The cave echoed with Finnlay's calls for help.

Jenn dipped the cloth into the bowl of water then set to scrubbing the table top. Even in the poor light, she could see the smears of mud she was making, the combination of layers and layers of cave dust and the water she was applying. Tonight they had thrown a cloth over it and ignored the dirt in favour of simply feeding themselves and getting the rest they all needed, but now Jenn was making up for it: for the foreseeable future, this bleak place would be her home.

The caves were quiet now. The children were all in bed asleep, along with most of the adults. Martha and Ronald were on Key duty, together creating a mask around its aura to ensure Nash wouldn't find them. Until they found some other alternative, they would each have to take turn at Key duty. They were all being trained how to do it, as each could hold the mask for only a few hours at a time. Fiona was on watch, sitting outside the cave, rugged up against the cold and Seeking periodically to ensure that there was indeed nobody in pursuit. Jenn would take her a cup of brew as soon as it came to the boil.

Robert was asleep. Jenn dipped her cloth back in the bowl again, rinsing the dirt from it, looking over at him as she did. He lay on his side on a makeshift cot pressed into a slight curve in the cave wall; even in the dim light she could see his exhausted face, the shadows under his eyes. One of his hands was under the covers, the other was by his cheek, clutching the blanket as though it were a lifeline. He had been almost incoherent when he'd arrived, rambling about Nash and monsters and riding and horses, and things none of them understood. It was a miracle he'd survived, another miracle he'd avoided Nash; a third miracle had brought him safe back, where he could finally rest and recover his strength.

'Jenn?' The whisper came from behind. She turned to find Finnlay standing in a narrow embrasure. All the others were asleep in other caves; where Finnlay now stood led only to a small enclosure through which a trickle of water ran. He held a lamp in his hand, lighting up the wall behind him.

'What is it?'

'Come and look at this.' He gestured, then disappeared behind rock. Sighing, Jenn followed. As she entered the enclosure, Finnlay pointed to a corner on her right where a thick black shadow ran from floor to ceiling.

'What?' She frowned, in no mood to play guessing games. She was awake only in case Robert needed something.

'Look.' He stepped forward and slid his hand into the shadow – followed by half his body. 'I didn't see it before, and everybody else was busy getting settled. I couldn't sleep, so I thought I'd explore. Come on, take a look.'

Suppressing another sigh, Jenn shooed him on with her hand. Finnlay disappeared behind the rock, but his lamp threw out enough light to see where she was putting her feet. Gingerly she pressed herself between the folds of rock, inching her feet along sideways. The space was very close, even for her, but she reached the end of it to find Finnlay scrambling down a curved slope where the cave roof was too low to stand.

Living in the Enclave for over ten years had given Jenn a healthy respect for caves and their eccentricities. She trod carefully, watching where she put her feet on the too-smooth surface. She was about to voice a complaint when she smelled something on the air: water. And then she was sliding the last few feet until she landed on a small platform. Finnlay was on her right where the cave opened out; when she reached his side she let out a low whistle.

'Why didn't Andrew mention this?' she murmured, aware of how noise travelled in unfurnished caves.

'I don't think he knew about it. He wasn't here for long – perhaps Robert didn't think to show him. Still, I'm glad I found it.'

'You won't be the only one.' Jenn took the lamp from him and stepped forward a little. She stood on a ledge which sat alongside a wide rock pool. The cave roof soared above to where the light couldn't reach. To her right, the ledge continued, almost following the pool to the other side of the cave. She knelt down –and gasped in surprise. The floor of the pool was green and glowed with light the closer she went. Before she could say a word, Finnlay was removing his boots and wading into the shallow area. He crouched down, his face alight with wonder. His fingers dipped into the water until they touched one of the glowing green things. Then he looked up, a crooked smile on his face.

'It's some kind of plant, I think. It's got fronds, like a feather, and it feels as soft. It seems to like the lamp. It's beautiful.'

'Is it safe?' Jenn whispered, now close enough to see that the entire floor of the pond was covered in the glowing green plants. 'Perhaps that's why Robert didn't tell Andrew.'

'Oh, I think if it had been dangerous, Robert would have warned Andrew to stay away. Besides, it hasn't killed me, has it?'

'So far.' Jenn smiled, and it felt good to do so. If this place was safe, then it would be a luxury they could all enjoy – and it would be a perfect salve for Robert's burns.

As though he'd heard her thoughts, Finnlay stepped back out of the water and picked up his boots. 'Let's go back. We'll ask Robert about it when he wakes up.'

This time Jenn went first, easily finding the way. When she reached the main cave again, she left the lamp on the table and knelt by Robert's side. Sometimes she hated having Healer's Sight, and knowing how badly he was hurt. She wished he could be free of injury for a while, just so he could enjoy health, enjoy feeling good.

'He'll sleep for a day at least,' Finnlay murmured from behind her, his voice a little ragged. Jenn looked up to find his eyes shadowed. He answered the question she hadn't asked. 'That was too close, Jenn. We won't be so lucky next time. All these years and we're still not ready. What more do we have to do?'

'Be patient.' Jenn got to her feet and went back to the table. She gave the lamp back to him and resumed her scrubbing. 'You've hardly spoken to him in years, Finn. Give him a chance to talk, to explain, to tell us his plans.'

'You're assuming he will.'

She was, and she didn't need Finnlay to tell her that assumption was a bold one. 'You've believed in him all these years, Finn. Don't start to doubt him now.'

He was silent a long time, then, without further word, he turned and left the cave, taking his lamp with him.

In the dim light of her single candle, Jenn continued removing dust from the table.

As soon as the rain stopped, Jenn went outside, walking through the woods where fresh leaves brightened the day and the spring wildflowers dotted the forest floor with colour. She still wore her boy's clothes, so no gown impeded her progress, and the simple pleasure of striding out into the fresh air was almost enough to make her laugh out loud. As the ground rose before her, she took bigger strides, breathing heavily before slipping and sliding down the other side.

They'd been here two days and so far, their Seekers had not found a single soul in any direction, let alone any sign of Nash. Jenn had decided to keep the Seekers out on regular shifts for another week, but if they were still wonderfully alone at the end of that, she would work out some other sentry schedule that would be a little easier on the Seekers.

Everybody was feeling the relief. For the first time this morning, the children had been allowed out to play. Inside the caves, they had to remain quiet because Robert was still sleeping, but out here, where the day was so fresh and welcoming, they could make all the noise they wanted.

All morning, she and Martha, Arlie and Maren had searched the lower caves, looking for spaces more suitable for habitation. Unlike the Enclave – or the Goleth caves, as she had to call them now – these were entirely natural, carved out of the mountain by rivers eons ago. Other than the one Robert had made his own, this place was full of tall, narrow caves with sharp, uneven floors and unpredictable passages. And until Robert woke up and was able to help them mould the stone, they would have to make do with what they had.

They had made use of the natural shape of the caves by stringing up hammock beds, which the children loved, although Lady Margaret had flatly refused to even consider getting into one; her expression had made them all laugh. The days were filled with endless activity: firewood to be collected, the horses watered and fed, foraging missions to catch rabbit, fish and anything else they might eat to be arranged by Murdoch and his nephews Edain and Braden.

Later, when it was safer, Jenn would send them to the nearest villages, but that would have to be done quietly and carefully: they couldn't allow their presence to be noticed by anyone. Robert had certainly chosen a good spot for his hideaway: in the middle of the country, but still isolated, giving him the freedom to come and go as he wished.

The damp forest smelled wonderful and Jenn breathed deeply; for the first time in a long time, she began to relax a little. Now all she needed was—

'Jenn? Jenn!' She turned to find Finnlay's youngest, Anna, running towards her, waving her arms and leaping over small bushes. 'Uncle Robert's awake, Uncle Robert's awake! Papa said to tell you!'

He was sitting up by the time she got to him. Finnlay was there, and Martha, and Arlie was applying his Healing talents to Robert's back. The moment she arrived, Martha caught Finnlay's arm and drew him out of the cave. Jenn couldn't read their expressions.

'You're right,' Arlie said, packing up his salves and bandages. 'The burns are no worse and are healing well. That sleep did you the power of good.' He looked up at Jenn, then exited quietly, leaving her alone with Robert.

He barely looked at her. Instead, he cast his gaze around the room, paying attention to detail, the things they'd changed, furniture they'd moved. Then he threw back his blankets, swung his feet out of bed and stood up slowly.

Jenn moved to help him, but he held his hand out to stay her. As soon as he was upright, he stretched and she heard his spine pop back into place. His shirt was grey and rumpled, his trousers splattered with mud. Even his bare feet looked tired. She watched him for a moment, then turned to pour them both a cup of brew from the pot hanging by the fireplace. She put his cup on the table, where he could reach it easily.

Robert pulled out a chair and sank into it slowly. With his elbows on the table, he ran his fingers through his hair, then picked up his brew and swallowed loudly. With his voice husky and tired, he asked, 'How did he regenerate? That's what we need to know. How did he get from being horribly crippled and unable to fight me, to being so strong he can stretch his Seeking across the country and find me struggling with the Key?' Robert emptied his cup. 'And how, in the name of Serin, did he manage to subdue the will of thirty and more Malachi so they would obey his every command?'

'Malachi?'

'His men, most of them were Malachi. Couldn't you tell? Finnlay said Nash practised a perversion of the Bonding – but it seems impossible that he's managed to get thirty-odd Malachi to consent to such a thing.' He didn't wait for her answer. Instead, he got to his feet, went to the fire and refilled his cup from the pot. Without thinking, Jenn moved to refill it and put in fresh leaves. She set the pot over the flames to boil.

She *hadn't* noticed the Malachi – but then, she hadn't actually got that close to Nash. And she had been concentrating too much on *him* to really think about the men behind him.

Robert stood beside her, his gaze centring on the fire, but reaching much further. 'I can't fight him like this.'

'Robert, you're exhausted and injured. When you're rested—'

'Even rested, at my very best, he's far more powerful than I am now. By rights—' He broke off to look into the flames. 'By rights, we should be equally matched. That would make sense to me: if we are destined to battle, then it should never have been a question of who was more powerful, but who was stronger . . . By the gods, I'm trying to make sense of the *Prophecy* now – I *must* be tired.'

'You are tired.' Jenn deliberately didn't reach out the way she wanted to. 'And so you're seeing the worst of everything, forgetting that you're not alone in this.'

He still didn't look at her. 'But I *am* alone in this. Nowhere in the

Prophecy does it say that you and I fight him together, or that I get help from any other quarter.'

'Robert, accepting the Prophecy doesn't mean you have to follow it to the letter!'

'But you said the Prophecy was the answer, not the question. So help me, Jenn, I can't find a single answer in it. At least, not the Prophecy we know. Perhaps Nash has a different version, but I can't imagine that will give *me* any hope or he wouldn't bother fighting this battle in the first place.'

Jenn swallowed. Robert's face reflected flickering shadows from the fire. She had promised him no more lies; even excepting the great lie about Andrew, she couldn't keep this from him. 'It wouldn't give you hope, no.'

At that, Robert finally turned to look at her, his gaze searching, hard, and she felt trapped, though he exerted no power.

'What did he say to you?' He asked with so little voice it felt as though Robert was as afraid of the question as he was of the answer. She saw the shadows in his eyes, heard the tremor in his voice.

She had spoken with Nash – and Robert had sent her to do it. Could he still trust her – assuming he had ever trusted her?

'He said,' she began carefully, breathing steadily to both still the catch in her voice and the shaking in her hands, 'that you were . . . destined to destroy me. That the only way you could avoid that fate would be to give me up to him.'

For a moment, Robert didn't move. He might have been made of stone. Then his gaze dropped back to the fire. He shuddered once, then ran a hand over his eyes. 'Serin's blood!' He turned away from the fire then and made for his chair by the table.

Almost without thinking, Jenn opened up one of the canvas bags and brought out one of the last loaves of bread and sliced some salted ham. She put these things on the table before him, and wished he'd had the foresight, at some point, to build a door over the entrance to this cave. These were not things she wanted anybody else to know – or perhaps Finnlay had known this and ensured everybody would be out working in the forest somewhere.

'I have no time left,' Robert said after a moment, his fingers idly pulling off bits of bread that he didn't eat. 'I can rest here perhaps one more day, but no more.'

'Then what happens?'

'Then I need to take Andrew with me and—'

'Sweet Mineah,' Jenn murmured, sinking into a chair opposite him. She was going to lose both of them, she knew it, and there was nothing she could do to stop it. Was that the whole point of the Prophecy, that she was merely a pawn to be held to ransom between Robert and Nash? That couldn't be it – and yet, that was exactly how Robert wished to view it. Nash had given him the knowledge of how he could be beaten, knowing full well that Robert would never give in.

'How does he know?'

'What?' Robert frowned, pulling off a sliver of ham and putting it in his mouth.

'How does he know that you need to give me up to him in order to beat him. How does he know that? That's not in our Prophecy, is it? Nor in anything else we've found.'

Robert's chewing slowed, then, abruptly, he got up from the table, barely hiding a wince, and went back to his bed. He rummaged under it for a moment, bringing out a small bag with something heavy in it, and a slim leather pouch. He brought both back to the table. 'Bring that lamp a little closer, will you?'

As Jenn moved the lamp towards him, he sat again, opening up the pouch to draw forth a piece of thick parchment, folded twice. He opened this and drew it close to the light.

'Robert? What is it?' If she'd promised no more lies, then he had to start telling her what he was doing – and why.

As though he'd heard her thoughts, he tilted the paper further towards the lamp. 'It's something Osbert gave me when I went to Marsay.'

'After you found the Calyx?'

'Well, after I found the book which turned out to be the Calyx, yes. He'd told me about rumours of a Prophecy that Kenrick had asked him to circulate about the city. He didn't elaborate, but it was obvious it was the same Prophecy. He was sure Kenrick had somehow stolen it from Nash and asked Osbert to translate it for him. I'd forgotten all about it until now.'

'Can you read it?'

Robert's frown deepened. His mouth formed words as he read, but he shook his head twice, closed his eyes a moment and tilted his head back, as though he were remembering something. Then he put the paper back on the table and used his finger to trace each word. 'If this is the original that Osbert translated from, then it's incomplete. Nash must have other sources to fill this in.'

'What does that say?'

'The language is very old, one I've seen only infrequently. This also seems to be a fragment of something larger, but I can't tell what. It mentions things like *Angel*, and *Prophecy*, *Bonding* and *eternity*. *Ally and Enemy*, and *dire consequences*. To be honest, I could rearrange them to suit a dozen meanings.'

'But?'

'But already knowing the Prophecy, I'm afraid it doesn't tell us anything new.' He dropped the paper and ran his hands through his hair. 'I've sent Patric to his death, I know it. But it seemed so possible that he would find something of use. Instead, I've just wasted the life of a good friend. Serin's blood, I only—'

Jenn left her seat and moved around behind him. Hesitating only a moment, she put her hands on his shoulders and pressed a little, massaging the tight muscles there. A heartbeat later, he was leaning back into her, his sigh barely audible, but enough to encourage her.

Then his hand came up to capture one of hers. He kissed the back of it, then turned in his seat, wrapped his arms around her waist and pressed his face against her belly.

She almost wept with relief, but instead, she drew in a breath to gather the strength she needed. When he spoke, his voice was muffled, but he didn't lift his head.

'I need to put a door on this room, don't I?'

'I think that would be a good idea. On a few other caves too.'

A pause then and Robert lifted his head and set her back a little. His green eyes were serious, but no longer dejected. 'We also need to do something permanent about the Key.'

'Permanent?' The very idea terrified her. She was still joined to it; maybe Robert had forgotten that.

'Yes, to protect it when I'm not here. Otherwise, I'm just as trapped as—'

'As I am?' Jenn removed his hands from her waist and returned to her own seat. This was not a subject she could trust herself on, not when he was so close and she so needful of him. Not when he was talking about the Key. 'So you don't mind *me* being trapped and tied to the Key, so long as you're not, is that it?'

Robert rolled his eyes and spread his hands on the table. 'Look, we need to protect the Key one way or the other. Once that's done, I don't see any reason why you can't leave it behind the way you did at the Enclave.'

'But you'd rather I stayed here.'

'Out of Nash's way, yes. Do you blame me?'

'After he's told both of us that the only way you can beat him is to give me up to him?'

'Oh, and you think I should?' Robert rose to his feet even as his voice rose. 'You think I should trust *his* word in this? Do you honestly think he'd willingly give me the one clue I needed to defeat him?'

'Considering how little credence you're giving it, I wouldn't be at all surprised if he did. After all, he would *expect* you not to believe him.'

'And with reason. The Prophecy doesn't support such a suggestion—'

'That you know of—'

'And how, in the name of Serin, could my handing you over to him help any of us?' Robert pushed his fists onto the table and leaned over her. 'Unless . . . unless you *want* to go.'

Jenn sprang to her feet. 'Damn it, Robert, don't you dare!'

'He said you're his Ally.'

'Robert, I'm warning you—'

'And you stopped me at Shan Moss. I could have ended it then, but you stopped me.' His eyes bored into her, but his face showed his fear, and through her anger, she could see clearly how hard it was, for him to finally ask the questions which had plagued him for almost nine years.

She could have tried to explain, but nine years down the line, none of it seemed to make sense any more. Except—

'You were about to use the Word. You would have killed yourself in the process. I couldn't . . . allow that.'

He blinked once, but his gaze didn't change. He simply straightened up. 'And I have no guarantee you won't do something like that again.'

She caught in a breath of surprise then, but she couldn't look away as he continued, 'You forced me to accept the Prophecy, to admit to myself that somewhere along the line, I might have to . . . to destroy you in order to save Lusara. Well, Jenny, if I have to accept that, then you must allow me the privilege of sacrificing my own life for the same reason. If you want us to be in this together, you have no choice.'

Jenn felt tears pricking at the back of her eyes, but she refused to acknowledge them. 'No matter what I say, you won't trust me, will you? Whatever you do to protect the Key, you'll make sure it means I have to stay here with it. You'll shut me out again, just as you've always done, after you promised that we—'

He almost broke then, his hands reaching out for her – but then he stopped, dropping his arms to his sides. He turned away and picked up the other bag. He held it in his hands a moment, and changed the subject completely. 'I think we might have enough information and enough talent here to create the kind of barrier the Key had around the Goleth. It won't need to be as big, nor as powerful, as the caves will provide some natural protection. But we'll need everyone to participate.' He paused, placing the bag back on the table.

'What's that?' Jenn asked levelly.

'This is the orb Kenrick was going to use with Helen's blood. I took it from him to make sure he didn't try something similar again.'

Jenn gasped, glaring at the bag. 'An orb? Like the ones Nash uses to regenerate?'

'Yes,' Robert said, his fingers lingering on the bag. 'It's made of the same material as the Key. As far as I can tell, the Cabal used orbs to transform power from one source to another. Nash has his absorb the blood of sorcerers, then he takes the power from the orb.'

When Robert didn't continue, Jenn guessed the rest. 'And you think that you can use the orb to create the kind of protection the Key gave us at the Goleth?'

'Yes.'

'And then what?'

But Robert ignored her question. 'We'll do it tomorrow night. I'll leave once it's set.'

14

Robert could feel the tension fluttering in his stomach. He was tempting fate with this plan; every time he'd tried that before he'd failed miserably, sometimes almost lethally. But, as usual, he had no choice: no matter what he did, what he said, it always came down to where he had no choice.

He had his back to the fireplace, where the coals had burned low. After three days of continual occupation, some of the caves were finally beginning to warm up, and the atmosphere was almost comfortable.

This particular cave was almost bare of furniture now, to create as much space as possible for this . . . working. Everybody was here, except for Martha and Ronald, who were masking the Key. The children stood with their parents in a circle, filling the cave, all facing the centre and the small orb he'd placed there. Years ago, the Key had given Jenn a vision of how it had been created by the Cabal at the Palace of Bu. The vision had been awesome in its detail, giving Robert as much help as possible. If he could create another like the Key – if *they*, working all together could – then the Key would be safe within these caves, and he could leave knowing Nash wouldn't come and get Jenn.

He didn't dare look at her; everything was so much harder now that he could no longer pretend he didn't love her, or she him. He could no longer ignore how she felt or thought; to break the bonds that joined them now was unthinkable. But still he had to hold to his plans, however harsh that might seem, or they would both be lost. He simply couldn't tell if Jenn fully understood that.

He took a deep breath and turned his focus on the orb sitting almost innocuously on the floor before them. The room was lit with three lamps suspended from the ceiling, which gave out enough light for him to see a little fear in all those there. The orb was the same one he'd taken from Kenrick, the one the monster King would have used to absorb Helen's blood. How perfect that it would now be used to help defeat him.

He had nothing but his instincts to guide him, but he had read much over the years, and observed even more, and his own experiments with the orb had suggested this would probably work. It appeared that the mechanism to create the protection existed in the orb itself, in how it had been constructed.

'Please, everyone, take a deep breath,' he began softly, 'and you'll find it easier if you close your eyes.' He waited until he was sure they were all ready before shutting his own. Instantly, the aura of the orb appeared before him, like a ghost, insubstantial, but present. In the darkness of his closed eyes, it cast a greater shadow on the floor.

The last time he'd tested it, the orb had absorbed some of his power, had tried to draw him in further, as though its goal was to swallow him whole, so he knew it would be dangerous for anyone to get too close, much less touch it. Perhaps this was how the Key had got the Word of Destruction: because one of the men making it knew the Word.

Robert stopped, his eyes snapping open. If that was the case, then how was he to prevent this orb from taking the Word from him? Perhaps it was simply a matter of control. When the Cabal had made the Key, they had intended it to be a power in itself, but Robert wanted this orb purely to provide protection.

He closed his eyes again; he would have to be extremely vigilant. The moment he felt *anything* dangerous, he'd have to pull out – and everyone along with him.

Of course, that assumed he'd be able to.

'Focus on the orb before you. You should be able to See it.' He knew Andrew would be frowning and shaking his head – that boy had powers coming out of his fingers, but he had no idea how to wake them up. Still, it would be a good experience for him, and who knew what it might do. 'Now, open your Senses to the orb. At first, you'll feel a little cold, but then it will get warmer as it begins to do its work.' He didn't elaborate on what that work was: he didn't want the children to misunderstand the concept of the orb absorbing their power.

He fell silent then, concentrating with his own Senses, but even though the ghost remained before him, nothing else happened: the orb felt entirely dormant, as if it was unwilling to absorb a single shred of power. This wasn't how it had worked before: though he had barely touched it, it had begun drawing in his power – and there was more than enough power in this room now for touch to be unnecessary.

So why wasn't it working?

He opened his Senses wider, taking in everyone in the room, recognising each aura, seeing each full of energy and bright, just as a Salti should be—

Except for one: his mother, Lady Margaret. She had a normal, human aura, gentle and soft, but entirely devoid of power, at least, of the arcane kind. Robert opened his eyes.

She was standing next to him and sensed his attention. She looked up at him and smiled a little. 'It's me, isn't it?'

'I'm sorry, Mother. I'd thought it would work with us all here.'

Her smile deepened and she squeezed his hand. 'I shall watch, and be here anyway.' With that, she stepped back out of the circle and moved to the arch of the doorway.

Robert closed his eyes again and continued his sweep of the group. Now all the auras glowed brightly. Once more he focused his attention on the orb, opening his Senses to it, waiting for the catch, the moment when it began to draw him in as it had done before.

Still nothing. Not a flicker. Not a breath's worth of attention. It was as though the orb was ignoring them, ignoring him because of some offence he could not—

Again he opened his eyes, but this time, he found Jenn's gaze upon him. Nobody else in the room moved. They were all focused on the orb.

I can't do this, Robert. Her words came to him soft and personal, as all mindspeech. The apology was in her eyes. *It won't let me in. Every time I open my Senses, it feels like the Key throws up a barrier of some kind. It must be because I'm joined to the Key already. Will it matter if I step out?*

What choice do we have? But if you do step out, you can still help. I need to be careful that the orb won't take control of this gathering. If you Sense anything like that building, or if I call you for help, will you—

I'll do what I can. Good luck.

He nodded and closed his eyes; this time he was there, almost instantly, in the darkness, *feeling* the contours of the orb, touching the depths of the ghostly shadow as though it were real and substantial. Now it was working. He could feel it, almost see it: a thin tendril of connection to each person standing in the circle. They'd begun with seventeen, now they had fifteen, but the Cabal had made the Key with twelve. Well, this orb seemed to think fifteen was enough.

So he could get it to absorb power – now the only problem was to persuade it to mask the Key. Certainly, he laughed silently. Easy.

And then the darkness crashed in.

Jenn found she was holding Margaret's hand, her grip so tight it must be causing bruises, but Margaret said nothing to stop her. Instead, their eyes were firmly fixed on the circle of intense faces, the children showing the strain the worst, but most of all, on Robert, who looked pale and tired and stretched too far to be trying this so soon.

And then he gasped, his features contorting in pain the others obviously did not feel.

Robert? He did not answer. *Robert? Are you all right?*

He said nothing, but gave a tiny shake of his head, so small she wouldn't have noticed it if she hadn't been watching so closely. Damn! All this effort just to protect the Key – why couldn't it keep protecting itself? Of course, she didn't dare ask it now that it was joined to the Calyx. She had no way of knowing what would happen if she placed that much strain on it.

The Key had given her this vision, of how it had been created – but in the vision, one of the creators had been killed by the Key, struck down even as he fought to keep his place in the circle. Her feet took an involuntary step forward, her hands out ready to pull Robert from the circle, but Margaret stopped her, pointing towards the orb.

'Look, it's glowing. Does that mean it's working?' she whispered.

'I don't know,' Jenn whispered back. That was the whole problem with this – they were relying on guesswork, never sure of anything until it was too late. When the Key had been created, there was no doubt nobody in that room really understood what it was they were doing. It would have come as a surprise to the man who'd been killed, and of course, the man who gave the Key the Word of —

'Serin's blood!' Jenn gasped, her gaze snapping back to Robert. If he couldn't control—

Robert let out a soft moan, then, without warning, he fell to his knees and the glow from the orb died. There was a heartbeat of silence, and then everyone was talking at once. Jenn ran to Robert's side, put one hand beneath his elbow, another on his cheek, drawing his face up to hers.

'Robert? Robert, talk to me. Are you—'

He gave her a slow grin, then opened his eyes. 'I wouldn't want to be doing that every day, but as far as I can tell, it worked.'

Jenn helped him to his feet as everyone gathered around. It was Finnlay, of course, who asked the obvious question. 'How can you tell if it *did* work?'

'When we joined the Key and Calyx together, I was right there, almost on the inside looking out. I got a very clear idea of how the barrier worked and this one looks exactly the same.'

'Really?' Murdoch said sceptically. 'Then perhaps later you can show a few of us what that looks like, just in case we need to reinstate it once you're gone.'

'Good idea,' Robert said. 'In the meantime, let's get the furniture back in here.'

As they began to move, Robert added, 'And it's time Andrew and I were moving on.'

Jenn caught an odd look from her son. Finnlay waited until everybody else was engaged in shifting furniture, then said quietly, 'I don't think you should go tonight – and I don't think you should go alone.'

Robert was obviously expecting opposition; he raised his eyebrows, his good humour still intact, and asked, 'Why not?'

'There are things we need to discuss: the Calyx and how we use it, and what exactly are you going to do with Andrew, and do you think it's such a good idea for you to take him away from here when you're still tired after such an exhausting working.'

'Oh.' Robert's smile became a little stilted.

'Please, Robert.' Jenn joined in the fight, prepared to do almost anything to keep him here as long as possible. 'Stay until tomorrow. You need the rest and Finnlay's right, we do have things we need to talk about.'

Robert's gaze landed on Andrew. He remained silent for a moment, then said, 'Very well. We'll leave tomorrow. Now let's put my bed back together, eh?'

Margaret sat on the stool Murdoch had made her and rested her back against the cave wall. Thanks to the vagaries of the cave floors here, she had a perfect place to rest her feet, on a ledge of rock jutting out from the wall. With a candle stuck to another tiny niche in the wall, she had enough light to see to her mending. Though the stitches were getting more fuzzy as each year wore on, her eyes were still good enough to make this shirt wearable for a bit longer.

Of course, how long depended entirely on what her elder son intended on doing in it.

She couldn't tell if he was avoiding her. She didn't want to believe it so, but he'd hardly said a word to her, and there was so much that needed to be said between them. And she was not afraid to admit how terrified she was for him. He took on so much, more than any one man should, and yet, was about to take on yet more. Only Finnlay and Jenn appeared to have any sway over him.

The truth was, it was Jenn's fear which really drove Margaret's. Though nobody else could or would see it, the fear sat clearly on Jenn's face, every time she looked at Robert, every time she spoke to him.

Robert, as usual, was utterly oblivious to it – as he should be. The last thing he needed was their fear to infect him; Margaret knew he had plenty of his own.

'So this is where they've hidden you.' Robert stood at the crooked entrance to her small cave, his head ducked down a little to peer in. The doorway was at least two feet shorter than he was; he bent double to step inside. 'Very cosy. Are you comfortable?'

Very well, so he was not avoiding her. 'As comfortable as I can be. I'm told the floor of this cave can be levelled a little to make walking around easier. For the moment, I'm just very careful where I put my feet.'

'And you have a bed on the floor, I see.' Robert smiled a little as he said this, hiding his merriment – he'd obviously heard the story. 'And tucked away down here, you have less need of a proper door in the short term.'

'I . . .' Margaret paused. Should she mention this or not? So far, nothing had been said. Nevertheless, 'I asked Edain if he would put up a curtain of some kind across the door to your room. So you can have a little privacy.'

He looked at her then, searching a little, but giving away nothing – as usual. Unrepentant, and rather enjoying herself, she continued, 'It must be uncomfortable having your bedroom in the same room we all cook and eat. If you were staying longer, I would suggest you choose another cave for your own.'

'Mother, what are you trying to say?'

'I thought I'd just said it – or weren't you listening?' He wasn't the only one who could be contrary when he wanted to be. 'Here, I finished mending your shirt. If you wash it out now, you can take it with you.'

She held it out to him, doing all she could to ignore the way her hands trembled, and the way he saw them. Without a word, he took the shirt, folding it as carefully as if it were silk. But he'd never treated silk so well, back in the days when— Suddenly swallowing was painful, and her eyes stung awfully. By the heart of Mineah, she hadn't wanted to do this to him.

But Robert read her better than she'd read herself. He put the shirt to one side and knelt before her, taking her hands in his and pressing a soft kiss to her cheek. 'Mother, I'm sorry. I'm so very sorry. I never meant to do this to you. I never meant for you to lose your home and everything, so you had to put up with all this. By the gods, Mother, I'm so sorry.'

Words bubbled up in her, desperate to break through and deny that he'd done anything bad at all. Nothing he'd done had come from malice, after all, so in reality, he had nothing to apologise for, but even as she accepted that, as she took a breath to tell him, so too did she know that this apology was as much for him as for her, that it was not just to her he was apologising, but to the whole of Lusara.

Her tears dried then and she drew him close, pressing a kiss to his forehead, squeezing his hand in her own. And then she did speak. 'Robert, we none of us know, when we're young, what life will make of us. You have had perhaps the toughest road of all, even with all your privilege. But neither I nor your father could have asked for more in a son, nor been more proud of you.'

He looked up at her, a little surprised, but before he could say anything, she continued, 'The night before you and your father left to fight Selar, he and I argued. I didn't want him to take you. I thought that, at fifteen, you were still too young. You weren't – but I feared to lose both of you in the same conflict. After an hour or so, I gave in and stopped fighting. I couldn't bear the thought of him leaving with us like that. But even as he rode through Dunlorn's gates the next morning, I resented the fact that I'd had to give in, just to get the peace we both needed. Robert,' she paused, feeling his gaze upon her, 'tomorrow when you leave, make sure she knows how much you love her, and make sure you know how much she loves you. For both of you, that memory might have to last a very long time.'

When he smiled at her, gently, she saw a light in his eyes that had been absent for so long she'd forgotten it had once been there all the time. He kissed the back of her hands and stood up straight. He picked up his shirt and turned for the door, pausing before ducking his head again to say, 'My father, for all his early death, was a very, very lucky man. And so, I might add, am I. Goodnight, Mother.'

'I don't understand why you can't just raise an army, Robert,' Finnlay said for the fourth time. 'If you do, the King will have to pay attention. That way you bring him out into the open, away from Nash, and hit him then.'

Robert raised his hands to quieten his brother. Edain had hung a spare blanket over the door, but Robert had also taken one of his deerskins and added to it, both to control the draft and to deaden the voices on the inside. He'd known this was going to be a battle of some kind.

'Hit him with what?' Murdoch answered before Robert could. 'I've been out in the country, Finnlay, I know what's out there and at the moment, coming off a hard winter, there's not enough will out there to raise an army, let alone fight Kenrick. I agree with Robert: stealth is the only way for the moment.'

'Then I'll go with you.' Finnlay turned his attention back to Robert, ignoring Martha, Jenn and Andrew in the process. 'You need help, Robert. If something happens to you, who's going to protect Andrew?'

'The fewer people we have with us, the smaller the risk – even you have to concede that.' Robert poured out ale into his cup, but took only a sip.

'But there's a point where you can have too few people – and this is it. Don't you trust me? Is that the problem?' Finnlay's eyes were hard. 'Why don't we ask Andrew? After all, he's going to be King, isn't he?'

Robert almost laughed at that, but then he looked at the boy and found him watching them carefully. His eyes dropped to where his hands rested on the table and Robert said, 'Look up, Andrew. If you have opinions, either keep them to yourself, or voice them with confidence.'

Andrew did look up then, and met his gaze with some surprise. Then he said, firmly, 'I would like Finnlay to come if it's not going to ruin anything.'

'You would *like* Finnlay to come?' Robert repeated, then bit his tongue to stop the sharp addition. Andrew was a sweet, genuine, honest boy – if he arrived on the throne like this, he would be eaten up by wolves within minutes.

Which was exactly the reason Robert didn't want anybody else going with them. He had work to do, and he couldn't allow any hindrances. On the other hand, Finnlay might be quite useful.

And it *would* be nice to have him along, if truth be told.

'Very well,' he said at last, 'Finnlay comes with us.'

'Thank you, Andrew,' Finnlay said pointedly. 'Now tell us, Robert, what do you plan to do first?'

'First of all,' Robert replied evenly, 'we need to find Micah.'

At the looks of surprise around the table, he could tell that, with all the excitement, they'd all forgotten that Micah was supposed to have joined them at the Enclave. Instead, all he would have found would have been the departing Salti. Where he would have gone to next was another matter: for all their problems, Robert couldn't simply leave him in the lurch. Micah had spent the last eight years by Andrew's side, protecting his future King, and such loyalty meant something was owed in return.

'And what about the Calyx?' Martha laced her fingers together and gave them all a smile. Robert had never seen her angry or flustered in all the years he'd known her. She was also the single most capable person he'd ever met. 'What do we do with it? Is there any way we can gain any information from it?'

Robert looked at Jenn, who shrugged. 'I don't think it's a good idea to do anything with the Key or Calyx until I get back,' he said.

'And when do you think that might be?' Murdoch asked without preamble. 'And, forgive me, what happens if you don't?'

'Don't worry, Murdoch.' Jenn patted his hand. 'I'll do a little work on my own first, so we have a grounding before Robert gets back. I don't think we *can* do much with it individually – it only seems to like both of us at the same time. It's certainly safe enough now we have the orb.'

'And it's still working without trouble?'

'Indeed it is,' Martha said. 'Every one of our Seekers tested it today and not one of them could See the Key from outside – or inside, for that matter.'

Robert opened his mouth to say something, and was interrupted by a violent yawn, which brought a smile to almost everyone – except Andrew, who was busily yawning himself. When they were done, they shared a chuckle, then Robert got to his feet. 'Time to get some sleep. If you have any more questions, we'll discuss them tomorrow before we go. Goodnight.'

Chairs and stools scraped across the cave floor as each of them stood and left, calling out goodnight as they went. Jenn lingered to gather up the cups and place them in the bucket by the water embrasure. Robert watched her. She returned to blow out two of the lamps, leaving the last one alight. Robert didn't let her reach the door. With an arm around her waist, he pulled her close, breathing deeply of her scent, pressing soft kisses to her throat as her arms wound around him.

'I can't say it, can I?' she whispered, even though they had all the privacy they could.

'Say what?'

'I wish you wouldn't go.'

He turned so he could kiss her properly, tasting her, reminding himself of what he had here, of what he was fighting for, and simply remembering all their past together. She tasted sweet, of memory and of the present, her body moulding up against his, so small and yet so very strong.

'I too wish,' he said when he could breathe again, 'that I didn't have to go.'

'They all know, you know. About us. Or at least, the adults do.'

'What about Andrew? Have you said anything to him?'

Jenn drew back a little then and looked up at him. Her gaze was troubled, and she drew her bottom lip between her teeth. 'I don't want to give him any more to add to his confusion. If we . . . if once this—'

Robert finished it for her. 'If we survive what's coming, then I'm going to marry you, Jenny, no matter what.'

'No!' She rose up on her toes, pressed her hand to his mouth to silence him. 'You can't say that. The Key would never allow it.'

Robert let his voice drop. 'I don't *care* what the Key thinks. I will make you my Duchess, one way or the other. When that happens, we'll tell Andrew.'

At that, Jenn's eyes glistened with tears she wouldn't shed, with words she would never say. Even now, he knew there were things she wasn't telling him, and the omission hurt. But just as they were keeping the truth from Andrew, perhaps these secrets were of the same nature.

Perhaps it was time he tried to trust her.

'Stay with me tonight,' he whispered into her ear. 'Let us have this much, if nothing more. Please, stay.'

He could feel the tension in her body as she debated the wisdom of sharing his bed while so many questions still hovered between them, but then she suddenly relaxed into him, hiding her face in the curve of his neck.

With a grin on his face, he nodded towards the lamp and the flame dropped to a tiny flicker. Then he wrapped his arms around her and he drew her to his bed, thankful that he'd made it big enough for two.

15

Lightning crackled along the top of the hills, making the forest even darker. Nash could smell rain on the air, but so far, it was dry where he stood.

If he could, he would have made the sky rain blood.

The view told him all he needed to know. He stood atop a crag, where harsh rock tumbled down the cliff into the gentle valley below. Sharp edges of wind slapped at his face, but he remained oblivious, keeping his gaze on the land below where his men rode at full pace, spread out, looking for something that wasn't there.

It *should* have been there. Reason demanded it be so—

But he'd been fooled. By reason, by hope, by destiny. Either way, he'd been fooled, and the knowledge of it burned his eyes and scorched his flesh.

He had to hold his breath to contain the fury. It leaked out of his fingertips in crackles of angry fire. He clasped them together, raised them before his face, tilted his head back and let out a roar. The sky around him flashed, the rock beneath his feet split in three and the wind howled in sympathy.

It was too late. Even being angry was too late. The Key was gone from his grasp again and the only thing he had left to do was to begin to look for it once more.

He'd tried scanning for it. For hours and hours, he'd gone into a deep trance, opening his Senses to the icy spring night, allowing for any possible tiny shred of aura to reach him, but there was nothing, nothing but the bitter taste of failure and loathing which remained in his mouth.

He gestured to Taymar, who stood behind him, to bring the men back. They would not find the Ally here, nor the Enemy, and most certainly not the Key. And it would be pointless trying to guess in which direction they had gone; this country was far too big and he'd been trying that for the last hundred years.

He couldn't bring himself to even consider the prospect of failure.

'You lost it.' Valena's voice broke his concentration. 'I told you to be careful of her, and you ignored me. You torture me to make me help you, and yet you pay no attention to what I say. How can you continue to place such blind faith in her?'

'The Prophecy—'

'The Prophecy does not say you will have the Key, does it? Because the Prophecy predates the Key. So why do you keep chasing it? Because to have power over the Key means you will have power over *her*?'

Nash barely moved, barely registered her hatred. It was nothing compared with his own rage. Instead, he watched as Taymar rode down into the pleasant valley, past the lake, and beyond the ruins of Elita.

She had been born here, and here, he had learned the Enemy's true face.

He knew not how he *could* continue to have such blind faith in the Prophecy. But what other choice did he have?

Nash turned then and walked back from the crag's edge. Valena stood by her horse, tied to it, her eyes dull from the drugs. He stood before her and pulled off his gloves. 'At what point,' he began softly, 'did you lose faith in me? In my ability to achieve my goals? I always told you it would take time, and yet you grew impatient and turned instead to DeMassey to protect you. Why?'

She met his gaze, lifting her chin in defiance, but she still had an air of indifference. She gave him no answer.

Nash lifted his hand to her face, caressed her cheek and felt her flinch beneath his touch. With a smile, he stepped back. Instantly, her hands flew to her face, fingers gingerly touching the scorch mark he'd left there, burned into her beauty.

'Betrayal brings scars, my dear.' Nash turned for his horse. 'And consequences.' He swung up into his saddle and turned back to face her two guards. 'Bring her when the others come back. We head due west. It's time I saw what they left behind at the Goleth.'

Brother Benedict held his hands up for silence, then moved quickly to his window. It was dark outside, but there was still life in the tavern on the other side of the village, enough life to make him sceptical, and careful. Even with the thunder rolling in the distant hills, there were plenty of people moving about, plenty of people to question.

He leaned out of his window far enough to make sure there was nobody standing close by, or deliberately eavesdropping. Since the Guilde had taken over the Hospice in Fenlock, the monastery had shrunk by half, but after so many years suffering dwindling numbers, over the last few months, new monks had started to arrive. But the Guilde still watched them closely – at times, a little too closely.

He turned back to find his monks waiting for him, those five who had been here the longest and formed the core of the current community. He pulled the shutter closed, moved away from the window and folded his hands into his sleeves, adopting his usual posture of patience. 'We must not say anything about this.'

'But I know what I saw, Brother,' Stanley replied, no less passionate than when he'd come in an hour before. 'How much longer can we ignore this? Sweet Mineah, Brother, *you* worked alongside Her Grace. Surely you were aware even then of—'

'There is no guarantee that what you saw had anything to do with the Lady Jennifer,' Benedict insisted, keeping his voice calm. The last thing he needed was hysteria. At it was, it was hard enough to contain the villagers and their nightly visits to the remains of the castle.

'But when you combine that with the other reports we've received—'

'We must notify the Bishop of what is happening here, Brother. There must be an investigation into the miracles—'

'We need to set up a shrine—'

'We need to say prayers—'

As the voices rose in excitement and reverence, Brother Benedict called once again for silence. Obediently, they quieted and he took a breath. 'You have seen these lights with your own eyes?'

Stanley nodded solemnly. 'Yes, Brother.'

There was nothing else for him to do. While he had to avoid hysteria, he also could not afford to ignore the growing signs. If they were true, then perhaps the country might finally have some real hope to hold onto. 'Very well, tomorrow I shall write to Bishop Godfrey and inform him of what we have seen here. We will await his judgment on whether the matter requires an Inquisitor. Until then, I ask you all to avoid speaking of this to the villagers. There are enough rumours flying around about the Lady as it is.'

As Stanley beamed at him, the other monks signed the trium and turned to leave his office. Stanley bowed low, then turned to go.

'Brother Stanley?' Benedict stopped him.

'Yes, Brother?'

'In the morning, please set me down a written account of all you did tonight which led you to seeing the lights on the crag.'

'And the figure on top of the crag, talking to the thunder?'

'Yes, all of it.'

'Brother Benedict, it would be my pleasure.'

Nash rode without mercy, without care and without repentance. He'd never really understood those concepts anyway, so doing without them as he raced across the country was no loss. He barely looked at his men, and he allowed himself to forget entirely about Valena. Instead, he changed horses whenever their speed began to flag, and stopped only when his bright, vibrant new body begged for rest.

He took all the roads he could, using their greater speed, enjoying, when he could, the pleasure of seeing the peasants scramble out of his way, of villages and towns scattering stock to clear his path, the chaos and the anger around him serving to feed his own. Not once did he stop, nor even so much as call out a warning. Explanations were for the weak.

Somebody had to pay. Why not Lusara?

That thought kept him amused for four days and nights, until he reached the foot of the Goleth mountains. Hills surrounded him, patched with plowed fields, woods and pasture. Before him rose the mountains, the highest in the country: all sharp edges and grey stone, still laced with white and bitter cold. An interesting place to hide a community of sorcerers, he thought, but they'd not been found for more than five hundred years, until *he* had come along.

Nash smiled and kicked his horse into motion; his men followed unquestioningly, as always. He had sent scouts out to discover the best route to the Goleth itself and this was it: a narrow trail winding up through the foothills until the land turned rocky and became a mountainside. A small monastery to the north was the only feature in the land. He smiled again at the thought of how horrified the monks would have been to discover there were all these sorcerers no more than half a day's ride away.

An hour into the mountains thick cloud descended, creating a uniform blanket of grey over everything. The air was moist with the possibility of rain, which then became a reality, falling softly and steadily until Nash was soaked to the skin. He did not pause for one moment, pressing on for hour after hour, never once checking over his shoulder to ensure he was still being followed. He almost didn't care. The rain was equally determined, crowding him onto the path, keeping his face down until the path turned a corner and he knew this was it.

He'd not seen this in his vision, nor found anybody in the valleys below to tell him what to look for, but if he'd wanted to hide in the mountains, this was how he'd do it: a huge rock, the size of a house, jutted out into the path, with a narrow space to slip behind it, and then a dark tunnel of some kind, too short to consider, too unimportant – because on the other side—

On the other side was – by the Blood!

Nash slipped down from his horse in awe. The tunnel had opened out onto the mountain top. Steep rocky walls framed a field of solid green, the rock rising in sharp fingers to the sky. The ground everywhere was trampled with recent footprints, though there was no sign of life. He didn't expect any.

It was perfect. No wonder they'd been so safe all these centuries.

There were more tunnels, and doors leading below ground. He left the horse and walked towards the nearest one. It was dark inside, and very cold. With a flick of his hand, he brought forth a light, bright enough to see where he was going. Even as he strode down the slope, he heard footsteps behind him, echoing into corners as yet unseen.

This place was incredible. Every step he took opened up another tunnel, another passageway. There were rooms leading off in every direction: living quarters with furniture left behind, kitchens, eating halls, washing areas, alcoves where peat was stored for fires, caves with shelves lining the walls, abandoned bottles of ale, lamps hanging from the ceiling, rugs on the floors, discarded clothing. So much had been deserted in the rush to leave before Nash could get here: so much was left behind for him to examine.

The caves went on endlessly. After an hour of wandering, he lost count of the beds he'd found, of the family rooms, of his estimation of how many people had once called this place their home. He'd had no idea of the size of the place.

He came to a halt at the entrance to the biggest cave of all, a huge cavern the roof of which rose further than his light could reach. This was a most unusual cave: on one side, a separate room was walled off with an ancient panel, carved with extraordinary workmanship. The room it hid was even more astonishing: the walls, from floor to ceiling, were painted with stories he barely had the patience to read, but that first glance showed he had to. This room told the story of the Salti, and how they had made this place their home.

With amazement, he sank down into a chair left in the corner of the room. Almost six hundred years before, Malachi and Salti had been one, the Cabal, escaping from war in the southern continent. They'd brought the Key with them, which had then split them into two warring groups. The Malachi had travelled further north and founded a great city on the edge of a windy plateau, giving it the name of Karakham. There they had prospered, and there Nash had spent many years, living under his true name of Carlan.

The Malachi had flourished, building towers and palaces, their artists more skilled than any in the world. The Chabanar was one of the most beautiful buildings he'd ever seen – and yet there was something so powerful about this one small cave that made all the riches of Karakham pale into insignificance.

This was determination: not only shield themselves from the Malachi, but also to live here, in caves underground, hidden in the bowels of the highest mountain in Lusara, apart from all the luxuries they could have demanded and yet, with these paintings, still able to keep their vibrant history alive. The Salti Pazar had not only survived these centuries, but had flourished, had developed such a strong community that it could up and leave literally at a moment's notice. He'd had no idea at all: he had never guessed that this place existed until a few short years ago, and yet, obviously, he'd known the Salti had the Key hidden somewhere. He had not expected this underground city.

Nash stared at the walls, shining his light on patches of colour here and there, tracing the major historical moments until he found one he recognised all too well, where the paint was a little fresher than the rest: a great forest, a clearing, two armies facing each other, and three figures in the clearing – two battling with awesome powers, the third standing to one side, her hands raised to stop the battle. Shan Moss, nine years before. Why *had* she stopped them? The Enemy had been about to use the Word of Destruction, which would not have killed Nash, but he would have heard it, learned eventually how to use it himself. She might have realised that, but how could she have known the Word wouldn't kill him?

Unless she'd been afraid it would kill the Douglas, and keeping him alive was more important to her than killing Nash. He had been such a fool – Douglas had called him that, before their battle, had said something about all the things Nash had missed along the way, details he should have paid attention to, and by the blood of Broleoch, he'd been right. So many opportunities lost because of his blind determination to achieve one thing, ignoring the often-true fact that sometimes the best way to get one thing is by focusing on another.

The light in the small cave shifted and changed as footsteps came towards him, echoing around the hard walls. Taymar appeared at the door, a lighted torch in one hand, two men behind him bearing lamps. There was no expression on Taymar's face, no wide-eyed surprise at what he'd seen in these caves, just the simple and predictable acceptance of any Bonded man.

Nash had been blind for too long. It was time to shine light on some corners of this world. He'd been given more than a new body with this regeneration; he had been given a fresh chance to finally achieve what none of his ancestors had, and he would die before he'd let anybody stop him – even himself.

He got to his feet and unhooked his cloak. Swinging it over the back of the chair, he gave out orders. 'Make sure the horses are brought inside and taken care of. Get fires lit in the kitchens and see if there's any food been left. Send somebody to find me a pen and some paper and ink and bring it to me here. After that, I want everybody except Valena's guards to go on a room-by-room search. I want to know exactly what has been left behind – especially any books. Go.'

Taymar took a lamp and handed it to Nash, then he and his comrades disappeared, leaving Nash alone listening to the echo of their voices around the caves. With the lamp held high, he began a careful examination of the paintings, the stories that were so important to the Salti that they wanted to be reminded of them every time they came into this chamber.

The Douglas had said he'd underestimated his enemies, would lose in the end because of this. But this was something he could change, and his first step would be to learn all he could about the people who had followed the Enemy, Robert Douglas, into battle against a King and the Angel of Darkness: to learn what he could about this remarkable and determined people – before he destroyed them utterly.

16

To Andrew's surprise, the weather was kind to them as they rode away from the mountain hideaway. Before they'd left, Jenn had given the caves the name of Sanctuary, because Robert had first been safe there, and now they and the Key were being protected. The orb's Mask, that he'd had a hand in creating, had so far protected the Key perfectly, though Jenn was determined to test it regularly, just in case.

But it was hard riding away, even though the sun was shining and there was just the smallest of breezes rippling through the treetops. Sanctuary had been just that, and as long as he was there, he wasn't following Robert to where they'd find Kenrick and Nash and . . .

He couldn't get the thought of his destiny out of his head; it was like a shadow which followed him around night and day, so no matter what else was happening, no matter if he was happy or sad, the shadow reminded him constantly of what he still had to do.

Finnlay rode in front, constantly scanning the landscape. Andrew couldn't help but remember what Finnlay had said to him about Kenrick, about being King, about killing. And about Helen, by the gods, how could he— He just couldn't work out why he didn't want to kill Kenrick, no matter how appalling Kenrick was. He could not stop thinking that the King was his cousin, his flesh and blood. They'd grown up together, and, in many ways, they were equally isolated. Though it was true that there was something about Kenrick that made Andrew's skin crawl, that didn't mean—

No. He was never going to understand this, but Robert was still going to make him do it, whether he thought he *could* or not. He would have had better luck getting his father to do it: it was just the kind of thing Eachern had excelled at – in fact, killing was the *only* thing he'd excelled at. How disappointed he would have been to find his own son baulking at such a prospect. He wondered what his father *would* have said, if he would have refused, touting family loyalty, or would he have done the deed without question and reaped the benefits? And why was he suddenly thinking about his father so much lately?

He rode in silence between Robert and Finnlay, cantering when he was told, saying nothing if he wasn't spoken to. The brothers chatted now and then, about inconsequential things, making Andrew wish he had a brother too, someone with whom he could share that kind of history, with whom he could enjoy the sort of bond the Douglas brothers had. Someone he could confide in, who would not think him a coward.

They stopped in a small town just after midday to purchase bread, a piece of salted bacon, hard cheese and some vegetables. Andrew took his share, packed it into his saddle-bags and mounted up, once more riding behind Finnlay until they were out of the town. He had no real idea of where he was. It felt like he'd been on horseback most of his life now. Apart from the few nights at the Sanctuary, and the one at the Enclave, he had been travelling for nearly two months, since he'd left Marsay what felt like a lifetime ago. At least his expertise on horseback was increasing with the practise.

'Andrew? Are you listening?'

He blinked and looked up to find Robert riding alongside him. They were following a road, the sun still high overhead. Finnlay was a little in front, riding in and out of the dappled shadows cast by the trees lining the road.

'What's wrong?' he asked, trying to clear his head. Whenever Robert spoke to him he felt like he was being tested; he'd already suffered for giving the wrong answers before.

'Nothing. I just want to set a few things in place, in case we need them.'

'Things?'

Robert pointed at the road. 'We'll be doing a lot of travelling, and I can promise you there'll be a few surprises along the way. If we get separated for any reason, then our standard response is to travel south for two leagues. After that, find the nearest church or tavern and wait. Think you can do that?'

Andrew shrugged. 'Yes. Wait for how long?'

'Six hours at most. If the separation is longer than that, then we have different meeting places. Dunlorn for the south, Ayr for the north-east, centrally, our cave Sanctuary, Elita for the east—'

'What about Maitland?'

'No,' Robert said emphatically. 'I don't want you going anywhere near Maitland – at least, not so anyone can see you.'

Andrew frowned, and noticed Finnlay watching over his shoulder. 'But there's no reason to think those Malachi might still be around, is there?'

'We don't know they're not waiting for you to come back. After all, we don't even know why they wanted to take you in the first place.'

'No,' Andrew said, looking down at his gloves. It was hard to go through a day without that all-encompassing weight on his chest, thinking about how Bella and Lawrence had died, and that he'd not even had a chance to say prayers for them, or for the others who had died. He didn't even know who had survived. They would wonder if he was dead, or they would think he'd gone into hiding, or was too much the coward to come back and face them. He had failed in his duty towards them; Lawrence would have been very disappointed in him. Both father and adopted father so disappointed in him: Andrew's face grew red at the thought.

'But things could get much worse than a simple separation,' Robert continued, oblivious to Andrew's pain. 'I'm sorry, Finn, but if you get captured, unless it's a straightforward situation, the chances are you'll have to get yourself free. I won't risk leaving Andrew without protection.'

Finnlay gave them a wry smile over his shoulder. 'I'll just have to make sure that doesn't happen. I know I'm expendable.'

'I didn't say that. If I get captured or killed, then you get out of Lusara completely – and immediately.'

'What?' Finnlay brought his horse to a halt and turned to face them both. 'Leave Lusara? And go where? You haven't even told us where we're going once we find Micah.'

Robert's voice was low and firm, almost matter-of-fact, and yet it was laced with a tension Andrew couldn't penetrate. 'Flan'har. Bleakstone Castle. I need to collect the men waiting for us there. After that, we have work to do.'

If Finnlay was surprised, he hid it well. 'Fine. And if you get captured?'

'Take Andrew to Bishop McCauly. He'll know what to do next.'

Finnlay gazed steadily at his brother, a gaze Robert returned without blinking. Then Finnlay drew in a short breath, gathered his reins together and looked away, obviously choosing not to say all the things racing around in his mind. Robert watched him as though he wished Finnlay *would* say them, no matter that he'd heard them before.

'You'll have to draw us a map,' Finnlay added, eventually.

'Of course.'

Finnlay turned his horse for the road and they began to move once more.

Silence ruled for a short while, then Robert turned to Andrew and asked, 'Can you think of any other places Micah would go if he found the Enclave empty?'

'Other places?'

'Well, would he make straight for Flan'har, to see his family, or would he find some other way to meet up with you? Did you ever set meeting places in case you were split up?'

'Well, yes, but—' Andrew frowned. There was a catch to Robert's voice that was quite distracting, as though he were asking one thing, but seeking to find out something else entirely.

'Andrew,' Finnlay interrupted, 'if you intend to become King, you'll have to learn to finish your sentences. If you leave them to other people, you never know what you might end up with.'

'And there,' Robert added, with a smile, 'speaks the voice of experience.'

'Oh, I couldn't agree more. After all, *you* were the one always finishing my sentences when I was a boy, if I recall correctly.'

'Your memory is notoriously bad. Even Andrew knows that.'

Despite himself, Andrew smiled at the brothers' silly banter, and even though a part of him knew they were doing it for his benefit, to make him feel more comfortable, such effort required some reward. He thought for a moment, then said, 'There was a place on the other side of Maitland, a huge dead tree, where the middle had been burned out by a lightning strike years ago. But that was if the Manor was attacked or something and we got separated. There was always the Enclave, and usually, his cottage. If we were coming from Marsay, then there was a tavern about five leagues off the road where we could meet. I just don't know that any of these would qualify.'

'Yes, well,' Finnlay peered over his shoulder, 'you're not the only one who thought the Enclave would never fall.'

Andrew chanced a glance at Robert, but his expression was entirely closed. It was obvious he was preparing to ask more questions, probably about things Andrew didn't want to talk about, so he did the only thing he could do – he went on the attack. 'You and Micah used to be close friends, didn't you?' Out of the corner of his eye, he saw Finnlay look up sharply, but Robert did no more than grunt. 'Why aren't you close friends now? When I told you he hated you, you weren't surprised. He stayed behind at Maitland because he didn't want to spend a week travelling with you to the Enclave – and yet now, even though I know you'd rather we went looking for Kenrick or something, instead, we're going to look for Micah. If he's not your friend any more, then why?' Andrew surprised himself at the passion in his voice. He didn't dare look at the other two for fear of what else they might see. 'What happened? Why aren't you friends any more?'

Robert said nothing for a few minutes, and Andrew didn't press him. They waited patiently for a cart and oxen to pass by in the opposite direction.

'What has Micah said you to about it?' Robert asked eventually.

'Nothing.'

'Really?'

'Why? What did you expect him to say?'

'Andrew,' Finnlay warned, 'you can exercise a little more respect than that.'

'I just—'

'Want to know something that's personal, between myself and Micah, is that it?'

Andrew opened his mouth to reply, but Finnlay beat him. 'I did warn you about not finishing your sentences.'

This time, Andrew didn't smile; he could feel the confusion building inside him, the evasions, the prospects, the awful possibilities of the future he would have no say in. 'Why shouldn't I ask?' He was shocked at his own temerity, but he couldn't stop the rest tumbling out. 'After all, you're about to ask me all about Kenrick, to tell you everything I've learned about him over the years, and I'm sorry, Finnlay, I know you don't want me to say his name, but, Robert, you're being loyal to somebody who used to be your friend and yet you think me a fool because I'm loyal to a cousin who I've already sworn allegiance to. If there's some fine distinction between the two, I'd really like to know what it is, because I certainly can't see it.' He was breathing heavily and he bit his lip to calm himself down. When he looked up, he found both brothers looking at him, then they exchanged a look and it was almost enough to set Andrew off again.

But Robert forestalled him, reading him correctly. He gestured towards his brother, saying, 'You never asked, either.'

'You wouldn't have told me. And when did I get a chance to ask?'

'I mean, you never asked Micah, did you?'

Finnlay shook his head. He slowed his horse a little so he could ride on the other side of Andrew. Oddly calmed by this gesture, Andrew wrapped the reins about his hands and kept his eyes on the road.

After another short pause, Robert began talking. 'There are moments when your resemblance to your mother is quite . . . unsettling.' Andrew frowned, but Robert clarified, 'But that's a good thing. Don't ever think otherwise.

'I can only tell you my side of it.' Robert began again, 'and that's with the distance of nine years. Micah was once my closest friend and I trusted him like no other, sometimes even to the exclusion of my own brother.'

Andrew felt his face redden, but he kept his eyes on the road.

'Micah fell in love with a Malachi girl. He should have told me about it, but he didn't. Not realising who she was, we captured her at Shan Moss. He was there when I questioned her and said nothing. The next day, her people rescued her and abducted Micah. When I found out, I went to rescue him and while I was helping him, she stabbed me.'

Andrew gasped, his head snapping around to see Robert's face. He felt he should have asked these questions a long time ago, especially when he found out about Sairead.

'Now wait, Robert,' Finnlay began, 'you're not trying to tell me that Micah deliberately betrayed you to Nash?'

'The truth is, I didn't have time to examine it. I had a knife in my shoulder, I was already wounded badly by Selar, I was surrounded by Malachi and there was Nash, waiting for me to fail. All I knew was Micah had lied to me, and his presence had brought me to that place.'

'And now?'

Andrew held his breath, waiting for the judgment.

'He's spent the last eight years watching over Andrew. He protected him against the Malachi attack. He knows Bleakstone. If his purpose had been to betray me to Nash, he could have done so a thousand times over the last few years.'

As Robert fell silent, Andrew looked from one brother to the other. Neither seemed to know anything about what had happened to Sairead. If he said nothing now, would Robert consider him just as disloyal? And of course, if he did say something, then this fragile new trust Robert had formed in Micah would be shattered, all of which really meant that it was up to Andrew to decide whether Micah could be trusted or not.

He trusted Micah to protect him, as he had never once done anything to suggest that he wouldn't, and he had saved Andrew's life on any number of occasions. But did he trust Micah to be loyal to Robert's cause? That was another matter and he had absolutely no idea.

There were no more revelations after that, and no more questions. It felt like he'd awakened memories that Robert needed to shake before they could move on. Andrew didn't mind. The longer he kept his silence about Kenrick, the longer he could avoid making his own choice.

Long before dark, Finnlay started looking for a useful place to spend the night. When he first saw the abandoned farm, he scanned the area as they approached, leaving Robert to Seek for danger. But the place was well away from the road, and although both farm house and stable were blackened with fire, there was some roof left on the stable, and all four walls. It was more than they usually had, and he was grateful for it.

By the time they reached it, the sun had set, leaving a pale glow in a western sky still devoid of clouds. Of course, now that the sun had gone, the night became bitterly cold and they set up their camp as quickly as possible. Finnlay immediately set a fire going on the hard dirt floor and pulled out his cooking pots.

Just as Andrew made for the door, however, Robert stopped him. 'Where are you going?' he asked.

Finnlay's heart sank, but he kept his head down.

'I was going to get some more firewood. That small pile won't last us through the night.'

'Leave it. Finnlay will take care of it.'

'Oh.'

Finnlay could hear the hesitation in Andrew's voice, and the command in Robert's.

'Where is your sword?'

'By my bed.'

'Bring it here. We'll have some practice.'

'Practice?'

'If you take much longer about it we can still be standing here at breakfast debating the issue.'

Andrew scrambled for his bed and returned with his sword still in its scabbard. As Finnlay poured water into a pot to make soup, Robert took the sword and slid it out, examining the blade up against a light he made himself. Andrew stood before him, still substantially shorter than his father, but nevertheless, no weakling. In another year or two he would be approaching Finnlay's height. Physically, there was no doubt where his blood came from.

And oddly, neither father nor son saw it – though Andrew had no idea of the history of his mother's relationship with Robert. It amazed Finnlay even now: that they could have an altercation like that on the road today, and all Robert could conclude was that Andrew was like his *mother*?

The truth was, he couldn't say exactly why he'd insisted on coming on this trip, except that he knew these two needed somebody to stand between them, to inject a little reason into the battles he knew were coming. And no matter which way he looked at it, that boy over there, watching with trepidation as Robert examined his sword for nicks and flaws, would one day be Finnlay's King. What man wouldn't want to be a part of something like that – especially when that King was also his nephew, the Kingmaker his own brother?

'This is blunt,' Robert announced, 'and the hilt is far from solid. Hold it and let me see your grip.'

Andrew took the sword and held it before him. Robert watched a moment, then walked around the boy, and only Finnlay would know how much of that was real, and how much designed to intimidate. There was not a man alive who knew more about intimidation than Robert.

As Finnlay dropped his carefully chopped carrots into the pot, Robert drew his own sword and brought it up before him. Without warning, he swung in a slow arc, and grunted with approval when Andrew raised his blade in defence. The clash of steel echoed oddly in the burned-out stable.

Again and again the plangent impact filled the building, each blow slow and deliberate, all done without words. And then, abruptly, Robert twisted his wrist, pricking Andrew's hand with the point of his sword and sending the boy's blade flying through the air to land by the horses, which stumbled away at the noise of the sudden impact.

'Pick it up,' Robert commanded, and Andrew rushed to obey.

It was odd, but the only command Andrew had ever fought was Robert's insistence that he kill Kenrick; at any other instruction, Andrew was more obedient than the most loyal servant. What would it take for him to rebel?

Finnlay no longer thought about telling Robert the truth about his son.

'Who taught you sword?'

'Um, Lawrence had a swordmaster come to the Manor three days a week. I trained with him half a day each time. I also trained with bow and pike, and staff. And then, when I go to Marsay, I train daily with K— with the court. Kenrick has the finest teachers.'

'I see,' Robert said. 'Is that all?'

'Oh, and Micah. He was really—'

'Exacting?'

'Yes.' Andrew fell silent and waited again.

Robert simply stared at him, his sword hanging easily in his fingers, pointing at the ground. Andrew watched him as though he should be doing something but couldn't work out what.

Finnlay added onions and turnips to the pot, threw in some corn and a heavy pinch of herbs. He could hardly bear to watch – and yet he couldn't look away.

Without warning, Robert swung his sword again, but this time hard and fast. Andrew barely brought his blade up in time, and certainly without enough force to combat the blow. He stumbled back, darting around a support pillar to give him a few extra seconds. Robert pursued him relentlessly, using his greater height, weight and speed to his advantage. It took no more than a few seconds before Andrew was pressed up against the opposite wall, his sword gone and Robert's blade pressed up against his throat.

Robert didn't employ any dramatics. 'Obviously Micah wasn't quite exacting enough. Come, pick up your sword and we'll go again.' He turned and headed back to their starting point. Andrew paused a moment, then fell to the ground to pick up his sword, and ran back to face Robert again, this time far more ready for the attack.

Or rather, he *thought* he was. As far as Finnlay could tell, Robert did everything exactly as he'd done the first time, and although Andrew met the blows with more power, moments later he was once again pressed against the wall, gasping for breath.

'Come, again.'

Again, and again. Finnlay lost count. He watched only because somebody had to bear witness, again and again, until Andrew slipped and fell and Robert's blade caught the bottom of his chin, drawing blood.

'Come, again.'

Andrew wiped the blood away and scrambled to his feet, running back to where Robert waited for him. Though he couldn't admit it out loud, Finnlay couldn't deny what a pleasure it was to be able to watch Robert in action. It wasn't often he got to see such consummate skill from a Master swordsman of Robert's calibre. Finnlay got comfortable. Again and again they faced off, and the result was always the same. Finnlay went outside and gathered more firewood, found a few hard apples on a tree and a dozen edible mushrooms around its base. When he returned, he found another bout just finished. As they regained their starting position, Robert paused, his voice showing no sign at all that he'd exerted himself.

'Well?'

'Well what?' Andrew replied, trying to pretend that he wasn't breathing hard.

'What have you learned so far?'

'That you're expecting me to give up.'

'I see. Are you?'

'No.'

'So you want to keep going all night?'

'If that's what you want.'

'You don't want me to win?'

Andrew didn't answer that, but lifted his chin a little, keeping his sword in front of him.

'Because it's a little late, that's all. How many bouts do you think we need before you *do* win?' Robert sheathed his sword and moved to stand over Andrew, not openly threatening; it was more subtle than that. 'I already know how determined you are, Andrew. I'm just not sure exactly what you are determined to *do*. Unfortunately, I don't think you are either. And if you think I was trying to get you to give up, then you need to look again at what you're trying to learn from me.'

'Me?' Andrew almost squeaked, lowering his sword. 'I never said I wanted to learn from—'

'No?' Robert smiled. 'Then why are you still standing there? Finnlay, what's for supper?'

'Soup, bread and bacon,' Finnlay replied evenly.

'Perfect. I'm hungry!'

This was going to be a long trip.

It started again before breakfast, before Finnlay had even woken up properly. The first thing he heard was a rhythmic thumping noise. He rolled out of bed to find Robert and Andrew gone. He absently poked some life into the fire, then went outside to find a discreet corner somewhere, only to discover the two of them hard at work.

Robert had found some old rag and had tied it to a tether post in the middle of the yard. He stood to one side as Andrew practised cuts at it, swinging to the count Robert made.

'Did you—' he asked on his way past.

'I last scanned about five minutes ago. There are a few convoys coming along the road, but apart from that, we're mostly on our own.'

'Good.' There was not a day went by when he didn't curse his inability to Seek. It was such a small thing in the grand scheme, but it never failed to irk him.

The thumping kept up for another hour, long after the sun came up, by which time Finnlay had made breakfast, eaten it, washed up, packed and was sitting on a discarded mill-wheel getting bored.

Or at least, that's what he wanted it to look like. Andrew was self-conscious enough as it was, under Robert's scrutiny. It wouldn't do either of them much good to know that Finnlay was watching them both carefully. The moment would come, not soon, but eventually, when the constant grating of one against the other would cause a flash point: Andrew *was* a Douglas, whether he knew it or not, and he was a Ross, even though he'd never really been allowed to be. So Finnlay watched and waited, pretending he was doing neither.

And then Robert was putting an end to the morning's training and getting ready to saddle up. He let Andrew go to wash up at the well, and Finnlay brought his horse up. 'If you're going to give me a lecture, Finn,' Robert grunted, 'do it now and do it quickly.'

'No, no lecture. Why would I do that?'

Robert looked aside at him while tightening the straps on his saddle. 'It's a compulsion with you.'

'Well, I have no lecture.' Finnlay put his hands behind his back, knowing he was looking smug, but unable to help it.

'You're probably saving it for later.'

'Robert,' Finnlay put his hand on his breast, 'I'm wounded you think that of me.'

'I'm sure you are,' Robert replied, but he laughed a little. He waited a moment until Andrew came back, then said to both of them, 'We'll get to Micah's cottage late this afternoon. I also want to have a look around while we're there. I'm sorry, Andrew, but I would like to know why your aunt and uncle were targeted by the Malachi once it was clear they weren't going to get you.'

Andrew just nodded slowly.

Finnlay asked, 'What do you expect to find?'

'I don't know – but there's no harm in looking. I'll go on my own.'

'Of course.'

'Then you don't think Micah can be trusted.' Andrew spoke quietly and thoughtfully.

'I don't know that Micah *can't* be trusted – but I do know that he has been close to Malachi in the past and they have more than proved their worth. In his favour, when the Malachi did attack us, his actions saved your life. I'm not going to risk it for anything, Andrew, so you'll stay with Finnlay, out of the way. With any luck, we'll find Micah waiting for us, and then we can continue in peace.'

Andrew searched Robert's face for a moment, then looked away, as though there were a host of things he wanted to ask but didn't dare. Robert appeared to be oblivious, but Finnlay wasn't so sure. So much of what Robert was doing, so much of what he said and how he schooled his expressions, were entirely for Andrew's benefit. For the most part, Finnlay wasn't sure what he was supposed to say or not. He'd corner Robert tonight, away from Andrew, and sort out exactly what Robert wanted from him.

His brother had already picked up a stick and, with his boot, smoothed out a patch of yard dirt. 'Finnlay, your map. Andrew, you need to look at this too.' Robert began to draw on the dirt, familiar lines that looked like rivers and lakes. 'Here is Maitland, and here, Dunlorn. This line is the border with Flan'har. I should have drawn you a proper map back at the cave, but this will have to do. Now, ten leagues over the border from here, you'll find St Julian's Monastery. The good Bishop spent most of the last eight or so years there, and the monks are good friends of our cause, taking in a large number of our refugees. If all else fails, you can find help there. But if you head due south from St Julian's, towards the sea, you will reach Bleakstone Castle. The Bishop, Payne, Owen, Daniel and Deverin are there, along with I don't know how many men who've found their way to us.'

'Just head due south?'

'Aye.' With his head still down, Robert put in a few more details. 'If you find there's trouble at Bleakstone, or find the Bishop is gone, or anything else, then head straight for the capital. I know Grant will do his best to hide you in the first instance, then get you on a ship in the second.' Robert added, 'Either way, Finn, you just get Andrew to Aiden.

'And you?' Robert turned to Andrew. 'Could you find your way to Bleakstone?'

Andrew frowned a little and turned to look at the map from different angles. Then he looked up again. 'Yes. What . . . what instructions have you left with the Bishop?'

That question made Robert laugh, slowly and deeply. 'The news is all bad, I'm afraid, my boy. His instructions are to give what aid he can to put you on the throne. And the men he has with him are just as heartless on this matter as I am. You'll find no mercy there. But if you do find you need to rely on him, I want you to trust him without question. He is more trustworthy than the rest of us put together. Now come, we need to get moving before we're *all* captured.'

He couldn't pinpoint why he kept his silence, but Robert found it more and more difficult to maintain an even mood the further they travelled. It might have been the shifting tides of the weather, tumbling between windy and warm to cold and wet, where clouds swept across the sky one moment, to be replaced by a sun almost too bright. It might also have been the company on the roads – one of the reasons he usually avoided them. For the most part, he found it too hard to see up close what Kenrick was doing to Lusara, and seeing the poor camped on the edge of a village, lining the road with their hands out for a copper so they could eat, or the child hanging from a rope at a crossroads, or the lost and dispossessed who, with bare and sometimes bloody feet, trudged from one side of the country to the other hoping for work, or a home, or some place where they could be safe, where what they had and who they were was not going to be stolen from them again.

He couldn't remember the last time he'd seen a Lusaran speak with pride about his own country, and so much of it was indirectly – and directly – his fault. If he had moved quicker, had not left Selar in the first place, or killed him when he could, or done just about anything over the last twenty years, things would be so much better than this. Travelling through his country was a proper reminder that he'd failed badly, and nothing Jenn nor anyone else could say would change the fact that if they thought he was the man to fix this now, then he was also the man who had failed to fix it previously.

But for the very same reason that he avoided looking and feeling these things, he knew he had to force Andrew to. He let the boy ride in front, alongside Finnlay, and he himself just watched, speaking only when asked something directly.

It was interesting how a boy as sensitive, as caring and gentle, as honest and unspoiled as Andrew could be so completely ignorant of what was going on literally at his feet.

As the morning approached zenith, Robert got them down from their horses, saying they needed the exercise for an hour, to rest their mounts, to get their own blood flowing. Finnlay made no comment, and although his gaze had lingered on the terrible sights, Andrew's demeanour had never changed. It was perhaps the single most disturbing thing Robert saw all day. This was never going to work. He had to be mad to think he could make this work: Andrew wouldn't get as far as fighting Kenrick, let alone taking the throne – and how, in the name of the gods, was Robert to beat Nash when Nash was already so much stronger? How was Andrew going to cure the ills of this blighted country when he was as blind to them as Kenrick?

Perhaps what Lusara really needed was for Robert to just let go – he shuddered at that thought, but neither Finnlay nor Andrew noticed. Why was he suddenly thinking Lusara would be better off without him, particularly surrounded by all this misery – he thought for a moment his demon might be rising, but he recognised that although it was there, it was a mere shadow of its former power, almost – *almost* – harmless. So if not the demon, then what? If he let go of this now, if he pulled back and did nothing more in this rebellion, it would most certainly fail, and horribly, and that could not possibly be better than this. So there would be no withdrawal, no more self-doubts, no more hesitations or procrastinations. This was it: since he *was* the man who had failed to fix it previously, then he was also the man who *had* to fix it now.

They stopped in a riverside village long enough to buy some fish for supper, then Robert began Seeking again. Throughout the afternoon he felt Finnlay's eyes on him, but he said nothing. And though he couldn't pinpoint the reason for it, his silence still grew. Perhaps he was simply missing Jenn: the last few weeks had been the longest time they'd spent together since they had first met, sixteen years ago. And now, to finally be allowed to touch her, to lose himself in her – no matter what else happened, he could not regret that. Perhaps he was afraid he would never see her again; he was moving further and further away from her, leaving her to the tenuous protection of an orb only newly made.

And perhaps he could Sense Malachi nearby.

For the fifth time in an hour he suppressed a sigh: there was no way to ignore it, and even Finnlay would be feeling it soon, even if he didn't Seek. He didn't know how Andrew would react, or even if it were safe for them to continue.

Were they walking into a trap?

Even so, he couldn't run: he needed to find Micah, and discover who had killed Bella and Lawrence, and why. If Nash had wanted Andrew, did that mean he was about to get rid of Kenrick for his own reasons – and in that case, should Robert be standing in his way? Of course, to encourage Nash to do that, he'd have to give him Andrew – which he would no more do than hand over his mother. But either way, he needed to know more. Knowledge was his only real weapon, especially now that Nash had regenerated.

'That's far enough,' he said quietly, his voice swallowed up by the thick pine forest they'd entered. Even the gentle steps of the horses were muffled, and their path almost invisible on the dry needle floor. 'You two can wait here, under cover. I'll check Micah's cottage.'

Andrew didn't look happy, but Finnlay agreed quietly. He and Robert exchanged looks, then Robert turned his horse, heading in the direction of the clearing and the cliff, Seeking again.

It was so much stronger now, a flavour in the air, like a trail of crumbs he could follow: just one, ahead of him, waiting. No sign of Micah. He wound his way through the thick pine forest until he reached the clearing. Micah's cottage stood on the other side, in the shadow of the cliff leaning over it like a sentinel. There was smoke coming from the chimney, and fresh firewood stacked outside the door. Somebody had made themselves at home.

He should just go; obviously Micah hadn't returned here after going to the Enclave, so he should collect Andrew and Finnlay and continue on his way – but if he did, he would never find out what he needed to know – and, damn it, who the hell was living in Micah's house?

He rode forward, stopped in the centre of the clearing and swung down from his saddle, keeping his hand on his sword, ready for battle. On the ground were fresh footprints made that day and, in the air, the scent of freshly baked bread. A fine thread of memory tingled down his spine, warning him, but then the door was thrown open and he was faced with Sairead, the woman who had taken Micah's soul, who had tried to kill Robert in Nash's service.

For a moment, real shock widened her eyes, then she was standing tall, ready to fight him. Robert had already brought his sword up. 'What have you done with him?'

He couldn't deny she was beautiful. She stood before him in a gown of delicate rose hue, a heavy fabric fit for riding. She had no weapons other than the ice-blue of her eyes, the gold of her hair. She stared at him for long seconds, as though measuring him, before she stepped clear of the door. 'Micah is not here. He has been captured. I'll take you to him.'

'You have him hostage?' Robert couldn't keep the hostility out of his voice. This woman had destroyed a friendship he'd thought indestructible. 'Am I his ransom?'

'If you want to look at it that way, then yes. But you must come with me nonetheless.'

'And if I don't?'

'Then I cannot be held responsible for what happens to him.'

'And you would pretend you care.'

Her eyes flashed at him then, and she took a step closer. 'He is my husband. I carry his child. His life is in danger and he sees you still as his friend. If you would help him, then you must come with me.'

There was no doubting the passion in her gaze, nor the gentle swell in her belly. But how could Micah have *married* her? She was Malachi, the sworn enemy of all Salti, people Micah had grown up with, people like Finnlay and Patric, and Robert himself.

'You would leave him to his fate?' Sairead asked, frowning, disbelieving. 'You will not help?'

'Why should I trust what you say? You're Malachi.'

'And you,' she said harshly, 'are Salti! You carry your own crimes. Micah has been captured, held against your return. I don't know any more than that. I have been waiting here in the hope that you would come looking for him, that you still care enough for him to aid him.'

'And where will you take me?'

'The longer we delay, the worse it will be.'

Robert frowned, sending his Senses out again to check if there were more Malachi around. 'How?'

'They'll know you're here and if you don't come with me—'

This was idiocy, and yet, he could not ignore this plea. Whatever Micah had done, Robert could never abandon him, even if this were just another trap. But if he left, he would do so without a word to Finnlay and Andrew. They would assume him captured, and Finnlay would ride with all speed to Bleakstone, where the Bishop – a man of his word, if nothing else – would take the first step in an avalanche which would be unstoppable. If this *were* a trap, as it undoubtedly was, then Andrew would need that help.

And there was no doubt in his mind that if she knew Andrew was with him, this woman would tell her people.

Fine, then. He sheathed his sword. This wasn't how he'd planned it, but again he had little choice. 'So be it. Let's go,' he said shortly.

Sairead's eyes widened in surprise, then she turned for the door. 'I'll put the fire out. We'll leave immediately.'

17

No matter what Robert had said, Finnlay couldn't just stand there and ignore the vibration in the air, the itching in his spine that said there were Malachi about. And perhaps Robert hadn't expected him to, because he neither looked back nor did anything to stop Finnlay following on foot at a distance, slowly and quietly. Andrew stuck by him, equally determined, as though he could read Finnlay's thoughts.

They crept towards the clearing, and paused when Robert did, but when he strode on up to the cottage, Finnlay kept Andrew back and set a Mask over them, casting a warning glance in Andrew's direction to stay quiet and still.

He wasn't surprised when the door of the cottage opened and a woman stepped out. She looked a little familiar, but he couldn't remember why. Robert appeared to know her and other than raising his sword initially, neither fought her nor fled, despite the fact that she was Malachi. What did surprise him was the gasp of horror from Andrew, the wide eyes and the sudden, urgent movement forward – which Finnlay stopped with a hard hand.

Andrew turned agonised eyes on him, but Finnlay held a finger to his lips for silence, then mouthed, 'Wait.'

Andrew's urgency abated a little, but his body still strained towards Robert. The two were talking, and though Finnlay guessed their words were heated, he could see only gestures, and heard nothing. For the hundredth time he wished he could mindspeak Robert.

Then, inexplicably, Robert sheathed his sword, and, as he swung back into the saddle, the woman ran inside, emerging a moment later with a cloak on. She shut the door and entered the stable to bring her own horse out. Without another word, she mounted and rode into the forest behind the house – and Robert followed her!

Finnlay swore and dropped the mask, ready to shadow the pair. But then he paused. Robert had given him orders, and no matter what else happened—

Andrew rushed forward, already calling out. Finnlay scrambled to stop him, holding the struggling boy with some difficulty. Fortunately, there was no sign the Malachi had heard him.

'Finnlay, you have to let me go! You don't understand! She's his wife! She promised she wouldn't . . . and now—'

'Just calm down, Andrew,' Finnlay held him firm, 'and tell me what this is about. Then we'll decide what to do.'

'We don't have time—'

'Enough!' Finnlay bellowed, and the boy froze, staring at him wide-eyed. His struggles ceased as Finnlay released him and stepped back. 'Tell me who she is.'

'Sairead. Micah's wife. She's the Malachi who stabbed Robert. Micah married her.'

'You knew this?'

'I found Micah with her last year and he admitted that they were married, and I didn't want to not trust him but he promised me she was no danger, that they'd been married for years and kept their marriage secret from both us and her people, and I'm so sorry, Finn, this is my fault, if they kill Robert, it's going to be my fault. We have to go after them! We have to get Robert back!'

'Why in the name of the gods didn't you say something about this before? You should have told Robert at least. Especially after yesterday and— Well, we can argue about this later. Let's go.'

Andrew didn't pause, but swung up into his saddle and turned ready to go after Robert, but Finnlay put his hand on Andrew's rein. 'No, we're going to Flan'har.'

'What?' Andrew's face, already white with shock, paled again. 'But what about—'

'Robert was no prisoner. By my guess, she's taking him to Micah, who's either being held by Malachi or Nash. Either way, Robert won't be back today, and will be better off if we leave him to do what he needs to do – so you and I are heading for Bleakstone.'

'But we can't just leave him!'

'Andrew.' Finnlay waited until the boy turned back to face him, then with as much confidence into his voice as he could, he said, 'There's not a Malachi alive powerful enough to best Robert – and they know that. You have to trust him.'

'Oh? And you're going to tell me that *you* don't want to go after him?'

'Of course I do, but we're still going to Bleakstone.' Finnlay herded Andrew's horse away from Robert and the mysterious Malachi.

'But, Finnlay—'

'If Robert had wanted us to wait, he would have given us some kind of signal when the woman went into the house. Now that's enough. We have some serious riding to do.'

Robert kept track on two different levels. At first, his sole desire was to Seek Finnlay and Andrew, to make sure that they got away cleanly with nobody following them, that they weren't going to make some idiot attempt at rescuing him, and that they were heading in the right direction. Then, once he was sure they were on their way safely, he began to pay more attention to where he was being taken, and the Malachi who hated him.

They turned south, climbing the hills behind the cottage and then making their way down the other side. They did not travel fast. It was obvious that even so early on in her pregnancy, riding hard was uncomfortable for Sairead, but still she wore an expression of strained urgency, and again his doubts shifted. Would she risk her life waiting for him if Micah wasn't really in danger?

'Where are we going?'

'Does it matter?'

'Yes.'

'Why should I tell you? Would you tell me, if our positions were reversed?'

'No,' Robert conceded with a half smile, 'I don't think I would.'

Another hour went by before he tried again. 'How long have you and Micah been married?' Micah being married at all was a strange concept, but even more strange was the reality that he'd married a Malachi, the same woman who had tried to kill Robert. And all this time, Micah had kept her at his cottage, so close to Andrew.

Had the boy known?

'We married a year after the Battle of Shan Moss, though why you should care, I know not.'

He nodded at her reply, barely registering the details and the tone of sheer disdain. But he had to keep her talking. 'This is your first child?' He had to hide his sudden and gut-wrenching fear: was Andrew's reticence about killing Kenrick and taking the throne based on more than a desire not to hurt his cousin and a wish not to be King? Was he already under the influence of Malachi, and, by association, Nash? It was hard to believe that Jenn's son could possibly— But he could also be influenced without him realising it. Could he possibly be so near a Malachi and not know – or if he did know, then why hadn't he said anything, especially when it was Malachi who had killed his aunt and uncle? None of it made sense.

He realised she was talking to him. 'Our first child, though it should be our third or fourth. Why are you asking these questions?'

Robert turned to look at her. 'Why are you answering?'

Her look had daggers in it. 'Because a long time ago, he idolised you.'

'And now he hates me.'

'Yes,' she whispered, 'he hates you.'

Andrew felt sick to the stomach. If Finnlay had let him pause long enough, he would have left his breakfast behind some bush somewhere. But instead, they rode as though there were a hundred demons chasing them, pausing only long enough to change horses, to grab some bread and refill water bottles. Then they were on the road again, leaving the road, taking paths across the countryside, constantly heading southeast, further and further away from Robert.

It was all his fault: now both Robert *and* Micah were in danger, and all because he couldn't tell when to trust somebody and when not to. Robert wanted him to be a King and he couldn't even do something like this the right way; he had been so sure she had not lied when she said she was no danger to Micah – but of course, that didn't mean she wasn't a danger to Robert. How, in the name of all that was holy, was he supposed to make good judgments when he was on the throne?

Once again, his stomach lurched and he swallowed hard to settle it. There was nothing he could do now, other than to keep up with Finnlay and head further east into another country, going to a place where people would all do their best to make him into something he didn't want to be.

'Are we going to travel all night?' Robert asked, looking up at the new-formed stars above. They were travelling across a hill where three small farms sat below in the valley – farms with warm fires and food and some place to rest. He was tired, still not fully recovered from his ordeal with the Key, and the picture of a warm bed was tantalising.

'No, not all night. Another hour, maybe more.'

Another hour – where would that put them? And what would he find when he got there?

How she hated him – for what? For being Micah's friend? When she'd stabbed him at Shan Moss, Nash had congratulated her and she'd said, '*Shut up, I didn't do it for you.*' The implication was that she'd done it for Micah, to free him of service to – who did she think he was? *What* did she think he was? If Sairead was so evil herself that she would think Nash better than Robert, then how could Micah, the best of men, want to be married to her?

It made no sense – unless Micah hated him so much that he had betrayed him to the Malachi; there was a thought Robert didn't dare touch. Micah had spent the last nine years protecting Andrew, it appeared at the cost of his marriage to Sairead. Such a man would not then betray Robert . . .

The moon came out as they descended the hill, washing the slope in grey light. Sairead looked tired, and rode holding herself rigidly, as though she was in pain and didn't dare admit it.

'Do you want to stop for a few minutes? To rest?'

She looked at him with that same ice-cold gaze, but she made no answer. Instead, she led him to a wood at the end of a lane, her mouth pinching as they wound their way around ancient trees.

'Come, Sairead, a few minutes' rest will help your baby.'

As though it was the last thing she wanted to do, she pulled on her reins, bringing the horse to a stop. Robert jumped down and stood beside her, offering her his hand so her dismount would be easier. She paused almost too long, then took his hand, easing herself down to the ground with a barely concealed gasp.

'Here,' Robert drew his cloak from his shoulders, 'lie down for a moment. I'll make us a brew.' Gradually, he got his reluctant patient lying on her side, her eyes closed and her lips in a thin line. She must be in some pain for her to give in so easily, especially to one she hated so much.

Robert grabbed enough wood to start a fire, and with a brief gesture, got it going. He pulled out a pot from his saddle-bag, filled it with water and a pinch from his pouch of dried leaves. He turned back to find her watching him without expression.

'How do you feel now? Any specific pain, or is it just fatigue?'

'Just fatigue. I'll be fine in a few minutes.'

'Good.'

'Good? Why are you helping me?'

'You think I'm the kind of monster who would enjoy your pain? That I would think nothing of endangering the life of your child?'

'I'm Malachi. My child will also be Malachi. We're your enemies.'

'Yes, and if you fight me, I'll fight back.' Robert turned back to the brew and poured it into a cup. He handed it to Sairead and helped her sit up so she could drink. 'If our positions were reversed, would you not help me?'

'No,' she said as she emptied the cup. 'I don't think I would.'

Robert got to his feet, stretching his back. What did he hope to achieve by talking to her? If she forgave him his crimes, would he be able to forgive himself?

Would Micah?

'What are you doing? You're not supposed to—' Sairead's voice had a thread of fear to it, making Robert turn quickly – but not quickly enough. The first blow hit him on the side of his head so hard he stumbled forward into his horse. Dizzy, nauseated, he struggled upright, glimpsing some men, Sairead pushing her way through them, and then something large and hard

169

swinging towards him again. He tried to duck, but not in time. The second blow sent him into oblivion.

Andrew lost track of time: he galloped when Finnlay did, trotted and walked when he was told. His horse was swift and obedient and every footstep was sure. They didn't talk, and Andrew knew why: if they did, then they'd have to talk about Robert and Andrew would just start feeling sick again. But clouds swallowed the sky and he lost track of the stars and even, after a while, the moon. When they entered a heavy forest, where the ground was rocky and treacherous, he prayed that somehow Finnlay was able to navigate.

It rained a little at some point, but not for long, just enough to put a chill into him, to refresh the horses and to give some texture to the night. Nothing else changed the unending vista until the faintest of glows filtered through the treetops, warning of a welcome dawn approaching.

At the next stream they found, Finnlay called a halt, ordering him to dismount and stretch his legs. He nearly fell off his horse, but Finnlay was there to catch him. 'Careful. We don't want you to break anything.'

Andrew asked bleakly, 'Where are we?'

'About a league from the border. We'll be across it within the hour.'

'The border?' That woke him up, but Finnlay was already leading their horses to the water.

As they drank, he continued, 'I asked directions the last time we changed horses. If the man was right, we can cut a whole day off the trip by going this way. We just need to be careful crossing the border. It's sometimes patrolled by Kenrick's men.'

Andrew started to feel sick again, as though the ground under his feet was shifting and rolling like the waves on a beach. 'I don't think I want to leave Lusara.'

'You think I do?' Finnlay looked up at him, then reached out a hand to squeeze his shoulder. 'It will be an adventure for both of us. Come, let's get moving. I want to be in Flan'har before dawn.'

Micah tried not to flinch at every noise that sounded out of place. He tried not to get up every few minutes and look outside, he tried to trust that Gilbert's Seeking would warn them in time – but trying got him nowhere. Some time in the middle of the night, the older man had given up telling him to go to sleep. Micah took to pacing, going out of the old mill to walk along the river, his ears pricked for some sign.

It was taking too long: Sairead should have been back a week ago. He should have found some other way to do this that wouldn't involve her – especially now.

He got to his feet again, going to the table to pour some ale into an earthenware mug. He drank a few swallows before putting the mug down and heading outside, where the air was clearer.

Gilbert had insisted they wait here, that Micah not be at the cottage, so that Robert's access to him would require distance, ensuring Robert came alone. They had to ensure that Robert could not Seek the Malachi until it was too late. All very reasonable, all very sensible and still unbearable. Gilbert was asleep upstairs, where some old hay gave him a comfortable mattress and where he wouldn't be disturbed by Micah's growing worry. His calm annoyed Micah – after all, Sairead was Gilbert's niece.

Of course, he also knew that Gilbert was right – there was little they could do but wait—

'Micah?'

The night was just on the edge of dawn, with just a frail edge of light in the sky. It was enough. 'Sairead?' He took off at a run, heading down the mill track as fast as he could, yelling out for Gilbert to come. He found her almost falling off her horse. Without a word, he gathered her into his arms carefully and turned back for the mill. Gilbert was there now, pulling his jacket on, running to grab the horse and bring it in.

Micah carefully took Sairead inside and laid her down on his own bed. Without asking, Gilbert brought a cup of wine and knelt down beside him. Sairead looked tired and ill and Micah knew he would never forgive himself for doing this to her. If she were to lose the baby . . .

'Drink a little,' he murmured, lifting the cup to her lips. She met his gaze, smiling enough to reassure him, then drank. She closed her eyes for a long moment, then tried to sit up. 'No, stay there. Just rest,' he told her tenderly.

'I can't rest. I—'

'What happened?' Gilbert asked levelly.

'Can't you see she's ill?' Micah frowned. 'Let her rest and then—'

'No, Micah, he's right. We don't have any time. Uncle, I was bringing him, but I lost him.'

'How could you lose him?'

'We'd stopped to rest a moment and they came out of the darkness. They knocked him out and took him.'

'Who?' Gilbert demanded. 'Don't tell me it was—'

'Felenor, yes. He wasn't there, but I know his men. Two of them stayed with me for an hour or more, and then left, telling me to go home. By the time they were gone, I couldn't follow the others.'

'Who?' Micah demanded equally strongly. First he'd endangered Sairead and their baby, and now Robert had fallen into the wrong hands. 'Who are we talking about?'

Gilbert laid a blanket over his niece and got to his feet. He went to the door and stood there, staring out into the growing dawn. 'Felenor Calenderi. We grew up together.'

'So you're friends?'

'I wouldn't say that.'

'Then what would you say?'

Gilbert turned to look at him. 'I'd say we have to hope that Douglas can get himself free.'

'Can't you Seek him? Surely we can find him, find some way to get Robert back.'

Gilbert shook his head. 'I doubt there's anything I can do.'

Micah got to his feet, surprised by the anger which coursed through him. 'Your grandfather is the Chabanar! How can Felenor disobey you?'

'He works for Kenrick.'

A cold shiver ran down Micah's back, dissolving his anger in one breath. Even so, he turned back to Sairead, determined at least to tend to her. 'So do you. We have to do something.'

'Felenor is a vicious killer.'

'I don't care. We still have to do something.'

It was dark: too dark to be night. Robert could open only one eye; the other felt glued shut. Gingerly he rolled onto his side, but it was awkward. His hands were bound behind him, his feet tied also, and there was a gag in his mouth that no amount of twisting would remove.

His head throbbed and his thirst was a desert waiting for rain. But he'd been here before and he knew his only hope of survival was small movements, careful and considered; that he needed to listen and learn so that when the time came, he would be ready.

Just to make sure, he tried extending his Senses, but he found nothing. The blow to his head had killed his powers, leaving him as blind and impotent as any human – which was, of course, why they'd taken him that way. He couldn't even see if Micah was in here with him.

Keeping his movements small, he shifted a little, swinging his legs forward, hoping to discover Micah in the darkness. All he found, however, was a wall, solid and uncompromising.

In the silence, he swore, the noise emerging as a grunt.

The door opened and before he could be blinded by light, Robert squeezed his eyes shut, giving them the chance to adjust. Two sets of footsteps drew closer and stopped before him. Carefully, he opened his eyes to find boots in front of him, an open doorway behind and bright sunshine streaming in.

He was indeed the only captive.

'So, you're awake. Do you know where you are? No? You should be able to recognise hell without too much trouble.'

Robert rolled onto his back until he could see the faces of the men standing over him. The one speaking was about his own age, tall and thin, with black hair and an eagle nose. Even the eyebrows gave him a hawkish look. The man beside him was harder to see, but had longer hair, curly and an expression of pure hatred on his face.

'Now,' said the first man. 'Are you going to tell me where you have hidden the Key?'

The Malachi and their obsession with finding the Key. Robert would have opened his mouth to voice a refusal, but he didn't get the opportunity. The second man simply swung his foot and kicked Robert in the side. Instantly, he doubled up, scrambling away from further attack, but both men pursued him.

'I didn't think you'd give in, so we need to make you understand that you won't get out of here alive unless you tell us.' They continued to kick him then, and the pain rattled through him, making him gasp and curl up into a ball. They didn't want any information out of him. They just wanted to hurt him.

He knew he was yelling at them to stop, but the gag drowned out any noise he made. They stopped only when he lost the strength to fight them, then he drifted down into the darkness again and felt nothing more.

18

Finnlay slept fitfully, waking every few minutes to sit up and look around, barely extending his Senses, checking Andrew – but there was never anything there. They had ridden through the night and all the next day; now they needed proper rest, so Finnlay had taken the risk and hired a room in a tavern for the two of them. The beds were hard, but the door had a lock on it, and there would be fresh horses ready for them in the morning.

The moment the first threads of sunlight hit his face, Finnlay sat up once more and ran his fingers through his hair. 'Andrew?' he called firmly, 'time to wake. We'll take breakfast before we go.'

The boy groaned before rolling over and opening his eyes. 'But we just went to sleep.'

'Come on. Get your boots on. I want to be on the road in half an hour.' Finnlay got out of bed, drew on his jacket, and splashed some water on his face. He gathered his things back into his saddle-bag and pulled his boots on. He could have given Andrew a few more minutes in bed, but a roiling urgency in his belly wouldn't let him be still. He headed for the door, calling, 'Downstairs in five minutes, Andrew, or you miss breakfast.'

He tried not to think about Robert, but there'd been so many images of him in Finnlay's dreams it was hard to forget. More times than he could count he'd considered mindspeaking Jenn to tell her what had happened, but since she could do no more than he, all he'd succeed in doing would be to make her worry more, as if she didn't have enough of that as it was.

Finnlay made it downstairs, dropped his bags on one of the empty tavern tables and headed out the back to the stable. He found a boy putting their saddles on two fresh horses and threw him a copper for his efforts. By the time he got back inside, Andrew was waiting for him, already tucking into a bowl of porridge thick with honey and cream. Finnlay's own mouth watered.

There was fresh sourdough bread, sizzling bacon and figs to eat as well. Finnlay was hungry, but he couldn't put away anything like the amount of food the boy consumed. Andrew ate as though he'd been starving for a month. By the time Finnlay was getting him on his feet to go, Andrew was still reaching for a last fig and the remaining crust of bread.

They headed south, without deviation. Finnlay had asked for directions, not to Bleakstone – for that would have attracted attention – but instead to the sea. So they rode into the morning, stopping again only to water the horses and to stretch their legs. As the afternoon wore on, the horses began to tire and Finnlay chose the next town to make a change.

They ate again, filling up on roast goose and sweet potatoes – a real treat. Finnlay bought some extra bread and gave it to Andrew before they mounted up again. He couldn't ignore the shadows under his nephew's eyes, nor the exhaustion in his movements, but he didn't dare stop unless they were ready to fall over.

It was so strange travelling in a foreign country. Flan'har had been an independent Duchy for so long that nobody remembered its origins. Its Dukes had always been the allies of the Earls of Dunlorn, and this Duke in particular, Grant Kavanagh, was a boyhood friend of Robert's. He'd long ago given Robert free use of Bleakstone Castle, along with the protection of his borders. Still, that didn't make this place the same as Lusara, and Finnlay couldn't help feeling a little lost in it. One look at Andrew and he knew he wasn't the only one.

They didn't rest that night: they were too tired, too restless, too close to breaking, and stopping now would only delay arrival at their destination. But the night was clear and Finnlay found a star to guide him and a road to follow. After that, his mind wandered, sleeping while he was awake, fuzzing over his aching muscles, his throbbing knees and the regrets which bounced around his mind. The night felt as long as three, but eventually, when he'd all but given up hope of seeing it, the sun rose, suddenly and sharply, over a view he'd never imagined. Stunned, he brought his horse to a halt, calling to Andrew to do the same.

Before them, just a few leagues away, was an immense ocean the size of which he couldn't begin to gauge. It stretched both east and west, and swept away to the horizon.

'What is it?' Andrew asked, rubbing his hands over his face. He peered over his shoulder and turned back to Finnlay.

'It's just been a long time since I saw the sea, that's all.' Finnlay breathed deeply, enjoying that odd tang in the air, letting it wake him up.

'Finn?'

'Yes?'

'Didn't Robert say we'd get to the castle *before* we reached the coast?'

'Uh, yes, he did.' Finnlay shook his head, apparently not yet awake enough.

'Then do you think that might be Bleakstone back there? The one we passed about an hour ago?'

Finnlay closed his eyes and took in another deep breath. Then he turned his horse to find Andrew's observation annoyingly accurate. They'd gone right past it in the darkness. 'Come on,' he said dryly, noting the smug smile on the boy's face. 'See if we can't miss it a second time.'

'I don't see how you missed it the first time.'

'*I* missed it? But you didn't?'

'I wonder what they'll have for breakfast,' was Andrew's only comment; Finnlay didn't argue; his stomach was making too much noise.

Robert didn't remember the gag being removed, but the next minute, something cold and refreshing was being poured into him. He swallowed convulsively, tasting water and something else perhaps, probably his own blood. He could hardly move. His hands were still tied behind his back, his feet still bound. He lay on his back, coughing as the water went down, hardly daring to open his eyes. The pain was . . .

He'd lost count of the attacks. They weren't trying to kill him, just to beat him to a pulp – and they were succeeding. Apart from that first time, they hadn't asked him a single question, though it was obvious they knew who he was. It was always the same man leading the attack, although the others changed. It was the leader who also seemed to enjoy the violence more than the others, as though Robert's only purpose was to provide him with entertainment. There was no doubting the hatred in their eyes. He could see that much, in the sweltering, clinging atmosphere in his hell-prison.

They were right, he did know this hell: this was where he'd lived for so many years, these men merely the physical personification of his demon. Was he not here because he'd wanted to help a man who'd once been his friend, as he'd tried to help a woman who was his enemy?

With a last desperate swallow, the water was gone. Robert licked his cracked lips, making the most of it, then looked up, hoping to see a friendly face. It was just another of the men who had kicked and beaten him; Robert looked away. The door didn't close as the man left, but instead, the leader came in, standing this time by Robert's feet so he could see better.

'My, we must be in some pain by now, eh? Well, there's plenty more of that when you're ready. But we must let you rest – though I doubt your stomach is interested in food, is it? I'll be back in a couple of hours, and we'll start the next session.'

As he turned to go, Robert took his only chance. 'Why?' he croaked. 'Why are you doing this?'

'Why? Because you're Salti. Because you're Robert Douglas, and you've terrified my people for a long time, and I want to show them how easily even you can be humbled. Because you know where the Key is and I'm going to get it from you and Nash be damned. Because I know you won't give it to me until you know in your soul there's no other way for you to get away from the pain, until your will is completely and utterly broken. Don't worry – I know how to keep a man alive for a long time like this.' With that he smiled warmly, turned and left, closing the door behind him with a loud bang.

Robert gasped and shut his eyes against the agony. This pain was everywhere, all around him, suffocating him, crying out to him for release. Should he let them kill him? Perhaps he could lie to them – but they would know. He could hold out for a long time, and by then, it probably wouldn't matter anyway – but it did matter, that what this was all about. It was so hard to concentrate around the pain, around the shadows dancing in the corners, laughing at him, celebrating the destruction of his dreams.

He thought perhaps it would be better if the rebellion continued without him; if he couldn't get himself free of this, if he couldn't withstand the pain, or hold onto his mind while they beat his body for idle sport, then perhaps it was only just punishment. He hated the Key, probably as much as these men hated him, and he wished he could give it up because, so far, it had brought him nothing but heartache: the Prophecy and Jenn, and so much else. But to give it to the Malachi would be like giving it to Nash: if the Salti didn't know how to use it properly after five hundred and seventy years, what would the Malachi do with it, other than abuse its power, especially now that it was joined to the Calyx, an artefact he'd opened long enough to know only that he wanted more.

So these Malachi would never get the Key, and Robert would die in this room. At least that was something he could hold onto.

'Your Grace! Your Grace!'

Aiden looked up from his book with a frown. It was far too early for Father John to be running around the castle in such a manner – assuming it was ever appropriate for him to do so. 'What's wrong?'

He arrived at Aiden's study with one hand on the door to prop him up, the other on his chest as he caught his breath. He almost wheezed his apology, 'Forgive me, Your Grace, but you must come down to the court-yard – there are new arrivals. You must come!'

It was impossible to miss the glint in John's eye, and although he'd asked not to be disturbed this morning, he put his book down and followed the priest. He took the stairs carefully, mindful of the two worn steps he'd nearly broken his neck on the day before. By the time he reached the bottom, the voices he heard were coming from the Hall. John, moving like a man in his teens, ran before him, opening doors and ushering him through. The moment he entered the hall, he realised why the priest was so excited.

'Finnlay?'

The younger man turned at his call, smiling a little as he came forward. His face was white with exhaustion, his eyes dull and ringed with grey. Still, he bent on one knee and kissed Aiden's hand where his Bishop's ring would have been. When he straightened up, he gestured.

And Aiden held his breath, his heart breaking in that moment.

'Your Grace, please allow me to present Andrew, Duke of Ayr and Earl of Elita. Andrew, His Grace, Aiden McCauly, Bishop of Lusara.'

Finnlay's voice, too, was grey with exhaustion, but he had brought the boy safely here, which meant—

Aiden bowed, biting his lip. When he straightened, he found a pair of huge blue eyes staring at him with a mixture of fear and awe. Andrew's resemblance to Lady Jennifer was striking, but the boy was already taller than her. And now that Aiden knew about it, he could see the strong resemblance to his father.

Aiden looked to Finnlay, unable to loosen the tightening in his throat; he was already forming prayers. 'What—' he swallowed hard, unable to control the blossoming grief, 'what of Robert? How did he die?'

'Die?' Finnlay said, bemused, as Andrew whirled around to look at him. 'Robert's not dead, Your Grace. At least, he wasn't when we left him.'

The relief that swept through Aiden almost made him dizzy. He took a steadying breath and said quickly, 'Forgive me, Andrew. Robert had told us you would not come here unless he was dead or dying.'

'He was captured,' Andrew replied, 'by Malachi. But Finnlay said we had to come here because we'd promised Robert.'

'My lord?' Aiden's colleagues were coming into the Hall, all of them old friends of Finnlay's. They greeted him with smiles and hugs, and there was much laughter for a few minutes, which calmed when Finnlay turned to introduce his young charge.

'Andrew, this is Everard Payne, Earl of Cannockburke, Sir Owen Fitzallan, Sir Alexander Deverin and Lord Daniel Courtenay. A finer group of loyal men you will never find.' All of them smiled at that, but Andrew's smile was decidedly faint. 'Gentlemen, this is Andrew,' Finnlay said, his voice softening, 'our future King of Lusara.'

Aiden watched carefully as the others studied Andrew, and how Andrew reacted. The boy seemed entirely without energy – and then Aiden was calling for servants. 'You young fool, Finnlay! You're both off your feet with exhaustion! I suppose you rode day and night to get here, didn't you?

Well, you both get up to bed – we'll find you somewhere to sleep and then once you're rested, we can talk.' He allowed only Deverin to help. Andrew was left in Father John's hands while Aiden helped Finnlay up the stairs.

As John took Andrew into his own rooms, Aiden turned to Finnlay, keeping his voice low. 'When you're rested, we have a lot to talk about. I don't know what Robert did at the Enclave, but we've had Salti arriving by the dozen for the last few weeks. They'll be thrilled to see you. But there's something else you should know – Patric has returned, and he has news for Robert.'

'Patric's here?' Finnlay smiled with only half his face. The other half appeared to have already gone to sleep. 'That's wonderful! Robert will be so—'

'Go, get your rest.'

With a strong hand, Deverin steered Finnlay down the Hall and into a room made up with a bed all ready. A moment later, the corridor was empty and silent; in that moment, Aiden let fly a prayer to heaven that his fear had been unfounded. And then he turned and headed back downstairs to give the order.

He could see strange spots of splashing colour, appearing and disappearing, swallowing the darkness and enlightening it, like an enormous ballet danced to music he could not hear. He reached out to touch each puddle with his finger, leaving behind a drop of blood, marking it with his own scars.

His body was on fire; these suns of colour were his agonies. But what was one pain when compared to another? Did his country care that this was a different tyrant to the last? Pain was pain was pain, all experienced and endured, and, ultimately, forgotten. That was the nature of pain; he knew; he could feel it with his own burning skin.

He breathed shallowly now, as he lay still, with his eyes open, watching the splashing colour, waiting for it to stop, as it would, waiting for it to become a memory, waiting for them to stop making him pay.

It grew inside him: his people *did* care that they had one tyrant after another. They couldn't forget the pain yet because they were still enduring it. It wasn't over, and it should have been. It wasn't finished yet, instead, barely started.

The demon inside him wasn't dead, but with each attack it was gathering its strength.

Micah ran forward at a crouch and sank to his knees behind a thick bush. Beside him knelt Gilbert, whose eyes remained fixed upon the house in the distance. It sat on the edge of a small town; the Malachi had taken two long days to find it. For a town house, it was quite big, with three rooms below and another two above. There was a cellar entrance at the back, heavily barred and locked, and a stable in a separate building, inside a fenced area. Micah was sure Robert was inside that house.

He felt a small movement behind him as Sairead joined them, leaving her hand on his lower back. She had recovered her strength and had refused to stay behind, no matter what he'd said, which was odd behaviour given how much she hated Robert.

But then, didn't *he*?

'Well?' he whispered. 'Are they still in there?'

'Nobody's left in the last hour.'

'Then let's go.'

'I still think this plan is flawed. There are only three of us, and you have no powers. By Sairead's count, there are six of them, not including Felenor.'

'By my count, Robert's been in there almost three days. If he's still alive it will be a miracle.'

'I can't Sense him.'

'How could you? You don't know him.'

'No, I mean, I can't Sense anybody but seven Malachi.'

Micah ignored his look. 'You'll never Sense him anyway. That doesn't mean he's not in there. We're wasting time.'

'You want to stick to your original plan, even now you've seen the place?'

'Yes, why not? Sairead can set fire to the building. As they all run out, you and I can go in via the cellar and get Robert. Simple.'

'Simple? You don't think they'll take him with them?'

'And risk their own lives? If he's at all able-bodied, he would use the confusion to escape anyway.'

'And if he's not?'

Micah paused and looked apologetically at Sairead. 'I'll go alone if I have to. I got him into this. No matter what, he doesn't deserve an end like this.' She returned his gaze without blinking; this came as no surprise to her. Wasn't this, after all, exactly why she hated Robert?

Gilbert sighed and agreed. 'Very well. As soon as we hear the midnight bell, we'll move. That way, they'll most likely be asleep and the fire will cause the most confusion. Let's move back until then. No point in giving ourselves away.'

'Sleep well?'

Father John came into the room with a jug of steaming water in his hands. He was followed by four servants, also carrying huge jugs, which were poured into a bath that had been placed before the fire. One by one the men left, and John closed the door behind them.

'How do you feel?'

'Better. I could sleep for a week, though.'

'I'm sure you could – but the Bishop has things he needs to talk to you both about, and some decisions need to be made. After that, I think you'll be allowed a little more sleep – although as it is, you've slept more than a day.'

Andrew swung his legs over the edge of the bed and sat up. With a stretch, he got to his feet and padded over to the fireplace and the bath. John had left out towels and clean clothes for him and the water looked inviting.

'Don't be too long,' John smiled, heading for the door. 'And call if you need help. I'll be back shortly to take you down to the Council Chamber.'

The moment the door was closed, Andrew stripped off his remaining clothes, awfully tempted to simply toss them into the flames, he'd been wearing them so long. No wonder John wanted him to have a bath.

He sighed as he sank down into the water and picked up a bar of yellow soap. This was luxury. The last time he'd had a bath like this had been at Marsay, just after—

Just before he'd left, after Kenrick had appeared in public with his facial scars miraculously healed.

No: He wasn't going to think about it any more!

He washed quickly, before the water could get cold, and was almost dressed by the time John came back to show him to the Council Chamber. They were halfway down the staircase when his stomach let out a growl loud enough for the priest to hear. John laughed, but although Andrew tried to laugh with him, it sounded false to him.

The Council Chamber was a beautiful room that Andrew knew he couldn't really appreciate because the long table was almost groaning under the weight of food. He could smell it the moment he walked in. Fortunately, Finnlay was there, already eating, and the sight of a friendly face was enough to make Andrew's appetite blossom even more. He sat down opposite Finnlay and tucked into to a bowl of porridge and sweet preserved fruit, augmented with hot rolls and fresh sliced ham and a mug of steaming brew. It took three helpings to sate his hunger, by which time, Finnlay had finished and the others had all arrived. They took seats and watched him.

Watched *him*, not Finnlay.

It made his skin crawl. Every time he looked up, someone was staring at him: what were they expecting – that he turn into a King in front of him? If Kenrick was such a bad King, then what was he supposed to do? How could he learn about being a King from anybody *but* Kenrick – and when he turned out the same, who would they get to replace him?

When the Bishop arrived, everybody stopped talking. Andrew got to his feet, but McCauly waved him back to his seat. There were smiles all around, even from Finnlay; it was like they were all talking this language he'd never learned, and they were never going to teach him. It was like they didn't want him to know what was going on; he was a stranger, and they didn't trust him.

'How do you feel now, Andrew?' McCauly asked kindly, pouring himself some brew. He didn't dress like a Bishop of course, but it didn't make any difference: there was something about the man, about his eyes, or the way he spoke – something that marked him as a priest. Both John and Godfrey had the same look and it was vaguely comforting. 'Do you feel rested? I see you've stopped eating.'

'Only for the moment,' Finnlay added with a grin Andrew couldn't quite match.

'Well, I'm afraid that you won't get to rest for much longer.'

'Why is that?' Finnlay asked, as if he were expecting trouble.

'Because we leave at midday.'

'Leave?' Finnlay looked first at Andrew, then at those seated along the table. 'Does this have something to do with Patric? Where is he?'

'You can see Patric when we're done here.' Aiden pulled up a chair beside Andrew. 'How much did Robert tell you about his plans? Not too much, I would guess.'

'Try just about nothing.'

'He told us very little, but he did at least leave us detailed instructions showing how he had orchestrated everything, so all we need to do is send off signals to people he's worked with throughout Lusara. There are also people here ready to go back, armed for the conflict, including some Salti. You have no idea how much work he's put into it, how we were both hoping for and dreading your arrival: dreading because he'd told us the signal would come only if he were dead, and hoping, because we knew it would be the beginning of the end for Nash and Kenrick.'

Andrew didn't understand any of this, and Finnlay was looking confused. 'I'm sorry, what signal? What plans?' he asked.

'Robert has set up across the country people who are willing to rise and fight against the tyrant, in pockets here and there. People able to fight and win a local battle, in areas where it is essential to Kenrick that he maintain power. This morning, the letters were sent telling them to begin.'

Andrew felt a cold wash across his stomach, tangling with the food he'd just eaten and heralding nausea. A moment later, he found he was standing, pushing his chair away from the table. 'Today? You . . . ss-sent letters?

As though he understood the terrible turmoil rattling through Andrew, Aiden continued solemnly, 'That was Robert's plan. That's why he told you to come to me: so that I could set it all in motion for him.'

'Set it in mm-motion?'

'Andrew,' Finnlay said, trying to calm him, 'you don't need to—'

'Yes, Andrew,' the Bishop interrupted, his eyes steady on Andrew's face, 'your rebellion has begun.'

19

Early morning mist rose off the river, thick white tendrils reaching for the ghostly sun, leaving the hill Kenrick was standing on seem like an isolated island amongst the clouds. Before him, laid out like a map, sat the Vitala River, and the capital, Marsay in its centre, connected only by the narrow causeway. From this distance, it all looked remarkably peaceful, clean and tidy.

'My lord, are you ready to begin now?'

Kenrick swung around to where Rayve stood a little down the other side of the hill, away from the city's view – assuming anybody could see this far. The King moved until he could stand beside the young Malachi. 'Very well. What are we doing today?'

'You need to learn how to move things: all sorcerers can move small things with barely a thought, and how well they do it depends on how much practice they do. But if you have substantial abilities, you are able to move larger items, sometimes quite impressive distances.'

'Really?' Kenrick found himself smiling in anticipation. 'So, if I was really strong, would I be able to, say, move a mountain?'

Rayve replied sternly, 'Nobody is strong enough to do that much. But I have seen huge rocks moved, carts, horses, even trees shifted beyond their natural capacity. Be warned, though, it takes a great deal of skill to be able to use this trick in combat, so don't start playing around with it or you may end up breaking something you can't fix.'

Kenrick chuckled. Rayve was the most grave of characters, and took absolutely everything utterly seriously. He did smile, but only when he thought it appropriate, not because he thought anything was actually funny. Kenrick was constantly tempted to poke fun at him; only the threat of losing him as a willing teacher stayed his hand. 'Very well, how do I begin?'

Rayve began to walk downhill a little. 'Moving objects requires using your imagination to picture your hand exercising the force required. I will set out some rocks here, and when I give the word, I want you to raise your hand and think about moving them. Not far, just a foot or so will be enough. Remember, it is important to practise the skill of shifting the object, not the distance nor the size – at least, not yet.'

Kenrick watched as Rayve moved around kicking up melon-sized rocks for him to practise with. 'When did you say this Felenor Calenderi was due back in Marsay?'

'He did not say, my lord. Only that he had important and urgent business to attend to in the south.'

'Sounds like he's trying to avoid me.'

Rayve straightened up, shaking his head earnestly. 'No, my lord. He is true to his word. Since DeMassey's death, he has taken responsibility for those D'Azzir working in Lusara. He has broken his ties with Nash and no longer wishes to support his plans.'

'But he's willing to support mine? I find his sudden change of heart disturbing.'

Rayve spread his hands. 'At least allow him to convince you himself, my lord. As soon as he returns, he will speak with you.'

'And if I make a proper alliance with him, and he has already declared himself against Nash, where does that leave me?'

Rayve put the last rock in place and came back to stand at Kenrick's side, his gaze sweeping down the hill to where Kenrick had left his guard, safely out of the way.

'My lord,' Rayve murmured against the cold, grey morning, 'you know of the process of Bonding?'

A band of tightness caught hold of Kenrick's stomach. 'Yes. Nash Bonded my father, and ruled him utterly, leaving him with no will of his own. I am sure Nash ordered my father to die by Douglas's sword, but I will never be able to prove it.' He turned to find the young Malachi's eyes on him.

'We believe that Nash has somehow found a way to Bond Malachi.'

'What?' Kenrick hissed, horrified.

'This breaks every promise he made to our people, violating the trust the Chabanar placed in him. More than that, this Bond is invisible. There is no deadness in the eyes to give it away, no noticeable change in personality. But we have heard enough whispers amongst our people, and seen enough young men and women fail to return home when they were supposed to, fail to carry out their duties with no discernable reason. And too many of them refused to return to Karakham with DeMassey's body, which for us is a sacred ritual. Felenor and I both received special permission to remain behind, given the circumstances.'

Kenrick turned to the rocks placed on the hillside and carefully pictured one having Nash's face. With a violent gesture, he swung his fist, pushing with whatever power he had inside. The rock jumped off the ground about three feet, moved down hill an inch or so and fell – like a rock.

'Damn it, you said this was easy!'

Rayve studied him. 'It is never wise to use your powers in anger, my lord. While they might be stronger, you have less control.'

'What difference does control make? If Nash has Bonded Malachi, we're all . . .' He didn't finish. The last thing he wanted right now was to lose his temper in front of Rayve. 'Fine. Let's get on with it.'

No wonder Calenderi didn't want anything more to do with Nash – neither did Kenrick. What other nasty surprises did Nash have waiting for him? With a private guard of Bonded Malachi, Nash was virtually invulnerable to any kind of attack – not that Kenrick had exactly planned one, but the idea had occasionally crossed his mind. Now he had no weapon at all – and even learning to use his abilities properly would not give him something to fight Nash with.

But Kenrick was not sure whether he wanted to fight Nash, or merely to survive against him; until the sorcerer returned to court, Kenrick had no idea where he stood with the old man. There was still no sign of Andrew, but that could mean that Nash had him away somewhere, turning him into something horrible, like himself.

But that was unthinkable: Andrew was impressionable, but he had never raised his voice in all the years Kenrick had known him, not once had he been rude, or cruel, despite how he'd been treated at court . . . Although there had been one time, many years ago, the first time Andrew had come to Marsay, for the funeral of his parents. He and Andrew had met for the first time, in the Basilica, and Andrew had reacted as though he'd seen a monster. At the time, Kenrick had been mortally offended and demanded his father put the boy to the sword immediately, but Selar had been busy planning his invasion of Mayenne and wouldn't take Kenrick seriously. So the boy had been allowed to go home unmolested, and Kenrick had promised vengeance on him at some later date, when Andrew had grown large enough to defend himself.

But that day had never really come, and Kenrick had long since forgotten the incident, and his desire for revenge, when faced with his ridiculously innocent cousin. It was impossible for him to remain angry with Andrew for more than a few minutes, and if Nash intended to use him in some manner, he would have to work very hard to get him to change his natural character. Perhaps in the end, Nash might even fail.

He glanced aside to find Rayve waiting patiently, as though able to read the scattered thoughts going on in Kenrick's head. Well, good luck to him. Kenrick raised his hand again, thinking about moving rocks, and pushed. To his surprise, the first one slid downhill about a dozen feet, then came to a sudden stop.

'Well done, my lord. Minimum effort for maximum results. Just remember that it is very dangerous to use too much power in one go when you are untrained. Your body is simply not capable of withstanding such strain.'

'How dangerous is it?' Kenrick frowned. Nash had said nothing of this over the years.

'Sorcerers have been known to die from overextending themselves. This is why we have training.'

'Of course.' Kenrick turned back to the rocks, pushing one after the other in exactly the same way, stopping only when he'd run out. Rayve left him to set up another line.

There was so much Nash had never told him: he did things in secret, ignoring the fact that they were supposed to be allies, working for the same goals. Nash had promised him that Tirone of Mayenne would find himself without a single son to inherit, and with the lovely Princess Olivia as Kenrick's bride, but the last boy was still alive, hidden away somewhere where even Nash's assassins had been unable to find him – and Olivia was no closer to being his than a year ago.

Of course, he could always pursue his original line of thinking and take her himself: after all, if he had Felenor Calenderi wanting an alliance, what better way for the Malachi to prove their loyalty than to bring him his fifteen-year-old cousin as his bride? He could even get Godfrey to marry them, and once he'd consummated the marriage, there would be nothing Tirone could do to stop him. That way, when the last boy died – as Kenrick knew he would – there would be no bar to him taking the throne of Mayenne, the way his own father had repeatedly failed to.

It was always satisfying creating a plan of his own, especially when it meant he didn't have to directly cross Nash to get what he wanted. He would talk to Calenderi when he returned to court.

Nash walked into the gallery in Ransem Castle and almost immediately sneezed at the dust lying everywhere. It had been almost four months since he'd last been here; so much had changed in that time – rather, *he* had changed. Still, the dust would have to go.

'Taymar!'

'Yes, Master?'

Nash continued walking down the gallery towards the rooms he used to sleep in, where he did his most secret work. 'Get this place cleaned out, and I want a bath and a meal in an hour. Have my bags brought up here and the long table cleaned off. I have work to do.'

'Of course, Master.' Taymar vanished; Nash could hear him calling out orders to the servants who were supposed to keep Ransem clean and functioning when he wasn't here. He'd returned without warning, but that was no excuse for sloppiness.

He sneezed again, and resisted the temptation to open one of the windows. Instead, he opened the door to his bedroom, to find this room at least somewhat free of dust, and fresh linens had been laid on the bed some time in the last week or so, which would do until he decided exactly where he was going to go next.

He did a quick scan to make sure he was alone, then moved behind the bed to the tiny hidden alcove in the wall. He flicked the invisible switch and reached inside to pull out the pouch he'd left there so long ago, then walked over to his desk and collected half a dozen books. By the time he returned to the gallery, the long table was cleaned of dust, tiny particles of which were dancing in the sunshine streaming through the windows. He waited only as long as it took for his bags to be brought up, then he sat down to work. He fished out the notes he'd taken down over the years, then spread out the maps he'd made from the stories on the cave wall. Slowly, he began to compare them, building up a composite picture.

He ate at his table and only stopped when his bath was ready. He left his notes then and returned to his bedroom where the tub sat before the fireplace, steaming and smelling of rose petals. In the past he had always preferred to bath alone, to hide the scars the Enemy had given him at Shan Moss, but those scars were gone now, and he undressed with relish. The water felt superb on his skin as he sank into it, revelling in the heat.

With a sigh, he slid down in the bath and doused his head under the water. He could hear nothing then but the steady thumping of his own heart. Blowing out bubbles, he surfaced and looked around at the room he'd lived in for so many years.

It was time to leave here and turn those caves into a fortress of his own. Time to return to court and prepare for the war to come – for he knew now there would be one, and soon, at that. So much that he had never understood before had become clear: no wonder he had failed in all his previous attempts to find the Key.

But now he understood: Robert Douglas was *not* simply the Enemy, and considering him as such had hindered Nash's thinking. First and foremost, Douglas was a Lusaran, and a Salti. His duty to his country and his people would always come before any duty towards a Prophecy he couldn't comprehend. By understanding the man who would destroy him, Nash could finally predict the future, and what they could expect to happen next. He could plan to meet the next blow head on, be ready to fight and this time, win.

That day inside those caves had been more than worth the time: the cool air, the darkness, breathing in the same air that had so recently swept around the Key and his Ally had felt almost surreal. Better still, now that he understood the Enemy, he knew exactly what he had to do with Kenrick. The boy would be feeling very suspicious – especially after Nash's sudden disappearance from Marsay, leaving no word. And no doubt Kenrick would have heard about the attack on Maitland, and the possible death of his cousin. Nash could be fairly certain that Kenrick was honestly concerned about young Andrew – an emotion Nash could cure him of without too much trouble.

Though he thought he was on the final run now, it was certainly not time to alienate Kenrick; on the contrary, it would be best to once more become indispensable to him – at least until he could perfect the ritual of Bonding without consent.

He laughed out loud at the thought of Bonding Kenrick and, shaking water from his hands, stood up in the bath, taking the towel Taymar had laid over a nearby chair. He stepped out of the tub and onto the thick rug in front of the roaring fire, no longer plagued by the cold as he'd once been. This body was not only better than before his injuries, but better than any he'd had before. Not a day went by when he didn't notice.

Drying himself thoroughly, he pulled on a robe and poured a cup of wine. He went to his door then and called out for Taymar. A moment later, the familiar face appeared at the opposite end of the gallery, and Nash told him, 'I want Valena in here. Now.'

As he waited, he carefully folded up his notes, sipping his wine and enjoying the warmth the bath had left through his entire body. Then two of his Malachi appeared at the door, Valena between them, now washed and dressed after her long and trying journey. Her eyes looked through him, as though he were made of the same glass as the gallery windows.

Without a word, his men took her through to his bedroom and he followed, leaving the papers on his table by the fire. Then he took a seat, refilled his wine and dismissed his men.

Valena waited with something that might have been patience if she'd cared at all. Instead, she found some place to rest her eyes and left them there, the only movement in her body that of her chest as it rose and fell with her breathing. The small scar on her cheek did little to mar her beauty; in fact, for him it served only to highlight it. He golden hair, shiny and clean, swept over one shoulder and down to her waist.

She was the first woman he'd known, the first who had called his attention away from his destiny long enough to learn about the pleasures of the flesh. A supreme seductress, even his iron will had bent before her beauty and the promise of delight it held. And not once had he been disappointed there either.

'You know,' he said, taking a last sip of his wine, 'you have almost outlived your usefulness.'

She didn't react, but he had not expected her to. He rose from his seat and put his cup down, then, standing before her, he held her face with one hand and examined her features, looking for the obvious signs of aging. There were few, not enough to make him regret.

'I have to say, I admire your courage. I honestly had not thought you would last this long, but then, you were always determined, weren't you?' Nash smiled. 'But then, so was I.'

He took her arm then, and led her to the bed. With little enough force, he pushed her down until she lay beneath him. He took her bound hands and tied them to the end of the bed, just in case, then proceeded to remove her clothes until all her smooth, creamy flesh was revealed to him.

Her belly, despite having borne a child, was as flat as he remembered it, no scar anywhere to suggest she wasn't a girl of twenty and he her first man. Her eyes were open, gazing unseeing at the canopy above.

'Where are you? Are you hiding from me? From this?'

When she did not answer, he slapped her face until she tore her gaze away and met his. She said nothing, but that small attention was all he wanted.

Or not quite all. He let his desire rise, his anger along with it, thrusting between her legs and into her, enjoying his own new body as much as hers. The pleasure was sweet indeed, but more so was her humiliation. Even as his pleasure peaked, he watched her face, saw her gaze flicker a moment, and that was enough for him.

Spent, he lay full length on top of her, his arms stretching out along hers, feeling the bonds holding her to the bed, to him. His teeth found the tender flesh along her shoulder and he bit down hard, drawing blood, tasting it. Not once did she move a muscle.

'Fear not, my dear,' Nash said with a smile. 'I neither expected you to fight me, nor wished it. Withdrawing from me means nothing.'

'And your entering me did?' she whispered suddenly, a laugh in her voice he'd never heard before. 'You are pathetic.'

He looked into the face that had been so withdrawn a moment ago; the effect of the drugs was clear in her eyes, but her will was by no means broken. 'You think me pathetic, yet you lie there and let me use you, as you allowed so many other men over the years.'

Again she laughed, and the sound made him feel ill. 'You are pathetic.

No real man would ever take a woman without her consent, for to do so proves that he would never gain that consent, never be good enough for her. You were never good enough for me, Sam. Never. That's why I was content to share Selar's bed, why, in the end, I had to go back to Luc. Do you know how long I've been expecting you to rape me like this? Since you took your own daughter's blood in a greater rape than any you could perpetuate on my tired body. You think you can hurt me like this? You think making me submit to your men would break me? If you think so, then you are less than even I realised.' Her laugh continued, and now he could feel it rattling through his body, unsettling him, setting him on fire in a completely different way.

With a growl, he caught hold of her face in both hands, and let that anger go, feeling it course through his new body with all the vengeance of the old, shaking him with the vicious power of it. He pushed it out through his fingers, his palms and let it join with her, listening to her screams as the balm to his hurts, enjoying it more than he'd ever enjoyed her body. Only when she fainted from the pain did he finally stop.

He rolled off her, grabbed his robe and threw open the door. His two Malachi were waiting for him.

'Get everyone in here, now, every Bonded Malachi I own. Now. Go!' As they ran down the gallery, they called out, and he listened to their voices as he poured another cup of wine, swallowing it all in one go. He was on his second when they arrived back, filling the gallery.

He stood before them, surveying their youth, their strength, and the promise of their undying efforts. He hated his own weakness for needing to remind them of their vow, but still he did so, shouting, 'You must not forget, ever, no matter what else happens. I have your vow: while I survive, regardless of all else that is going on around you, you carry out my orders to the letter, sacrificing whatever you have to in order to achieve them. Do you understand? Do you?'

'Yes, Master!' They answered as one, in a single shout, the echo rattling down the gallery, but doing little to ease him.

He gestured to the bed in his room. 'Get rid of her. Keep her alive, but I no longer care about her comfort. Use her if you wish, just make sure she lives until I'm ready to kill her.'

As his men turned for the bedroom, he headed for the nearest garderobe and emptied his supper down the smelly hole.

It was no longer a comfort to know he could kill her whenever he liked. He would have to find a more fitting way to exact his revenge.

20

A knife. They'd promised him a knife next time, that they'd cut him, slicing his skin apart, so he could bleed. At least he could breathe then, his skin could breathe, and that would let the pressure out because it was building too high in here, getting too dark and too stuffy. Now, when he rolled, the pain didn't change, didn't get worse, it just stayed the same, making him long for them to come back, long for the knife, the blade they'd promised as they laughed at him as he'd laughed back.

They were going to break him, that's what they said, like a twig, snap him in two until he said anything they wanted him to say. He wanted to tell them, oh yes he did, that it was too late, that he'd been broken decades ago, by something they would dearly love to have but never would. He really wanted to tell them that it was too late, that he'd already been broken by an expert.

His head lolled back and he laughed around the gag. They put it back on now, to shut him up. He wanted to talk to them; they didn't want to listen. He kept egging them on, telling them where to kick him, where it would hurt the most, where it would make him bleed – but they shut him up, like they didn't want his advice, didn't want to be told how to torture, that it was a skill at its best when self-taught.

They'd promised him the knife but they hadn't brought it yet and that made them late. Late, late, late. Much too late. Well, he would just find some other way to make the pain flare and then he would go to sleep and damn them.

He lifted his head and cracked it back against the floor, feeling the pain rattle through him, welcome. He hissed in pleasure, diving into it where it was warmer than usual, he breathed in deeply, finding the demon and wrapping himself in it, so warm, so perfect, like when he'd killed Selar, when he'd simply let the demon run free and he'd put his sword into a man he'd once called friend and felt the blood flow through his fingers and into the ground.

The demon. *His* Enemy, as though born of his own private prophecy. That dank, sweating, slithering core of his soul that hated everything and everybody, that dogged him with its stinking righteousness, driving him on further, holding him together, making him whole and torn apart at the same time.

He couldn't live without it.

He started to laugh again, at the irony, the sweet, vicious inevitability of it all. The demon drove him to madness, yet kept him sane. The Prophecy had never seen that, had it? If he was going to be damned, why not for this as well? Failure was a skill he knew inside out and could repeat it at will.

Such a hopeless failure.

He laughed again. Too hot now, choking him, screaming through him with voices that didn't belong to him. And then light, but they weren't bringing the blade, though they'd promised . . . lifting him, talking to him, using words he was now beyond understanding.

But when they got him to his feet, when the blood cleared from his eyes, when they carried him between them, up stairs he'd never seen, into the darkness, past the witch who had betrayed him, when they ran through the night, holding him between them, when the pain rose up like a living, fire-breathing demon, he gasped and cried out for the first time. The movement stopped, but it was too late, then, too late, as the other darkness, the soft, welcoming darkness inside opened its arms and enveloped him.

For the first time in his life, he embraced it in return.

Finnlay had to admit he was impressed. After living in the Enclave for so long, dealing with the efficiencies of Martha and her fellow councillors, he'd grown accustomed to seeing things well-organised, but this was something else again: a complex pattern so finely balanced as to be almost poetic. And his own brother had devised the entire thing by himself.

He read as he rode, keeping a good hold of each page, tucking them inside his cloak if it looked like the wind was playing up. When he had questions, he'd direct them to Owen or Payne and if he had suggestions to make, Deverin would nod and repeat them to himself until he was sure he'd remember them. It took him the better part of the morning to read through the summaries, and an afternoon to finish debating them. By nightfall, he was confident he had a good grounding, certainly enough to carry on without instruction.

It was the most amazing feeling: to be part of this gathering of men, this little army heading towards a goal all of them feared but none would run away from. Only Andrew seemed unhappy, though he did his best to hide it. Finnlay wanted to talk to him, but the boy had thrown up a wall around himself, smiling at everyone and saying little.

If this army was the avalanche, then Andrew was surely the snow driven down the mountain.

At the tavern, Finnlay collected a plate of food and sat down beside Patric. They'd talked a little that morning, but it had been nine years since Finnlay had seen him; they had a lot of ground to cover. He couldn't help looking over at Patric's young friend, Joshi, who sat on the other side of the table, eating in peace, disturbing nobody. Finnlay admitted to himself that he was burning with curiosity, but this wasn't the time to indulge in such things.

'You must be sick of the saddle by now,' Patric said, using a finger to ensure he had food on his spoon. He brought it to his mouth, ate and began chewing, smiling as he did so. 'I would think Andrew would feel that too.'

'Yes, well, I don't want to think about that.'

'You know,' Patric said, wonderingly, 'I can't believe you've got three children now. And Jenn's Jaibir! And finding the Calyx – Finn, that's so much more than I expected. So much has happened. I know John tried to fill me in, but he knew only the things from court, and what he'd read in letters from Murdoch – but you, you were there at the Battle of Shan Moss, weren't you? You saw Robert fight with Nash?'

The memories were all still so strong. 'Yes, I did.'

'And Jenn stopped it, didn't she? She split them up, and Nash survived?'

'He did, and it took him nine years to regenerate from his wounds.' Finnlay sighed. 'What are you going to tell Robert?'

Patric laughed. 'And what would you do if I told you?'

Groaning, Finnlay rolled his eyes, realising belatedly that Patric would not see it. Joshi did however, and smiled a little at his expression. It was the first time Finnlay had seen the young man smile. 'Look, Patric, I know you've come a long way, but—'

'But you can't wait a few more days for me to tell Robert in person.'

'You don't know he'll be at Elita to meet us.'

'Why wouldn't he be? I'm sure he's managed to get away from those Malachi, and he knows you brought Andrew to Bleakstone. Therefore he would know to meet the Bishop at Elita. Sounds very straightforward to me. No, it's nothing that can't wait until we meet up with Robert.'

'But you said it was urgent.'

'It is.' Patric put another spoonful of food in his mouth and began munching, still with a grin on his face. Finnlay flicked a look at Joshi to see him quickly hiding his own smile.

'Fine,' Finnlay grunted. 'Have it your own way.'

Micah stoked up the fire again, putting on more logs. The old mill was awfully cold and Robert wouldn't stop shivering. Satisfied, Micah returned to his side and picked up another makeshift bandage. It had taken him more than an hour to wash off all the wounds, the blood and dirt caked on him. Now he was dressing all those he could, thankful Robert hadn't woken up yet.

His body was a mess. The first look had almost turned Micah's stomach, and even Gilbert had looked away. Micah couldn't tell if Robert would survive. He'd seen worse wounds, deep, horrible wounds, and Robert had survived all of them. But this time, his mind had travelled as well, as though to stay and suffer with his body had been too much.

As he wrapped the injuries, he saw the fine print of boots on Robert's thighs, on his chest, but he had found no bones broken, and the cuts were all small – all but the old wound on Robert's left side, the one Selar had given him all those years before. He couldn't think about why, in nine years, it hadn't healed.

Who knew Robert better than he did? But he had not known that Robert would banish him. The thought had never occurred to him, mostly because he'd believed there was no way Robert would ever find out that Sairead was Malachi. But then he had, and Micah's whole world had fallen apart.

'Why do you do this?' Sairead spoke from the doorway. Her hair was down, her face a little flushed as though she'd just woken. 'Isn't he going to die?'

'I don't think so. The wounds just look bad. He won't be able to move for a few days, though. And after that—'

'What after that?'

He couldn't speak. How could he tell her what he was thinking without hurting her?

'You blame me that he was taken?'

'No, of course not.' He finished wrapping the last bandage then pulled the blanket over Robert's shivering body. He gathered the rest of his things together and put them away, then he washed his hands in the rest of the water, tipping it out through the open window. Once he'd completed his tasks, he found Sairead still there, waiting for him, her eyes dark and serious.

'I don't blame you,' he repeated. 'I blame myself. None of this should have happened. If I'd had the courage—'

She came up to stand close to him, placing her hands on either side of his face. 'You know you cannot change the past. You must not hate yourself for what's gone. You no longer have that luxury, not when you will soon be a father. Please, Micah, leave him and come to bed.'

With a sigh, he kissed her softly, then caught her hands, steering her to the door to the other room. 'You go and get some rest. I'll stay with him, in case he needs something.'

'What can a man like him need?'

'In case he wakes.'

She gave him a small smile. Then she was gone and the door closed softly behind her.

Pools of colour surrounded him, but the brightness was fading. He could move, but he no longer wanted to. His body was encased in thick mud, viscous and sickly. It slowed everything down, even his breathing.

This new nightmare smelled different too: of old hay, and familiarity, of pine and fresh moisture in the air. There were shapes in the darkness, urging him to return, to embrace the light, to give back what he'd taken, but he ignored them all. He was not going to be fooled again. Trust was too thin, the consequences too wide to avoid.

He understood now what it was he'd been running from all these years. Finally he understood the nature of the demon inside him: he had seen it in the men who'd come to him with it blazing in their eyes. All these years he'd been fooled, but no more: as long as he stayed here, inside the demon, he was immune to its hate.

And so was the rest of the world.

'Is he any better?'

Micah looked up as Gilbert carried a bulging saddle-bag into the room. In his other hand he held a loaf of bread and two large carrots.

'He still hasn't woken up, but I think his sleep is more restful now.'

'And the bleeding?'

'Has stopped at last. I was getting worried.'

'Well, it's been two days. He should be awake by now.' Gilbert put the food on the small makeshift tables they'd made and drew off his cloak. 'Where is Sairead?'

'Bathing down by the rock pool.'

'What are you going to do once this is over?'

Micah sighed, though he didn't want to. 'I don't know. I wish I did.'

'You should take your wife to Karakham, like any good husband would do. Let her live in comfort for the next months. Be a father to your son.'

'Son?' Micah turned back to look at Robert, and the awful bruises purpling one side of his face. Micah's father had disowned him because he'd chosen to serve this man. What kind of father would he be with such an example to follow? 'I could as easily have a daughter.'

'Ah, Micah, you are such a fool.'

He stood and washed his hands in the water he'd brought from the stream. 'What do you want from me? You think I should forget who I am, what I am? What I've spent my life doing? All because I fell in love with a Malachi? Would you? If that's so, then why are you here, Gilbert?'

The older man watched him for a moment, then said, 'I'll go and find some more firewood. Call if he wakes.'

The last time Aiden had seen Elita had been with Robert, almost ten years ago, when they'd come here asking rebel lords for help to fight Selar's invasion of Mayenne. The place had changed little; it looked to be even more of a ruin than ever before. As then, he couldn't help but picture it as it had once been: a large and prosperous castle jutting out into the lake, where hundreds of people lived and worked. But then Robert had come, chased by Malachi, and he'd used the Word of Destruction, flattening everything within half a league, leaving nothing of the castle but the main keep. All else was a mess of ruined rock scattered across a barren landscape.

'It was beautiful once.' Finnlay was staring out at the same view. They were both sheltered within the forest, but the lake and the ruins and escarpment above were compelling.

'I'm sure it was.' Aiden put his hands behind his back. 'Perhaps one day Andrew will rebuild it.'

'Possibly.'

'You don't sound convinced.'

At that, Finnlay frowned and looked back the way they had come, although their camp was invisible from here. 'I don't know. That boy . . .'

'What about him?' Aiden held his breath. He'd been watching Andrew and for the journey here, had deliberately kept his distance. Andrew seemed too easily overwhelmed, and very unsettled. Only returning to Lusara had given him some of his confidence back. 'I would appreciate it if you would be candid. I'm sure you understand my concerns.'

'Of course,' Finnlay said. 'I share them.'

'Does Robert?'

'Robert keeps his own counsel – as usual.' With a sigh, Finnlay spread his arms. 'Andrew is a wonderful boy. He's kind and honest, tries so hard at everything, is more willing to help than anybody I've ever met, and if you ask him to do something, he won't settle until it's done. He's got a fine mind, but some days he's reluctant to use it. Since I first met him, I've done all I can to get him to develop his powers, even just to wake up his Senses, but while he seems to understand what I'm saying, there is this wall between him and success. He's had the best teachers, I'm sure he knows more about sorcery than any boy his age – and yet, still nothing.'

When Finnlay stopped, Aiden looked back once more to ensure they were alone. 'Will he need such powers to fight Kenrick?'

Finnlay's eyes returned to Elita. 'Yes.'

'How is Robert with him?'

'Oh.' Finnlay's expression shifted a moment, and then settled, as though he were putting his mind around a completely different question. 'Robert drives him like a slave master, but never with cruelty. Andrew just idolises him, would bend over backwards if Robert asked him – and yet, Andrew battles valiantly with him about his part in all this.'

'Robert asked him?'

'I believe so – but Andrew's answer all along has been no.'

'No?'

'He doesn't want to kill his own cousin.'

'I see.' Aiden folded his arms and leaned up against a sturdy sapling. With his eyes steady on Finnlay, he asked softly, 'And do you think there is any love there, between father and son?'

Finnlay didn't react immediately, but then turned a look of feigned puzzlement on Aiden, who saw through it instantly, giving him the confirmation he hadn't realised he'd needed.

'I'm sorry, Bishop, I'm not sure what you mean.'

'You know exactly what I mean.'

For a moment, Finnlay stared at him hard, and then he swore. He came closer and whispered, 'You can't say anything to either of them! Damn it, Father, how did you know?'

'Father John told me.'

'And how many others are going to guess? If the people know he's Robert's son, that he's a b—'

Aiden held up a hand. 'Never say that! By church law, Andrew was born within the sanctity of marriage – he is not illegitimate and therefore there is no bar him taking the throne.' When Finnlay raised his eyebrows in surprise, Aiden shrugged. 'I did some research, just to make sure.'

'Then you expect others will notice the resemblance?'

'No, I doubt it. You need to know it's there to see it. And you say Robert has no idea?'

'None. If he did, I doubt he'd be going to all this trouble to put his own son on the throne.'

'No, of course he wouldn't.' The silence grew between them.

'So,' Finnlay said eventually, 'do you think you can help with Andrew?'

'Are you expecting a miracle?'

Finnlay laughed. 'Well, you are a priest. You're far more qualified than me.'

'A miracle would require a saint.'

'Well, that definitely leaves me out.'

Aiden could only laugh as well. Miracles were not his forte – daily life was hard enough as it was. 'Can you go back and see if you can ask Father John to join me? He knows Andrew well. I'd like to talk to him.'

'Of course.' With a wave, Finnlay disappeared down the track and Aiden turned back to the view. None of the others had said anything so far, but he knew they would. They'd all given Robert their oaths, and nothing would change that, but he could see their questions in their eyes. Andrew was not the boy they'd been hoping for, and certainly not the potential King Lusara needed. All of them had made the effort to speak to him, and while he'd been polite and nice, there had been no spark in the boy, no sign there was anything more than what was visible on the surface. Aiden could almost taste the disappointment in the air.

And he knew Andrew could as well.

'You wanted to see me, Father?' John approached quietly, dressed in browns enough to make him blend into the background. The journey here had required subterfuge, with their large group broken into smaller ones, and even their camp had been spread out in pockets through the forest so they could be as invisible as possible.

It felt so very, *very* good to be back in Lusara.

'Tell me, Father,' Aiden began, studying the priest carefully. This man had, until few weeks ago, been the boy's chaplain and teacher. His insight would be invaluable. 'How do you think Andrew is coping with all this?'

'I can't say exactly.' John shrugged apologetically. 'I can't get close enough to talk to him. He says what he thinks I want him to say, and little else. I don't think he's . . . '

'What?'

'Come to any decision yet.'

'I see.' Aiden had the same impression. 'Do you think he will make a good King?' Aiden could see loyalties warring within the priest, and was pleased to note it.

'I think . . . yes. One day, he will become a great King.'

'One day?'

Once more, John shrugged. 'The idea is still new to him. I think he's confused and a little lost. And—'

Aiden could see there was sorrow in the priest's eyes and pressed him for more. 'And what?'

'His foster parents were murdered by the Malachi just a few weeks ago. I don't think he's begun to mourn yet.'

'His foster parents? That would be Jennifer's sister and her husband? By the mass, I had no idea!' Aiden leaned back against the tree, annoyed that this was the first he'd heard of the tragedy. No wonder the boy was so confused. So much had happened to him in such a little time; he'd had no chance to adjust.

'Thank you, Father.'

'Do you think you can help him?'

'I don't know. But I can at least try.'

As the priest turned back for the camp, Aiden added, 'Only if he'll let me, though.' And if he was anything like his father, Andrew would be very hard to help indeed.

He could hear voices and after a moment, he could even understand the words.

'I just don't think it would be wise to linger here much longer.'

'I can't move him until he wakes up.'

'And how long will that take? His wounds seem to be healing. Felenor is going to know the fire was a rescue, and it won't take him too long to work out who was responsible. If he finds us—'

'How did he find us in the first place? How did he know where Sairead was? You said only your most trusted people knew about this. How did Felenor know to wait for Sairead there? You can't tell me it was an accident.'

'Of course it wasn't an accident, and at the first opportunity, I will demand an explanation from him – but that doesn't change the fact that you can't sit there with him for ever. We need to move from this place. Soon.'

'We'll move when he wakes up, and not before.'

'By the Blood!'

Footsteps then, and a door slamming, wooden walls shaking a little, then quiet, with a background of rushing water, some forest birds and, closer by, a crackling fire.

'My lord?'

That voice was closer now, closer than it had been for a long time. It tempted him, asking for things, making him wake.

'My lord, you need to open your eyes. It's safe here, I promise you.'

A promise too easily made.

He opened his eyes. The roof above him was dark, shadowed, with old beams gnarled and knotted, spider webs crisscrossing the corners. The last of the day's light filtered through some window somewhere, augmented by a lamp hung close by.

'My lord?' There was a smile there now, one he could not afford. 'How do you feel?'

Robert moved his head, his muscles waking up painfully. He held his breath, then remembered not to. With a groan, he got an elbow under himself and half-sat up, Micah's hands immediately reaching to help him.

'Don't try too much too soon. You've been out three days. Just take it slowly.'

Robert kept moving, ignoring the throbbing in his head and the warning in his belly, until he was sitting on the side of the cot bed, stars in his eyes, wheezing. That would do for the moment. He could stand in a minute, once he'd caught his breath.

'How do you feel?'

Yes, it wasn't too bad. He could live with this. It would get better and in a little while, he'd be fit enough to travel. Then he had work to do.

'My lord?' The silence filled the empty spaces, making them brighter. 'How do you feel?'

'How do I feel?' His voice came out as a rasp, but not without strength. It was enough to make him smile. 'How do I feel? Well, Micah, I'm not sure how I feel. What do you think?'

'My lord?'

'How do you think I feel?'

'Well . . . you look a lot better.'

'So, I should feel better.' Robert placed his hands on the cot either side of himself and used the leverage to get to his feet. This time the dizziness brought black patches to his sight, but after a moment, they vanished, leaving him standing. 'Where are they?'

'Who?'

'Your Malachi friends.'

Micah scrambled to stand in front of him, holding up his hands. For the first time, Robert turned to look at him, finding some considerable fear in those familiar blue eyes. Micah had aged a little over the years, his hair showing some grey here and there, his face developing more freckles, and losing some of its old sunniness in the process. This Micah had seen more, had been more than the old one. It wasn't enough to give Robert pause.

'Where are they?'

'My lord, you need to listen before you do anything.'

'What makes you think I'm going to do anything?'

'They beat you up, and your body's still healing. You need to rest and recover before you—'

Robert reached out with one hand and grabbed Micah's throat, tightening his grip just enough to make his point felt. 'Where are they?'

Micah froze, his eyes wide with real fear now. Still, he struggled to explain. 'Please, just wait, I beg you. This is not what it looks like. Let me call Gilbert and he can talk to you. Please, just—'

Robert let him go. Micah stared at him a moment, then strode to the door, called out Gilbert's name, then turned back. 'Gilbert had nothing to do with your torture. Those were other Malachi, nothing to do with him.'

'Why,' Robert said clearly, looking around the room, 'do you think I care one way or the other?' There was nothing here he could use. On the other hand, there had to be horses somewhere around. This place looked like a disused mill – just another building emptied and ruined thanks to the monster he'd left on the throne.

He spied a water-bottle by the bed and retrieved it, pulling the stopper to drink long and deep. Water had never tasted so sweet.

'Ah, you're awake!'

He could feel it, burning his skin as it always did, that unmistakable stench of Malachi blood close by. The Key had been right to banish them, right to drive them from this land. It was fitting that they were the tools of Nash. They worked so well together.

Robert turned slowly and took a look at the man facing him. This one was his own height, with rust-red hair streaked with strands of silver. The hair was kept long and plaited down the man's back, in a fashion Robert hadn't seen on this continent. The face, however, was the most striking thing: an ugliness Robert could honestly appreciate, skin marked with some childhood disease, black eyebrows, a huge nose almost comical, and teeth not knowing in which direction to grow. The combination was instantly unforgettable.

'My lord,' Micah began, standing between them as though he still trusted that Robert wouldn't hurt him, 'this is Gilbert Dusan. He's the grandson of Aamin, the Chabanar – he's like the Jaibir, the leader of the Malachi. Gilbert wanted to talk to you, that's all. Please, hear him out.'

Robert started laughing. 'I was right, you didn't know what you were doing.' Robert pushed past them both and walked out the open door. The evening was drawing down, bringing cool air and blessed darkness. He looked around for the expected stable and found it on his right, not far from the stream.

The other two ran after him, Micah still doing his best. 'The group who took you, they work for Kenrick. That's why Gilbert is here. This isn't what you think it is. Gilbert helped rescue you. He saved your life! You need to listen.'

Robert was listening. Very carefully. He listened as he found a suitable horse, and a saddle. He had no sword, but he didn't need one for the moment. He took the saddle and swung it up onto the horse, his hand immediately tying up straps and buckles. The pain rattling through his body only made him move faster.

'Forget it, Micah.' Gilbert spoke for himself at last. 'He doesn't want to listen.'

'Listen to what?' Robert said, ducking under the horse's neck to make more adjustments. 'I've heard nothing of interest so far. Was there any other reason you brought me out here and nearly got me killed? No? Fine. I'll be leaving in that case.'

Both men stood aside as he led the horse from the stable. He gathered the reins together and turned to face Micah, who was standing there shaking his head sadly, as though he were witnessing something he'd never thought possible. Robert almost laughed at the idea. Nothing was impossible. He had learned that if nothing else.

'Where's your *wife*?'

Instantly, Micah's expression changed. His face hardened and he stuck out his jaw.

Not really expecting an answer, Robert continued, 'I'm going to let her live for one reason and one reason only. She carries a Maclean child and I owe your father one. But I warn you, if she comes near me again, I will kill her without a thought.'

Done now, he swung up into the saddle and kicked the horse hard. He turned straight into the track, and, with a look up at the stars, chose his direction. Not once did he look back.

21

'How long do we wait? In another week, our letters will have reached their destinations and things will start to happen. How are we to move if we're sitting here waiting for Robert to appear?' Finnlay looked from Payne, to Deverin and on, from one man to the other. This was Robert's council, the men he had entrusted with helping Andrew rule once he had taken the throne. Finnlay could not fault Robert's choices, but they were all getting very edgy. They'd been encamped within the thick forest around Elita for two days now, and Finnlay had nothing to tell them. He couldn't Seek, and John didn't know Robert well enough to try.

If Robert didn't appear soon, he'd have to mindspeak Jenn and see if she could find Robert, but that was an option he wanted to leave until last.

'We can afford to give him one more day,' Daniel said; 'after that, we'll lose the advantage of surprise.'

'I agree,' Payne said, then asked Finnlay, 'Do you think he'll be here?'

'If he can, he will be.'

'And if he can't?'

He hated to admit it, but he had no choice. 'If he can't, there's no point in waiting longer.' They all had the grace to at least not mention the possibility that if Robert couldn't come, then he was most likely dead – and if he was dead, they had no real hope of fighting Nash, or of winning.

With a deep breath, Finnlay looked across the camp to where Andrew was sitting on his own, reading from a book the Bishop had given him.

'He's not what I expected,' Payne said quietly, careful that nobody outside this group should hear him. 'What does McCauly say?' They were all waiting on Finnlay's answer.

The uncle in him rose to Andrew's defence, even though he knew he shouldn't. 'He can see some difficulties, but he doesn't believe they are insurmountable. Andrew is young and he—'

'Will be ruling this country before the end of summer,' Payne finished for him, obviously none too happy with the idea. 'I told Robert—'

'For good or ill, my lord,' Deverin imposed his firm voice on them all, 'Andrew will be our King. All else is *our* responsibility.'

Finnlay smiled at the big man. 'Exactly what I was thinking. Now, anyone interested in a cup of ale?'

Micah rode hard, probably harder than he'd ever ridden before, and still he couldn't catch up with Robert. Every time he stopped, he crouched to the ground and found the tracks so he could be sure he was heading in the right direction, but he never drew any closer.

Robert had to know he was following. A sorcerer of Robert's ability couldn't possibly not know he was being tailed, but there was no sign of it, no suggestion that he'd stopped and looked, nor even done anything to lose Micah.

So Micah kept riding, managing to change his horse once at a prosperous farm. After that, he didn't stop unless he had to.

Robert had had no more than an hour's head-start on him. Micah had waited just long enough for Sairead to return, to give her a hurried explanation, to beg Gilbert to look after her, then he'd leapt on his own horse and ridden off at a gallop. He couldn't leave it like this, couldn't just make these mistakes and do nothing about them. He wasn't that kind of man. He wouldn't be the man Sairead loved if he did.

So he rode on and never tought of stopping.

Aiden waited until after supper, when things were being cleaned up and fires stoked against morning. Sure that nobody was paying him any attention, he made his way down the gentle slope towards the river where a narrow track followed the water to the ruin of a mill left there centuries ago.

As though he had no other plan, he wandered, his hands behind his back, breathing deeply of the sweet Lusaran air, listening to the call of night birds newly returned from the south. It was good to be back. With a little luck, and many prayers, perhaps he would never need to leave again.

He found the ruin without difficulty. Finnlay had told him about this place, and a little of its history. In the darkness, with fine threads of moonlight falling on its ruined walls, there was definitely a ghostly beauty about it.

Andrew was there, where he'd expected to find him, sitting just outside the ruin, on moss-covered rock, his back against a wall, one knee raised, his eyes lost in the forest opposite.

What was he looking for? What did he expect to find that he had to be on his own?

This was Robert's son, he reminded himself. By this age, Robert had already fought a battle, had seen his father die at his feet, his country fall to the usurper. And though he appeared to be the innocent, Andrew too had seen his share of evil.

'It's a nice evening,' he began gently.

Andrew started, jumping up from his seat, eyes wide with surprise. 'Oh, Your Grace . . . I didn't hear you—'

'Generally the others call me Father. In the current climate, I think it's also probably safer.'

'Of course! I'm sorry.'

And he did look sorry, genuinely sorry, and Aiden felt sorry for him in return. What an amazing ability that was, to so completely generate pity in another person. A quality rare amongst Kings, but not without its uses. His own cynicism made him smile. 'Please, sit. I was just taking a walk. The weather has been unusually pleasant – at least, it is as far as I can recall. It's been a long time since I spent a spring in Lusara.'

'Yes,' Andrew sat down again, though this time he kept his hands on the rock beside his legs and kicked his feet against it. 'Are you glad to be back?'

'Very much, though of course I wish the circumstances were better. What about you?'

'Me?'

'Are you glad to be back?'

'Oh, yes!'

'But you were only gone a few days. Were they so bad?' While he awaited Andrew's answer, Aiden wandered around the ruin a little, enjoying the moonlight and the fact that it wasn't so cold he needed fifteen layers to combat the chill.

'Not bad, no. I just didn't want to leave Lusara.'

'None of us do, my boy.' Aiden found a suitable rock to sit on himself, a wide flat stone with dried lichen on top. He dusted it down then sat facing Andrew. 'So tell me,' he began without changing his tone. 'What do you make of all this?'

Andrew's mouth dropped open at the question. 'I'm not the best person to ask, Father. You should know that I—'

'Yes, Finnlay has explained your reluctance to kill your cousin.' Aiden waved his hand, deliberately dismissing the issue before Andrew could get bogged down in it. 'I meant the rest of it. The rebellion, the prospect of being King, the need to have your powers, the expectations of you. What do you make of all that?'

For a moment, Andrew didn't answer. Then his eyes dropped to his hands and he shrugged. 'I don't know. I'm sure you've all talked about it a lot. I didn't know anything about it until I met Robert, and that was only a few weeks ago. You've already sent letters out, so the rebellion can't be stopped. I suppose everything will happen one way or the other.'

There was something so fragile in Andrew's tone that Aiden couldn't miss it; he knew he had to address it now, or it would become a monster on its own. He stood and made his way to Andrew's side. The boy watched him as he sat on the same piece of wall, laced his fingers together in the same way. 'Do you know what's going to happen when you become King?'

Andrew shook his head slowly.

'Well, the country will be a mess, that's for sure. I mean, it's already a mess, so a rebellion isn't going to fix it up at all. Not without help. And the people will be a mess – again, so many of them are already – and as King, you will be responsible for making their lives better.'

The boy's eyes remained wide, and not a little frightened.

'Can you imagine, however, what would happen if we just left it all to one person? You, or even Robert? We would have an even bigger mess on our hands – which would defeat the entire purpose of the rebellion. And that's why we're here. Your Council: Deverin, Owen, Payne and Daniel, me, even Finnlay. We're all here to help you. So you can learn from us, so we can take a lot of the work from you – because we're all older, and wiser, and we've done much of this before. But even if you were thirty years old, even if you had done it all before and knew everything there was to know about being a King, we'd still be here to help you.'

'Why?' The shy question almost made Aiden cry.

'Because,' he replied quietly and solemnly, 'you are a Ross by birth, and the last of our Lusaran royal line. You are our true King.'

'But I don't know what being a King means. I mean, if Kenrick is so bad, then what else can a King do?'

Aiden smiled. 'Learn.'

'Learn?'

'A good King is always learning. You're young, you've been taught well so far. Just keep going.'

'That's all?'

'For the most part, yes. The more you learn, the more you'll learn. But whatever you do, don't try to make it all happen now. All that business with fighting Kenrick and the rebellion and making your powers develop – worry about those as they come. For the moment, the single best thing you can do is to talk to us, your councillors. Ask questions. Learn. That's what we're here for.'

Andrew's eyes searched his for several heartbeats, then the boy nodded.

Knowing he'd breached those emotional walls Andrew had barricaded himself within, Aiden now began to mend them. 'You know how long I reigned as Bishop? About three hours. Long enough to celebrate mass and consider the enormous role I had just taken on. After that, I was put in a cell, with a nice locked door, and told I would never see daylight again. Two years later I did, thanks to Payne, and your Father John, and a number of others. After I met Robert, things changed again. He drew me into this entire adventure, and he's never let me go since. During all that time, no matter my pleas, he has always called me Bishop – even when I threatened to hit him.' Andrew smiled a little at that. 'I can see you know what I mean. You see, he wanted me to remember. He wanted me to never forget that I did have a role to play – and an important one at that. And here I am, more a Bishop every day, and you know, I still don't know how to do it. More than that, it scares me more as each day goes by. One day soon, I'll stand before my congregation in the Basilica and I will have to show them what they've been waiting for. The very idea frightens me half to death.'

Andrew frowned. He slipped off the wall and moved away a few steps. Without turning, he said, 'You think I'm afraid.'

'I'm saying *I'm* afraid.'

'No, you think I'm afraid.' Andrew turned then and looked up, his eyes meeting Aiden's openly.

Once more, Aiden shook his head, 'I don't think you're afraid—'

'Don't.' Andrew held up his hands. 'Please, Father, I know you're lying. If you want me to trust you, and if we're going to do all this then I need to know you won't lie to me.'

Aiden held his breath in shock. By the gods, this boy *could* tell the truth from a lie! Was that why he'd been so determined to keep himself apart from everyone else? Because he could see the lies they would speak to him?

Dear Mineah, then he would know how disappointed they were, that they had expected so much more. And could this be the first of his powers beginning to show? He'd have to ask Finnlay.

'Yes,' he admitted, laying himself open as he did. 'I do think you're afraid. I also think you've every reason to be and I don't think there's a man alive who, in your position, wouldn't be afraid. I also think,' Aiden paused, standing up straight and stretching, 'that being afraid is not the worst thing in the world. I know for a fact that Robert is afraid all the time.'

Andrew scoffed at that. 'He is not.'

'I promise you he is. Ask him.'

'He'd never tell me.'

'I think you'd be surprised.' Aiden looked back at the path winding along beside the water. 'It's still early. Do you know this area at all? Is it safe to keep walking?'

'If I come with you it will be.'

'Very well. Lead the way.' Aiden's smile wasn't just for the boy's benefit. This was definitely Robert's son: beneath that gentle, beguiling exterior was a heart of pure steel. Deverin was right: Robert had chosen well.

Micah didn't see the trip wire until it was too late and he was tumbling from his horse, landing heavily. He rolled twice, out of breath, but he still managed to come up in a crouch, ducking out of the way of his panicked horse. He had a dagger in his hand, ready to confront his attacker – but he needn't have bothered.

Robert stood over him, Micah's own sword pointed towards him, inches from his throat. 'Give me one good reason why I shouldn't just kill you.'

Micah waited a heartbeat then dropped his dagger. 'I don't have a reason for you.' He looked up, not wanting to see what he knew would be there in Robert's eyes. The moonlight was bright, almost enough to read by. This stretch of the path was open enough and he could see clearly. The darkness came entirely from Robert's eyes and sent a shiver of profound shock through Micah from head to foot.

He'd known this man from the age of six and not once, in all that time, had he ever seen Robert angry. Until now.

'I'm not going to go away,' Micah began carefully, not trying to hide anything in his voice. He couldn't hide anything from Robert anyway and they both knew it. 'I want a part of this. I *am* a part of this.'

'That's why you stayed with Andrew, was it? So you could hold some sway over him?'

'No! I stayed with him to teach him, to protect him. I thought you'd want it.'

'Oh, I did – until I found out you'd married a Malachi! And you kept her there, so close to Andrew, knowing full well what he was all along.'

'No, I had nothing to do with the attack, so don't even go saying it.'

'I'm still waiting for that reason.'

Carefully, slowly, Micah climbed to his feet, noting how Robert simply followed him up, using the sword when his powers would do the job better but less painfully. 'Lusara is my country. My father had to die on foreign soil. You owe *me* a Maclean.'

Robert didn't answer immediately. His eyes didn't waver, nor did his threat. Then, abruptly, he stepped back, twisted the sword and tossed it to Micah hilt-first.

'Fine. But what I said about your wife still stands. And one other thing.' Robert turned away, pulling his gloves on absently. 'If I suspect you will betray Andrew or anyone in our cause, I will kill you without question and you will consider it a blessing.'

'Robert—'

'No.' He turned and faced Micah squarely, anger written in every line of his face. 'You gave up the right to call me that when you agreed to that deception.'

'I had no choice!'

With a bitter laugh, Robert strode to the side of the path where his horse was tethered. 'Welcome to my world.' With that, he mounted up and rode away, leaving Micah to scramble to catch his mount and follow. And though so much had changed in ten years, it all felt exactly the same.

Finnlay used the moonlight to his advantage. With the night so bright, the shadows were doubly dark, and hiding in them was so much easier. But he didn't need to get too close to Elita's main keep to see the villagers, to hear them praying.

They gathered some time around midnight, on the road approaching the castle. Roughly about where the outer postern gate had stood, where huge blocks of stone still lay, the villagers held their gathering. There was only a dozen of them, and they sang softly, but with passion. Less than half an hour later, they were walking back down the road towards Fenlock, gleaming smiles on their faces as though they'd been blessed by the goddess herself.

There was simply no accounting for some people. How could anybody think Jenn was the incarnation of the goddess? Certainly she'd done a number of miraculous things, but they could all be attributed to her powers. It was true that none of these people would know that she was a sorcerer – although it was possible that some had recognised her at Shan Moss and knew what she'd done, and it was ironic that they would credit her with this status when Mineah was last known for putting down the sorcerer's rebellion – but should that make a difference?

Still deeply puzzled, Finnlay backed away from the road, found more shadows to hide in and gradually made his way back to the camp. He'd posted sentries and checked each before finding his bed and sinking into it with gratitude.

More waiting. In particular, more waiting for Robert. He had no trouble assuming Robert was still alive; he had to be. Since Robert and Jenn were together now, he couldn't imagine Robert – in whatever dire straits – not finding the power at least to mindspeak Jenn to say goodbye, not after they'd waited so long to be together.

And now they were here, ready, waiting, the rebellion in its first precious hours. It had taken so long to arrive at this point, so much had happened, but there was so much still to happen. And though he had all the faith he could muster in a brother who was still not here, and a nephew who didn't want to be here, there was not enough faith in him yet to believe that they had a real chance for victory. The one thing he did know, however, was that this would be their last try. If they didn't win this time, then the loss would be final.

'Damn it!' he whispered to himself. He hated thinking things like this when he was trying to get to sleep. When he woke in the morning, he'd be cranky, without really being able to say why.

He rolled over, found a more comfortable position and closed his eyes. Breathing deeply, he listened to the sounds of the camp, to Deverin snoring and the horses stamping. He tried not to listen to the river below; that would just make him want to get up to relieve himself. The ground was comfortable enough, his blanket adequate against the cool of the night, and the moon soft enough to make him feel at home, such a powerful blue glow—

His eyes snapped open – then widened. By the gods – was he dreaming? He sat up, looking around to make sure he was the only one awake. He was, and the sentries were a good distance away, so they shouldn't see this.

Careful to keep his movements as quiet as possible, Finnlay peeled his blanket back and returned his eyes to his nephew. Andrew was lying not far away, beside an old tree trunk struck down by lightning. He had a blanket over his shoulder, with just his face and his left hand protruding from the cloth: both of which were glowing a vivid blue, as though the moon had condensed itself onto his skin.

Finnlay would have danced with joy, but he knew Andrew wouldn't appreciate it. Instead, he crept over to the boy and knelt beside him. Carefully, he laid a hand on Andrew's shoulder, giving it a friendly squeeze, as he had done a thousand times over the years. The only words he spoke were, 'That's it, Andrew, relax. Just sleep. Don't worry about anything. Just relax.'

It took a little time, but slowly the glow subsided, and by the time Finnlay got back into bed, Andrew once more appeared to be an ordinary boy not far off turning fifteen. A boy who had a powerful sorcerer for a father, another powerful sorcerer for a mother – who some believed to be the incarnation of the goddess – and who would one day assume the throne of his ancestors. A very ordinary boy who must at last be coming into his powers. This *had* to be it, didn't it?

Finnlay went to sleep with a smile on his face.

And woke up to rain pouring down on his face, icy needles of water, and swearing. He would have buried his head and simply suffered it, but it was morning and there was somebody standing in front of him who hadn't been there last night.

'Micah?'

'None other.'

With a faint groan, Finnlay rolled to his feet, clapping Micah on the shoulder in welcome. 'It's good to see you're still in one piece. We were worried. And where's Robert?'

Micah blinked once then turned so Finnlay could see. There was his brother, seated by the fire, beneath the small shelter they'd made the day before, a cup of brew in one hand, a piece of pie in the other, regaling the sentries with outrageous stories of his travels. Laughter filled the camp, waking everybody, driving away the rain.

The last ten years might never have happened.

'Don't be fooled,' Micah murmured when Finnlay would have gone forward. 'He was captured and tortured. I don't know how his body is healing, but it is. As for his mind—'

A shiver of icy fear rattled down Finnlay's back. 'He looks fine.'

'Yes,' Micah said. 'He does *look* fine. Come on. I'm hungry.'

22

'Again.'

Hard rain spattered against the window; the constant noise made Kenrick's head hurt, but since Rayve was standing before him with his sword raised, Kenrick could only respond in kind. As he'd been taught, he felt the power flow from the pit of his stomach, out through his limbs, into the blade he held. Forgetting all he had learned about conventional combat, he lifted the sword and swung hard and fast, clashing against the other blade in a flash that could have been mistaken for lightning.

They stayed like that, hilt against hilt, Kenrick holding the power where it needed to be, concentrating to make it flow evenly, watching out for some other move against him, trying to keep his balance against the answering force of Rayve's power, trying to—

'Breathe, my lord. You must breathe or you will fall over.'

Ah, breathing – he had forgotten again. With his head spinning and his chest aching, Kenrick tried to ease air into himself, but it upset his entire balance and everything fell apart. A grinding noise came from somewhere; there was another flash and he was thrown back, stumbling to land on the ground – in about the same place he'd landed the last dozen times.

'Damn it!' he swore again, only this time he didn't bother getting up. His head hurt too much and this whole thing was starting to really annoy him. Was Rayve a bad teacher, or he a bad student? All that really mattered to him was that he learn, and quickly, but it wasn't happening anywhere near quickly enough.

Rayve stood in the same place, though his sword was now sheathed. 'You are improving, my lord. If you can remember to breathe, you will find your stamina will treble.'

'But I *can't* remember to breathe,' Kenrick said, tossing his sword away and watching it slide across the cold tiled floor, spinning slightly until it stopped short of the fireplace, pointing towards the door.

'A little more practice, my lord. That's all you need.' Rayve always called him 'my lord', as though acknowledging the crown he wore by calling him Sire would be too much.

'I'm sick of practising. We practise every day, morning and night, and

I'm weary of it.' He winced as another splat of rain hit the glass and pressed his thumbs to his temples. With every practice came this pain, and it got worse every day. Sometimes he could dull it with a little sweet wine, but that just slowed him down when they were practising sword work, defeating the purpose.

He heard Rayve walking away from him and he scrambled to his feet. 'Wait!'

The young Malachi turned, his face as impassive and emotionless as always. 'If you no longer wish to learn, then I will return to my people.'

'I do want to learn, but that doesn't mean I'm not sick of it. And that doesn't mean I've given you leave to go.'

Rayve looked at him as though daring Kenrick to stop him.

'You'll go when I say you go,' Kenrick growled, but even he could hear the weakness in words that needed to be repeated like that.

For some reason, however, Rayve did not laugh at him. 'My lord, you are trying to learn in a few weeks what we take years to master. That's why you experience pain. To lose the pain means you must stop practising.'

'But I *have* to practise!' Kenrick bellowed, then winced again as his own volume was echoed around the room at him. 'I have to,' he added in a whisper. With a sigh, he turned and made for the fireplace, and the table beside it. The fire chased away the cold of the morning; the wine softened the headache. 'Tell me,' Kenrick went on as he sank into a soft-covered chair, resting his head against the back, 'tell me about the D'Azzir.'

He watched the young Malachi debating with himself, then waved his hand at a chair. 'Sit. Tell me about the D'Azzir and DeMassey.'

Rayve sat on a chair opposite, carefully moving his sword out of the way. Even so, he sat upright and rigid, as though to allow himself to be comfortable was another form of weakness. The Baron DeMassey had been a hard master.

'The D'Azzir were always the army of the Cabal,' he began quietly, looking not at Kenrick, but at a spot on the wall behind him. 'In the beginning, they were merely soldiers, skilled in the use of weapons, whereas the other Cabal were artists or farmers, priests or blacksmiths. But over hundreds of years, the Cabal practised manual labour less and less, instead trading their expertise for gold. The Cabal became very wealthy, but the demands on the D'Azzir increased as a result. Palaces were often attacked, and traders travelled with armed guards. The Cabal needed some means to ensure their survival which could never be challenged by any of the Princes they aided. So the D'Azzir began to develop skills which blended sorcery and sword fighting. Within twenty years, they had cultivated such a reputation as to prevent any further attacks on Palaces, and they were the finest warriors anywhere.'

Kenrick could hear the pride in the young man's voice, felt a ripple of it himself. Weren't these, after all, his ancestors as well?

'It was a D'Azzir who first developed the process called *Folinet aro Shar*.'

'What's that?' Kenrick perked up and watched Rayve closely.

'It's the Feeding Blood. It was originally developed so a D'Azzir could use the blood of a vanquished foe to strengthen himself, and help heal his wounds. It was to be used only in extreme circumstances and only in battle.'

'But now Nash uses it to regenerate.'

'Yes, or a form of it. What he does takes days rather than minutes, and he uses—'

'The blood of sorcerers,' Kenrick interposed. *He'd* used such blood, to heal his scars, and would have used the blood of the Douglas girl if he'd had the chance. He knew so little about it, but it was obvious that the stronger the sorcerer, the greater the regeneration. 'Tell me about Nash and DeMassey.'

'They were enemies,' he said baldly.

Kenrick laughed a little. 'Does Nash have friends?'

'DeMassey did – still does.'

'So how did they work together if they were enemies?'

'Their goals were the same, or so the Baron thought. They used each other to further those goals, but in recent years . . . '

'What?' Kenrick's gaze narrowed. There was a story here and he needed to hear it.

'The Lady Valena – my master loved her, and we believe she loved him. He would often leave and visit her, when Nash was unlikely to notice. We believe that somehow the Lady Valena was involved in my master's death.'

Kenrick remembered Valena; she had shared his father's bed, she had been his constant companion; he remembered how she would sometimes whisper in a corner with Nash. But his father had been Bonded to Nash, and unable to make any real choices of his own. And what kind of woman would sleep with a man on the orders of another?

Then he asked, 'But you said DeMassey died here.'

'He did – but I think he did so to protect her.'

'Do you think he succeeded?'

Rayve's eyes dropped to his hands. 'We will avenge my master and the Lady Valena if we must. If she is with Nash, there is nothing we can to do free her. She can only free herself.'

Kenrick snorted at that, then, steeling himself against the response, said, 'So do you know how to find out when Nash will return to Marsay?'

There was a long silence as Rayve rose from his chair. He turned, his hand lingering on the back of the seat, then said, 'He has been seen returning to Ransem Castle. I think it may only be days before he returns here.'

'And when he does?'

There was no expression on the young Malachi's face. Instead, he walked towards the door, saying quietly, 'Good day, my lord.' And then he was gone, with only the echo of his hatred filling the corners of the room.

'I need to know what you are going to do, Osbert.' Godfrey put his hands on his hips and turned to look out the window, into the cloister below, where he wished he was now. But they couldn't have this conversation in the open air, at least, not in this city, not when the subject was treason.

'Why must I decide now? Do you know something?'

Godfrey groaned. 'Why must you persist with this reckless position? We are already damned, you and I. One day Nash will return and he'll remember what I did and assume you rescued me.'

'Then surely that means you should leave the city?'

'And leave the Church and my brothers at a time like this – and when I have been placed in the position of Bishop, with so much faith?' Godfrey studied the man he sometimes despaired of. Osbert sat in a chair with his legs crossed, his robes draped elegantly, the very image of a man with few cares. But the image died on inspection of his eyes, where the constant fear he lived with was imprinted. It was to that fear that Godfrey made his plea. 'You *must* decide now if you hope to carry out any constructive acts. You need to be planning what you will do, so you will have time to make provision.'

'Again I ask, do you know something?'

'I know that one day – whether it be tomorrow or next year – there will be a war between Robert Douglas and Kenrick. Before that day, you need to decide which side you will fight on. And don't dream of saying the winning side or I will have you thrown into the street!' Osbert began to chuckle as Godfrey added, 'If you think I'm joking—'

Osbert's smile shifted only a little. 'Godfrey, just as you cannot rule the conscience of every priest in your flock—'

'Would that I could.'

'So I cannot rule the minds of all my Guildesmen. My predecessor, Vaughn, had their hearts, and he whipped up their loyalty with a hatred of sorcery. Since his disappearance, and Kenrick's ascension, Guildesmen everywhere have voiced their confusion. I don't have answers for them. I can't openly declare against Kenrick, and yet that's what they want me to do. I don't have Vaughn's personality, his flare for the dramatic—'

'His evil and twisted imagination.'

Osbert stood before him, his voice dropping. 'I can't lead them where they don't want to go.'

'But that's exactly what you *must* do. At the very least, you should prepare your soldiers.'

'So they can be used *against* your cause?'

Godfrey looked away, frowning. This argument always ended the same way. 'You're going to run out of time one day, Osbert – and I won't be there to help you wrestle with your conscience.'

'Well, if you're right and Nash comes for us both, that day's not so far away then, is it?'

'Perhaps.' Godfrey went to his desk and picked up a letter he'd received that morning. It had made him lose his appetite. 'You know the village of Fenlock?'

'No,' Osbert said as he returned to his seat. 'Should I?

'It stands not far from the ruins of the castle of Elita, and has always been loyal to the Earls of Elita. In the village there's a monastery which, until the Guilde takeover of hospice work, ministered to the needs of the community and environs. Over the last years, obviously, the number of monks has decreased – but in the last six months or so, the numbers have more than doubled.'

Osbert raised his eyebrows, though he did not see the significance. Godfrey continued, his eyes dancing over the paper in his hand, picking up phrases here and there, 'It seems there have been a number of miraculous happenings at the ruins of Elita: mysterious lights at night, ghostly figures seen moving about, faces which appear and vanish, voices heard, footprints appearing in the snow.'

With a start, Osbert was on his feet again, all pretence of carefreeness now gone. 'But you yourself said you once met with Douglas and McCauly and the others there. Surely these are just—'

'And about a week ago, one of the monks himself saw a figure on the ridge overlooking the castle. He saw lightning flickering from the figure's hands, and then a great flash of light in the sky overhead.' Godfrey ignored Osbert's growing agitation and went on, 'Then there are the miracles. Barren women who have conceived, a blind child now sighted, fevers cured, wounds healed. One story after another, and I know, deep in my heart, Osbert, that this is merely the beginning.'

'How?' Osbert whispered like a man afraid.

'I am requested to send an emissary to investigate these happenings, to see if I can attribute them to the new incarnation of Mineah—'

Osbert closed his eyes. 'Jennifer Ross.'

'Over and over again I am reminded that the Hermit of Shan Moss has been preaching for years now that her return is imminent, that she will appear to fight against the darkness, that this is her time. I receive reports from every source possible; every monk wishing to become a mystic has sent me a vision in the last few weeks. It's as though they are *willing* it to happen.'

Osbert met his gaze. 'She didn't die in the fire at Clonnet. She was at Shan Moss – and too many people saw her, so they know she's alive. But they also saw her use sorcery.'

'Did they? Was it sorcery she used? Or was it something else?'

'Oh, come on, Godfrey, don't tell me you believe all this? She's a *sorcerer*! How can she be the incarnation of Mineah if—'

'I don't know,' Godfrey said, putting the paper back down, 'but this I can tell you: if Jennifer Ross is the goddess, then this war is about to begin, and you, my friend, need to decide whether you are prepared to die for nothing, or for a *noble* cause.'

With a groan, Osbert ran his hands though his thinning hair. 'Can't I choose not to die?' Godfrey said nothing; after a moment, Osbert gathered his robes about him and turned his face in profile. 'I can't lead them where they don't want to go.'

'Osbert,' Godfrey said, smiling a little, 'they can't go if you *don't* lead them.'

Nash waited until it was dark: he had always preferred entering Marsay from the river, at night. That way, he could sneak up on the unsuspecting city – and in this particular instance, an unsuspecting King.

He sat in the longboat listening to the oars dip and glide, watching the lights of other boats ripple across the water. He heard voices call out from one to the other as they made their way downriver, towards the coast, to take on cargo, or to offload it: coming and going, a circular trade. And then there were the lights of the city, damp from the day's rain, and subdued, as though in need of summer to brighten up.

He studied the view until the black walls of the city rose before him, towering over him, making him look up and remember. 'Taymar?'

'Yes, Master?'

'The Envoy will be waiting for me?'

'Yes, Master. And he has brought the gold.'

'Good.' The boat began to rock a little as it approached the narrow dock. The oarsmen stopped rowing and it glided to a halt, then was quickly roped and tied off. The moment Nash stepped ashore, Taymar and his men followed behind; together they entered the alley and climbed the stairs leading up to the castle.

The Envoy was waiting for him outside the watergate, as arranged. The man looked wholly uncomfortable, not to mention cold; the robes of a southern lord were not suited to this country. By this time, after so many of these transactions, this man should have known to dress according to the climate rather than his own customs.

'Greetings,' the Envoy said as he gave a slight bow, as though he didn't really feel Nash deserved it.

Nash went straight to business. 'The gold?'

There were four massive chests at the Envoy's feet; Nash waved to his men and all but two moved forward to collect them. As they were carried off, he gestured at the two men remaining. 'These were going to be yours,' he told the Envoy.

'*Were?*' The Envoy frowned.

'But I think now I need them here more than your master does.'

'Then I will take my gold and return home.' The Envoy drew himself up to his full height and glared at the smaller man.

'No, I don't think you will,' Nash said, and smiled. 'You see, I need the gold as much as I need these men. But I promise you, nobody will miss you, and in a few months, when you fail to return home, they will send another in your place, and I will be able to tell them that you never arrived. They will wonder if you disappeared with the gold you were to give me, and then they will continue with the business of slavery, just as you have done over the last few years.'

'But – but you can't do that!' the Envoy stuttered. 'I'm—'

'A casualty of war,' Nash said to the men. 'Dispose of the body so nobody can find it.' And without looking back at the frightened Envoy, he began to move up the stairs, taking them two at a time, and smiling when he heard the scuffle behind him abruptly silenced.

It was a shame to sever such a useful connection, but between Kenrick, and the probably vengeful Malachi – and the Enemy soon to be knocking on their door – he needed every man he could get; it would be increasingly difficult to recruit Malachi to be Bonded. The gold would come in useful, though; armies were very expensive.

When he reached the base of his favourite tower apartments, he almost sighed with pleasure. His men had lit a fire and candles, and had opened windows to air the rooms. He wanted to run his hands through the gold which would pay for his new army, and he wished to visit Valena in her new accommodation, but he had something else he had to do first.

Keeping Taymar with him – no man of any worth travelled in the city entirely without retinue, and he couldn't afford to flash his Bonded Malachi around too much until the regular kind returned in force, in case somebody noticed – he strode through the smaller courtyard and then into the larger. There were soldiers about, and other people moving in the damp spring evening, though nobody paid him too much attention.

He took the steps in the hall two at a time, enjoying the fact that Taymar, a man of only thirty, was struggling to keep up with him. This new body felt so incredible; would immortality feel like this every day?

When he reached the first landing, he paused long enough to ask a guard where the King was, then he took off down that corridor, nodding and smiling at those he passed, all of whom stopped and frowned at his back.

And when he arrived at the King's door, he waved it open before him, not bothering with ceremony, enjoying the wide eyes of the guards standing on either side of it. He strode into the room. There was a fire roaring, beating back the cold evening, and a table laden with sweet-smelling foods. A few of Kenrick's listless lordlings were lounging about, sipping wine and pining for a damned good battle of some kind. When he found the King, Kenrick's eyes widened with shock and, Nash was pleased to note, not a little horror.

He had to admit, almost everything qualified as a weapon these days. With a flourish, he bowed deeply. 'Greetings, Sire. I am returned to court.' Considering he'd never asked permission to leave in the first place, he enjoyed the hypocrisy of his greeting.

But it was Kenrick's face which made the trip worthwhile, the very reason he'd come himself, rather than have Kenrick find out through some other means. The King was staring at him, face white, mouth open, as though interrupted mid-thought.

'Sire? Are you well?' Nash feigned concern and approached, almost laughing when Kenrick took a step back.

'Yes.' Kenrick gathered himself, but could not control the colour in his face. 'I am quite well. And wondering where you have been these last weeks.'

Nash allowed a broad smile to crease his new face. 'Working for you, Sire.'

'Really?' Kenrick walked past him, deliberately knocking his shoulder, making Nash move. As he reached the table, he poured himself a large goblet of wine and emptied it in one swallow. His men watched him with wary eyes.

'Yes, Sire, really.' Nash spread his arms wide, deliberately including all those useless men in his gesture. 'I have returned just in time, too. I have uncovered a plot, Sire.'

Kenrick almost rolled his eyes, but stopped himself in time. Instead, he gestured for Nash to continue.

'I suggest you put out a call to arms, Sire.'

'To what end?' Kenrick finally snapped, slamming his goblet down on the table. 'You would have me empty the treasury by keeping a standing army against every tiny threat you imagine?'

'Oh, but this is a very real threat. It comes from the Rebel, Robert Douglas.'

At that, Kenrick froze. 'What of him?' he asked.

'Treason, Sire.' Nash paused deliberately. 'He has your cousin, Andrew, Duke of Ayr – and he plans to put him on your throne.'

23

The vision felt different: hard and mean, and full of something so horrible he couldn't look at it. There were scrapes of blood all around on the hard floor, and thick slimy moss growing on the walls that reached so far up they vanished into infinity. But the deeper he looked, the more the walls grew into trees, with huge thick trunks and deep green bows reaching down to touch him, to warm him, to shelter him.

He sat up, blinking in the sudden bright light. It was hot and very dry and not at all what he was expecting. There was a sword on the ground at his feet, pointing towards a door. To his left, a wide open space, filled with desert, golden and red, achingly empty. He could hear them coming, through the floor, through the walls, scraping across the blood, clashing their swords.

The noise woke him.

For a moment, he couldn't see the roof of his cave properly. It was afternoon, and the sun was coming from the wrong direction. But he blinked and gradually the rough edges of the walls and ceiling appeared to him and he smiled a little. He was getting old; they weren't so sharp now as they had once been.

Slowly, he sat up, rolling a little over his bad shoulder, doing his best not to gasp at the pain; instead, whispering a small prayer of thanks that he could use it at all. Once he had his legs over the bed, his feet resting on the floor, he murmured another prayer, holding his hands together in obeisance, bowing his head. Once his cave fell silent again, he took his walking stick and used it to get to his feet.

He could walk well enough, but his right knee always ached worse in the afternoon, as though complaining that it had done its share and now wanted nothing more than rest. Feeling better for his nap, he stood in the doorway and breathed deeply. Spring had most certainly arrived in the forest, leaving the air richly scented with wildflowers and other growing things.

He'd smelled spring in the air in that vision. So often scent played a huge part in what he saw, and now it was telling him something he could not ignore.

Looking down to where he was putting his feet, he stepped out onto the flatstone path embedded into soft earth. He followed it around to the left of the hill, away from his cave, to where the ground flattened out and the forest was filled with young saplings dotted with fresh leaves. There, beyond his patches of vegetable garden, stood his boundary, the edge of the hermitage, on the other side, two monks and a donkey. The animal had baskets brimming over with goods strapped to its back.

'Good afternoon, Brothers,' he called, waving to them. 'Come in, come in. We have so much to do.'

He smiled at them as they followed the path towards him, towing the donkey behind. They were both young and had been to visit him before, so he knew he would not have to show them around, nor tell them what needed to be done. Besides, there was no more work to be done.

'Come, down this way. I shall put some water on to make a brew for us all as we prepare.'

'Prepare, Brother?' the older of the two asked. His name was Edward, and he came often to visit to listen to the visions, to learn to understand them. 'You have had another vision?'

'I have had so many I can't begin to tell you,' he laughed, clapping the young man on the back. 'But we must not waste time like this. I will make you a brew and you will help me prepare. I cannot move the way I used to.'

He chuckled at their puzzled frowns as he took them back to the cave. The other monk set about removing the baskets from the donkey's back while the kettle boiled and Edward questioned him. Normally, Edward would write down what there was to report and take it back to his Abbot. From there, notice would be sent to the Bishop and to all the other houses of note.

But not today.

He leaned on his stick to take the water from the fire. He poured it into a pot and let it sit, taking three earthenware mugs down from hooks on the cave wall.

'Forgive me, Brother,' Edward began, obviously not comfortable. 'But your visions – they have told you something new? Something important?'

'Very important, Brother Edward. So important that I cannot stay here any longer.'

Edward's eyebrows rose. 'Not stay? But where will you go?'

He smiled, poured the brew and gestured outwards, past the door, past the forest. 'Out there. To where it's all going to happen. To where she is.'

'She?'

He laughed again, saying, 'Take the other cup out to our friend doing all the work. Then we must pack up my notes and some small things for the journey. Then we must leave.'

'Forgive me, Brother.' Edward put down his cup and clasped his hands together, the essence of patience. 'But you can understand my confusion – you have never left your hermitage. There has been a hermit here for almost two hundred years.'

'Longer.'

'And you want to leave?'

'Want is not a word a monk should use, Brother. I have no wants. I merely go where the Goddess directs me, and she is leading me out of here. So far, I do not understand why, but I know my visions will tell me when the time comes. Now, I do need to leave today. I appreciate you need to speak to the Abbot before you can accompany me, so this night we will spend at the Abbey, and tomorrow, properly provisioned, we will set out to cross the mountains.'

Edward's eyes grew wide, a little excited, a little hopeful, and a little fearful, all at the same time.

'Come, let's begin.' And he left Edward to take the other cup out to the younger monk.

24

Andrew woke with a headache. He could feel it before he even opened his eyes and for a moment he lay there, remembering the luxurious comfort of his own bed, in his own room, a place where rain didn't fall inside; a place where, if he'd wanted, he could have remained buried for a whole day while he read a book.

Of course, the book would have been one supplied by Robert, and to stay in bed in such a manner would require him obtaining permission from an uncle now dead, and the bed he missed so much no longer existed, it was, in fact, little more than a charred remnant.

Fine thoughts to be starting a new day with – and what was all that noise? They were all supposed to be as quiet and invisible as possible while they were in hiding in the forest around Elita.

He opened his eyes and sat up, pulling his blankets away. A fine rain was falling, leaving everything damp and cold, though the fallen tree where he'd put his bed was keeping him relatively sheltered and—

The voice finally penetrated his foggy waking haze and he frowned. Robert. Then his frown turned to a smile and he leapt up and ran across the camp, never happier to see anyone ever before. Robert saw him approaching and gave his own open smile in return, which turned into laughter as he pointed at Andrew's bare feet: in his haste, he had forgotten to put on his boots.

'What happened? Where's Micah? Is he all right? Did you get away from the Malachi?' Andrew was full of questions, knowing he was going to get his own interrogation sooner or later, but the horrible tension of the last ten days felt like it was unravelling in his stomach.

Robert stood and drew him under the shelter, away from the rain. Most of the men he'd been talking to had done sentry duty all night; they bid farewell and went to their beds as the newly arisen crew began to prepare breakfast.

'I see you brought back reinforcements,' Robert began, pouring himself some more brew from beside the fire.

'The Bishop said that's what you wanted us to do. And Finnlay said that's why—'

As he sat down again, Robert interjected, 'You'd better go put your boots on before your feet freeze.'

'Robert!' Finnlay approached, grinning, with Micah, though Micah stayed back, which made Andrew frown a little.

'It's good to see you back.'

'I can't leave you alone for five minutes, can I, brother? Now you've gone and started a rebellion. Some people can't be trusted.'

'Oh, well,' Finnlay laughed, spreading his hands, 'if I get to take credit for it, I'm not going to complain. Though I might just go and wake up the Bishop, as he was the one who gave the order.'

Robert looked around the camp: everyone was spread out, neatly bedded beneath sheltering bushes and trees. 'He's here too?'

'Everyone is here, Robert,' Finnlay said, a little more soberly. 'Including Patric.'

A flash of something indescribable appeared on Robert's face and then as quickly disappeared. He sprang to his feet urgently, though his voice was as calm as ever. 'He's here? I thought he'd have to be dead by now. I—'

'How about I go and wake everybody up while you have some breakfast? I suppose you rode all night? No, don't bother answering, I know that look.' Finnlay turned to Andrew and added, 'And you can do as you're told and put your boots on. You should also do something with that hair before it walks off on its own.'

Instantly, Andrew's hands flew to his hair and his face warmed a little as Robert chuckled again, but Andrew found he was smiling as well as he ran back to his bed.

As he sat down on the dead tree trunk, Micah approached him, a little hesitantly. 'Good morning, my lord,' he said quietly.

Andrew pulled his boots on, then knelt down to roll up his bedding. He tucked it neatly inside the trunk and hoped it would stay protected from the rain. Then he stood, looking over his shoulder to where Robert was paying them no attention.

'What's going on? What happened? Why did—' he paused, with another quick look around to make sure nobody would hear him. 'Why did Robert leave with Sairead? Where were you?'

Micah met his gaze steadily, as though he were looking for something in Andrew. He couldn't guess what. 'I can't explain it to you.'

'Why not?'

'Because I promised I wouldn't.'

Andrew's gaze narrowed. 'Promised who?'

Micah's eyes left Andrew's to light on a place behind him. They lingered there a moment, then he looked away, a flash of pain on his normally sunny face. 'I almost got him killed. I'm only here because he—'

Dry pain pressed against Andrew's chest, making it hard to breathe. He watched Micah force air into his own lungs, and did the same. He needed an answer, and so did Robert. 'He doesn't trust you, does he?'

Micah just shook his head.

'Should he?'

At that, Micah looked up, at first wounded that Andrew would ask such a question, and then a little surprised, for the same reason. His answer was simple. 'Yes. You both should.'

Andrew looked harder, and deeper, but there was nothing else there but the truth. That was all he wanted. 'I believe you.'

For a moment, Micah just stared at him, blinking slowly, then again he looked away until a pleased smile wiped some of the darkness from his eyes. 'Thank you, my lord,' he whispered.

'Come on, let's eat. Finnlay says Robert rode all night. Did you?'

'Aye, we did.'

'Food, and then some sleep. Then I'll fill you in on everything you missed.'

'Just don't forget to do something about your hair.'

Finnlay certainly planned to wake everybody up, but in reality, he went straight to where Patric's bed was sheltered by an arrowhead of bushes. Joshi's bed made up the third side, protecting Patric even while he was sleeping.

His friend was already awake, and Joshi was packing up his bed, ready for the day. The young man eyed Finnlay warily, but Finnlay simply smiled. He was going to enjoy this – especially after Robert's reaction.

'Patric, you need to get up. Robert's back and he's waiting to see you.'

Almost instantly, Patric was up, pulling on his cloak. 'I feel the cold so much more now. I wish I didn't but—' Then he was out of bed, feeling for his boots and pushing his feet into them. 'I always remembered spring in Lusara as being much warmer than this.' He stepped over his bedding, reaching out a hand to Joshi to guide him as he usually did. His smile reached and filled his blind eyes. He'd more than recovered from his fever now and Finnlay found watching him move about quite strange.

'Well? Where is he?'

'Here.'

Finnlay turned to find his brother standing there, horror and amazement fighting for domination on his face. He was deathly pale, his mouth open in surprise. He took a short step forward, but the ring of steel on steel slapped him out of his shock.

Joshi held his sword pointed at Robert's belly, his stance clear enough to everyone. Before Robert even moved, Finnlay knew what he was about to do—

'Robert, don't! Just—'

But Patric was already talking, speaking aloud to Joshi in a language Finnlay could have sworn he understood – but he didn't. Then Joshi, normally so quiet, answered back, his voice a growl, his gaze never once deviating from Robert's face.

'Finn?' Robert asked for clarification in one word, but Finnlay waited.

Again Patric spoke, his voice hard, his attention all on his friend. Joshi grunted, sheathed his sword and turned back to Patric. He said something else, his eyes blazing in anger; Patric snapped back, shutting up the young man with a word. There was silence for a moment, then Joshi turned and walked away, leaving the three of them alone.

Finnlay watched, amazed. In the week and more since he'd arrived at Bleakstone, he'd not seen Joshi more than a few yards from Patric – and now he was stalking off to the river without looking back.

'Robert?' One word, and then Patric was being swept up in a fierce hug by Robert. Then Robert was stepping back, gesturing at Patric's eyes.

'In the name of Serin, Pat, what happened? I thought you had to be dead! It's so long since we heard anything from you and—'

'And it's been almost a year since I heard anything about you. The only way I knew you were alive was that I was sure I'd hear if you'd died. You're a hard man to find, Robert.'

'You're not the only one who's said that,' Finnlay laughed.

'Look, come back to the fire and have some breakfast,' Robert began. His voice seemed completely normal, but his face, for once, showed his shock and concern.

'If you don't mind, Robert,' Patric interrupted, 'I think perhaps we would be more comfortable discussing things in a more private manner.'

Robert's gaze hardened. 'Of course. Finn? Could you—'

'There's the old ruin, where the mill used to be. We could have some privacy there.'

For a moment, he thought Robert would refuse, but then he said slowly, 'Very well.'

'Are you going to ask McCauly as well?'

'Why don't we just invite everyone?' Robert said sourly. He looked uphill to where McCauly was talking to Father John, and added, 'I suppose I'd better, or he'll never leave me alone. Finn, could you take Patric down to the ruin, and I'll retrieve the good priest.'

Aiden saw Robert approach, trying to both hide a grin and look nonchalant at the same time. His tall, imposing figure seemed completely at home in this setting, his powerful shoulders counterpoint to the strength in the trees, his long dark hair, weathered tan skin and green eyes almost a part of the forest itself. Aiden composed his own features, laced his fingers together in a gesture of contemplation, and waited for Robert to speak.

'Did I say to bring *everybody*?'

'You said to bring everybody who wanted to come. These, I'm afraid, are only the men who could get away in the short notice I gave.'

'Oh.' Robert reached up to scratch the back of his head.

'I like the boy.'

'Boy?' Robert's gaze shifted a little, but then focused again. 'He's impossible not to like. If you could rule a country with popularity alone, he'd be the most successful King in the history of the world.'

'Not only that, but I think he has some kind of power buried somewhere in him.'

'That's what I'm told – though how do you know?'

'He has the uncanny ability to know when somebody's telling the truth or lying.'

'That's just guesswork.' Robert began to wave off the suggestion, but Aiden pressed on.

'I don't think so. And it's not just me. A number of us have tried to lie to him and he gets it right every time.'

Robert narrowed his gaze, then said, 'Well, even if you're right, that's not going to do him a lot of good on its own.'

'He's young,' Aiden began, but Robert forestalled him.

'It seems Patric wants to talk – and I don't think that what he has to say can wait. I need to know what he's learned before—'

'Before what?'

Robert shook his head. 'Look, do you want to hear this or not?'

'Fine, lead the way. I just thought we might at least get breakfast.'

With a flat gaze, Robert said, 'They're down at the mill. You go, I'll collect food. Will that shut you up?'

Completely deadpan, Aiden replied, 'I'll let you know.'

Robert turned for the fire then, murmuring something about people obsessed with eating.

Despite his grumblings, Aiden couldn't help but notice that it was in fact

Robert who did most of the eating. He'd brought back boiled eggs, two loaves of bread, a small pot of honey and a large pot of brew, along with cups and some dried apricots. All but the brew had been slung in his cloak, so that when he arrived in the ruin, he found a flat stone on which he spread out the cloth.

Patric ate a little, sipped a little and, for a blind man, did a remarkable impression of watching Robert. And Robert did his own watching, wiping out the worst of his hunger before finding a piece of fallen dressed stone to sit on. Then he munched on another piece of bread and said, 'Go ahead. Give me the bad news.'

Patric raised his eyebrows. 'You assume it's bad?'

'Well, if it was good, I think you would have found a way to tell me by now.'

Tilting his head to one side, Patric seemed to be listening to something. 'Well, I won't say whether it's bad news or not. I'll leave that to you to decide. But first off, I need to tell you – well, ask you, really – are you and Jenn Bonded?'

Robert had just taken a mouthful of brew and instantly began choking on it. Finnlay leapt to his aid, thumping him on the back a few times as Robert's eyes watered and he tried to breathe.

'I'm sorry, I didn't realise you were about to drink.' Patric grimaced. 'Next time—'

'Next time warn me,' Robert coughed one last time. 'What's this about Bonding?'

Patric swallowed. 'It's not actually about Bonding – but about you and Jenn. I . . . we don't have time to go into all the details now, but—'

'Robert,' Finnlay interrupted, 'for the last four years or so, Patric has lived with the people you sent him to find – the Generet. A lot of what he's found has come from carvings on their walls, and some from what they told him. He had to learn their language, and the language on the walls.'

Robert turned back to Patric, 'And your friend, he's Generet, isn't he?'

'Ah, yes.' Patric grimaced a little. 'I'm sorry about that – but that group you encountered at Bu had warned him about you, that they believed you were—'

'The Angel of Darkness.'

'How did you know?'

'Jenn could hear them mindspeaking at Bu. That's why we left there so quickly. So your friend thinks I'm the enemy?' Robert smiled a little. 'I mean, the enemy rather than *the* Enemy?'

'His name's Joshi – and yes. But don't worry about him, honestly. He was just trying to protect me.'

'He's done a good job.'

With another nod, Patric continued, 'I learned a lot about Bonding – and about mindspeaking, since all the Generet can do it. By the mass, Robert, there's so much you need to know, I don't know where to start.'

'Just stay with Bonding for the moment. Why did you ask about Jenn and me?'

'Because if you can mindspeak with her, you're supposed to be Bonded.' There was silence in the ruin as Aiden looked at Robert and then his brother. Patric continued, 'Mindspeaking is a product of the Bonding, just like the Key said.'

'But,' Robert interrupted, 'you just said all the Generet could mindspeak. You're saying they're all Bonded to each other?'

'No, I'm saying *you* and *Jenn* are supposed to be Bonded. For the Generet, the relationship between Bonding and mindspeaking is different.'

'Why? Why is there one rule for them and one for us?'

'Because,' Patric paused, reaching out and feeling for where he'd put his cup, 'because you and Jenn were mentioned in the Prophecy. The Generet have almost nothing to do with it except as the keepers of it.'

'I'm sorry,' Finnlay interrupted. 'They were supposed to keep the Prophecy? Who gave it to them?'

'Amar Thraxis.'

A clatter on the ground made Aiden start. He turned to find Robert had dropped his cup. It rolled on the hard ground until he noticed it. Picking it up, he absently shook the last of the brew out of it, then busied himself getting up and refilling it. He took the pot around to the others and refilled theirs as well. When he sat, he was composed again, though looking a little tired after his night ride.

Patric remained silent and then took up his story once Robert regained his seat. 'Amar Thraxis is the father of the Generet.'

'Wasn't he a Guildesman?'

'Yes, one of great skill. He was also known in some texts as the Marklord, just as you suspected, Robert.'

'How do you know this?' Robert was mystified. 'How could the Generet know? There were hundreds of years separating the records of the Marklord and Thraxis. Yes, some of our findings pointed towards them being one and the same man, but there was nothing conclusive.'

'I'm sorry,' Aiden interrupted. 'I'm confused – why is it important who Thraxis and this Marklord were?'

There was silence a moment, as they each waited for somebody else to answer the question. In the end, it was Finnlay's impatience which broke first. 'Father, all children born to one of the twenty-three great Houses of Lusara are born with a House Mark.'

'Yes, I know that.'

'Well, Patric has always believed that the Marks and sorcery were linked somehow, but until Robert was born, no children with abilities were born to any of the Houses. But then there was Robert, and me, then Jenn – and then a host of others that we now know Nash abducted. We believe that he was looking for Robert but failed because Robert was the wrong age or something – and he *did* abduct Jenn. And Robert and Jenn have been labelled by the Key as being the figures in this Prophecy. The only things linking them together are their powers – and their House Marks. We knew Thraxis was involved in sorcery because he wrote some books on the subject, and was considered an authority at the time. And the Marklord was the man who is believed to have created the House Marks.'

Aiden picked up the threads and continued, 'So you're saying that Thraxis created this Prophecy, then made the House Marks so he could keep track of the ancestors of the people who would make the Prophecy come true?'

Finnlay turned then to Patric, as did Robert. '*Is* that what you're saying? That it was Amar Thraxis who created the Prophecy in the first place?'

Patric grimaced. 'Yes.'

'And the Generet have this written down somewhere? This isn't just what they have in folklore? It's carved in stone?'

Again, Patric grimaced. 'Yes. It's carved in the stone of his tomb.'

'Serin's blood!' It was Finnlay's swearing, but Robert was the one who sprang to his feet.

He paced up and down a little before musing aloud, 'Then that means . . . of course, I should have seen that before. But if he's got the same Prophecy as the one from Bu, then that could— Yes, and the Key was—' Robert looked up, his whole body suffused with an energy that Aiden marvelled at. 'Pat, the Prophecy – that's why there was the split with the rest of the Cabal, right?'

'Oh, yes, exactly. They each had a version carved into a wall. After the last battle—'

'The one at Bu was destroyed, I know, I saw it. No, what I mean is, that the reason was the differences, right? That there *were* differences and that was the cause for the split?'

Patric didn't answer immediately. Then he ran his hands through his bleached white hair, pulling it back from his face. 'Look, Robert, the differences are minimal, in terms of meaning and interpretation. The Generet Prophecy is simply more than the Key's.'

'Then why the split?'

'Because the Generet were the keepers, and they believed that the Cabal were using the Prophecy for their own ends, to threaten the Kings and Princes of the day, to ensure their position and rank were maintained. There's no mention of it, but I think that's also why the Word of Destruction was created – so it could be used as an ultimate weapon nobody else could counteract.'

'So the Prophecy . . .' Robert became utterly still and Aiden's heart went out to him. It was so clear that he needed this answer to be something else entirely, and yet, he already knew it wasn't. 'So the Prophecy doesn't change? From start to finish—'

'No, it doesn't.'

'Robert,' Aiden murmured, 'Patric never knew the ending the Key gave to you.'

Robert's gaze darted to him for a moment, then back to Patric. 'How does it end?'

Swallowing hard, Patric quoted, *'By these very means, born unto these hands, will be the instrument of ruin, dividing that which is by that which should never be. In the act of salvation, this will become desolation itself, destroying that which it would love most, and laying waste all that was created.'*

'That's not exactly the same, Robert,' Aiden added quietly. 'There are substantial differences. Laying waste all that was created isn't the same as—'

Robert just held up his hand. 'Go on, Pat.'

There was a pause before Patric continued in the same subdued voice, 'There was originally more to the Prophecy. Generet folklore says that he wrote it over the later years of his life, then tore it up into pieces because he was afraid of what he'd written. Then in his last days, he put it back together again, but some of it was lost. Because of that, he wrote a little more and decided that it would do as it was. It is accepted that the final Prophecy is the same as what was carved on the Generet wall, and at Bu, though I would imagine some degradation due to age would inevitably occur, not to mention difficulties with translation and language, and the sheer number of years involved. Robert, you need to understand: this Prophecy is merely one of hundreds that have appeared in so many cultures over the last millennium. It's the nature of Prophecy that it foretells something terrible to happen – otherwise, there'd be no point.'

Robert stood before them gazing out through a gap in the wall to his right, leaving them with only a profile to watch, a jaw firm against his last hope dashed. When he spoke, his voice was quiet, contained, intimate. 'Of course, though none of the others was created by the man who made the Marks and was the father of a group of people who mindspeak and seem to have sorcerers' auras but don't. And yet,' his voice dropped to a whisper, his words seeming to be for himself only, 'I can mindspeak with her, I am supposed to be Bonded with her and all I can do is kill—'

Finnlay sat forward, making his own try. 'Robert, the Prophecy predates both the Word of Destruction and the Key. It can't possibly include either of them.'

'And yet it seems to, as though it foretold their creation as well.' Robert frowned slightly, his tone speculative. 'In both cases, the men creating them did so in the attempt to save their people, and in the end, they destroyed them. I can't see how I can hope to better their efforts.'

'There is one other place you can try. Robert. You can't assume anything until you've exhausted all possibilities. There's one more place—'

'What's the point?' Robert kept his gaze steady for a moment, then shifted himself back into the room, his eyes showing more than his exhaustion. 'I've lost count of the number of sources I've found for this damned Prophecy, and all say essentially the same thing.'

'That's because they've all come from the same source.'

'Exactly. So why bother looking any further?'

'Because there's one place where we might find the whole Prophecy, in its original form.'

'A place where time hasn't degraded it? Where there isn't the same problem with language? A place we can find some time in the next few days, Pat? Because that's all I've got. A few days. I have a rebellion to fight. I've waited long enough. I can't sacrifice my country because—'

Patric surged to his feet, his hands reaching out to find Robert in his darkness. 'Robert, listen to me. Thraxis made the Calyx! Remember? If he made the Calyx, there's a good chance he put the Prophecy into it.'

At that, Robert froze for a moment, then started laughing, a little bitter, a little exhausted. 'Fine, Patric, fine. We'll ask the Calyx – though I don't care too much for our chances of getting an answer considering what happened the last time I went near it.'

With that, Robert turned and strode out of the ruin. Aiden gave him a moment before chasing after him.

'Robert, wait, I'm too old to run. Please slow down.'

He didn't, but it gave Aiden an excuse to puff a little when he did catch up. 'Look, you can't—'

'Please, Bishop, spare me your platitudes. I have no more hope to waste on this venture. I have a war to organise. If we're going to stop off to talk to the Calyx then I need to get these men moving today. If you want to talk, we can do it later, but not now.'

'But—'

Robert held out a hand, stopping in the centre of Aiden's chest. He turned a fathomless gaze on Aiden, shadows framing the green, the face pale beneath a tan won of years living a rough life. 'Trust me, Bishop. The freedom of Lusara does not depend on how I *feel*. We'll talk later. In the meantime, you can help me get these men organised.'

25

Finnlay organised the sentries, making sure they were close enough to hear what Robert had to say, while still being able to keep watch for anyone approaching. It was always tricky covering the presence of what amounted to a small army – especially in these times – but with the help of a few Salti and their ability to nudge a man's thoughts away from a particular subject, they were left alone on their last morning in the forests of Elita.

He could only hope that they had been equally invisible for the rest of their stay: the people of Fenlock didn't need to see anything more to convince them of strange occurrences up at the castle.

Robert, despite his lack of sleep, the injuries he kept concealed beneath his clothes and the most recent destruction of his meagre hopes, was at his best, as he always was when in front of people who were as willing as he to do whatever was needed to bring freedom to his country – even if there was a dark glint to his eye only the practised observer would notice.

It had never ceased to amaze Finnlay that Robert could do this: he could put aside what he was thinking and feeling and become this other, public person who looked as though he'd never experienced a day's self-doubt in his life. His confidence in himself and his people was supreme. He looked into each face, into every man's eyes, letting them know he knew how much they wanted to fight and win, that he felt the same way, and their victory would depend on that same passion. His open smile, his strong bearing and rich voice created an image that remained in people's minds. It was this, he knew, more than any other characteristic, that made Robert the leader of legend that he was, the reason why no other rebel had ever commanded the same respect, following or adoration. And it would be this quality that would be remembered long after they were all dead and gone.

And so they sat or stood, listening to him as he outlined what they were each to do, though keeping their actual assignments secret from one group to the next, in case anyone was captured. Of the almost sixty men, he created five groups of ten, keeping the remaining ten for himself. Each group had a leader he trusted, and a good range of skills. How he had arranged all this in such a short space of time, Finnlay had no idea, though the Bishop was sitting there reading names from a list that looked very rushed.

Then Robert was addressing them all and Finnlay felt a shiver of something run down his spine, making his feet cold.

'You must remember that the goal here is not to wage a battle, but to win a war. Your missions will reflect that. You go in, do what you must, and get out, escape to fight another day. I don't want any massacres and I don't want any martyrs. I want you all to work together, those who are Salti, and those who have never met a sorcerer before in their lives. Today, and for the length of this war, there are no differences between us. We have all had our lives torn from us, we've all been dispossessed. We have suffered indignity, oppression and tyranny – but despite all we've been through, we are still strong enough to gather and fight this enemy. That speaks of a pride which runs through our blood. A pride we can give our fellow Lusarans the day we take back our country. And on that day, I will stand with you all and remind you that you were here, at the beginning, when nobody but us thought it could be done.'

There was no cheering, no stomping of feet, but Finnlay saw every chest swell, every heart grow a little with those words. Then Robert was calling for each of the leaders to come forth one at a time to receive their assignments, while the rest began to break camp. The chaos which ensued was organised: everybody seemed to know what they were doing, except for Finnlay.

But then his attention was taken by the sight of one fourteen-year-old boy with wide eyes watching a man he couldn't know was his father; Finnlay didn't need special powers to see what was going on in that mind.

For a long time, he'd been bound by his promise to Jenn not to tell Andrew about his father, accepting her reasons, though he never really understood them. But when it had been suggested that Andrew was as involved in the Prophecy as his parents, it grew harder to keep the secret. Now he wasn't so sure it was such a good idea. Andrew was confused. He was too quiet for his normal self, full of doubt and buried anger, with no real direction despite the considerable minds attached to educating him. Without a greater confidence, what kind of King would he be – assuming he was even capable of beating Kenrick? Surely he would benefit from knowing about his father; even with all that had happened, he still appeared to idolise Robert. They would all be better off if the truth was known.

But he couldn't tell. He'd made that damn promise and no amount of reasoning was going to make it disappear, but perhaps next time he saw Jenn, it could be worth discussing. Perhaps now that she and Robert were together, it might be a good time to tell.

Enough of this introspection. There were things to be done.

'Andrew?' he shouted to his nephew.

The boy started and then his face flushed, as though he should be ashamed of watching Robert. 'Yes?'

'I think the Bishop needs some help with those papers.' Finnlay himself headed for where Robert and McCauly stood together, talking with each group leader as he arrived for his mission.

'Owen, you'll take the barges at Casterlane. I want them bottomed, but not destroyed. Don't try to save the cargo and target any you see trying to flee.'

'And if we have no choice but to destroy them?'

Robert said, 'Then do it. We need to cut Kenrick's supply and this will take out a quarter of it in one go. Once you're done, head for Sawell, using standard evasion tactics. Chances are on the first strike you won't be pursued for long. After that we'll all have a lot more trouble. I'll leave a message for you at Sawell, at the tailor's. Rest there only as long as it takes to have the wounded cared for. There are Healers there you can trust. Then proceed with your next mission.'

Something of a smile creased Owen's face.

'Any questions?'

Owen shook his head. 'No, my lord. And thank you.'

Robert looked puzzled. 'For what?'

With a short bow to McCauley, Owen said, 'Good luck.' And then he was walking away, showing none of his sixty-odd years.

Deverin immediately took his place, anticipation almost dripping from his massive shoulders.

'Ah, Deverin.' Robert looked at the list McCauly held up for him. 'Yes, the border fort at Trowbridge. I need it gone. As long as it's there, most of our refugees can't get back across the border – and we need them. You'll also need to create a garrison capable of holding it for the next couple of months – but I'm sure as soon as you've knocked out Kenrick's men, you'll be spoiled for volunteers. Unfortunately, I can't spare you more than ten men to take the place, so you'll have to use subterfuge rather than brute force – and besides, you'll need to keep the fortifications intact as I'm sure once Kenrick realises what you've done, he'll send some reinforcements.'

'Aye, he will.'

'After that, head for Rona.' Robert looked up with a smile. 'Any questions?'

'I think that about covers it.'

'Good luck.'

Deverin grinned at Robert and McCauly, 'My lord, Father.' Then he turned deliberately to Andrew. 'Good luck, Your Grace.'

'Thank you,' Andrew replied in a surprisingly firm voice. 'And to you.'

His smile widening, Deverin made for his men, leaving a space Daniel immediately stepped into.

'What's he so happy about?'

'I think,' said McCauly with a straight face, 'that he's just been given what he's always wanted. That's bound to make a man smile.'

'Indeed,' Daniel laughed. 'Well, Robert, what do you want me and my motley crew to do?'

'Fiddech wool mills. Burn them to the ground.'

That wiped the smile from Daniel's face. He looked at Finnlay then replied, 'But that's going to bring that whole area to a—'

'Standstill, yes, I know. I want the entire country to come to a halt. I don't want a single penny more to make it into Kenrick's coffers, or to those merchants from Mayenne taking all our wealth and putting nothing in its place. It doesn't belong to any of them. I want Kenrick cut off at the knees.' Robert looked up with a smile, but there was a truly feral shadow to his eyes. 'Any questions?'

Daniel took a moment, then straightened. 'No. Consider it done.'

'Good luck.'

And then there was just Payne. Before Robert could continue, Micah appeared between them, with a tray of cups steaming and scented with fresh brew. They all helped themselves, and Robert, in between sips, outlined the last of his plans.

'Payne, you and your men will stay with me once I get back from this short side-trip.'

'How long will you be gone?'

'If we push it, about six hours' ride one way. We'll be there no more than a day, so we should return in two days.'

'Here?'

Robert paused, his gaze drifting over to where everyone was packing up and to where the first groups were actually leaving. 'No. We've left too much of a mark here already. If you follow the river east for a league or so, there's a bridge with a ford beside it. Cross and go south for two more leagues. There's a wood there mostly deserted these days. Used to be used for hunting, but its owner was exiled by Selar and he hasn't been back since. You should be safe there for the next two days.'

'And if we have to move? Or something happens to you?'

'Then go ahead with your mission regardless. We're running on a schedule with this.'

As though he could read Robert's mind, Payne began shaking his head. 'You're not serious. That's more heavily armed than Kenrick's bedchamber! How, in the name of Serin do you—'

'That's why we'll be using two groups.'

'That's still only twenty men—'

Robert looked up, pinning the Earl with a hard gaze. 'Kenrick's tax collectors will never get that gold to Marsay. He will need that money to pay for the army that will undoubtedly come after us. Don't worry about the ratio of men. You'll have both me and Finnlay on this one – and we're worth at least . . . oh, two men between us.'

'More like two and a half,' Finnlay added, following Robert's lead and injecting a little humour into the conversation.

Payne studied them both for a moment, then said, resigned, 'Very well, two days. Where will we ambush them?'

'On the road from Kilphedir, at dusk.'

Finnlay could see the grudging respect in Payne's eyes, mixed with a little surprise, as though he'd forgotten what it was like working with Robert.

The earl grunted, 'I'll get started. See you in two days.'

Already moving on, Robert turned away. 'Finn, I'll be taking you, the Bishop here, Patric, Joshi and Andrew to the Sanctuary. All the rest will go with Payne.'

Finnlay opened his mouth to ask about Micah, but he paused at the flicker in Robert's eyes. Perhaps this time it would be best left untouched. So be it. 'On my way. Andrew?'

Andrew hurried after Finnlay, trying not to trip over tree roots on his way. His head was so full of words and voices and looks and movement, it was hard to form words of his own, but he tried. 'Finnlay, the wood Payne and the others will be hiding in – who owns it?'

'Robert, of course.'

'And how many men guard the tax caravan?'

'Usually around fifty, sometimes more depending on the time of year. After harvest, it's closer to a hundred.'

'Fifty? How will they manage to ambush with only twenty men?'

'We, Andrew. We. And you don't think we have the skills to ambush a mere fifty men?'

He would have asked another question, but they'd arrived at Patric's area.

'Can you both be ready to leave in fifteen minutes?'

'Of course.'

Joshi was already turning to saddle their horses when Finnlay strode away, making Andrew rush to catch up with him again. 'Why are we going back to the Sanctuary?'

'Because Robert needs to talk to your mother about something, and they need to do some work on the Calyx.'

'Because of the Prophecy?'

'Yes. Go collect your bedding. I'll bring your horse over to mine and we'll be ready by the time Robert wants to move. You can saddle his as well.'

Andrew jumped over his dead log and reached inside for his bedding, but it caught on something, and as he pulled, he felt—

He paused, looking down to where his hand reached into the blackened bole. Only it wasn't black, it was glowing . . . glowing blue.

He snatched his hand away, hurriedly looking up at Finnlay to see if he'd noticed. Fortunately, he was packing up his own bedding and hadn't seen a thing.

What was happening? Why was the tree glowing? It had never glowed before, so why now?

Shifting so Finnlay couldn't see anything, he gingerly slipped his hand back in until he could touch his bedding. Nothing happened. He must have imagined it. Trees – especially dead ones – didn't just start glowing for no reason at all.

Sighing with relief, he grabbed his bedding and pulled again, but it snagged again and the harder he pulled, the more the tree glowed blue. He twisted and tugged, his heart pounding, until, with a mighty pull, the blanket broke free. Andrew fell back with a grunt, eyes on the tree trunk – but the glow had gone again.

He couldn't have imagined it a second time. And it was all perfectly normal now. But was it the tree – or *him*?

'What's wrong?'

Andrew flinched, springing to his feet. 'Nothing.'

'Good, then bring your saddle around here and get to work.'

By mid-afternoon, the light rain that had plagued them all day finally stopped, but was replaced by a wind which gusted and stopped, gusted and stopped. Finnlay found it irritating in the extreme, and the horses hated it. They rode hard, taking the long flat valleys and every bit of forest shelter they could find. As the day wore on, Finnlay could see McCauly tiring and called to Robert for a rest.

They didn't stop. Instead, Robert said a few words to the Bishop, who growled back, and Robert only laughed. Of course, Robert hadn't had any sleep either, and the wounds Micah had hinted at were telling in the way Robert sat on his horse, how little energy he used when he didn't need to.

He knew they were near by the way the trees were placed and he paid close attention so he would know it even better next time. And then, just on dark, they rode in single file up the narrow gully leading to the Sanctuary.

Martha was waiting for them with the door stone open. Without any fuss, they made their way inside to find some of the boys on hand to take care of the horses.

'You'll have to go through to the main cave. None of the others are big enough for all of you at once.' Martha smiled at all of them, adding, for Robert, 'Jenn's waiting for you.'

He strode past her, leaving Finnlay to follow with the others, answering questions as he went. By the time he got to the main cave, Jenn was at the door, a smile on her face.

'Patric?' she launched herself forward and wrapped her arms around him, kissing both his cheeks as they both laughed in genuine pleasure. 'None of us thought we'd ever see you again! When really, you were just off enjoying yourself in the sun, weren't you?'

'You guessed my secret.'

'And who's this?' Jenn let go of Patric to find Joshi kneeling at her feet. She looked up at Finnlay in enquiry, but it was Robert's growl from behind her that made her move. She bent down to take his elbow and make him stand, and together they straightened.

'That's Joshi,' Robert added flatly. 'He's from the Generet. Martha, could you help everyone get settled? We'll need a meal soon, and beds for tonight. We'll talk in the morning.'

'Everything's ready, Robert.'

As Martha began to usher the others away, McCauly reached Finnlay's side, his gaze raking over the inside of the cave, and the others, his expression one of sheer wonder.

'Was the Enclave like this?'

Finnlay grinned. 'Physically, no, nothing like it at all. But in reality, yes, exactly like it.'

'How so?'

Dropping his voice, he replied, 'The moment Robert arrives, he causes chaos. I'll see you at supper, Father. I'm going to go find my wife and daughters.'

The cool air of the caves made Jenn forget that it was spring, would soon be summer. She could almost hear the faint swish of people asleep, their heartbeats joining that of the mountain which shielded them.

This was nothing like the Enclave. Everything they did here was a struggle, every triumph came at a high price. This was not a place they could live in for too long, nor with too many people. As a safe haven for Robert, it could not have been better, but as a sanctuary for her and the Key and twenty others, it was too small, too dark and too dangerous.

But it would do them for the moment, until freedom came – in whatever guise.

She turned in her bed, closing her eyes again, though sleep refused to take her. *He* was back here again, and it was so very hard to pretend he wasn't, so hard to forget that every time she said goodbye to him could be the last, so hard to remember that the country needed him more than she did.

Breathing deeply, she let her Senses roam to find him, as they could with no other person. She was powerful in ways that others could never be, but with this simple trick, she was handicapped, except when it came to finding Robert.

But he was not in his bed asleep, as she'd thought. He'd curled up moments after supper and would not be disturbed, no matter the noise in the caves. But now he was up and moving, while everyone else was fast asleep.

With a smile, Jenn got out of bed and drew a robe over her nightdress. In bare feet, she padded out of her small cave, through another and past the alcove where Andrew was sleeping. Turning another narrow corner, she ducked under a low wall of rock and stepped into the main cave. Robert's bed was empty, but she knew where he was. Walking quickly but quietly, she stepped through to the water embrasure and behind the second wall to the passage leading to the green pool. The moment she moved around the wall, she could hear him, hear the water moving around him.

She kept her footsteps silent now, hoping to see him before he knew she was there. When she emerged, she paused by the wall, keeping perfectly still. Robert stood neck-deep in the water, the green glow lighting him softly, making the lines on his face disappear as he dipped his head back, closing his eyes. A moment later, he straightened up, his hair drenched, water cascading down his face, his chest and back into the pool.

He watched her with an unwary gaze, making her move. She slipped off her robe and stepped down into the water, finding places for her feet with great care. She kept going until the pool was too deep for her to walk and her nightdress billowed in the mild current, tangling in her legs.

He was there, his arms slipping around her, holding her steady, keeping her head high enough for her to breathe. His eyes rested on hers as easily, locking them together as though the whole world could not split them apart. It had always felt this way when they were together, invincible, one.

'I thought you'd gone to sleep,' he whispered. 'I thought I'd have this pool to myself.'

'Then I'll go,' she whispered in return. There was no privacy in these caves, even with the few doors they'd made. 'I'll leave you to your peace and quiet.'

'Yes, go,' he replied, his arm still like a vice around her. And then his mouth descended on hers and she lost all ability to think. When he let her breathe again, his hands roamed along her body, setting her alight, the fine cotton of her nightdress no hindrance to him.

'Where did these bruises come from?' she asked, fingering the few she could see purpling his chest. Gently, she kissed each one she found. 'Why can't they just leave you alone?'

He gave her half a smile as he ducked to kiss along her throat. 'Everybody wants me, I suppose.'

'Yes,' she moaned softly, 'everybody does.'

'Why is it that when I touch you now,' he whispered again, giving his hands free rein, 'there is no blue light? Does that mean we are no longer Bonded?'

'I have no idea,' she smiled against his chest, sliding her arms around him in the warm water, pressing her body up against his, knowing it would distract him even more.

'There was only that once,' and though she could hear the faint hesitation in his whisper, she couldn't address it, not tonight, 'and never again since. Perhaps that means that we *weren't* Bonded, or that we haven't yet, or—' He kissed her again, deeply, so she moved her hands in a way that would make him forget everything.

He moaned into her mouth and slipped her nightdress over her shoulders, drawing it away. The press of him against her then shut out all other thought.

The darkness gave away no sign of the fresh morning. Robert stood on the threshold of the cave and let out a low whistle. 'How did you find this?'

Jenn moved ahead of him, using her hand to steady the way down the rocky path. 'It was actually the girls who found it. Damaris and Helen were exploring without their parents' permission, as usual. Still, it's so far away from all the other caves that it seemed like the best place to put the Key. That way,' she paused, frowning into the darkness on her right before a lamp burst into life, 'if these caves are found, and he does have some way to find the Key, he can virtually reach it without killing everybody on the way.'

'Jenn,' Robert chided as he followed her into the huge cave, 'part of the reason they're all here is to protect the Key from Nash.'

'And they will – there's no way you can even get to this cave without going through the others we inhabit – it's just that, if there *is* a way, then—'

'Fine,' Robert sighed, looking up – and up. The left wall of the cave rose like a wave ready to crash on an unsuspecting shore, curving from the floor, out and up into darkness. The opposite side was equally smooth, the floor beyond the rocks was deep sand, grey and ashen in colour. The entire cave was almost as long as the great cavern at the Enclave. 'Did you knock the door in?'

'No, they found it that way.'

'And you've checked that there's no other way in here?'

She turned and faced him, hands on her hips, one side of her face in darkness, the other side lit by more than the lamp. He wanted to reach out, gather her up, find some corner in this mountain and hide there until Nash was consumed by his own evil.

'Are you feeling all right?' she asked, frowning suddenly.

'Of course. Why wouldn't I be?' He turned away then, clambering over the last of the rocks to land on the sand floor beside her. He made immediately for the box at the other end of the cave, deliberately not giving her the chance to read more into . . . whatever it was she was reading. There was so much he couldn't afford to tell her, so much she would know anyway, and even more he knew she could see, like the demon filling his belly. He knew what she was going to say, but he couldn't afford to listen to it. Not any more. 'Now, assuming Patric is right—'

'And you don't believe for one minute that he is.'

'But assuming he knows what he's talking about, Thraxis made this thing – the Calyx so that he could . . . what?'

'It's a library, Robert.' Jenn stood beside him looking down at the box and the object it contained. It sat neatly shelled in a willow-woven box, supported on a bed of hay so that it couldn't roll around. The Key was visible on top, the round surface of the orb still huge and commanding. At the bottom, seemingly moulded into the stone, were the gold arms, petals almost, of the Calyx. Fine silver decorated the edges and other small points. Patric had voiced his wish to see it, but Robert had immediately vetoed his suggestion to feel it instead.

'Where's the other orb?'

'In that corner, there. I wanted to keep them as far apart from each other as possible – since we don't know what would happen if they were put together.'

'Good thinking.'

'Thank you.'

'So you haven't touched this since I left?'

'Not touched, no. I have been down here, trying to get some sense out of the Key.'

'You're still joined to it?'

'Very much so.'

'How so?' Robert couldn't help asking, studying her profile as she kept her gaze on the Key.

'Robert, so far you're not a threat to it, so it doesn't mind us being together. But mar— what you want is completely different. It would mean,' she paused, pulling in a breath before turning to face him, 'that my—'

'That your loyalty would be entirely to me.' Even as he said the words, his heart sank. He turned to face the Key/Calyx and deliberately changed the subject. 'So how do you suggest we try activating the Calyx so that we don't alert Nash as to where we are?'

'Well, after talking to Patric and Joshi, I get the impression that we were right in the beginning. Both you and I are supposed to be touching it at the same time and that if we do, the writing becomes readable to both of us, and nobody else.'

'Suggesting that if Thraxis indeed made this, he did so to give us information – you and me in particular.'

'That's what I was thinking, yes.'

'And what happens if we fail?'

She looked up. 'In what way?'

'If the orb fails to mask the Key – what do we do if Nash comes after us again?'

Jenn didn't move for a moment, then she reached out and took his hand, holding it between her own. 'Then we stand and fight him. We're as ready as we can be.'

'Even not knowing the real Prophecy?'

She squeezed his hand. 'Robert, I know you don't want to hear this, but my life is nothing compared to what Nash is, what he has done, what he will do. You know this. Just because you love me, that doesn't change it. That's why we're locked into the Prophecy, why despite all the shifting landscapes over the last decades, we're still standing here, waiting for that last battle. Nothing will change it.' She brushed his cheek with her fingers, her voice softening. 'Not even you.'

His throat grew tight, and though he wanted to drown in the deep sea of her eyes, he pulled back and looked away. 'No. I'll find another way. I will. And if Patric thinks there's one here, then let's try to find it.'

She paused only a moment before turning back to the box. She reached out towards the Calyx. 'I think we need to make sure we don't touch the Key at all. I think it's highly likely that the reason everything fell apart last time was because the Key and Calyx were joining and you were trying to separate them.'

'You're probably right. Now, just to be on the safe side, we'll touch the Calyx only briefly once, first, just to test it. Agreed?'

'Agreed.'

Ignoring all the voices inside him, Robert put an arm around her waist and pulled her close, taking her right hand in his. Then, with their hands joined, he lowered them until they could just touch the Calyx.

Instantly the surface of the gold changed – then stopped the moment they withdrew. At an encouraging glance from Jenn, Robert put their hands down again and the surface shifted more, like oil moving over water. Colour swirled together, gliding up over the Calyx and onto the surface of the Key. It was like looking into a gilded mirror that never showed the same face twice.

'It's beautiful,' Jenn whispered. 'Nothing terrible is happening, is it?'

'No, not so far.' Robert didn't dare extend his Senses beyond the entrance to the cave. He'd left Finnlay, Arlie, Martha and Fiona out there, ready if there should be any mishap, out of the way in case of a backlash. They knew too little about this to be frivolous with safety a second time.

'So, what do we do now?'

'What do you usually do when you talk to the Key?'

'I think a question towards it.'

'And it answers?'

'If it feels like it.'

'And thinking a question, is that like mindspeaking?'

'Not really.'

'Then ask a question.'

'Which one?'

Robert laughed a little, knowing they were both avoiding the moment. 'Ask it what it is.'

'Why me?'

'Because you're joined to the Key.'

'Oh. All right.' She closed her eyes and he could instantly hear her voice, as though she were speaking from inside his head. To him, this sounded like mindspeaking – but then, when he did it, he thought of her to make the connection, and the Key wasn't a person. Perhaps that was what was different.

What are you?

There was no answer, but the swirling surface on the Key changed colours, growing darker, developing more depth.

What are you?

Robert kept his eyes open, his instincts trained on the Key in particular. Jenn was joined to it, a part of it in every sense of the word except the physical. It needed her to survive, and probably did so even now that it was joined to the Calyx. But that didn't mean he trusted it. Why should he? It had brought him nothing but grief his whole life, and now even prevented him from marrying the woman he loved, for whatever time they had left together.

Can you answer any questions?

And yet, there had been married Jaibirs before now. Fiona's father, Marcus, had been married to Ayn without difficulty. Jaibirs, male and female throughout the history of the Enclave, had enjoyed long married lives without it once interfering with the joining to the Key. So why was it a problem now? Was it because the Key hated him as much as he hated it? Was it just being vindictive? Or was it because of the Prophecy? Although the damned Prophecy *had* said he must not leave her alone, and that would suggest to him that marrying her was a damned fine way of making sure she was never alone – but that didn't seem to affect the way the Key looked at it. No, it wanted Jenn's sole loyalty no matter what.

Why – what difference would it make? If they were all supposed to be on the same side, then why would it matter if she shifted the bulk of her loyalty to her own husband? The black pit of hatred in his belly rose up, choking him, forcing him to gasp air to get it back down again, before it could drown him as it had almost done with Micah.

No, not yet. Not yet, but soon, so soon.

He held his breath, using the stillness to fill him, to control him, to let him see the truth.

Jenn wasn't moving. Nor was she speaking. He turned to find she wasn't even breathing – and in that moment, she sagged against him, her eyes rolling into her head.

Jenny!

26

The noise drummed through him, scraping skin from his fingers, burning him in the fiery darkness. He could see his mother, her pale face, her dark hair streaming down her back, eyes puffy with bruises, blood on her hands, her face, holding herself, while above her the black waves of smoke rolled heavenwards.

He called out to her, but she couldn't reach him. He ran towards her, but he was small and didn't have the strength. He was afraid for her, but couldn't say that, didn't dare even show himself.

She was dying and he was frozen with fear. He could see her fading in front of him, until no more than her bright blue eyes rimmed red with sadness remained. There was so much sadness he couldn't look any more.

The stone was hard against his face, but he turned away, shaking.

Andrew woke with another headache, this one worse than yesterday's. And instead of getting up this time, he just rolled over, wrapped his arms over his head and wished it would go away. But he wasn't allowed any peace; instead, he had to listen to Joey, Guy, Edain and Braden getting out of bed, talking to each other, laughing and joking and getting on with the day like it was any other.

He really wanted to yell at them to be quiet, but the thought of the questions such behaviour would raise almost made his headache throb harder, so he kept his silence, stuck his fingers in his ears and waited until they were dressed and gone.

It was his own fault. He shouldn't have sat in the shadows last night, listening to Finnlay, Fiona, the Bishop and Patric talking. And Lady Margaret had been there too, listening, occasionally murmuring agreement, but saying little, and he'd had the distinct impression she'd known he was there – but she'd kept her silence, and he'd kept listening, learning all sorts of things he didn't want to know about.

They'd been talking about the Troubles, more than thirty years ago, how Robert and Finnlay's father, Earl Trevor, had worked to bring peace to the warring Houses, and how only Selar's invasion had really brought an end to the bloodshed – by killing most of those involved. And then they'd gone on to talk about Selar's invasion, and the stories of courage they'd witnessed, or heard about, touching only briefly on the death of Lady Margaret's husband. Even then, he'd heard the still-raw sorrow in her voice as she remembered him.

There'd been more, bringing to life real experiences, things he'd only ever read about from books. He shouldn't have been listening, but the Bishop had told him to learn what he could, to use what others had learned before him to explore his own skills.

He just hadn't realised it would give him a headache like this. And then, of course, his stomach chose that moment to growl. By the gods! Was he to be tortured on every level?

A laugh escaped him. How, in the name of the gods, could he think *this* was torture? After what Robert had obviously just gone through with the Malachi, and before that, with the Key? How could Andrew lie in bed moaning about a little pain in his head when Robert was probably already up and moving around, doing whatever work he needed to do with the Key, before they launched off again into the rebellion.

He opened his eyes and stared up at the low roof of the cave above. That speech yesterday, the way Robert had given out orders, the way he'd moved, and spoken, looked at everybody—

It was just horrifying. There was no way, no matter how many years he practised, that he would ever be able to lead anybody like that – and if he couldn't, how was he ever to be a good King?

No, the best way around this was for Robert to take the crown. Somehow or other Andrew would make sure it happened that way, no matter what.

His headache seemed to have subsided a little, so he tested it out by sitting up. It gave one vicious throb and then vanished, leaving him able to get up without any further trouble. One of the others had lit a lamp and he used this to find his clothes, pulling on his boots before brushing his hair. He probably should be getting it cut, but if he let it grow longer, it would be more like Robert's.

Dressed, he turned back and tidied his bedding. With his stomach growling even louder now, he headed for the doorway – but the cave was suddenly plunged into darkness.

He froze, listening hard, but there was nothing there now that hadn't been there before. He could hear the faint noise of other voices echoing around the Sanctuary, the rustle of horses not far away and, if he really tried, the trickle of water from the pool cave – but that was all: no exceptional wind, no physical reason for the lamp to suddenly go out – unless it had simply run out of oil.

Breathing a sigh of relief, he turned back and with his hand on the wall, carefully retraced his steps so he could collect the lamp and refill it. But the moment he drew level with it, it sprang back into life.

He jumped back, letting out a yelp. His heart pounding hard, he stared at the flame, but it barely flickered. It simply stood there, on the small rock shelf he'd chipped out himself for that exact purpose. The glass bowl around the frame let out the light without impediment and nothing looked even remotely strange.

'I'm going crazy,' he murmured to himself. 'Blue glows, lamps going on and off.'

Carefully, he stepped back, keeping his eyes on the lamp. One step towards the door, then another, and on the third, the lamp died again. Holding his breath, he shifted his weight onto his back foot and, miracle of miracles, the lamp sprang back into life. He tested it once more and on the third success, he simply kept going out of the cave.

He didn't want to think about this. Ever.

'Arlie! Quickly!' Robert picked up Jenn in both arms and carried her to the other end of the cave, as far from the Key as possible. By the time he set her down, Arlie and Martha had rushed inside, the Healer immediately kneeling beside Jenn, one hand going to her throat.

'She's not breathing,' Robert groaned, not letting go of her. 'It's the Key. It's done something to her, I know it. It's my fault, I shouldn't have agreed to this. If she—'

He didn't keep going. His curses and promises would mean nothing if Jenn never breathed again. But he did know it was the Key, he could feel it under his skin, as though it was laughing at him, taunting him like this, knowing how precious she was to him, but reminding him that ultimately she would die by his hand.

'Robert, can you mindspeak her?'

Serin's blood, he hadn't even tried that! *Jenny? Jenny, answer me! Please, breathe. That's all you have to do, just breathe. Please, Jenn, just breathe for me.*

'Robert, look!'

He opened his eyes and felt her shudder at the same time. He held her tighter as Arlie continued to check on her.

'I can't see anything wrong exactly, but she's breathing without difficulty now. What were you doing?'

'We were touching the Calyx, and she was asking it a question, that's all. Nothing more dangerous than that, and this is what happens.' Bile made him swallow hard, but he kept his attention on Jenn, watching her breathing, her fluttering eyelids, until the moment they finally opened.

He'd been thinking about marrying her, and how the Key was deliberately trying to keep them apart. How was this for proof? The Key didn't want her dead – at least, not yet. It just wanted him to remember how powerless he was to stop what he was fated to do.

Damn it! How, in the name of Serin, could the Key have this kind of determination when it *postdated* the Prophecy? Why was it so necessary that he destroy Jenn in order to kill Nash? Why was she a part of this in the first place? And why, after all these years, was he no closer to answering that question?

'Arlie?' Jenn murmured, opening her eyes.

'Just keep still,' Arlie replied. 'You're fine, nothing wrong with you, but you stopped breathing for a moment and I just want to be sure there's no damage.'

'Can you See anything?' Martha asked, holding Jenn's other hand.

Her husband shook his head. 'No, nothing in particular. I think she'll be fine.'

After another few minutes, Arlie let Jenn first sit, then stand up. Only then did she turn to look at Robert. She appeared unharmed despite her collapse.

With the colour already back in her cheeks, he asked, 'Do you know what happened?'

She shrugged. 'I suppose I asked the wrong question. It wouldn't be the first time.'

'Perhaps, but it will be the last.'

'Oh, Robert, whatever it did, it wasn't deliberate.'

'No? I suppose destroying the Enclave's protection wasn't deliberate either. I tell you Jenn, it was *very* deliberate, and for a reason. It doesn't want us asking questions. It just wants us to follow the Prophecy. If we try to deviate from it, it will make you pay and, in turn, me. So yes, this is the last time. Until this is over, neither you nor I will go anywhere near the Calyx. This is all the Key's doing and if you still can't see that, then you're blind.'

'But, Robert—'

'No!' His shout reverberated around the cave, silencing everyone. Instantly, he felt their eyes on him, knew their shocked expressions without looking. Robert never got angry, never lost his temper, never showed *anything* that wasn't carefully controlled. But that was before he'd seen the truth; now he just didn't give a damn.

'I mean it, Jenn,' he added, his voice hard and uncompromising. 'Talk to the Key if you must – and only if you must – but stay away from the Calyx.'

With that, he turned and leaped up the slope to the entrance, leaving before he could say anything else, before he could let anything else loose, before she could see the thing she wasn't supposed to know about.

But it hurt, walking away from her like that. It hurt a lot.

Jenn watched Robert go, tempted only for a moment to follow him. She felt fine, but the moment she went to move, a wave of dizziness washed over her, and Martha immediately reached out a hand in support.

'What happened to him?' she murmured. 'Finn? He was fine when he left here two weeks ago. What happened? Did you find Micah?'

She turned to look at him, but he said only, 'All I know is that Micah has somehow become involved with Malachi. Robert went to help, thinking Micah was in trouble, and Robert was captured and tortured. I don't know what they did to him, or how he got free. But Micah is with the rest of the men. I know Robert didn't want to bring him here.'

Tortured. She'd seen the bruises, hadn't she? And he'd told her nothing, as usual. Even now, with them as close as they were, there were still huge walls separating them. He would trust her with some things, not with others. And she, damn it, she was no better!

But the demon was there again, inside him, growing every day as though it was trying to make up for lost time, as though it had double the power over him, as though he *wanted*—

She pulled in a breath and straightened; she felt better now, at least after her collapse. Now she felt well enough to find a nice hard cave wall to bash her head against.

'Did he say when you'd be leaving?'

Finnlay replied, already heading for the corridor, 'At a guess, I'd say we're probably leaving now.' He shrugged and disappeared, leaving her to the scrutiny of Arlie and Martha.

'Are you sure you feel all right now?'

'Yes, thank you. There's nothing wrong with me?'

'I didn't say that.' Arlie half-smiled. 'No. Whatever happened didn't actually do you any damage.'

'Good, then there's no reason I can't go with them, is there?'

Martha let out a loud chuckle. 'You mean, other than Robert refusing to let you?'

Jenn headed for the entrance. 'It won't be the first time he's tried to stop me from doing something.'

'And it won't be the last,' Martha finished for her, the words fading quickly as Jenn almost ran down to her room. If she didn't move fast, Robert would leave without her, and this time, she wasn't going to be left behind to worry. She could do that and be with him at the same time.

Much more efficient.

Finnlay paused one last time to look around the small cave he shared with Fiona. It didn't look like he'd left anything important behind, but that didn't stop the feeling that he had. Even so, he finished tying the laces on his saddle-bag, drawing them tight, making sure the few things he did take wouldn't fall out, knowing in the back of his mind that he was also drawing the moment out, reluctant to leave. He was indeed leaving something behind.

He turned to find her watching him. He said nothing.

'This is the last time, isn't it?' Fiona murmured. 'Robert will kill the beast who murdered my mother, and you won't go traipsing off after him any more. Will you?'

'Yes, it's the last time.'

'And then you'll come home, won't you? Come home and—'

He could feel her throat tightening as she tried to find the words and he knew he couldn't address the fear inside her. She'd always known this would happen one day – hadn't there already been so many of these days? But this time it was the last time, and if he returned safely, she would never have to feel like this again.

'I'll come home,' he whispered. 'No matter what happens, I'll come back.'

She nodded then, looking around, as though she'd forgotten something as well. He knew her too well to ignore such a sign. With a sigh, he stepped forward and wrapped his arms around her, enjoying the comfort of her, the absolute knowledge that she loved him. When she lifted her head, her eyes were closed and she kissed him hard. Then she stepped back, as though holding on longer would diminish his chances of returning alive.

'The girls are waiting with the horses. Helen is very upset that Andrew is going with you but she can't. Whatever you do, don't tell her she's too young. You know how attached she is to that boy.'

Finnlay took her hand, kissed her palm, grabbed his bag and left, feeling the weight of the caves pressing down on him. He barely saw where he was going when he reached the horses. His eyes would only find his girls, Helen, Bronwyn and Anna. He held each one, kissed each one and lingered with Helen, even though he knew he shouldn't. He wanted to whisper to her that he would make sure Kenrick would never live to threaten anyone again, but the promise died on his lips against the sight of her tears. Turning away from her was almost impossible. But she knew better. She stepped back, wiped her eyes with her sleeve and handed him his reins with a smile.

'Make Andrew King, Papa.'

He had no choice then but to smile back at her, and at his younger daughters. Then he took his reins and led the horse away towards the cave entrance, completely in awe of his family's courage. It was a fine gift to take with him.

'No.'

Jenn sat upon her horse, deliberately looking up at the sky to see what the weather might do. Robert mounted his in front of her, drawing up beside her, leaning over, making sure she heard him the second time. He kept his voice low, so it wouldn't look to the others like they were having the argument they were having.

'No. You are not coming with us.'

By the look of it, there could be rain that night, but for the moment, it was clear, if a little chilly. It was a good thing she'd brought a warmer jacket.

'Andrew, would you mind taking the others down the gully? I'll catch up with you shortly.'

As Jenn kicked her horse to follow them, Robert reached out and grabbed her bridle, holding her horse in place and his words in check until the last sign of them had disappeared down the hill.

'What are you doing?' His tone was light, a little mystified, more than a little determined. 'At what point do you finally accept that you could lose your life if you don't stay put? I don't want you with us. I can't concentrate on watching out for you and keep everything else—'

'You're assuming I want you to watch out for me.'

'Oh, by the gods,' Robert groaned, releasing the bridle. His horse stamped as though in sympathy. 'What do I have to do, Jenn? How can I keep you safe?'

She met his gaze squarely. 'That's simple. You can't. What's more, you never should have tried. Robert, what do *I* have to do, what do I have to say to make you understand – *I have a part in this, too*! I have a say in what happens. I'm mentioned more times in the Prophecy than you. I have a role to play, and I can't do it hiding in some cave waiting for it all to be over. I can't do that to myself, and I certainly can't do that to you! You think it's fun sitting in there, worrying about you? Worrying about my son? You think that's what the Prophecy meant when it said not to leave me alone? Well, I think it means you're supposed to keep me with you and, by the gods, Robert, you *will* keep me with you! I'm not going to let you shut me out any more!' Jenn gulped in a breath, startled to find tears stinging her eyes.

Robert saw them too, but it didn't soften his expression, at least, not immediately. When the silence drew out, he dropped his gaze to his gloves, and he sighed once. 'You were well chosen, that much is sure.'

'Oh? And what does that mean?' Jenn growled back, not sure if she'd won or not. But when he looked up, her victory was written in his eyes, in pleasure and sadness in equal measure.

'It means that you are a very formidable Ally.' With that, he reached out, took her hand and kissed the back of it. 'Come on, let's get moving. We have a tax collector to meet.'

'They're late.'

'It doesn't matter. How many carts?'

'Just two.'

'And men?'

'Mounted, forty. There are another six for each cart, three at the front, three behind. Draft horses pulling both carts, teams of four each. All look fairly young and strong. They're also fresh, so we can push them hard for a day at least.'

'We won't need anywhere near that long.' Robert looked up at the sky, breathing deeply, but there was no scent of moisture in the air. 'It will be a clear sunset, but as they're running late, it will be dark before they reach us here. So we'll have to make a few alterations.'

He stepped back, gesturing for the others to make some room. He knelt down and, with the tip of his dagger, drew the road in the dirt, the side of the hill it was wrapped around, the house-sized rock and the two ancient oaks. 'Payne, you and your men will wait here, just around this corner. There's plenty of cover, and the moment you see the vanguard turn here, I want you to attack. This will panic the men behind, forcing them back. At that point in the road, there's very little room for them to manoeuvre. We'll have archers ready, but it will still be a hand-fight. Just keep a watch out and make sure those horses don't bolt and take the carts over the side of the hill. I don't want to be cleaning up the mess.'

He looked up, finding their eyes on him: Finnlay, Andrew, Payne, his lieutenant, Micah, Joshi, McCauly and Jenn. He straightened up, putting his dagger away. 'Jenn, Patric, the Bishop and Father John will remain on the hilltop as lookouts and will not fight.' He deliberately didn't pause but continued on, ensuring she couldn't argue, at least, not in front of everybody, 'Micah, you stay with Payne's group. I'll keep Andrew with me. Everyone is to stay well back from the road until we receive the signal that the advance riders have passed. Only then do you take up your positions. Any questions?'

A few looked once more at his map, but everybody shook their heads.

'Good, go make yourselves comfortable. I estimate we have about an hour.'

Without hesitation, they all turned and made for their respective positions; even Jenn left with McCauly, tucking her hand in his elbow and chatting to him, making him laugh.

Then Robert was left alone with Andrew, standing a few feet from the side of the road, where a long line of twisted elms sheltered both sides of the hill. 'Come on,' he said and, with a touch to the boy's shoulder, he headed across the road, into the thicket on the uphill side. He chose his spot carefully, where bushes hid their bodies, but where he could clearly see the road about half a league back. He made himself comfortable, looked over once at Andrew then turned his gaze on the road and kept it there.

'Are you comfortable?' he asked eventually, quietly, no wish to alert the others in hiding that he was having this conversation with their future King. Unfortunately, he'd not had the time with Andrew that he'd planned. How was the boy going to react to the fighting? He'd done well at Maitland, during the Malachi attack, but that hadn't been anywhere near as chaotic as this was going to be. And chances were, at some point today, Andrew was going to have to kill for the first time, whether he wanted to or not.

'Yes,' was Andrew's only reply, his voice soft in the late afternoon.

'You understand what you have to do?'

'Yes.'

Robert raised his eyebrows, but didn't move his eyes from the road. 'Do you understand why?'

There was a pause before he got an answer: 'Do I need to?'

For a moment, Robert struggled with disbelief that he could ask such a question, but seconds later, he knew he was being tested – and that knowledge calmed him instantly. 'Say I get killed in this battle. You will look on these minutes as being your last chance to learn what you can from me. Are you going to waste it so frivolously?'

'You won't d-d-die,' Andrew replied with half-hearted scorn.

Robert didn't say anything else then, leaving the boy to think all on his own; he would have no choice in the silence. There was still so much to be done with him, so much he had to learn, so many things Robert needed to open up. There was still no sign of his powers, and it was getting perilously late. Though the Bishop had mentioned Andrew's ability to tell truth from lie, and Finnlay's story about the blue glow were encouraging, it was all very little. He didn't dare say anything to Andrew about it, but the chances were, there would be a clash with Kenrick's soldiers – and possibly the King himself – in no more than a month. Once Kenrick began to feel the effects of Robert's rebels, retaliation would be only a heartbeat away.

Noticeably, Andrew hadn't seen that for himself.

He'd had great hopes of spending months with the boy, of being able to take his time and teach the way he needed to – but there was Tirone's threat looming above them all; if Tirone didn't think he was doing enough to stop Kenrick, then they would all have to deal with another invasion from Mayenne – and that would be the end of the rebellion and any hopes Robert would ever have of freeing Lusara.

'If Kenrick loses this gold, his ability to build a sufficiently dangerous army to fight us is limited.' Andrew's voice never rose above a whisper, but Robert listened carefully. 'Without this gold, he won't be able to afford to bring in mercenaries, and will have to rely more on drawing soldiers from his vassals, most of whom will be untrained and unprepared to fight a war in the middle of spring, without any warning. Drawing soldiers from the land will be difficult in the extreme, as most men will be heavily involved in spring planting, and unable to comply. On top of that, most men won't want to fight, and with so many over the border, in exile, Kenrick will find it more and more difficult to bring an armed response against us. His actions, therefore, will be limited, and instead, he will fortify existing strongholds, and reinforce areas he considers to be our most likely targets.'

Andrew paused then, as though he wasn't sure whether to continue.

'And?'

'We should then deliberately shift our attack away from such targets and instead, focus on those goals he has taken resources away from. This will—'

'Go on.'

'This will draw him out, stretching his men further from their strong-holds, leaving them open to attack. Fighting in such a manner means we in turn have no need for one large army which is difficult to maintain and feed, not to mention hide, but instead, we can work in small groups which are easy to hide and can move much more quickly. For larger missions, two or more groups can join up, and then split afterwards. Depending on how effective the soldiers are, a war fought in such a manner can last a fraction of time compared to a traditional war. Or—'

'Or?' Robert did his best to hide his smile of triumph.

'Or it could last ten times longer.'

With his Senses telling him nothing of the approaching caravan, Robert risked a look down at the boy. He sat there with his legs up, his arms wrapped around them, his chin resting on his knees. He looked up when Robert met his gaze. 'The Bishop told me to listen and learn.'

'And where did you hear all that?'

'I didn't really. But—'

Robert turned back to the road. 'Don't apologise. You have read the situation very well. You'll make an excellent strategist one day.' He could almost hear the boy's pleased smile, but he said nothing else.

The analysis had indeed been impressive considering how he'd been thrown into all this – but his manner was still so tentative, as though he constantly needed to apologise for being there. Aiden had said he'd seen metal in the boy, but Robert had found precious little evidence so far. And he needed to have such metal if he was to survive the next few weeks – or indeed, the next few hours. Serin's teeth, Andrew was Jenn's son! Surely he'd inherited her steely determination. How could he have missed out on that?

And they needed to find out what the hell was going on with his powers! Without them, Kenrick was going to flay him alive.

Robert's breath caught as the demon rose snapping and hissing inside him. He swallowed hard, forcing it down. Now was not the time, not yet. But it was definitely time to push Andrew a little and see how far they got.

'You stay right by my side no matter what.' He changed the subject, his tone remaining level. 'If something happens to me, find Finnlay and stick with him. Failing that, you go to your mother. She'll protect you against the gods themselves.'

And he said nothing after that; there was more than enough to rattle around in the boy's head.

Andrew closed his eyes, but even then he could see the afternoon turn into evening, feel the change of warmth to coolness, the sounds shift into night. If only time would stand still. If only he could make everything stop long enough to think about all this.

But Robert's presence at his side was like a wall of rock, impenetrable, immobile, dark and determined. He couldn't escape it. To be honest, he wasn't sure he wanted to escape. He wanted—

He heard it before the first signal, before even Robert stiffened on his seat. Some faint shift in the balance of rural noises, the thud of one heavy hoof after another onto a hard-packed road. Before he could even move, the signal came and Robert shifted, inching forward on the balls of his feet, his momentum taking Andrew with him.

Andrew felt ill. His stomach tumbled and turned, grumbled and groaned, leaving him giddy and unwilling to move. But even as the vanguard trotted down the road towards the ambush, even as he almost felt those around him ready to attack, even though he knew, as a loyal citizen, that he should give these soldiers the alarm, warn them they were about to be attacked, he knew he would never do it, and in fact, as Robert rose and the first cry of attack filled the night, he went with them, his sword high, his feet running downhill, taking him to the first man, pulling him from his horse, fighting him.

Breathless, he swung, deafened by the cries, shouts, orders, panic all around. He twisted his ankle on something, but kept his balance, ducked a wildly flung sword aimed for his head, heard Robert call out some order to someone, smelled the blood and fear, and turned again to face the man before him who was determined to kill him for what he was doing.

And it was Robert and his sword practice, the same rhythm, the same shifts in balance, the same thudding of steel against steel, and the face he couldn't see because it was too dark, and the man before him stumbled back and Andrew's sword pierced his side, but he couldn't stop because they were outnumbered two to one and he had to get rid of his share or he wouldn't be able to look anyone in the eye, so he turned for the next one, jumping over the first, meeting this man's blade before it could be raised, and the hilt in his hand began to grow hot, making him feel every single blow, every crease in his palm, every notch in the handle. He took a double grip as the man before him began to call him names, but it was a language he couldn't understand, this language of hate, so he just went on, swinging and fighting and fighting and feeling the sword get hotter and hotter and hotter until—

He stopped, his blade buried to the hilt in the man's gut, his hands still holding it, withdrawing it, burning him until he dropped the sword in horror.

'Andrew, look out!'

27

Robert ran, the demon flowing through him with vengeance. With one shoulder, he pushed Andrew back out of the way, with the other, he swung hard, cutting the soldier down with one stroke. With a single fluid movement, he spun, swooped to grab Andrew's sword and tossed it to him, meeting the blow of the next attacker at the same time, his blade glowing with a power he struggled to contain. This man was too big to stop his momentum, meeting Robert's sword before he could swing his own again, flames flaring across his body. With a gasp, Robert pushed, crushing the demon, forcing it to obey, forcing it back to where it couldn't do Andrew any harm. The soldier fell, dead, leaving Robert breathless, turning to Andrew, saying, 'What's wrong with you?'

For a second, he thought the boy had frozen, but then he dived back in the fight. Robert had no more time for him then, other than keeping him close to the left wherever he moved.

And the fight went on, horses and men and blood and anger pouring over him like a balm to his demon, easing it, feeding it, living off it. So vicious, so cruel, so very, very black. And how the demon loved it all.

He heard a voice calling, and as the man before him fell, he paused long enough to look up. Here and there were pockets of resistance, but for the most part, the road was clear of soldiers and full of bodies. It was Payne calling him, somebody else passing on the word. The carts were secure and it seemed nobody had escaped.

The demon inside him crowed, but he resisted the urge to laugh out loud. Somehow he knew Jenn would hear it.

He moved forward, ready to begin the clean-up, and found Andrew standing at the edge of the road, looking back towards Kilphedir, wearing a frown, spatters of blood on his face, his hands, his clothes. Then he looked down at his hands, wiped them on his jacket and looked again, as though he were expecting to see something else there.

'Andrew, come here.'

The boy started, as though surprised to see Robert. Then he came to himself and moved, stepping over bodies the way he'd moved uncaring around beggars on the road – and suddenly it struck Robert what it was he was seeing, and the realisation sent an icy grip of fear clutching at his stomach.

No, not this boy, too. Not when he had to be King.

Never. He would not allow it, and tomorrow, he would begin to take steps to make sure it stopped here and now.

'You did well,' he said, in a voice too wooden for his liking. 'Go find Finnlay and Micah and we'll get this mess cleaned up.'

Finnlay took one last look around the hayloft, content that everyone was either asleep, or at least, close, then climbed down the ladder to the stable. The farmer had turned out all his animals into fields nearby, leaving the building for the rebels, giving them fresh straw to sleep on. It was probably the most comfortable bed they would enjoy for a while.

It was a big barn, holding twenty horses down one end, leaving the other end to sleep a few more weary fighters. Payne's men had taken the stolen gold to Casterlane, where Owen was hiding a barge to ship it south. Where it would be hidden after that, Finnlay didn't know. He just knew his body was aching, exhausted, and needed to get horizontal as quickly as possible.

He paused at the door and glanced outside to where the fire was no more than a handful of glowing coals. Robert sat there, staring into them, his eyes reflecting red. Opposite him was McCauly, frowning down at a notebook he was trying to read. After a moment, he gave up, got to his feet and said something to Robert. Robert looked up, nodded and smiled, and let the Bishop go to his bed.

Finnlay turned and made for his own, close by the door, the first line of defence should they be attacked. The straw was sweet and fresh, soft enough to make him sink down into it. He wrapped his blanket about him, rolled onto his side and let out a long, deep breath.

'Finn?'

The whisper was timid, almost inaudible, but it came from Andrew lying close beside him. 'Yes?'

'Is everybody all right?'

'I think so. Why?'

'Just wondering.' A pause, then, 'What about Robert?'

'He's sitting by the fire.' Finnlay kept his whisper as quiet as possible – there were tired men here who needed their rest before their next mission. 'He'll be in shortly.'

'Good.'

'Goodnight, then.'

'Goodnight, Finnlay.'

He closed his eyes a moment, then opened them again. 'Are you all right?'

'Of course,' Andrew replied, a little too quickly.

'Well, if you're not, you just say so.'

'I will. Goodnight.'

'Goodnight.' Finnlay readjusted his blankets again, closed his eyes and let his mind wander.

But try as he might, sleep would not visit him so quickly. How could it? Today had seen, after so many years, the first strike in the rebellion. For the first time in his life, Finnlay was at last fighting the war his heart had longed for since the day his father had died and Selar had claimed the crown. How could mere sleep compare to that?

The smoke was choking him, tasting hard and sharp and revolting. But he had to keep breathing it. The flames grew as tall as the sky, brilliant, orange, yellow, violent and deafening. He was burning up, attacked from all sides. But at least this time she was out of it. His mother stood apart from the flames, wounded, pale, hurting, eyes wide with fear, but she was alive and not dying. But this time, he was. On top of the tower, black smoke and blood, flames driving him up, flames inside him, burning his soul, leaving a blackened husk. Below a sheer drop, and he would fall, would fall to his death if she moved, if she stopped watching.

Aiden collected his small bag and picked a path through the bracken down towards the stream. He had no idea how far it was, but since he could hear it, he couldn't be breaking Robert's rules about going too far when they stopped to rest.

The ground became rocky beneath his feet, so he slowed down, turned around a big tree – and came up against the edge of the stream. Fresh sparkling water made him thirsty and he dropped his bag, knelt down, dipped his hands in the water and took a long, deep drink.

It was bitingly cold, but wonderfully refreshing. Quickly, before Robert could call everyone back, he dipped his hands in the water again and splashed it over his face, again and over his hair, rubbing in his ears, along his forearms, around his neck. It was almost as good as taking a bath.

Done with his quick wash, he rummaged through his bag for a towel and was rubbing it over his hair when he realised he wasn't alone. Micah Maclean knelt a dozen feet away, doing much the same as he was.

Micah looked up, gave him a quiet smile and said, 'You have to take your chances where you can.'

'That much is true. Does Robert have something against washing?'

'He never used to,' Micah replied, the smile vanishing as he got to his feet. He dried his face and hands and did up the buttons to his jacket. 'I'm surprised he hasn't insisted you go back to Bleakstone. How did you change his mind?'

Aiden said, 'I didn't.' And he hadn't. In fact, Robert hadn't said a word to him about how he shouldn't be there, which was completely unlike him. Why? He certainly had enough to say about Andrew's safety, and Jenn's, and he'd been particularly specific about Patric remaining with them until he'd seen Joshi with a sword. But this time, for some reason, Robert had made no point of telling Aiden it was time to go home.

'Ready?'

Aiden followed behind the younger man, seeing determination and not a little sorrow in the set of his shoulders. He hated seeing Micah like this, and could remember the friendship he'd had with Robert only too well – but he knew both men enough to know neither he nor anyone else could mend the rift between them. Only they could heal what they'd broken.

'How long do we ride today?' Aiden asked, more for conversation than anything else. Robert had forbidden idle chatter while they were travelling, in case somebody should hear them as they rode by. 'Where is the next destination?'

'We'll ride all day today, then another hour or so tomorrow. Tomorrow we hit the silver mine at Tereg Targgam. After that? Well, we hope we don't get caught.'

'Or killed,' Aiden added with a laugh. They'd arrived at the clearing as everybody was mounting up. Though he felt Robert's eyes on him, he studiously didn't look back. He simply put the bag on the horse, untethered the reins and hauled himself into the saddle.

One thing was certain: when he'd taken his final vows so many years ago, and pledged himself to be a priest, he'd had no idea that plying his devotion would require him to ride so many leagues behind a rebel who questioned everybody's motives but his own.

'When you hear that bell, you retreat. Don't stop to look back, just get out of there and get to the meeting point by whatever route you can. If you don't, you'll likely be trapped in the mine and nobody will be stopping to get you out.'

Aiden copied the map Robert had drawn into his notebook and spoke without looking up, 'But how are you going to get in?'

'Andrew and I will take care of that. Once the gate is open, you all know what to do.'

Robert paused but it was actually Jenn who asked the next question. 'What will they have in the way of guards?'

'Well,' Robert looked down at his dirt map. 'I haven't been there for more than a year, and then there was a garrison of fifty Guilde soldiers. It's possible there could be more now.'

'A garrison?' came one voice.

'Fifty Guildesmen?' came another.

'But I wouldn't worry too much about that,' Robert said, and Aiden could see how his confidence soaked into everyone else. 'We'll have some help from the villagers. Just remember, we're not there to wipe out the Guilde presence, just to close down the mine. If you have any questions, we'll cover them over breakfast. Goodnight, all.'

As the group began to break up, Aiden collected his notebook and headed for his bed. He'd chosen a good spot, between two raised roots of some kind of fir tree. The ground was covered in thick needles and the scent of the place was wonderful. Of course, the ground was still hard and his hips always hurt by morning, but what more could he expect at his age? Most men of sixty-two were crippled or bed-ridden. He still had excellent health, so he had no convenient excuse.

He put his book away, shook out his blanket and sat, ready to remove his boots. He knew he shouldn't, that if they needed to run during the night, then he'd likely have to do it barefoot, but he simply couldn't wear his boots all day and then all night, not even to save his feet in an emergency.

He paused when he heard a brush of cloth, the tell-tale snapping of a twig. Without looking up, he said, 'I had a feeling I was being stalked.'

Robert's voice emerged from the darkness. 'Then you should have challenged me.'

'What? Only to have you laugh in my face? I think not.'

But Robert's chuckle reached him anyway. It grew closer and then the face itself appeared as Robert stepped over one of the raised roots and sat down on it. 'You've found yourself a nice spot here. Much more comfortable than my lumpy bed.'

'Well, I'm not swapping. Move your feet before you get my blanket muddy.'

'Are you always this grumpy in the evenings, or is it a show just to impress me?'

'Don't you have a rebellion to fight? Surely you have more important things to do than harass an innocent priest.'

Robert snorted in laughter, then held up his hands, his expression – what Aiden could see of it – open and equally innocent.

Aiden sat on the other tree root. He clasped his hands together and studied the man who had become a son to him, no matter their ages, nor their wildly different lives. 'What's wrong?'

'Wrong?' Robert frowned, his aspect entirely one of a man who had no concerns at all. 'Why should something be wrong before I come to talk to you? I was simply wondering how you were coping with the travelling. Whether you had any questions you wanted to ask without everybody listening. You usually do.'

'Oh?' Aiden said, not believing the innocent act at all. 'Very well. In that case, why am I here?'

Robert frowned quizzically. 'Haven't we had this conversation before? You're the priest, you should know all the philosophical answers to that question.'

'If you don't stop it, Robert, I will hit you, I swear.'

'Says a man of the cloth.'

Aiden could only laugh with him, the soft sound gentle as the fir needles beneath his feet. Eventually, he asked again in the quiet, hoping this time for the answer he needed. 'Why am I here?'

'Don't you want to be?'

'Of course I do. And I'm not complaining. I just don't yet understand what you want from me this time. Usually I have no trouble seeing my role, but now?'

'You tend to our wounded, say prayers for us every morning.'

'John can and does all that too.'

'John wouldn't be here without you.'

'True. But none of these are things he *can't* do. So why am *I* here? You don't need me as you once did.'

'Don't fool yourself, Bishop.' Robert looked away, and a faint touch of firelight reflected in his eyes, glinting in the darkness, and Aiden could see so many other things reflected there. 'But you're right. You're not here because of me.'

It didn't take Aiden long to find his answer. 'Andrew?'

Robert looked down at his hands and for a moment, Aiden thought that might be the end of their conversation, that Robert would stand, bid him goodnight and go – but he didn't. He lingered, and Aiden was not so sure that Robert didn't need him after all. When he spoke, however, Aiden was surprised at the question.

'As a priest, is what I say to you held in confidence?'

'Of course.'

'Then could I discuss with you something to do with your role as a priest?'

'What is it?' Both concern and worry filled Aiden then. Robert had never spoken to him like this, not in all the years they'd known each other.

'If I asked you—' Robert paused, the question obviously not easy for him for reasons Aiden could only guess at, he continued, 'Would you be able to perform a marriage?'

'Marriage?' Aiden queried, 'Who—'

Robert's head lifted, his face lit faintly on one side, his expression so hopeful it tore Aiden's heart in two.

'You and Jenn?' Aiden already began to smile as Robert nodded. 'When?'

'Well,' he sighed, 'I have to get her to say yes.'

'You haven't asked her?'

'Oh, I've asked, she just keeps telling me the Key won't let me get that close to her.'

'But you won't let that stop you.'

'No.'

'Well, of course, if she says yes, I'd be delighted to marry you two! I've been waiting for years for you to ask me.'

'Well, just be ready, you know, for when the time comes. And nobody knows about it just yet. Not even Andrew.'

Aiden frowned; he couldn't say anything. Andrew's true parentage wasn't his secret to tell. 'Perhaps you should tell him sooner rather than later.'

'There's too much going on in his head at the moment. He has other questions that need to be addressed first. If I confuse him any more, he'll combust. Besides, I don't want him trying to guess my motives for everything. He needs to be able to trust me.'

'And of course he'll do that when he finds out you've had designs on his mother all this time.' Aiden bit his tongue then. He was not one to be lecturing Robert on being honest and open. 'Just be careful with him.'

'Oh, I can't afford to be careful, Aiden. That's what you're here for.'

'Well, in that case,' Aiden said, phrasing his question carefully, 'I want to do more than tend wounds and be careful with Andrew. I need to be seen.' Aiden continued softly, already hearing Robert's objections, 'All these years I've spent in safety in Flan'har, writing all those books and essays on sorcery and how everyone should accept it as a gift and the like. But I haven't been here, with our people, suffering as they have – and they know it. If I am to have any effect on how they think, how they feel about you, about Andrew, about all Salti, they need to see me, hear my voice directly and not just through rumour and hearsay.'

'They need to know I didn't coerce you into saying all those things.' For a moment, Robert stared at him, then he looked away. 'You know I don't want you in any danger, I would rather ensure nobody recognised you until this whole war was over, but—'

'That's as much my risk to take as yours, Robert. This is my country, too. I would rather die fighting for freedom here than of old age in Flan'har.'

'Wouldn't we all,' Robert whispered. 'Just be careful – and take somebody reliable with you.' He got to his feet, stepping carefully over the tree root. 'Sleep well.'

'You too.' A brush of fabric, a cracked twig, and Aiden was alone again.

'But, Mother,' Andrew bit his lip and deliberately lowered his voice, 'you *can't* fight!'

'Why not? I have combat skills. Finnlay made sure I was very well trained. I'm at least as good as he is. There's no reason I shouldn't fight.'

'Except that Robert won't let you.'

'I don't always do what Robert says.'

'But you must!' Again Andrew paused, looking around, but it seemed everyone else was either already in bed, or in small groups talking. He dropped his voice even lower. He said nothing of the dreams, nothing about what he saw when he closed his eyes at night. 'Robert is the leader of this rebellion, Mother. You can't challenge that.'

She raised her eyebrows at him, but her expression didn't change. 'And I'm the Jaibir. That doesn't stop him challenging me whenever he wants to.'

'That's different.'

'Is it?'

He opened his mouth, caught the look in her eye and shut it again.

'I will fight, Andrew. You need to remember, this is my country too. You're my son. Your claim to the throne comes through my blood. I was fighting for Lusara's freedom for two years before you were born – and I did so alongside Robert. If he doesn't want me to fight, he'll tell me. Then we'll discuss it.'

Andrew didn't need to hear that discussion to guess exactly how it would go.

'And what about you,' she continued without missing a beat. 'You fought yesterday. Robert said you fought well.'

He blinked at her, some part of him shutting a door. He couldn't talk about it, not even to his own mother. Especially not her. Instead, he said the things he'd heard the other men say. 'We won, that's the main point. And we didn't lose any men. Payne's taking the gold, we're off to another mission.'

'I see,' she nodded, her gaze a little penetrating, but she didn't ask further. 'Well, I don't know about you, but I'm in need of some rest. And you?'

'Robert wants me to get up early for more practice.'

'Then go to bed now.'

Andrew smiled. No matter how old he got, nor how he fought to gain a throne he didn't want, she would still be his mother, telling him when to go to bed. 'Goodnight, Mother.'

She leaned over and kissed him on the forehead. 'Goodnight, my love.' With that, she lay down on her own bed, pulled the blankets over her and shut her eyes.

Andrew watched her for a moment, then turned for his bed as well.

He didn't want to dream again – at least, not *those* dreams. But they came nonetheless, every now and then, when he didn't expect them, when he didn't know what to do with them. So now they were a little more vivid, but in truth, he barely remembered the details most of the time. All he usually recalled was that his mother was in danger, and that there was fire.

And when he wasn't thinking, when he wasn't talking, or doing anything else, he knew that fire terrified him more than anything else. The fire – and the face he could see inside it: his father's face.

He lay back, searching for stars between the trees above, then rolled to his side. With his voice a soft whisper, he said, 'I'm glad you're here, Mother.'

And she replied, 'So am I.'

They left their horses at the tavern, which was not as close to the mine gates as Andrew would have liked. As a result, they had to walk through the length of the ugliest village he'd ever seen anywhere. Like the surrounding countryside, it was devoid of trees, most of which had been cut down long ago to fuel the smelting fires. The houses here were made entirely of stone, with grey slate roofs and grey stone cobbles in the streets. With a metal grey sky above, it was hard to make out any specific features – until he spied the wall at the end of the village.

It spliced off a corner in the valley, with two round hills rising behind it. In the centre was a great wooden gate, solidly locked. It was only opened twice a day, to let the workers in and out, and once a week, to send off shipments of precious metal and to dump cartloads of leftover rock into the land behind the village. Only the Guilde yellow badge on the gate gave away who ruled here.

It was a cold morning, but they were without cloaks, so they'd look more like locals and not so much like strangers. Robert certainly greeted people in the streets like he knew them, and Andrew took that as an example, remembering that at least some of these people were prepared to fight the Guilde when the mine collapsed.

'This way.' Robert ushered him inside a cheesemaker's, where it was even cooler and sheltered from the morning's sun. No sooner was he inside, however, than the shopkeeper waved them into the back. Robert moved quickly, making Andrew almost run to keep up. Without a word, they went through the back room and then into a stone corridor. They paused before a door and the shopkeeper pulled out a key to unlock it. He pushed the door wide then turned to Robert.

'How long will it take?'

'Not long. Can you be ready?'

'Your Grace, we've been ready for years.'

Robert gave the man a grin, clapped a hand on his shoulder and headed through the door, leaving Andrew to hurry after him. Then the door was locked shut behind them and Robert brought a pale light to bear.

'Let your eyes adjust, and be careful where you put your feet.' Robert moved forward briskly and Andrew followed, his fingers trailing along the wall for balance. The tunnel was rough-hewn, with a ceiling so low Robert had to duck his head to keep from losing it. Inches of water and filth swirled around his boots, and every few steps he almost tripped over support beams that had fallen, or other detritus he didn't care to think about. The further they went, the darker it got. They turned a corner, continued on for another dozen paces, then Robert came to a halt.

Andrew blinked. There was the smallest amount of light here, filtering down from a shaft above.

'There's a door up there I need you to get open. You're the only one of us small enough to get through it.'

Andrew squinted up but could see nothing but the finest strips of light which blinded him to the rest of the detail. 'I can't see anything.'

'Don't worry, I'll get you a little closer.' Robert extinguished his own light and tilted his head back, stepping sideways as though tracing something.

'How do you know where everything is here?' Andrew whispered.

'I used to own the mine, before Selar made me an outlaw and the Guilde claimed it as compensation. I worked here for a month, when I was your age.'

Then, right before Andrew's eyes, Robert swung his arms, and jumped high into the air, further than he'd thought possible, and clung onto a beam crossing the shaft. He swung there a moment, then hauled himself up onto the beam. There was a few seconds of rustling, and then something hit Andrew's face, making him jump.

A rope.

'Quickly.'

Hand over hand Andrew climbed, until Robert caught his arm and pulled him onto the beam. He pointed up. The door was not far overhead, close enough for him to stand and reach, but it was a tight fit.

'That small door is unlocked. You need to get through it and unlatch the larger one so I can climb up.'

'Is there anyone on the other side?'

'Damn it, Andrew, you should be able to Sense for yourself!'

'But—'

'Close your eyes,' Robert hissed, 'and imagine yourself on the other side.'

Andrew put his hand out to the wall and carefully stood up. The door was immediately above him, just waiting for him. All he had to do was reach up and push it open. He closed his eyes, thought of the door, of what might be on the other side, of whether there could be Guildesmen or—

He opened his eyes to find Robert standing beside him, eyes hard and unforgiving.

'It's safe. Get moving,' he said with a finality that made Andrew's heart sink. Without a word, he reached up and pressed against the door.

'Jenn?'

'What?'

'Where are you going?' The Bishop waited, standing beside his horse, far enough down the valley to be safely away from the action. But that didn't mean he wasn't involved. Some days he was too much like a watchdog.

'I'm going to get a little closer. I don't like being this far away.'

'Being closer won't help anybody.'

But she couldn't sit still. Her skin felt like her clothes had ants in them. That said only one thing to her: Malachi. But should she go? Or should she stay by McCauly in case he was the one in danger? Though both John and Patric were Salti, neither were exactly her first choice if it came to a fight – and Robert had asked her to stay with the Bishop.

Damn it: she should have known he'd do this to her!

Robert?

What is it?

Sorry, but I think there's Malachi in the area.

Are you in danger?

No, and don't worry, we'll move if we have to. I just wanted to warn you. Do you Sense anything from the mine?

Not so far – but I will stay alert. It could just be somebody passing through. Stay low and keep watch.

Be careful.

'You can't keep ignoring it, Andrew.'

He scrambled aside as Robert slid the larger door closed and removed all sign of them having been there.

'When you face Kenrick, you'll need every weapon you can bring to bear. Do you think he won't use everything against you? Eh?' Robert stood, placing his back against the wall of the empty room. There were two windows looking out onto the work yard, and two doors, one obviously going outside. 'If you don't do anything about it now, by the time you need them, you won't have a clue how to use your powers. Come on, this way.'

Robert darted under the window and across to the other interior door. Andrew ran at a crouch to end up behind him, watching closely as Robert held his hand over the lock. He heard a loud grinding, then a hard click, and Robert was opening the door.

On the other side was a narrow, steep staircase. Robert climbed up it, still moving quickly. Andrew's heart pounded in his chest as they reached the top and emerged into a room where they could clearly hear voices.

They froze, but the voices were in the next room and a moment later, Robert was dragging him through a low doorway into a room with a barred pit in the floor. He closed the door behind them, holding his hand over the lock as it clicked into place.

They were now locked in.

Robert pointed to the pit and the huge chain hanging through the ceiling next to it. 'Take a hold of that. When I release the bars holding the gate closed, you need to pull that chain to open the gate. Don't stop until it's all the way open or the guard will be able to close it too easily. Once it's open, we'll fuse the chain so they can't get it closed again.'

As Robert crouched by the pit, Andrew realised they were in fact directly over the gate. He took hold of the chain, hearing the voices beyond the door grow louder and closer. Robert ignored them. He simply held out his hand, did something Andrew couldn't see, and below them, the huge wooden beams barring the gate began to lift out of their chocks, silently.

They were nearly clear when a big hand tried to open their door and, finding it locked, the guard called out, shouting to his mates, and banged on the door. Andrew's heart stopped in his throat as a boot was kicked into the door, and splinters of solid wood went flying across the room.

'Hurry!' Andrew hissed – but it was too late. With one great crash, the door burst into pieces.

28

As the first wave crashed over Jenn, she stumbled under the sheer force of it. Instantly, she felt hands catch her, help her keep her balance, and questioning faces peering down at her, but she couldn't place any of them where she needed.

This was so big, so overwhelming, so awful. Never before had she felt this terror, this horrible failure . . . so much – too much—

'Jenn! What's wrong? What do you see?'

Another wave came sweeping down, drowning her, making her fight for air, numbing her fingers, making her hands shake. This wasn't real; how could she be simply a little worried one minute and then—

'Jenn?' It was Patric's voice now, steady and firm, comforting and enquiring at the same time. 'Just tell us what you're feeling. You're fine, there's nobody close who could be a threat. Just talk.'

'Terror,' she gasped, closing her eyes against the dizziness of it. 'Can't see anything. So strong. Never felt this before.'

'Is it Nash?'

Jenn reached in, reached out and felt nothing familiar to say it was Nash. Relief filled her then, but it wasn't strong enough to filter out the other. 'No, not Nash. Just—'

And as quickly as it had appeared, the suffocating terror vanished. A moment later, she was breathing normally, opening her eyes to find three worried faces against a flat grey sky. 'I'm fine,' she managed.

'What happened?' Aiden asked, 'Were you mindspeaking?'

'No,' Jenn began to say when, abruptly, an image of Andrew flashed before her. 'By the gods,' she whispered. It was Andrew. He was projecting what he was feeling! How could he do that? Surely she had it wrong . . . but then he'd done the same thing when the Malachi had attacked. Robert had been called back to them not by words, but by a blinding, overwhelming wave of terror. Somehow Andrew had found another way of calling for help. He probably didn't even know he was doing it.

Jenn turned for her horse, but the Bishop stood in front of her. 'I have to go! Something's wrong. Andrew's in trouble. I can't just leave him—'

Aiden's gestures, his voice were calm. 'Are you still feeling this terror?'

273

She looked at him, then at John and Patric. 'That doesn't mean he's not still in trouble.'

'No, but it might mean that Robert has it under control, or Finnlay or Micah, or any of the others – all of whom are very capable of protecting him. Please, Jenn.'

She held the reins for a moment longer, but it was true: there was no great sense of anything now that there hadn't been before. Even the warning of Malachi seemed to have vanished. With a sigh, she put the reins in McCauly's hand. 'Very well. But if it happens again, I'm going.'

Andrew dropped the chain and, in one movement, drew his sword, clashing directly into the blade aimed at Robert's neck. With a great shove, he pushed the man back, filling the doorway with his body, meeting each new blow with his sword, desperately, knowing his resistance could only last a moment or two.

They were too late for secrecy now. The alarm had been raised. Over the noise of the fight, he could hear shouts from outside, and something else he couldn't identify. After that, he didn't have time to wonder. The first man was thrust back into the room, falling on his face, only to be followed by two more, brandishing swords, flashing Guilde colours onto the grey walls. Andrew swung first one way, then the other, trying not to trip over his feet, trying just to keep them back, so Robert would have time to—

The floor vanished beneath his feet and, with arms and legs flying, he tumbled downwards to be caught awkwardly by a pair of strong arms and a grunted, 'Quickly!'

His feet were barely on the cobbled yard when Robert was already running, dodging one guard after another, and only then did Andrew realise that their men were swarming through the open gate, taking on the Guilde, fighting to let Robert get to the mine.

For a moment, Andrew was seized with an insane desire to laugh, but instead he ran after Robert, catching up in time to deflect an attack from the right. The yard was filled with small stone buildings, some of which were belching smoke and flames. Others were taller and piles of crushed stone sat against their walls, making grey mud where water trickled past. There were carts and dogs, people and horses, and the further they ran, the more chaos flurried around them. He could hear shouting, cries, clashes of swords and other weapons, people running and he laughed through it all. The laughter scared him more than anything.

Robert ducked around two Guildesmen determined to stop him, leaving Andrew to face them. Without hesitation, he cut back at the first one, shoving hard until the man unbalanced and stumbled into his colleague. As he was picking himself up from the mud, Andrew sliced at the other man, wounding him from shoulder to shoulder. He spun in time to put a cut on the first man's arm, then ran again, determined to stick behind Robert no matter what.

He found him shouting at people to get out of the mine. Dozens of folk, all blackened with mud, their eyes wide and disbelieving, were running out of a long tunnel wormed into the hillside. Andrew followed in blindly, helping those who had fallen get back to their feet. They kept going until the flood of people became a trickle, until they were so deep into the mine that the entrance was no more than a small dot.

The roof was too low for either of them to stand here. Other tunnels ran off at angles from the central one, all sloped downwards, all braced with rickety wooden beams, making the place look horribly unsafe.

'This is far enough.' Robert looked around, panting. 'This will do. The mine's empty. Go back now. Left of the entrance is a bell tower. When you get there, start ringing.'

'But what about you?'

'Just go!'

Andrew backed away, watching until the last minute as Robert pressed his hands against the roof of rock above him. Then he turned and ran, unable to miss the profound rumble beneath his feet, echoing all around him. With his heart in his mouth, he pelted out of the tunnel, skidded to the left and raced to the bell tower. Without even pausing for breath, he hauled on the rope and the great bell began to swing. He hauled again, putting his whole body into it, feeling the tower tremble around him. On the third pull, the bell finally began to ring, and he kept pulling, swinging from the rope, watching the entrance of the tunnel, whispering prayers he didn't realise he even knew.

The first crack seemed to come from the centre of the earth, rending the air with a power he'd never thought could exist. Then the hill itself began to groan, rumbling in displeasure, shuddering beneath his feet and coughing out dust and smoke through the tunnel entrance. Andrew rang the bell once more, then ran back to the tunnel entrance, but the next wave shoved him out of the way and he rolled, coughing against the dust. He scrambled to his feet to see the face of the hill above shift and change completely, then another great groan, an almighty crack, and Robert was running towards him, shouting for him to get out of the way.

He scrambled to his feet, turned to his left and started running himself, not stopping even when he was overtaken by a thick cloud of dust, or when rocks began to fall out of the air. Robert gained his side, grabbing his elbow, and the two of them raced across the now-empty yard, through the gate and along the village street until they reached the tavern. Only then did they stop, coughing, gasping for air, aching all over.

Some kind person handed them each a cup of something, and some *un*kind person doused them both with a bucket of water, but Andrew didn't care. He shook the water out of his hair and looked up to find Robert laughing at him.

'Come on, we have to get out of here before the Guilde decide to chase us.'

'They're coming.'

Jenn started, looking from Patric to Father John for his confirming nod. She sprang to her feet, running around the back of the ruined church until she could see the road. There was nothing there, but a moment later, Patric joined her.

'I can hear them. Two horses.'

Jenn frowned, and then heard it for herself. They were galloping, but John confirmed that there was no pursuit. At least, none so far.

And then they were rounding the corner in the road, Robert on his horse, dark hair flying, dust and grime all over him from head to foot, and Andrew, younger, smaller, but equally dirty. Jenn resisted the momentary urge to run to her son and instead moved to hold his horse as he came to a halt.

'Are you ready to move?' Robert asked, his expression utterly unreadable, which didn't comfort her at all.

'How did it go?' Jenn asked, already moving back to where they'd left the horses.

'The mine is closed; the Guilde will be on our tails soon enough.'

A few moments later, and they were mounted up, ready to go. And then Patric turned his head, the movement alerting Jenn.

'Guilde?'

He nodded, listening with the preternaturally sharp ears of a blind man. 'Ten, perhaps fifteen horses.'

'In other words, trouble.' Robert finished for him. He took a moment to peer around. 'Jenn, any further sign of those Malachi?'

'No, not for a while.'

'Good, we go this way.' With that, he was off around the ruined church heading away from the road, across farmland that gave them little cover.

Keeping an eye on the Bishop, Jenn rode flat to her horse, urging it to greater speed, watching the undulations of the ground and shifting her weight to compensate. Soon they were strung out in a long line, with John and McCauly at the back. Jenn slowed a little, pulling up behind them both, ready to react if necessary.

The land sloped down, and Robert rode on, leading them over hedges and stone fences, splashing through a shallow stream and up the opposite bank. Now there was the cover of a few stringy trees, and then they were curving around the side of another hill. As they gained height, Jenn chanced a look over her shoulder.

Robert, they're gaining on us. About a dozen. They've seen us.

There's no cover. Not enough to chance hiding with a mask. Don't turn unless you have to, and tell me if you do. I'll come back and let Andrew take the others on.

Fortunately, their horses were well-rested and took the gallop without complaint. On the other side of the hill was a winding river, lined with willow and elm. Robert made straight for them, using the cover as best he could.

Jenn, there's a wood not far. Keep the group together. Once we're inside, we'll stop and mask. If it doesn't work, we'll have to fight.

Jenn came up behind McCauly and slapped the rump of his horse. They needed to be more of a group before entering the wood or there wouldn't be time to get the horses still enough to make the mask work.

The Bishop wasn't comfortable, she could tell that much, but he made no effort to slow down, and in fact just tried to go harder. As soon as Jenn saw the wood, she took another sighting of the Guildesmen over her shoulder.

We have two minutes, no more.

Robert had already vanished into the wood. Seconds later, Jenn plunged into its darkness, following the shadows in front of her, only slowing when she saw Robert's face. As soon as she reached him, she jumped from her horse, turning immediately to calm it, quieten its breathing, get it to be as still as possible. Everyone else was doing the same. Any movement beneath a mask would ruin the layer of invisibility Robert would place over them.

Jenn heard them before Patric could signal, her gaze going to the edge of the wood where the light was bright and she could see the flash of gaudy yellow against the grey landscape. The Guildesmen were heading straight for the wood, right for where they were waiting, probably following tracks as much as what they'd seen.

Jenn groaned inwardly. They would have to fight after all, and only three of them could – against a dozen soldiers.

Robert, what do we do now? They'll be on us in a moment!

Wait till I give the word, then push out to get around the rear of them. Andrew and I will take the first—

Jenn stared, mouth open, at the Guildesmen as they stopped at the edge of the wood, horses snorting and wild-eyed, confusion filling every movement. Then, over the top of everything else, she could see other horses to her left, horses she'd never seen before. With a great show, they abruptly turned and galloped back out into the countryside. Instantly the Guildesmen shouted, kicked their mounts and gave chase. Within minutes, they were gone and the wood was quiet.

By the gods, why hadn't she thought of that? And when had Robert learned to make such a convincing image without telling her? With half a smile, and not a little pride, she turned her gaze on him.

To find him turning the exact same gaze back on her.

'Don't look at me,' Jenn said. 'I had nothing to do with it.'

Robert opened his mouth to speak, but it was Patric who said, 'Did what? And why were those Malachi hiding in this wood? Why did they direct the Guilde away from us?'

'Malachi?' Robert stared in the direction the horses had gone. He was still a moment, then he said, 'No matter. Let's get going. The others will be wondering what's happened to us.'

One by one they arrived, and Aiden saw to them first, checking over their injuries and wounds before leaving them in John's hands to bandage. It was dark before the last got in: Micah had a cut on his cheek that wouldn't stop bleeding, not to mention a look from Robert that didn't help it any.

But Aiden did finally get the bleeding to stop and by the time he was finished and cleaned up, supper was ready by the big fire Jenn had lit when they'd arrived.

He'd lost track of how many forests they'd found shelter in. This one seemed devoid of clearings, but instead grew its trees in clumps of three or four at a time. With the branches all crossing over in the central space, there remained a very comfortable natural shelter big enough for two or three to sleep without trouble.

There were worse places to spend the night.

Around the fire were little more than the sounds of eating, occasional requests for a second helping. But the moment the most urgent hunger was satisfied, the men began to talk, commenting on the day's battle, pointing out things others might have missed, admiring the bravery of the villagers who had fought, but who also had to face the wrath of the Guilde in the morning. And then the inevitable question was asked. 'So how will those villagers live without the mine?'

The query was directed at Robert, but his attention was elsewhere. He stared off into the forest as though he were on the other side of Lusara.

After a moment, however, he blinked and looked back, realising that they were all waiting for his answer.

'Oh, sorry. It's not really going to be a problem for long. I only collapsed the main tunnel – or at least, I hope I did. It will take them months to dig it out and regain the ground they've just lost. But they'll do it because the mine is incredibly rich in mineral deposits, you see. And they'll have to pay the villagers to do the digging – so the Guilde not only loses the income from the mine, but must pay for the repairs.' Robert gave them half a smile. 'See? Simple.'

'But the Guilde will take revenge on the villagers, won't it?'

'I doubt it will be too bad. It was their choice to shut down the mine, and to involve themselves in the fight. I had very little say in the matter.'

There was a pause then, before Andrew, sitting with his back to a tree trunk, picked up a stick and began picking at his boot with it. 'You used to own that mine, didn't you? And you had an interest in the barge-building yards at Casterlane. Your father owned two wool mills at Fiddech. You have personal interests in most of the other rebel missions as well, don't you?'

Aiden sat up. Though he'd kept rein on Robert's personal finances over the last few years, that had happened only *after* Robert had lost all his assets in Lusara. He'd never noticed the pattern there.

'Yes, that's true.' Robert's tone remained neutral.

Andrew looked up then, very aware that everyone in camp was listening to his questions – his challenge. 'It's going to look to Kenrick as though you're only doing all this to regain your own personal fortune.'

'Is it?'

'And the people of Lusara are going to think the same as well.'

'Are they?' Andrew flinched a little under Robert's gaze, but didn't back down. 'And what would be wrong with Kenrick thinking I'm doing all this for personal reasons?'

'Because you're not.'

'So?'

Andrew looked around as though he would get help, but everybody – even his mother – remained solidly silent. He bit in his lip for a moment, then chirped up – Aiden admired the boy's courage – 'Because he's going to be able to work out what you're going to hit next, and given enough time, we'll end up on the wrong end of an ambush. There's no point in fighting a war like this if your movements are entirely predictable.'

'There is if at some point you *want* to be caught.'

Andrew came to a halt, eyes wide, but again, he didn't back down. 'Or . . . or if you want to make it look like you were following a pattern only so you could break it completely.'

Aiden could see Robert fighting hard to contain a smile, though he doubted anybody else but Jenn and Finnlay could read it. For some reason, Robert didn't yet want Andrew to know how pleased he was. Instead, Robert nodded slowly, turning away again to stare at the forest, ending the conversation.

People took that as a perfect moment to move and soon all was activity as wooden bowls were washed off in the river and bedding was rolled out for the night. With the chores finally completed, Aiden looked around for Andrew and found him checking on the horses hobbled on one side of the camp.

'Your questions are getting more interesting,' he began softly, to give the boy warning of his approach. 'Not to mention entertaining.'

'Yes, well.' Andrew shrugged a shoulder, turning back to the horse he was patting. 'It never seems to make a difference. He's never satisfied no matter how hard I try.'

'Oh, so you want him to be satisfied?'

'Doesn't everybody?'

Aiden surreptitiously glanced over his shoulder to where Robert was seated beside Jenn, both of them talking and moving as though there was nothing going on between them. 'He did say you fought well at the ambush.'

'He lied.'

'Oh?'

'I . . . I froze. He had to save my life by killing a man. I didn't do well at all and I wish he hadn't said anything!'

'But what about today?'

'Today I did everything right, except—' Andrew paused, then looked up to Aiden. 'He keeps pushing me to use powers I don't have, and then he gets annoyed when I fail. And tomorrow we've got another mission, and another for the day after that and you heard him tonight – one day he *wants* us to get caught. You know what that means? That he wants Kenrick to catch up with us so I can fight him.' Andrew's eyed turned dark, his voice quiet and hard. 'How can I fight without—'

'Sometimes,' Aiden began carefully, 'the answers are all there, right in front of us, at our fingertips the moment we need them. And other times, we don't see the answers at all, until long after the question has become unimportant. No matter what other skills you have at your disposal, you will fight Kenrick with courage. Perhaps that is all it will take.'

Andrew turned to stare at him. 'You don't think Kenrick has courage?'

'No.' Aiden was utterly positive of this, if nothing else. 'No, I don't think he has any courage at all.'

Robert put his head back against the tree trunk, toyed with the palm full of pebbles he'd collected and began tossing them out into the darkness in front of Jenn, one by one. 'And you're sure it was Andrew? It couldn't have come from anywhere else?'

'Didn't you feel something similar when we were under attack at Maitland? Isn't that why you came back?'

'Yes, but that doesn't mean it was Andrew. But even if it is, I think you're right – he has no idea he's doing it. As a result, I don't think we should say anything to him.'

'I agree. Do you think perhaps this might be a sign that his powers are emerging?'

Robert sighed. 'All we seem to be getting are signs, with very little substance. Whatever he has he needs to be trained to use it before he can expect any success in combat. You know that as well as I do.'

'I remember . . .' Jenn's voice drifted off, with a smile in her tone, 'I remember you telling me I was a sorcerer, how I wouldn't believe you until you let me see your *ayarn*.'

With a small laugh, he said, 'Yes, I remember the headache afterwards.'

He listened to the night for a few moments, before looking aside at her, as if trying to burn her profile onto his memory. 'Do you have any idea,' he began softly, careful to keep their conversation private, 'how much I hate being this close to you and not being able to touch you?'

'And it's so damned hard not smiling when you say things like that.'

'Perhaps we should be mindspeaking?'

'So people would wonder why we were sitting so close without saying a word?' Jenn shook her head. Robert could feel the movement faintly against his shoulder, where it met hers.

'Well, we could always just tell everyone. At least that would give us a modicum of privacy.'

'A modicum is all it would give us. Unless there are walls in this forest my eyes are unable to see.'

'Trust me, if there were, I'd be taking you behind one now—'

'Robert!'

He took the opportunity to laugh, and knowing she was sitting beside him laughing as well was enough for the moment to do without that privacy. And when the laughter had gone, he said, 'You haven't demanded that I leave your son alone.'

Jenn was quiet a moment before replying, 'Would you prefer that I object?'

'You weren't happy when I took him.'

'And what would you have done if I'd done the same to you?'

'I just wanted you to know that I had noticed, nothing more.'

'In that case, thank you for noticing.'

'Is that all you want to say?'

'Aloud, yes.'

There was a crunch of pebbles from behind as Finnlay approached their spot. He stood before them, hands on his hips, staring out into the night as they had done. Then he turned and crouched down, his expression open and entirely smug. 'I thought I should come over and disturb the peace before anybody else noticed how much there was in this corner.'

Robert sniggered and Jenn elbowed him.

'Do we,' Finnlay continued, his voice a little louder, 'have another early start in the morning?'

'Not too early,' Robert replied, bringing his knees up to clasp his hands around them. 'Our next mission is not until the day after and the distance isn't too great. Besides, I have another training session with Andrew at dawn.' He deliberately didn't say any more about that. The less these two knew about what he was doing the better.

'So, it's the water wheels at Dunfress? And after that?'

'After that, we'll see. It's not a race, you know.'

'Oh? Then what is it?' Finnlay had a sparkle in his eye, but his question was serious.

'Come, Finn, don't start claiming you don't approve of my methods.'

'I've *never* approved of your methods, brother – and if you haven't noticed that by now, then obviously I wasn't arguing loudly enough.'

'Oh, trust me, you were.' Robert watched Jenn, who had her head back, her eyes half closed and studying the stars. In profile, she looked almost more beautiful than he could bear.

He tore his gaze away when Finnlay cleared his throat. Duly chastened, Robert addressed himself to Finnlay's next question.

'And what do you think that was all about today, with the Malachi?'

Ah, yes, the Malachi. 'Do you think they saw us?'

'How could they not?'

'They definitely saw us,' Jenn added.

'So maybe they were running from us,' Finnlay said.

'Yes, perhaps,' Robert agreed. Or perhaps they were trying something else infinitely more dangerous. Without thinking, his gaze shifted and turned, sweeping across the camp to where Micah lay on his bed, curled up on his right side so the cut on his face wouldn't get dirty. And in the darkness, his sight, enhanced so much by his powers, could see everything so clearly.

Micah had his eyes open, and he was staring directly at Robert.

There was somebody there, in the darkness, where the flames were worst. He couldn't see who it was, but there was danger flooding across the floor, splitting the burning boards, shaking the ground beneath their feet. He looked up, but his mother couldn't see. Her blue eyes were pasted white, as blind as the night. He reached up to take her hand, but it was cold and unmoving. The fiery shadow drew closer and, terrified now, he began to shake her, to make her wake up, to make her open her eyes and—

Andrew woke with a gasp. He sat up, but there was no enemy sneaking into the camp, no attack happening around him. For a moment longer, his blood pounded hard through his body, then with a silent sigh, he sank back down. He rolled onto his side again to watch his mother. She lay peacefully asleep. He could see her small movements, and if he listened hard enough, he could hear her breathing.

So she was fine. She was alive. He didn't have to worry. He didn't have to fear.

He closed his eyes and did his best to go back to sleep.

'Again.'

Andrew closed his eyes and swung the staff. Late into the swing, he finally hit the tree and the unexpectedness of the collision jarred his elbows. He opened his eyes, frowned at the trunk, stepped back and started again.

'What are you doing now?'

'Trying again.'

'Why?'

Andrew opened his eyes. Robert was standing to his right with his arms folded, his gaze driving straight through Andrew the way it always did. There was no way that Andrew could read what was expected of him next.

'Because I didn't do it right the first time. Isn't that what I'm supposed to do?'

'Why didn't you do it right the first time?'

'I don't know. I just—'

Robert moved forward and snatched the staff away from him. Without pausing, he closed his eyes, turned three times and immediately swung at the tree, hitting it squarely six times in a row. He then turned again, stepped to his right, turned a second time and again struck the tree right on the mark. Done, he opened his eyes and tossed the staff back at Andrew. 'Always know where you are. Your surroundings are going to change, everything in your life is going to change. If you don't know where *you* are, you'll just get lost every time you turn around. Now, try again and this time, know where you are.' The words emerged with a fine edge to them, spoken in the early morning before even the birds had awoken. Dawn was about to break, however, and although they were some small distance from the camp, their privacy and quiet wouldn't last much longer.

How was he to know where he was? What did that mean? And what was the point in trying? Even if he did get it right, Robert would never say so, would never deign to praise him. He'd just come up with some new task even more impossible and still expect Andrew to do as he was told.

'Are we going to wait until Caslemas before you make another attempt?'

Andrew grunted and got back into position. 'I was just working out where I was.'

'Oh?' Robert murmured. 'And where would that be?'

Andrew didn't answer. He just closed his eyes, took in a deep breath and tried to remember where the trunk was. This really shouldn't be that hard considering it hadn't moved.

And then he saw it, bright red flashing in front of his eyes, even though they were closed. It flashed again and before it could move, he swung, hitting it squarely. He swung again, hitting it from the other side. Triumphant, he opened his eyes and turned to Robert.

'And what, you've killed it, have you? With those two blows?'

'Damn it,' Andrew tossed down the staff, 'you're never satisfied! Nothing I do ever pleases you!'

'Why are you trying to please me?'

'What?' Andrew stared at him disbelieving. After everything – he could ask a question like that? 'You're the one who keeps testing me, keeps giving me all these skills I have to learn. And why? So that when I fight Kenrick I will have a better chance at winning?'

Robert came closer, his voice low and menacing. 'Would you rather I stand by and let you get killed?'

'I'd rather I didn't have to fight him at all!'

With one eyebrow raised, there was mockery written all over Robert's face. 'Don't you get tired of repeating yourself? I certainly do.'

Fury flooded through Andrew then, making his heart pound dangerously. He wanted to lash out, to hit Robert, to wipe that smug smile off his face, to stop him from *pushing* all the time – but if he did—

He bit his tongue, forcing it back so he could swallow his fury down.

'See,' Robert continued, shaking his head, 'that's the part I find so difficult to master. I always find it much easier not to get angry in the first place, but to be honest, to get angry and then not do anything about it is simply a waste.'

'You want me to get angry?' Andrew gaped at him. 'Why? So you can

284

laugh at me? So you can tell me exactly how bad my swordsmanship is when I lose my temper? Why am I listening to you?'

'Because I know more than you do.' With that, Robert turned and picked up the staff. He held one end and swung the other slowly, turning until it pressed against Andrew's stomach. 'You need to stop asking me questions and start asking them of yourself. For instance, why do you want to please me? Surely you should be pleasing yourself. And another – why do you try so badly? Every test I give you ends in failure. Is that because you're afraid to succeed? Or is it that you go into it expecting me to be disappointed? And lastly.' Robert pressed until Andrew stumbled back and fell onto the ground; he then dropped the staff and stood over Andrew like a nightmare. 'Lastly, what is it about fighting Kenrick that scares you so much, eh? Is it really because he's your cousin?'

'I don't want to—'

'Don't,' Robert silenced him. 'I'm not forcing you to fight him, Andrew. You're free to go any time you like. But I don't see you running away.'

Stunned, Andrew couldn't move for a moment. Then Robert stepped back. 'Go and help prepare breakfast. We'll practise again tomorrow morning.'

Andrew scrambled to his feet, his face red with – he didn't know what. He grabbed the staff, his fingers clenching around it. He wished he could break it in half, wished he dared swing it and, and . . . But Robert would kill him if he tried. Robert would break *him* in half. There was one weapon he could use, though.

'I hate you!' he hissed, moving away, his feet taking him in the direction of the camp. 'I hate you.' And then he turned and ran, and the freedom of it almost made him feel ill.

Finnlay heard the words, even though he didn't want to, and shouldn't have. But he'd been watching from the bushes uphill, needing to see with his own eyes what Robert was doing, so he couldn't miss the heartbreak in the boy's voice, the flushed face, the abject disappointment that his hero of all these years had turned out to be such a tyrant himself.

He left his hiding place and approached his brother slowly. He'd lost count of the times he'd longed to tell Robert that the boy he was trying so desperately to train was his own son. Years ago, he'd even threatened Jenn that if she didn't tell Robert, then he would – but he'd kept his silence. And now it was entirely probable that Robert would never know that the boy he would put on the throne was his own flesh and blood, the child he'd always longed for, the heir he believed would never be his.

'I wanted to tell you what a wonderful teacher you are,' Finnlay began, also noticing in the quiet morning how Robert's head hung low after his son's angry departure. Now it rose sharply and a frown creased Robert's face.

'You think I *enjoy* doing that to him?' Robert spread his arms wide, appealing to the whole world. 'You think I want him to hate me? Kenrick is going to slice him to shreds if he doesn't—'

'But he seems to be doing so well—'

'Yes, he is. But he's got it all here—' Robert thumped his own chest, 'and it needs to be up here, in his head, where he can believe in it. Oh, Finn,' Robert sighed, 'you should have seen him yesterday, at the mine. I was so proud of him. But his father was a monster who beat his wife for sport, who enjoyed killing people weaker than himself. Andrew is going to be *King*, Finn. I have to push him—'

'And until he pushes *you*—' Finnlay didn't finish that comment. Robert was already walking away.

'Don't interfere, Finn. Not if you want him to live.'

29

Godfrey hurried up the stairs, flanked by his Guilde escort. It had been a long time since he'd been inside the Guilde Hall and this occasion filled him with no confidence whatsoever.

Osbert had been unusually silent for the last few days, declining Godfrey's weekly invitation to dinner with some excuse of pressing work. Since Godfrey had more than he could manage of his own, he'd not thought too much about it, but now – now he knew there was something wrong.

The bells of the Basilica were still ringing the end of evening mass, and as he passed by the narrow windows on the staircase, he could see the people of Marsay streaming out into the square, pulling cloaks around their shoulders against the cool spring evening. They'd been blessed with some warmer weather the last week, but it had rained all day today and he'd done his best not to think of it as a bad omen.

He wished there was some way he could know what was going on. He could – and did – send messages, to McCauly at St Julian's, and he felt confident that they would be passed on, but there was no way McCauly could send any messages back. Godfrey was cursed with living in doubt, only hoping that he was helping and not hindering.

His escort turned a corner, taking him down a wide corridor where impressive double doors led off to both right and left. To his knowledge, he was the only non-Guildesman ever to have been allowed this far into the Hall. Every other time he'd been there had left him filled with dread.

But he held his head high as he paused before the smaller, less impressive door at the end of the passage and waited for the guard to open it for him. He was announced and ushered inside.

Osbert's study was a wide, open, panelled room with two fireplaces, and a huge oval table in the centre. The Proctor himself had lost weight over the last months, and there were shadows under his eyes that had never been there before. With a bark at the guards to wait outside, Osbert dismissed his men and waved Godfrey closer. He sat at the table, where books, papers, scrolls and parchments were scattered everywhere, with seemingly no order to them at all. Two heavy candlesticks sat at either end, thick with melted wax, yellow with use. Osbert himself looked no better. His face was as pale as the wax, the lines around his eyes as baggy. With his elbows on the table, his hair lank around his ears, he planted his hands on the papers.

'By the mass, Godfrey, just look at this.'

'At what?' Godfrey hesitated to move closer – this was Guilde business and he wasn't sure he wanted to know.

'Don't you know? Can't you see? Have you heard nothing at all?'

That heavy hand of dread pressed against his chest once more. 'Heard what?'

There must have been something in his tone that made the Proctor look up. It took a moment for his eyes to focus, and then, with his voice harsh with an emotion Godfrey couldn't name, he said, 'It's started.'

'Started?' Godfrey's eyes widened, his blood rushing to his face. But he didn't dare hope, not yet, not without proof. 'What has started?'

But Osbert had seen his reaction and simply shook his head. 'The rebellion.'

'I don't give a damn what you suggest!' Kenrick took his cup and threw it against the opposite wall, splashing red wine against the grey stone. He took one look at the blood-red stain then turned back to his council arranged around the table. They were all watching him with ill-concealed trepidation. Were they really more afraid of him than they were of the Douglas?

'I don't want suggestions, I want facts! I want solutions! I want somebody to tell me how in Serin's name twenty *peasants*—' he spat out the word like it was poison, '—managed to capture a fort manned with seventy trained soldiers! That border is now open wide! Do you have any idea how many malcontents will have crossed over by now? Enough to take two more border posts at least!'

He stalked the length of the table, eyeing each man opposite him, noting who cringed and who met his gaze. 'Where is my army? I want this – this petty rebellion crushed!'

'Sire,' his Chancellor objected, raising his hands in supplication, 'with the loss of those taxes, keeping an army for more than a few weeks will be impossible.'

'I won't need it for more than a few weeks!' he bellowed, ready to let loose more than mere anger. 'Just do it! The man who brings me the head of Robert Douglas will become the wealthiest man in the country! Now go!'

Almost as one, they all scrambled to their feet, bowing profusely and backing out of the door faster than Kenrick had thought possible. Their cowering frames so incensed him he picked up the wine jug and threw it after them. It clattered to the ground, leaving wine streaked across the tiled floor.

And then the room was empty.

He stood at the head of the table, where written reports and accounts of the attacks nearly covered the ancient wooden surface. Somewhere in there was a letter from Tirone, confirming that, under the circumstances, he would not give his permission for Kenrick to marry his daughter, Olivia. Until Lusara was peaceful, until Kenrick succeeded in quashing this rebellion, Tirone would admit no further Embassies on the subject.

Of course, what Tirone didn't consider was that without Olivia and the dowry she would bring, without Mayenne's wealth behind him, Kenrick was in no position to guarantee the damn girl's safety. Well, so be it. Gilbert was due back at court tomorrow – that would be his first task, to get that girl away from her greedy father!

'This is all your fault,' he ground out, not turning to face the man he knew had entered the room in silence.

'My fault, Sire?'

Kenrick pressed his fists to the table and waited until Nash passed him, his pace idle, his urgency nonexistent, as though he didn't give a damn if Kenrick lost the throne.

And perhaps he didn't any more.

'Yes, your fault. For ten years you've kept promising to teach me about sorcery – and yet, what have I learned from you?'

'You think that would have prevented this uprising?'

'It's not an uprising! It's just a few idle peasants stirring up trouble, using *my* gold! Douglas is testing me, no more.'

'So you don't intend to take this seriously.'

'I'm taking it a lot more seriously than you. You were the one who kept telling me that I should wait to press my suit with Olivia. So I did, and now look what's happened! Douglas has overtaken us! You promised me you'd get rid of Tirone's last son – and yet, the boy still lives and Tirone has no need of either me, or the protection I could give Mayenne. And without his support, I'm left stripped bare! This *is* your fault, damn it, Nash. I demand you do something about it!'

Nash reached the jug still lying on the floor, and picked it up, setting it on the table. Then he collected a fresh goblet, pulled the stopper out of a flask of his favourite wine and poured some out. 'What exactly would you have me do? I am at your disposal, of course. I have already supplied you with vital information.'

'What? In telling me my own cousin has now changed sides and is fighting with the Rebel? Why should I take your word? You were the one who ordered the Malachi down there to abduct him in the first place.'

Nash took a mouthful of wine, savoured it, then swallowed. 'Sire, I assure you, my purpose was to get the boy to safety. I had suspected Douglas would try to take him for his own reasons. I thought to bring him back here, where you yourself could protect him. Alas, DeMassey failed in that regard, and nobody has seen the boy since.'

'Which only proves that he is missing, not that he is with Douglas. Why would he become a rebel, eh? He's always had my love. He's my cousin, the closest thing I have to an heir – and he knows that. It would be in his best interests to remain my friend. Besides, Andrew is a child, too meek to go looking for a crown on his own.'

'But certainly malleable enough to allow somebody else to put him there, a personality as strong as Robert Douglas, perhaps?' Nash paused, holding up his hand to beg for peace. 'Sire, I have tried to explain to you what I have learned. I warned you Douglas would attack like this, with mosquito bites all around the country, that he was no longer in a position to field a large army. I also warned you that McCauly has been working on the people, warming them to the idea of sorcery, and now Andrew's mother appears to them to be the new incarnation of the goddess Mineah. This is indeed a serious situation, and yet you refuse to listen to me. I cannot see how I may help you if you don't.'

Kenrick stared at Nash, knowing hatred flowed out of his gaze and into the air between them. He couldn't help it and gave up trying to stop it. Instead, he looked away, back down at the maps and papers on the table before him. He had to ask. If he didn't, he could regret it for the rest of his life – which wouldn't be that long.

'What do you suggest, then?' he asked ungraciously.

'How long until your army can be ready?'

'I'm told another week. Osbert will have a thousand men ready to ride by then as well.'

'Fine. Send them out in bands of two hundred, in every different direction. Keep yourself another five hundred. Your first priority is for the people to see you, see your men, see the Guilde and know that although the rebel has drawn first blood, you are by no means unable to respond. By all accounts, each of his bands is small, two dozen men at most. You go first to intimidate, second to capture.'

'And what good will that do, other than have my men running all over the country?'

'Oh, so you know where Douglas is, do you? You know where to send your army?'

Kenrick blinked once, then stabbed his finger on the map. 'I must not leave Marsay unprotected.'

'Why?' Nash moved closer to pour himself some more wine. 'Afraid your cousin might slip in behind your back and take your throne?'

'Andrew would never do that,' Kenrick replied, with a puzzling certainty. 'If I send my men out like that, how do I fight Douglas?'

'By taking hostage the only thing he really cares about. Send your men to the places his rebels have already hit, collect a dozen innocent locals in each place and put them to the sword. Send out word that unless Douglas submits himself to your justice, you will execute fifty or a hundred in each town. If nothing else, that will reduce the number of raids he and his men make.'

Kenrick had to admit, it was a solid plan. 'And then what – because you know he won't give himself up.'

'No, he won't – but he will keep going, and when the rest of his men don't, you'll be able to track him down eventually. The people will turn from him because of your justice. It will only be a matter of time before you will see the end of him.' Nash coughed a little and drained the rest of his wine, wincing as he did.

'This could take months. I don't have the finances to keep armies in the field that long, and you know it.'

Nash nodded, his eyes dropping to the table. After a moment, he looked up. 'Fortunately, I have been preparing for this day for a long time. There is gold available to pay your armies—'

'And?' Kenrick prompted.

'If we had Malachi to help—'

'So it's Malachi you need to work with, is it?' Kenrick strode to the door and yelled. 'Rayve!'

Moments later, the young man appeared, his usual somber face giving nothing away as he bowed and looked at Nash. For his part, Nash raised his eyebrows, betraying his surprise.

'I know you, don't I? You were one of DeMassey's men, weren't you?'

'Yes,' Rayve agreed. 'I was his student, and proud to serve under in the D'Azzir.'

'I had thought you had all returned home with DeMassey's body.'

'Yes,' Rayve refrained from answering the question. 'Your absence was noted. We were also saddened to see you were not able to allow the Lady Valena to accompany the Baron's body home.'

Kenrick noted with some pleasure how Nash stiffened at that, though he gave nothing else away.

'Sad, yes,' Nash agreed, 'but alas, it was not possible to free her from her duties for so long.'

'We understand,' Rayve said. His face might have been carved from stone.

'And so sad too,' Nash added, almost as an afterthought, 'for DeMassey to die of his injuries in that manner.'

'Indeed.'

Nash appeared to have exhausted his conversation with the young man, so Kenrick took the moment to intervene. 'Rayve has offered to contact his brothers and inform them that they are still welcome at court, though of course, without DeMassey, you will need to lead them a little more directly. We can send at least one Malachi out with every squad of soldiers, increasing the chances of them finding the rebels.'

Nash didn't respond. Instead, he blinked rapidly, his colour several shades lighter than it had been when he had come into the council room. He opened his mouth to speak, then stumbled, his hand reaching out to the back of a nearby chair.

Kenrick frowned. 'What is it?'

Shaking his head again, Nash coughed a little, then his legs collapsed beneath him and he fell to the floor. Only then did Kenrick move, walking the length of the table to stand over Nash's prone body. Rayve was still standing in the open doorway, his face as impassive as ever.

'You,' Nash gasped, 'poisoned me.'

'I?' Kenrick raised his eyebrows in the same way he'd seen Nash do a thousand times. 'Why would I do that? I need your help to rid my country of Robert Douglas. You and I have always been friends, have we not? We pledged our allegiance many years ago. *I* have no reason to kill you.' This was incredible! Had somebody poisoned Nash? If so, did that mean he might be rid of this creature without any further effort? 'You don't know the poison wasn't meant for me. Should I call a doctor?'

Nash's glazed eyes darted from Kenrick to the young man by the door. Then, with an enormous act of willpower, he rolled to his side, clutching his stomach. 'Won't work.'

'I'm pleased to hear that,' Kenrick lied.

'Can't . . . poison me.' Nash closed his eyes a moment, his skin ashen, his lips blue. He breathed in deeply through his nose, then opened his eyes again. 'Can't kill me.'

'No?' Kenrick tried to keep his disappointment out of his voice, only barely succeeding. 'Oh, of course, that's because you only just regenerated, isn't it? Good. Still, Rayve, call the doctor and get some help for Nash. No doubt he will be more comfortable in his own rooms.' Kenrick made it as far as the door before he threw one look back at the man he hated more than any other. Then he walked away. Though he would have paid almost anything to be able to stand there and watch Nash in such pain, he couldn't afford to risk so much so quickly.

But a little fear could only be a healthy thing, couldn't it? Even for a man who thought he was immortal?

'So what are you going to do?' Godfrey stood before the table, arms folded, waiting. For so many years he'd kept faith with this man, knowing he needed help, trying so hard to help him and yet, always falling short of the mark. Now it was time for Osbert to help Godfrey – or rather, his own country. Whether Osbert saw that was, however, another matter.

'I don't think I'm going to get a choice, Godfrey.' Osbert hauled himself to his feet and almost staggered over to the fireplace. He picked up a pot of something that looked like honey and milk and poured some into a cup. With his hands wrapped around it, he sipped. 'Kenrick's ordered me to ready an army of Guilde soldiers. I need a thousand men ready to march next week. How can I not obey? They go to march on a man who is a known sorcerer, who has already demonstrated his skills to the whole country. The Guilde will always support a fight against sorcery, no matter what I say.'

'And it doesn't matter to your brethren that Kenrick is also a sorcerer? That he is a tyrant and a monster? Doesn't that count? Do they not see the difference between Robert and Kenrick?'

'Better the demon you know, Godfrey, than the one you would have replace him.'

'The people love Robert!'

'Damn it, Godfrey, this isn't about love – it's about power! How much power do you think the Guilde would have under Robert Douglas? The same as we have now? After all that Vaughn did to destroy Robert? After all we've done since? You don't think ordinary Guildesmen can see that conflict for themselves? Open your eyes, Godfrey.'

For a moment, Godfrey said nothing. Then he approached the Proctor, keeping his voice low, his hands clasped together in a gesture of peace he meant with all his heart. 'Oh, my eyes are wide open, Osbert. Has the Guilde really sunk so low? Has your Sacred Vow become so transparent? The Guilde was always to be the people's wisdom, holding and saving precious knowledge, working to build and construct, to teach and learn, to *share*. And instead, the Guilde is now nothing more than a private army, jealously guarding the knowledge of a nation in desperate need of enlightenment. The very thing Robert Douglas fought against in the beginning.'

Osbert's gaze was low and hooded.

Godfrey continued, 'And the saddest thing of all is that you know this to be true in your heart. That's why you wanted to replace Vaughn's bigotry with your own wisdom, why you've remained friends with me all these years – because I could remind you with only my presence that the Guilde was always meant for better things than these tyrants have made of it.' Godfrey paused, taking a breath. 'You know all this to be true.'

Osbert watched him in silence, then slowly shook his head. 'I know nothing.'

Disappointment welling up inside him, Godfrey took a step back. All his efforts to save this man's soul had failed. There was nothing more he could do. 'Very well, Osbert,' he said, 'It seems you have finally made your choice. So be it.'

Godfrey turned then and left the room, walking down the corridor as his escort hurried to catch up with him. As he passed by the stair windows, he saw that the rain had finally stopped.

Nash shook off the solicitous but insincere hands of young Rayve and the doctor he'd called. He got to his feet on his own, though the world spun and tilted around him like some dizzy game, and he nearly emptied the contents of his stomach all over the nice tiled floor beneath his feet.

This had to be the work of Malachi. Only they would know which was his favourite wine, which poison would cause him the most agony. Kenrick wouldn't dare – and even the Malachi probably knew it wouldn't kill him.

But by the blood of Broleoch, it hurt!

He took a few minutes to steady himself so he could at least walk, hold his head up high, could get himself through the castle and into his tower. Only then would he allow himself the luxury of giving in to the poison.

His sight was muffled, blurry and stinging, but he elbowed his way out of the council room and into the corridor. He knew people were staring at him as he walked past, but he refused to comment, or to give any sign that he cared at all. They might see him affected, but he could never afford to let them think he was weakened by it. This city was terrified of him, and now was not the time to break that hard-won image.

One careful step after another took him downstairs, along the corridors, out of doors and into the open. The cold bite of fresh air was almost enough to make him faint, but he spent a moment clinging onto the stone wall before straightening.

He could *feel* Rayve behind him, watching him, as though he cared, as though he was just making sure Nash got to his rooms safely – but Nash knew better. Rayve had been one of DeMassey's brightest. Revenge often came in a poison bottle.

The cobbles of the courtyard almost beat him, but he kept his dizzy gaze on the gate and the smaller yard beyond it. After that, his own faithful Malachi met him and escorted him inside, shutting and bolting the door behind him, just in case.

He let his men carry him upstairs. They were Bonded – he didn't need to care what they thought.

Fever burned him, racking his body with a shaking that would not be stilled. His head pounded in counterpoint to his racing heart, giving him not a moment's peace. But this couldn't kill him. He wouldn't let it, not when he was so close.

What poison had they used? One designed to kill, or simply to maim? It was hours since he'd lost the contents of his stomach, his body purging itself of everything, and then still going on, as though it would turn him inside out. The pain from those wrenchings alone was enough to make him want to die.

He didn't dare take any of the unguents Taymar brought him, would only drink water his own Malachi had drawn from the well themselves – after they had tasted it – but even that he could not keep down. The bedclothes around him scraped against his skin, like particles of sharp sand, leaving his joints bloodied. He only knew the days were passing because he saw darkness fill the windows now and then. All else was one long, agonising death.

He *couldn't* die from this. Hadn't his regeneration been of his own blood? His own power combined with Valena's, from his own daughter? Their compound strength should have been enough to make him immortal – and if not, then closer than this.

So if his own daughter's blood wasn't strong enough to resist this poison, was it possible he could die?

No!

But he couldn't ignore the pain, the soiled bedding Taymar changed every few hours, the weakness in his limbs, the sweat, the desperate need for the torture to be over. He *was* dying. All the regeneration had given him was more time to suffer. If he didn't act soon, he would be too weak to save his own life.

'Taymar,' he whispered, and the man appeared.

'Master?'

'Valena. Prepare her.'

'I have her ready, Master. She has been without the drug for two days now, without food or water for the same time. We have her in chains in the next room. Her blood will save you.'

Nash could only nod weakly, then lie back and wait for them to bring her in. He barely looked at her as they placed her down on the table, on her back, winding the chains around her arms, her legs, her belly, around her neck. She could not escape, no more than he could.

When all was ready, Nash got out of bed, using the strong arms of two men to help him, getting him to the side of the table so he could look upon her face once more, so he himself could make the cut.

She watched him with eyes open and awake, all too aware of what was about to happen. She smiled. 'So you are humbled again. So my child died in vain. You have made my death a happy one.'

'Yet you will help me survive,' Nash gasped, holding on to what little strength he had left. He would not fall in front of her – not *her*, of all people. All along he'd known that this would be her end. He would make her fear him at the last if it killed him.

'You know,' she smiled again, 'in the beginning, I did love you. But you gave all your soul to Jennifer Ross, leaving me with this as my destiny, pretending all along that you cared. My own fault, I know.'

Her confession sounded wrong to his ears, but he had no time to tell why.

'Come, Samdon, kiss me one last time. Though you have ruined my beauty, I forgive you. Though you have taken everything from me, I forgive you.'

'Why?'

'I wish to go to my death free of the anger and hatred that flow through your veins. Kiss me, Samdon, then kill me.'

Though her face was twisted and scarred from his anger, her eyes still held him. He could only take the kiss she offered. He leaned down, bracing himself on the table, his arms shaking with the effort. But as his lips touched hers, he felt something else, something awful happening inside him, like a burning, like a glowing white-hot coal deep in his groin. With a cry, he sprang back, caught by his men.

'You witch!'

Her laughter filled the room. 'You fool! Oh, Sam, you fool! A kiss? Why would I forgive you? You are the destroyer – only now you will destroy no more of your own children. I have made you as barren as the earth you would rape. And come what may, you will never sire your own immortality on the Ally! You are impotent, Samdon Nash, and now you can't even pretend you are a real man!'

Nash roared, strength coming from somewhere to hold his body upright. He grabbed the dagger from Taymar, took her arm and sliced down the entire inside length, pushing it over her head to drop bright red blood into the calyx on the floor. Then he took the other arm and did the same, not caring if any was spilt now. He would have her blood, he would have her dead and he would do it now!

He dropped the knife, listening to her laughter soften as her blood drained from her body into the calyx, taking life from her and giving it back to him.

'You fool,' she whispered, her smile unmoving, 'fool. Wanted death. Longed for it . . . Thank you . . . Oh, Luc—'

And then she was still.

30

Andrew ran down the alley as fast as he could, but when he skidded around the corner, all he could hear was a voice calling, 'Look out!'

He saw the figure lunge towards him and he ducked, rolling down the slope until he landed hard against a water trough. Before he could get up, he heard the slice of steel against chain-mail, saw a flash against the moonlight, and then a grunt as the man fell to the ground.

'This way!'

He was up and running then, following Robert step for step, listening hard for the next sounds of pursuit. This attack had all gone so wrong, but they weren't caught yet, and they'd still managed to collapse the walls of the grain store. The chaos was perfect for their getaway too, even though they'd been caught in the act, though Andrew had a long cut in his arm, Robert was injured and he couldn't remember if he'd seen Micah get away or not. What mattered was that the walls of the grain store had fallen and the people of this town were now attacking that stockpile with barrels and baskets, and he knew by morning there would be nothing left for the Guilde to sell back to the people who'd given it as tithe.

'Stay here.' Robert pressed his arm against Andrew's chest, forcing him back into the shadows. Then he readied himself to run across and empty square on his own, to the tavern where he'd left their horses.

'Wait!' Andrew hissed, 'I'll go. You're limping.'

'Are you going to question every order I give you?'

'No, I—'

But Robert was gone, his figure a dark splash against the damp cobbles. Then there was stillness, and silence. He listened hard, hoping for a miracle, but it seemed the Guilde was more interested in trying to save the grain than catch the culprits.

Robert came back across the square, already mounted up, hauling Andrew's horse behind him. Without pausing, Andrew vaulted up into the saddle, but before he could even kick his horse into action, Robert had his say.

'When I need you to treat me like an invalid, I'll tell you. Until that day, you follow my orders without question. Understood?' He didn't wait for a reply. A moment later, they were galloping across the square, heading for the edge of town and the open country beyond.

It wasn't until they'd left the road an hour later that Andrew was able to get the reins to stop burning his hands, and for the trees all around them to stop appearing like blood-spattered ghosts every time he blinked.

Jenn tipped out the bowl of water, rinsed it from the well, then refilled and took it back to the stable where the wounded were being treated. It was dark, but they had two lamps burning; a luxury these days, like the loft they were sleeping in tonight, and the fresh bread the farmer had promised them for breakfast. Sometimes the generosity of these poor folk made her weep with admiration, considering the risk they took hiding and helping a group of condemned rebels.

Robert was waiting for her, sitting on a mounting stool, shirt off, yet another scar bleeding from his shoulder, one more on his calf. At least the old wound in his side was looking much better, despite all the stress he had been putting on it over the last few months.

In one way, she could see and appreciate why the Key had done what it had, to prevent both of them from ageing. Robert was forty-five now and should be slowing down. But no: the Key had interfered in some some way she had never been able to discern, and instead of greying hair, Robert's was still a mane of near-black, his face without lines, his body as strong, and his gaze the same clear green as it had been the day she'd met him almost seventeen years before.

But in another way, she wished the Key hadn't touched him, because he *was* forty-five and he *should* be slowing down now, not still riding hard, fighting harder and working like the demon inside him to win a war begun thirty years ago. Though the country had known peace in that time, Robert never had.

'It's not bad,' he said, twisting his neck so he could see the cut on his shoulder.

'Really?' Jenn asked quietly. 'I just don't understand why you won't wear mail. Is that too much to ask?'

'Oh, come on,' he laughed softly, just for her. 'You think the Key is going to let me die from some small cut with a sword? No, it has much more important ways for me to expire.'

'Don't joke about it!'

He caught her hand, turning his body to shield the movement from the others in the stable. As usual, Robert and Andrew were almost the last in, so the others were on the point of going to their beds.

'I'm sorry,' he whispered, his gaze catching hers, holding it, giving her something to drown in. 'I can't move properly in mail, not for these missions, at least. I have to make a choice between armour and flexibility. I'm not being reckless, I promise.'

And she could see the honesty in his eyes. So many times he *had* been reckless, not caring if he died, because at least then he wouldn't be plagued by the Prophecy any more – but this was different. Now he was working towards the end of the Prophecy as though he still believed he could defeat it.

'I know,' she said, and he let go her hand. She dipped a clean cloth in the water and washed the wound. He didn't flinch, but instead, watched her face, making her blush a little. 'You shouldn't do that.'

'But I love doing it,' he murmured. *I love you, and I miss being able to say it to your face.*

And one day when you do, I'm going to shock everyone by kissing you in front of them – and where would that leave us?

He didn't answer that, and when she finished washing the wound, she looked up to find his eyes sparkling and a cheeky grin on his face. She had to bite a lip and turn away quickly to stop herself from laughing out loud.

'Here, hold that,' she said as she came back with a dressing, taking his right hand and pressing it against the wound. Then she busied herself with looking at his calf. This wound was smaller but deeper, looking like a pike had stabbed into it rather than a sword.

Such a wonderful skill to have, the ability to recognise which weapon had caused which wound. Fortunately, this one was clean and no longer bleeding. Her Healer's Sight told her all she needed, so she wrapped a bandage around it and let him put his boot back on. She wound another around his shoulder, knowing full well he'd take it off in the morning before the next mission.

Then he was standing and thanking her and moving away and instantly she missed him, as though somebody had carved a piece out of her. How had she lived so long without him? Why was it that the more time they spent together – especially now that they *were* together – that each separation was a terrible wrenching she didn't think she could bear?

She busied herself with cleaning up, making sure that nobody else needed help, trying to ignore the look from the Bishop and the way her eyes stung as she tried not to think about the man who had just walked away from her because he had to.

'Jenn?'

She swallowed hard and looked back at McCauly, who was finishing the last of his own bandaging for the night. 'Do you need help?'

'I wanted to make up a tonic for this lad here. I left my medicines bag on my horse. Would you retrieve it for me?'

'Of course.' Jenn left her things where they were and headed outside, and around the back of the stable—

Where she was caught by arms she knew so well, swept up into the darkness where they both belonged.

'This is crazy,' she whispered against his lips. 'If somebody should walk by—'

'They won't.'

'You'll be missed.'

'Not for a few minutes, I won't.' And then he didn't give her the opportunity to object further. Instead, he kissed her and she tasted the rich warmth of him, felt the love in the arms that held her fast against him, in the way he breathed in time with her, the way he shielded her body against the stable wall in case she was cold.

It was impossible now to remember what it had been like in the awful years when she hadn't seen him at all, when he'd hated her, or she'd hated him. But had they ever really hated each other? Or had it just been this, in some other, isolated, frustrated, convoluted form?

No, they had always been like this. Even before they'd acknowledged it, and seventeen years of heartache hadn't changed it. Not even Nash could destroy this.

That thought alone was enough to make her smile. He felt the movement and shifted back a little. It was completely black where they were, but she knew he could see her.

'You smile. Why?'

'You brought me back here to talk?'

She felt his laughter and joined in again until he kissed her, more deeply this time, drying up the laughter, but leaving joy behind.

'When this is all over,' he murmured, holding her close again, 'I will marry you no matter what you say.'

'What makes you think I want to be a Douglas?'

'The fact that you're not exactly squirming to be let go.'

'I can squirm if I want to.'

'Oh? Well, go ahead.'

'But you won't let me go, will you?'

He kissed her hard then, his whisper fierce and hot against her throat. 'I'll *never* let you go, Jenny. Never.'

'Oh, I see,' the Bishop's voice came to them, purposefully louder than it really needed to be. 'I'm pretty certain Robert went off to have a scout around the farm, but he'll probably be back in a few minutes. Why don't you talk to him about it then?'

Jenn sprang back from Robert. A moment later, the voices were gone, leaving them alone again. But this time, she didn't go into his arms. This time she could only cling to the memory of his warmth and of what he was fighting, the darkness inside him more whole than this night. If only she could do something to stop it.

'Robert, you can't hold on for ever.'

'I can,' he whispered back, knowing exactly what she was talking about. 'I can hold on for as long as it takes.'

'But the demon is growing again. I can see it.'

'Then stop looking.'

'But—'

'Please.' And then he pulled her close again. 'I can't fight with you any more. I can barely stand to be apart from you. Don't—'

She could only kiss him and hold him. They were both lost, both found, both as trapped as they could be, and just as free. Words weren't going to change anything.

Then she said, 'You'd better go and ensure the Bishop wasn't lying. I'll go get his medicine bag.'

He vanished into the darkness like a wraith.

This time the wrenching almost tore her in two.

Micah moved through the quiet loft and collected together the water-bottles each man carried with him during the day. Most of the men were here, asleep, exhausted, or wide awake with the agony of their wounds. Robert had already been amongst them and deadened what pain he could, but this feeling went bone-deep, and Micah couldn't ignore it.

For his own part, he had received little more than scratches, and he'd worked as best he could towards the success of each mission. For the rest, he kept his thoughts to himself and the remainder of him out of Robert's sight.

He laid the strap for each bottle over one shoulder and skinned down the ladder into the dark farm yard. To his left, sheltered by other buildings, was the last of the fires they'd lit and he could see familiar faces sitting around it: the Bishop, Patric, Joshi and Robert. Jenn had already gone to bed, it appeared.

Micah turned away and padded silently through the farmyard, past the house, opening one gate after another, until he reached the long lane heading north. The hedge was thick here, fresh with spring leaves and evening dew. Then the lane opened out onto a wide lake, sprinkled with dappled moonlight and very pretty. He couldn't help but stand and stare at it for a moment, hiding in the shadows of trees pressed close to his left.

A movement by the lake made him freeze, frowning into the darkness to make out the shape. For a moment, he thought it must be a dog or something, but the shape moved and there was enough light to see somebody crouched by the water, splashing handfuls on his face.

Micah cleared his throat. 'My lord, are you all right?'

Andrew started, almost tumbling over. Then he almost as quickly turned back, using the crook of his elbow to dry his face. 'Yes, I'm fine,' he grunted, getting to his feet and shaking the water from his hands.

'Are you sure?'

'Yes, of course.' And the tone was almost normal.

'You shouldn't really be out here, not at this time of night, not on your own.'

'I know, I'm sorry.' Andrew's head dropped, his voice emerged contrite. 'I'll go back.'

'There's no hurry. You can help me with these if you like.'

Andrew looked up, as though Micah had just given him some breath of hope in a wasteland of darkness. 'Of course.' He surged forward and took the bottles from Micah, kneeling down by the lake to refill one after the other with the sparkling water.

Micah knew he shouldn't, but he'd been guardian of this boy for eight years; he knew him too well to ignore the signs. 'How goes your training?'

Andrew shrugged and pushed the stopper into a bottle. His tone emerged cool and a little too calm. 'I'm a disappointment. I should be a skilled and powerful sorcerer by now, ready to fight and kill Kenrick. Instead, I'm a weakling who doesn't care enough about his country to try as hard as it takes in order to remove a tyrant. But other than that, it's quite fun. What about you? How are you enjoying your exile?'

Micah blinked a moment, then busied himself with another water-bottle. 'My best friend won't talk to me and as a result, everybody treats me as some kind of traitor except for you, the Bishop and Jenn. I miss my wife and I worry about her carrying this child on her own, but essentially, you're right, this is all a lot of fun.'

He finished with the last bottle and put it to one side, then looked up to find Andrew's gaze on him, eyes wide with wonder.

'Child? She's . . . you're going to be a father?'

Micah couldn't help it. His face broke into a grin he was sure was half delight, half terror. 'Yes. Seems strange, doesn't it?'

Andrew's own smile warmed the cool night. 'Congratulations, Micah. I don't care if – just – congratulations. You'll make a good father.'

'You think so?' Micah stood and bent to gather the bottles together, handing half to Andrew.

'I do. You played the father often enough with me. You've had plenty of practice.'

But that wasn't all that made a father. Micah knew that much. 'I hope you're right. My own father was—' He stopped, not sure whether he even wanted to think about how he'd given up his relationship with his father so he could follow Robert. But it had been more than that. He'd given up his father's principles in favour of Robert's friendship, Robert's opposing principles. His father had never forgiven him that betrayal.

'Your father?' Andrew was standing in front of him, water-bottles forgotten, staring at him with that same shadowy need.

'My father should have listened more. And I should have been prepared to talk.'

Andrew searched his gaze, myriad thoughts scuttling across his face. 'My father—'

Micah held his breath. This was the first time he'd ever heard Andrew voluntarily mention Eachern, the man the world believed was his sire.

'My father didn't listen to anyone either. He used to . . . he would hit my mother if she disagreed with him.' Andrew swallowed hard, but continued bravely, 'My father beat everybody who got in his way – except me. Uncle Lawrence, though, he never lifted a hand against anybody.'

'Your uncle was a good man.'

'But my father wasn't.' And then Andrew looked away, revealing his face in full moonlight. He spoke softly, as if to himself. 'You'll be a good father, Micah. You're a good man, and your children will be lucky to have you.'

Andrew fell silent then, his gaze lost in the distance. Micah left him with the quiet for a moment, then swung the water-bottles over his shoulder. 'We should move back now. It's getting late and Finnlay should return soon with the messages.'

'Oh, yes,' Andrew said, as though nothing was wrong, and followed Micah back to the farm.

Even in the darkness, Micah could see where the farm had once been prosperous and was now suffering. Though there should have been animals noises all around, now there was just the sound of a few pigs snuffling in the sty and in the field beyond, a few sheep, but that was all.

Andrew walked with his head down, silence sitting around him like a shroud.

They took the water up to the loft, leaving bottles beside each man, ready for the morning. Just as they were finished, Micah heard the unmistakable sound of a horse approaching and stood to peer out of one of the holes in the loft roof. He relaxed when he saw that it was Finnlay. He turned to find Andrew helping a wounded soldier drink.

'We'd better go down.'

Finnlay's back ached. Too many hours in the saddle, too much time spent looking over his shoulder. But it was good to reach camp at last.

He brought his horse to a stop just inside the farm gate. Micah took the animal and as he got to the fire, Robert handed him a cup of warmed spiced wine. Finnlay wrapped his tired hands around the cup and sank to an empty seat by the fire.

'How did you go today?' was his first question. The Bishop was there, sitting on a firewood stump, his back to the stable, and Andrew sat on the opposite side of the fire, watching him warily.

Robert reached forward to stir up the fire. 'We opened the grain store but we were discovered before we could get away cleanly and we have two more injuries that need some attention. What about you? You're very late back. Did you have trouble?'

Finnlay drained his cup and said, 'There's a lot of Guilde activity in the north. I had to go back three times before it was clear to do the pick-up. Things are getting more dangerous by the day.' Their missions took them from one side of the country to the other, never further west than the Goleth Mountains, but even so, their path was taking them inexorably north, towards Marsay, Kenrick and Nash. The opposition was only going to get worse from here.

'Were there any messages?' Robert had a few message points set up around the country, safe places where his contacts could leave coded notes. So far, they'd been very lucky about keeping the drop points secret. They'd lost only two to date, and those without any real trauma.

'Three.' He reached into his jacket and pulled out a pouch, tossing it in Robert's direction. Robert didn't open it immediately, gesturing for Finnlay to continue. 'Owen says the raid in Brigham went well, though he's lost two men and has another too badly injured to continue. He does say that he's had five volunteers join his group, so his numbers are still functional. Expects to have a full complement to bring to Rona.'

Robert's gaze darkened a little.

'Daniel has had a lot of trouble with Kenrick's soldiers; he had to go back over the border once already to escape them. He returned by a different route, undiscovered – but he wanted to tell you that there are a lot of refugees returning, and that we'll encounter them on our travels. He's worried about them coming back while Kenrick's still on the throne.'

Robert shrugged. 'There's nothing we can do to stop them. We need the borders open.'

'Oh, I agree. He also said he'd see us at Rona.' Finnlay fell silent then, staring into his cup a moment before taking a large swallow. Then his eyes lifted to Micah as he finished with Finnlay's horse and returned to sit with them. Micah caught the look and raised his eyebrows in question.

Robert knew them both too well to miss such signals. 'What aren't you telling me? You said there were three messages.'

Finnlay nodded. 'Yes.' It would have been better if he'd lost the last message – but then, Robert had always been bound to find out about this one day. He'd just hoped that it wouldn't be him who had to break the news. 'There's a letter in there from Godfrey. He warns that Kenrick has ordered an army, which by now will be in the field. There's also a thousand Guildesmen on their way south.'

'All of which we expected,' Robert added quietly. 'And?'

Taking a deep breath, Finnlay continued, 'And he mentions a . . . well, I don't know how else to put this, but the monks at Fenlock, they've asked Godfrey to investigate several miracles occurring at Elita. Apparently, the entire area is abuzz with rumours and tales of wondrous sights. And it appears that, as a result of certain other coincidental events, the people of the area, including the monks, believe that it is all a result of the fact that . . . er, that the new incarnation of Mineah has come—'

'You're not serious!'

'They think Jenn is Mineah, yes.' Finnlay looked first at Micah, then at Robert. Lastly, he looked to Andrew who sat with his eyes wide open, face golden in the firelight.

'They think Mother is—' Andrew got to his feet, but a glance from Robert brought him back down to his seat. 'How can they think that?'

McCauly answered him. 'The Hermit of Shan Moss has been foretelling she would come for a long time, almost twenty years. And people believe that – oh, by the mass!' His voice trailed off in an odd combination of awe and wonder, enough to draw Robert's cynical gaze.

'You're not going to tell me you believe this, are you? You know full well the kinds of things the villagers have seen – sorcery, of one kind or another – some of which wasn't even Jenn! I can see how they might arrive at that conclusion, not knowing what's really going on, but you don't have that same excuse, Bishop. You *know* Jenn. She's not the goddess.'

Andrew looked at Robert then, almost clinging to the certainty in his voice.

McCauly raised his eyebrows, neither offended nor amused. 'And why couldn't she be the goddess? Each incarnation of Mineah takes on a different form, for a different reason. Patric has virtually confirmed that the last incarnation, fighting at Alusia against the Cabal, was in fact a woman from the Generet. You yourself have tried to convince me of exactly that—'

'I didn't. I just tried to suggest that it *might* be.'

'Which is exactly what I'm doing. I take it Godfrey is intending to investigate?'

Finnlay nodded, keeping his head down while sitting between the two men. Nobody liked to get in the middle of an argument between Robert and the Bishop. But the tightness in his gut didn't ease and he knew he'd have to tell them the rest. 'Godfrey has sent somebody down to take a look, but he thinks it's already too late.'

'Too late?' Robert asked faintly.

'He received word, just before he wrote, that a group of six nuns had made a pilgrimage to Elita and had already founded a religious house in the keep. He says that by the time we get the letter, word of it will have spread across the country.'

'Oh, by Serin's blood!' Robert ran both hands over his face. 'They know she's alive. They can't know she killed Eachern, but too many people saw and recognised her at Shan Moss and now they're . . . damn it!' Robert got to his feet and began to pace. 'We have to stop this. If people take this to heart then this will look more like a religious war – and how will Salti take it if the people think their own Jaibir is the incarnation of the same goddess who defeated the Cabal five hundred years ago? Serin's blood, they'll think she's about to betray them a—'

Robert stopped then, half turned away from the fire, so that Finnlay was the only one who saw his face pale, his eyes widen in abrupt and violent understanding of something. The moment seemed to stretch, but barely a heartbeat later, Robert had recovered and turned back to the fire. He resumed his seat and took the pot of warming wine, lifting it to refill Finnlay's cup.

'But, Father,' Andrew was shaking his head, still a little dazed by the news, 'You *know* my mother isn't the goddess. She *can't* be! Those people just *want* somebody to help them, that's all. They think if the goddess is here then everything will be fixed soon. They think it's Mother because she's the only woman alive who has stood up to Selar and Nash. And because she's a Ross, and they want to believe a Ross would still be watching over them. It's all just a lot of wishes and no real substance. I know her, Father, my mother is *not* the goddess.'

There was silence at this impassioned plea, and Finnlay could see he wasn't the only one who heard the note of desperation in the boy's voice, though it was Micah who spoke to it. 'You know Godfrey, my lord. He will treat all with unstinting fairness.'

Andrew visibly relaxed the worst of his tension. He turned his attention to the fire.

'What are you going to do?' McCauly ventured.

'Do?' Robert's expression was hard, his eyes glittering. 'Nothing. There's nothing we can do. People will believe what they want to believe regardless of what we say.'

'We have to tell her.'

'Yes. But *I'll* do it, if you don't mind, Bishop.'

'What? Afraid I'll contaminate it with too much religious significance?' Finnlay never seen the Bishop so close to being truly offended.

For a moment, Robert appeared completely lost at the question, as though he hadn't understood it at all. Then, his tone bemused, he asked, 'When have I ever given you that impression? What have I ever done to make you think that? How do you think she's going to feel, being told people think she's a goddess? You've just heard how her son feels about it. I just think it would be better coming from me, that's all.'

McCauly studied him, then sat back. 'I'm sorry.'

Although Finnlay saw Robert accepted the apology, he also knew Robert was holding something back that none of them were likely to hear about.

'So,' Finnlay dived into the uncomfortable silence, suddenly unafraid. 'What are we doing tomorrow?'

There was clear relief in Robert's voice as he started to reply, 'Well, the bridge at—'

'Nothing.'

They both looked up at Andrew, who was deliberately poking at the fire with a twig, ignoring the surprised attention of his elders.

'Care to elaborate?' Robert volunteered, though not very kindly.

'I don't think we should do anything,' Andrew replied, his voice only a little unsteady. 'I think the men are exhausted and need some rest. I think the wounded need to see a proper Healer. I think everybody needs to sleep in a proper bed for a change, and eat a reasonable meal or two. I think they all deserve to laugh and listen to some music and I think that if we don't do this now, our success rate will plummet and we'll have more casualties than either of us really want. So, I think tomorrow we should do nothing. And the next day. After that, we can pull down any bridge you care to name.'

Stunned silence surrounded the little fire for a moment, then Robert's gravelly voice intruded. 'That's a good idea. Perhaps we could send a message to Kenrick and ask him to hold off his armies because we're having a few days' rest. Perhaps we could ask the entire country to endure their misery for another two days because we're a little too tired to be bothered helping them.'

Andrew's head snapped up, fury in his eyes. 'And how are we to go on helping them if everybody is too tired to pay close enough attention to what they're doing? You've trained all these men very well, Robert, but they need a rest. We've been on the road for more than a month, and almost every day we've made one hit or another, or travelled great distances. Two more days won't make a difference to Lusara – but it could be the difference between these men living and dying in the next mission. They need to rest. Especially if—'

'What?'

'Especially if Kenrick is headed south. His troops will be fresh. Ours will barely remember the last night's full sleep they had.'

Robert sat up straight. His voice emerged soft and full of warning. 'How many chances do you think we have, eh? Do you think this country can survive for ever waiting for us to save it? Do you think the people have an infinite number of times they can support a rebellion? Whatever you *think*, Andrew, you need to understand right now that this is the last time we can do this. Another failure and any faith they had in us will die and they won't invest in anyone else again. Ultimately, Kenrick and Nash will win because we failed to try hard enough.'

'You think that I . . .' Andrew's mouth was open in shock.

'You've never agreed to fight him. What else am I to think?'

'But I've done everything—'

'He's coming, Andrew.' Robert got to his feet, tossing the dregs of his wine into the flames, making them sputter and flare blue and yellow. 'Kenrick is on his way to fight *you*. You want to rest? Fine, we'll rest. But you need to remember: *you're* the one who needs to make sure he's ready for that day. It's not just your life, your conscience that's at stake here. The entire country is holding its breath for you.'

With that, Robert tossed his cup to Micah and nodded at Finnlay and McCauly. 'I'll speak to everyone in the morning. Goodnight.' And then he was gone, leaving the air chilly and empty in his wake.

Micah heard the first noise, faint and harsh in the night. At the second noise, he sat up and looked over to Andrew lying beside him. The loft was mostly dark, but the full moon gave enough light through the cracks to let him see the faint sheen of sweat over the boy's face.

Another nightmare.

They'd plagued Andrew most of his life, though not often enough to be a real problem, and for the most part, he never remembered what was in them. But lately, there'd been more, coming hard and shocking in the middle of the night.

This one was no different. Andrew panted, then grunted and twisted restlessly in his blankets, mouthing words nobody could hear.

Then abruptly, the boy's eyes snapped open – but after a moment, Micah realised he could see nothing. Micah scrambled out of his blankets, squatting beside Andrew, already reaching out to calm him. But at the first touch, Andrew slapped his hand away, pulling back with terror in his eyes. Then, suddenly, he gasped, his hands flying up to shield his face.

'Andrew!' Micah whispered, desperate to stop the boy waking everybody in the loft. 'Please, wake. It's only a dream.'

'No, no, no, no! Mother, no!' With his voice strangled in his throat, Andrew sat up, his whole body shaking, his eyes blinking as he slowly came to himself. Micah sat by, holding his elbow, reaching for a bottle of water, ready with comfort.

He didn't get the opportunity. He opened his mouth to speak – and stopped when a vice-like grip took hold of his arm.

It was Robert, crouched beside him, dressed, sword in hand, alert and ready for danger. Instantly, Micah tensed.

'Get him ready,' Robert hissed. 'And wake Finnlay. Armed and down-stairs. One minute.'

Micah nodded, forgetting everything else in the urgency. 'What is it?'

'Danger approaching.' Robert was already moving away. 'Malachi.'

31

Robert could feel it, sitting like an itch beneath his skin; the warning all Salti felt when Malachi were near. He couldn't deny there was a part of him that had been expecting this.

He slipped down the stairs to the yard, pressing his body against the wall, melting into the shadows while he waited for the others to join him. He probably shouldn't have ordered Andrew to follow, but he'd vowed not to let the boy out of his sight – and after the attack on Maitland, he was not about to leave him alone and relatively unprotected in the loft sleeping while there were Malachi prowling around outside.

How had they been found?

Faint noises from above and he counted the footsteps coming down the ladder until Finnlay, Micah and Andrew stopped beside him, each looking out into the moonlight-drenched darkness, each listening, each tense, waiting for the next move.

'This way,' Robert whispered, gesturing to Finnlay to take up the rear. He moved quickly across the open yard, along the shadows of the stable, and into the narrow lane heading towards the lake. His Senses rolled before him like a tidal wave, giving the night a peculiar taint.

The lake sat alone in the landscape, waters flat and sparkling against the moon. The beach glistened with tiny lights in the places where shadows weren't cast by the scraggly trees. Robert made for those shadows, hand already on his sword.

They were not alone.

A small movement, a familiar shape, and then she stepped out into the light. She looked a little different, her belly more swollen, her clothes chosen for comfort. Her hair cascaded down to her shoulders, alive and silver in the night. Even before his mind registered her presence, Robert felt Micah shift and step forward. Robert stopped him with an arm across his chest.

'If you go, you may never come back.'

'By the mass!' Micah hissed. 'She's my *wife*!'

'You were not forced to marry her.'

'And you have had so much control over who *you* love?'

311

Robert snapped his gaze to his old friend. He could not stop now and argue; the time for that had passed six or seven years ago. 'I told you what would happen if she came near me again.'

Micah pushed past him until he stood in the space between them, a part of neither world. 'I won't let you—'

'Micah.' Sairead kept her voice low, but she spoke with the same determination as her husband. 'Stand aside. He cannot kill me and he knows it.'

'Don't believe it.' Micah remained where he was, his eyes not moving from Robert. 'I would once have thought him incapable of such a thing, but now . . .'

Another movement from the darkness drew Robert's attention, his sword drawn from reflex as much as anything else. It was the same man he'd seen before, the ugly man with the plaited braid and the crooked teeth: Gilbert Dusan, grandson of the leader of these people.

'There is no need for any violence,' Dusan said, holding his hands up and away from his body, displaying that he was unarmed – as though that made a difference to Malachi.

But even as he stepped further into the moonlight, Robert's Senses warned him that there were more people in the shadows, perhaps another seven or eight. The witch had brought reinforcements with her.

'If there's no need for violence, then why is she here? You heard what I said.' Robert moved until he was standing in front of Andrew, feeling Finnlay move to protect their rear. 'If you try to take the boy, you will all die. You have one chance now to leave with your lives. Take it.'

'My lord, please!' Micah stepped forward, his face anguished. 'They don't want Andrew. Please, just listen.'

'To what?' Robert's anger was already leaking out into the demon, making his sword glow softly. It took so little now to set it off. 'These are Malachi, Micah! They have, for more than five hundred years, done their best to slaughter every Salti alive! They have slaved under Nash's guidance to set a tyrant on our throne and rob us of the Key. What, in the name of Serin, could they have to say to me that I would want to hear? An apology?'

'A proposal of peace.'

The voice rattled across the sandy beach and fell into the darkness. Robert turned to Dusan and shook his head.

'A proposal of peace? Between whom? Are you saying Nash wants peace? Or Kenrick?'

'Just the Malachi.'

'The same Malachi who tried to abduct this boy here, who murdered his family?'

'And you are blameless in the war between our peoples?' Dusan stalked around Sairead, pushing Micah to one side to stand before Robert's sword, not once looking at it. 'You, the man who, in one moment, killed three hundred Malachi at Elita? This is not the time to be counting wounds, Robert of Dunlorn. Instead, it is the time to be considering who is your real enemy, and who could be your friend.'

Robert could only laugh, though the sound was harsh even to his own ears. 'And of course, I would trust anything you told me.'

'Such trust works both ways! You think *my* people want an alliance with such as you? There are not so many of us that every Malachi could fail to be touched by your actions at Elita. Surely that is enough reason to at least listen.'

'If those Malachi at Elita hadn't been in the service of Nash, they wouldn't have died. Nothing you can say will ever make me trust you.'

'No!' the ugly man spat back, his eyes narrowing. 'Your pigheadedness will bring us all to our doom. I will not leave until you have heard what I came to say. And if you think you can—'

The threat was all Robert wanted to hear. His entire body sang with satisfaction as he gave way to the desire. The demon leaped inside him, pushing forth with a power he never used deliberately. The invisible blow shoved the man backwards, lifting him off the ground before dropping him like a stone. Robert advanced until he could place the point of his sword at the man's throat. He was insanely delighted to see the flicker of fear where there had been nothing but arrogance before.

'I gave you the opportunity to flee.'

That flicker of fear wavered for a moment, but did not leave. Still Dusan spread his hands, vulnerable now on his back. 'I will not fight you, Robert of Dunlorn. If you wish me dead, you will have to murder me.'

The words drove the demon up into his throat, making his hand shake with a desire that was delicious and almost overwhelming. Malachi had always aided Nash, in full knowledge of what he was, what he was doing – and they'd supported him in his evil just because they'd wanted to get the Key, not caring who was murdered along the way, nor the misery that would be inflicted on a whole nation. 'You think the threat of murder would stop me? So be it!'

He raised his sword, letting loose the dark power of the demon to course through it. He heard voices rise along with it, Finnlay, Micah, even Sairead – though none of the other Malachi said a word. Running with the freedom of the demon, he swung down, aiming to strike off Dusan's head – but his blow was blocked by another sword.

'Don't,' Andrew whispered, struggling with both hands to hold off Robert's blade. 'Please.'

He turned and looked at the boy, at his mother's eyes in the masculine face, the qualities she possessed – and those he had gained from that monster of a father. The gaze never wavered, never changed, making him remember so much that he'd wanted desperately to forget.

This boy's mother . . . and this boy's father.

The demon dried up inside him, subsiding to sit in his belly again, lying in wait. Robert let up his sword and Andrew stepped back, relief filling his eyes, but keeping his silence.

While he stood there, Micah rushed forward and helped Dusan to his feet. Micah addressed Andrew. 'My lord, this is Gilbert Dusan, grandson of Aamin, Blood of the Chabanar.'

Andrew turned to face him, eyebrows raised in surprise at the name and title. 'Blood of the Chabanar?'

'Like the Jaibir, my lord.'

Robert faced Dusan. 'You speak for your people?'

'I speak for my grandfather. He speaks for my people.'

'All your people?'

Dusan nodded. 'All but those who abducted and tortured you.'

'Of course.' Robert gave him a dark smile. 'And what about those who tried to take Andrew? Who did murder his family?'

Giving him a measuring look, Dusan said, 'The abduction was at Nash's order. The men themselves were D'Azzir, led by the Baron DeMassey. He died of the wounds you gave him. Most of the men who served him, who made the subsequent attack on Maitland, now work for Felenor Calenderi, the man who abducted and tortured you. I should point out that your rescue was entirely driven by Micah, at extreme danger to ourselves.'

Robert absorbed this information silently. 'And why did he want me?'

'To find out where the Key is, of course. He has tired of Nash's promises, he feels threatened because his protector, DeMassey, is dead. He has formed some kind of alliance with Kenrick. He must have discovered that my niece was bringing you to meet me and decided to intervene. I had nothing to do with his plans. I have refused to speak to him for more than fifteen years, since he killed your Queen without cause.'

Bitter cold trickled down Robert's chest and sat in his stomach, keeping the demon company. '*He* killed Rosalind?'

'What does he look like?' Finnlay had appeared at Robert's side, as ready as any Lusaran to mete out justice.

But Robert held up his hand. If they were going to do this, they needed to get something fundamental perfectly clear – and as yet, he had not decided whether they *were* going to do this. 'This Felenor Calenderi wanted me to give him the Key?'

'That's right.'

'And what do *you* want?'

Dusan paused, his eyes going from Micah, to Finnlay, to Robert, and finally, to Andrew. 'Peace. We want peace between Malachi and Salti.'

'And you no longer want the Key?'

'If I said we had lost our desire for it, I would be lying. However, the last twenty years has drained us of our brightest lights, our best minds, and most powerful fighters. We can no longer afford to have the Key as our sole purpose in life. But even if we did, supporting Nash would bring us nothing but despair. If he gets his hands on the Key—'

'He'll never give it to you.'

Dusan shook his head sadly. 'No.'

'Then why?' Robert slid his sword home, spreading his arms wide. 'Why have you supported him all these years?'

'We didn't – officially. But our young men and women wanted the glory he promised, and they were prepared to do anything to be the one to return the Key to our people. None of use really understood what Nash was until it was too late.' Dusan's gaze turned inwards. 'For twenty years I have worked with him, appearing to do much more than I did, so that I could learn from him, glean his secrets, report back to my grandfather on our hopes for the Key. The longer I stayed with Nash, the more I realised that we were hopelessly naïve to think we could get the Key from him, or fight him for it. There was only one person alive who could do that.'

Robert allowed his Senses to roam into the shadows, then he gestured to the other Malachi standing there to come out into the open. One by one they emerged, pride in their eyes, the set of their shoulders.

If only they could have talked like this twenty years ago.

He couldn't forget what these people had done, nor what they could still do – but there was an air of desperate hope in their appearance. They found this as distasteful as he, and yet, they were here. They had done nothing when he'd gone to kill Dusan – and Sairead, for all the years she'd been married to Micah, had not once taken advantage of her proximity to Andrew. But was all that enough foundation to begin peace between them?

Andrew seemed to think so. And hadn't McCauly spoken about Andrew's ability to discern truth from a lie? Was he able to See somehow that Dusan and the others were here in honesty?

'And how,' Robert said quietly, 'do you propose to ensure peace between Salti and Malachi? Will you fight alongside us?'

'I don't think that's possible – no matter how much I would like to say yes. There are centuries of bad blood between us, and it will take more than a midnight meeting between you and me to change that. But we will offer support where we can, and in places you cannot reach.'

Intrigued, Robert asked Dusan, 'How?'

'Felenor Calenderi. His men. Kenrick has grown to rely on them, is sharpening his skills with their aid. I intend to stop them.'

Robert looked at the men behind Dusan, saw the truth in their eyes as well. 'And what about after this is over? Will you then try to wrest the Key from us again?'

Dusan's gaze deepened then, and he shook his head slowly. 'My people have spent half a millennium trying to regain something that never wanted them in the first place. It is time we let it go, and put our efforts into building what was lost when the Cabal fought the Empire. Aamin wishes us to return to Bu, though he is old and most likely will not survive to see it.'

'Leaving you to make it happen?'

Dusan murmured, 'I must replace one dream with another. Such a task will take time.'

The Malachi fell silent then, and the quiet spread over all of them. The night was heavy with expectation. Robert, unwilling to move, turned to Andrew standing on his left, finding the boy's eyes on him, waiting. Then, as though Robert had asked a question, Andrew nodded, so slightly nobody else would have noticed.

And Robert knew that was what he'd been waiting for. 'Very well.' He turned back to Dusan. 'We have a truce between us. All else will be resolved after Nash can no longer plague any of us.'

With a smile on his ugly face, and barely contained relief in his eyes, Dusan said, 'Good. You will not be disappointed.'

'I'll make sure of it,' Robert added easily. He waited as the Malachi drew back, listening as some mounted up on horses he could barely discern on the edge of the shadows. Dusan waited a moment longer, then he too turned and vanished into the darkness. Robert put a hand on Andrew's shoulder and steered him back towards the farm, hearing Finnlay fall in behind.

But he paused when he reached the lane. 'Finn, take Andrew back, will you? I want to talk to Micah.'

'What are you going to say?' Andrew stood before him, belligerence in his whole body. 'Are you going to punish him because he wanted to arrange a peace between Malachi and Salti? Are you?'

Robert gave a hard laugh. 'You think because I told you some of the facts that you understand my relationship with Micah? What I have to say to him is none of your business.'

'But he was only trying to do the right thing! He married Sairead years ago, and she came to the cottage every now and then. Despite the fact that she knew who I was, she never did a single thing against me, even when she worked out I was Salti. You can't make Micah pay for that, you can't!'

With one long stride, Robert stood before the boy, deliberately towering over him, seeing only the mulish cut of his father's chin, the stubbornness in his eyes. 'Don't you *dare* talk to me like that – this is none of your business! Now get to bed!'

Andrew's eyes widened, his mouth opened, but nothing came out. Then, without another word, he turned and fled, pelting down the lane as though there were a dozen demons at his back.

And weren't there?

'Well done, brother,' Finnlay murmured in the silence. 'Keep pushing him like that and soon he'll lose all faith in you. Or is that exactly what you want?' Finnlay reached out and put a hand on Robert's shoulder, squeezing to emphasise his words. 'Now and then, you should try asking what the rest of us think. Goodnight.'

Robert closed his eyes then, tuning out the moonlight and the sparkling lake, the rumbling inside and the shaking in his hands.

He couldn't ask – because none of them would understand. How could he talk about the demon, the darkness, and all that Andrew needed to be, all that he wasn't? The need that drove him couldn't be voiced, nor the determination to succeed.

He waited a moment longer before heading back to the lake and its glistening beach. He found them together, as he'd expected. Micah turned to face him, keeping hold of his wife's hand. There was fear in Micah's eyes; that alone was enough to cut Robert in two.

Why had he allowed this to happen between them? Why had Micah not believed in him; not said something about the Malachi girl he'd fallen in love with? All questions he could no longer ask. Whatever wounds Micah had inflicted, he had doubled them in return: it was a tangled web of betrayal no words would mend now.

'Do you plan to stay with us?'

Micah looked at Sairead before lifting his chin at Robert. 'Am I not banished?'

'The question,' Robert murmured, 'was directed at your wife.'

Micah's eyes widened in disbelief, then he glanced again at Sairead before he replied, 'No. She is returning with her uncle. I don't want her riding so much in her condit—'

'I'm not an invalid.'

'It's a wise decision,' Robert said. 'But if you go, you will not see each other again until this is all over. I can't afford anybody close enough to track our path. Not even you.'

'You're still threatening me?'

Robert moved closer, noting with some satisfaction that Micah no longer stood defensively. 'Why do you hate me?' he asked the girl. 'I never offered you anything but friendship.'

'Why do you think?' she said bitterly. 'He's my husband – but year after year, he chose you over me. How could I not hate you?' With that, she placed her hands either side of Micah's face and kissed him hard. Then she drew back, her gaze only on him. After a moment, she was gone, leaving Micah staring at the shadows, listening to her ride away.

'You know, Micah,' Robert murmured, not wanting to disturb the peace, 'you should never have done that. You should never have chosen me over her.'

'I know.' Micah turned back for the farm with his hands in his pockets. 'Believe me, I know.'

The noise of the market was as welcome to Jenn as the sun shining on her face, and the luxury of being able to enjoy it free from guilt. She walked along lanes of stalls burdened with cloth, vegetables, farm-tools and rugs. She kept away from the butchers; the smell alone was enough to sour the sunny day. Instead, she followed sweeter smells and bought twenty lemon cakes and some rosewater-flavoured jelly cubes she'd never seen before. The men would enjoy them once they were on the road again.

She'd been surprised when Robert had set them all free that morning, though a few minutes with Finnlay had opened her eyes. That Andrew had stood up to Robert was one thing – that Robert had agreed to a truce with the Malachi was news she still couldn't grasp. The idea that they were willing to give up the Key seemed impossible, and some part of her instantly rejected the concept – most likely the part joined to the Key.

For most of the morning, she'd sat alone, her eyes closed, listening to the shifts in her mind where the Key moved and lived, making sure she could still feel it, even if it wouldn't – or couldn't – talk to her any more.

The truth was, the news was worrying and there was no other way to look at it. She'd not been there, and so had missed seeing whatever honesty might have been in Dusan's eyes – not to mention Sairead's – but to trust these people at a time like this could possibly ensure their defeat at Nash's hands.

But an hour wandering through the town, another through the market, had helped clear her head. Besides, Robert had promised her a room in a tavern tonight, a real bed, and some precious time alone. But despite all his promises, she had declined to spend the day with him and instead, had hooked her arm in Andrew's and suggested they go into town.

His response had been slow, but his eyes had told her all she needed to know. He needed this break as much as anybody, perhaps more. She also resolved not to talk about anything to do with rebellion or Kenrick, unless Andrew broached the subject first. After the first hour, he seemed to relax a little and even enjoy himself.

But as she walked around the market with the midday sun following overhead, she couldn't help but look at him wandering along behind her, paying occasional attention to one stall here and another there. For the last few weeks, he had grown more and more removed from her, detached even from Finnlay and Micah. Worse still, she knew that to try to get close to him could quite possibly undo all Robert's work. She understood too little of what he was doing to chance that. She couldn't ask Robert directly what he was doing; the peace between them existed solely because she *didn't* interfere, and she knew that above all else, if there was no peace between her and Robert, their cause was lost.

That didn't mean her heart didn't bleed for her boy, the boy who looked to have grown four inches since the winter.

'Have a lemon cake.' She waved the cloth-covered bundle under his nose and smiled when he drew in a deep breath.

'Smells wonderful – though I'd rather wait until we had something more substantial to eat. There was a tavern back in the main street that looked fairly popular. We could get a plate of something there.'

'Well, you have such an appetite to you now, don't you?' She smiled and took his arm again. 'You're growing so fast, you'll be as tall as Finnlay before the end of summer.'

'You think so?' He raised his eyebrows but looked away, and the faint breath of awe in his voice was gone. Silently, Jenn mourned the loss of the boy, even as she rejoiced in the arrival of the man. 'Is that fish I smell?'

She turned to look in the direction he was pointing. 'Looks like it.'

He grinned at her. 'You remember the grilled fish at Ayr? Nothing like it. Do you want one?'

'No, you go ahead. I'll meet you at the village green.'

He nodded, then gave her cheek a brief but determined kiss. As he hurried through the crowds, she almost wept with the loss. What was happening to her? It was just the same with Robert: as though some part of her soul was waiting to lose them both permanently, as though her soul knew it was inevitable.

The end was close. She could feel it creeping up on them like a shadow, a tide none of them could stop. Robert felt it too, she could see it in his eyes. And now that she thought about it, perhaps that was the source of Andrew's quiet. They had weeks, possibly only days. When Kenrick's army arrived, the waiting would finally be over.

She turned and continued up the lane, pausing to admire a bolt of cloth she would once have purchased without question. It felt soft to her roughened fingers, and reminded her of how much time had passed since she'd last done this. Then she put the cloth down, smiled at the woman selling it, and continued on.

At the end of the lane, she moved to take the next, only to find Micah standing there, a bundle of his own purchases under his arm, a look of expectation in his eyes. He'd been waiting for her.

'Is something wrong?'

He shook his head, smiling a little. 'No, but I saw you coming and thought I'd walk with you a bit.'

'I see.' Jenn kept her pace slow as he walked beside her, steering her through the busy crowds. 'How is Sairead?'

'She's well. Doesn't seem to be suffering unduly, though I wish she wouldn't ride so much. Soon she'll barely be able to get on a horse and I won't be comfortable until that day.'

'You'll be a good father. You've been good with Andrew.'

'He said as much, himself. In fact,' Micah peered around them as though looking for something, 'I actually wanted to talk to you about that. Can we sit for a moment?'

'Of course.'

He led her through the crowds to the village green where benches were set out on the grass, catered for by the tavern across the road. He waited for her to sit before joining her on the bench. He framed his words carefully, beginning, 'Andrew has nightmares about you. About something terrible happening to you. I think that's part of why he's grown so distant. He's having the nightmares almost every night now. I had to wake him up last night, just before Sairead arrived. He won't talk about them, but I know he's very upset. And on top of everything else—'

'What?' Jenn frowned. Why would Andrew be getting such nightmares? She was in absolutely no danger at all – Robert always made sure of that.

'Well, I think it's time you told him about his father.'

Jenn froze. 'What? Why? I thought you said we couldn't do that now, not when we've—' she struggled for words, only too aware that their conversation could be overheard. 'You said that was impossible now.'

'No. I said it was impossible to tell Robert. I think it's becoming more and more important to Andrew. I think he's having nightmares about the night Eachern was killed. I think the events of that night are . . . weighing heavily on him.'

'He was so young—' The night she'd killed Eachern. The night her powers had wrenched out of her, blasting the life from him because it looked like he would kill Robert. Andrew had seen it all – though he'd never spoken about it. 'Micah, I don't know. If I tell him . . . with Robert so—'

Micah looked up, his eyes holding hers, beseeching her. 'He needs to know, Jenn. What Robert is doing will make more sense to him, will help him take the next steps without faltering. Apart from anything else, it will tell him that Kenrick is not his cousin. Please, Jenn. I beg you to think about it. There are things he needs to know about his father, things that will have a bearing on what he does in the future. He needs to know.'

She saw the honesty in his gaze and the reality sent a flicker of horror through her so hard her hands shook. And then she looked up to find Andrew coming towards them, finishing off a piece of grilled fish, licking his fingers.

She looked at him now and only saw Robert, though he had her looks, the shape of her face, her blue eyes. There was so much of Robert *inside* Andrew, and yet neither of them could see it.

Could she shatter the last of his illusions? He would never look at her the same way again, but if Micah was right, and that hatred of Eachern was holding back his last steps to maturity— But how could she say those words, after so long keeping them silent in her heart? What if it was enough to turn him against her – and against Robert? Could she take that risk, to place his personal needs before those of their country?

She couldn't, not until she was sure of the outcome.

'What's that about my father?' He stood before her, wiping his mouth with his sleeve, some faint smile on his face which did not reach to his eyes. But the comment alone was enough to make Jenn's heart thump, and she did her best to hide it.

'Nothing. Micah was just saying that you'll be as tall as him at least.'

His gaze flickered from hers to Micah and back. Then he nodded, pretending to be convinced. 'Are you ready for food yet?'

'But you just ate.' Jenn managed a smile in reply. 'Besides, there are other things to feed yourself with. I believe this town has a very pretty church. Why don't we go and say a few prayers for those of us who are injured, and then we'll go to the tavern?'

Andrew sighed, but without rancour. 'Yes, Mother. Are you joining us, Micah?'

'I'll meet you at the tavern.'

'Well, then let's go.'

The chapel was small, old and desperate for attention. But it was also out in the middle of nowhere, alone and used only on alternating weeks for mass for the poor farmers in the area. Even so, Aiden saw charm, the love in the spring wildflowers placed on the altar, the swept stone floor, the weedless path. He also saw the grim determination in the eyes of the men and women gathered before him, the hope flowing from the young priest who had welcomed him, and asked these people to meet him.

They had questions, many of them, and he worked hard to answer them all. Not all of their queries were about sorcery, and he had to be careful about what he said of Robert's plans, of what would happen next, and how it would be achieved. But this was not the first church he'd visited, and certainly not the most difficult audience he'd faced. Even so, he could tell from the look on John's face that the young priest was glad *he* wasn't expected to make a reply.

'One way or the other,' Aiden continued, taking in as many of the faces as he could, 'you must follow your own hearts in these matters.'

'But you're the Bishop, Your Grace,' a man of his own years said, expressing his confusion rather than his doubt. 'You've studied these things. How are we to know that what is in our hearts is right?'

'The same way any of us do,' Aiden replied with a smile.

'I don't know,' an old woman at the back said. 'These things all sound more than we can deal with. We're simple folk. We don't understand why there's sorcerers here and nowhere else. Why is it Lusara now? Couldn't they have stayed on the southern continent?'

'They've been here a long time. They are all born in Lusara, as were their fathers and grandfathers—'

'And grandmothers?'

Aiden laughed a little. 'Yes, grandmothers as well.'

'And you say this boy, Lady Jennifer's son, he'll be King when this is all over?'

'Yes, he will.'

'Another sorcerer?'

Aiden swallowed. What else could he say? Be it now or later, Andrew would eventually develop his abilities and there was no point in hiding it from a people already lied to for decades. 'Andrew Ross is a boy of great integrity and honour, true to his Lusaran blood. I know you remember his father, but Eachern died when Andrew was a young child and his influence was limited even then. This is why Robert Douglas has chosen him for the throne – because it is his by right.'

There was silence at this, but on every face he could see a touch of that same awe reserved for the mention of Robert's name. It was like a sorcery all of its own kind and Aiden tried not to overuse it. Still, these people, and all the others he'd spoken to, found the prospect of a rebellion driven by a legend enough to quell their biggest fears.

How patient they were, how steadfast, and deserving of more than they had been allowed. And he wanted them to have their freedom, to allow them the prosperity to build up their farms and their families, so that worshipping in this church was no longer an act of desperation, but instead, an act of thanksgiving.

He rose to his feet. 'I'm afraid I must leave you. We're expected in Rona in two days. I have another stop I need to make before nightfall and it's dangerous for me to travel on the roads at night.'

Instantly, they all got to their feet, anxious for him to be away safely. One by one they came up to him and kissed the ring he didn't wear, and at the end, he waved a blessing over all of them. Then, with Father John at his side, he walked out into the afternoon, to find Edain and Braden waiting with the horses.

'It's all clear, Father,' Edain said, handing him his reins. 'Do we go on, or back to town?'

'We go on. The more people I can speak to, the stronger this rebellion.' And with that, he swung up into the saddle and turned his horse. He found them all waiting outside the church, their faces speaking more to him than any words they'd uttered in the last hour. He raised his hand and signed the trium in the air, then turned away, leaving hope in his wake – and taking some with him.

Finnlay slid into the booth beside Joshi and handed out the tankards of ale he'd just bought. The young Generet held his between both hands and sipped, collecting a line of froth on his top lip before licking it off with a grin of satisfaction.

'I see Joshi has adapted to life in Lusara without too much trouble,' Finnlay directed the question at Patric before taking his own sip.

'He's finding the adventure more interesting as each day goes by,' the blind man replied. 'As am I.'

'Well, you know life with Robert is never dull,' Finnlay added dryly, checking that they were alone in their corner. He'd deliberately chosen this alehouse rather than the larger tavern in an effort to avoid the others. 'So tell me, what you were saying about the Marklord? That you thought he was trying to keep track of sorcery in each generation?'

'Yes. What about it?'

'Well, it doesn't make sense as to why he would want to keep track. I mean, even if you take the Prophecy into consideration, there's just no reason to do any of it, is there?'

'I suppose it depends on how you view the Prophecy. To some, it's merely a suggestion of what *could* happen. Jenn believes that it's a direction given to make sense of current events. Robert thinks it's a curse. Others would say it is a divine gift of prescience, a warning of what will happen if we're not wary. It could even be the description of a vision, such as that had by the Hermit of Shan Moss.'

'And if Thraxis genuinely had a vision, wrote it down as the Prophecy, then basically, we're in a lot of trouble.'

Patric sighed. 'We are if you believe visions are a true depiction of the future.'

'But so much of the Prophecy has already come true – and we can't forget the role the Key is playing—'

'Which seems to follow no discernible rules. Look, Finnlay, I can't give you any answers. I have told you all that I learned and still, even with your knowledge of what's happened while I was gone, *you* can't tell me what I need to know. And perhaps that's the point. Have you ever considered the possibility that we aren't supposed to know too much before it happens?'

'Pat, you haven't spent the last ten years worrying about my brother. I think you've forgotten what that's like.'

'He's withdrawing again.'

'Yes, he is, and he's doing it because he believes there aren't any answers to be had. Can you imagine how that's playing on his conscience?'

Patric took another mouthful off his ale and savoured it before swallowing. For a moment, he turned his head slightly and Finnlay knew he was mindspeaking with Joshi, saw it in the faint nod, the minuscule smile that followed it. Not for the first time, Finnlay wondered about how Patric could have learned to mindspeak when it was supposed to be something only the Generet could do – and of course, Robert and Jenn. And him.

'You know,' Patric said after a moment, 'Joshi says you shouldn't worry too much.'

'That's very kind of him,' Finnlay said dryly. Despite his strangeness, Joshi was easy to like. 'He just wants me to buy him more ale.'

'Well, that's true,' Patric conceded. 'But he also wanted me to point out that amongst the Generet, Jenn's family line was given another name.'

'Jenn's?'

'Yes, the Ally. Her line, or House, was called something else.'

'By whom?'

'He doesn't know, though he believes it is very old.'

'What was the other name?'

'Elite.'

Finnlay choked on his next mouthful and nearly expired as Joshi thumped his back hard. Bleary-eyed, he waved his hands and gasped for mercy. 'I give up, Pat, honestly I do. I can't keep up with this any more. I'm too old.'

'Not old,' Joshi spoke up, his voice rough with lack of use. 'Age good.' With that, he gave Finnlay another thump on the back and rose to get them all some more ale.

Finnlay watched him go, saying, 'All I can say is, I'm glad he's on our side.'

'Yes,' Patric grinned. 'So am I.'

The singing started up not long after dark and Robert, sitting in disguise in his corner, couldn't help but tap his foot to it, swaying with the other men at his table. All part of the disguise, but Andrew had been right about how good it was to listen to music again. It was just a pity that he couldn't do it in the open, but instead had to sit here wearing this heavy hooded cloak, listening in while his countrymen gossiped.

It was amazing how much he'd learned over the years in this very manner – and the technique did not let him down this time, either. For a start, it appeared that Godfrey had been right about the rumours and the new nunnery at Elita. It was currently one of two favourite topics: it appeared nobody had any doubts at all that Jenn was the incarnation of Mineah. He heard many impossible and outrageous miracles attributed to her, without a single shred of evidence – but these were people desperate for those very miracles, and the hope they brought. If believing that Mineah was finally amongst them meant their misery was almost over, how could they not wish it to be true?

He, himself, of course, was the subject of many other rumours. Word had spread about the rebellion, and they were all happy to share what they'd each seen or heard about. This was just as he'd wanted: it served his purpose for word to fly ahead of him, although the more rumours flew about, the less he was likely to maintain any secrecy – and some time in the next few days, he was going to need it.

As the song rolled on around him, he got slowly to his feet, maintaining the appearance of a man of seventy, crouched over with a bad back and a limp. He made his way to the door of the tavern and stepped out into the darkness.

He hated the disguise, but this town had a Guildhall and although he'd never spent any time in this place, that didn't mean people wouldn't recognise him. He kept to the shadows as he paced the length of the tavern, then hobbled across the street, heading slowly for the Guildehall. It stood by the church, a fine example of wealth abused, with its stone walls, tiled roof and hardbaked wooden fence all around it.

The gates were still open, though guarded by four men heavily armed. Robert kept going, hobbling around the corner until he was completely out of sight. In that moment, he straightened up, reached inside and bullied up his powers. With a held breath, he concentrated, taking the required dimensional step sideways to make himself invisible. Done, he turned to the wooden fence, scaling it in seconds, dropping down on the inside noiselessly.

He took a moment to scout the layout of the compound, but most rural Guildehalls were built the same and he had no trouble finding what he was looking for. Dodging Guildesmen, he followed one inside the main building, slipping down the corridor unseen. He found the Master's study with its door open wide. With a smile nobody else would see, he stepped inside.

The Master was sitting behind his desk, reading a message someone had obviously just given him. Robert kept his distance. It was one thing to move about knowing he was invisible, but if he got too close, somebody would notice the air moving, and if they reached out they would touch him and he would be lost.

So he stood and listened, and after a few more minutes, turned and made his way quickly out of the Guildehall. He exited behind a firewood cart, ran across the road and headed back towards the tavern. Only when he reached the stables did he find another shadow. There he released the shift, returned to his stoop and limp and hurried up the stairs going up to the second floor.

The room was on his right, over the kitchens, far from the tap room and all its noise. He paused at the door only long enough to send his Senses inside. Then, with a last look around to ensure his presence hadn't been detected by anybody, he opened the door and slipped inside.

Jenn's expression was precious as she surveyed his attire and the rest of his disguise. It wasn't the first time she'd seen it, but last time she'd been unable to react. Now she came up, her eyebrows raised, her mouth set in a determined line, her eyes sparkling with the laughter she was subduing. Without any preamble, she removed his hat and wig, tore off the beard he wore, then rose on her toes and kissed him.

With a groan, he wrapped his arms around her, lifting her off the ground so he could walk them both towards the bed. He collapsed on it with a grunt, not releasing her from the kiss.

How had they come to this? How had he allowed himself to be so bewitched by her that a moment alone with her was worth more than anything else in his world? Where had he changed so much that he – who had remained celibate for so many years – needed only to touch her and he was set alight?

He'd had no idea that love would be like this.

'I missed you today,' she purred, her hands sliding down his back, pulling him closer.

'And I missed you,' he whispered back, admitting the truth of it, even though he didn't want to. How could he continue with this rebellion, with this war, when she was such a weakness for him? If Nash knew – but Nash already knew enough to damn them all. 'I'm sorry, Jenny, but we can't stay after all.'

She opened her eyes, moving back a little to see his face. 'What? Why? What's wrong?'

He sat them both up, straightening her bodice with trembling hands. 'I just stopped in at the Guildehall. I'm afraid we have less time than we thought. Osbert's on his way – and if we don't leave tonight, we'll be surrounded by them tomorrow.'

She didn't move for a moment, but studied his face. 'And Kenrick?'

'Won't be far behind.'

'So we need to run?'

Robert let her go and stood up, crossing the room to pick up the disguise she'd dropped. 'Andrew needs more time. I have to give it to him.' He couldn't begin to say how close he was to failure with the boy. There was so much promise there, and yet, so little result so far. If Andrew didn't make some move soon, it would be impossible for Robert to convince anyone that he would make a King preferable to Kenrick. If Andrew didn't kill Kenrick – or couldn't – then nothing Robert could do would free Lusara.

'How much more time?'

'Another month perhaps – but even I can't guarantee him more than that.'

'You think Tirone will be content with what you've done so far?'

Robert nodded, looking up at her, his breath catching for a moment. With her hair a little messed, her cheeks a little flushed, her lips red from his kisses, she looked almost more beautiful than he could bear.

Unable to resist, he returned to her, pushing her back to the bed, kissing her again, trying to tell her all that he could never say aloud. Then he drew back, regret in every line of his body. 'I'm sorry. I promised you—'

She put two fingers over his mouth, then kissed him softly. Done, she rolled over and got off the bed. She moved to pick up her cloak – and froze at an urgent rap on the door. She looked at Robert, but he shook his head.

'Finnlay.'

As Robert got up, Jenn crossed to the door and opened it. Finnlay stepped inside quickly, closing it behind him. His face was ashen, his eyes wide with an unspoken fear.

'You have to come quickly! It's Andrew. He's in trouble!'

32

The rumble of horses travelling together echoed through the warm spring night. All but a few birds skittered away from the encroaching hordes; even the ground shuddered at the passage of heavily laden carts pulled by workhorses. In the darkness, they were all the same shadow, their uniforms of yellow dulled and without lustre.

Osbert pulled away from the main body, turning his horse onto a high place beside the road. The line of soldiers ran all the way into the darkness on his left, and he could not yet see when the last of them would pass him.

Another horse turned from the road, its rider joining him with a small bow from the saddle. Though he could not see a face in this shadow, he knew full well who it was. Lyle followed him as a precaution, as a testimony and as an unvoiced comfort.

'We have made good time, my lord,' Lyle began easily. 'The weather has been kind. If it keeps up like this, we will arrive by midday tomorrow.'

Osbert was surprised. 'We're that close? But I thought we were still a full day away.'

'We were, however, having the second ferry allowed us to cross the river much quicker than expected and marching through the night like this, making the most of the mild weather, has given us many hours we did not anticipate.'

'Do we have further word of the rebels?'

'No, my lord, but our information was accurate last time. The rebels had been there—'

'They'd just left long before we could get to them. Do you have any idea how pointless it is running around *after* them? Is there no way to guess where they'll go before they get there?'

'The King—'

'The King wouldn't know—' Osbert stopped abruptly and bit his lip, drawing blood. Kenrick ordered them here and there, chasing halfway across the country looking for phantoms before pulling them back. And now they had a clear report, a raid on a grain silo, and only the day before. The rebels were most definitely in this area and, come what may, Osbert

329

would be responsible for catching at least some of them, if nothing else. He would have something to show Kenrick if it killed him!

And something to show Nash.

As it had done a thousand times since he'd left Marsay, Osbert found Godfrey's voice rattling around in his head, warning him of what would happen if he followed this path, asking him to reconsider, to choose more wisely – but Godfrey had not lived in the shadow of fear the way Osbert had. He had no idea what it was like to face Nash on a daily basis, knowing the sorcerer had ways to see into a man's mind. Osbert had struggled for years to find a way to beat Nash, but all along he knew Nash would one day be the death of him. There was only one way to stave off that day.

'When will you order camp, my lord?' Lyle prepared to ride away.

'I won't.' Osbert decided on the spur. 'We ride through the night. A league from the town, I want the horses rested for an hour and then the men split into three groups. The first will head east around the town, the second west. I will remain with the third and head directly south. Have the men search every farm, every tavern, every building on the outskirts of town. If there are still rebels in this area, we will flush them out by morning. Let the captains know.'

Lyle smiled and bowed again. 'Of course, my lord.' And then he was riding away, happy to have this purpose in his life.

Happiness was something Osbert didn't understand at all.

Jenn pulled on her reins, making the horse skid to a halt beside Finnlay's. Her heart pounding, she jumped down and ran forward into the thicket. She barely heard Robert ordering Micah to round up the other men, the Guilde was closing in and they had to move on, now. All she could focus on was the noise in the distance, and the fear in Finnlay's eyes.

'What happened?'

When he didn't answer immediately, she turned, only barely stopping herself from running towards Andrew. Finnlay waited until Robert joined them, then said, 'I don't know what happened exactly. He and Micah were having supper at the tavern. I had just gone in to join them when Micah grabbed Andrew and hauled him outside. He pulled a cloak over the boy's face and told me we had to get him out of town immediately. We rode as far as we could, but Andrew seemed to be in pain and wouldn't answer when I spoke to him. We got to this wood, but he couldn't travel any further. He stopped and dismounted, then ran in here. Every time I try to get close, he warns me away.'

'Warns?' Robert growled. 'What kind of game is this? We don't have time to play here! The damned Guilde is on our tails! Micah, go back to the town and warn all our people. If we don't get clear—'

But Jenn held up her hand, seeing something in the darkness that didn't make sense. 'What's that?'

Finnlay took one look at the faint blue glow to the night and said, 'I noticed it a few weeks ago. I thought it was his powers beginning to emerge but nothing else happened. It flares up and fades down. He has no control at all. And that's the problem.' Finnlay turned his gaze on Robert. 'That's why we can't get close.'

'But why is this happening now?' Jenn murmured, inching forward despite Finnlay's warning.

'Why is it happening now?' Finnlay repeated, incredulous. 'After the way he's been pushed around by my pushy brother here? I tell you, that boy is in there because he's terrified of what's happening to him. And he's terrified because he no longer trusts any of us.'

Jenn stiffened at that. 'He trusts me! I'll go in.'

'Jenn, no!' Robert reached out to stop her, but she squirmed away from him, picking up her feet so she didn't trip on the uneven ground.

She followed the blue glow, tracing the flares in it, how it faded before emerging again. Of Andrew she could see nothing, but she could hear him, gasping in pain, occasionally thumping his fist on a tree or something. 'Andrew?' she began softly, not wanting to scare him further. And he would be scared, as Finnlay said. All these years they'd waited for these powers to emerge, and now that they had, he didn't know what to do with them. 'Andrew, can you hear me?'

'Stay away, Mother!' His anguished rasp reached her, making her heart bleed. 'Just stay away! It's too dangerous!'

Before he'd even finished speaking, she heard a great crack and a nearby tree shuddered and toppled, falling to the forest floor with an almighty crash. The ground beneath her feet shook, making her reach out to steady herself, but she didn't turn back. 'Please, Andrew, you don't need to be afraid. I can help.'

'No, you can't. Nobody can help. I can't control this. Every time I move, I—'

And another crash split the night. Jenn heard Robert calling her, but she just waved at him to keep his ground. The last thing Andrew needed right now was another confrontation with Robert.

She inched forward, listening hard for any more disruptions. Moving to her left, she swung around the area most illuminated by the glow, until she could see her son crouched on the forest floor, his back against a tree, arms wrapped around his stomach as though his belly ached. Every now and then, his fist would hit the ground and the earth beneath him would ripple like a wave, leaving cracks in the dirt like shattered glass. And then he opened his eyes.

Jenn gasped and took a step back. His eyes were black, all the colour absorbed. His face was white, covered by a sheen of sweat. His mouth was open as he panted, needing air. She wanted to go to him, but didn't dare.

'Andrew, please listen to me. I can help, I promise you. I can help you control this. You just need to listen.'

'No, Mother, please leave me! I'll just hurt you! I know I will – and I can't do that, don't you understand? I can't!'

'Of course you won't hurt me. I know that. You could never hurt me.'

'I would. *He* hurt you even though he said he wouldn't. But he hurt you and you – Please Mother, you have to go now!' Another thump against the ground and the soil rippled higher this time, enough to make her stumble and almost lose her balance.

Such power! So like his f—

Just as that Prophecy had said. *And one shall be born to raise his armies, increasing his faithful tenfold . . .*

But she'd known all along he wouldn't be spared. That was why she'd done all that work, in the hope that she would find something to prove her wrong. But all that time spent researching had only given up more evidence that this *was* all preordained.

Which meant that Andrew was just as much a part of the Prophecy as she and Robert, and that in the end—

'Andrew, I want you to listen to me. I can teach you how to control the power. I understand how you're feeling. I know how frightening this can be when it first happens.'

'No, Mother, please! You can't help me. Nobody can.'

'But I can teach you.'

'How? The same way you killed my father?'

The fire flickered every time Osbert peered through the trees, tantalising his imagination, making him hungry. But he knew what it was. Even though he didn't want to, even though he could wish with all his heart that it was anything but.

Osbert rode without questioning. He kept the firelight to his left, his attention on staying awake in the saddle, on getting his men to their destination without mishap. But the fire flickering in the corner of his eye grew bigger and he knew he wouldn't be allowed to ignore it the way he wanted to.

He turned a corner in the road and found exactly what he'd expected: an open fire, a dozen men with their horses tied to trees standing back out of the way, another man seated with his feet and hands warming at the flames, while a third cooked a meal before him.

The seated man looked up as Osbert appeared. A smile spread across his face and Osbert accepted the inevitability. He turned off the road and took his horse up to the edge of the firelight. For a moment he considered not dismounting, but he would be made to pay for that. So he swung his leg over the back of the horse and slid to the ground. Miraculously, another chair was brought for him, his horse taken by one of the men and a cup placed in his hand.

'Sit, Osbert. I won't bite. At least, not before supper.' Nash stared into the flames for a moment, then laughed a little at his own humour. 'Sit, sit! If you're good, I'll even see to feeding you.'

Osbert kept his silence, holding his cup but not drinking from it. Who could tell what it might contain? He, along with many others, had heard of the poison in Nash's wine, of how it had made him ill for a week but had not killed him, despite the enormous amounts that had been poured into the bottle.

Nobody knew who'd been responsible, and it seemed even Nash was at a loss, as there had been no sudden executions or even disappearances over that week. But he was here now, alive, perfectly well, in fact, better than Osbert had ever remembered seeing him.

Sorcery. Just as Godfrey had told him, Nash had used the blood of his own daughter to regenerate, to heal all his wounds, to increase his powers, to give him immortality. What could Robert Douglas hope to do to beat that?

A plate was handed to him, filled with a delicious stew and fresh bread. His own travel-fare had long since been consumed, and he'd refused exactly this kind of meal in order to hurry his army along the road.

But if he didn't eat, again he would pay. Nash was simply looking for an excuse to punish him. They'd been treading this path for a long time, and Osbert could only attribute his continued survival to the fact that he'd never given Nash any real reason to kill him.

He ate. Nash watched him with wry amusement.

'You think I would poison you? When I have so many other choices at my disposal? How unimaginative you must think me.'

Osbert swallowed, saying nothing. The food went down with difficulty, but he cleared the plate, ignoring his stomach protesting. He handed the plate back to the servant and got to his feet. 'If you don't mind, I will continue on my way.'

'Anxious to get there, are you? Do you know something I don't?'

'I am indeed anxious to catch these rebels – as you should be.'

Nash stalked around the fire until he stood only inches from Osbert.

'Why are you here?' Osbert muttered, unwilling, even now, to admit total defeat.

'I'm looking for something called the Key and I think it's somewhere in this region. If you see it, let me know.'

'A key? To what?'

'Ah, now that's the real question, isn't it? A Key to what. But we were never told, so I can't answer you. What I can tell you is that this Key is an orb, about this big—' He made a shape with his arms. 'It's incredibly powerful, but could kill a normal man with its touch – so as I said, if you see it, let me know.'

Osbert met his dark gaze for a moment longer, then nodded and gestured for his horse. He mounted up, wrapping the reins about his hands and turning for the road where his men still marched by.

'Good luck hunting your rebels,' Nash called after him. 'Make sure you don't go changing sides.'

Jenn froze, her throat so tight she could hardly breathe. 'What?'

Andrew didn't look at her, but his face betrayed his pain. He struggled to his feet, the tree behind him shuddering with his effort. Then he began to pace a few steps up and down, still holding his stomach with one arm, the other gesturing wildly, making branches fall from trees in every direction. The entire forest was under attack.

'Thought I'd forgotten. Thought the nightmares would . . . but they kept telling me, warning me and I wouldn't listen. You're in danger. My father tried to kill you. He hit you, I remember. I saw it. I wanted to stop him but I couldn't, I was so . . . so helpless – but you could have stopped him. Why didn't you, Mother? Why didn't you?'

'Because he would have known the truth about me. He hated sorcerers more than anything—'

'But you could have done *something*, Mother, you could have. But he beat you and you killed him! You struck out at him, and you killed him, so that Robert wouldn't die. But you didn't control that power, did you? You couldn't. Nobody can. That power is . . . is – it's not supposed to be controlled. It's evil. I've got *your* power and *his* evil inside me and the two together shouldn't be allowed to survive. Just get away, Mother. You can't help me. I don't want to hurt you.'

'Oh, Andrew, of course you can control that power – and it's not evil!' Jenn took another step closer, lacing her fingers together to stop herself from reaching out to him. Each step he took made her shake inside, each grimace of pain echoed inside her. This was all her fault. He remembered everything, though she had always hoped the memories would never return. But she couldn't take back that night, couldn't take back the fact that she had killed Eachern, and she *had* done it to save Robert's life.

This was her own fault. She should have insisted on talking to him years ago, before it could come to this. This must be the reason his powers had not developed before: because he thought such power was responsible for his father's death.

Serin's blood! Jenn came to a halt. Andrew was still pacing, his skin flashing a ghostly blue glow into the night, and behind the tree she could see Robert in the distance, Finnlay a little behind him, both watching, waiting for her to—

Just as she'd hoped Andrew would be free of the Prophecy, she'd hoped this day would never come. And with it, hand in hand, came acceptance that the Prophecy did rule their lives. Andrew had been born to them for a reason, they were each there for a reason, and so too the Prophecy's ending had a reason. For all that she had tried to get Robert to accept that fact, she had never really looked at it herself, had never really accepted that it would probably mean her own death.

Once more she looked back at Robert, tall, strong, determined and passionate. Never once had he failed to give everything he had to his cause – but she had always held back, afraid of too many things, of what might be and what couldn't be. For years she'd kept truths from him and paid for that, made them both pay for that.

But she couldn't do that any more. The time had arrived for her to sacrifice what little control she'd had over their futures. She could not hold onto the truth and let this beautiful boy of hers destroy himself over a lie.

And she couldn't let that beautiful man destroy himself over his fate.

'Andrew,' she began, her voice thick, her eyes stinging with tears she'd never before shed. 'This is not what you think.'

'Please, Mother!' he groaned and faced her, his eyes boring holes into her. 'Go! I can't hold it in much longer. I don't want to hurt you. I don't want to hurt anybody! Tell Robert I'm sorry. I can't be King for him. I never could. I don't know why he wanted me when my father was such a monster! I don't want somebody like me to be King of Lusara. Now please, Mother—'

'Andrew, listen!' Jenn came forward again, reaching out a hand to him, desperately praying he would hold still. 'Your father . . . he—' She swallowed hard, finding the words was suddenly difficult. She had rehearsed this moment so many times over the years, but never once imagined these circumstances. 'Your father wasn't—'

'He was a monster and I'm glad you killed him!' Andrew's glow flared then, and the ground groaned beneath his feet, making her stumble. She fell forward and on instinct, he reached out to catch her.

His skin burned under her hands, but she didn't step back. She held on tight. There was no turning back now.

With her voice little more than an ugly whisper, she said, 'Oh, Andrew, do you honestly think I would let Robert put you on the throne if your father had really been Eachern?'

Breathing hard, he swallowed, her meaning unclear to him. That mystification was enough to make the tears tumble down her face, and he reached up to brush them away, a gentle gesture that only produced more.

'Your . . . real father would never hurt me, Andrew. He would die first. You don't have Eachern's evil inside you, I promise you.'

Andrew's frown deepened, his gaze searching her face. 'My *real* father? What does that mean? Who is my *real* father?'

Jenn opened her mouth to speak, but a familiar voice intervened—

'I am.'

Micah left his horse at the end of town, and ran first to the ale house. He found Patric, Joshi and two others there, gave them the word and headed directly over to the tavern. One by one he found the men, giving them Robert's orders. The haste of their exit caused a few interested looks, but he couldn't do anything about that now. They had no time left.

He paused in the shadows near his horse then, going back in his mind, counting each of the men, making sure they were all accounted for. And even as he waited, they rode past, in twos and threes, taking the road at first before cutting away into the countryside.

They were well trained, had been taught all Robert knew about how to evade capture, how to blend into the natural surroundings, how to look like a local. If they had any time at all, the men would definitely get away.

Sure now that he had spoken to everyone, Micah mounted up and turned for the road back to where he'd left Andrew. But in the corner of his eye, he caught a flash of familiar colour, illuminated by the moonlight.

Guilde! The vanguard arriving already! They must be marching through the night. By Serin's blood!

With that, he threw caution to the wind, and kicked his horse hard. After a few minutes, he glanced over his shoulder, but there was no pursuit. With his heart thumping madly in his chest, he kicked his horse harder, pressing himself to its back to encourage greater speed.

'Father! Come quickly!'

Aiden stood and made his way across the ruined barn to where Braden was crouched by an empty window. Behind him he could hear John and Edain saddling horses, putting out the fire and gathering up their belongings.

'What is it?'

'Guilde! Look. There're at least fifty of them. By the gods! Come on, we have to ride!'

His arm was grabbed and in one swift movement, he was almost dragged across the small space to the wide door on the other side of the building. He finished saddling his own horse, his fingers fumbling the buckles and straps, while Braden checked outside to make sure they had a clean path out.

'Hurry! Damn it, Robert is going to kill me!'

Moving as fast as he could, Aiden grabbed his reins and followed John and Edain out into the night, holding his breath to listen as voices on the other side of the building grew louder.

'They're not supposed to be this far south yet!' Edain hissed.

'Come on!' Braden whispered in reply. 'We'll argue about it later.' With that, he led them along the side of the barn – but there was nowhere for them to go. Soldiers were already dismounting and running into the empty farm buildings, holding torches high in the darkness. As Aiden's heart leapt into his throat, a shout came from behind them.

In an instant, both Salti turned and faced the assault, their swords drawn ready to fight. It took the Guildesmen no time to swarm around them, surrounding them and hemming them in.

His guards were ready to fight, but Aiden could tell it was already too late. 'Please, put your swords down. They'll just kill you.'

'But, Father, we have orders you're not to be taken.'

'No.' Aiden moved forward and stood between them, making them lower their weapons.

'Father, are you sure?' John hissed from behind.

He was. Very sure, though thoroughly surprised to discover this so late in the day. 'Yes. I am.'

And then he turned to face the Guildesmen surrounding them, seeing dawning recognition in the eyes of more than one man.

'By the mass,' somebody whispered. 'It's the Bishop himself!'

Jenn started at Robert's words, panic flooding through her, making her heart flutter.

'Step back,' he said, moving closer to them. 'Now, Jenn.'

Some deep part of her was afraid for Andrew, but he wouldn't hurt his own son, would he?

Had he known? All this time, had he known Andrew was his? She could see nothing in his face, his eyes, his body, nothing at all to indicate his thoughts. Instead, his gaze was fixed entirely on Andrew, and Andrew's on his.

'Step back, Jenn. Now.' And that tone would not be brooked. Trembling, Jenn released Andrew and moved back.

Robert stood there, his eyes dark and unfathomable, holding Andrew in place, ignoring the pulse of blue rippling along his skin, the tremor in the forest from powers still uncontrolled.

Robert spoke, and where Jenn was expecting compassion, she found the exact opposite. 'You have your father's evil, do you? Is that the problem here? Or is it that you're too scared to face it? How old are you? Fourteen, nearly fifteen, and you're still too afraid to ask those questions. What kind of man do you expect to be?'

Andrew looked up at Robert, his face as open as Jenn had ever seen it. Never before had Andrew been so vulnerable, never before had Robert been so merciless.

Robert advanced, making Andrew back away. 'You wanted to know about evil? You only needed to ask. I can tell you everything you need to know. I can tell you all about how it sits in the pit of your stomach, like a sickness, black and seething, breeding upon itself with every tidbit thrown its way. And you live with it hour after hour, day after day, hoping and praying that you won't lose control, that it won't rise up like a viper and do your killing for you, or worse still, kill somebody you love, because it can do that, without any qualms at all. That's how your mother killed Eachern, you know. You saw it, you know that's true.'

'Yes,' Andrew whispered, as though Robert's words were water to his thirst. 'Yes, I saw it.'

'And you know how much you wished that it had been you throwing that power, don't you?'

'Yes!'

'You can still feel it, can't you? Still feel the fear of that night, with the castle in flames around you, and the Malachi there to kill you, and that man, that *monster*—' Robert spat the word out like it was poison. 'He was there to stop us, to stop your mother, and all you wanted to do was—'

'Kill him!'

Robert stopped advancing, no longer driving. Instead, his next question came out almost gently. 'Why didn't you?'

'I—'

'You were afraid, weren't you? Afraid of him, of what he might do to you

338

if he knew you were a sorcerer. He was your father and you hated him. When he died you rejoiced. You're right, Andrew, you *are* evil!'

Andrew reacted as though he'd been slapped. His head snapped up, his feet stumbled back until he caught himself against a sapling. 'But she—'

Instantly, Robert changed again, his voice unrelenting, the demon inside him barely contained, 'You can't blame it on anyone but yourself. You did nothing to help her that night and instead, forced her to do something she's regretted ever since. She never asked you about that night – but did you ever ask her how she felt about it? No. That was the first time she'd ever killed anyone. She didn't just do it to save my life, but yours as well, to save you from any more years under that man's roof! But you didn't care about that, did you? And you didn't care about the sacrifices she made to ensure you grew up knowing your own country. She would have given almost anything to have you with her at the Enclave, but she sacrificed that need so that you could have a normal life, so that some day you would develop a love for Lusara like hers, that you would want to care for it, would be prepared to fight for it, to die for it!'

Robert pulled in a breath, his fists curling as though he were ready to strike at the horror in Andrew's eyes. And then Jenn saw it, saw the demon inside Robert flare and rise, battling for freedom. Robert's voice rose with it. 'But you did nothing like that, did you? All the sacrifices she made for you, your aunt and uncle, Finnlay, *Micah* – all this and for nothing! Because deep down inside, you *are* evil, you *don't* care, and you *never will*!'

At that, Andrew let out a roar, threw his hands up in front of him and flames sprang from the ground, an inferno of rage and terror, all aimed at the man in front of him. 'Stop it! I won't listen to you any more! You twist everything around so that it does come out evil. I won't listen! You're wrong! And if you don't stop, I'll make you!' The power of the flames became a pulse, flattening the grass at his feet and everything around him.

Instinctively, Jenn took a step forward, but the heat was incredible, searing her flesh as she stood there.

Robert didn't move, didn't so much as lift an eyebrow. Instead, his expression changed, along with his voice. In a whisper, he said, 'Look inside, Andrew. Is it all black and stinking with evil?'

It took a moment for his words to penetrate Andrew's rage, but then he paused, blinking, frowning.

'Look inside, son.' Robert's voice grew warm, a smile there, if not yet on his face. 'What do you see?'

Eyes wide, Andrew looked back at him, tilting his head. Then he shook it a little. 'Nothing. I see . . . nothing.'

'Because you *can't* be evil. That's why you were born. That's why you have this power – because it can't be corrupted.'

Andrew stood there, chest heaving, trying to breathe, trying to comprehend.

'It's safe now, Andrew. You can let it go. You can't hurt me or your mother. Our power won't let us hurt each other. Let it go.'

'Please,' Andrew whispered, and then, abruptly, the flames fell, Andrew's eyes rolled up into his head and he collapsed forward, caught in Robert's arms. Sinking to the ground with his burden, Robert cradled Andrew's head against his shoulder, kissing his forehead, holding him against the pain.

'Just let it go, son,' Robert whispered, closing his eyes. 'You're safe now.'

Then the forest was silent once more.

33

Finnlay started forward when he saw Andrew collapse in Robert's arms, but in that same instant, he heard the urgent thunder of a horse approaching. Micah careened to a halt, his breath coming in gusts.

'Have to leave now – Guilde coming; we'll be surrounded within the hour!'

'Get the horses,' he cried, and ran towards Robert and Jenn, though unwilling to break the moment. Only Jenn appeared to see him, and that through a veil of tears. 'We need to move now,' he told her.

She wiped a hand across her eyes, then got up and took her horse from Micah as Finnlay turned to Robert.

His brother was already moving. 'Can you help me? I don't think he's able to walk.'

'Walk?' Finnlay grunted, taking half Andrew's weight as Robert stood up. 'I don't think he's capable of speech at the moment.'

'Don't worry, I'll carry him. Just help me get him onto the horse.'

It was a struggle, but eventually, Robert was mounted up, his son half lying across the saddle in front of him, his head on Robert's shoulder, Robert's arms holding him in place as he held his reins. Then Finnlay got onto his own mount and followed as Robert led the way into the woods.

'Did you find the others?' Robert asked of Micah.

'Yes. McCauly and John had already gone on earlier in the day.'

'Alone?'

'Edain and Braden were with him. All the others got away before I left the town. As I was leaving I saw Osbert's advance guard. If he follows standard practice, he'll split his troops into three and send some in this direction. We'll need to be very careful.'

'Aye, we will at that.'

'Where should we go?' Finnlay asked, pulling up to ride alongside Robert. Andrew lay unconscious against him, unaware of anything.

'I don't think we have a choice.' Robert indicated the direction they were already heading. 'We've run out of time, and Kenrick is forcing our hand. The others are all on their way, and we should be too.'

Finnlay's heart sank. He knew as well as any what that meant. Long ago Robert had picked out the site for this battle, this last confrontation between tyrant and rebels. All the other groups, having caused their share of mayhem, having provoked Kenrick to leave the safety of his capital, were now making their way towards Rona.

In his research for the origins of the Prophecy and of sorcery, Finnlay had once come across an odd story about Rona, about an old man who'd saved everything he had to give his daughter a dowry fit for a lord. The night before her wedding, his baggage train had been robbed crossing Rona. He lost everything and, with a broken heart, died then and there. It was said that his ghost still haunted the wilds of Rona and that all who went there with thievery in their hearts would perish.

Finnlay hoped that the stories were true.

He brought his horse to a halt as Robert held up his hand and let his Senses roam at will, coursing through the night until they reached the road. Jenn sat in silence, her face white, her eyes only shadows. She gripped her reins as though they were her last chance of life. She kept her eyes steadfastly ahead, looking at nobody. Finnlay desperately wanted to give her a hug, but she would have to deal with this on her own. Micah, wary for his own reasons, glanced at Robert; though he'd missed the drama, he was well aware that something momentous had happened.

'There're at least three hundred of them,' Robert whispered after a moment. 'Godfrey said a thousand in total. They're not actively looking for us, so we'll wait for them to pass.'

Finnlay settled, keeping his own Senses open, listening for the soldiers, feeling their quiet comments, their exhaustion, their fear and trepidation of this coming war. And then they were gone and the night regained its calm – at least, on the outside.

'This way,' Robert murmured, kicking his horse into movement.

They all followed, keeping silent still in the night, ignoring tiredness and yawns, the sounds of the land around them, small lights in the distance marking the occasional farmstead.

When dawn rose hours later, Finnlay knew he'd been dozing in the saddle. Robert called a halt to water the horses and to swop onto Andrew's, so his own could rest; the double burden was heavy on the animal. Andrew slept still, there was little conversation and, an hour later, they were on the road again, travelling north-east towards Rona.

Halfway through the day, Micah left them to buy food from a nearby market, but they didn't stop to eat. More than once, Finnlay offered to carry Andrew, but Robert shook his head, his lips set in a grim line, as silent in his determination as Jenn. Though Andrew still hadn't woken, he could only assume that if Jenn had seen something bad with her Healer's Sight, she would have said so.

For so many years he'd wanted his brother to know the truth about Andrew, but he'd never thought for one moment that it would happen like this, now, when they could least afford such a distraction.

Would Andrew recover, and if he did, would he hate both his parents, or be dangerously alienated from one or the other? Neither Finnlay nor Micah could afford to claim ignorance either; there would be a reckoning with Robert on that score as well.

But if nothing else, at last Finnlay would at last be allowed to be openly proud of his nephew. At least within this circle.

They zigzagged across the country, taking what cover they could, keeping well away from Kenrick's troops marching south. Soon enough they would return, and then there would be no more avoidance.

By nightfall, they were all ready to drop, but still Robert kept going, leading them along the narrow valley and up to the pass of Rona. On the higher ground he paused, did a final sweep of the area and pronounced it safe. Then they headed downhill a little to the copse he'd chosen as a meeting place for his rebels.

They were welcomed by Owen, Deverin and all their men, together with those who'd joined up since. In all there were almost one hundred of them ready to fight, the core of an army that would probably not survive the week.

Robert said very little to anyone, leaving Finnlay to take charge while he took Andrew to where there was shade beneath an old oak, built a small fire and wrapped blankets around the boy. An hour later, Finnlay found him still there, taking him a plate of food and a cup of ale. Robert had barely moved, sitting with his back to a tree, his hand on Andrew's head, now and then smoothing the hair down.

Andrew was not the only one who needed time.

Finnlay put the plate down beside Robert, then, without asking, he sat as well. Andrew's eyes were still closed.

'Is he going to be all right?'

'Yes,' Robert said, then as though he'd just awakened, he noticed the plate beside him. 'Thanks. I'm hungry.' With that, he picked it up and began spooning chicken stew into his mouth like it was the first food he'd had in a year.

Finnlay waited until Robert was wiping the last of the juices with a crust of bread before saying, 'The Prophecy never said anything directly.' Robert didn't react. Instead, he put his plate down and returned to his former position, with his hand on his son's head.

Finnlay continued, the words falling into the quiet night, 'That was the whole point of the Bonding, so that Andrew would be conceived, so that he would be this boy, this man, this King. That's why Thraxis created the Marks, so he could keep track of each Bonding through the ages, until this one between you and Jenn. And now that he's born, Andrew has no need of a Mark, because he's what was planned all along.'

Robert said nothing, but turned to look down at Andrew's still form. 'And just like me,' he whispered eventually, 'he has no choice about what he is, what he will do with his life.'

There was silence a moment, then Robert said, 'I don't want to leave him alone until he wakes, until we can be sure his powers are under control. Will you sit with him for a few minutes?'

'Of course.'

Robert rose slowly, as though reluctant to leave, and then, without another word, he turned and headed towards the camp, his head bowed as though he had been once more beaten and tortured.

She'd thought of simply running, but that cowardice was beyond her. She'd made the decision a long time ago: if there were awful consequences, she would face them, come what may. She would make him understand. She had to.

She wasn't surprised when she looked up from making her bed to find Robert walking across the camp towards her. Though it was late, there were enough men still up to notice his passage, though none seemed willing to stop him. From the look on his face, she didn't blame them.

When he reached her, he looked not at her, but instead, at the place where she'd laid out her blankets, her saddle and other meagre possessions. Then he gestured, and said, 'Come with me.'

She followed him away from camp, not caring now what people might say about them. After all, what could they say that wasn't true?

Robert came to a halt at the edge of the last trees, where the brook trickled out into open moorland. Though the moon was three-quarters full now, there was still enough light to be had between the skipping clouds silver-lined by it. Fear flooded through her.

He kept his back to her as he said, 'I was supposed to tell you: it seems the people of Fenlock and the surrounds of Elita believe you to be the new incarnation of Mineah. There are already nuns who have set up a religious order dedicated to you in what I left of your father's keep. At some point in the future, you may want to visit them and disabuse them of the idea that you are . . . at all related to the goddess.'

Robert fell silent then, leaving Jenn to unravel this ridiculous announcement, then he finally turned, allowing his eyes to rise and meet hers. What she saw there turned her heart to ice. How could she ever make him understand?

'I see now what it was you've been hiding from me all these years. I suppose I have you to thank also for Finnlay and Micah? Who else? At a guess I'd say Fiona, possibly Martha and Arlie. And of course, your sister and her husband. Any others I should know about?'

Jenn kept her silence. He stared at her, as though he still couldn't believe she'd done this. His face was clouded, his voice thick, his eyes dangerously moist.

'I had so much trouble convincing myself to trust you, but I always thought that the moment you joined the Key, you would be under its influence, and therefore, I couldn't be sure of anything you did or said. But this goes way beyond that. This lie has been between us for more than fifteen years, long before you joined with the Key, and despite your promises, you still kept it from me. You must have known that I would have willingly taken responsibility for him, and yet you— Did you think I would not be fit to be his father? That he would be better off not knowing me?' He swallowed hard; the struggle to keep his composure showed in every line of his body. Finally, he said, 'Tomorrow you will go back to the Sanctuary. I don't want to see you again.'

Shock and horror swept through her like a maelstrom, but her protest died on her lips as he held up his hand, blinking hard. 'You are such a weakness to me, do you know that? Such a distraction. The Prophecy kept telling me we were on opposite sides and I didn't want to know. What man would want to know that the woman he loved would one day . . .' He stopped, his voice fading at the last. Then he straightened up, putting on that public face so many saw and so few really understood.

He walked past her then, but she stopped him, determined to at least try. 'I was married, Robert. How could I have told you? But you never asked. Not once. Even when you could, even when it no longer mattered. Not once in fifteen years did you ask. You know you should have, you know I would have answered you honestly – but you didn't. Answer me that, Robert. Why didn't you ask me if Andrew was your son?'

'What difference would it have made?'

'I didn't know if you *wanted* him!'

Robert stared at her a moment, then growled, 'You go in the morning. Don't ever come back.'

'No, Robert,' she said quietly, as stubborn as he. 'I won't go. Not this time. It doesn't matter if you hate me – it's no longer your decision alone. I'm staying. There is too much at stake for us to be split apart like this.'

'You should have thought about that before you decided to keep this lie.' And with that, he was gone.

Sounds came to him softly, like they were wrapped up in silk clothing and dressed for a summer's day. He breathed deeply, allowing the fresh scent to fill him, to wake him properly, to draw into his body and bring him back to life. But when had he died?

Andrew opened his eyes. There were trees above him, littered with newborn leaves, dancing in some faint breeze, and above that, heavy clouds threatening rain soon. He sat up, feeling no discomfort, no pain, not even any memory – until he felt the hand resting on his arm and turned to find Robert asleep beside him, a blanket rolled up as a pillow, his face lined with exhaustion.

And in the space of one breath, he remembered it all.

Robert was his father. Not Eachern, Kenrick's father's cousin. Not the monster all Lusarans hated as a butcher and a murderer, but Robert. Robert Douglas, Duke of Haddon. Which made Finnlay his uncle, Fiona his aunt – Helen and the girls his cousins, Lady Margaret his grandmother.

And his mother a liar.

Or did it? Had she lied to him? Had he ever asked, is Eachern my father? No, of course not, but a lie of omission was still a lie. She'd never told him, never told Robert, and so by definition, she had lied.

Why?

He could *feel* her, at the edge of his awareness. She'd always been there – but this was the first time he'd noticed, the first time he realised he could feel it. He had Senses at last, and they were wide awake.

But they couldn't tell him why she'd lied.

Carefully, he disengaged Robert's hand from his arm, placing it down on the ground beside him. He tipped off his own blankets, laying them over the sleeping man. He stood then, stretching to wake up stiff muscles, looking around at the rest of the camp.

So this must be the wilds of Rona. He'd skirted this country a dozen times on his way home to Maitland, but never had he actually been up onto the plateau. There wasn't too much of it, but it was enough to defend, enough to make a stand. It would do.

He wasn't the only one awake, either. There were fires stoked up, more than one pot of brew on the go and somebody somewhere was cruelly cooking up bacon. It wasn't until he saw Deverin, however, that he decided to leave Robert to his rest.

Deverin welcomed him with a smile. 'How are you feeling this morning, my lord?'

'Well, thank you.' Andrew smiled back. 'I don't suppose you have a drop of brew spare, do you? I don't think I ate yesterday.'

'Not from what I heard, no.' Deverin gestured to Micah who immediately passed along a cup of fresh brew and Andrew sipped it, blowing on it to cool it so it wouldn't burn his mouth.

'Is everybody here yet?' he asked, looking around, trying to distinguish the various sleeping mounds.

'We're still waiting for Payne and Daniel, plus a few others. With luck, they'll be here by sunset. If not—'

Andrew looked up, but Deverin was giving nothing more away. He frowned, taking another look around the camp. 'Where's the Bishop? And Father John, Braden and Edain?'

Deverin held his gaze steadily. 'They have not yet arrived. I've sent men out to look for them. The Bishop may not travel as fast as you.'

Andrew heard the concern in the older man's voice and nodded. He could hardly bear thinking about losing McCauly and John. Surely they were still on their way.

He knew they were all watching him, not just Deverin and Micah, but everyone already awake: watching him and waiting, though none of them could know the truth about—

'Do we have sentries posted?' he asked as Owen approached.

'We do. Four men at each path up to the plateau, and two Seekers, one ranging north, the other south.'

'What shifts?'

'Four on, four off.'

'Change it to two on, two off. Everyone needs to take a spell. And we need a group to head down the northern pass into the nearest town – what's it called? Ana Rona? We'll need supplies. Just tell them to be careful not to get caught – but they can be as obvious as they like, and if they left a clear trail up here, then they would be doing a good day's work. Is this our only water supply?'

He ignored the swiftly hidden surprise and waited for an answer. Deverin was the first to recover, pointing towards the thin brook and saying, 'Yes, my lord. Though we do have barrels stored here, under cover.'

'Then we need to start filling them today. We have no idea how long we're going to be here and the last thing we need to worry about is water.'

'Will you take breakfast, my lord?' Micah asked quietly as Andrew handed him the empty cup.

'No. I'll wait until Robert wakes up. Right now, I'm going to wash.' He almost laughed as he walked away. The looks on their faces were a picture.

There were rocks on the ground he hadn't noticed the night before. Or perhaps he had noticed them and simply decided they weren't worth the bother of moving. Only now they left sharp-edged indentations in his ribs, recalling certain other bruises only recently healed. Next time he would learn to just move and be done with it.

He could hear he was the last to wake. It sounded like there was an awful lot of activity going on considering nothing much was happening as yet. But if he opened his eyes, he'd have to move, get up and really feel all the bruises from the rocks. He'd have to deal with more than that as well.

'Are you going to sleep all day, my lord, or are you going to remember that you're supposed to be leading this ragged army?'

Robert opened one eye to find the Micah staring down at him. More surprisingly, Micah was actually smiling – something he hadn't seen in more years than he could remember. He opened the other eye, just to be sure he wasn't still dreaming.

'Are we under attack?'

'Not at this moment, no.'

'Then yes, I plan on sleeping all day.'

'We'd rather you didn't. Just in case we do come under attack.'

'Oh, very well,' Robert sighed, making it sound like his rising was a personal favour. He sat up, his head aching a little at first. Then he accepted the cup of brew that Micah held out and took a good mouthful, breathing hard when he realised how hot it was. 'Any more arrivals?'

'A few, though not all we're expecting. We're still waiting for McCauly to arrive.'

Robert looked up with a frown. 'Is he late yet?'

'Not really, but Deverin has already sent out men to see if they can find him on the road. I'm afraid a missing Bishop is enough to make everybody a little nervous.'

'Including the enemy, I'm sure.'

'How long do you think it will take Kenrick to find us?'

'Two, perhaps three days. Four if he's not paying attention to all the clues I left for him.' Robert shifted until he could sit up against the tree, twisting to get the kinks out of his back. 'Where's Andrew?'

'Oh, well, that's anybody's guess. He hasn't sat still since he woke up. He's already reorganised the sentries, sent out foraging parties, arranged for water storage and fodder for the horses, not to mention the building of a shelter for the wounded. Everybody's been waiting for you to wake up so you can save us from him.'

Robert stared at his old friend, seeing more there than he had in a long time. 'You mean Andrew? The same Andrew we brought in last night?'

'Your son, Andrew, yes.' Micah said this quietly, folding his hands together, making himself ready for Robert's censure.

'Ah,' Robert nodded, withdrawing a little. 'So you heard.'

'Finnlay thought it wise I should know, though I confess, I had to assume something like that had happened.'

Robert knew he had to ask the question, though with their newly gained peace, it was hard to take that step out on another limb. 'How long have you known?'

Micah crouched down on the ground before him, picking at a raised tree root with little attention. 'I guessed, before Andrew was born. How could I not? I was at Elita the night before her wedding. It was not hard to guess why you'd sent yourself into exile. I knew you wouldn't be able to forgive yourself for . . . for failing to deny the Bonding.'

Robert stared at Micah. How could this man, who had been apart from him for so long, still care enough to say something like that? 'I need to ask. Why didn't you tell me?'

Micah pursed his lips. 'You never asked me. Jenn always knew that if you did, I would have told you.'

No, he hadn't asked. 'By the gods!' Robert breathed, putting his head back against the trunk.

'She's still here.'

'I know.'

Micah looked away out over the moor. 'I'd like to offer my congratulations on your becoming a father at last. I'm probably the first to do so.'

Robert couldn't help but smile. Despite everything else, Micah was right: he was a father, no matter how little he deserved such an honour. 'Thank you. Now I think it's time I went and found my son.' Few words had ever tasted so good.

'I don't think you'll have to look far.'

Turning, Robert caught sight of Andrew jogging across the moor towards him, wind-blown hair across his face.

'You need to decide what you're going to do,' Micah added, keeping his voice low as Andrew came to a halt beside them.

'Good morning,' Robert began carefully, getting to his feet. He had no way to guess what Andrew was thinking or feeling today.

Andrew didn't respond immediately, and Robert could sense that Micah was on the point of withdrawing. Then the boy replied, 'Good morning. You slept.'

'Not nearly as much as you.'

'Was that sleep?'

'I hope so. Besides, you're not dead, so what else was it?'

Andrew's eyebrows rose. 'You don't know?'

'Well, actually, at a guess I'd say that you stretched yourself a little too far the first time you used your abilities. Normally we begin by learning how to use an *ayarn*, which helps to focus and shield you from such overuse, but considering the fact that your mother never needed one and . . .' he faltered then, but recovered quickly, 'and I haven't needed one for years, it's not surprising that you didn't require one either. How do you feel now?'

With a shrug, Andrew grinned. 'Like nothing happened.'

'Well, something did happen, and don't you forget it. Later, once I've eaten, we'll find some quiet area and do some testing and training. I don't want a repeat of the other night.'

'No.' Andrew's smile faded and Robert knew he should broach the other subject, but he himself needed a little more time to absorb it first. Besides, there was something else he needed to say.

'You realise this changes everything.'

'How?'

Robert sighed, looking at Micah before saying, 'I can't put you on the throne.'

Instantly, Andrew was on the defensive. 'Why not?'

'Because you're my son, that's why,' Robert said, only too mindful of the men at work not so far away. An errant gust of wind would take his words much further than he was ready for.

'Why should that make a difference?'

'My lord,' Micah interrupted, 'the Bishop did some research. As far as the rest of the country is concerned, Andrew is Duke of Ayr, son to Teige Eachern and Jennifer Ross. You said yourself he was staking his claim through his mother's blood, not his father's, but even if he wasn't, you as his father only increases the strength of his claim to the throne of Lusara, since Eachern was Mayenne-born.'

'The Bishop knows as well?' Robert rolled his eyes, not appreciating having his own history and arguments quoted back to him. 'Micah,' he dropped his voice, none too comfortable about this, 'need I remind you of the simple fact that, well, that Jenn and I have never been married?' He felt his face reddening at saying this in front of Andrew, but it couldn't be helped.

Micah said, 'I'm afraid that actually doesn't make a difference in the eyes of the law – nor in the eyes of the Church. It doesn't matter if Eachern wasn't his actual father, what matters is that Eachern and Jenn were married at the time Andrew was born. I can assure you, Robert, that Andrew will not be the first King to have such interesting parentage when he ascends the throne.'

'You, of all people, are telling me to ignore the truth?'

There was an unmistakable sparkle in Micah's pale blue eyes which Robert had sorely missed. 'No, I'm telling you to listen to your son.'

Robert stared at him for a moment before it occurred to him to look at Andrew. The boy was almost bouncing on the balls of his feet, desperate to say something. As Robert turned, Andrew's arguments almost gushed out. 'You can't change your mind now! Everybody's expecting this, and if you go back on it now, they're going to wonder why. If you can't give them a reason, and I don't think you will, what *are* you going to say? There are thousands of people involved here, people who've placed their trust in you. All the reasons you used on me when you first abducted me, none of them have changed. If I hear right, we're two or three days away from this battle. You can't change the rules now.'

Andrew's enthusiasm, the sparkle in his blue eyes, the very passion leaking out of every pore, served to remind Robert of what was really at stake here: not just a crown, but the defeat of evil. Without giving an answer, he asked Micah, 'Would you mind giving us a moment?'

And as he moved away, Robert faced Andrew again. Almost immediately, the boy sobered. 'First,' Robert began carefully, 'I want you to know, I didn't mean what I said that night. I was trying to provoke you. I have never thought you a coward.'

There was a faint flicker of relief at that.

'Second, I need you to tell me why you've changed your mind.'

For a moment, Andrew said nothing. Then he drew in a breath and dropped his head. 'I *was* scared. Afraid that I would just be another . . . Kenrick, that it was in my blood and with my mother's powers. I—' He swallowed and looked up again. 'You said I didn't care, but I do; I just didn't know what to do.'

'And now you do? Now you're ready to kill Kenrick?' It was a harsh question, but Robert needed to hear the answer from his son's lips.

'No,' Andrew said, 'I don't think I'll ever be ready to kill him. But I am ready to fight him, and that's all we need, isn't it?'

Robert reached out, hooked an arm around the boy's shoulders and drew him close. As Andrew hugged him back, Robert felt a wave of emotion pass over him. Then he let his son go and announced, 'If I don't get some breakfast, I'm going to fall over.'

'Well, the bad news is that you're too late for breakfast as it's already past midday,' Andrew grinned. 'But Finnlay insisted on saving something for you. If you want to go and wash, I'll make sure it's ready.'

With that, the boy ran off towards the cook fire, leaving Robert reeling for the second time in two days.

Since they weren't hiding and they had no intention of dying quietly, Finnlay's suggestion that they have a little music after supper was greeted with cheers. Everyone gathered together around the fire and, led by those who could play an instrument or hold a tune, brought a little light and laughter to the wilds of Rona.

It was almost fun. But even with the music and the camaraderie, Finnlay could see the underlying tension in the eyes of the men singing along to the music, or tapping their toes. They all knew what was at stake. Though Kenrick wouldn't be able to get his entire army up onto the plateau, if Robert didn't receive substantial reinforcements soon, then they were all doomed.

But something had changed somewhere, and he was not the only one to notice it. It was Owen who found words for it. 'We know where we're heading now,' he said under the noise of the music. 'Somehow Andrew has found us a direction. It's amazing what can happen when a boy finds out who he is, where he came from. Amazing how it opens his eyes.'

Finnlay hadn't reacted to that – to his knowledge, Owen didn't know the great secret – but as he glanced at the old man, he could see that perhaps there were people who didn't need to be told. They were prepared to have faith, no matter what.

Andrew sat on the other side of the fire, spending more time watching his father than anything else. Jenn had always watched Robert in the same manner, and with the same eyes. The unfairness of it all made Finnlay's belly ache; more, he longed to be able to kiss his own wife, to hug his own daughters. But his contemplative mood was broken by one of the sentries, who ran towards the fire, his face white with shock. He came to a halt before Robert, who stood, quickly.

'What is it?' he asked.

'The Bishop, my lord,' the sentry stuttered, out of breath, 'he's been captured!'

34

'Where are we?' John's soft query was silenced immediately by the Guildesman's order to be quiet.

Aiden needed help getting down from his horse – it wasn't too easy moving about with his hands tied behind his back. It was too dark for him to see much more than John standing beside him and the two brothers just behind.

'This way.' A Guildesman grabbed Aiden's elbow and took him further into the darkness, towards a vague shape in the distance, where thick twisted trees overshadowed what looked like a group of tents, lit from within. As they approached, he could see from the corner of his eye people moving about, some hunched down around small campfires. The night had started out clear with some moonlight, but now, so close to morning, clouds had blanketed even that small comfort.

This was an army in wartime, hiding its numbers from the rebels Aiden represented.

'In here.' He was shoved into a tent so hard that he stumbled. John was immediately at his side, using his own shoulder so the older man could steady himself.

A single oil lamp hung from the apex of the tent, giving enough light for Aiden to see the faces of the men who had captured them, and his fellow prisoners. Though their fear was largely hidden, they were all too aware that this could – and probably would – be their deaths.

'Sit down,' the Guildesman ordered, then turned and left them. Aiden could hear him leaving instructions with guards outside, then his footsteps as he walked off.

'By the gods, Father, I'm so sorry,' Braden murmured, deep regret filling his voice as he stood by the door, hands bound behind him. 'I should have been Seeking more often. I should have seen them approaching.'

'No, it's my fault, brother,' Edain contradicted him as he moved about the small tent, looking for something he could use as a weapon other than his own powers. 'You're not the Seeker – I am. It was my responsibility to warn of dangers, and I failed.'

'Robert will kill both of us.'

'Aye, that he will.'

'Robert won't kill either of you,' Aiden replied firmly, finding a stool to sit on. He was so tired he could hardly think straight. 'If we live long enough to see him again, he'll be too relieved to do either of you any harm. Please, sit and rest. We need to be ready.'

'For what?' John sat cross-legged on the floor, while the brothers found places at either end of the tent – still in guard formation – but none of them did so in comfort.

'For whatever the gods send us,' Aiden replied calmly, wishing he really felt that inside. But even if he didn't, he wasn't going to show these men, his brothers, his fear, much less any Guildesmen, not after all these years of quietly fighting their bigotry and greed. If he was to die, then at least he had had the opportunity to do it fighting, to help to shape the people's minds against such things.

'How long do you think they'll hold us here?' Edain whispered, turning to listen to the noises of the camp. 'I should think there's close to a thousand men out there. Do you think the others will have escaped?'

'I'm sure of it, or we would have heard by now.'

Edain grinned wryly and settled back to rest.

Aiden moved to do the same, but a shout from outside put him instantly on guard. There was the unmistakable sound of horses galloping into the camp, and other noises he could not decipher. Immediately, the brothers were on their feet, if necessary ready to use the powers Aiden had forbidden them in order to protect him.

Aiden kept his seat, gesturing to John to do the same. He was in the company of three Salti, but if any of them were to exercise their powers to free him, these Guildesmen would crush them, giving in to the fear the Guilde had always fostered towards sorcerers. Too many would be hurt, and ultimately, for no reason. This war was not about victory, but about freedom, in whatever form it took.

'Where is he?'

Aiden blinked hard at that voice, and came to his feet to face the man who stormed into the tent. He looked around at all of them, his frown deepening, then turned to the soldiers he'd brought in with him.

'Take those bindings off the priest!'

Instantly his men rushed to comply, and Aiden's wrists were finally free. He suppressed a groan at the sudden release and started rubbing the skin to get back circulation.

'Leave us!' The men scrambled out of the tent, leaving Aiden alone with his fellow prisoners, and Osbert.

For a moment, the Proctor said nothing, but just stood there with his hands on his hips, shaking his head from side to side. Then he turned his gaze on Aiden, his anger evident.

'What, in the name of insanity, possessed you to go out on your own? Have you no concept of what's going on here? This is war, McCauly! You are damned lucky my men didn't behead you the moment they caught you! That's the King's order, you know. You've been under sentence of death from Selar's time, and Kenrick's done nothing to change that.' He looked at the others, his anger undiminished. 'Father John, I see. And these two, no doubt, are some of Robert's sorcerers. Well, a fat lot of good they've been to you, McCauly. And what was Robert doing allowing you out without his protection? I just can't believe this is happening!'

Aiden blinked. This was certainly not the reaction he'd been expecting. He drew in a breath, not entirely sure how to deal with this: it had been seventeen years since he had last seen Osbert, and back then, Vaughn had been Proctor, and this man an ambitious Governor looking to improve his position. What he saw now was startlingly different. Osbert had aged, and not at all well. He'd obviously put on some weight, but lost it recently and too quickly. There were grey bags under his eyes and a pallor to his skin that did not look healthy. His face, the way he moved, his anger: so many things spoke of a man who was working under too many pressures, and had been for a long time.

'What am I going to do with you?'

'I wasn't aware there was a question involved,' Aiden replied. He put a hand on Braden's shoulder, gently urging him to sit down again. None of them were in danger at this minute.

'Where is Robert?'

'Robert who?'

Osbert rolled his eyes. He took a step forward, huffing with anger. 'The same damned Robert you've been working with for the last seventeen years to wreak havoc and rebellion, that's who! The man who's made my life a misery! Now tell me where he is!'

'I don't know why you're asking me,' Aiden replied calmly. 'I haven't seen him for months. I have no part in any rebellion, and I certainly have no desire to make your life a misery.'

'Damn it, McCauly, you have no idea what you're playing with here.' Osbert dropped his voice to barely above a whisper. 'Nash is in camp this very minute and if he finds out you're here, you are a dead man. The only hope you have is if I send you off to Kenrick – and I have no choice about that. If I don't send you, then *I* am a dead man.'

'Then you must do your duty.'

'Oh, don't you start, too. Damned priests.' Osbert moved away, running his hands through his thinning, greying hair. Stress almost emanated from him in waves. 'If Nash gets hold of you now, he'll find out every secret you know about Robert, the rebellion, everything. If I send you to Kenrick, he'll try to get you to talk, but he'll give up. He doesn't have Nash's skill for torture. And if I send you to him, Nash won't suspect me of trying to get in his way. But Kenrick is three days' march from here. Anything could happen to you along the way. Anything.'

Osbert came to a halt, his deep frown creasing his face like a shadow. 'I can't keep you here. If I do, Nash will hear about it. I'll send in some food. Eat quickly. You'll leave inside the hour.'

As Osbert turned for the door, one of his men shouted to him, 'My lord! More priests!'

Aiden frowned at John and, without hesitation, followed Osbert to the tent opening. There before him were two dozen Guilde soldiers, four holding flaming torches up in the night. On the ground kneeling between them were two monks, and behind, another Guildesman holding onto a donkey.

'What's this idiocy?' Osbert snapped. 'Are you stupid enough to go around arresting every priest in the country? Are we suddenly at war with the Church?'

'My lord, these men were asking for you. The older one there, said he had a message for you.'

Aiden felt Osbert sigh rather than heard it. It seemed he wasn't the only man here who'd had a long night.

'Well, monk, what's your message?'

The older of the two men lifted his head and with his bound hands, signed the trium in the air before him . . .

'Oh, by the gods—' the words were out of Aiden before he could stop himself. A cold wash of shock swept over him.

Kneeling there, his face raised in hope, his eyes open in pure innocence, was Vaughn, Osbert's predecessor, presumed dead nine years before.

'What is this?' Osbert whispered, horror and shock shaking his voice. 'Is this some kind of joke?'

The younger monk raised his head and quickly got to his feet, holding out his bound hands in supplication. 'Forgive us, my lord. This is not a joke. We did not mean to offend. This is . . . this is the Hermit, my lord.'

'The Hermit?'

'Of Shan Moss.' The young monk looked from Osbert to Aiden and back, as though unsure to whom he should be speaking. Osbert appeared to have forgotten Aiden was even there. 'We have travelled many weeks and endured much hardship. The Hermit—'

But Osbert was shaking his head, saying, 'This is no hermit! This is—'

Aiden reached out a hand to Osbert's arm, but even he could see recognition in the eyes of a number of the men gathered around them staring at the Hermit. The Guildesmen were looking first to their Proctor, then each other. It would take no time at all for word of this to fly about Osbert's carefully constructed army.

'You see me and know me,' the Hermit smiled warmly. 'The goddess said it would be so. She said you would know me as I do not know myself. I have come to the place she intended.'

'No,' Osbert hissed, his face horribly white. 'This is insanity. This is a trick of some kind, some ghost sent to haunt me, some—'

Aiden gripped Osbert's arm firmly, shaking a little until he got the Proctor's attention. Wide-eyed, Osbert turned to him, as though he had no comprehension of what was expected of him. Aiden waited a moment for Osbert's shock to subside, then spoke. 'He does not remember. Look into his eyes. This is not the Vaughn we once knew. Look. This is no trick.'

Osbert frowned, then whispered to Aiden, 'Nash told us he'd been murdered, but we never found a body. All these years, somehow he survived. The Hermit must have taken him in or something. But it was Nash who . . . So that I could take over. Serin's blood! I played right into—' With groan, Osbert turned his back on his men, facing the tent, closing his eyes for a moment.

'I have a message for you,' the Hermit spoke again, his voice so different to that which Osbert recalled so clearly, but then, this was a different man: he was old, infirm, his eyes a little blind. All that he was, all that he remembered of himself was gone. Of course he would sound different. 'The goddess gave me a vision. To warn you. She is amongst us and begs that you forgive.'

'Forgive?' Aiden asked the question as Osbert appeared unable to take anything in.

'Forgive, yes. She says the Guilde has a strong heart and must be ready to open it. There are wounds which need to be healed, and only the Guilde can begin this work of hers. She says that this above all, is the Guilde's Sacred Duty.'

'That's your message?'

The Hermit smiled again. It was a little hard to take in that Vaughn was that same Hermit who had, for so many years, given Lusara the visions her people clung to for hope.

'Osbert,' Aiden murmured, 'you have to—'

'No!' Osbert looked up, his gaze hollow. 'I am so sick of priests telling me what I have to do. Get back inside.' He turned to his men. 'Call Lyle and bring him to me. Put these two in with the others and make sure nobody escapes.'

With that, Osbert stalked off, the weight on his shoulders increased tenfold.

Nash breathed deeply, letting his eyes open with the movement, feeling his body relax against the carpet beneath him as the cool pre-dawn air surrounded and caressed him. He'd been gone for hours this time, draining precious strength, leaving him empty and hungry. The darkness had always helped his Seeking, always given him a cushion he could rest upon as his Senses swept across the country, but this time he'd stayed out too long, and now his eyes could only see the interior of his tent, the lamp hanging above, the soft glow of the brazier.

He rolled to his side and sat up. Dizziness swept through him, making him pause, then he stood, grabbing the thick robe he'd dropped the night before, covering his nakedness in warm wool and silk. He reached for wine and drank a full cup before pausing for breath. He sipped another as he walked to the door of his tent.

'Taymar?'

His servant lay wrapped in his own blankets beneath a canvas lean-to. Hearing Nash's call, he sat up, blinking to wake properly. 'Yes, Master?'

'I need some food. Then begin to pack. We'll leave to rejoin the King.' Nash left him to his work and pulled a chair up to the brazier. He'd always hated the cold, and in the long years of his incapacitation, he'd grown particularly vulnerable to chills and drafts. Though his regeneration had changed all that, tonight – or rather, this morning – it was as though nothing had changed.

Never before had he felt so old, never had he drifted so close to outright failure. Every night for weeks now he'd spent his time Seeking across the country, looking for any sign at all of the Key, the Enemy, the Ally, but there was nothing. It was as though they'd all simply disappeared, or had never existed anywhere but in his imagination.

How had he managed to make that contact with the Key in the first place? Or had the contact been with the Enemy? But if it had, he'd been in close contact with the Key, as he'd been sure of the doubling and trebling of layers beneath, and absolutely positive that he'd actually touched the Key himself, after more than a hundred years searching for it.

It must have been the regeneration, because he'd just emerged, fresh and new, bristling with a power he could now barely remember. But even if he found another's blood to use in such a manner – assuming he could find somebody powerful enough, soon enough – there was no guarantee he could recreate that connection and without that connection, he could not find the Key. Without the Key, he could not—

He drained his wine again, resting his head on the back of the chair. That poison had nearly achieved what Prophecy, a hundred years, a dozen wars and the Enemy had failed to do. Did the Malachi have any idea just how close he'd come to death? No, they couldn't have, for if they had, there was no doubt they would have tried it again by now. He'd been so sure he was invulnerable to anything since his regeneration, but alas, he'd jumped too soon: a child of his and Valena's blood had given extraordinary strength, but everything he'd ever read had confirmed the Prophecy: that it would be only a child of the Enemy and Ally who could give him immortality.

Or a child of the Ally, fathered by *him* – a child that would never now be conceived. The art of the seductress, Valena's one great power was to make a man fulfill his potential – or to destroy it completely. He had forgotten. In the depths of his illness, he had let down his barriers and lost the one thing she had given him.

Now he had only one hope left: the Key. There was enough power in the Key to undo what she'd done, to heal all his wounds, to perhaps grant him immortality on its own. And the only way to the Key was through the Enemy.

So be it.

Nash got out of his chair, threw off his robe and began to dress. Taymar appeared with food on a tray and he ate in silence. An hour later, he was mounted and riding into the dawn.

The sound of horses woke Aiden from a fitful, yet comfortable sleep. They'd been brought blankets, but with five men in the tent, there was barely enough room for them all to lie down. Despite his curiosity, he had resisted the urge to speak to Vaughn. They all needed rest if they were to be shipped off to see Kenrick. It would be interesting to see what the King made of the Hermit of Shan Moss. It was hard enough at the best of times living with a legend – and Aiden knew all about that – but it was another thing altogether when that legend comes upon you, bringing pronouncements from the gods.

He could hear voices from the other side of the canvas wall, hushed and rapid words spilled out into the early morning. Then the flap was pulled back and Osbert appeared. His eyes turned first to Aiden, then he stood aside, ushering another man in.

'Wake up, all of you.' Though Osbert's voice was quiet, it held the weight of urgency.

Aiden carefully got to his feet, joints protesting the night's harsh treatment. As the others rose they stood back so the unknown man could deposit a large cloth bundle on the floor. With little fuss, he undid the rope holding it closed and let it open before them.

It was full of Guilde robes, as bright a yellow as the sun. Aiden looked to Osbert for answers.

The Proctor started speaking, quickly and urgently, 'Nash has gone to join Kenrick. He knows nothing about you being here. Everyone is to wear one of these, and make sure it looks genuine. There are horses waiting outside for you. I want you all gone before sunrise.'

'Gone?' Aiden queried, even as the others were already sorting out the robes and dressing. 'But what about—'

'Go back to Robert, McCauly, and take this—' he gestured at Vaughn, 'with you. This is more trouble than I can – or want – to deal with. He's the great hero, let him make what he can of this so-called hermit. Since he's failed to come and rescue you, I'm going to assume he's already left this region, and if that's the case, there's no point in my staying, either. So we're all off to meet up with Kenrick. He's marching to Rona because he thinks he'll find all the rebels there in one place, though why, I couldn't tell you. I can say, in all sincerity, that I hope never to see any of you again.'

With a last look around, Osbert turned and left the tent, leaving Aiden amazed.

'Quickly, Father,' Lyle said as he handed him a robe roughly his size. 'We have very little time.'

35

'This doesn't make any sense.' Robert opened his eyes. In front of him sat Andrew, Jenn and Patric.

'What doesn't make sense?' Andrew looked up, his eyes tired.

'I thought I had Braden before, but now I can't find Finnlay.'

'Robert,' Jenn ventured, almost not caring whether he listened or not, 'you need to rest. You've been at this almost all night. We have other Seekers who can take over for a few hours. You don't have to do everything yourself.'

He didn't look at her. Instead, he got up again, stretching his neck this way and that. 'I sent Finnlay out there, and now I can't find him. I should never have let the Bishop go out on his own. If something happens to Finn as well—'

Jenn stood too. 'He's shielding, that's all.'

'Shielding? From even me? He's never been that strong before.'

'He's had years to practise, Robert. I'm sure he's putting every effort possible into it because he knows Nash is around and probably looking for the Key. Remember, Nash knows Finn's aura too.'

It was a moment before she knew she'd got through to him. Robert stopped his pacing and drew in a deep breath.

'I'll go and get some brew,' Andrew volunteered, getting to his feet.

Jenn could hear the men behind them, waking into the morning, talking quietly, stirring up fires ready for the day. The night had been subdued; nobody liked the idea that, on the brink of battle, they'd lost their spiritual leader, least of all Robert. Of course, his first instinct had been to go out and mount a rescue himself, but he refused to either leave Andrew here, or to take him. So Finnlay had volunteered to go, along with twenty of their best men, and that had left Robert spending half the night trying to Seek Edain or Braden and, in the last hour, Finnlay himself.

His lack of success drove him to increasingly greater efforts, which in turn made him worry more and focus less. He was too tired, and all of them knew it, but none would say it. Robert had spent the last two months fighting, running, hiding, getting wounded and worrying about an entire country, turning a boy into a King, and doing it all on only a few short hours' sleep each night.

And soon he would have to face Nash.

'Robert, you need to rest,' she repeated, but he ignored her, as he usually did now. It only made her more angry. 'By the gods, why do you have to be so damned stubborn?' she muttered.

His eyes shot up to hers then and she almost flinched. 'You should just be damned grateful I am this stubborn, or else—' He broke off abruptly as Andrew returned with cups of brew for them all. As Jenn took hers, she tried to get Andrew to meet her gaze, but, like his father, he couldn't quite do it.

Had she really lost them both? So quickly? Jenn wasn't going to allow herself to get bogged down in this when there were other lives at stake. They could solve their personal differences later, when they could afford the luxury of time. 'I'm sorry, Patric, Andrew, I need to speak to Robert alone for a moment. Perhaps you could go and see if there is any breakfast yet.'

She watched Andrew looked once to Robert. Patric got to his feet and, with a hand on Andrew's shoulder, followed him back to the main camp where fires were already warming the cold day.

'I told you I wanted you to go,' Robert began, his voice low and venomous, but also reeking with exhaustion.

'And I told you I'm staying. Are we going to have this argument every hour?'

'Until you go, yes.'

'Fine. In the meantime, I'll do your thinking for you, shall I?' Jenn leaned against the nearest tree and folded her arms, never once taking her eyes off him. 'You are pushing yourself up to and beyond your limits. And don't even think you can fool me, of all people. I know you better than you know yourself. I know you're tired, I know you're worried, and I damn sure know you're scared. But if you don't rest, if you don't take the time to heal, when Nash comes, you won't have an ounce of energy left to fight him. Your reactions will be slow and your ability to think will be halved. You're already having trouble Seeking Braden, when, just a few hours ago, you found him without too much trouble. Robert Douglas, I have absolutely every possible faith in you to beat Nash, but you need to allow yourself to do it. And clinging stubbornly to your hatred of me as an excuse not to listen is a piece of stupidity the like of which I had never thought you capable.'

He looked not at her, but out across the wild moor, where crusty knots of trees were bent against a wind from previous years. 'I don't hate you,' he said, though his tone belied that statement, as cold and frosty as any winter. 'But I can't trust anything you say any more.'

'Why? Because I didn't tell you the child you gave me was yours? Because you disappeared an hour after he was conceived, and didn't return until an hour before he was born? Because I knew you *would* acknowledge him – and I was already married to Eachern? Because every minute of your life from the moment you spoke the Word, you've been fighting this rebellion, and haven't known a single moment's peace since, and have blamed yourself for every ill this country's ever known? Because I refused to add another to it? Because I knew you would blame yourself for leaving me with your child? Is that why you can't trust me, Robert? Is it?' Jenn swallowed the lump in her throat, determined not to cry in front of him.

How could he love her and not understand? How could he swear his life for hers and yet make no effort to see that she had done it for him?

'What would you have done with a son, Robert? What kind of life would he have had? You think I didn't know what he was heir to? If you had taken him, he *would* have been branded a bastard and you would now have no new King to place on that throne.'

'That's hindsight, and you know it!' he broke in, angrily.

'To you, perhaps it is – but you forget, I've known all along that he was yours.'

'And you think I would have ruined his life if I had acknowledged him? There have been bastards on thrones before now – or is it you don't think I would have been a fit father for him? Did you want him all for yourself? Or have you some other scheme in mind?'

'Robert,' Jenn sighed, seeing the glowing darkness in him growing stronger with every word, 'I'm just saying you need to rest. That's all. If Finnlay were here, or the Bishop, they'd say the same.'

He turned and looked at her then, and there was nothing familiar in his gaze. 'The Bishop thinks it's entirely possible you're the incarnation of Mineah. I should not need to remind you that the last time Mineah came to us, she fought against the Cabal in favour of the Empire, and was responsible for almost wiping out sorcerers from the face of the world.' He walked towards her, using his height to make her look up. 'Everything you say makes perfect sense to me, and yet all I keep thinking is that a few weeks ago, at the Enclave, we promised each other that we would have no more lies between us, because we both knew we'd be in this position one day, readying ourselves to face Nash. We made that promise, both of us, and yet, you never meant it, and that is what I do not understand. Why say such a thing when you didn't mean it? See, these are the questions I have to ask myself because we're not talking about how my love for you seems to mean absolutely nothing to you, but instead, we're talking about the future of this country, and perhaps the whole world, if Nash gets his hands on the

Key. So you tell me, Jenny,' Robert paused, his voice breaking at the last, 'do you really think I should trust anything you say?'

She could find no words, nothing to show him the light to the darkness inside him. From the moment she'd joined with the Key, she'd broken his trust, and even now, when it was so important they be united, he couldn't even acknowledge a simple fact he knew to be true, because she was the one saying it.

She turned away then, swallowing again, pushing down the pain, though it had nowhere to go. But as she moved, she saw Andrew standing near by – close enough to have heard at least a little of what Robert had said. He looked bewildered, and horribly lost. She looked back to Robert, ready to say something, anything to make it right for them, but Andrew didn't wait.

'Father?'

It might have been the Word of Destruction for the effect it had on Robert. He shuddered and closed his eyes. Then, his voice a whisper, he said, for her ears only, 'Please, Jenny, just go. I'll rest, I promise. Just leave me.'

Jenn pulled in a breath to ease her tight throat, then walked away from her lover and her son, out onto the moors. She heard Andrew calling to her, but she couldn't face him now. When the wind picked up, it turned the tears on her cheeks to ice.

'Father, are you going to tell me—'

'No, I'm not,' Robert said, shaking his head, which was enough to make him sway on his feet. 'And you can't call me that.'

'Why not?'

He refused to watch her walk away, refused to face her accusations, her lies, her sacrifices. He could barely stand as it was. 'Because if everybody knows who you are, they're going to think—'

'That I'm the bastard son of Robert Douglas and Jennifer Ross – which happens to be the truth. Or am I not good enough to be your son?'

Robert's head snapped around. 'Don't be ridiculous,' he said, but then he paused, seeing much in the boy's eyes that hadn't been there a few weeks ago. 'Oh, by the mass, you are your mother's son.'

'I am my father's son, too,' Andrew lifted his chin, and there was absolutely no fear in him now, where not too long ago, there had been too much. 'Know where you are, my father said to me, because everything around you can change at any minute. I know exactly where I am, Father. I just need to know where you are.'

Stunned, Robert found words failed him. Andrew raised his eyebrows and moved closer. 'You still love my mother, don't you?'

Did he? Or was it something else after all?

'Don't you?'

'Yes.'

'Because of the Prophecy?'

And then he did look away, to where her figure was retreating into the distance. She would return later, when they had both calmed down and could work together again. 'No, not because of the Prophecy. I can't not love her.'

'Me neither.' Robert looked back to his son then, to find compassion in his eyes. 'Please, Father, get some rest. I'll make sure nobody wakes you. There's nothing you need to do for a while. At midday, I'll ask Mother to try mindspeaking Finnlay. You might be able to Seek him by then.'

'Andrew—'

But the boy grinned cheekily. 'When you make me into a King, I'll be your King too, so you'll have to obey my orders. This is a wonderful opportunity for you to get a little practice.'

Robert found a smile creasing his face. 'Very well, sleep it is. But wake me at midday.'

'If necessary.'

'I mean it.'

'Yes, Father, whatever you say.' And with that, Andrew also turned and walked away, leaving Robert remembering that exact tone, and when he'd used it on his own father.

Jenn walked and walked, leaving all the heaviness behind, making for the edge of the plateau, letting the wind cool her mind, dry her tears and leave her soothed and empty. Perhaps she should have gone, and left Robert with that relative peace. The last thing he needed right now was to deal with all this, and the constant reminder of her lie. But if she left, she would be deserting both him and Andrew – and the cause of freedom in her country. That was something she could not do.

Thick heather on the ground made walking an energetic exercise, forcing her to lift her feet with every step. By the time she reached the edge, the sun was truly up, warming the cold, brightening the landscape. The slope down to the valley was steep, which was why Robert had chosen this place. It was almost a fort in itself, and much easier to defend than a forest.

She continued following the edge, where the heather was shorter, battered by the wind. The country below was beautiful indeed and, even ignoring the circumstances, more than worth the effort of the climb.

Feeling better with each step, she finally reached the first of the three approaches to the plateau, where half a dozen men stood guard, hunched down in the heather, out of the wind, keeping watch in every direction. They all looked up as she reached them, but only Micah stood to welcome her, and he did so with a smile.

'There are easier ways to get exercise,' he said, gesturing to where he was sitting, and she accepted the invitation with a faint smile of her own.

'I take it all is quiet?'

'You would know otherwise.'

'Good.' Jenn let her gaze wander over the valley again, and north, to the hills and mountains of Nanmoor, just visible in the distance. The Key was there, safely away from Nash, and Robert was wishing she was there with it.

'Any news?'

'About McCauly? No, not yet. Robert's tried Seeking Braden and Finnlay, but he's a little too tired to achieve much. I believe he's resting at the moment. He'll try again later.'

Micah grunted, but she felt his eyes on her as he asked, 'He didn't take the news well, did he?'

Jenn casually glanced around; the other men were far too close for her to be too explicit in her reply. 'Not well, no. At least, not to my part. The rest – well, he couldn't be happier.'

'Yes, that much was obvious. For both of them.'

'You think so?'

'Absolutely. Andrew is changed.'

Jenn looked up at him then, finding a smile in Micah's eyes and wishing she had one in her own.

'Micah? There's another group approaching.'

The voice came from their left; one of the sentries was raising his arm and pointing at ten men on horseback, riding steadily, in no particular hurry, yet obviously aiming for Rona. They slowed as they arrived at the bottom of the track, moving into single file, walking.

'They've been trickling through since we got here,' Micah said. 'I don't know how much good they'll do us, but it's nice to have them.'

'They could make all the difference. You can never tell what's going to happen.'

'Unless you have Prophecy,' Micah murmured in reply. 'And now we wait?'

'Now we wait.'

'Robert knows what he's doing.'

'Robert always knows what he's doing.' Jenn said this as much for Micah as herself, as much for the men sitting around her guarding the track, and for the men riding up the slope towards them—

'Serin's blood!' Micah froze where he sat, making Jenn look at him. His eyes widened in deep shock, and then he was on his feet. 'No, it can't be! I must be seeing things!'

'What is it?' Jenn rose, all ready to call the alarm to Robert.

Micah went to take a step forward, checked himself, then took it after all. As the first rider broached the top of the hill, Micah broke into the biggest smile she'd ever seen on her face. 'My brothers! All of them! Every single damned one of them!'

He ran forward then, to drag the first one down from his horse. With laughter, the others arrived, jumping down to embrace their youngest sibling, smiles and grins on the faces of every man present.

After a few minutes, Micah rushed back to her. 'Come, please, you have to meet them or I'll be thinking I am imagining this,' he said as he took her hand and dragged her down to the group: all the men looked like Micah in one way or another. She had known he came from a big family, but this was ridiculous.

'Jenn, these are my brothers, Talcott, Ralph, Lambert, Kaniel and Durrill. These other two, Ian and Timor, are my sister's husbands. The young ones are my nephews, Peron and Savin.'

'We would have brought more of the clan with us,' Durrill grinned, sharing a look with his brothers, 'but we needed to leave somebody behind to look after the women.'

This statement was greeted with so much laughter, Jenn was left in very little doubt as to how much looking after was actually required.

'This is—' Micah went to continue his introduction, but Durrill interrupted.

'This isn't your wife, is it? Only, I never thought you had so much good taste, Micah.'

Another round of laughter ensued, which Jenn couldn't help but join in with. She'd only met Micah's father once, and none of his brothers. Micah seemed to have grown a permanent smile at their arrival.

'My wife?'

'Mother told us you'd married.'

'Oh, no.' Micah grimaced a little in apology to Jenn. 'My wife is not here. This is . . . um—'

Before he could mangle up the introduction any further, Jenn intervened. 'I'm Jenn,' she said, smiling.

Almost as one, they bowed, with the younger ones giggling and elbowing each other. But then – was it Talcott? – frowned a little. 'Jenn? As in Jennifer Ross?'

'The same.'

'Oh.'

'Why?'

'Nothing. We've just heard a lot about you,' Talcott said, recovering quickly.

'From Micah,' Durrill added.

'His letters home,' Ralph clarified.

'Of course,' Jenn agreed, knowing full well they were all lying, at least a little. Still, not that it mattered; after all—

Jenn? Can you hear me?

She closed her eyes and shut out the smiling faces and the noise, concentrating on the voice in her head, holding onto it, strengthening the connection. *Yes, Finn, I can hear you. Are you all right? Robert couldn't Seek you and he's been worried.*

I'm fine – and I found McCauly. You'd be surprised how good he looks in Guilde yellow, though he says it makes him look jaundiced.

Is he well?

Completely unscathed. John, Braden and Edain are fine as well. They were already on their way to rejoin us. It appears Osbert let them go, and organised the Guilde uniforms so they could travel unmolested.

Any idea why?

No – but he's collected a – a souvenir on the way, but you'll see that for yourself when we return. I just wanted to let you know that we're all fine. That and . . . well, Osbert told the Bishop that Kenrick is on his way.

On his way?

To Rona.

So it was happening. *I'll tell Robert. When do you expect to be back?*

Tonight some time. We haven't stopped except to change horses. The poor Bishop's about ready to collapse, but he doesn't want to rest until he reaches Rona.

We'll be ready with a heather mattress for him.

I'll tell him.

Take care.

Jenn opened her eyes to find a dozen men staring at her, anticipation heavy in the air. 'The Bishop is safe. They're on their way back.' At their smiles, she turned and began walking back to camp. *Robert? Are you awake?*

I'm supposed to be asleep.

Good – I've just heard from Finnlay. He has McCauly and they'll be back tonight. They're all fine. And Kenrick is heading for Rona.

There was a long silence, broken finally when he replied, *Thank you.* And then he was gone.

'No. If you do it like that, he'll have you in the first few minutes.' Robert

368

changed Andrew's grip on his sword, then stepped back again. 'Now, you need to remember that your powers are a part of you. They come from inside, and only emerge when you want them to. If you retain control, you can do just about anything with them. If you lose control, they could just as easily kill you as anyone around you. Believe me, it has happened. Retaining control is a matter of concentration and patience – and over all, you have to believe you can do it. Most importantly, you need to control your emotions. This much is the same for any fighting skills, arcane or otherwise: you can't allow your anger to rule your actions. For a sorcerer, losing control of your emotions will lose you control of your power. Being afraid of your abilities will only make you question your judgment.'

'But I hardly know what my abilities are.' Andrew widened his stance a little, peering up to where the sun sat low on the horizon. 'How do I know I can even fight?'

Robert drew his own sword again and stepped back, ready to engage. 'As far as I can tell, just about everybody can fight. How good they are is a matter of training.'

'Of which I have almost none.'

'Of which you will have plenty if you stop talking and start practising.'

Andrew grinned. 'Well, go on then,' he challenged.

Sighing dramatically, Robert brought his sword up, feeling the power flow through him in a familiar manner, a grim, but necessary comfort. Almost instantly, his blade began to glow a little, just enough to make Andrew's smile widen.

'This isn't a game.'

The smile vanished immediately, and Andrew began to concentrate. Without warning, Robert swung his sword, as they had done hundreds of times over the last weeks, and Andrew parried, the ring of steel clear in the late afternoon, cushioned by the heather around them, and the small wind still blowing.

Deliberately, Robert pushed a little harder, making his blade glow more brightly, letting Andrew get a feel for what he was doing – and then in one rush, he pushed as hard as he could.

With a grunt, Andrew was lifted into the air and thrown back a dozen feet. He landed in a tangle of arms and legs. Robert said nothing and held his breath as Andrew got back on his feet and returned with his sword up and ready, all suggestion of fun gone from his visage.

'How much chance is there that he's going to be as strong as you?'

'Kenrick? I couldn't say – but people have been telling me for years that I'm stronger than anyone else. I've never fought Kenrick, though I'd suggest that he's had some training.'

'From Nash?'

'I doubt it. For all that they're allies, they're also rivals. If I were Nash, I'd severely limit the amount of training I'd give Kenrick.'

'And we're very glad you're not Nash.' Andrew studied the end of his sword a moment, then met Robert's eyes again. 'Are you going to use that much force each time?'

'Why?'

'It's just that I think I'll change position so I land in the heather next time.'

Robert could only laugh. 'Come on. It's almost dark. We've still got a lot to do before bed time.'

Jenn was about to get up to wash out her bowl, but it was taken from her before she could move. As the soldier moved away, she smiled. 'I'm starting to feel a little useless.'

'Why?' Patric tilted his head. 'Because they won't let you do any work?'

'Yes.'

'Well, that just says to me they think you have much more important things to do than wash dishes.'

'Like what?'

'Keeping me entertained?'

'Which would be true if I were more entertaining.' Jenn leaned back on her hands and started to turn her head, to look for the tenth time to where Robert and Andrew were.

'They're still at it,' Patric said.

'They've been at it all day.' Though it was dark, she could see their movements clearly, lit as they were by the light of their glowing swords. It gave her some comfort to see that Andrew's was as bright as Robert's. On the other hand, she would have felt a whole lot better if they had allowed her a little closer.

With a sigh, she lay back on the blanket and looked up at the stars showing faintly through the film of cloud. 'The weather has been so good. After the last winter, I was expecting constant rain.'

'It's taken me a while to get used to the cold again. The longer I'm here, the more I miss the warmth of Alusia.' Patric sat cross-legged on the ground, plaiting pieces of rope by touch alone. On the other side of him sat Joshi, cleaning his sword by the light of fires and what little moon they had left.

'Do you think you'll go back, after this is all over?' she asked her old friend.

'That largely depends on whether I live through it, I suppose.'

Joshi looked up at that, but then gave Jenn a half-smile and returned to his work.

'Does Joshi want to go home?'

'For all that the Generet live in one city, they are still nomadic by nature. Joshi knows where he came from, and certainly misses his family and friends, but he feels no desperate need to return just yet.'

'And what about you? Where is home for you now?'

Patric, a puzzled frown on his face, thought a moment before answering, 'I don't really know. I'm sure I wouldn't want to go back to the Enclave, even if I could. But apart from that, I honestly haven't thought about it.'

Jenn watched the two of them a moment, and the obvious bond between them, knowing they were mindspeaking. Patric habitually relayed the contents of every conversation had in his presence. It appeared the young Generet had no gift with learning the language. Or perhaps it was just a problem with spoken language.

'How does Robert plan to fight this army coming towards us? Our numbers are pitiful compared with theirs.'

Jenn looked around, but most of the men were involved in evening chores of one kind or another. Their numbers had increased noticeably during the day. Now there were campfires scattered across a third of the plateau, leaving the pleasant scent of peat burning in the air. Keeping her voice low, she replied, 'Knowing Robert, he has a dozen tactical tricks he'll play to make the most of our small numbers, and of course, the terrain is in our favour. He'll separate Kenrick and Nash. If he doesn't, Nash will just kill Andrew.'

'But how does he plan to separate them?'

'I don't know. He's not actually talking to me at the moment.'

'Because you lied to him about Andrew?'

Jenn's eyes widened. 'Pardon?'

'Forgive me,' Patric said, 'but it was impossible to mistake the tension in the air between you – especially after everything seemed so good; a little judicious prodding of Finnlay got my answer. I wasn't trying to pry, but you know I'm interested in all things to do with the Prophecy. Finnlay told me about your other research suggesting Andrew was also involved in the Prophecy. I confess, I found similar suggestions myself.'

'Suggestions of what?'

'Oh, so much! For example, that ancient Prophecy that said something was supposed to happen about three hundred years ago? Well, I think it would have if the Cabal and Empire hadn't battled. I suspect what's happening now was supposed to happen then. See, the odd thing about Prophecy is that it seems to recreate itself, over and over. Bits of it survive in the oddest places, out of context, being applied to different things. The moment you start to travel, to see the world through the eyes of others, it's hard to hold onto your old ideas and prejudices, beliefs that you would have sworn were absolute.'

'For example?'

'That to be blind is to be crippled.'

'But Joshi is your eyes.'

'Exactly.'

Jenn laughed a little, and looked away, her gaze sweeping over the men, at their makeshift beds, their practical movements. Some faint echo of laughter floated towards her and she knew that came from the Maclean camp.

'I wonder, have you asked yourself why the Key chose that moment to drop its protection?'

With a frown, Jenn turned back to Patric, who stopped his plaiting and faced her, his eyes wide open but seeing nothing. 'What do you mean?' she asked. ' It was joining itself to the Calyx. Robert tried to split them apart—'

'Yes, but he didn't break the protection, did he?'

'No.'

'And the Calyx couldn't – so it had to be the Key. Why? Why, after more than five hundred years of protecting us all, would it suddenly choose that moment to make us completely vulnerable, exposing us to not only the rest of the country, but especially to Nash?'

A prickle of fear ran down her back and she sat up again. To keep her hands busy, she reached back and pulled her braid over her shoulder, undoing the tie to release her hair. 'Why do you think it did?'

'Robert's always fought the Key, because it gave him the Prophecy, and the ending of the Prophecy, along with the Word of Destruction. It basically told him he'd use the Word to destroy everything he loved. He considered it a curse and has mistrusted the Key ever since.'

'True.'

'The Key knows this.'

Jenn's hands froze. 'You're saying the Key did it deliberately? To force Robert into—'

'To force Robert into moving on with the Prophecy. To force us out into the open, to force *you* out into the open. Yes. I think that's exactly what happened.' Patric resumed his own plaiting. 'We need to consider why the Key was made, what purpose it had at the time of its creation. Now, after so long, it has become an object of great power, but back then, I think it was made to hold the Prophecy, so that those who were leaving the Cabal would be able to take it with them.'

'But—'

'As far as I can tell, every single Cabal palace had a wall with the same Prophecy carved onto it. We're talking about something wholly central to all sorcerers, our very reason for existence. There is no way they could leave something that important behind without carrying a permanent copy of it with them. I think that's the real reason why the Malachi wanted the Key back, because without it, they couldn't claim to be the new Cabal, and they would lose the major part of their heritage.'

'By the gods,' Jenn breathed, stunned to her core. All that had seemed incomprehensible made sense now. 'I never thought—'

Patric laughed a little. 'None of us did. We were all too close to it, too desperate to find the answers that were right in front of us.'

'So how did *you* see the answers?'

For a moment, Patric chewed his bottom lip and Jenn realised Joshi was watching him very closely. 'There's one other way of looking at the Prophecy: Amar Thraxis was father of the Generet, possibly of us all. What if, instead of the Prophecy being some vague instruction of what we should do if certain things happened, it was instead, the result of some kind of plan? What if he set all this in motion deliberately and left the Prophecy to warn us of what was happening – because he made sure it would?'

Jenn rose to her knees, her attention fixed on the two men in the distance, still battling, still circling, still trying to win. 'When Robert and I tried to ask the Calyx for the Prophecy, the Key stopped my breathing, making Robert withdraw. He said it was deliberate, that it was just trying to prove to him that he had no choice in what happened, that it was entirely in control.'

'You and Robert,' Patric continued in a whisper, 'were Bonded. Sixteen years ago, when Andrew was conceived, the Prophecy took the first step and brought you together. But it wasn't the first step. If Thraxis did indeed plan it, Andrew's conception was the first of the final steps. We're about to take the rest.'

Robert was right – he had been right all along. None of them had any choice at all: they had all been born to do this, created to reach one final goal – whatever that was.

But she knew what that was: the same thing Robert had dreaded and feared and fought against all his life, because he loved her, because Thraxis had Bonded them together. And Bonding existed to make sure certain people married, made sure they would have children who would Bond with others. All along the line until she was born, and Robert. And between them, they had their son.

She closed her eyes, fighting back the swell of horrified emotion that threatened to choke her, fighting for control.

You are the Key.

That's what it had said, long ago, when she'd joined with it, when Robert had tried to stop it, when he'd been caught by it as well. Together in the nothingness inside it, the Key had worked on them, changed them, altered their bodies and healed all their old scars, preventing them from ageing so they would survive long enough to make the Prophecy happen. And at the end, it had told her that. *You are the Key.*

She felt Patric's hand on hers and she opened her eyes, squeezing back to reassure him, though reassurance meant nothing now.

'You can't tell him,' she whispered, rapidly pulling her hair together again, winding it around until it sat at the back of her head, out of the wind. 'Don't tell anybody.'

For a moment, she thought Patric would refuse, but then he asked, 'You'll take us with you?'

She stared at him, then at Joshi briskly putting his sword and cleaning things away. 'Are you sure?'

'Yes. I think Joshi needs to be there.'

Jenn met the young man's gaze a moment, then got to her feet. 'I'll be back. We'll wait until everybody's gone to bed.' She drew in a deep breath, then headed off into the dark, towards the two men who were the centre of her world.

36

Robert had chosen a spot far enough away not to be disturbed, but close enough for all their men to see Andrew at work, so they could know and feel confident in him. Still, it was a long walk to Jenn, a walk of seventeen years. The closer she got, the more she could hear above the clashing of swords: the questions, the instructions, the complaints, the responses.

Would they have been like this if she'd not separated them all those years ago? Had she hampered Andrew's chances of survival by giving him so little time with the one man who could teach him how to live?

It was too late now for those questions – at least for her. Now she only had time for answers.

She came to a halt on the periphery of their space, watching as they completed a set, as they launched into another. She could tell that although they were both tired, they were also both awake and alert, as though their purpose alone was supplying them with strength. Would that be enough to ensure they both lived?

This last bout came to an end, leaving Andrew breathing hard, but Robert without a sweat. Andrew glanced at her, as though he were ready to smile, but it faded at the last minute. She couldn't bear to think what Robert had said to him about her.

'What is it?' Robert asked, his tone civil enough. She wished it wasn't just for Andrew's benefit.

'I need to talk to you. Both of you.'

'Why?'

She didn't hesitate. 'I've decided to go.'

'What?' Andrew put away his sword and moved towards her. Without that light, it was hard to see his face, but she could hear the confusion in his voice. 'Why? What's wrong? Is it because . . . because Father—'

'No, it's nothing to do with your father. Or rather, it has everything to do with him.' This boy of hers could tell truth from a lie, so she had to be very careful. 'He made a vow, many years ago, that he would protect me. If I stay, then his fight with Nash could be compromised. None of us wants him to be distracted. I don't want to leave, but really,' she paused, hearing something inevitable echo in her voice, 'I don't have much choice.'

Andrew remained immobile for a moment, then he came towards her and wrapped his arms around her. As she held him in return, her eyes began to sting again; she almost broke then. She felt Robert's eyes on her and looked up, unable to read him at all.

Then she kissed her son's forehead, touching the sides of his face with her hands. 'I'm so very proud of you,' she whispered. 'You will be the greatest King this land has ever seen. You are already a man others will look up to.' She kissed him once more and let him go.

She could see him biting his lip, but there were no tears from her boy. There never had been. Not once in his entire life had he ever cried.

'Go and get some supper,' Robert murmured.

Andrew stayed still for a moment, then left them alone together.

Jenn took a breath but didn't move.

'He would rather you stayed.'

'But you want me gone.'

He was silent at that for a moment, then replied, 'I no longer know what I want. No, that's not true.' He came and stood close, but she didn't look up. She couldn't. 'I want to hear you tell me you love me.'

'Oh, Robert,' she sighed, 'I've told you that every day for the last seventeen years – but the Prophecy keeps drowning me out.'

'I want to hear the words.'

'But you won't believe anything I say any more, will you?'

She heard him hiss in a breath then and looked up to find him facing the camp.

'I suppose I deserved that.' He ran a hand through his tousled hair. 'Are you going alone?'

'Patric and Joshi will keep me company. We'll go once everyone's gone to bed. I don't want to cause any kind of fuss.'

He looked down at her, his face softening a little. She wanted to say it then, she desperately wanted him to know it for sure, so that no matter what happened, he would carry that with him – but she didn't dare. That softening in his gaze warned her: if she did, he would bend, she would break – and she would never be able to leave.

She had no choice at all – which was how she was sure she was doing the right thing.

But he had no such thoughts, and it appeared he didn't need to hear the words after all. He bent his head and kissed her, softly, briefly. Then he straightened up, took her hand and led her back to the camp, and through all the tenderness, she knew he had not forgiven her.

Joshi had saddled horses for them and packed up their sleeping blankets, gathering a little food for the journey. Since everyone was used to him moving around on his own, nobody questioned his actions, but by the time Jenn reached him, most of the men had gone to their beds anyway. Only Deverin remained by the fire, trying to read a book by the light of the flames. He looked up when Jenn and Robert approached, saw their joined hands and gave them a little smile. She gave him one in return, leaning down to kiss his cheek as she passed.

She wanted to say goodbye to Micah too, but it would take her an age to find him. Robert stood by and watched her mount up, putting his arm around Andrew's shoulder when he joined them. As Patric and Joshi brought their horses alongside her, she took one last look at the tiny army that would free Lusara.

But she was denied such a clean departure. Before she could turn her horse for the track, she heard riders coming towards her.

'Finnlay.' Robert moved forward into the firelight.

Jenn saw them a moment later, all weary, saddle-sore and more than ready to arrive. She pulled her horse out of the way, shying away from the puzzled look Finnlay threw her when he saw her mounted.

'Welcome back.' Robert gave them something like a smile, but kept his voice quiet so as not to disturb the men sleeping. 'A little detour, Bishop?'

'You could say that.' Aiden grimaced as he slid from his horse. He grunted when he hit the ground and Robert stepped forward to steady him. 'Thank you. Next time, I'll thank you not to let me go out on my own. Obviously I am not to be trusted.' He looked briefly at Jenn, but instead of asking what was going on, he said to Robert, 'I . . . er, brought you a surprise.'

'A surprise?'

'Yes. While I was with Osbert—'

He got to say no more as one of the last horses rushed forward, and an old man slipped to the ground. With a soft cry, he fell to his knees before Jenn's horse, murmuring words she couldn't quite hear.

'Who's this?'

'This is the Hermit of Shan Moss,' Aiden replied quietly. 'You'll also know him by his former name—'

Jenn knew it before he said it, knew it even as the old man raised his face towards her.

'—of Vaughn.'

'Oh, blessed be the goddess Mineah, divine in her every creation. We sing praises down on your merciful head, and beseech you bless us with your presence for many years to come. Surely we are gifted with a righteous victory with only the blessing of your smile.'

'Vaughn?' In a flash, Robert was there, hauling the old man to his feet, turning him around, exposing him to a light Robert fashioned from his powers. 'Serin's blood, it is! Damn it, Aiden, where did you find him?'

'I didn't. He found me – or rather, he found Osbert. I believe he's been looking for . . . um, Jenn.'

'The goddess, yes, she is—'

Robert clapped a hand over the old man's mouth. He didn't struggle. 'Andrew, get Deverin to bring me a gag. I want this criminal bound and anchored to a tree.'

'Robert,' Aiden protested. 'He's an old man!'

'He's an old man who conspired to put you in prison, would have had you executed, who led a murderous pursuit of sorcerers across Lusara, who drove a wedge between me and Selar to the point where I deserted my own country simply to keep the damned peace! If I'd been able to maintain control over Selar, none of this would ever have happened, so don't go telling me about how he's a feeble old man!'

'What are you going to do?'

'I'm going to restrain him, gag him and in the morning, I'll talk to him. In the meantime, I suggest you all get some food and some rest.'

Deverin returned then with the gag, tying it around Vaughn's mouth before binding his hands together in front of him. Then Deverin took him away, leaving Aiden shocked and Robert pale.

In the silence, Jenn took her last look at Andrew, and then at Robert. Without a word – for only one word had the power to change them – she turned her horse and rode away, knowing Patric and Joshi were following her.

The silence of the night swallowed her up, a balm to the aches inside, giving her a little unexpected peace from all expectation, all demands, all failure. For now, there was only the present and the future. The past was, literally, behind her.

The sentries bid her goodnight as she rode by and she sent a silent prayer after them, turning her horse onto the track with great care. After that, she simply rode, keeping her thoughts on the path, her Senses stretched to the maximum and everything else tamped down in that same place where she'd pushed the anger.

Long after midnight, she paused to water the horses, dismounting to stretch her legs and wake up her numb feet. Joshi helped Patric do the same, wordlessly, silently. She'd once thought they were mindspeaking all the time, but having watched them for some weeks now, she knew it had very little to do with speech and everything to do with love.

'Is Joshi a Seeker?'

'All Generet can Seek, most are very competent. He can provide what you require.'

'Good.'

'How far do we go?'

'Up to the approach. I want to be sure you can find it again.'

'We'll be there by dawn?'

'No later.'

'Fine. Then we should eat now.'

The food tasted like sand, but she ate it anyway. Then they mounted up again and continued on. She listened to the night sounds, studied the faint stars and a little before dawn felt the first rain they'd had in weeks – retribution for her comment about the good weather.

Finally, when the sky cleared a little, she called a halt. 'Is this far enough?'

'Yes,' Patric said. 'How long will you need?'

'How long will it take?'

'Before midnight tonight.'

'I'll be waiting.'

'Only stay as long as you need, Pat. As soon as you're done, leave.'

Patric opened his mouth to reply, but it was Joshi who spoke. 'No. We stay.' He met her eyes and repeated, 'We stay.'

She smiled back. 'Good luck.'

Patric said nothing, but a moment later, he allowed Joshi to lead him back down the hill. Jenn waited until they were gone, then continued on alone. It took her only a short time before she reached the end of the ravine and there she finally dismounted. She waited for the sun to rise, for it to reach the edge of the cliff above, to move down until it touched her face. She closed her eyes, smiled up into the warmth for the last time, then turned and went into the Sanctuary.

37

Despite his exhaustion, Finnlay rose early, only to find that almost everybody else had as well, the exceptions being the Bishop and Vaughn, whose presence still puzzled him. But he gave it little thought as he rolled his aching body out of his blankets, struggled to his hands and knees and hung his head, waiting for the dizziness to subside.

He was getting much too old for this.

With a grunt of determination, he braced himself on his little tree-trunk and pushed his feet into his boots, wincing as he found the previous day's blisters. Why was it that shoes he'd worn almost continuously for the last six months, suddenly chose a day like today to develop blisters?

'So you're up at last?'

Finnlay cringed at the sound of that voice, and worse, the tone. 'Yes, dear brother, I'm up. Why, have you another mad rescue you need me to perform?'

'Why – do you only do mad rescues, or can I request a sane one?'

A cup of steaming brew was passed in front of his nose and he took it quickly, before it could be snatched away. He gave it a quick blow, then took a sip. It tasted good; he sighed loudly in contentment before facing his brother. 'So, any news?'

'Kenrick's a day closer. Is that what you wanted to hear?' Robert raised his eyebrows. 'We'll engage today some time, though I'm afraid I can't be more precise than that.'

'You're slipping then. See, that's old age for you.'

'Well, apparently I don't have that problem.'

'That's what you think,' Finnlay grumbled as he took another sip. What really annoyed him about the whole age thing wasn't that Robert now looked like his younger brother, but that he would eventually look like Finnlay's son, and then his grandson. Perhaps he could have a chat to the Key after all this was over, see if they could come to some sort of agreement – he was Robert's brother, after all.

'Feeling better now?' Robert was poised on the balls of his feet, as though ready to pounce the moment the word was given, which, of course, he had to be.

'Yes, actually. Where's Jenn?'

Robert became unnaturally still. 'Gone.'

'Is she coming back?'

'No.'

'But she has to!' Finnlay downed the rest of his brew, then finished getting dressed. 'You have no idea the effect she's had on the men. They all think she's—'

'I know what they think she is, but ultimately, that's got nothing to do with it. Them thinking she's the incarnation of Mineah isn't going to help defy the Prophecy, nor fight Nash.'

'So you've got her safely out of the way.'

'Don't start, Finn—'

'Because she lied to you about Andrew? I can't believe you—'

'Damn it, Finn—'

Finnlay stepped close, dropping his voice. 'You love her, Robert, with your heart and soul. Do you have any idea how happy you've been over the last few weeks, finally being together with her? The two of you . . . Serin's blood, you waited so long, and now you're just going to throw it all away because she was afraid to tell you?'

'What do you mean, she was afraid? Jenn's never known a moment's fear in her whole life.'

Finnlay blinked. 'You are joking, aren't you?'

Robert stared at him for a moment, then stepped back. 'Look, I don't have time to discuss this right now. I have a battle to prepare for. Whether I forgive her or not no longer matters. She's where I want her, safely out of Nash's way.'

'You have to forgive her, Robert,' Finnlay murmured, 'or you'll never forgive yourself.'

He got another sharp look for that, but no direct reply. Instead, he received his orders. 'I have too much to do this morning to spend any more time training Andrew. You know more about combat than anyone else here. Take Deverin if you need a hand. I want Andrew training all day, without a break – and I don't care how tired he gets. He'll be a damn sight more tired by the time we're finished with this war. Can you do that? Can you help your nephew take his throne?'

The challenge in Robert's words were unmistakable, but there was a lot more there that made Finnlay smile. 'Most certainly I can, brother. It will be an honour.'

As he walked off to obey, a last comment floated towards him, 'Damned right it will be, brother.'

Grinning, Finnlay made directly for the camp kitchens, which had grown considerably since they'd arrived a few days ago. Their numbers had increased again overnight; at a glance, he'd have to say they probably had five, perhaps six hundred men. Woefully few in comparison, of course, but it was certainly good to see the Maclean brothers, along with a number of other faces he recognised.

He found Andrew with a piece of bread in his hand, about to take a bite. Finnlay snatched it from him on his way past, taking a mouthful and admonishing his nephew, 'You should never exercise on a full stomach. Come on, we've got work to do. Deverin!'

'Yes, my lord?'

'Bring your sword.'

'Aye, my lord.'

'But, Finn, I'm hun—'

He stopped and fixed his nephew with a flat stare. 'Yes, Your Grace?'

Andrew flicked a glance to the men around them and lifted his chin. 'Nothing. Robert and I were practising over there yesterday. It's out of the way.'

'Then it will do us fine today. Pass me that jug of ale. This will be thirsty work.'

'Wait,' Andrew said as Deverin came up behind him, ready for work, 'is that Micah?'

Finnlay turned around to find Micah galloping towards the camp with scant regard for the uneven terrain or the steadiness of his horse. 'Where's Robert?' he called out as he approached. More than a few stopped their work and looked up, in time for Robert to appear. Finnlay held his breath.

'You need to come. Take a horse. And Duke Andrew as well.'

'What is it?'

'Good news, my lord. Come!'

There were saddled horses all around; the three of them mounted up and kicked the animals into motion. After all the hours Finnlay had spent on a horse over the last few days, his aches and pains rattled through him against his protesting muscles: *definitely* getting too old for this. After this war, he'd most certainly retire, go home to Dunlorn, sit down and write a book that nobody would read. And then he could spend his time doing truly useful things like choosing which crops to plant, which young men were most worthy of his daughters. And he'd do it all from his bed, without moving an inch except to bathe.

The fantasy kept him amused all the way across the plateau, with the thunder of hooves as counterpoint. Then Micah was drawing his horse to a halt, swinging down from the saddle and gesturing that they follow him.

It wasn't until they were right on the edge of the hill that he saw why. He caught his breath, his jaw dropping in sheer amazement. 'I'm still asleep, aren't I?'

'No, my lord,' Micah whispered in reverence.

Finnlay turned to Robert and was stunned a second time. His brother, pale-faced and powerful, had tears in his eyes at the sight before him.

'They began arriving just after dusk,' Micah supplied. 'None of them wanted to try climbing up here in the dark, so they camped on the plain.'

When neither Robert nor Andrew said anything, Finnlay turned back to the unbelievable view. Spread out, from one side of the narrow plain to the other, were fighting men, preparing for the day's battle around small camp-fires dotted here and there. And walking between them, giving aid and food, was the Guilde.

'How many?' he murmured.

'A thousand Guilde, close on two thousand others.'

A thousand Guilde? That was all Osbert had brought with him – and that would mean that in number alone, their force was greater than Kenrick's.

'Don't get too excited, brother.' Robert swallowed hard, blinking to hide his tears. 'These men are mostly untrained. They're farmers and black-smiths. Their weapons are pitchforks and anvils.'

'They have come to fight, Father,' Andrew said to Robert. 'As have we. They know the risks, but they come to fight for you and for their country. I for one won't deny them the right to fight for their own freedom.'

'But where have they come from?' Robert mused.

'I sent scouts down there when I first saw them.' Micah supplied. 'Some are returned refugees, like my brothers, wanting to do what they can. Others are people from the villages and towns we've been helping over the last few months. Some have travelled across the country, hoping to find some fight they could join.'

'They should not have come,' Robert whispered, his voice still full of awe. 'They fight their own countrymen. I never wanted this.'

'You may lead us, Father,' Andrew smiled, 'but this is *their* rebellion.'

'Aye, that it is,' Robert said, coming to himself. 'So be it. Finn, get back to that training with Andrew. I have a few other arrangements to make and then I'll take him down.' He looked at each of them then, a smile growing on his face. 'They've come to put my boy on the throne; the least we can do is show them what he looks like.'

'Except that they don't know that he is your boy.'

'No – but they do think he's the son of a goddess. I think that will do them for the moment. Come, let's get moving.'

Aiden listened carefully to each instruction Robert laid out, taking notes now, just in case they would be needed later. As usual, Robert held his council of war in the heart of his small captive army, listening to every thought and idea before addressing each one. Then he would continue on, incorporating changes, strengthening his strategy, charming them all with his confidence and his courage. Piece by piece the battle plan came together and, not for the first time, Aiden was amazed at Robert's brilliance – and by the look of it, he wasn't the only one.

Andrew did his best not to sit there wide-eyed in wonderment, but every now and then, Robert would point out some other forgotten point, and the boy would half-smile to himself, then look up again with rapt attention.

Micah had told the Bishop: he'd heard all the awful details, along with the good news, not long after he'd risen. It was a lot to absorb, but he left most of his questions for another time. Today they would fight a battle, regardless of the hour. Today, Lusara's history would change for ever, one way or the other.

So he took his notes, writing down the names of those present, men who had been there last time, at Shan Moss – like Bergan Dunn, and Daniel Courtenay, Payne and Owen, and those for whom this battle was their first, and hopefully, their last – like Andrew. And in the end, Robert gave no great speech as he usually did, but instead, asked Aiden to say a prayer. He did, his voice abruptly thick, and he felt more than heard the rumbled Amen at the end of it.

Then they were all moving, each man to his task, each life to its goal. By the time he closed his notebook, Robert was already moving away.

'Robert, wait.'

He hurried to catch up and found Robert waiting, wariness in his eyes. 'Is this about Jenn? Are you going to berate me as well?'

'I don't know, should I?'

For a moment, Robert searched his face, then said, more calmly, 'She's safe. That's all I care about.'

'Then I'll save my berating for later. In the meantime, I beg of you, please set Vaughn free. He remembers nothing of his previous self, of the things you accuse him of. He takes your censure because he is a peaceful man and bears you no ill will. Can you condemn a man for crimes he doesn't remember committing?'

'Can I, in all justice, set him free? He would compound his errors by moving amongst my army, giving them hopes of divine intervention. What will they do when Jenn doesn't appear, ready to split the ground asunder, as she did last time? Will they then find that cause to lose hope?'

Aiden replied, 'You assume he is mistaken about her.'

'Oh, please, Aiden, let's not get into that again. You know how I feel.'

'Better than you know. It scares you to think that she might be the incarnation, doesn't it? That she might be so far beyond even your control?'

'Trust me, Aiden, she's never been under my control.' Robert sighed heavily and ran his hands over his face, bracing himself against the tiredness he could not afford. How many hours had he slept last night? If he'd slept at all . . .

'Vaughn can do no harm. An army that believes it can win has a greater chance of winning than otherwise.'

'Fine,' Robert threw up his hands. 'Release him, take off his gag – but keep him out of my way. I might forget that *he's* forgotten and put my sword through him anyway. But whatever happens, you take responsibility for him. Understood?'

'Thank you.'

'Don't thank me. I just don't want anyone around here wasting time by feeding him when they'll have wounded men to deal with. Now, do you have any other last requests, or do you think you might trouble yourself to come with me and my— me and Andrew down to see this ragged army of farmers and Guildesmen? You might enjoy seeing the look on Osbert's face when I tell him his future King will be a sorcerer as well.'

Aiden chuckled at Robert's dry humour, glad to see it still present. 'As long as we don't tell them Andrew takes after his father, I don't see they'll have a problem.'

'Why? What's wrong with his—' Robert came to a sudden halt, things ticking over in his head. 'You heard.'

'From Micah.'

'And?'

'And I'll berate you about Jenn later.'

'That's it?'

'And congratulations.'

'That's what Micah said.'

'Are we going?'

'Damned pushy priests.'

'That's what Osbert said.'

'Nobody's original any more.'

Osbert didn't need to give out too many orders after the first shocking few. His Guildesmen had taken his defection almost without comment, changing sides as though they'd believed this was a tactic they'd all been planning for months. It was a sentiment that irked him without measure.

How could they know what he'd planned when he hadn't known

himself? Or perhaps they hadn't known until he'd made the decision for them. What had Godfrey said? *They cannot go unless you do lead them.*

No matter what they'd thought – he'd led and they'd followed him here, to this god-forsaken moor, where his yellow-clad Guildesmen calmly handed out provisions meant for the royal army, fed peasants and farmers, blacksmiths and fishermen alike. His only concern now was Godfrey. He'd tried, but there was no way he'd been able to get the Bishop away safely without anybody noticing. Still, knowing Godfrey, he would rather be left behind and have Osbert's men join the rebels. Either way, when Osbert saw him again, he would be able to look at those dark, all-seeing eyes and do so without shame.

He didn't want to think about never seeing Godfrey again, but as he looked up and saw Robert Douglas riding towards him, he knew there would be questions he couldn't answer. But for the moment, he simply stood his ground, alone before his small tent, the spread of the peasant army arranged before him.

Robert did not come alone. Behind him were other faces, most of which he recognised, but it was Robert's gaze which held him as the Duke brought his horse to a halt, and he swung down to the ground. For a moment, he glanced around, pulling his gloves off, ignoring the stares of all those who recognised him and instead, seeing and appraising, before turning back to Osbert.

'You had to leave Godfrey behind.'

Startled, Osbert nodded. 'I'm sorry, Robert, I had no—'

'Choice? No, I don't suppose you did. But . . . *this* choice, this was a good one. You do know that, don't you?'

He did – but it wouldn't feel like it until the battle was done, until it was all over, until Kenrick and Nash were dead. Until he had the chance to look at Godfrey without shame.

It seemed Robert wasn't waiting for an answer. Instead, he gestured, and one of his companions rode forward. Osbert paid attention this time, and he was unsurprised to find young Andrew watching him steadily. Without a word, the boy slipped to the ground and moved to stand before Osbert.

'My lord Proctor,' Robert began evenly, 'will you accept Andrew, Duke of Ayr as my candidate for the throne of Lusara? Will you support him and swear him your fealty, giving your loyalty to him alone?'

And that was the question, wasn't it, for deep inside, Osbert knew this boy was most likely a sorcerer – how could he not be with that mother? So it would be one sorcerer King over another.

'You cannot swear, can you?' Andrew asked quietly, obviously reading Osbert's dilemma. 'But you know that it isn't a question of sorcery, but a question of good and evil. It always was. A long time ago, you pledged yourself to a cause, not questioning if it was evil or not. You're right to wish to avoid making the same mistake again. So I will give you this promise: if you do swear to me, and you find I am evil, then I will not hold you to your vow. For you, the Guilde, have no right to serve anyone other than the people. And *that* cause cannot be evil.'

'Your Grace,' Osbert began, then paused, taking in a breath and lacing his fingers together. 'I am here. My men are here. We will fight.'

Andrew simply shook his head, and Osbert could see all too clearly why this boy had been chosen. 'We *must* be united, my lord. We, Lusara, sorcerers and all others must be as one to fight this enemy. You must choose, Osbert, and you must choose *me*.'

The simple, open authority in that voice, the same in the blue eyes was somehow exactly what Osbert needed to hear. Without a word, he eased down to one knee and bowed his head. 'I swear, Your Grace. The Guilde is yours.'

Andrew tried to keep his head up, tried to see with his own eyes as many of these men who had travelled so far, mostly on foot, to join this army, tried to imagine what it had been like for them, tried to ride along each of their rows so that they could all see him pass by – but it was impossible. After the first few minutes, he pulled up and jumped down to the ground. Immediately, the four men entrusted with the role as his personal guard surrounded him – but he waved them off. He simply couldn't lead this army onto the battlefield without having spoken with any of them at all.

So he did. One here, one there, asking where they were from, their names, how long it had taken to travel, why they had come – only he stopped asking that one after the first few times. The answer was always the same.

He felt his father's eyes on him as he walked, but Robert said nothing to him, simply rode along behind, with Micah on one side, and Finnlay on the other. The Bishop rode behind, with Osbert at his side.

But these men here weren't so impressed with titles and positions. They had one single passion in common: freedom, a luxury Andrew had always enjoyed – or at least, up until the last few weeks when he'd turned himself into a rebel.

There were so many of them, untrained, but willing to give up their lives. At least there, he did have something in common with them.

'Your Grace?'

Andrew stopped and turned around. Hearing those words from Robert seemed wholly unreal – and yet, he *had* uttered them, changing for ever the roles they would play.

But it wasn't just the words. There, in the eyes of Robert Douglas, the legend, was honest respect. The sight shocked him a little.

'It's time to march.'

Andrew took the reins of his horse and climbed up into the saddle. As they turned back towards the head of the army, a cheer began to rise among those he'd seen, and it filtered out across the mass, thrumming the air with its energy. Andrew wanted to laugh, to gallop forward, to shout with the wonder of it all – but he didn't. Now he had no trouble riding with his head held high, taking in the sight of all these men who had joined this rebel's army; he felt as if he were one of them.

The rest of his council were waiting at the top of a small rise, mounted and ready to march. As the cheers died down, Robert turned his horse to face them and Andrew drew alongside.

'Robert, will you give the order to march?' asked the Bishop, finally wearing the robes of a priest; he looked like a man who had at last found home.

'No,' Andrew replied without looking at his father. 'I will.' With that, he raised his arm, held it aloft for a preternaturally long second. Then he dropped it. With a ceremonious thud, drums began to beat and the head of the army began to move forward, leading out of the plain and into the valley where Kenrick was awaiting them.

Awaiting *him*.

Robert remained at his side as they turned to parallel the march, with the others falling in behind. Andrew, his voice lowered, asked, 'Is it always like this?'

'Always?' Robert replied. 'I couldn't tell you. But don't let yourself get carried away with it. The thrill only lasts until the moment you step onto the battlefield.'

'And after that?'

'You live in hell until it's over, or until you die. There are worse ways to die, believe me. On the other hand, there are also better ways to die. I've always preferred the ideal of old age, but it appears I might not be allowed that.'

For a moment, Andrew frowned, but then he remembered the Key's work on both his parents. 'You're expecting the volunteers to break lines?'

'They've had little or no training, and it's certainly possible a large number of them fought at Shan Moss – though their training there was minimal too. Still, they were fairly disciplined on the field. That's why I want to keep the Guilde in amongst them. Besides, it's time the Guilde remembered who they are supposed to be serving.'

'I can't believe they're here at all.'

Robert laughed a little. 'If that's Godfrey's work, then I'll personally nominate him for sainthood.'

They fell silent for a while and Andrew watched his army marching diligently towards the battlefield. Within an hour, perhaps two, first blood would be shed, and the very thought sent a shiver down his spine.

Was he ready to do this – did he even want to?

'What are your planned tactics with Kenrick?'

The question hit straight to the heart of his fear and he almost flinched.

'Come, son,' Robert said, encouragingly, 'Always know where you are. Once you do, you'll know where Kenrick is.'

'Do you think I can beat him?' Andrew whispered, too scared to really voice his fear.

'Do you think I can beat Nash?'

Andrew started. In the flurry to get himself ready, he'd forgotten all about that – and Robert had had so little rest, yet he was ready to fight for more than just his life.

'Promise me something?' Andrew returned to a whisper. He looked behind, but only the Bishop was close enough to hear, and he was deliberately holding back, knowing Andrew and Robert would need to talk. 'I don't know why my mother did what she did. And I can't say I'm not angry that she never said anything to me, because I am. She knew how I— It mattered to me that I knew, and she said nothing. So I understand being angry. But the only time I've ever seen her happy has been . . .'

Robert stared at his son. When he finally looked away, Andrew continued, 'Please promise me that if you live through this, if she does, that you'll try to forgive her?'

Robert was silent for a long time then, finally, he murmured his answer. 'You need to be prepared for the fact that, in all likelihood, neither your mother nor I will survive.'

'But if you do?'

'Forgiveness is not the problem. But if it was, then yes, I would promise.'

'But—'

'Please, Andrew, I am only what I am.'

As Robert's whisper died away, Andrew swallowed hard around the tightness in his throat. Silence was the only way he could show his love.

38

Kenrick picked up the empty wine jug and threw it across the tent at the feet of his Chancellor. The man stumbled back to get out of the way of the heavy silver.

'What do you mean you just found out? How can you just find out something like that? Didn't anybody notice there were no Guildesmen in our camp this morning? Where is Osbert? I want him here now!'

'H-he is with them, sire.'

'With them? They're *all* gone?'

'Yes, sire.'

Nash glanced over his shoulder at the poor Chancellor still standing by the door, shaking like a leaf. 'Are you saying all the baggage-carts are gone, too?'

'No, my lord. Only the provisions.'

'How?'

'Yes, how?' Kenrick snarled, sending Nash a vicious glare that bounced off him.

'When the Proctor and his army joined us yesterday, they took responsibility for the provisions, as is the Guilde's duty. Some time in the night—'

'Some time in the night?' Nash sat forward in his chair, dropping his feet from the stool where they'd been resting. 'Nobody noticed until this morning? Is that why I didn't get any breakfast?'

'Damn it, Nash, this is serious!'

'Oh, of course, sire. My apologies.' Nash sat back again and put his feet up on the stool. He rested his elbows on the chair arms and steepled his fingers together, doing all he could to pretend that he didn't feel the Enemy drawing closer, as though there was no tremble in the air, no shaking inside him. Instead, he watched this silly farce, and out of the corner of his eye, kept track of the good Bishop's reactions. None of the other Councillors dared show their faces.

'What provisions do we have?' Kenrick snapped.

'Enough for a day, no more.'

'Fine, then we send out raiding parties tonight.'

'But, sire, today we fight a battle. The men will not be in a condition to . . . and to forage on your own territory is—'

'What? What?' Kenrick stormed forward and slammed his fists down on the table. 'These Lusarans have stolen from *me*, Chancellor. I will take back what is mine! And when I see Osbert, I will slit his throat myself. As of this moment, he and his entire army are traitors and outlaws. Now get out of my sight!'

As the man rushed to get out of the tent with his life intact, Nash could not stop the rumble of laughter from emerging into the heavy air. 'Oh, Osbert! Finally he chooses a side! I never thought he had it in him. And with such a grand gesture, too. I am impressed. Unless, of course, our good Bishop here has been the one to make a man out of him.'

Godfrey met his gaze without flinching, and without fear; Nash respected that. This priest was perhaps the only man in this entire country who could do so – except of course, the Enemy. For that alone he would die.

'If Osbert has chosen to follow his own conscience, then I would not be one to condemn him.'

'Even if his conscience leads him to treason?' Kenrick demanded. 'He's joined the rebel army, Godfrey! Don't you even care about that?'

'Of course, sire,' Godfrey bowed, but his long-faced expression did not change, making Nash laugh again.

'I wouldn't bother trying if I were you, Kenrick. This man is not one who will break for you.'

'Oh? And I suppose you could break him, could you?'

'Oh, yes, I could,' Nash allowed a smile to spread across his face, relishing the prospect.

'Why? What do you know?'

'I know—' Nash broke off, but there was still no sign of fear on the priest's face. Interesting. 'I know that Godfrey has secretly been spying for the rebels for years now.'

'What?' Kenrick froze. 'You knew and you did nothing?'

'He was enjoying himself so much.' Actually, he hadn't known – but it was a good guess.

'What were you—'

'Yes, yes – but did you know that our saintly priest here is also guilty of the crime of—'

'Murder.' Godfrey said the word himself, without flinching, though the disgust was clear in his voice.

'Yes, murder.' Nash tapped his fingers against his chin. 'This man murdered my daughter.'

'Your daughter?' Kenrick began, but Godfrey ignored him.

'And you used her blood to regenerate, didn't you? No doubt hoping it would bring you immortality. If I hadn't killed her, you would have.'

'But I didn't. And this time, your great friend Osbert won't come back and rescue you.' Nash swung his feet down and stood. 'And when I kill you, you will wish the pain in your conscience was all you had to worry about.'

'Nash, stop!' Kenrick bellowed. 'You have no right—'

Nash raised his hand, letting loose a fist of power aimed at Kenrick's throat. Kenrick was dragged up into the air and left suspended there, his hands grabbing at his neck as though to release a rope. In an instant, Nash was at his side, looking up at him. 'I've had enough of you, you brat. You only live because I can't be bothered with the day-to-day rule of a pathetic country like this. *You* serve *me*, do you understand that, boy? You've slaved with your Malachi teacher to give you enough power to keep your throne – well, let me tell you, the battle you have to fight today will not decide whether you live or die. Your life is in *my* hands every minute you breathe! Another word out of you, and I will extinguish you easier than I would a candle! Now cut your whining and call your army out. The Enemy marches to face you and you are whinging about lost provisions and a murdered child you care nothing about.'

Nash didn't even bother waiting for Kenrick to reply. Instead, he released the King. A satisfying thud accompanied his withdrawal. He walked back around the table, making a small gesture at the priest. 'You will come with me.'

He stalked out of the King's pavilion and across the short space to his own. Taymar stood there waiting, the only person who did not vex him in any manner. Would that he had a thousand such men.

'Sit there,' he ordered Godfrey, and the priest, unable to exercise his will over his own body, sat in the chair indicated. 'Taymar, where are my Malachi?'

'In position, Master.'

'Good. As soon as that boy marches out onto the battlefield, I want him bound and trussed and brought back here. I myself will take care of the Enemy.'

'Yes, Master.' Taymar should have left, but he hesitated.

'What is it?'

'There are two men waiting to see you.'

'Who?' Who indeed? Was it Felenor ready to crawl back to him now that the poison had failed?

'They would not give their names. They only said to tell you that *she* had sent them.'

Nash froze. He took a breath. 'Bring them in.'

'Yes, Master.'

As Taymar vanished, Nash unlocked a chest by the opposite wall and withdrew a flask of wine he had sealed himself. He pulled out the stopper and drank deeply. He turned back to the priest. 'You may speak.'

'I have nothing to say to you.'

'No? Not even to beg my forgiveness?'

'You murdered the girl's mother as well, didn't you? That's how you survived the poison. So your own daughter didn't give you immortality; how disappointed you must be.'

'I see the idea of victory in your eyes, Father. That's why you can remain so calm.'

'No,' Godfrey whispered, 'I see salvation. Robert will destroy you and you will be no more. My death, my torture is nothing.'

'Really? Well, we can test that, if you like.' Nash laughed and stepped aside as Taymar returned with the two strangers.

He knew neither of them. One was obviously blind, the other his guide. Both were tanned as though they had recently arrived from the southern continent. There was something odd in the aura of the younger man, something vaguely familiar. 'What do you want?' he asked.

'She sent us to bring you to her. You must come now,' the blind man answered.

'She?'

'The Ally.'

'And I am supposed to believe this is not a trap?'

'She seeks to save her country by giving you what you want. The Enemy is on the battlefield. What trap can there be?'

Nash laughed again, louder this time, but both men remained unmoved. 'Why would she suddenly change her mind? Her son has an army out there. Why doesn't she just wait and see what happens? Has she so little faith in him?'

'She said to tell you that it is not about victory, but about the Key. She has pledged to give it to you, if you spare her son, her country and her lover.'

Nash bristled. Her lover? Robert Douglas? It had to be, for she would take no other. By the blood, how had that happened? But she would know her rebels would be hard-pressed to win this battle, even with Guilde soldiers augmenting their numbers. Even if it *was* a trap, he could not refuse this. All he needed to do was to get close to the Key, then she would be unable to stop him – though she couldn't know that. And with the Enemy on the field, fighting for his country . . .

'Where is she?'

'We will take you to her.'

'Am I to come alone?'

'You may bring what men you wish. She has no means to stop you.'

'No?' This *had* to be a trap of some kind – but he would be prepared, with fifty Bonded Malachi. He would worry about the boy later. If he did indeed get the Key, neither Andrew, nor even the Enemy would be able to stop him. 'Taymar, is my horse ready?'

'Yes, Master.'

'Then call my Malachi. We go to take posession of the Key!'

Kenrick burned. Inside him, flames of hatred consumed him, almost lifting him off the floor; he was incandescent with rage.

He got to his feet, still gasping for breath, his throat burning, the same fire as that which ran inside him. With a bellow, he called for his horse, and for his army to line up on the battlefield.

Suddenly he was surrounded by activity as his servants finished with his armour, as his Council clarified orders for the battle, as he kept the fire inside banked and ready. When they were finished, something white and mocking caught his eye, and he turned towards it, knowing in his heart that it was time.

Forb'ez stood by the door as the rest of Kenrick's servants flowed out. He waited with a patience Kenrick hated, with an innocence he could no longer afford to believe. 'Why are you here?'

'Sire?'

'You deserted my father on the field. Why are you still here now?'

The older man's eyes widened, as though it surprised him that Kenrick knew about it. 'Sire, I . . . I promise you, I—'

But the last word died in the man's throat as his eyes widened impossibly further. Kenrick merely stood and watched as Forb'ez looked down to the dagger his king had just plunged into his belly. The soldier sank to his knees, then fell forward. There was something deliciously satisfying in hearing his last breath draw out. Kenrick smiled.

Then he was outside, walking to his horse, mounting up. The animal was frisky, prancing and shying from the noise and colour. All around, men shouted, marched, horses galloped, all heading towards the east.

Where the rebels were.

Kenrick turned his own horse, riding through the camp, standard-bearer riding before him, magnates riding behind. On either side of him, everywhere he looked, were his Malachi, now sworn enemies of Nash, ready to help him defeat anybody. Ahead, he could see the field, bright in afternoon sunshine, colourful, almost festive. It was too late in the day to be starting a battle, but the rebels were approaching and there was only one way to stop them. But his soldiers were trained, skilled and, thanks to Nash's gold, paid well.

It took more than an hour for his army to be ready, thrust upon the battle as they were. But he could see the enemy lining up before him, lines of peasants, traitor Guildesmen, Robert Douglas – and his own cousin, Andrew.

Nash had lived by hatred, had succeeded by it. Now Kenrick finally understood what a power it was.

'Micah?' Robert gestured towards the forming armies taking their places on the gently sloped valley. 'Your friend Gilbert: is he planning to make an appearance? Kenrick's forces reek with Malachi. We have perhaps a hundred combat-trained Salti. If it comes down to a pitched battle between us, we're going to be in a lot of trouble.'

'He gave you his word, my lord.'

'That he did.' Robert surveyed his own lines of archers, foot soldiers, the pitiful number of mounted cavalry, too few of them properly armoured. And the hundreds and hundreds of ordinary men and boys, armed with anything they could find, grim determination in their eyes.

'They're afraid.' Andrew appeared at his side, his words softly spoken. Robert looked at him and saw the same fear there. As it should be.

'Most men are afraid before a battle.'

Andrew turned and faced the enemy. 'Where's Nash?' he asked.

'Oh, he won't show himself for a while. At least, that's usually the coward's way out. Last time he waited until I was already badly wounded. A fair fight between us would terrify him.' The words sounded like bluster, but in his heart, he knew they were true. Why would Nash want a fair fight? He cared only about winning, not honour, nor truth – like all other noble concepts, they were wholly expendable. 'I dare say Kenrick will want to talk first. Do you want to see him yourself?'

'Do I have a choice?'

'Well, yes. I could go out there for you.'

'He's terrified of you.'

'Which could be a good reason for me to go.'

'Or a good reason for me to go instead.'

'Why? Do you think you can talk him out of his throne?'

Andrew frowned, as though seriously considering Robert's suggestion. 'I need to tell him why I'm here.'

'No, you don't.'

'You spoke to Selar at Shan Moss.'

'In the hope that I could see something of Nash.'

'In the hope that you could convince him not to fight at all.' With a grunt, he swung up into his saddle. He turned to Micah and said, 'Find me a white flag. I want to talk, even if he doesn't.'

'Aye, Your Grace.'

He rode away then, missing the grim smile left on Robert's face.

'Damn it, Rayve, where's Nash?'

'I have no idea, my lord. He never said he would fight in this battle. His argument is only with Douglas.'

'But he needs to be here! I need him here!'

'My lord, my people have not seen him for more than an hour. They questioned the Bishop, who told them Nash had left with his men before you called for the army to line up.'

'Left?' Kenrick turned a glare on the young Malachi. 'Left? How could he have left?'

He was deserting Kenrick. Hadn't he said he'd had enough, that Kenrick only lived by his grace? Was this the point at which he withdrew that support?

'Fine, he's best out of the way. We can easily dispatch this rabble without him.'

'Sire?' His Chancellor rode towards him, pointing back across the field. 'The rebels want to treat with you.'

A rider with a white flag was trotting into the centre of the empty battleground. Behind him were four other riders, but at this distance, he could recognise only the bright yellow of Guilde robes.

'Good!' he snapped. He kicked his horse and almost ran the Chancellor down, riding out onto the field on his own, just as Robert Douglas had done to his father. Well, he wasn't the only man who could bluff.

Away from the noise of his army, the battlefield felt cold and empty, despite the spring sunshine – or was it summer now? He came to a halt in the centre, his head held high, waiting for the others to reach him, casting his gaze from one face to the other.

Yes, there was Osbert, that frightened look missing from his face now, despite the bad company he was keeping. Another older man he didn't recognise, and a third who looked familiar enough to send a shiver down his spine. The old man would have to be McCauly, riding like he'd been born in the saddle. The other couldn't be Robert Douglas, but would be his brother.

And between them, looking awfully small and pathetic, was his foolish cousin.

'If you'd wanted an army,' Kenrick began the moment they came to a halt, 'you should have said. I could have given you something to play with. Instead, you've allowed yourself to be swayed by these traitors. Come with me now and I will forgive you. You are, after all, still my heir.'

Andrew looked quickly at the sombre men beside him, then lifted his chin. As he replied, his voice was shaky, as though he were trying desperately to appear their equal. Kenrick remembered the cheerful and innocent boy at his court, who had given him milk and honey drinks to ease his headaches, who had always treated him with kindness. A wave of anger swept over him that these mercenary rebels had used this boy in such a way as to cause this conflict in him.

'Your offer,' Andrew said, swallowing hard, 'is appreciated, but I must decline. In return, I offer you exile if you disband your army now and leave Lusara for ever. You fight an unjust war and your t-tyranny will no longer be tolerated.'

Kenrick laughed a little. 'We were always friends, you and I. Come, we can be so again. I don't know what these men have told you, but you know I am no tyrant.'

Andrew flushed, his eyes dropping to his hands where he twisted his reins together. None of the others moved a muscle, keeping their attention focused entirely on Kenrick, as though, despite the white flag, they didn't trust him to keep the truce.

'If you ch-choose not to t-take exile,' Andrew continued, as though his speech was prepared, 'then I offer you single combat.'

'Single combat?' Kenrick did laugh outright then. 'What, you think you can beat me?' It was more tempting than he could have imagined. It would give him an opportunity to finish this quickly and painlessly – and with the boy beaten at his feet, he could then afford to be magnanimous. A few months in prison would be enough punishment. 'Would you give me up your rebel leaders if I did win?'

Andrew's gaze rose then, as though trying to read his cousin. 'They are not mine to surrender.'

For the first time in his life, Kenrick felt pity, and it was an interesting feeling. Still, he had a war to win, and he couldn't afford to be swayed. 'Then our armies will decide for us. Just remember: I did make the offer.' With that, he pulled his horse around and galloped back to his lines.

The rest of them could die, but he would give the order for the boy to be kept alive. With the right influences, he could be a strong ally, and Kenrick needed all of those he could get.

Robert waited on the lines, holding his breath and telling himself he was foolish to do so. Andrew was capapble of looking after himself, and he'd taken Finnlay with him, who would die for his nephew. So why could he not stand still; why did he have to use brute force to keep the demon down, to stop himself riding out there and strangling the life out of that monster before anything else could happen?

But this wasn't his fight, it was Andrew's – and he had to win it for himself.

Still Robert watched the parlay party, wishing he could mindspeak Finnlay to know what was being said. Of course, they weren't out there long. Only a few minutes, and then they were riding back towards him, allowing Robert to finally breathe, to get the demon under control.

Their expressions, when they arrived, were a bizarre mixture: Osbert showed profound relief; Robert couldn't blame him, since he shared that feeling. Aiden's was one of unconcealed respect. Finnlay jumped down from his horse and walked towards Robert, a combination of bleak fury and stunned incredulity at war on his face.

'That boy,' Finnlay kept his voice down, standing close to Robert while the others remained mounted around him, 'if I'd not known who his mother was, then—'

'What happened?'

Andrew threw Finnlay a look of warning. 'Nothing. But he refused the challenge of single combat.'

Another shiver ran down Robert's spine. 'Single combat? When did we discuss that?'

'We didn't,' Andrew replied without moving. 'It doesn't matter anyway now.'

Robert looked up at his son. Andrew met his gaze steadily and in that moment Robert *knew*. Until then, he'd never quite been sure, but now he did. This boy of his, of Jenn's would become a great king indeed. He hid his thoughts with a nod, turning to his horse. 'We fight?'

'Yes,' Andrew agreed. 'We fight.'

All through the ride, Nash kept watch, Seeking constantly for the ambush he knew had to be there – but nothing happened. He knew they rode north, passing through woods and past farms, but he could not think of a specific destination they could be heading for.

But it hadn't been too far from here that he'd lost the Key, all those weeks ago, when he'd been so certain he could get it from her. They must have found a hiding place somewhere close. She had never been able to lie to him. Her anger and her honesty were too close to the surface, and he had all those years behind him, when he'd got to know her in the innocence of friendship, before she'd known who he was. Back then, she'd been very fond of him, and he'd allowed himself to love her from a relatively safe distance. But desire and need had stayed his hand – too long, as it happened. Still, he rode towards her now, and he would be waiting no longer.

Nevertheless, he kept Seeking. *She* might not be able to lie to him – but the Enemy was capable of *anything*.

The caves were not as silent as she'd thought they would be once everybody had left. It had taken her a long time to convince Martha and Fiona and Lady Margaret that they had to go, using every ounce of persuasion she could muster – not to mention every lie she'd ever known – but for them to stay would guarantee their deaths, and she couldn't allow that. In the end, it had been the safety of the children that had swayed Martha. They'd packed a few belongings and left hours ago, leaving Jenn alone in the not-so-silent caves.

She spent time making herself a meal she couldn't eat. Then she wandered from one cave to another, looking at the home they'd made in such a short time, unable to stop the memories filling her of that other cave life she'd helped to destroy. Quite deliberately, she kept away from the Key.

Did those people really think her to be the incarnation of Mineah? Were they so desperate for hope that they would believe such a thing, that they could interpret her actions in such a manner?

Were they expecting her to turn against sorcerers, as Mineah had done five hundred years before?

No. It was impossible, far too scary a thought to consider – especially on this, of all days.

With still hours to wait, she collected clean clothes and made her way to the green pool, allowing the memories to sweep over her. The force of them drove her to her knees, clutching the gown to her as though it could give her the comfort she needed. But only one person had ever been able to give her that.

She remembered as she stepped naked into the water, as it swirled around her, warm and soft.

And in the darkness, alone, she opened up her mind and reached out as far as she needed.

Robert had exactly one hundred archers; it was they who started the battle. With fifty on either side of the army, their arrows rained havoc down on Kenrick's foot soldiers, while his own backed away from arrows flying in return towards them, ducking behind layers of solid shields.

'How long do we hold this?' Andrew's voice betrayed his strain.

'As long as they do. We have a good supply of arrows, thanks to Osbert.'

'It's still Lusaran fighting Lusaran.'

'Yes, but there's only one way out of that.' Robert felt his own words haunt him then.

'We don't have a choice, is that what you're saying?'

'That's exactly what—'

Robert?

He turned away from Andrew, gesturing to Finnlay to come close, just in case. *Jenn? What is it? What's wrong?*

I'm sorry.

His breath caught, but the noise of battle swirled around him like a heady aroma. *Jenn, we've started the battle.*

I know. I just wanted you to know I'm sorry. For everything.

There was definitely something wrong. The tone was almost foreign, as though—

Jenn, what's going on? Are you all right?

Nash is coming. He'll be here soon.

What? How did he find you?

I told him. I'm going to give him the Key. That's the only way we can end this. I'm sorry. Take care of our son.

Jenny? Damn it, Jenny, answer me! He called again and again, but she was gone, shutting him out as he had done to her so many times before.

Nash. She was going to give him the Key – no! He opened his eyes and spun around to find Finnlay and Andrew watching him, Aiden behind them, stern and prepared for anything.

To Andrew he said, 'I have to go. Now. Finn, I leave you the army. You know how to command, you've memorised all my plans. Trust your instincts.'

'Why, what's happened?'

'Nash is on his way to the Sanctuary.' Robert waved for his horse to be brought up. 'Andrew,' he paused then, seeing real fear for the first time in the boy's eyes that day. Robert caught his breath a moment, stilling the urge to panic and let the demon loose. He put his hands on his son's shoulders and met his gaze, shutting out the whole world. 'I have to go, son. If I don't survive, you rely on Aiden. You rely on Finnlay, and the rest of the Council. You learn from them and you grow. You become a part of your family, and let them be a part of you. Kiss your grandmother for me, and tell her I love her. Find a woman to love and marry her, have lots of children. And do it all . . . knowing I was proud that you were my son, if only for a few days.'

With that, he placed a kiss on Andrew's forehead, then turned for his horse. He climbed up into the saddle, and turned to the Bishop, knowing all that he could never say. 'Good luck,' he called softly, and then Robert turned and rode away, pulling behind the back of their lines until he had a clear path north. Without hesitation, he kicked the horse hard, pushing with his power to gain greater speed. He bent flat against the animal's back and became one with it, using only the smallest of commands to control it.

With terror in his heart, he raced towards the day he'd feared all his life: the culmination of the Prophecy.

39

With a bellow into the sharp wind, Kenrick ordered the charge. Two thousand disciplined men raised their swords against the rebels and marched forward, the tattoo rattling across their lines. The very sound of it struck joy and terror into his heart and he laughed out loud.

The valley was filled with colour and movement; the gentle hills on either side shutting out the rest of the world. Everything real existed here and now. Kenrick kicked his horse into action, then gave it its head as they plowed into the mêlée. He swung his sword left and right, slicing into flesh and bone, ignoring the blood that spurted into the air, over his hands, his legs, into the dusty earth. The noise was deafening; already there was a sickly stink of those who had already died, and those who would soon join them.

He could smell the fear, too, rising from the roaring crowds, flooding across the valley and reaching high into the sky. He was made for this.

Andrew shuddered, ducking another blade swinging at him. He'd lost his horse in the first hour and hadn't found even a minute to climb onto the replacement Micah appropriated for him. Finnlay fought on his right, Micah on his left, and Deverin, despite his age, guarded his rear. But the men in front, the soldiers pushing through his own lines, were trained, hardened warriors; they kept on, making him fight them, making him kill, again and again.

He'd had no real idea: when Robert had said battle was hell, he thought he'd understood, but he hadn't – and now he knew why Robert had said so little. This was not something a man could ever love, but it was something he could survive.

He ducked again, slipping on ground sodden with blood. He pushed forward again, heaving his shoulder into one man while he swung to cut down another. On his left, Micah stumbled, a bleeding slash on his left arm, and Finnlay had blood smeared from his cheek down to his hip. He was covered in it himself.

How long would they last? The volunteer force had broken ranks, but he couldn't see how anybody was doing now. He couldn't even look back to see if the Bishop was still watching from the hill. There was only the swing of the sword, the bone-jarring clash of metal on metal, the stench of blood, and the deep, soul-wrenching terror that swept through him with each step he advanced.

They couldn't last, not like this. In another few hours, this battlefield would be covered in bodies, and most of them would be his men. Without Robert's leadership, they were blind. Without Robert, this army had little chance of survival, even with Finnlay as its general.

Andrew stumbled again and fell, his face landing in a puddle of blood, leaving him choking and retching. He heard a shout of warning and rolled, just as a blade stabbed into the ground where he'd been lying. Continuing the roll, he got back on his feet, sweeping in a curve to slice his blade across the stomach of the soldier trying to kill him.

Each step was hell. Each swing, each cut, echoed every minute he'd spent training with Robert, but it was only when he saw the clouds banking up in the distance, forming a backdrop to Kenrick's camp, that he finally realised what he had to do.

Nash slowed as they began the incline. There was something familiar about this place, though he could swear he'd never been here before. By the look of his guides, they were getting close, and he wanted to be extra careful about the danger of ambush. His Seeking still revealed nothing, but his eyes and ears told him enough. Above were steep high cliffs, beyond which was Nanmoor. The ravine grew more narrow as they travelled, following a tiny watercourse, little more than a trickle of water. There were plenty of trees, all in full foliage now, settling in to the promise of summer, but no matter where he looked, or how hard he listened, he could not penetrate the unnatural silence which blanketed the entire gorge.

This was certainly the right place for a trap.

He looked up at the sky, where a line of dangerous grey cloud spread across the blue, promising thunder, lightning and rain to come. His men followed behind, saying nothing, but as alert as he was, watching for what they could not see.

In front, the blind man took the lead, as though he didn't need eyes to see where he was going, and his companion kept close behind him, as though protecting from some danger Nash had not yet come upon.

And then, finally, they came to a halt. The blind man dismounted and put his hand out in front of him, head tilted on one side as though he were listening. He moved toward the cliff face and a wall of solid rock. As his palm flattened against it, Nash heard the grinding of ponderous weight, a shuddering in the earth beneath his feet.

This was no trap. If there was to be an attack, or an ambush, then it would have happened by now.

Agonisingly slowly the face of rock slid to the left, revealing a dark chamber beyond that spilled cool air out into the evening. With a gesture, the blind man stepped aside, offering Nash entrance to the underground world.

He hesitated only a moment before ordering his men to dismount. Still he Sensed no danger – though he definitely Sensed *something* – but it was hard to say what it was. The closer he got to the door, the more that something prickled at the back of his neck, the more it drew him in further.

Perhaps it was destiny, calling him on to glory. He smiled to himself, and stepped into the darkness.

Instantly, he felt the cold air, smelled cooking, horses, other traces he couldn't name. A faint breeze touched his face and was gone. Four of his men were left at the entrance as sentries; the rest of his Malachi drew their swords and followed him into the darkness. Passing him, they cautiously moved up the long cavern, exploring each side-fissure and alcove. They reached the end without incident. With a clenched fist, Nash made his own light, and moved forward.

He'd hoped she would be waiting for him. Perhaps she was in the cave where she kept the Key.

With a gesture, he ordered his men to move out into the other caves, and it wasn't long before he was called. He turned to his left, following an uneven fissure, down a short slope until it opened into a comfortable room. There was a bed, a long table, cooking implements and even a fire crackling away.

She'd been here recently. He could *feel* her presence in the air. He began to feel as if his blood was rushing through his body, making him ready for something he had only ever dreamed about.

A Malachi waited for him at the end of the room, gesturing towards another fissure. He followed this one, stepped behind a wall of rock and traversed a low, sloped tunnel until it opened out into a room that almost made him gasp in surprise. A pool in the middle of the rock chamber glowed green with light from some invisible source.

And standing there, looking more beautiful than he had remembered, was the Ally.

With a final lunge, Andrew made it to the top of the slope and fell to his knees. His left arm stung badly from a cut he'd received an hour before. No sooner had he come to a halt than McCauly was at his side, putting a cup of

404

wine in his hand and urging him to drink. Before he could say a word, the Bishop was winding a bandage around his wound.

'Don't. It's nothing and there are other men hurt worse than me.'

'Just keep still,' Finnlay grunted from his left. 'They're being tended to.'

'How goes it?' McCauly asked, his expression grim as he tied one knot after another.

'I don't know,' Andrew murmured, looking over his shoulder at the unholy mess of battle still raging behind him. For the first hour or so, it had been easy to see the demarcation line of where his forces met Kenrick's, but now it was just a sea of heaving, fighting bodies, and an even bigger sea of dead ones. 'We have to stop this,' he said.

'We can still win,' Finnlay said, helping him to his feet. 'If we call a retreat, and regroup, Robert's strategies can still rout this army. Don't lose hope.'

'I haven't,' Andrew said, and looked up at his uncle, at the Bishop, and at Micah and Deverin, who stood close by. All around him were men lying wounded and dying, being tended to by priests, Guilde Healers and Owen. Not too much further down the valley the battle filled the view, and the bleak, pewter clouds in the distance spattered lightning across an almost-black sky. 'That's not what I mean. I mean, we can't let this battle continue. This is wrong. Robert knew it all along. That's why he spent so many years avoiding doing exactly this, why he didn't want the volunteers.'

'We're fighting ourselves,' McCauly whispered, obviously echoing words he'd heard from Robert.

'Yes,' Andrew agreed, weariness flooding through his whole body. But he had no time for exhaustion. This was his responsibility. 'It doesn't matter that Kenrick is driving them to it, those are still Lusarans out on that battlefield. If we don't stop the killing, even if we do win, there'll be so many enemies made out there today, there'll still be no peace afterwards. These men should all be fighting for the same cause.'

'They probably think they are.'

Andrew looked at Finnlay. 'They've been told I'm the upstart cousin of the King, who has nothing more than a few greedy, malcontented rebels at his back to push his claim to the throne?'

Finnlay gave him a grim smile. 'Aye, exactly. Damn it, Micah! Where's Gilbert and his Malachi? He said he'd be here. We could use his help.'

'I don't know where he is. Kenrick or even Nash could have stopped him somehow. I can only promise you that if he can, he *will* be here.'

'It doesn't matter.' Andrew turned back to the battle. 'I need to get to Kenrick. Can you see him?'

'What are you going to do?' McCauly was immediately at his side.

'I'm going to finish this.' And he felt like such a *child*: he still couldn't say it, not even now, when there was only one way he *could* finish it. 'I need half a dozen Salti, Finn.'

'I'll go with you,' Micah protested.

'No, not this time,' Andrew shook his head. 'Finn?'

'I'll be back in a minute. Micah, Deverin, get us some horses, the freshest you can find, and if they have any armour, all the better.'

While he waited, Andrew moved amongst the wounded, sharing a few words with them, doing what he could, no matter how little that felt, or how futile. All he knew was that he hated seeing them like this, hated that they'd been given no choice.

That's what Robert had told him: that he would have no choice when it came to Kenrick, that he would do what needed to be done, that Robert wouldn't need to force him. And Robert, as always, was exactly right: here he was, doing it because he had no choice.

He reached out to a soldier lying on the ground before him, bleeding from a bad leg wound too quickly bandaged. The man grimaced in pain, then tried to produce a smile for him. As Andrew grasped his hand however, he found his was shaking.

'Son of the goddess,' the man whispered, 'give me your blessing.'

Andrew's stomach flipped over then, but he didn't hesitate. Instead, he let his hand move, signing the trium from the man's shoulder to his forehead, then to his other shoulder. At the last touch, the man smiled a little and closed his eyes, his breathing easing. Speechless, Andrew got to his feet to find Finnlay waiting for him, five bloodied and grim Salti standing behind him, each with their own horse. Micah had another for Andrew.

Andrew clenched his fists against the shaking and strode over to his uncle. 'Classic arrow shape formation. I just want to get to Kenrick and live long enough to bring this corruption to an end. We don't stop for anything – but there're Malachi surrounding Kenrick, and I'll need you to keep them away from me.'

Finnlay's expression was grim, but his eyes were shining. 'Let's go,' he said.

The green light from the pool softened the shape of the cavern walls which reached up into the darkness beyond and were lost somewhere in the distance. Nash followed them with his eyes until he could see no more, then traced them down again, before turning his attention once more upon the Ally.

She wore a simple white shirt, a boy's trousers and boots, similar to the last time he'd seen her. But now she was rested, and her hair, shining and loose, cascaded down her back in long thick waves. He'd never seen it displayed like this before, and his hands itched to bury themselves in that rich softness.

She waited for him as though he had taken an eon to arrive. Oddly enough, he had.

'As always, it is delightful to see you. I had thought you would be waiting for me at the entrance, but now I see why you waited here. The colour from the pool enhances the beauty of your eyes.' And here he lied – because it didn't enhance them at all; in fact, the green drowned out her natural bright blue and instead, served only to remind him of the Enemy's eyes, which was not something he wanted to think about now, at his moment of triumph. 'You said you were ready to give me the Key?'

Her eyes were empty of everything but sadness. 'You agree to my terms?' she asked quietly.

'Terms?' Nash raised his eyebrows and smiled. 'Your friend said you wanted your son spared. And your country.'

'And Robert.'

'Ah, well, there I'm afraid I can't help you. For the other two, I don't care one way or the other. One King is the same to me as the next. Kenrick is already outliving his usefulness. I had planned to kill him myself and put your boy on the throne, so we can be in complete agreement on that score. But as to the Enemy?' He shrugged, and continued, 'Alas, he and I may not exist without fighting. We are drawn to each other, as are you and I. If I spare him, then he will never rest until he kills me – which of course, I couldn't allow. No, I'm afraid the only way your beloved country will have any peace is if the Enemy dies.'

She stared at him, then started blinking rapidly, as though her eyes had suddenly begun to sting. Then she lifted her chin. 'Come.'

The battlefield parted before them; Andrew's hands still hadn't stopped shaking. He was crazy to try this, when his powers were only days old, and with so little training, but he could not let all these men die just because Kenrick was too stubborn, too much the coward.

He felt the resistance even before he got close enough to see it. Kenrick's Malachi, seeing his approach, had formed a circle around their patron. They outnumbered Andrew's Salti three to one; Andrew didn't have a hope, and he'd been foolish and immature to think that anything he could do would make a difference. So what if he was Robert's son – or even the son of the damned goddess – that didn't make him a King, and even if it did, what did he know about any of this? Four months ago, he'd never even met Robert; he was still at court, believing he was Kenrick's cousin, that—

A sword glowing with orange fire swung towards his head, threatening to decapitate him. Without a thought, he raised his hand, pushing hard, punching his anguish into the air. The sword was wrenched out of the Malachi's hand and flew into the air, landing where he couldn't see. Another Malachi took his place, but Finnlay blocked that blow, the rest of his Salti fighting around him, staying close. Andrew turned his horse to break through the circle, but he met more resistance. He swung and cut, one eye on the figure in the centre of the circle, waiting for him, but no sooner had he dealt with the next Malachi than another took his place. They were outnumbered. Already he had lost two of his Salti. They were going to lose: the Malachi would overcome him and he would die, leaving his country with no hope for a future free from tyranny.

Another glowing blade stabbed towards him, and he parried, gathering his powers the way his father had taught him, pushing back, giving his sword arm more strength. He just needed to get to Kenrick, that's all, and if he could do that, then he could end all this—

His thoughts distracted, the Malachi succeeded in pushing him back, and his horse stumbled. Andrew struggled to regain control of it, but now another Malachi had joined the first, deliberately targeting him, determined to kill him. His men were pressed hard and he had no choice but to fight. He swung both left and right, but he knew he couldn't keep it up for long—

Then another, deeper sound pierced the battle roar. For a moment, he thought it was the promised thunder, but instead, he saw two dozen horsemen galloping towards them. He heard Finnlay's shout to retreat, but he couldn't go until there was absolutely no chance at all. Robert was right about him having no choice about being here, but he did have one choice left: he could surrender.

All he needed to do to bring this carnage to a halt was to condemn these men to living under Kenrick's rule for ever.

And that he could never do.

Andrew swung again, using his other hand to push at the second Malachi, making him fall back into the tight crowd around him. But then they were surrounded by the new soldiers and Andrew shouted in triumph: he recognised Gilbert Dusan – and they weren't fighting the Salti, but their own Malachi brothers.

Suddenly the odds were a lot more even, but as Gilbert pushed himself between Andrew and his Malachi attackers, Andrew's horse bucked and reared. With his hands covered in blood, he lost the reins and, with a yell, he tumbled to the ground, losing his sword in the process.

For a moment, he couldn't breathe, or make anything move at all. But then he drew a noisy breath in, and though his whole body ached with the impact, he knew he was still whole and intact. As the noise of battle rose around him once more, he lifted his head—

And found Kenrick standing over him with a blade to his throat.

Nash almost trembled as he walked behind the Ally. He ordered his men to stand watch, to allow nobody through the entrance. He kept his hands at his sides, fists clenched to hide the shaking, the physical need to find this ending, to reach this promised goal after so very long.

Jenn walked in front of him, saying nothing, taking each turn with her face immobile, as though, at the last, she had given up all sense of who she was. Nash paid no attention to where she was taking him, but instead, reached out, desperately Seeking, even though he already knew he would find nothing.

Her footsteps slowed and once she glanced over her shoulder, her eyes not meeting his, as though making sure he was still there, as though hoping he wasn't. Of course, she would be reluctant to do this. She, of all people, understood the nature of the Key, being joined to it herself. But understanding the nature of the Key also showed her that this was the only way forward for all of them. He smiled at the thought.

With what might have been a sigh, she made a final turn, leading him into a low passage where the floor was steeply uneven, requiring both hands to keep balance. At the end was another opening, and here she ducked inside and then started climbing down onto the cave floor.

This was it. He knew it without looking: this was his destiny right here.

He barely noticed the approach, or the uneven slope to the floor. He could see only the box at the end of the long cave, and at his end, another orb, sitting alone on a piece of cloth.

This was how they'd masked the Key, how they'd hidden it from him since their flight from the Goleth. This was the orb he'd given Kenrick, that the Enemy had stolen: somehow, they'd been clever enough to make a shield out of it, using abilities he had not guessed they possessed. But it made no difference now, because at the other end of the cave was—

Jenn had moved. She now stood between him and the box, her hands clasped together before her, her eyes almost black in the shadowy cave which was lit by a lamp suspended from one wall, the light Nash produced himself, and a glow coming from the box behind her, which made her hair shimmer.

'Promise me,' she said firmly, 'my son and Lusara will be free. You will not have the Key unless you promise.'

'Promise? Why would you believe me? Or is it that you just don't want to feel that you have betrayed your lover for nothing?'

'I am only what I am. You said I am the Ally.'

'Ah.' Nash moved forward a few steps. 'But whose Ally are you? Mine? The Enemy's?'

'Your promise, or you will not have the Key.'

'My dear Jenn, do you honestly think you can stop me now, promise or no? All I ever needed was to be in the same room with it – and the Key knows that. Why do you think it's done nothing to stop me? We both know it has the power to.'

'I am joined to the Key, Carlan. I control it.'

'No, you don't.' Nash smiled ironically at her use of his real name. 'I thought you understood: it controls you. It always has. That's why it was created.'

'So the Prophecy would come true, yes, I know that. But that doesn't mean I can't control it.'

'Really?' Nash moved forward a little more. 'Is that why you had to make another orb mask the Key's aura? Because you couldn't get the Key to shield itself from me?'

She had no answer to that and he moved again; now he was only a dozen feet from her. 'Please,' she whispered, 'please promise.'

And though he had intended only to take, Jenn's beauty once again spoke to him. The Key would reverse Valena's curse and the Ally would be his completely – once he'd killed the Enemy. She would be far more pliant if he had saved her useless son.

'Very well, I promise,' he said, savouring his power over her.

She shuddered then, closing her eyes a moment. Then she stepped aside, revealing the simple wooden box with the faint glow coming from it. Still he could not Sense anything, but that would no longer matter in a moment. With his whole body tingling with excitement, he circled the box, always keeping Jenn in his line of sight, until he stood behind it and saw what it was she had been hiding from him.

They had found the Calyx.

He began to laugh. 'That's how I found you, wasn't it? You joined the Key and the Calyx together. If you had asked me, my love, I would have told you it would not work. The Key has too much power for the Calyx, it would do everything to protect it from you. Ah, my dear Jenn. Promises or no, you have lost, despite all your efforts otherwise. And your lover is nowhere in sight to save you.'

Nash reached out then, spreading his hands towards the curve of the Key. In truth, he had no idea how long it would take to absorb this power, but that didn't matter, for the moment he touched it, he would control its power and nothing anyone could do would stop it.

'My lover,' Jenn said, her voice abruptly different, harder, as though she had a secret, 'is taking care of his son.'

The orb's shell glistened at him, the dappled surface shining as though covered in dew. His palms began to burn as he lowered them towards it, but her words penetrated his concentration. He looked up to find her smiling at him in a way wholly unlike her.

Son?

The Enemy's son?

'You couldn't be Bonded!' The words flew out: part desperation, part impatience. 'You could not be here doing this if you had Bonded with the Enemy!'

'We did Bond, long enough to conceive Andrew. Why? Didn't you know?'

He took in her malice and forced a laugh. 'There is nothing you can do to stop me now – and my promise means nothing. The Enemy is not here to stop me.' With that, he pressed forward, his hands reaching out and grasping the Key, taking what had been promised to him centuries before.

He barely heard her shouted 'No!' as shock suffused his entire body. The Key's glow covered him, taking his breath away, making him blind. The power blazed across his skin; his face felt like it was melting. Oh, but it was so magnificent! He could feel his body remade, his power increased a thousandfold. The glow burned brighter, lighting the whole cave: after all these centuries, the Prophecy had come true and he was heading for immortality.

No matter what trick she thought she'd played, it was too late for her to stop him now. In a few hours, he would have absorbed the entire power of the Key and his thoughts alone would tear down this mountain.

He had won; his triumph made him roar with unholy laughter.

'Please, don't,' Andrew whispered, his gaze deliberately moving up the bloody steel until it reached Kenrick's eyes. He put all his fear, all his desperation into those two words, letting his whole body speak his terror.

It was enough.

Kenrick hesitated, and in that moment, Andrew *pushed*, forcing the blade away. He rolled to his side and sprang to his feet, grabbing the first sword he could find. Betrayed, Kenrick roared and swung to cut him down, but Andrew brought his blade up and the two met with a dull clang, before power rattled through them both and brought their swords to life. Around them, Malachi and Salti still fought, giving them room, leaving them to each other.

'Why?' Kenrick hissed, incomprehension in his face. 'We were friends. I never harmed you.'

'You harmed my country,' Andrew replied, maintaining the power, holding his emotions where he could control them. 'I am my country, as is any man here. You cannot be King any longer.'

'Fool, traitor!' Kenrick pushed and swung again, but once more, Andrew's blade caught his, holding it off, keeping the stalemate. Kenrick was older and bigger, but he had not had Robert Douglas to teach him. 'You think Nash will let you live?'

'My father will kill Nash,' Andrew replied, forcing his eyes to meet Kenrick's. 'You fear him, don't you?'

'Father?' For a moment, Andrew almost felt sorry for his cousin – cousin no longer, though – but Kenrick's voice was filled with contempt and hatred. 'Douglas,' he spat. 'Then your mother is a whore!'

The words tore through Andrew as power surged into his blade, enough to drive Kenrick back, to make him stumble – but then the King recovered, driving Andrew back with his greater weight.

'You should have stopped him years ago,' Andrew continued, using the fear that he saw in Kenrick's face. He saw into Kenrick the way he always had, even as a child; all he had to do was reach in and pull out what he had Seen and hated, even when he had not understood it. 'You could have stopped him, but you were too scared,' Andrew continued. 'You were always scared, weren't you, Kenrick? Scared of your mother, then your father, of your sister and her marriage to my father, and now of Nash. Your whole life is fear and it's driven you to the most disgusting acts, all in an effort to hide your fear even from yourself.' Andrew parried another thrust that would have cut him in half. 'But *I* know. *I* can see it in you – but you were never afraid of me.'

The force of his words and a sudden lunge made Kenrick stumble again; this time the King stepped back, staring, wide-eyed with shock. Andrew took a breath, lowering his own sword, keeping the glow, knowing even then that he would win, *had* already won, no matter what happened next.

The thought brought him no joy at all, only sorrow.

He did not want to kill Kenrick – but he didn't know what he *did* he want to do.

'I did love you,' he whispered, knowing Kenrick would hear him even over the deafening noise of battle. 'I did love you, but you would have murdered me in the end, destroying even that love because it scared you.

But love is no weakness, Kenrick, it's a strength – and it could have saved you.'

'You – it's *you*, in the Prophecy: you're the one—' Kenrick stared at Andrew, his face draining of colour. In his eyes was a horror Andrew had never seen before, and it broke something inside him.

'I'm sorry,' he whispered, shocked to find tears falling down his face.

Kenrick saw the tears and nodded, his sword slipping from his fingers. Without pausing, Andrew's own sword rose, as though he had no control over it. With a cry wrenched from his heart, he brought his glowing blade down across Kenrick's body, slicing him diagonally from shoulder to hip. Before he could even fall, Andrew swung again, and pierced his chest through and through. For a moment, Kenrick stood there, blood bubbling up over the steel, and from the corner of his mouth—

Then Andrew pulled the blade away and Kenrick fell to his knees, landing face-down in the bloodied mud.

With a wrenching cry, Andrew landed beside him, his sword forgotten. Kenrick's eyes were still open. Andrew reached out and placed his hand on the blond head, holding his cousin as his heartbeat slowed and then faded completely.

And from behind him, the call was taken up, spreading far and fast.

'The King is dead! Long live the King!'

For the first time in his life, Andrew cried.

With the horse almost dead beneath him, Robert galloped up the rise to the top of the ravine. Gasping for breath, fear almost ready to shake him to pieces, he jumped from the poor animal and landed before the entrance.

Patric and Joshi waited for him, the bodies of four dead men lying to the right.

'What happened?'

Patric said, 'There are another fifty or so still inside. They got here an hour ago. You have to hurry.'

Drawing his sword, Robert told them, 'You stay here.'

'No.' Joshi moved to stand at his side.

'It's too dangerous.'

'No. We go.' The determination was unmistakable.

Robert acquiesced and ran inside, to be met almost immediately by Nash's Bonded Malachi who rushed forward, their swords glowing, ready to defend their master to the last. But Robert was not about to be stopped by anybody, least of all Bonded men with no minds of their own. With his own sword blazing, he pushed forward, his whole body pulsing with a desperate need to get to the Key before Nash could, though he knew he was probably too late.

Swinging, hacking, thrusting, barely knowing what he was doing: every step made the demon inside him stronger, bubbling up in him until it burst forth, spewing fire from the end of his sword, blinding him, and killing the Malachi before him.

Robert staggered to contain it, broke through the line of defenders and, leaving Patric and Joshi to it, he ran towards the end of the entrance cave and then into the tunnels, leaping over rocks in his way, skidding on the sandy floor, ducking and rolling through low doorways, descending further into the morass of caves. He knew he was being pursued, but nothing mattered now except getting to the Key, and stopping Jenn.

Damn it, damn her, how could she do this, how could she betray him again? Why hadn't he stopped her? Why hadn't he given in to the Bonding and made sure they were one for life? Because he'd been afraid, and now his fear was coming back to haunt him.

Jenn had tried to make him understand, and Nash had told him she was *his* Ally, and everything he'd ever learned about the Prophecy said that he couldn't trust her. But his heart thought differently, and always had, and now it was too late to stop what should never have happened in the first place.

His heart pounding, he ran the last few yards and came to a halt at the entrance to the Key's cave.

Too late indeed.

The whole cave was lit with an unholy glow emanating from Nash, who was frozen in his stance at the opposite end. Light coursed through him, rising up the sloping wall and into the tall distance beyond. He had his hands on the Key, his flesh was red and burned, but sustaining the power. Robert could feel it without difficulty. The air tingled with it, the floor beneath his feet thrummed as though the mountain was alive.

'No!' The shout was barely out of him before he saw Jenn, standing before Nash, backing away from him. She turned to see Robert standing there, and her whole face lit up with hope. That one look was enough to make him pause.

'You did this deliberately,' he whispered harshly.

She took two steps towards him, her hand reaching out to him. 'Yes, I had to. Robert, we don't have much time—'

'Why?' he whispered. 'Why did you—' But he couldn't find the words. The demon filled his chest, swelling inside him, closing his throat, making his whole body vibrate with an anger he had kept reined in all his life, an anger he'd ignored and denied, knowing that to let it free would be to ensure that the Prophecy—

414

It *was* too late. And she had known it would be. She had risked everything to force him to this point, to make sure he would be here, at this time, in this moment, ready to use the power the Prophecy had given him.

Even though it would mean her own death.

'No,' he whispered this time, his feet taking him down the rocky slope until he was standing before her. Though all the light was behind her, he could see her clearly.

'You don't have a choice.' She looked up at him, her eyes deep blue. She was ready and that knowledge chilled him. 'We should do it because we *don't* have a choice. Every time we have choices, we've made the wrong decisions. This is what we were born for, Robert. This is what the Key made us to do.'

'No,' he said, shaking his head, though a quick look at Nash rippled horror through him.

'Yes,' Jenn whispered urgently, her hands taking his and holding them around the sword hilt. 'Thraxis made us, gave mankind sorcery, and at the same time, he knew that one day, someone like Nash would rise. But he also knew that we would be able to defeat him, given enough time, enough power. You and I were *made* to do this. We were Bonded so that we would conceive Andrew, so that he would rule after us—'

'We can't know that for sure.'

'It's true,' she urged. 'Please, Robert, we don't have much time. The more power he absorbs, the more difficult this will become. If we don't stop him now, it will be too late. If he absorbs all the power from the Key, he'll also have all the knowledge in the Calyx – and the Word of Destruction – then nothing we can do will ever stop him.'

'No. I won't believe it. There has to be another way.' With that, he put her behind him, raising his sword, feeling the air rippling around him, buzzing with a power that was too close now. Jenn was right about one thing – if he didn't stop Nash now, then it would be too late. And if he got the Word—

'Robert, please, don't—'

Only once before had he been this close to the Angel of Darkness, and now, as then, his skin crawled, itched and burned, screaming at him, lighting the darkness inside him. Who was the Angel here, and who was the demon? Light fell off Nash, in thick, sickly waves, his body stiff and immobile, his face twisted in some sort of agony – but there was life there, and recognition – and *laughter*.

A blast of something icy split the air of the cave. Robert brought his sword up just in time, defending by instinct alone – but that touch was

415

more than enough. Without thought, the demon inside him howled in triumph and in a heartbeat, blossomed forth in a blaze of fire that consumed the man before him. For the first time since the demon had been born, he made no attempt to stop it, to contain the flow. It felt too good, absolute. He would destroy both of them utterly, in the one deadly furnace. His hands shook with the effort of holding his sword, keeping the blast at full strength, his eyes stinging with staring at the white-hot incandescence. He could do it . . . he *would* do it. He would—

Another icy blast struck his sword, followed by another, and another. Each blast grew in strength, making Robert back away, still protecting Jenn behind him.

'Robert, please, no!'

Her hand touched his arm and, abruptly, the fire was gone. Dizzy, he almost stumbled then. He looked at her and then at Nash. No longer under attack, the Angel of Darkness had ceased his own defence; his concentration had returned to absorbing the Key's power.

He appeared completely untouched by Robert's power.

'You can't destroy him that way. You know it's true. You've tried before; by the gods, he's told you himself that it won't work. There's only one way we can beat him.'

'Jenny, you don't understand that I can't do this, I can't. I love you.' The words were wrenched out of him, draining him.

'Oh, Robert, it's because you love me that we *can* do this, that it will work.'

'No,' he murmured yet again and pulled her to him, dropping his sword and wrapping his arms around her. They were beyond forgiveness now, beyond begging for it. He had failed and he knew it. Nothing he said now would change that, nothing would save her.

She shook in his arms, burying her face against his chest, holding him as tightly as he held her.

And he felt her love then, felt it flowing through him, filling him with wonder and joy, despair and sorrow; with all that weight on him, he said, 'How?'

Her face was invisible to Nash, her words beyond his hearing. 'Complete the Bonding.'

'By the gods!' If he did that, he would feel everything he did to her, he would *feel* her death . . . but his objection died in the steady glow of Nash's rise. Looking once more upon his enemy, the enemy of all life, he nodded.

He had never had a choice – but she had understood that all along. Perhaps that was her role, to believe, where he would always have doubted. That was why she'd drawn him here, knowing that he would come.

He drew away from her a little, until he could see her face, her eyes glistening with tears she was too brave to shed. She smiled at him, but this time he didn't give in. There was nowhere left for him to run.

'I love you,' he said firmly, his voice deliberately loud to fill the glowing cavern. And then he kissed her.

Instantly, he felt it as he allowed himself to be drawn into her, just like that first night so many years ago. He was no less afraid of it now than he had been then, but at least this time he understood what it was doing to them. He kissed her again, opening his eyes enough to catch a glimpse of the blue glow emanating from their bodies, then shut them again, choosing now to go where she led, to go to that place where they were one, where they were together, where nothing could ever separate them.

I'm so sorry, Jenny, for all that I have done to you. I should have listened, should have asked about Andrew, but I was afraid that he was my son, that I would have failed to defy the Prophecy so much that I left you with our child, in Eachern's care, and by the gods, I hated him so much, hated that I wasn't the one to kill him, hated the possibility that Andrew was his son and not mine, that Eachern had you and I didn't—

She drew him down further, into that place where words died away and only peace could reign.

And there she was, exactly where she should be, smiling at him, glowing with a love he had never really understood, until now. She had sacrificed absolutely everything she had ever held dear in order to protect him, to help him, to make sure that he would survive so that he could find this place and still have the strength to do what had to be done.

We are one, Robert. We will always be one.

He opened his eyes. She watched him. He smiled and she replied with her own smile. He could *feel* the Bond between them, making them one, allowing him to almost read her thoughts, but she spoke them anyway.

Use the Word, Robert.

Yes. Even in the joy of finding her, he would let her go. She was ready to sacrifice this; he could not refuse her.

He took her face in his hands, giving her one last soft kiss, knowing she understood the love with which he gave it.

Then he let her go. As he did, he let his shoulders slump in defeat, only partly feigned.

Though she turned and walked away from him, the Bond between them was still strong, and would be until the moment she died. It tied them; her heart beat with his, she breathed in time with him; they were two halves of a perfect whole. She walked towards Nash. Bound up with the Key, he could barely move; but Nash watched her nonetheless, his eyes wide with disgusting pleasure. He knew what this was, knew her surrender was his success – Robert could see all that in Nash's face.

With his heart swelling with pride at her courage, Robert watched her move to Nash's side, reach up and touch his face, turning his head towards her. Trapped between the Key and the Ally, Nash could do nothing to stop her – but at the last, horror filled his eyes as he saw what she was about to do.

Jenn smiled. Then she stood on her toes, opened her mouth a little and pressed a kiss to Nash's lips.

And in that moment, Robert let loose the demon, let it flow across the Bond joining him with Jenn, let it flood her as it flooded him, let the desperation and the fury course white-hot until it reached its destination.

With the last breath of Prophecy, Robert opened himself and, using the mindspeech he'd shared with Jenn for so many years, spoke the Word of Destruction.

40

The ground rumbled beneath his feet; the mountain groaned with the power he'd unleashed. Choking dust trickled down from the ceiling, making Robert cough, but before he could move, he was knocked down by a blast of wind tearing through the cave. The shuddering grew stronger as ancient stone ground together, unable to contain the force of the Word; Robert tried to cover his head to avoid the falling stones and rubble.

Then the power hit them. Blinding white light flared and blossomed, consuming both Nash and Jenn, and though he'd known it would happen, Robert cried out, staggering to his feet, reaching forward to save her from it, even though he could no longer see her.

'Jenny!'

The roaring wind knocked him sideways as it fed the incandescent fire before him, making it grow brighter, stronger, until it almost consumed the cave. But he wouldn't leave: if he was destroyed by it as well, then so be it. The ground beneath his feet heaved and groaned, then split suddenly as a gaping hole appeared in the floor between them. He fell back again, but pulled himself up onto his feet, ready to leap across the divide. More rocks fell around him now, threatening to collapse the cave completely, but he stayed, unable to leave Jenn to Nash.

And then he heard a sound that sent a chill down his spine: a scream, low at first, and deep, seeming to pierce the very rock itself, coming from Nash, alongside another voice that could only be Jenn. And the sound was pure terror, an inescapable agony, a pain Robert could feel inside him. The screams rose and rose, joining with the groaning mountain, with the flaring white light, until, with a deafening explosion, the cave erupted.

Rock showered down from above, knocking him over, making him roll in a ball, forcing his powers up to protect him, though why he should care if he lived, he didn't know. Still the wind seared the feeling from his flesh, blinded him, tore the breath from him.

And then, suddenly, it stopped.

For a moment, silence reigned; even as he uncurled himself and looked up, the ceiling again began to crumble, and he rose to his feet, stumbling forward, leaping over the crack in the floor.

There, half-hidden by the blinding dust, sat the box containing the Key and the Calyx, all glow from it gone. And beside it lay Jenn, her body still, her face white, her chest not moving.

Nash was gone.

Robert didn't pause. He ran forward and picked up Jenn, putting her over his shoulder so he could grab the Key/Calyx. Then he turned and ran, leaping over the hole, dodging boulders that hadn't been there when he came in. Hardly stopping to breathe, he ran up the slope and kept going, hearing the cave crash and crumble behind him, deafening as, in one mighty explosion, the roof fell in. Dust flew past him in a cloud, but he kept going, gasping for air now with the effort, running uphill, racing against time. He turned one corner after another, paying no real attention to where he was going, letting his feet decide, until finally he saw light, and the entrance.

Patric and Joshi stood there waiting for him, both bloodied and injured. With a warning yell, Robert ran past them and the bodies of dead Malachi, going on until his legs would no longer hold him up. Then he collapsed to the ground, dropping the Key so he could place Jenn's body on the ground carefully. Patric and Joshi were not far behind as the mountain moved again, spewing more dust out of the entrance. Another groan and suddenly there was silence.

Robert knelt on the ground, one hand holding Jenn's, gasping for air that wouldn't fill his lungs, blinking against tears that drove the dust out of his eyes. As he came to, he found Patric and Joshi crouched next to Jenn, both breathing heavily too.

'Malachi?' Robert managed to croak out.

'Gone. The last just turned and ran.' Patric swallowed. 'About twenty of them, Joshi says. And Nash?'

Robert wiped dust from his mouth. 'Dead.'

Joshi said something then, in a language Robert thought he should understand but didn't. Patric translated. 'Joshi says it's over.'

'Yes,' Robert said, looking down at Jenn. 'Yes, it's over.'

Grief rose in him then, like a tidal wave, but before it could consume him, he saw something he had never expected: a faint movement in her chest. It was all the hope he needed. With a cry, he pressed his fingers to her throat and felt the tiniest pulse there; placing his ear down on her breast to listen, he could hear a beat: there it was, faint but strong, and most definitely alive.

'By the gods!' The words came out choked and thick, his throat still full of dust and fear, but he pulled her up until he could hold her, until he could wrap his arms around her and bring her back. 'Jenny, oh, Jenny,' he whispered. This time he was never going to let her go, not ever. No matter what happened, she was never going to be out of his sight for more than a few minutes, and he would kill anybody who tried to take her from him.

He closed his eyes then, rocking her gently, feeling her heart beat stronger with each minute, her breathing getting steadier until she started to cough. Then he felt a hand on his shoulder, squeezing to get his attention. He looked up to find Joshi standing over him, a bottle of water in his hand. Robert took it and held it to Jenn's lips, letting only a few drops in before he took a long drink himself. Joshi returned a moment later with a dripping-wet cloth, which he used to wipe some of the dust from her face before encouraging her to drink again.

He settled down to hold her gently until she was ready to surface on her own, watching as Joshi bound Patric's wounded shoulder, and Patric in turn wound a torn bandage around Joshi's left hand, and another around a badly wounded thigh. Both men moved as though they were decades older, slowly and painfully.

Finally, Robert spoke.

'Thank you,' he said hoarsely.

It brought a smile to Patric's grimy face, but it was Joshi who replied, 'Thank you, Enemy. Joshi happy. Generet happy.' He looked at Patric and added, 'Thraxis happy.'

Godfrey felt it the moment it stopped, and that pain was enough to make him gasp out loud. But he wasn't the only one. The young man guarding him, who Nash had called Taymar, stopped in that same moment, frozen, his eyes wide with some unnamed fear. Then, as though he were made of crumbling stone, he collapsed onto the floor of the tent, on his knees, arms wrapped around his middle.

Godfrey still couldn't move, but now it was only ropes that bound him to the chair. The power that had controlled his body and kept him frozen all these hours had suddenly gone; he prayed that it meant Nash was dead, that Robert had finally defeated him.

He listened to the noises outside as he had for the last hours of the battle. Unable to leave the tent, listening was all he had. But now the noises changed, shifted, the cries of pain closer and softer, the cries of anger and fury all but gone.

Was it over? Did he dare hope that the decades of torment were finally at an end?

Then he heard something else, a voice he knew, calling, 'Godfrey! Godfrey, where are you? Godfrey!'

Did he dare hope?

After hours of being held in Nash's power, he had little voice left; he shouted out weakly, but his voice not loud enough to fill the tent, let alone reach further. He need not have worried: the tent flap was pushed open, and Osbert appeared, a sword in his hand, his glorious Guilde yellow besmirched with blood and gore, his eyes more alive and alert than Godfrey could ever remember.

'There you are! Thank the gods!' In an instant, Osbert had cut the ropes tying him, helping him to stand, though a little unsteadily. 'Are you injured? Do you require a Healer?'

'No, I'm fine,' Godfrey croaked. 'Just a little stiff and sore. Nash wasn't around long enough to do anything.'

'I'm so sorry I left you, I promise you. If I could have taken you with me I—'

'Don't worry about it,' Godfrey smiled, almost laughing at the complete change in his friend. 'We survived – but what happened?'

'Kenrick is dead,' Osbert said baldly, looking around the tent and noticing Taymar on the floor, rocking back and forth. 'Andrew is King. Of Robert, we have no word.'

'Well,' Godfrey took a deep breath, 'if this young man's reaction is anything to go by, I think Nash might well be dead, too.'

Osbert looked properly at Taymar, then turned slowly to Godfrey. 'Really?' he asked.

'I believe Taymar was Bonded to Nash. I think that Bond is now broken.'

Osbert peered out of the tent and called out orders to one of his men, adding to Godfrey, 'Nevertheless, we'll put him in chains until Robert gets back. He'll know if the boy is a danger. Now come, McCauly is looking for you.'

'He is?' A smile took control of Godfrey's face then, followed by a sudden shaking in his whole body. 'Is it really over?'

'Yes, my friend.' Osbert took his elbow and matched his smile. 'It's finally over. Come, there is celebrating to do.'

'Wait,' Godfrey said, 'I really need to know: what made you change your mind?'

'My mind?' For a moment, Osbert frowned, not understanding, then comprehension flooded across his face. 'Oh, that. Well, that fool Vaughn and his stupid visions, actually.'

'Stupid visions?'

'What was it you said? If I didn't lead them, they couldn't follow? Well, I told my Guildesmen that if the goddess was fighting on the side of the rebels, then we were fighting on the wrong side. I don't think it took them that long to make the decision. It was a choice between two sorcerers, but one has a goddess for a mother.'

'Or so Vaughn believes.'

'Does it matter?' Osbert said. 'It would kill the old Vaughn to think that he gave me the opportunity to redeem the Guilde by fighting beside Robert.'

'Nash laughed.'

'Did he?' For a moment, there was a shadow in the man's eyes, an echo of his former living fear. 'Well, I'll wager he's not laughing now. Come on, Godfrey. We have a King to crown.'

Godfrey emerged from the tent into night. Thunderous clouds were heavy in the west, flashing constant lightning from one point to another, though there was no rain as yet.

The camp he walked through was very different to the one he'd last seen. Here, every pavilion had its sides raised, where the wounded and dying were being treated by monks who appeared to have arrived en masse from the gods knew where. Amongst them were Guilde Healers, and the overall feeling was one of relief, of release, and – he finally dared to think it – of freedom.

Osbert led him through the camp, not giving him a chance to linger, however much he might have been tempted. Instead, he was taken to the edge of the battlefield, where there were so many dead, but there were many still alive too, taking care of the bodies.

In front of him was a sight that nearly made him stop in his tracks: a huge bonfire had already been built, and on a bier lying at its heart, was Kenrick's body. Even from here, Godfrey could see the blood spattered across the costly robes. And then he looked to the right, where men he knew and some he didn't stood waiting for him. The sight of Aiden McCauly brought tears to his eyes. McCauly smiled and strode over to him, not pausing until he'd embraced Godfrey, slapping him on the back half a dozen times, expressing what words never could. 'Oh, Father, I am so glad to see you alive. I had feared that – but no matter. You're here now. Well done, Osbert, I knew you'd find him.'

'Godfrey?'

McCauly released him and stepped back and Godfrey was swept up in another embrace, this time from a young, but apparently relieved King. 'We've been looking for you for hours! Where were you?'

Godfrey breathed deeply, ready to answer, but Osbert broke in, saying, 'Nash's pavilion, bound and held by some power of Nash's. But – well, it seems that power suddenly died. Taymar, Nash's Bonded servant, is rambling now, incapable of speech. We think that – it could mean Nash is dead.'

Andrew's eyes widened, but they filled with sorrow at the same time, making Godfrey frown. But Aiden was there, with a hand on the boy's shoulder. 'Don't think the worst, Sire. There's no reason to think they did not survive.'

Andrew turned to him, hope in his face, then abruptly called out, 'Finnlay? Can you mindspeak my mother?'

Finnlay came to stand with them. 'I'll try, sire,' he told his nephew.

Godfrey barely understood what was going on, so he kept his silence. He had spent too many years apart from all these people, while they'd all been fighting for the same cause.

Eventually, Finnlay shook his head a little. 'I can't get through to her. But that doesn't mean anything bad has happened. She might be shutting me out, or she could be—'

'Unconscious?' Andrew interrupted, almost bouncing with urgency, 'Can you try Seeking her? If Nash is dead, he can't Sense you any more – and if he isn't, well, he doesn't need to Sense you to know where you are now. Or if you can't find her, try for m— for Robert.'

Finnlay's expression softened, reminding Godfrey of the man's brother. 'I'll try, though I'm a bit rusty these days.'

Again, they all fell silent, waiting as Finnlay closed his eyes, a small stone emerging in his left hand, gripped lightly. Godfrey ignored the dozens of questions that he had.

Then, abruptly, a smile flooded across Finnlay's face. He opened his eyes. 'I found Robert, and Patric and I think, Joshi, too. I can't find Jenn, but—'

Andrew held up a hand. 'I know the ending of the Prophecy, Finn. We'll wait until they return. Right now we have other work to do.'

Finnlay smiled briefly and stepped back.

His expression now grim, Andrew walked past him until he stopped by the quiet bonfire. He stared up at Kenrick's body for a moment, then raised both his hands. Godfrey held his breath as fire flashed out of the boy's hands, setting the bonfire alight. The flames spread quickly, forcing them all to step back from the heat. All but Andrew, who stood close by until the flames finally licked around Kenrick's body, and only then did he turn and walk back to McCauly.

The Bishop gazed with compassion on the young King, then reached into his robe and brought forth a narrow silver circlet.

'This was found amongst Kenrick's things. It's not the coronation crown, but it will do until we reach Marsay, the people need to see something. Consider it a symbol, if nothing else. We'll have a proper coronation within a week.'

Andrew didn't say anything, but his expression was sombre. He knelt before McCauly, but the Bishop didn't place the circlet on his head immediately. Instead, he turned to Godfrey. Gently, he took Godfrey's hand and placed it on the circlet, so they were both touching it as it reached the boy's head.

'By the blessings of Divine Mineah and Serinleth,' McCauly began solemnly, 'and in the sight of Broleoch, we crown thee, Andrew, King of Lusara.'

From all around, the sound started quietly, building as Andrew rose to his feet, until it was a cheer more deafening than the sounds of battle had been. Blinking hard, the boy kept his place as first McCauly, then Godfrey traced the trium on his shoulders and forehead. Then Finnlay took up the chant.

'Long live the King!'

Andrew hadn't felt like eating anything, but Micah had insisted, pushing a plate into his hands, and warning him that if he didn't clean it completely, then there would be half a dozen burly men who would be willing to hold him down while Micah force-fed him. Andrew decided to give in graciously; after the first mouthful, however, he found his appetite had returned and the rest was devoured within minutes, leaving Micah standing before him on the other side of the table with a smug grin on his face. He'd had the table removed from Kenrick's pavilion and set up outside, so the men could see him no matter where he was, or what he was doing.

'Any more?' Andrew said without inflection.

Micah just took the plate from him, returning moments later with more bread and the remains of the stew. 'That's all there is, I'm afraid. Osbert's already sent parties out to the nearby towns to find us more food. Too many mouths to feed.'

'That's not a bad thing,' Andrew said around the bread dipped in gravy. 'The more mouths, the more survivors.' He had barely finished when a yawn overtook him and he almost dropped the plate.

'You should get some sleep,' Micah said, pointing towards what had been Kenrick's pavilion. It was late, and the entire camp was doing its best to bed down for the night, although there were some defiant souls still up, sitting around a campfire nearby, playing on flute and drum. The music was light and easy.

'They'll be here soon, sire,' Micah added, soothingly.

The title still sat uneasily on him: all he had done was kill Kenrick. Was that all one needed to do to become King? Was that all a King was?

There was still much to be done: there were so many wounded, on both sides – sides that were now one. Healers worked by lamp and candlelight while the storm rumbled in the distance, apparently unwilling either to move closer or to die away completely. Gilbert's Malachi patrolled the perimeter, on the watch in case Godfrey had guessed wrong and Nash still survived. How could he sleep when there was still these questions hanging over him?

Andrew could barely contemplate the possibility that Robert hadn't saved his mother, and yet, he'd been fairly warned, had known for a long time that it was likely that she would die along with Nash, and yet—

'Sire?'

The intonation in Micah's voice hit him and he leapt to his feet, turning to the north to watch the approach of four horses, three mounted. Even through the darkness he could make out Patric and Joshi, and then Robert emerged, with his mother across the saddle in front of him. His feet took him forward without thought – and then Micah was helping her down from the saddle and she was smiling at Andrew, walking into his arms and holding him close.

He could hardly speak as she held onto him, her whispers making no sense to him until he remembered that she hadn't known that he had survived either. Then she was kissing his face, leaning back to look at him, before pulling him close again, tears falling down her face.

'Don't cry, Mother,' he murmured, his own throat tight. 'We're fine. All of us. We're fine.'

He felt her finally loosen her grip on him, then let him go to embrace first Micah, then Finnlay who had joined them, leaving Andrew to face his father. There was something in Robert's eyes then that he'd never seen before. Though it was dark, there were torches lit around the camp, and plenty of lamps and flickering candles. The deep green of Robert's gaze held him: Andrew didn't know what to say, and was afraid that his voice would betray him. But Robert didn't need words; he reached out and embraced Andrew, holding him as tightly as his mother had, and Andrew held him back.

'Thank you,' Andrew whispered. He would have said more, but he knew he didn't need to.

'Come,' Micah interrupted them all. 'I'll go see if I can get Osbert to find us some more food. I think he was saving something for you. You must be starving.'

Robert greeted that with a laugh. 'You have no idea.' Then, without hesitating, he took Jenn's hand, put his arm around Andrew's shoulder and led his family towards the table.

There were drops from the last downpour still sticking to the diamond window-panes. From inside the warm room, Aiden raised a hand to one of them, tracing its descent as it glistened in the new sunshine. For some reason, today the weather couldn't seem to make up its mind. For most of the night, blustery showers had gripped the city, and then from dawn onwards, there'd been these short, sharp patches of rain, followed by an hour or more of clear, uninterrupted sunshine. Aiden looked up at the now-clear sky. Perhaps it was simply all the seasons coming out to herald a new era.

'Do you think the weather will hold when he rides into the city?' Godfrey brought two cups of brew into the study.

'The people will come out regardless of the rain. They want to see him the first time he rides into his capital,' Aiden replied.

Godfrey wrapped his hands around his cup, his gaze going out to the street below where people were already gathering. 'But do they come to see their new King, or the man who gave him the throne?'

Aiden smiled. 'Does it matter? Robert and Andrew will enter the city together, and this evening, before them all, we will place a crown on that poor boy's head. After that, it won't matter a damn who put him on the throne, only what he does with it.'

'And the people will come out to see both of them, regardless of the weather,' Godfrey said briskly and returned to the long table where they'd been working for the last few days. It was covered in piles of scrolls, papers, some books, tally sheets and various other things Aiden couldn't possibly concentrate on right now. 'What do you want to do about the smaller monasteries? Over the last year, income has dropped considerably, but Brome was so unpopular with the people, I'm sure some churches suffered because of that. Still, in the short term—'

Aiden moved away from the window and stopped beside the younger Bishop, placing his hand on Godfrey's arm. 'In the short term, we can leave this work for another day.'

Godfrey began to shake his head firmly, but Aiden squeezed his arm until he looked up. With a smile, he added, 'I'll grant you, I've only known Andrew a few months, but I think I can assure you he will not be the kind of tyrant King who will execute us for not having this work done before his coronation.'

For a moment, Godfrey blinked at him and then, abruptly, some colour appeared on his cheeks. Aiden let him go and instead wandered around the room a little, peering out of the windows on the other side at a different street, also full of people, and the noise rising up to the windows had an air of excitement to it.

'Forgive me, Your Grace,' Godfrey murmured eventually. 'It's just that—'

'Forgive you?' Aiden turned to face him. 'For what? For holding fast against untold dangers? For keeping the faith? For having the courage to stand where so many others gave way? Please, Father, never underestimate the role you have played here, nor how important it was to our cause.'

Godfrey frowned. 'I could have done more.'

'Don't worry, you still have your chance.'

'How?'

'Do you honestly think I'm going to be able to cope with all this work on my own? It's seventeen years and more since I last set foot in Marsay; I've been either a prisoner or exiled for all that time. You know full well I can't simply walk back into this position and be able to pick up—'

'Of course, Your Grace, I never expected—'

'And even if I could, there's far more work available here than one poor Bishop can handle in a lifetime – which is why I have decided that, regardless of what protests you might make, I will not allow you to step down from the mitre.' Aiden went on, deliberately ignoring Godfrey's reaction, 'Lusara is a great and mighty country. We have an enormous task on our hands undoing Brome's mistakes, Kenrick's tyranny – and on top of that, we still have to convince the people that sorcery is not the work of Broleoch himself! It's time we had two bishops.'

'But – but I—'

Aiden, purposely imperious, said, 'No, I'm sorry, Godfrey. Nothing you can say will change my mind. Now, let us leave all this here and go and find something to eat. We'll have to begin robing for the coronation soon, and then they won't let us bring food near our robes.'

'Your Grace.' Godfrey's face had regained its colour, and his eyes held a real smile. 'You should not underestimate the effect your work has had on the people's understanding of sorcery. They gather outside today because they're no longer afraid of it as they once were. That was your doing.'

Aiden still found that hard to believe, so he put his cup down and frowned. 'Well, you'll have to stop doing that for a start.'

'What?'

'From now on, you will call me Aiden, and I shall call you Godfrey.'

'My,' came a voice from the door, 'this is all very cosy.'

Aiden turned and immediately smiled in pleased surprise. 'Finnlay? Micah? What are you doing here?'

Finnlay led the other man into the room, looking around as he did so, appraising the elegant furnishings. 'I always knew you bishops lived in luxury. Now I see it was all true.'

'You do know,' Aiden folded his hands together, 'that envy is a sin, don't you?'

'Pay no attention to him, Your Grace,' Micah gestured. 'He's been doing that all day.'

'So, er, what *are* you doing here?'

'Oh.' Finnlay finished his wandering and paused in the centre of the room, looking a little sheepish. 'It appears we're your escort.'

'Escort?'

'It was all Father John's idea,' Micah added. 'He wants the entire Council waiting before the doors of the Basilica when Andrew and Robert ride up. Finnlay has papers, Father Godfrey, naming you officially as a member of his Council as well. We're to go down together.'

Finnlay fished in his jacket for the documents, 'There. Now, is there any chance of getting something to eat before we get started? Micah's been up since before dawn making sure all his enormous family are quartered in the castle, and I've been running around after my daughters and haven't eaten since yesterday. If I don't get something soon, I'm going to faint some time between the procession and the coronation mass.'

Aiden didn't answer him immediately; instead, his eyes remained fixed on Godfrey, and the way he turned the papers over in his hand without opening them. Then he gathered himself together and said, 'Well, this is what happens when you let Father John organise the coronation. Come, I'm sure we can find some food somewhere.'

Andrew could still hear the noise from outside, but here, within the Basilica, it remained a soft echo, a reminder no more, of the music and laughter, the celebrations still rolling along the streets of Marsay. In all the years he'd lived here, he could never remember seeing anything so overwhelming. They had all worked hard to make the coronation something the people could be a part of. The Basilica doors had remained open all day, and the folk of Marsay had crowded in, making Andrew feel very small as the crown was placed on his head. But he'd looked up and seen his family – his parents – watching him, and he knew he was never going to be so small he would be crushed by the weight.

The cheering afterwards had been deafening; even now, hours later, the memory brought a smile to his face. But he kept his footsteps quiet as he made his way through the Basilica, listening carefully, allowing his still-new Senses to spread out before him. There was something delicious about creeping around this late at night, with nobody watching him and, for the moment, no responsibilities other than to celebrate attaining a throne he'd never desired.

But there would be a time later for such concerns. Right now, he had another mystery to solve. Not more than half an hour ago, he'd noticed his parents had left the banquet table, along with McCauly, and it had required every ounce of his fledgling abilities to track them here. Now he held his breath as he heard voices from a tiny chapel beside the vestry. He crept closer, pressing himself to the wall, hoping his presence would not be noticed.

The voices became clearer; as he turned around the corner, he saw an altar, lit by a dozen candles. Bishop McCauly, his expression sombre, his voice low and rich, was signing the trium in the air over the two people kneeling before him. Though Andrew was close, he could scarcely hear the whispered words, but the ceremony was unmistakable: questions were asked and responses given, then McCauly signed the trium in the air once more and his face creased in a broad smile.

Andrew's throat tightened as Robert got to his feet, bringing Jenn with him. There was just enough light to see the look in Robert's eyes, and the answering expression in Jenn's. And then he could see no more as Robert held his bride close and kissed her. With his heart pounding, Andrew slipped back into the shadows, no longer watching, but bearing witness nonetheless. A smile broke out on his face too, and he almost laughed aloud.

It was just like them to get married now, *after* he'd become King.

Still smiling, he slipped away, heading back to his banquet, his Council, his people and his country.

As McCauly made his way out of the chapel, Robert turned to Jenn, keeping her within the circle of his arms, delighting in how good it felt. 'Are you sure about the Key?' he asked her.

'There's nothing there. I keep trying, but whatever presence I used to Sense before has gone. It may grow again, I don't know – but for the moment, it's just a shell. And besides, it didn't interfere with the ceremony, did it?'

'I still find it hard to believe you actually married me. You put up such a fight for so damned long I really thought I would have to drag you, bound and gagged, before a priest.'

Jenn began to laugh softly to herself.

'I had the men ready and organised, the plan laid. All I needed was just one more refusal from you and that would have been it.' Robert paused, a small frown creasing his forehead, then he went on, 'But then, for some strange reason I'll never understand, you actually said yes. You can imagine my surprise, my disappointment: all that effort, all that organising – all for nothing. You gave in without a fight. Anybody would have thought you'd *wanted* to marry me. Hardly like you at all.'

'Perhaps you don't know me as well as you thought,' Jenn said, grinning.

'Oh, yes I do.' With that, he pulled her to him. 'I know you better than anyone in the world. Better than you do.'

She laughed again. Then her hands came up and cradled his face, her soft touch sending shivers down his spine. 'My dear, sweet, darling Robert. I have something I must tell you.'

'You don't need to tell me, my love,' he murmured, lifting a strand of hair from her forehead. 'We're Bonded, remember? I already know.'

'How?' she whispered, her eyes searching his face.

'I felt you die, Jenny.' Robert's voice dropped low and he shook his head. 'I felt you die and the demon with you. We are Bonded for life. I couldn't miss something like that.'

'I don't understand how it happened.'

'Nor I – but what can we do but accept it for the miracle it is?'

'No miracle, Robert. You said it yourself to Andrew: our powers can't hurt each other. How many times have you and I shielded each other, survived blasts that would have killed anyone else?'

'Then it's not a miracle,' he said. 'You know? I don't care. I have you, and there is no more Prophecy. Our son is on the throne and Lusara is free.'

'More than that,' she whispered, '*you* are free.'

'As long as I am with you.'

Her eyes danced in the candlelight. 'There's something else I have to tell you.'

Feigning horror, Robert frowned. 'What is it? Are you going to tell me you're having my child?'

He could feel her laughter. 'Well, now that you mention it, perhaps I am. No, actually, it was something else. Something important.'

'Well, go on. If we don't get back soon, people will start to talk and we can't have that.'

She burst out laughing; the sound lifted his heart. 'Oh, Robert, I love you.'

For a second, he thought he'd misheard. For another second, he thought he was dreaming. For a final second, he thought he might be delirious.

'What?' he whispered. 'What did you just say?'

For a moment she concentrated on slipping her hands beneath the folds of his shirt.

'Don't do this to me, wife! After seventeen years, I think I deserve to hear it at least once more.'

In response, she touched his face. 'Robert Douglas, Earl of Dunlorn, Duke of Haddon and father of my son, I love you. I love you and I will always love you. And in case you're still wondering, that's the only reason I married you, you fool. Did you think I was after your money?'

Robert began to laugh, a rumble which grew from his belly, filling his whole body. He gazed down at her as if for the first time.

She was watching him gravely. 'We should go back now and join the others. They'll be wondering where we are.'

'No.' Robert said, 'they won't be wondering at all. I should think they're all drunk by now. I don't care anyway. For once, Jenny, you and I are going to do exactly what *we* want.'

And with that, he took her hand, leading her out of the Basilica and into a world that was already waiting for them.

Epilogue

THE SECRET HISTORY OF LUSARA
Ruel

Despite the efforts of many of the protagonists, rumours that Jennifer Ross was indeed the incarnation of the goddess Mineah continued to abound. There is little doubt now that what happened to her would be considered a miracle by most people; this was the second re-birth she had experienced as far as the common populace was concerned. The word spread like wildfire across the country; Andrew did nothing to stop it. He would neither confirm nor deny that the woman who had helped kill Nash and bring down a mountain was his mother. There is a possibility that secretly he wished the memory of his mother to live long after, in the legends of Elita.

Of Robert and Jennifer, little was heard after those first few weeks. They left Marsay after their son's coronation, and returned to Dunlorn with the rest of Robert's family, determined to bring the castle back to life.

They were not much seen at the new Enclave, founded the following year by Patric and Joshi. The new school was more open than the previous one, though its location was kept secret, using the age-old Seal. Patric spent many years developing techniques which could copy the Key's protection and, to this day, few folk have any idea where the Enclave is, though it continues to flourish now that Seeking for new members is done openly and is, for the most part, welcomed by the populace. Every year, a dozen Generet arrive to train in the Salti manner, and a dozen Salti head to Felkri, in Alusia, the better to understand their cousins.

What is most interesting to those sorcerers who were involved from the beginning is that what was foretold actually came to pass. They were set free from their prison and now live amongst the people, accepted and no longer feared. Even the Malachi, under the leadership of Gilbert Dusan, worked hard with those of the Enclave to remove the old prejudices, and to allow a reunification of their people, giving Lusara an opportunity to see that sorcerers of different persuasions could all live in peace.

And so, in a voice of hope, ends this Secret History, along with the prayer that peace will now reign in Lusara for all the future yet to come.

Ruel

Finnlay paced up and down the dark corridor, rubbing his hands together against the damp chill this place always engendered. Why Patric had chosen such a gloomy place as this was a question he had never answered convincingly. All along the stone walls, moisture glistened in the light of oil lamps suspended from the ceiling. There weren't even any rushes on the floor to give the illusion of warmth. Finnlay would have to speak to him about that. How on earth could he expect new candidates to welcome living in a place like this for the years it would take them to become adept? The gods alone knew how the Generet could stand living here after the heat of Alusia.

He reached up and pulled the collar of his cloak further around his neck, then turned again and retraced his steps, walking away from the door. A sound in the distance made him look up. From the depths of the dark passage a figure came towards him, a midnight blue cape trailing behind. The woman walked swiftly, as though her journey was a matter of urgency. Before she even reached him, she was asking him questions.

'Any word yet?'

'Not a sound,' Finnlay replied, looking at the door. It remained as shut as it had been all morning.

'I don't understand. What can be taking so long?'

Finnlay smiled gently and reached out to the girl's shoulder. 'I know this is hard, my dear, but we always knew this part couldn't be hurried. Patience, that's the key. Patience.'

'You sound like you know what's going to happen. I thought you said this was the biggest gamble of all.'

Finnlay shrugged. 'At my age, every day is a gamble for another few hours of life.'

The girl relaxed a little and a short laugh escaped. She drew the cloak hood back from her face, revealing dark auburn hair plaited and tied with a single ribbon. 'And you're so feeble, too, aren't you, Finnlay? You can hardly get on a horse, let alone keep up with those reckelss grandchildren of yours.'

Finnlay drew himself up to his full height. 'My grandchildren are not reckless – just adventurous, that's all. I may be old but I'm certainly not feeble.'

She stood on her toes and kissed his cheek. 'At fifty-seven, Finnlay, you're not even old.'

Finnlay kept up his stiff stance. There was no need to make this girl think he wasn't actually offended. 'And what about Andrew? Is he here yet?'

The girl raised her fine, dark eyebrows in mock surprise. 'Why, Finnlay, you're the great Seeker. Can't you sense his presence within the Enclave?'

'If you're not careful, girl, I'll make you sorry for your lack of respect. I don't know where you learned it.'

'I'll give you one guess.' She turned around just in time for Finnlay to see his nephew come down the corridor towards them.

'Any word yet?' the King asked quietly.

'Do you think we'd be standing out here in the cold if there were?' Finlay said wryly.

'Oh, I don't know,' Andrew replied, deadpan. 'You always did like to have something to complain about.'

'Hell.' Finnlay eyed the two of them acidly. 'You're both as bad as one another. I know you're King, Andrew, but I sincerely hope you don't treat your subjects as badly as you treat the members of your own family.'

'Oh, come, Uncle,' Andrew smiled, putting his arm around the waist of the girl. 'I treat Ruel here very well indeed. Don't I?'

Ruel frowned prettily. 'I'm sorry, sire, is that one of those commands that sounds like a question but isn't?'

Finnlay laughed. 'You brought that one down on your own head, my boy. Look, I'm sick of standing out here. My bones are starting to freeze together. Where's your brother?'

'I thought he was in there,' Ruel said. 'Haven't you seen him?'

'Not for a while. Let's go in and see what's happening.'

Without waiting, Finnlay strode to the door, knocked once and pushed it open. He held it as Andrew and Ruel followed him in then closed it, automatically waving a hand over it with a warning. Then he made his way to the fireplace and stood with his back to it, warming his body against the heat. Andrew and Ruel were less comfortable. They stood on either side of the table-end, looking somewhat lost. By the window, curled up on a huge seat with a small book, was Ruel's brother. He looked up once, gave them all a smile, then returned to his reading as though it were the most important thing in the world.

The room was compact, but saved from being small by a huge fireplace and a deep bay diamond-paned glass window that looked out upon the hill. Dark panelling gave the walls warmth; the Alusian rug was a gift from Joshi's family. The long table was strewn with piles of papers, two silver goblets and a carafe. On the other side, facing Finnlay, Jenn sat with her eyes still intent on the page before her. She paid no attention to their entrance, but kept reading. Robert stood by the long windows, one hand resting high on the stone, his gaze focused on the grey view beyond the Enclave.

A rustle of paper drew Finnlay's attention back to Jenn as she turned the last page over onto its face. Then she sat back and clasped her hands together on her lap. She looked at none of them. Watching her, Finnlay was still surprised by how little she'd aged over the years; though now she looked like a woman of thirty-five or so. It seemed now the Prophecy was done with them, they were finally beginning to age, albeit slowly. Even so, they had taken the extra years granted to them, living them to the full; it was impossible to mistake their happiness.

'Well?' Andrew said into the silence. 'What do you think?'

Finnlay almost smiled at the question: it was brave of the young King to be the first to ask. Neither he nor Ruel dared to broach the subject; they were both so involved.

'I think,' Jenn replied quietly, 'that Ruel and Finnlay have put a lot of work into this. There is hardly a thing I can fault. I'm surprised, Finn. I hadn't realised your memory was so good.'

'It isn't.'

'Ah,' Jenn said, turning to Ruel. 'You had other help – from whom?'

Ruel looked first at Finnlay, then at Robert, who was standing alone by the window with his back to them. 'From Micah and Andrew and a few others.'

'Did you speak to Lady Margaret?'

Ruel nodded.

'I see.'

There was another long silence and Finnlay could see Ruel was getting more and more agitated – she was still very young, despite her education and worldliness, and the tension of the moment was almost too much for her. She took a step forward. 'Is that all?'

'What else is there?'

'But . . . what do you think of it?'

'It's a very good history, my dear,' Jenn replied warmly. 'I'm proud of your efforts to write such a thing. I could never have done it.'

'But do you approve?'

Jenn just raised her eyebrows.

Ruel turned from her and half-crossed the room. 'Father?'

Robert said nothing for a moment. Then, he lifted his hand and pointed to something out the window. 'You know, there's a farmer who keeps sheep on that hill over there. One day, during a storm, he went out onto the moor to bring his flock together to take them to saftey. He had trouble finding them in the downpour. Cloud had decended over the hill and the white sheep melted into the grey. For hours he searched, growing exhausted, until he slipped and fell down the hill. He landed against a tree, hitting his head. When he came to, he thought it was night, but it was only when he got to his feet that he realised he'd lost his sight. The storm still howled around him and he could hear the terrified bleating of his sheep. Afraid, but knowing what he had to do, the farmer set out again, blindly, up the hill. Carefully he gathered all his sheep together, by the sound of their bleating alone. He brought them back to his farm and into the shelter they needed.'

Robert took a deep breath. 'But for a simple accident, he would have lost half his flock. Some would have said the gods had guided him, others that his own foolishness led him to a greater insight than he could otherwise have known. Maybe the man was fated to lose his sight – the occasion alone was the only variable.'

Ruel took another step forward, then asked Jenn, 'Are you angry that I didn't ask for your permission to write the story?'

Jenn came to her feet and placed her hands on the back of her chair. 'He's angry. But he's also proud of you, aren't you, Robert?'

At this, he finally turned around from the window. 'Of course I'm proud of you. I'm afraid I can't be so generous about my brother's contribution, however.'

Finnlay dropped his head and tried to hide his smile.

'But what do you think of it?' Ruel asked again. She had her father's green eyes, but they lacked his intensity, even now.

Robert shrugged. 'As your mother says, it's a fine history. You've done well to find out so much of what is, in effect, a very great secret. I just want to know one thing. Why write it? Why put down on paper the truth about Carlan? About Selar and Kenrick? More to the point, why tell the truth about your own brother's parentage? Do you not think that is a secret worth keeping?'

'I don't mind the truth being known, Father,' Andrew said evenly. 'I'm not sure it even matters now.'

Robert turned his full attention on his oldest son. 'You've been on the throne almost ninteen years. In that time you've put down – what, three insurrections from Kenrick's old supporters? You've had border incursions from both Sadlan and Tusina, and if it were not for the fact that you had the sense to marry Tirone's daughter, I dare say Mayenne might even have joined in.'

'Lusara has had no armed attack from any side for the last thirteen years, Father, and you know it.'

'And I also know that Selar was on his throne a little longer than you before he got himself into serious trouble.'

'But Selar's biggest mistake was making an enemy of you, Father. I personally would never be that stupid.'

Finnlay had to bury his face in his hands to stifle his laughter. This meeting was turning out to be more entertaining than he'd expected.

Andrew went on, 'Really, Father, I can't see that it can do me that much damage after all this time. I named my son and heir after you and people believed it was to honour the man who fought so long for my throne.'

'You mean it wasn't?' Finnlay murmured, but a glance from both father and son shut him up.

Jenn interrupted, 'Both you and your sister were conceived before your father and I were married. Does that mean nothing to you?'

'I was conceived on the eve of a battle that put my brother on the throne and rid this country of its greatest evil for ever. That means a lot to me, yes.'

'But Andrew inherited titles and lands that do not belong to him. So has David. By openly publishing this history you would throw so much into confusion where there is no need. You would destablise a country that has only recently begun to enjoy its peace. And to what purpose? So you could tell a story that was never meant to be told? And don't mistake me. It can't affect Robert and me. We have no public role and most people have forgotten we even exist. Our lives won't change with this book, but yours will.'

Ruel turned to her father, but his eyes were on Jenn. In the back of his mind, Finnlay could hear what the others would hear: the faint echo of a whisper, the trail of mindspeech passing between Robert and Jenn. Only the blood-tie allowed him to hear that much; more was impossible.

'Please.' Ruel moved forward to stand before her father. 'I want you to understand: I'm not trying to destroy all you worked for. On the contrary, I want everyone to know the sacrifices you made to bring it all about. Nobody knows what really happened – especially in the battle with Carlan. Nobody was there but you and Mother. The rest of us only know because you told us. You would never write such a history because for so long you blamed yourself for failing and then hated yourself for not acting sooner. There are people in Lusara who need to understand why you didn't act for so long. They need to know why the whole thing happened in the first place. There is a greater, deeper truth that can be learned from this story, something the whole country can benefit from. Is it so wrong to want that? I know it will cause ructions here and there and people will look at Andrew, David and me quite differently, but that's a sacrifice we're all willing to make. You taught me that.'

Robert raised his eyebrows and looked at Jenn. 'She's your daughter, all right.'

Jenn's luminous blue eyes betrayed a smile. 'Don't blame me, Robert. You're the one who said she and David should know the truth. You suggested she should live in Marsay with her brother. Can I help it if she can twist you around her little finger?'

'Well, you could stop giving her an example to follow,' Robert replied, trying to hide his own smile. He turned back to his daughter and took her hands between his. 'Don't for one moment think I don't appreciate what you are trying to do. I've had many advocates through my life, but never before have I had one who has acted so passionately from hearsay alone.'

'But—'

'Let me finish,' Robert murmured gently. 'You forget in your history the suffering my actions and inactions caused, the pain and confusion my people went through, all because I tried to run from something that was in my blood. This peace you so lightly value is something a lot of people in this country have never experienced before. We changed the face of the land, but there are still many people alive today who remember what it was like before, and what it cost them to banish the evil. So many didn't live to see this peace – and many of those were people I loved.'

Ruel's gaze didn't leave her father. 'Then you won't let me publish it?'

Robert shook his head slowly. 'No. I know it may sound harsh to you, but I want you to understand something. You're right about one thing. There is a deeper lesson to learn from history, a greater understanding of who we are, and why. But you need to ask yourself: if Amar Thraxis had just told us what we were in the beginning, what would we have done? Would we have blindly followed instructions based on a magic we couldn't begin to understand? We are, all of us in this room, the product of a work he began more than a thousand years ago. He knew it would take a long time – but he was wise enough not to tell us why.'

He drew Ruel to a chair by the end of the table and sat her down. He pulled out another one and sat opposite her, keeping hold of her hands.

'You don't think people will understand?' Ruel asked quietly.

'No,' Robert said, 'I think it's too soon to ask them to. This goes back so many centuries, and we, as sorcerers, were created to be guardians over them. How will they feel to know they were left out? Will all the old prejudices and fears erupt again because they feel inferior?'

439

'But you do think one day they will be ready?'

'I hope so,' Robert replied, lifting her hand to kiss it. 'I'm so very proud of the courage you've shown in writing it all down, knowing we might be angry. It really is far superior to anything so far written about those years, and one day perhaps, when it *is* published, we will live to regret that because we've been plagued by all the questions it would engender. However, you've shown an insight not common in someone your age. There *is* a lesson to be learned: the most important lesson of all, that our differences are our strengths, and it is those strengths that keep evil away. It's just that I'm not sure we've learned it properly yet.'

Ruel looked at her mother and Jenn came around the table. 'In this, I agree with your father. Believe it or not, there are some things about which we do not constantly argue.'

Robert glanced over his shoulder, an eyebrow arched. 'There are?'

Jenn laughed and stood behind his chair, placing a hand on his shoulder, which he grasped immediately. 'But your work will not be in vain. Nor will it be lost.'

'What do you mean?'

'We will put it in the safest place possible, where it can be read when the time is right. Robert and I will code it for inclusion in the Calyx.'

Ruel's eyes widened. 'You can do that?'

Finnlay moved away from the fireplace and gently drew Ruel to her feet. 'I'm quite sure you should have noticed by now that your damned parents can – and usually do – do anything they want to do. At least we won't have wasted our time, even if you did get all the praise. I suppose my contribution will never be remembered.'

'Nor should it be,' Robert replied instantly. 'I think that's the penance you should pay for all those years you harassed me.'

'See?' Finnlay turned to Ruel for support, then to Andrew. 'All that hard work, fifty years supporting a brother who never understood the meaning of gratitude. I spend two years helping his daughter write a book that makes him out to be a hero and what do I get?'

Andrew was already laughing. 'As I said, you're always happier when you have something to complain about.'

'And,' Robert murmured, coming to his feet with a smile, 'what kind of brother would I be if I didn't constantly try and give you the means to be happy? Really, Finn, what do you think of my sense of duty?'

He placed his arm around Jenn's waist and favoured them all with his usual charming smile. 'Come, let's gather up the rest of our cursed family and go and get some dinner. Micah, Sairead and the boys should have arrived by now. I'm sure the Queen is tired of being beleaguered by my grandchildren running wild – not to mention those wayward grandchildren of yours, Finn; I don't know how Fiona puts up with them.'

Jenn grinned at them both, 'That's because she knows where they got it from.'

Robert chuckled and turned to the boy in the chair. 'David? Please put the book down and come play with your family.'

At twelve, David was only just starting to grow, but even so, his father towered over him. With a grin, the boy slid off the chair, tucked the book under his arm and ran out of the room ahead of the adults.

'And you worry about *my* grandchildren, Robert,' Finnlay murmured. 'Personally, I think it's *your* progeny who are going to cause us the most trouble.'

'That's as it should be, brother,' Robert replied with a laugh. 'Exactly as it should be.'

HERE ENDS THE
FINAL BOOK OF ELITA